NO LONGER THE PROPERTY OF
BALDWIN PUBLIC LIBRARY

NANCY KRESS

This special signed edition is limited to 1000 numbered copies.

This is copy 416.

THE BEST OF NANCY KRESS

THE BEST OF NANCY KRESS

NANCY KRESS

SUBTERRANEAN PRESS 2015

First Edition

ISBN
978-1-59606-721-9

See pages 557-558 for individual story credits.

Subterranean Press
PO Box 190106
Burton, MI 48519

subterraneanpress.com

TABLE OF CONTENTS

INTRODUCTION

How do you choose the best stories an author ever wrote? And why should the author be the one doing the choosing?

These are not trivial questions, because they bring along, like the debris unavoidably entangled in a comet's tail, all the much-debated issues about "standards" in art. Are there objective criteria for judging a story "good"? If so, what are they? Or is the entire question of value purely a subjective one? I once had a woman say to me, "If I like it, it's good." Well—what if you like it and I don't? Can a work of fiction be both good and bad at the same time? That makes nonsense of the very words.

Unless...

I think that stories are usually good in parts. Some have compelling, realistic, fascinating characters but the plot is predictable. Others are amazingly inventive in narrative but the writing is pedestrian: it never surprises, never soars. Others, especially in science fiction, explore fascinating ideas, but the characters have all the depth of a solar sail. Every once in a while a story has everything—character, idea, plot, language—and we gasp in admiration. But there are still readers out there who will hate it. This doesn't imply the absence of standards or even the presence of wholly individual standards; rather, it means that some readers care only about one of the parts of fiction (a hero I care about! Weird aliens! A new scientific idea!). The other parts just don't register, as all wavelengths of light not near 475 nanometers will be thrown back by an object that is "blue." Nothing not-blue is absorbed.

I know readers like this. Sometimes I *am* a reader like this, disappointed by a story that does not satisfy the standards I happen to value most, even as I can recognize that the story includes other excellences.

Sometimes this is true of a writer's entire output. I'm not going to name names; I want to keep my friends.

The stories in this book try to do different things. Some, such as "People Like Us," are predominately idea stories. Some, like "Laws of Survival," are mostly interested in what a character would do in an impossible situation. Some, like "Unto the Daughters," were written because I enjoyed writing the voice. At least one, "Casey's Empire," is a comment on writing science fiction: why, how, and at what cost one may become an SF writer. Just as I had different motivations for writing these stories, the stories themselves meet different standards of "good." Or else they don't—you, the reader, must judge that for yourself.

As to why the author was the one to choose her "best" from among over a hundred stories: because, after decades of waiting for editors to accept or reject manuscripts, it was just so much *fun* to finally be the one doing the choosing. A few favorite but very long novellas had to be left out due to length, notably "The Erdmann Nexus" (which won me my second Hugo) and "Fountain of Age" (a Nebula). But for the most part, for better or worse, these are the stories of my own that I like the best.

Now the judging is up to you.

AND WILD FOR TO HOLD

The demon came to her first in the long gallery at Hever Castle. She had gone there to watch Henry ride away, magnificent on his huge charger, the horse's legs barely visible through the summer dust raised by the king's entourage. But Henry himself was visible. He rose in his stirrups to half-turn his gaze back to the manor house, searching its sun-glazed windows to see if she watched. The spurned lover, riding off, watching over his shoulder the effect he himself made. She knew just how his eyes would look, small blue eyes under the curling red-gold hair. Mournful. Shrewd. Undeterred.

Anne Boleyn was not moved. Let him ride. She had not wanted him at Hever in the first place.

As she turned from the gallery window, a glint of light in the far corner caught her eye, and there for the first time was the demon.

It was made all of light, which did not surprise her. Was not Satan himself called Lucifer? The light was square, a perfectly square box such as no light had ever been before. Anne crossed herself and stepped forward. The box of light brightened, then winked out.

Anne stood perfectly still. She was not afraid; very little made her afraid. But nonetheless she crossed herself again and uttered a prayer. It would be unfortunate if a demon took up residence at Hever. Demons could be dangerous.

Like kings.

Lambert half-turned from her console toward Culhane, working across the room. "Culhane—they said she was a witch."

"Yes? So?" Culhane said. "In the 1500s they said any powerful woman was a witch."

"No, it was more. They said it *before* she became powerful." Culhane didn't answer. After a moment Lambert said quietly, "The Rahvoli equations keep flagging her."

Culhane grew very still. Finally he said, "Let me see." He crossed the bare, small room to Lambert's console. She steadied the picture on the central square. At the moment the console appeared in this location as a series of interlocking squares mounting from floor to ceiling. Some of the squares were solid real-time alloys; some were holo simulations; some were not there at all, neither in space nor time, although they appeared to be. The project focus square, which *was* there, said:

TIME RESCUE PROJECT

UNITED FEDERATION OF UPPER SLIB, EARTH

FOCUS: ANNE BOLEYN

HEVER CASTLE, KENT, ENGLAND, EUROPE

1525:645:89:3

CHURCH OF THE HOLY HOSTAGE TEMPORARY PERMIT #4592

In the time-jump square was framed a young girl, dark hair just visible below her coif, her hand arrested at her long, slender neck in the act of signing the cross.

Lambert said, as if to herself, "She considered herself a good Catholic."

Culhane stared at the image. His head had been freshly shaved, in honor of his promotion to project head. He wore, Lambert thought, his new importance as if it were a fragile implant, liable to be rejected. She found that touching.

Lambert said, "The Rahvoli probability is .798. She's a definite key."

Culhane sucked in his cheeks. The dye on them had barely dried. He said, "So is the other. I think we should talk to Brill."

The serving women had finally left. The priests had left, the doctors, the courtiers, the nurses, taking with them the baby. Even Henry had left, gone...where? To play cards with Harry Norris? To his latest mistress? Never mind—they had all at last left her alone.

A girl.

Anne rolled over in her bed and pounded her fists on the pillow. A girl. Not a prince, not the son that England needed, that she needed...a girl. And Henry growing colder every day, she could feel it, he no longer desired her, no longer loved her. He would bed with her—oh, that, most certainly, if it would get him his boy, but her power was going. Was gone. The power she had hated, despised, but had used nonetheless because it was there and Henry should feel it, as he had made her feel his power over and over again...her power was going. She was queen of England, but her power was slipping away like the Thames at ebb tide, and she just as helpless to stop it as to stop the tide itself. The only thing that could have preserved her power was a son. And she had borne a girl. Strong, lusty, with Henry's own red, curling hair...but a girl.

Anne rolled over on her back, painfully. Elizabeth was already a month old, but everything in Anne hurt. She had contracted white-leg, so much less dreaded than childbed fever but still weakening, and for the whole month had not left her bedchamber. Servants and ladies and musicians came and went, while Anne lay feverish, trying to plan.

Henry had as yet made no move. He had even seemed to take the baby's sex well: "She seems a lusty wench. I pray God will send her a brother in the same good shape." But Anne knew. She always knew. She had known when Henry's eye first fell upon her. Had known to a shade the exact intensity of his longing during the nine years she had kept him waiting: nine years of celibacy, of denial. She had known the exact moment when that hard mind behind the small blue eyes had decided: *It is worth it. I will divorce Katherine and make Anne queen*. Anne had known before he did when he decided it had all been a mistake. The price for making her queen had been too high. She was not worth it. Unless she gave him a son.

And if she did not...

In the darkness Anne squeezed her eyes shut. This was but an attack of childbed vapors; it signified nothing. She was never afraid, not she. This was only a night terror, and when she opened her eyes it would pass, because it must. She must go on fighting, must get herself heavy with a son, must safeguard her crown. And her daughter. There was no one else to do it for her, and there was no way out.

When she opened her eyes a demon, shaped like a square of light, glowed in the corner of the curtained bedchamber.

Lambert dipped her head respectfully as the high priest passed.

She was tall and wore no external augments. Eyes, arms, ears, shaved head, legs under the gray-green ceremonial robe—all were her own, as required by the charter of the Church of the Holy Hostage. Lambert had heard a rumor that before her election to high priest she had had brilliant, violet-augmented eyes and gamma-strength arms, but on her election had had both removed and the originals restored. The free representative of all the hostages in the solar system could not walk around enjoying high-maintenance augments. Hostages could, of course, but the person in charge of their spiritual and material welfare must appear human to any hostage she chose to visit. A four-handed spacer held in a free-fall chamber on Mars must find the high priest as human as did a genetically altered flier of Ipsu being held hostage by the New Trien Republic. The only way to do that was to forego external augments.

Internals, of course, were a different thing.

Beside the high priest walked the director of the Time Research Institute, Toshio Brill. No ban on externals for *him*: Brill wore gold-plated sensors in his shaved black head, a display Lambert found slightly ostentatious. Also puzzling: Brill was not ordinarily a flamboyant man. Perhaps he was differentiating himself from Her Holiness. Behind Brill his project heads, including Culhane, stood silent, not speaking unless spoken to. Culhane looked nervous: He was ambitious, Lambert knew. She sometimes wondered why she was not.

"So far I am impressed," the high priest said. "Impeccable hostage conditions on the material side."

Brill murmured, "Of course, the spiritual is difficult. The three hostages are so different from each other, and even for culture specialists and historians.... The hostages arrive here very upset."

"As would you or I," the high priest said, not smiling, "in similar circumstances."

"Yes, Your Holiness."

"And now you wish to add a fourth hostage, from a fourth time stream."

"Yes."

The high priest looked slowly around at the main console; Lambert noticed that she looked right past the time-jump square itself. Not trained in peripheral vision techniques. But she looked a long time at the stasis square. They all did; outsiders were unduly fascinated by the idea that the whole building existed between time streams. Or maybe Her

Holiness merely objected to the fact that the Time Research Institute, like some larger but hardly richer institutions, was exempt from the all-world taxation that supported the Church. Real-estate outside time was also outside taxation.

The high priest said, "I cannot give permission for such a political disruption without understanding fully every possible detail. Tell me again."

Lambert hid a grin. The high priest did not need to hear it again. She knew the whole argument, had pored over it for days, most likely, with her advisers. And she would agree—why wouldn't she? It could only add to her power. Brill knew that. He was being asked to explain only to show that the high priest could force him to do it, again and again, until she—not he—decided the explanation was sufficient and the Church of the Holy Hostage issued a permanent hostage permit to hold one Anne Boleyn, of England Time Delta, for the altruistic purpose of preventing a demonstrable, Class One war.

Brill showed no outward recognition that he was being humbled. "Your Holiness, this woman is a fulcrum. The Rahvoli equations, developed in the last century by—"

"I know the Rahvoli equations," the high priest said. And smiled sweetly.

"Then Your Holiness knows that any person identified by the equations as a fulcrum is directly responsible for the course of history. Even if he or she seems powerless in local time. Mistress Boleyn was the second wife of Henry the Eighth of England. In order to marry her, he divorced his first wife, Katherine of Aragon, and in order to do that, he took all of England out of the Catholic Church. Protestantism was—"

"And what, again, was that?" Her Holiness said, and even Culhane glanced sideways at Lambert, appalled. The high priest was *playing*. With a research director. Lambert hid her smile. Did Culhane know that high seriousness opened one to the charge of pomposity? Probably not.

"Protestantism was another branch of Christianity," the director said patiently. So far, by refusing to be provoked, he was winning. "It was warlike, as was Catholicism. In 1642 various branches of Protestantism were contending for political power within England, as was a Catholic faction. King Charles was Catholic, in fact. Contention led to civil war. Thousands of people died fighting, starved to death, were hung as traitors, were tortured as betrayers..."

Lambert saw Her Holiness wince. She must hear this all the time, Lambert thought. What else was her office for? Yet the wince looked genuine.

Brill pressed his point. "Children were reduced to eating rats to survive. In Cornwall, rebels' hands and feet were cut off, gibbets were erected in market squares and men hung on them alive, and—"

"Enough," the high priest said. "This is why the Church exists. To promote the holy hostages that prevent war."

"And that is what we wish to do," Brill said swiftly, "in other time streams, now that our own has been brought to peace. In Stream Delta, which has only reached the sixteenth century—Your Holiness knows that each stream progresses at a different relative rate—"

The high priest made a gesture of impatience.

"—the woman Anne Boleyn is the fulcrum. If she can be taken hostage after the birth of her daughter Elizabeth, who will act throughout a very long reign to preserve peace, and before Henry declares the Act of Supremacy that opens the door to religious divisiveness in England, we can prevent great loss of life. The Rahvoli equations show a 79.8% probability that history will be changed in the direction of greater peace, right up through the following two centuries. Religious wars often—"

"There are other, bloodier religious wars to prevent than the English civil war."

"True, Your Holiness," the director said humbly. At least it looked like humility to Lambert. "But ours is a young science. Identifying other time streams, focusing on one, identifying historical fulcra—it is such a new science. We do what we can, in the name of peace."

Everyone in the room looked pious. Lambert hid a smile. In the name of peace—and of prestigious scientific research, attended by rich financial support and richer academic reputations.

"And it is peace we seek," Brill pressed, "as much as the Church itself does. With a permanent permit to take Anne Boleyn hostage, we can save countless lives in this other time stream, just as the Church preserves peace in our own."

The high priest played with the sleeve of her robe. Lambert could not see her face. But when she looked up, she was smiling.

"I'll recommend to the All-World Forum that your hostage permit be granted, Director. I will return in two months to make an official check on the holy hostage."

Brill, Lambert saw, didn't quite stop himself in time from frowning. "Two months? But with the entire solar system of hostages to supervise—"

"Two months, Director," Her Holiness said. "The week before the All-World Forum convenes to vote on revenue and taxation."

"I—"

"Now I would like to inspect the three holy hostages you already hold for the altruistic prevention of war."

Later, Culhane said to Lambert, "He did not explain it very well. It could have been made so much more urgent…it *is* urgent. Those bodies rotting in Cornwall…" He shuddered.

Lambert looked at him. "You care. You genuinely do."

He looked back at her in astonishment. "And you don't? You must, to work on this project!"

"I care," Lambert said. "But not like that."

"Like what?"

She tried to clarify it for him, for herself. "The bodies rotting…I see them. But it's not our own history—"

"What does that matter? They're still human!"

He was so earnest. Intensity burned on him like skin tinglers. Did Culhane even use skin tinglers? Fellow researchers spoke of him as an ascetic, giving all his energy, all his time to the project. A woman in his domicile had told Lambert he even lived chaste, doing a voluntary celibacy mission for the entire length of his research grant. Lambert had never met anyone who actually did that. It was intriguing.

She said, "Are you thinking of the priesthood once the project is over, Culhane?"

He flushed. Color mounted from the dyed cheeks, light blue since he had been promoted to project head, to pink on the fine skin of his shaved temples.

"I'm thinking of it."

"And doing a celibacy mission now?"

"Yes. Why?" His tone was belligerent: A celibacy mission was slightly old-fashioned. Lambert studied his body: tall, well-made, strong. Augments? Muscular, maybe. He had beautiful muscles.

"No reason," she said, bending back to her console until she heard him walk away.

The demon advanced. Anne, lying feeble on her curtained bed, tried to call out. But her voice would not come, and who would hear her anyway? The bedclothes were thick, muffling sound; her ladies would all have retired for the night, alone or otherwise; the guards would be drinking the ale Henry had provided all of London to celebrate Elizabeth's christening. And Henry...he was not beside her. She had failed him of his son.

"Be gone," she said weakly to the demon. It moved closer.

They had called her a witch. Because of her little sixth finger, because of the dog named Urian, because she had kept Henry under her spell so long without bedding him. But if I were really a witch, she thought, I could send this demon away. More: I could hold Henry, could keep him from watching that whey-faced Jane Seymour, could keep him in my bed...She was not a witch.

Therefore, it followed that there was nothing she could do about this demon. If it was come for her, it was come. If Satan, Master of Lies, was decided to have her, to punish her for taking the husband of another woman, and for...How much could demons know?

"This was all none of my wishing," she said aloud to the demon. "I wanted to marry someone else." The demon continued to advance.

Very well, then, let it take her. She would not scream. She never had—she prided herself on it. Not when they had told her she could not marry Harry Percy. Not when she had been sent home from the court, peremptorily and without explanation. Not when she had discovered the explanation: Henry wished to have her out of London so he could bed his latest mistress away from Katherine's eyes. She had not screamed when a crowd of whores had burst into the palace where she was supping, demanding Nan Bullen, who they said was one of them. She had escaped across the Thames in a barge, and not a cry had escaped her lips. They had admired her for her courage: Wyatt, Norris, Weston, Henry himself. She would not scream now.

The box of light grew larger as it approached. She had just time to say to it, "I have been God's faithful and true servant, and my husband, the king's," before it was upon her.

"The place where a war starts," Lambert said to the faces assembled below her in the Hall of Time, "is long before the first missile, or the first bullet, or the first spear."

She looked down at the faces. It was part of her responsibility as an intern researcher to teach a class of young, some of whom would become historians. The class was always taught in the Hall of Time. The expense was enormous: keeping the hall in stasis for nearly an hour, bringing the students in through the force field, activating all the squares at once. Her lecture would be replayed for them later, when they could pay attention to it. Lambert did not blame them for barely glancing at her now. Why should they? The walls of the circular room, which were only there in a virtual sense, were lined with squares that were not really there at all. The squares showed actual, local-time scenes from wars that had been there, were there now, somewhere, in someone's reality.

Men died writhing in the mud, arrows through intestines and neck and groin, at Agincourt.

Women lay flung across the bloody bodies of their children at Cawnpore.

In the hot sun the flies crawled thick upon the split faces of the heroes of Marathon.

Figures staggered, their faces burned off, away from Hiroshima.

Breathing bodies, their perfect faces untouched and their brains turned to mush by spekaline, sat in orderly rows under the ripped dome on Io-One.

Only one face turned toward Lambert, jerked as if on a string, a boy with wide violet eyes brimming with anguish. Lambert obligingly started again.

"The place where a war starts is long before the first missile, or the first bullet, or the first spear. There are always many forces causing a war: economic, political, religious, cultural. Nonetheless, it is the great historical discovery of our time that if you trace each of these back—through the records, through the eyewitness accounts, through the entire burden of data only Rahvoli equations can handle—you come to a fulcrum. A single event or act or person. It is like a decision tree with a thousand thousand generations of decisions: Somewhere there was one first yes/no. The place where the war started and where it could have been prevented.

"The great surprise of time rescue work has been how often that place was female.

"Men fought wars, when there were wars. Men controlled the gold and the weapons and the tariffs and sea rights and religions that have caused wars, and the men controlled the bodies of other men who did the actual fighting. But men are men. They acted at the fulcrum of history, but often what tipped their actions one way or another was what they loved. A woman. A child. She became the passive, powerless weight he chose to lift, and the balance tipped. She, not he, is the branching place, where the decision tree splits and the war begins."

The boy with the violet eyes was still watching her. Lambert stayed silent until he turned to watch the squares—which was the reason he had been brought here. Then she watched him. Anguished, passionate, able to feel what war meant—he might be a good candidate for the time rescue team when his preliminary studies were done. He reminded her a little of Culhane.

Who right now, as project head, was interviewing the new hostage, not lecturing to children.

Lambert stifled her jealousy. It was unworthy. And shortsighted: She remembered what this glimpse of human misery had meant to her three years ago, when she was an historian candidate. She had had nightmares for weeks. She had thought the event was pivotal to her life, a dividing point past which she would never be the same person again. How could she? She had been shown the depths to which humanity, without the Church of the Holy Hostage and the All-World Concordance, could descend. Burning eye sockets, mutilated genitals, a general who stood on a hill and said, "How I love to see the arms and legs fly!" It had been shattering. She had been shattered, as the orientation intended she should be.

The boy with the violet eyes was crying. Lambert wanted to step down from the platform and go to him. She wanted to put her arms around him and hold his head against her shoulder...but was that because of compassion, or was that because of his violet eyes?

She said silently to him, without leaving the podium, *You will be all right. Human beings are not as mutable as you think. When this is over, nothing permanent about you will have changed at all.*

Anne opened her eyes. Satan leaned over her.

His head was shaved, and he wore strange garb of an ugly blue-green. His cheeks were stained with dye. In one ear, metal glittered and swung. Anne crossed herself.

"Hello," Satan said, and the voice was not human.

She struggled to sit up; if this be damnation, she would not lie prone for it. Her heart hammered in her throat. But the act of sitting brought the Prince of Darkness into focus, and her eyes widened. He looked like a man. Painted, made ugly, hung around with metal boxes that could be tools of evil—but a man.

"My name is Culhane."

A man. And she had faced men. Bishops, nobles, Chancellor Wolsey. She had outfaced Henry, Prince of England and France, Defender of the Faith.

"Don't be frightened, Mistress Boleyn. I will explain to you where you are and how you came to be here."

She saw now that the voice came not from his mouth, although his mouth moved, but from the box hung around his neck. How could that be? Was there then a demon in the box? But then she realized something else, something real to hold on to.

"Do not call me Mistress Boleyn. Address me as Your Grace. I am the queen."

The something that moved behind his eyes convinced her, finally, that he was a mortal man. She was used to reading men's eyes. But why should this one look at her like that? With pity? With admiration?

She struggled to stand, rising off the low pallet. It was carved of good English oak. The room was paneled in dark wood and hung with tapestries of embroidered wool. Small-paned windows shed brilliant light over carved chairs, table, chest. On the table rested a writing desk and a lute. Reassured, Anne pushed down the heavy cloth of her nightshift and rose.

The man, seated on a low stool, rose, too. He was taller than Henry—she had never seen a man taller than Henry—and superbly muscled. A soldier? Fright fluttered again, and she put her hand to her throat. This man, watching her—watching her *throat*. Was he then an executioner? Was she under arrest, drugged and brought by some secret method into the Tower of London? Had someone brought evidence against her? Or was Henry that disappointed that she had not borne a son that he was eager to supplant her already?

As steadily as she could, Anne walked to the window.

The Tower Bridge did not lie beyond in the sunshine. Nor the river, nor the gabled roofs of Greenwich Palace. Instead there was a sort of yard, with huge beasts of metal growling softly. On the grass naked young men and women jumped up and down, waving their arms, running in place and smiling and sweating as if they did not know either that they were uncovered or crazed.

Anne took firm hold of the windowsill. It was slippery in her hands, and she saw that it was not wood at all but some material made to resemble wood. She closed her eyes, then opened them. She was a queen. She had fought hard to become a queen, defending a virtue nobody believed she still had, against a man who claimed that to destroy that virtue was love. She had won, making the crown the price of her virtue. She had conquered a king, brought down a chancellor of England, outfaced a pope. She would not show fear to this executioner in this place of the damned, whatever it was.

She turned from the window, her head high. "Please begin your explanation, Master…"

"Culhane."

"Master Culhane. We are eager to hear what you have to say. And we do not like waiting."

She swept aside her long nightdress as if it were court dress and seated herself in the not-wooden chair carved like a throne.

"I am a hostage," Anne repeated. "In a time that has not yet happened."

From beside the window, Lambert watched. She was fascinated. Anne Boleyn had, according to Culhane's report, listened in silence to the entire explanation of the time rescue, that explanation so carefully crafted and revised a dozen times to fit what the sixteenth-century mind could understand of the twenty-second. Queen Anne had not become hysterical. She had not cried, nor fainted, nor professed disbelief. She had asked no questions. When Culhane had finished, she had requested, calmly and with staggering dignity, to see the ruler of this place, with his ministers. Toshio Brill, watching on monitor because the wisdom was that at first new hostages would find it easier to deal with one consistent researcher, had hastily summoned Lambert and two others. They had all dressed in the floor-length robes used for grand academic ceremonies and never else. And they had marched solemnly into the ersatz sixteenth-century room, bowing their heads.

Only their heads. No curtsies. Anne Boleyn was going to learn that no one curtsied anymore.

Covertly Lambert studied her, their fourth time hostage, so different from the other three. She had not risen from her chair, but even seated she was astonishingly tiny. Thin, delicate bones, great dark eyes, masses of silky black hair loose on her white nightdress. She was not pretty by the standards of this century; she had not even been counted pretty by the standards of her own. But she was compelling. Lambert had to give her that.

"And I am prisoner here," Anne Boleyn said. Lambert turned up her translator; the words were just familiar, but the accent so strange she could not catch them without electronic help.

"Not prisoner," the director said. "Hostage."

"Lord Brill, if I cannot leave, then I am a prisoner. Let us not mince words. I cannot leave this castle?"

"You cannot."

"Please address me as 'Your Grace.' Is there to be a ransom?"

"No, Your Grace. But because of your presence here thousands of men will live who would have otherwise died."

With a shock, Lambert saw Anne shrug; the deaths of thousands of men evidently did not interest her. It was true, then. They really were moral barbarians, even the women. The students should see this. That small shrug said more than all the battles viewed in squares. Lambert felt her sympathy for the abducted woman lessen, a physical sensation like the emptying of a bladder, and was relieved to feel it. It meant she, Lambert, still had her own moral sense.

"How long must I stay here?"

"For life, Your Grace," Brill said bluntly.

Anne made no reaction; her control was aweing.

"And how long will that be, Lord Brill?"

"No person knows the length of his or her life, Your Grace."

"But if you can read the future, as you claim, you must know what the length of mine would have been."

Lambert thought: We must not underestimate her. This hostage is not like the last one.

Brill said, with the same bluntness that honored Anne's comprehension—did she realize that?—"If we had not brought you here, you would have died May 19, 1536."

"How?"

"It does not matter. You are no longer part of that future, and so now events there will—"

"How?"

Brill didn't answer.

Anne Boleyn rose and walked to the window, absurdly small, Lambert thought, in the trailing nightdress. Over her shoulder she said, "Is this castle in England?"

"No," Brill said. Lambert saw him exchange glances with Culhane.

"In France?"

"It is not in any place on Earth," Brill said, "although it can be entered from three places on Earth. It is outside of time."

She could not possibly have understood, but she said nothing, only went on staring out the window. Over her shoulder Lambert saw the exercise court, empty now, and the antimatter power generators. Two technicians crawled over them with a robot monitor. What did Anne Boleyn make of them?

"God alone knows if I had merited death," Anne said. Lambert saw Culhane start.

Brill stepped forward. "Your Grace—"

"Leave me now," she said without turning.

They did. Of course, she would be monitored constantly—everything from brain scans to the output of her bowels. Although she would never know this. But if suicide was in that life-defying mind, it would not be possible. If Her Holiness ever learned of the suicide of a time hostage... Lambert's last glimpse before the door closed was of Anne Boleyn's back, still by the window, straight as a spear as she gazed out at antimatter power generators in a building in permanent stasis.

"Culhane, meeting in ten minutes," Brill said. Lambert guessed the time lapse was to let the director change into working clothes. Toshio Brill had come away from the interview with Anne Boleyn somehow diminished. He even looked shorter, although shouldn't her small stature have instead augmented his?

Culhane stood still in the corridor outside Anne's locked room (would she try the door?). His face was turned away from Lambert's. Lambert said, "Culhane...you jumped a moment in there. When she said God alone knew if she had merited death."

"It was what she said at her trial," Culhane said. "When the verdict was announced. Almost the exact words."

He still had not moved so much as a muscle of that magnificent body. Lambert said, probing, "You found her impressive, then. Despite her scrawniness, and beyond the undeniable pathos of her situation."

He looked at her then, his eyes blazing: Culhane, the research engine. "I found her magnificent."

She never smiled. That was one of the things she knew they remarked upon among themselves: She had overheard them in the walled garden. *Anne Boleyn never smiles.* Alone, they did not call her Queen Anne, or Her Grace, or even the Marquis of Rochford, the title Henry had conferred upon her, the only female peeress in her own right in all of England. No, they called her Anne Boleyn, as if the marriage to Henry had never happened, as if she had never borne Elizabeth. And they said she never smiled.

What cause was there to smile, in this place that was neither life nor death?

Anne stitched deftly at a piece of amber velvet. She was not badly treated. They had given her a servant, cloth to make dresses—she had always been clever with a needle, and the skill had not deserted her when she could afford to order any dresses she chose. They had given her books, the writing Latin but the pictures curiously flat, with no raised ink or painting. They let her go into any unlocked room in the castle, out to the gardens, into the yards. She was a holy hostage.

When the amber velvet gown was finished, she put it on. They let her have a mirror. A lute. Writing paper and quills. Whatever she asked for, as generous as Henry had been in the early days of his passion, when he had divided her from her love Harry Percy and had kept her loving hostage to his own fancy.

Cages came in many sizes. Many shapes. And, if what Master Culhane and the Lady Mary Lambert said was true, in many times.

"I am not a lady," Lady Lambert had protested. She needn't have bothered. Of course she was not a lady—she was a commoner, like the others, and so perverted was this place that the woman sounded insulted to be called a lady. Lambert did not like her, Anne knew, although she had not yet found out why. The woman was unsexed, like all of them, working on her books and machines all day, exercising naked with men who thus no more looked at their bodies than they would those of fellow soldiers in the roughest camp. So it pleased Anne to call Lambert a lady when she did not want to be one, as Anne was now so many things she had never wanted to be. "Anne Boleyn." Who never smiled.

"I will create you a Lady," she said to Lambert. "I confer on you the rank of baroness. Who will gainsay me? I am the queen, and in this place there is no king."

And Mary Lambert had stared at her with the unsexed bad manners of a common drab.

Anne knotted her thread and cut it with silver scissors. The gown was finished. She slipped it over her head and struggled with the buttons in the back, rather than call the stupid girl who was her servant. The girl could not even dress hair. Anne smoothed her hair herself, then looked critically at her reflection in the fine mirror they had brought her.

For a woman a month and a half from childbed, she looked strong. They had put medicines in her food, they said. Her complexion, that creamy dark skin that seldom varied in color, was well set off by the amber velvet. She had often worn amber, or tawny. Her hair, loose since she had no headdress and did not know how to make one, streamed over her shoulders. Her hands, long and slim despite the tiny extra finger, carried a rose brought to her by Master Culhane. She toyed with the rose to show off the beautiful hands, and lifted her head high.

She was going to have an audience with Her Holiness, a female pope. And she had a request to make.

"She will ask, Your Holiness, to be told the future. Her future, the one Anne Boleyn experienced in her own time stream, after the point we took her hostage to ours. And the future of England." Brill's face had darkened; Lambert could see that he hated this. To forewarn his political rival that a hostage would complain about her treatment. A *hostage*, that person turned sacred object through the sacrifice of personal freedom to global peace. When Tullio Amaden Koyushi had been hostage from Mars Three to the Republic of China, he had told the Church official in charge of his case that he was not being allowed sufficient exercise. The resulting intersystem furor had lost the Republic of China two trade contracts, both important. There was no other way to maintain the necessary reverence for the hostage political system. The Church of the Holy Hostage was powerful because it must be, if the solar system was to stay at peace. Brill knew that.

So did Her Holiness.

She wore full state robes today, gorgeous with hundreds of tiny mirrors sent to her by the grateful across all worlds. Her head was newly shaved. Perfect, synthetic jewels glittered in her ears. Listening to Brill's apology-in-advance, Her Holiness smiled. Lambert saw the smile, and even across the room she felt Brill's polite, concealed frustration.

"Then if this is so," Her Holiness said, "why cannot Lady Anne Boleyn be told her future? Hers and England's?"

Lambert knew that the high priest already knew the answer. She wanted to make Brill say it.

Brill said, "It is not thought wise, Your Holiness. If you remember, we did that once before."

"Ah, yes, your last hostage. I will see her, too, of course, on this visit. Has Queen Helen's condition improved?"

"No," Brill said shortly.

"And no therapeutic brain drugs or electronic treatments have helped? She still is insane from the shock of finding herself with us?"

"Nothing has helped."

"You understand how reluctant I was to let you proceed with another time rescue at all," Her Holiness said, and even Lambert stifled a gasp. The high priest did not make those determinations; only the All-World Forum could authorize or disallow a hostage-taking—across space or time. The Church of the Holy Hostage was responsible only for the inspection and continuation of permits granted by the Forum. For the high priest to claim political power she did not possess...

The director's eyes gleamed angrily. But before he could reply, the door opened and Culhane escorted in Anne Boleyn.

Lambert pressed her lips together tightly. The woman had sewn herself a gown, a sweeping, ridiculous confection of amber velvet so tight at the breasts and waist she must hardly be able to breathe. How had women conducted their lives in such trappings? The dress narrowed her waist to nearly nothing; above the square neckline her collarbones were delicate as a bird's. Culhane hovered beside her, huge and protective. Anne walked straight to the high priest, knelt, and raised her face.

She was looking for a ring to kiss.

Lambert didn't bother to hide her smile. A high priest wore no jewelry except earrings, ever. The pompous little hostage had made a social error, no doubt significant in her own time.

Anne smiled up at Her Holiness, the first time anyone had seen her smile at all. It changed her face, lighting it with mischief, lending luster to the great dark eyes. A phrase came to Lambert, penned by the poet Thomas Wyatt to describe his cousin Anne: *And wild for to hold, though I seem tame.*

Anne said, in that sprightly yet aloof manner that Lambert was coming to associate with her, "It seems, Your Holiness, that we have reached for what is not there. But the lack is ours, not yours, and we hope it will not be repeated in the request we come to make of you."

Direct. Graceful, even through the translator and despite the ludicrous imperial plural. Lambert glanced at Culhane, who was gazing down at Anne as at a rare and fragile flower. How could he? That skinny body, without muscle tone, let alone augments, that plain face, the mole on her neck...This was not the sixteenth century. Culhane was a fool.

As Thomas Wyatt had been. And Sir Harry Percy. And Henry, king of England. All caught not by beauty but by that strange elusive charm.

Her Holiness laughed. "Stand up, Your Grace. We don't kneel to officials here." *Your Grace.* The high priest always addressed hostages by the honorifics of their own state, but in this case it could only impede Anne's adjustment.

And what do I care about her adjustment? Lambert jeered at herself. *Nothing. What I care about is Culhane's infatuation, and only because he rejected me first.* Rejection, it seemed, was a great whetter of appetite—in any century.

Anne rose. Her Holiness said, "I'm going to ask you some questions, Your Grace. You are free to answer any way you wish. My function is to ensure that you are well treated and that the noble science of the prevention of war, which has made you a holy hostage, is also well served. Do you understand?"

"We do."

"Have you received everything you need for your material comfort?"

"Yes," Anne said.

"Have you received everything you've requested for your mental comfort? Books, objects of any description, company?"

"No," Anne said. Lambert saw Brill stiffen.

Her Holiness said, "No?"

"It is necessary for the comfort of our mind—and for our material comfort as well—to understand our situation as fully as possible. Any rational creature requires such understanding to reach ease of mind."

Brill said, "You have been told everything related to your situation. What you ask is to know about situations that now, because you are here, will never happen."

"Situations that *have* happened, Lord Brill, else no one could know of them. You could not."

"In your time stream they will not happen," Brill said. Lambert could hear the suppressed anger in his voice and wondered if the high priest could. Anne Boleyn couldn't know how serious it was to be charged by Her Holiness with a breach of hostage treatment. If Brill was ambitious—and why wouldn't he be?—such charges could hurt his future.

Anne said swiftly, "Our time is now your time. You have made it so. The situation was none of our choosing. And if your time is now ours, then surely we are entitled to the knowledge that accompanies our time." She looked at the high priest. "For the comfort of our mind."

Brill said, "Your Holiness—"

"No, Queen Anne is correct. Her argument is valid. You will designate a qualified researcher to answer any questions she has—any at all—about the life she might have had, or the course of events England took when the queen did not become a sacred hostage."

Brill nodded stiffly.

"Good-bye, Your Grace," Her Holiness said. "I shall return in two weeks to inspect your situation again."

Two weeks? The high priest was not due for another inspection for six months. Lambert glanced at Culhane to see his reaction to this blatant political fault-hunting, but he was gazing at the floor, to which Anne Boleyn had sunk in another of her embarrassing curtsies, the amber velvet of her skirts spread around her like gold.

They sent a commoner to explain her life to her, and the life she had lost. A commoner. And he had as well the nerve to be besotted with her. Anne always knew. She tolerated such fellows, like that upstart musician Smeaton, when they were useful to her. If this Master Culhane dared to make any sort of declaration, he would receive the same sort of snub Smeaton once had. Inferior persons should not look to be spoken to as noblemen.

He sat on a straight-backed chair in her tower room, looking humble enough, while Anne sat in the great carved chair with her hands tightly folded to keep them from shaking.

"Tell me how I came to die in 1536." God's blood! Had ever before there been such a sentence uttered?

Culhane said, "You were beheaded. Found guilty of treason." He stopped and flushed.

She knew, then. In a queen, there was one cause for a charge of treason. "He charged me with adultery. To remove me, so he could marry again."

"Yes."

"To Jane Seymour."

"Yes."

"Had I first given him a son?"

"No," Culhane said.

"Did Jane Seymour give him a son?"

"Yes. Edward the Sixth. But he died at sixteen, a few years after Henry."

There was vindication in that, but not enough to stem the sick feeling in her gut. Treason. And no son...There must have been more than desire for the Seymour bitch. Henry must have hated her. Adultery...

"With whom?"

Again the oaf flushed. "With five men, Your Grace. Everyone knew the charges were false, created merely to excuse his own cuckoldry—even your enemies admitted such."

"Who were they?"

"Sir Henry Morris. Sir Francis Weston. William Brereton. Mark Smeaton. And...and your brother George."

For a moment she thought she would be sick. Each name fell like a blow, the last like the ax itself. George. Her beloved brother, so talented at music, so high-spirited and witty...Henry Norris, the king's friend. Weston and Brereton, young and lighthearted but always, to her, respectful and careful...and Mark Smeaton, the oaf made courtier because he could play the virginals.

The long, beautiful hands clutched the sides of the chair. But the moment passed, and she could say with dignity, "They denied the charges?"

"Smeaton confessed, but he was tortured into it. The others denied the charges completely. Henry Norris offered to defend your honor in single combat."

Yes, that was like Harry: so old-fashioned, so principled. She said, "They all died." It was not a question: If she had died for treason, they would have, too. And not alone; no one died alone. "Who else?"

Culhane said, "Maybe we should wait for the rest of this, Your—"

"Who else? My father?"

"No. Sir Thomas More, John Fisher—"

"More? For my..." She could not say *adultery*.

"Because he would not swear to the Oath of Supremacy, which made the king and not the pope head of the church in England. That act opened the door to religious dissension in England."

"It did not. The heretics were already strong in England. History cannot fault that to me!"

"Not as strong as they would become," Culhane said almost apologetically. "Queen Mary was known as Bloody Mary for burning heretics who used the Act of Supremacy to break from— Your Grace! Are you all right...Anne?"

"Do not touch me," she said. Queen Mary. Then her own daughter Elizabeth had been disinherited, or killed...Had Henry become so warped that he would kill a child? His own child? Unless he had come to believe…

She whispered, "Elizabeth?"

Comprehension flooded his eye. "Oh. No, Anne! No! Mary ruled first, as the elder, but when she died heirless, Elizabeth was only twenty-five. Elizabeth became the greatest ruler England had ever known! She ruled for forty-four years, and under her England became a great power."

The greatest ruler. Her baby Elizabeth. Anne could feel her hands unknotting on the ugly artificial chair. Henry had not repudiated Elizabeth, nor had her killed. She had become the greatest ruler England had ever known.

Culhane said, "This is why we thought it best not to tell you all this."

She said coldly, "I will be the judge of that."

"I'm sorry." He sat stiffly, hands dangling awkwardly between his knees. He looked like a plowman, like that oaf Smeaton…She remembered what Henry had done, and rage returned.

"I stood accused. With five men. With George. And the charges were false." Something in his face changed. Anne faced him steadily. "Unless… were they false, Master Culhane? You who know so much of history. Does history say…" She could not finish. To beg for history's judgment from a man like this… No humiliation had ever been greater. Not even the Spanish ambassador, referring to her as "the concubine," had ever humiliated her so.

Culhane said carefully, "History is silent on the subject, Your Grace. What your conduct was…would have been…is known only to you."

"As it should be. It was…would have been…mine," she said viciously, mocking his tones perfectly. He looked at her like a wounded puppy, like that lout Smeaton when she had snubbed him. "Tell me this, Master Culhane. You have changed history as it would have been, you tell me. Will my daughter Elizabeth still become the greatest ruler England has ever seen—in *my* 'time stream'? Or will that be altered, too, by your quest for peace at any cost?"

"We don't know. I explained to you… We can only watch your time stream now as it unfolds. It had only reached October 1533, which is why after analyzing our own history we—"

"You have explained all that. It will be sixty years from now before you know if my daughter will still be great. Or if you have changed that as well by abducting me and ruining my life."

"Abducting! You were going to be killed! Accused, beheaded—"

"And you have prevented that." She rose, in a greater fury than ever she had been with Henry, with Wolsey, with anyone. "You have also robbed me of my remaining three years as surely as Henry would have robbed me of my old age. And you have mayhap robbed my daughter as well, as Henry sought to do with his Seymour-get prince. So what is the difference between you, Master Culhane, that you are a saint and Henry a villain? He held me in the Tower until my soul could be commended to God; you hold me here in this castle you say I can never leave, where time does not exist, and mayhap God neither. Who has done me the worse injury? Henry gave me the crown. You—all you and my Lord Brill have given me is a living death, and then given my daughter's crown a danger and uncertainty that without you she would not have known! Who has done to Elizabeth and me the worse turn? And in the name of preventing war! You have made war upon *me*! Get out, get out!"

"Your—"

"Get out! I never want to see you again! If I am in hell, let there be one less demon!"

Lambert slipped from her monitor to run down the corridor. Culhane flew from the room; behind him the sound of something heavy struck the door. Culhane slumped against it, his face pasty around his cheek dye. Lambert could almost find it in herself to pity him. Almost.

She said softly, "I told you so."

"She's like a wild thing."

"You knew she could be. It's documented enough, Culhane. I've put a suicide watch on her."

"Yes. Good. I...she was like a wild thing."

Lambert peered at him. "You still want her! After that!"

That sobered him; he straightened and looked at her coldly. "She is a holy hostage, Lambert."

"I remember that. Do you?"

"Don't insult me, intern."

He moved angrily away; she caught his sleeve. "Culhane—don't be angry. I only meant that the sixteenth century was so different from our own, but—"

"Do you think I don't know that? I was doing historical research while you were learning to read, Lambert. Don't instruct me."

He stalked off. Lambert bit down hard on her own fury and stared at Anne Boleyn's closed door. No sound came from behind it. To the soundless door she finished her sentence: "—but some traps don't change."

The door didn't answer. Lambert shrugged. It had nothing to do with her. She didn't care what happened to Anne Boleyn, in this century or that other one. Or to Culhane, either. Why should she? There were other men. She was no Henry VIII, to bring down her world for passion. What was the good of being a time researcher if you could not even learn from times past?

She leaned thoughtfully against the door, trying to remember the name of the beautiful boy in her orientation lecture, the one with the violet eyes.

She was still there, thinking, when Toshio Brill called a staff meeting to announce, his voice stiff with anger, that Her Holiness of the Church of the Holy Hostage had filed a motion with the All-World Forum that the Time Research Institute, because of the essentially reverent nature of the time rescue program, be removed from administration by the Forum and placed instead under the direct control of the Church.

She had to think. It was important to think, as she had thought through her denial of Henry's ardor, and her actions when that ardor waned. Thought was all.

She could not return to her London, to Elizabeth. They had told her that. But did she know beyond doubt that it was true?

Anne left her apartments. At the top of the stairs she usually took to the garden, she instead turned and opened another door. It opened easily. She walked along a different corridor. Apparently even now no one was going to stop her.

And if they did, what could they do to her? They did not use the scaffold or the rack; she had determined this from talking to that oaf Culhane and that huge ungainly woman, Lady Mary Lambert. They did not believe in violence, in punishment, in death. (How could you not believe in death? Even they must one day die.) The most they could do to her was shut her up in her rooms, and there the female pope would come to see she was well treated.

Essentially they were powerless.

The corridor was lined with doors, most set with small windows. She peered in: rooms with desks and machines, rooms without desks and machines, rooms with people seated around a table talking, kitchens, still rooms. No one stopped her. At the end of the corridor she came to a room without a window and tried the door. It was locked, but as she stood there, her hand still on the knob, the door opened from within.

"Lady Anne! Oh!"

Could no one in this accursed place get her name right? The woman who stood there was clearly a servant, although she wore the same ugly gray-green tunic as everyone else. Perhaps, like Lady Mary, she was really an apprentice. She was of no interest, but behind her was the last thing Anne expected to see in this place: a child.

She pushed past the servant and entered the room. It was a little boy, his dress strange but clearly a uniform of some sort. He had dark eyes, curling dark hair, a bright smile. How old? Perhaps four. There was an air about him that was unmistakable; she would have wagered her life this child was royal.

"Who are you, little one?"

He answered her with an outpouring of a language she did not know. The servant scrambled to some device on the wall; in a moment Culhane stood before her.

"You said you didn't want to see me, Your Grace. But I was closest to answer Kiti's summons..."

Anne looked at him. It seemed to her that she looked clear through him, to all that he was: Desire, and pride of his pitiful strange learning, and smugness of his holy mission that had brought her life to wreck. Hers, and perhaps Elizabeth's as well. She saw Culhane's conviction, shared by Lord Director Brill and even by such as Lady Mary, that what they did was right because they did it. She knew that look well: It had been Cardinal Wolsey's, Henry's right-hand man and chancellor of England, the man who had advised Henry to separate Anne from Harry Percy. And advised Henry against marrying her. Until she, Anne Boleyn, upstart Tom Boleyn's powerless daughter, had turned Henry against Wolsey and had the cardinal brought to trial. She.

In that minute she made her decision.

"I was wrong, Master Culhane. I spoke in anger. Forgive me." She smiled and held out her hand, and she had the satisfaction of watching Culhane turn color.

How old was he? Not in his first youth. But neither had Henry.

He said, "Of course, Your Grace. Kiti said you talked to the Tsarevitch."

She made a face, still smiling at him. She had often mocked Henry thus. Even Harry Percy, so long ago, a lifetime ago… No. Two lifetimes ago. "The what?"

"The Tsarevitch." He indicated the child.

Was the dye on his face permanent, or would it wash off?

She said, not asking, "He is another time hostage. He, too, in his small person, prevents a war."

Culhane nodded, clearly unsure of her mood. Anne looked wonderingly at the child, then winningly at Culhane. "I would have you tell me about him. What language does he speak? Who is he?"

"Russian. He is—was—the future emperor. He suffers from a terrible disease: You called it the bleeding sickness. Because his mother, the empress, was so driven with worry over him, she fell under the influence of a holy man who led her to make some disastrous decisions while she was acting for her husband, the emperor, who was away at war."

Anne said, "And the bad decisions brought about another war."

"They made more bloody than necessary a major rebellion."

"You prevent rebellions as well as wars? Rebellions against a monarchy?"

"Yes, it—history did not go in the direction of monarchies."

That made little sense. How could history go other than in the direction of those who were divinely anointed, those who held the power? Royalty won. In the end, they always won.

But there could be many casualties before the end.

She said, with that combination of liquid dark gaze and aloof body that had so intrigued Henry—and Norris, and Wyatt, and even presumptuous Smeaton, God damn his soul—"I find I wish to know more about this child and his country's history. Will you tell me?"

"Yes," Culhane said. She caught the nature of his smile: relieved, still uncertain how far he had been forgiven, eager to find out. Familiar, all so familiar.

She was careful not to let her body touch his as they passed through the doorway. But she went first, so he could catch the smell of her hair.

"Master Culhane—you are listed on the demon machine as 'M. Culhane.'"

"The…oh, the computer. I didn't know you ever looked at one."

"I did. Through a window."

"It's not a demon, Your Grace."

She let the words pass; what did she care what it was? But his tone told her something. He liked reassuring her. In this world where women did the same work as men and where female bodies were to be seen uncovered in the exercise yard so often that even turning your head to look must become a bore, this oaf nonetheless liked reassuring her.

She said, "What does the 'M' mean?"

He smiled. "Michael. Why?"

As the door closed, the captive royal child began to wail.

Anne smiled, too. "An idle fancy. I wondered if it stood for Mark."

"What argument has the Church filed with the All-World Forum?" a senior researcher asked.

Brill said irritably, as if it were an answer, "Where is Mahjoub?"

Lambert spoke up promptly. "He is with Helen of Troy, Director, and the doctor. The queen had another seizure last night." Enzio Mahjoub had been the unfortunate project head for their last time rescue.

Brill ran his hand over the back of his neck. His skull needed shaving, and his cheek dye was sloppily applied. He said, "Then we will begin without Mahjoub. The argument of Her Holiness is that the primary function of this institute is no longer pure time research but practical application, and that the primary practical application is time rescue. As such, we exist to take hostages, and thus should come under the direct control of the Church of the Holy Hostage. Her secondary argument is that the time hostages are not receiving treatment up to intersystem standards as specified by the All-World Accord of 2154."

Lambert's eyes darted around the room. Cassia Kohambu, project head for the institute's greatest success, sat up straight, looking outraged. "Our hostages are—on what are these charges allegedly based?"

Brill said, "No formal charges as yet. Instead, Her Holiness has requested an investigation. She claims we have hundreds of potential hostages pinpointed by the Rahvoli equations, and the ones we have chosen do not meet standards for either internal psychic stability or benefit accrued to the hostages themselves, as specified in the All-World Accord. We have chosen to please ourselves, with flagrant disregard for the welfare of the hostages."

"Flagrant disregard!" It was Culhane, already on his feet. Beneath the face dye, his cheeks flamed. Lambert eyed him carefully. "How can Her Holiness charge flagrant disregard when without us the Tsarevitch Alexis would have been in constant pain from hemophiliac episodes, Queen Helen would have been abducted and raped, Herr Hitler blown up in an underground bunker, and Queen Anne Boleyn beheaded!"

Brill said bluntly, "Because the Tsarevitch cries constantly for his mother, the Lady Helen is mad, and Mistress Boleyn tells the church she has been made war upon!"

Well, Lambert thought, that still left Herr Hitler. She was just as appalled as anyone at Her Holiness's charges, but Culhane had clearly violated both good manners and good sense. Brill never appreciated being upstaged.

Brill continued, "An investigative committee from the All-World Forum will arrive here next month. It will be small: Delegates Soshiru, Vlakhav, and Tullio. In three days the institute staff will meet again at oh-seven hundred, and by that time I want each project group to have prepared an argument in favor of the hostage you hold. Use the prepermit justifications, including all the mathematical models, but go far beyond that in documenting benefits to the hostages themselves since they arrived here. Are there any questions?"

Only one, Lambert thought. She stood. "Director—were the three delegates who will investigate us chosen by the All-World Forum or requested by Her Holiness? To whom do they already owe their allegiance?"

Brill looked annoyed. He said austerely, "I think we can rely upon the All-World delegates to file a fair report, Intern Lambert," and Lambert lowered her eyes. Evidently she still had much to learn. The question should not have been asked aloud.

Would Mistress Boleyn have known that?

Anne took the hand of the little boy. "Come, Alexis," she said. "We walk now."

The prince looked up at her. How handsome he was, with his thick, curling hair and beautiful eyes almost as dark as her own. If she had given Henry such a child... She pushed the thought away. She spoke to Alexis in her rudimentary Russian, without using the translator box hung like a peculiarly ugly pendant around her neck. He answered with a stream of words she couldn't follow and she waited for the box to translate.

"Why should we walk? I like it here in the garden."

"The garden is very beautiful," Anne agreed. "But I have something interesting to show you."

Alexis trotted beside her obediently then. It had not been hard to win his trust—had no one here ever passed time with children? Wash off the scary cheek paint, play for him songs on the lute—an instrument he could understand, not like the terrifying sounds coming without musicians from yet another box—learn a few phrases of his language. She had always been good at languages.

Anne led the child through the far gate of the walled garden, into the yard. Machinery hummed; naked men and women "exercised" together on the grass. Alexis watched them curiously, but Anne ignored them. Servants. Her long, full skirts, tawny silk, trailed on the ground.

At the far end of the yard she started down the short path to that other gate, the one that ended at nothing.

Queen Isabella of Spain, Henry had told Anne once, had sent an expedition of sailors to circumnavigate the globe. They were supposed to find a faster way to India. They had not done so, but neither had they fallen off the edge of the world, which many had prophesied for them. Anne had not shown much interest in the story, because Isabella had, after all, been Katherine's mother. The edge of the world.

The gate ended with a wall of nothing. Nothing to see, or smell, or taste—Anne had tried. To the touch the wall was solid enough, and faintly tingly. A "force field," Culhane said. Out of time as we experience it; out of space. The gate, one of three, led to a place called Upper Slib, in what had once been Egypt.

Anne lifted Alexis. He was heavier than even a month ago; since she had been attending him every day he had begun to eat better, play more, cease crying for his mother. Except at night. "Look, Alexis, a gate. Touch it."

The little boy did, then drew back his hand at the tingling. Anne laughed, and after a moment Alexis laughed, too.

The alarms sounded.

"Why, Your Grace?" Culhane said. "Why again?"

"I wished to see if the gate was unlocked," Anne said coolly. "We both wished to see." This was a lie. She knew it. Did he? Not yet, perhaps.

"I told you, Your Grace, it is not a gate that can be left locked or unlocked, as you understand the terms. It must be activated by the stasis square."

"Then do so; the prince and I wish for an outing."

Culhane's eyes darkened; each time he was in more anguish. And each time, he came running. However much he might wish to avoid her, commanding his henchmen to talk to her most of the time, he must come when there was an emergency because he was her gaoler, appointed by Lord Brill. So much had Anne discovered in a month of careful trials. He said now, "I told you, Your Grace, you can't move past the force field, no more than I could move into your palace at Greenwich. In the time stream beyond that gate—*my* time stream—you don't exist. The second you crossed the force field you'd disintegrate into nothingness."

Nothingness again. To Alexis she said sadly in Russian, "He will never let us out. Never, never."

The child began to cry. Anne held him closer, looking reproachfully at Culhane, who was shifting toward anger. She caught him just before the shift was complete, befuddling him with unlooked-for wistfulness: "It is just that there is so little we can do here, in this time we do not belong. You can understand that, can you not, Master Culhane? Would it not be the same for you, in my court of England?"

Emotions warred on his face. Anne put her free hand gently on his arm. He looked down: the long, slim fingers with their delicate tendons, the tawny silk against his drab uniform. He choked out, "Anything in my power, anything within the rules, Your Grace..."

She had not yet gotten him to blurt out "Anne," as he had the day she'd thrown a candlestick after him at the door.

She removed her hand, shifted the sobbing child against her neck, spoke so softly he could not hear her.

He leaned forward, toward her. "What did you say, Your Grace?"

"Would you come again tonight to accompany my lute on your guitar? For Alexis and me?"

Culhane stepped back. His eyes looked trapped.

"Please, Master Culhane?"

Culhane nodded.

Lambert stared at the monitor. It showed the hospital suite, barred windows and low white pallets, where Helen of Troy was housed. The queen sat quiescent on the floor, as she usually did, except for the brief and terrifying periods when she erupted, shrieking and tearing at her incredible hair. There had never been a single coherent word in the eruptions, not since the first moment they had told Helen where she was, and why. Or maybe that fragile mind, already quivering under the strain of her affair with Paris, had snapped too completely even to hear them. Helen, Lambert thought, was no Anne Boleyn.

Anne sat close to the mad Greek queen, her silk skirts overlapping Helen's white tunic, her slender body leaning so far forward that her hair, too, mingled with Helen's, straight black waterfall with masses of springing black curls. Before she could stop herself, Lambert had run her hand over her own shaved head.

What was Mistress Anne trying to say to Helen? The words were too low for the microphones to pick up, and the double curtain of hair hid Anne's lips. Yet Lambert was as certain as death that Anne was talking. And Helen, quiescent—was she nonetheless hearing? What could it matter if she were, words in a tongue that from her point of view would not exist for another two millennia?

Yet the Boleyn woman visited her every day, right after she left the Tsarevitch. How good was Anne, from a time almost as barbaric as Helen's own, at nonverbal coercion of the crazed?

Culhane entered, glanced at the monitor, and winced.

Lambert said levelly, "You're a fool, Culhane."

He didn't answer.

"You go whenever she summons. You—"

He suddenly strode across the room, two strides at a time. Grabbing Lambert, he pulled her from her chair and yanked her to her feet. For an astonished moment she thought he was actually going to hit her—researchers *hitting* each other. She tensed to slug him back. But abruptly he dropped her, giving a little shove so that she tumbled gracelessly back into her chair.

"You feel like a fat stone."

Lambert stared at him. Indifferently he activated his own console and began work. Something rose in her, so cold the vertebrae of her back felt fused in ice. Stiffly she rose from the chair, left the room, and walked along the corridor.

A fat stone. Heavy, stolid yet doughy, the flesh yielding like a slug or a maggot. Bulky, without grace, without beauty, almost without individuality, as stones were all alike. A fat stone.

Anne Boleyn was just leaving Helen's chamber. In the corridor, back to the monitor, Lambert faced her. Her voice was low like a subterranean growl. "Leave him alone."

Anne looked at her coolly. She did not ask whom Lambert meant.

"Don't you know you are watched every minute? That you can't so much as use your chamber pot without being taped? How do you ever expect to get him to your bed? Or to do anything with poor Helen?"

Anne's eyes widened. She said loudly, "Even when I use the chamber pot? Watched? Have I not even the privacy of the beasts in the field?"

Lambert clenched her fists. Anne was acting. Someone had already told her, or she had guessed, about the surveillance. Lambert could see that she was acting—but not why. A part of her mind noted coldly that she had never wanted to kill anyone before. So this, finally, was what it felt like, all those emotions she had researched throughout time: fury and jealousy and the desire to destroy. The emotions that started wars.

Anne cried, even more loudly, "I had been better had you never told me!" and rushed toward her own apartments.

Lambert walked slowly back to her work area, a fat stone.

Anne lay on the grass between the two massive power generators. It was a poor excuse for grass; although green enough, it had no smell. No dew formed on it, not even at night. Culhane had explained that it was bred to withstand disease, and that no dew formed because the air had little moisture. He explained, too, that the night was as man-bred as the grass; there was no natural night here. Henry would have been highly interested in such things; she was not. But she had listened carefully, as she listened to everything Michael said.

She lay completely still, waiting. Eventually the head of a researcher thrust around the corner of the towering machinery: a purposeful thrust. "Your Grace? What are you doing?"

Anne did not answer. Getting to her feet, she walked back toward the castle. The place between the generators was no good: The woman had already known where Anne was.

The three delegates from the All-World Forum arrived at the Time Research Institute looking apprehensive. Lambert could understand this; for those who had never left their own time-space continuum, it probably seemed significant to step through a force field to a place that did not exist in any accepted sense of the word. The delegates looked at the ground, and inspected the facilities, and asked the same kinds of questions visitors always asked, before they settled down actually to investigate anything.

They were given an hour's overview of the time rescue program, presented by the director himself. Lambert, who had not helped write this, listened to the careful sentiments about the prevention of war, the nobility of hostages, the deep understanding the Time Research Institute held of the All-World Accord of 2154, the altruistic extension of the Holy Mission of Peace into other time streams. Brill then moved on to discuss the four time hostages, dwelling heavily on the first. In the four years since Herr Hitler had become a hostage, the National Socialist Party had all but collapsed in Germany. President Paul von Hindenburg had died on schedule, and the new moderate chancellors were slowly bringing order to Germany. The economy was still very bad and unrest was widespread, but no one was arresting Jews or Gypsies or homosexuals or Jehovah's Witnesses or... Lambert stopped listening. The delegates knew all this. The entire solar system knew all this. Hitler had been a tremendous popular success as a hostage, the reason the Institute had obtained permits for the next three. Herr Hitler was kept in his locked suite, where he spent his time reading power-fantasy novels whose authors had not been born when the bunker under Berlin was detonated.

"Very impressive, Director," Goro Soshiru said. He was small, thin, elongated, a typical free-fall spacer, with a sharp mind and a reputation for incorruptibility. "May we now talk to the hostages, one at a time?"

"Without any monitors. That is our instruction," said Anna Vlakhav. She was the senior member of the investigative team, a sleek, gray-haired Chinese who refused all augments. Her left hand, Lambert noticed, trembled constantly. She belonged to the All-World Forum's Inner Council and had once been a hostage herself for three years.

"Please," Soren Tullio said with a smile. He was young, handsome, very wealthy. Disposable, added by the Forum to fill out the committee, with few recorded views of his own. Insomuch as they existed, however, they were not tinged with any bias toward the Church. Her Holiness had not succeeded in naming the members of the investigative committee—if indeed she had tried.

"Certainly," Brill said. "We've set aside the private conference room for your use. As specified by the Church, it is a sanctuary: There are no monitors of any kind. I would recommend, however, that you allow the bodyguard to remain with Herr Hitler, although, of course, you will make up your own minds."

Delegate Vlakhav said, "The bodyguard may stay. Herr Hitler is not our concern here."

Surprise, Lambert thought. Guess who is?

The delegates kept Hitler only ten minutes, the catatonic Helen only three. They said the queen did not speak. They talked to the little Tsarevitch a half hour. They kept Anne Boleyn in the sanctuary conference room four hours and twenty-three minutes.

She came out calm, blank-faced, and proceeded to her own apartments. Behind her the three delegates were tight-lipped and silent.

Anna Vlakhav, the former hostage, said to Toshio Brill, "We have no comment at this time. You will be informed."

Brill's eyes narrowed. He said nothing.

The next day, Director Toshio Brill was subpoenaed to appear before the All-World Forum on the gravest of all charges: mistreating holy hostages detained to keep peace. The tribunal would consist of the full Inner Council of the All-World Forum. Since Director Brill had the right to confront those who accused him, the investigation would be held at the Time Research Institute.

How? Lambert wondered. They would not take her unsupported word. How had the woman done it?

She said to Culhane, "The delegates evidently make no distinction between political hostages on our own world, and time hostages snatched from shadowy parallel ones."

"Why should they?" coldly said Culhane. The idealist. And where had it brought him?

Lambert was assigned that night to monitor the Tsarevitch, who was asleep in his crib. She sat in her office, her screen turned to Anne Boleyn's chambers, watching her play on the lute and sing softly to herself the songs written for her by Henry VIII when his passion was new and fresh six hundred years before.

Anne sat embroidering a sleeve cover of cinnamon velvet. In strands of black silk she worked intertwined H and A: Henry and Anne. Let their spying machines make of that what they would.

The door opened and, without permission, Culhane entered. He stood by her chair and looked down into her face. "Why, Anne? Why?"

She laughed. He had finally called her by her Christian name. Now, when it could not possibly matter.

When he saw that she would not answer, his manner grew formal. "A lawyer has been assigned to you. He arrives tomorrow."

A lawyer. Thomas Cromwell had been a lawyer, and Sir Thomas More. Dead, both of them, at Henry's hand. So had Master Culhane told her, and yet he still believed that protection was afforded by the law.

"The lawyer will review all the monitor records. What you did, what you said, every minute."

She smiled at him mockingly. "Why tell me this now?"

"It is your right to know."

"And you are concerned with rights. Almost as much as with death." She knotted the end of her thread and cut it. "How is it that you command so many machines and yet do not command the knowledge that every man must die?"

"We know that," Culhane said evenly. His desire for her had at last been killed; she could feel its absence, like an empty well. The use of her name had been but the last drop of living water. "But we try to prevent death when we can."

"Ah, but you can't. 'Prevent death'—as if it were a fever. You can only postpone it, Master Culhane, and you never even ask if that is worth doing."

"I only came to tell you about the lawyer," Culhane said stiffly. "Good night, Mistress Boleyn."

"Good night, Michael," she said, and started to laugh. She was still laughing when the door closed behind him.

The Hall of Time, designed to hold three hundred, was packed.

Lambert remembered the day she had given the orientation lecture to the history candidates, among them what's-his-name of the violet eyes. Twenty young people huddled together against horror in the middle of squares, virtual and simulated but not really present. Today the squares were absent and the middle of the floor was empty, while all four sides were lined ten-deep with All-World Inner Council members on high polished benches, archbishops and lamas and shamans of the Church of the

Holy Hostage, and reporters from every major newsgrid in the solar system. Her Holiness the high priest sat among her followers, pretending she wanted to be inconspicuous. Toshio Brill sat in a chair alone, facing the current premier of the All-World Council, Dagar Krenya of Mars.

Anne Boleyn was led to a seat. She walked with her head high, her long black skirts sweeping the floor.

Lambert remembered that she had worn black to her trial for treason, in 1536.

"This investigation will begin," Premier Krenya said. He wore his hair to his shoulders; fashions must have changed again on Mars. Lambert looked at the shaved heads of her colleagues, at the long, loose black hair of Anne Boleyn. To Culhane, seated beside her, she whispered, "We'll be growing our hair again soon." He looked at her as if she were crazy.

It *was* a kind of crazy, to live everything twice: once in research, once in the flesh. Did it seem so to Anne Boleyn? Lambert knew her frivolity was misplaced, and she thought of the frivolity of Anne in the Tower, awaiting execution: "They will have no trouble finding a name for me. I shall be Queen Anne Lackhead." At the memory, Lambert's hatred burst out fresh. She had the memory, and now Anne never would. But in bequeathing it forward in time to Lambert, the memory had become secondhand. That was Anne Boleyn's real crime, for which she would never be tried: She had made this whole proceeding, so important to Lambert and Brill and Culhane, a mere reenactment. Prescripted. Secondhand. She had robbed them of their own, unused time.

Krenya said, "The charges are as follows: That the Time Research Institute has mistreated the holy hostage Anne Boleyn, held hostage against war. Three counts of mistreatment are under consideration this day: First, that researchers willfully increased a hostage's mental anguish by dwelling on the pain of those left behind by the hostage's confinement, and on those aspects of confinement that cause emotional unease. Second, that researchers failed to choose a hostage who would truly prevent war. Third, that researchers willfully used a hostage for sexual gratification."

Lambert felt herself go very still. Beside her, Culhane rose to his feet, then sat down again slowly, his face rigid. Was it possible he had... No. He had been infatuated, but not to the extent of throwing away his career. He was not Henry, any more than Lambert had been over him.

The spectators buzzed, an uneven sound like malfunctioning equipment. Krenya rapped for order. "Director Brill: How do you answer these charges?"

"False, Premier. Every one."

"Then let us hear the evidence against the Institute."

Anne Boleyn was called. She took the chair in which Brill had been sitting. *"She made an entry as though she were going to a great triumph and sat down with elegance"*...But that was the other time, the first time. Lambert groped for Culhane's hand. It felt limp.

"Mistress Boleyn," Krenya said—he had evidently not been told that she insisted on being addressed as a queen, and the omission gave Lambert a mean pleasure—"in what ways was your anguish willfully increased by researchers at this Institute?"

Anne held out her hand. To Lambert's astonishment, her lawyer put into it a lute. At an official All-World Forum investigation—a *lute*. Anne began to play, the tune high and plaintive. Her unbound black hair fell forward; her slight body made a poignant contrast to the torment in the words:

> "Defiled is my name, full sore,
> Through cruel spite and false report,
> That I may say forever more,
> Farewell to joy, adieu comfort.
> "Oh, death, rock me asleep,
> Bring on my quiet rest,
> Let pass my very guiltless ghost
> Out of my careful breast.
> "Ring out the doleful knell,
> Let its sound my death tell,
> For I must die, There is no remedy,
> For now I die!"

The last notes faded. Anne looked directly at Krenya. "I wrote that, my Lords, in my other life. Master Culhane of this place played it for me, along with death songs written by my...my brother..."

"Mistress Boleyn—"

"No, I recover myself. George's death tune was hard for me to hear, my Lords. Accused and condemned because of me, who always loved him well."

Krenya said to the lawyer whose staff had spent a month reviewing every moment of monitor records, "Culhane made her listen to these?"

"Yes," the lawyer said. Beside Lambert, Culhane sat unmoving.

"Go on," Krenya said to Anne.

"He told me that I was made to suffer watching the men accused with me die. How I was led to a window overlooking the block, how my brother George kneeled, putting his head on the block, how the ax was raised..." She stopped, shuddering. A murmur ran over the room. It sounded like cruelty, Lambert thought. But whose?

"Worst of all, my Lords," Anne said, "was that I was told I had bastardized my own child. I chose to sign a paper declaring no valid marriage had ever existed because I had been precontracted to Sir Henry Percy, so my daughter Elizabeth was illegitimate and thus barred from her throne. I was taunted with the fact that I had done this, ruining the prospects of my own child. He said it over and over, Master Culhane did..."

Krenya said to the lawyer, "Is this in the visuals?"

"Yes."

Krenya turned back to Anne. "But Mistress Boleyn—these are things that because of your time rescue did *not* happen. Will not happen in your time stream. How can they thus increase your anguish for relatives left behind?"

Anne stood. She took one step forward, then stopped. Her voice was low and passionate. "My good Lord—do you not understand? It is because you took me here that these things did not happen. Left to my own time, I *would have been responsible for them all*. For my brother's death, for the other four brave men, for my daughter's bastardization, for the torment in my own music...I have escaped them only because of you. To tell me them in such detail, not the mere provision of facts that I myself requested but agonizing detail of mind and heart—is to tell me that I alone, in my own character, am evil, giving pain to those I love most. And that in this time stream you have brought me to, I did these things, felt them, feel them still. You have made me guilty of them. My Lord Premier, have you ever been a hostage yourself? Do you know, or can you imagine, the torment that comes from imagining the grief of those who love you? And to know you have caused this grief, not merely loss but death, blood, the pain of disinheritance—that you have caused it, and are now being told of the anguish you cause? Told over and over? In words, in song even—can you imagine what that feels like to one such as I, who cannot return at will and comfort those hurt by my actions?"

The room was silent. Who, Lambert wondered, had told Anne Boleyn that Premier Krenya had once served as a holy hostage?

"Forgive me, my Lords," Anne said dully. "I forget myself."

"Your testimony may take whatever form you choose," Krenya said, and it seemed to Lambert that there were shades and depths in his voice.

The questioning continued. A researcher, said Anne, had taunted her with being spied on even at her chamber pot—Lambert leaned slowly forward—which had made Anne cry out, "It had been better had you never told me!" Since then, modesty had made her reluctant even to answer nature, "so that there is every hour a most wretched twisting and churning in my bowels."

Asked why she thought the Institute had chosen the wrong hostage, Anne said she had been told so by my Lord Brill. The room exploded into sound, and Krenya rapped for quiet. "That visual now, please." On a square created in the center of the room, the visuals replayed on three sides:

"My Lord Brill...was there no other person you could take but I to prevent this war you say is a hundred years off? This civil war in England?"

"The mathematics identified you as the best hostage, your Grace."

"The best? Best for what, my Lord? If you had taken Henry himself, then he could not have issued the Act of Supremacy. His supposed death would have served the purpose as well as mine."

"Yes. But for Henry the Eighth to disappear from history while his heir is but a month old...we did not know if that might not have started a civil war in itself. Between the factions supporting Elizabeth and those for Queen Katherine, who was still alive."

"What did your mathematical learning tell you?"

"That it probably would not," Brill said.

"And yet choosing me instead of Henry left him free to behead yet another wife, as you yourself have told me, my cousin Catherine Howard!"

Brill shifted on his chair. "That is true, Your Grace."

"Then why not Henry instead of me?"

"I'm afraid Your Grace does not have sufficient grasp of the science of probabilities for me to explain, Your Grace."

Anne was silent. Finally she said, "I think that the probability is that you would find it easier to deal with a deposed woman than with Henry of England, whom no man can withstand in either a passion or a temper."

Brill did not answer. The visual rolled—ten seconds, fifteen—and he did not answer.

"Mr. Premier," Brill said in a choked voice, "Mr. Premier—"

"You will have time to address these issues soon, Mr. Director," Krenya said. "Mistress Boleyn, this third charge—sexual abuse..."

The term had not existed in the sixteenth century, thought Lambert.

Yet Anne understood it. She said, "I was frightened, my Lord, by the strangeness of this place. I was afraid for my life. I didn't know then that a woman may refuse those in power, may—"

"That is why sexual contact with hostages is universally forbidden," Krenya said. "Tell us what you think happened."

Not what did happen—what you *think* happened. Lambert took heart.

Anne said, "Master Culhane bade me meet him at a place...it is a small alcove beside a short flight of stairs near the kitchens...He bade me meet him there at night. Frightened, I went."

"Visuals," Krenya said in a tight voice.

The virtual square reappeared. Anne, in the same white nightdress in which she had been taken hostage, crept from her chamber and along the corridor, her body heat registering in infrared. Down the stairs, around to the kitchens, into the cubbyhole formed by the flight of steps, themselves oddly angled as if they had been added, or altered, after the main structure was built, after the monitoring system installed...Anne dropped to her knees and crept forward beside the isolated stairs. And disappeared.

Lambert gasped. A time hostage was under constant surveillance. That was a basic condition of their permit; there was no way the Boleyn bitch could escape constant monitoring. But she had.

"Master Culhane was already there," Anne said in a dull voice. "He... he used me ill there."

The room was awash with sound. Krenya said over it, "Mistress Boleyn—there is no visual evidence that Master Culhane was there. He has sworn he was not. Can you offer any proof that he met you there? Anything at all?"

"Yes. Two arguments, my Lord. First: How would I know there were not spying devices in but this one hidden alcove? I did not design this castle; it is not mine."

Krenya's face showed nothing. "And the other argument?"

"I am pregnant with Master Culhane's child."

Pandemonium. Krenya rapped for order. When it was finally restored, he said to Brill, "Did you know of this?"

"No, I...it was a hostage's right by the Accord to refuse intrusive medical treatment... She has been healthy."

"Mistress Boleyn, you will be examined by a doctor immediately."

She nodded assent. Watching her, Lambert knew it was true. Anne Boleyn was pregnant, and had defeated herself thereby. But she did not know it yet.

Lambert fingered the knowledge, seeing it as a tangible thing, cold as steel.

"How do we know," Krenya said, "that you were not pregnant before you were taken hostage?"

"It was but a month after my daughter Elizabeth's birth, and I had the white-leg. Ask one of your experts if a woman would bed a man then. Ask a woman expert in the women of my time. Ask Lady Mary Lambert."

Heads in the room turned. Ask whom? Krenya said, "Ask whom?" An aide leaned toward him and whispered something. He said, "We will have her put on the witness list."

Anne said, "I carry Michael Culhane's child. I, who could not carry a prince for the king."

Krenya said, almost powerlessly, "That last has nothing to do with this investigation, Mistress Boleyn."

She only looked at him.

They called Brill to testify, and he threw up clouds of probability equations that did nothing to clarify the choice of Anne over Henry as holy hostage. Was the woman right? Had there been a staff meeting to choose between the candidates identified by the Rahvoli applications, and had someone said of two very close candidates, "We should think about the effect on the Institute as well as on history..."? Had someone been developing a master theory based on a percentage of women influencing history? Had someone had an infatuation with the period, and chosen by that what should be altered? Lambert would never know. She was an intern.

Had been an intern.

Culhane was called. He denied seducing Anne Boleyn. The songs on the lute, the descriptions of her brother's death, the bastardization of Elizabeth—all done to convince her that what she had been saved from was worse than where she had been saved to. Culhane felt so much that he made a poor witness, stumbling over his words, protesting too much.

Lambert was called. As neutrally as possible she said, "Yes, Mr. Premier, historical accounts show that Queen Anne was taken with white-leg after Elizabeth's birth. It is a childbed illness. The legs swell up and ache painfully. It can last from a few weeks to months. We don't know how long it lasted—would have lasted—for Mistress Boleyn."

"And would a woman with this disease be inclined to sexual activity?"

"'Inclined'—no."

"Thank you, Researcher Lambert."

Lambert returned to her seat. The committee next looked at visuals, hours of visuals—Culhane, flushed and tender, making a fool of himself with Anne. Anne with the little Tsarevitch, an exile trying to comfort a child torn from his mother. Helen of Troy, mad and pathetic. Brill, telling newsgrids around the solar system that the time rescue program, savior of countless lives, was run strictly in conformance with the All-World Accord of 2154. And all the time, through all the visuals, Lambert waited for what was known to everyone in that room except Anne Boleyn: She could not pull off in this century what she might have in Henry's. The paternity of a child could be genotyped in the womb. Who? Mark Smeaton, after all? Another miscarriage from Henry, precipitately gotten and unrecorded by history? Thomas Wyatt, her most faithful cousin and cavalier?

After the committee had satisfied itself that it had heard enough, everyone but Forum delegates was dismissed. Anne, Lambert saw, was led away by a doctor. Lambert smiled to herself. It was already over. The Boleyn bitch was defeated.

The All-World Forum investigative committee deliberated for less than a day. Then it issued a statement: The child carried by holy hostage Anne Boleyn had not been sired by Researcher Michael Culhane. Its genotypes matched no one's at the Institute for Time Research. The Institute, however, was guilty of two counts of hostage mistreatment. The Institute's charter as an independent, tax-exempt organization was revoked. Toshio Brill was released from his position, as were Project Head Michael Culhane and intern Mary Lambert. The Institute stewardship was reassigned to the Church of the Holy Hostage under the direct care of Her Holiness the high priest.

Lambert slipped through the outside door to the walled garden. It was dusk. On a seat at the far end a figure sat, skirts spread wide, a darker shape against the dark wall. As Lambert approached, Anne looked up without surprise.

"Culhane's gone. I leave tomorrow. Neither of us will ever work in time research again."

Anne went on gazing upward. Those great dark eyes, that slim neck, so vulnerable...Lambert clasped her hands together hard.

"*Why?*" Lambert said. "Why do it all again? Last time use a king to bring down the power of the church, this time use a church to—before, at least you gained a crown. Why do it here, when you gain nothing?"

"You could have taken Henry. He deserved it; I did not."

"But we didn't take Henry!" Lambert shouted. "So why?"

Anne did not answer. She put out one hand to point behind her. Her sleeve fell away, and Lambert saw clearly the small sixth finger that had marked her as a witch. A tech came running across the half-lit garden. "Researcher Lambert—"

"What is it?"

"They want you inside. Everybody. The queen—the other one, Helen—she's killed herself."

The garden blurred, straightened. "How?"

"Stabbed with a silver sewing scissors hidden in her tunic. It was so quick, the researchers saw it on the monitor but couldn't get there in time."

"Tell them I'm coming."

Lambert looked at Anne Boleyn. "You did this."

Anne laughed. *This lady*, wrote the Tower constable, *hath much joy in death*. Anne said, "Lady Mary—every birth is a sentence of death. Your age has forgotten that."

"Helen didn't need to die yet. And the Time Research Institute didn't need to be dismantled—it *will* be dismantled. Completely. But somewhere, sometime, you will be punished for this. I'll see to that!"

"Punished, Lady Mary? And mayhap beheaded?"

Lambert looked at Anne: the magnificent black eyes, the sixth finger, the slim neck. Lambert said slowly, "You want your own death. As you had it before."

"What else did you leave me?" Anne Boleyn said. "Except the power to live the life that is mine?"

"You will never get it. We don't kill here!"

Anne smiled. "Then how will you 'punish' me—'sometime, somehow'?"

Lambert didn't answer. She walked back across the walled garden, toward the looming walls gray in the dusk, toward the chamber where lay the other dead queen.

Afterword to "And Wild For to Hold"

This is my Anne Boleyn story. It was inevitable that eventually I would write an Anne Boleyn story because she has fascinated me for forty years. Here is a woman who dared to pit her desires against those of a king, using the only weapon available to her: her sexuality. Henry VIII wanted a mistress; Anne wanted a crown. She won, and then lost it all. None of this is politically correct by the standards of our day, of course. But Anne did not have the options open to her that women have today. She could not go to college, become a stockbroker, and buy a condo in her own name.

But how to fit Anne into a science fiction—not fantasy—story? I didn't want to have a future time-traveler visit Anne's time. It took far longer than it should have for me to hit on the reverse: bring Anne to the future. But why? And with what consequences?

So that she could do the same thing again: use her sexuality to bring down a ruler and a church.

Once I had these ideas firm in my mind, it was great fun to devise the parallels between Tudor history and my invented future. Those parallels are not exact, of course; for one thing, nobody is beheaded. Still, Culhane is Mark Smeaton, Toshio Brill is Wolsey, Her Holiness is Pope Clement. And Anne is, eternally, herself.

"And Wild For To Hold" was nominated for the 1992 Hugo. However, it lost—to "Beggars in Spain." I was not unhappy.

OUT OF ALL THEM BRIGHT STARS

So I'm filling the catsup bottles at the end of the night, and I'm listening to the radio Charlie has stuck up on top of a movable panel in the ceiling, when the door opens and one of them walks in. I know right away it's one of them—no chance to make a mistake about that—even though it's got on a nice suit and a brim hat like Humphrey Bogart used to wear in *Casablanca*. But there's nobody with it, no professor or government men like on the TV show or even any students. It's all alone. And we're a long way out on the highway from the college.

It stands in the doorway, blinking a little, with rain dripping off its hat. Kathy, who's supposed to be cleaning the coffee machine behind the counter, freezes and stares with one hand holding the filter up in the air like she's never going to move again. Just then Charlie calls out from the kitchen, "Hey, Kathy, you ask anybody who won the Trifecta?" and she doesn't even answer him. Just goes on staring with her mouth open like she's thinking of screaming but forgot how. And the old couple in the corner booth, the only ones left from the crowd when the movie got out, stop chewing their chocolate cream pie and stare too. Kathy closes her mouth and opens it again and a noise comes out like "Uh—errrgh..."

Well, that got me annoyed. Maybe she tried to say "ugh" and maybe she didn't, but here it is standing in the doorway with rain falling around it in little drops and we're staring at it like it's a clothes dummy and not a customer. So I think that's not right and maybe we're even making it feel a little bad, I wouldn't like Kathy staring at me like that, and I dry my hands on my towel and go over.

"Yes, sir, can I help you?" I say.

"Table for one," it says, like Charlie's is some nice steak house in town. But I suppose that's the kind of place the government men mostly take them to. And besides, its voice is polite and easy to understand, with a sort of accent but not as bad as some we get from the college. I can tell what it's saying. I lead him to a booth in the corner opposite the old couple, who come in every Friday night and haven't left a tip yet.

He sits down slowly. I notice he keeps his hands on his lap, but I can't tell if that's because he doesn't know what to do with them or because he thinks I won't want to see them. But I've seen the close-ups on TV—they don't look so weird to me like they do to some. Charlie says they make his stomach turn, but I can't see it. You think he'd of seen worse meat in Vietnam. He talks enough like he did, on and on, and sometimes we even believe him.

I say, "Coffee, sir?"

He makes a kind of movement with his eyes. I can't tell what the movement means, but he says in that polite voice, "No, thank you. I am unable to drink coffee," and I think that's a good thing because I suddenly remember Kathy's got the filter out. But then he says, "May I have a green salad, please? With no dressing, please?"

The rain is still dripping off his hat. I figure the government people never told him to take off his hat in a restaurant, and for some reason that tickles me and makes me feel real bold. This polite blue guy isn't going to bother nobody, and that fool Charlie was just spouting off his mouth again.

"The salad's not too fresh, sir," I say, experimental-like, just to see what he'll say next. And it's the truth—the salad is left over from yesterday. But the guy answers like I asked something else.

"What is your name?" he says, so polite I know he's really curious and not trying to start anything. And what could he start anyway, blue and with those hands? Still, you never know.

"Sally," I say, "Sally Gourley."

"I am John," he says, and makes that movement again with his eyes. All of a sudden it tickles me—"John!" For this blue guy! So I laugh, and right away I feel sorry, like I might have hurt his feelings or something. How could you tell?

"Hey, I'm sorry," I say, and he takes off his hat. He does it real slow, like taking off the hat is important and means something, but all there is underneath is a bald blue head. Nothing weird like with the hands.

"Do not apologize," John says. "I have another name, of course, but in my own language."

"What is it?" I say, bold as brass, because all of a sudden I picture myself telling all this to my sister Mary Ellen and her listening real hard.

John makes some noises with his mouth, and I feel my own mouth open because it's not a word he says at all, it's a beautiful sound, like a bird call only sadder. It's just that I wasn't expecting it, that beautiful sound right here in Charlie's diner. It surprised me, coming out of that bald blue head. That's all it was: surprise.

I don't say anything. John looks at me and says, "It has a meaning that can be translated. It means—" but before he can say what it means Charlie comes charging out of the kitchen, Kathy right behind him. He's still got the racing form in one hand, like he's been studying the Trifecta, and he pushes right up against the booth and looks red and furious. Then I see the old couple scuttling out the door, their jackets clutched to their fronts, and the chocolate pie half-eaten on their plates. I see they're going to stiff me for the check, but before I can stop them Charlie grabs my arm and squeezes so hard his nails slice into my skin.

"What the hell do you think you're doing?" he says right to me. Not so much as a look at John, but Kathy can't stop looking and her fist is pushed up to her mouth.

I drag my arm away and rub it. Once I saw Charlie push his wife so hard she went down and hit her head and had to have four stitches. It was me that drove her to the emergency room.

Charlie says, "What the hell do you think you're doing?"

"I'm serving my table. He wants a salad. Large." I can't remember if John said a large or a small salad, but I figure a large order would make Charlie feel better. But Charlie don't want to feel better.

"You get him out of here," Charlie hisses. He still doesn't look at John. "You hear me, Sally? You get him out. The government says I gotta serve spics and niggers but it don't say I gotta serve him!"

I look at John. He's putting on his hat, ramming it onto his bald head, and half standing in the booth. He can't get out because Charlie and me are both in the way. I expect John to look mad or upset, but except that he's holding the muscles of his face in some different way I can't see any change of expression. But I figure he's got to feel something bad, and all of a sudden I'm mad at Charlie, who's a bully and who's got the feelings of a scumbag. I open my mouth to tell him so, plus one or two other little things I been saving up, when the door flies open and in bursts four men, and damn if they aren't all wearing hats like Humphrey Bogart in *Casablanca*. As soon as the first guy sees John, his walk changes and he comes over slower but more purposeful-like, and then he's talking to John and Charlie in a sincere voice like a TV anchorman giving out the news.

I see the situation now belongs to him, so I go back to the catsup bottles. I'm still plenty burned though, about Charlie manhandling me and about Kathy rushing into the kitchen to get Charlie. She's a flake and always has been.

Charlie is scowling and nodding. The harder he scowls, the nicer the government guy's voice gets. Pretty soon the government guy is smiling sweet as pie. Charlie slinks back into the kitchen, and the four men move toward the door with John in the middle of them like some high school football huddle. Next to the real men he looks stranger than he did before, and I see how really flat his face is. But then when the huddle's right opposite my table with the catsup bottles, John breaks away and comes over to me.

"I am sorry, Sally Gourley," he says. And then, "I seldom have the chance to show our friendliness to an ordinary Earth person. I make so little difference!"

Well, that throws me. His voice sounds so sad, and besides I never thought of myself as an ordinary Earth person. Who would? So I just shrug and wipe off a catsup bottle with my towel. But then John does a weird thing. He just touches my arm where Charlie squeezed it, just touches it with the palm of one of those hands. And the palm's not slimy at all—dry, and sort of cool, and I don't jump or anything. Instead I remember that beautiful noise when he said his other name. Then he goes out with three of the men and the door bangs behind them on a gust of rain because Charlie never fixed the air-stop from when some kids horsing around broke it last spring.

The fourth man stays and questions me: what did the alien say, what did I say. I tell him, but then he starts asking the exact same questions all over again, like he didn't believe me the first time, and that gets me mad. Also he has this snotty voice, and I see how his eyebrows move when I slip once and say, "He don't." I might not know what John's muscles mean but I sure as hell can read those eyebrows. So I get miffed and pretty soon he leaves and the door bangs behind him.

I finish the catsup and mustard bottles and Kathy finishes the coffee machine. The radio in the ceiling plays something instrumental, no words, real sad. Kathy and me start to wash down the booths with disinfectant, and because we're doing the same work together and nobody comes in, I finally say to her, "It's funny."

She says, "What's funny?"

"Charlie called that guy 'him' right off. 'I don't got to serve him,' he said. And I thought of him as 'it' at first, leastways until I had a name to use. But Charlie's the one who threw him out."

Kathy swipes at the back of her booth. "And Charlie's right. That thing scared me half to death, coming in here like that. And where there's food being served, too." She snorts and sprays on more disinfectant.

Well, she's a flake. Always has been.

"The *National Enquirer*," Kathy goes on, "told how they have all this firepower up in the big ship that hasn't landed yet. My husband says they could blow us all to smithereens, they're so powerful. I don't know why they even came here. We don't want them. I don't even know why they came, all that way."

"They want to make a difference," I say, but Kathy barrels on ahead, not listening.

"The Pentagon will hold them off, it doesn't matter how much firepower they got up there or how much they insist on seeing about our defenses, the Pentagon won't let them get any toeholds on Earth. That's what my husband says. Blue bastards."

I say, "Will you please shut up?"

She gives me a dirty look and flounces off. I don't care. None of it is anything to me. Only, standing there with the disinfectant in my hand, looking at the dark windows and listening to the music wordless and slow on the radio, I remember that touch on my arm. And I think, they didn't come here with any firepower to blow us all to smithereens. I just don't believe it. So why did they come? Why come all that way from another star to walk into Charlie's diner and order a green salad with no dressing from an ordinary Earth person?

Charlie comes out with his keys to unlock the cash register and go over the tapes. I remember the old couple who stiffed me and I curse to myself. Only pie and coffee, but it still comes off my salary. The radio starts playing something else, not the sad song, but nothing snappy neither. It's a love song, about some guy giving and giving and getting treated like dirt. I don't like it much.

"Charlie," I say, "what did those government men say to you?"

He looks up from his tapes and scowls. "What do you care?"

"I just want to know."

"And maybe I don't want you to know," he says, and smiles nasty-like. Me asking has put him in a better mood, the creep. All of a sudden

I remember what his wife said when she got the stitches: "The only way to get something from Charlie is to let him smack me around a little, and then ask him when I'm down. He'll give me anything when I'm down. He gives me shit if he thinks I'm on top."

I think again about the blue guy. John.

I do the rest of the clean-up without saying anything. Charlie swears at the night's take—I know from my tips that it's not much. Kathy teases her hair in front of the mirror behind doughnuts and pies, and I put down the breakfast menus. But all the time I'm thinking, and I don't much like my thoughts.

Charlie locks up and we all leave. Outside it's stopped raining but it's still misty and soft, real pretty but too cold. I pull my sweater around myself and in the parking lot, after Kathy's gone, I say, "Charlie."

He stops walking toward his truck. "Yeah?"

I lick my lips. They're all of a sudden dry. It's an experiment, like, what I'm going to say. It's an experiment.

"Charlie. What if those government men hadn't come just then and the...the blue guy hadn't been willing to leave? What would you have done?"

"What do you care?"

I shrug. "I don't. Just curious. It's your place."

"Damn straight it's my place!" Through the mist I can see him scowl. "I'd of squashed him flat!"

"And then what? After you squashed him flat, what if the men came then and made a stink?"

"Too bad. It'd be too late by then, huh?" He laughs and I can see how he's seeing it: the blue guy bleeding on the linoleum and Charlie standing over him, dusting his hands together.

Charlie laughs again and goes off to his truck, whistling. He has a little bounce in his step. He's still seeing it, almost like it really had happened. Over his shoulder he calls to me, "They're built like wimps. Or girls. All bone, no muscle. Even you must of seen that," and his voice is cheerful. It doesn't have any more anger in it, or hatred, or anything but a kind of friendliness. I hear him whistle some more, until the truck engine starts up and he peels out of the parking lot, laying rubber like a kid.

I unlock my Chevy. But before I get in, I look up at the sky. Which is really stupid because of course I can't see anything, with all the mist and clouds. No stars.

Maybe Kathy's husband is right. Maybe they do want to blow us all to smithereens. I don't think so, but what the hell difference does it ever make what I think? And all at once I'm furious at John, furious mad, as mad as I've ever been in my life.

Why does he have to come here, with his bird calls and his politeness? Why can't they all go someplace else besides here? There must be lots of other places they can go, out of all them bright stars up there behind the clouds. They don't need to come here, here where I need this job and so that means I need Charlie. He's a bully, but I want to look at him and see nothing else but a bully. Nothing else but that. That's all I want to see in Charlie, in the government men—just small-time bullies, nothing special, not a mirror of anything, not a future of anything. Just Charlie. That's all. I won't see nothing else.

I won't.

"I make so little difference," he says.

Yeah. Sure.

Afterword to "Out of All Them Bright Stars"

This was a "gift story," one of those rare occasions where the whole story occurs to me at once, I wrote it in one sitting, and little editing was required. In another sense, however, a lifetime had prepared me to write it: I had been a waitress in a diner, and since childhood I had hoped to meet an alien. So far this has not happened (although I do know some pretty strange people).

"Out of All Them Bright Stars" won the 1986 Nebula. I had not expected to win; the buzz (such as it was in those pre-Internet days) favored someone else. But I went to San Francisco for the award ceremony, and at lunch that day at Maxwell Plum's, Connie Willis was appalled that I had not written any sort of acceptance speech. She pushed a napkin toward me, produced a pen, and said, "You write something right now, just in case!" So I did. It does not do to argue with Connie.

PATHWAYS

The Chinese clinic warn't like I expected. It warn't even Chinese.

I got there afore it opened. I was hoping to get inside afore anybody else came, any neighbors who knew us or busybodies from Blaine. But Carrie Campbell was already parked in her truck, the baby on her lap. We nodded to each other but didn't speak. The Campbells are better off than us—Dave works in the mine up to Allington—but old Gacy Campbell been feuding with Dr. Harman for decades and Carrie was probably glad to have someplace else to take the baby. He didn't look good, snuffling and whimpering.

When the doors opened, I went in first, afore Carrie was even out of the truck. It was going to take her a while. She was pregnant again.

"Yes?" said the woman behind the desk. Just a cheap metal desk, which steadied me some. The room was nothing special, just a few chairs, some pictures on the wall, a clothes basket of toys in the corner. What really surprised me was that the woman warn't Chinese. Blue eyes, brown hair, middle-aged. She looked a bit like Granmama, but she had all her teeth. "Can I help you?"

"I want to see a doctor."

"Certainly." She smiled. Yeah, all her teeth. "What seems to be the problem, miss?"

"No problem." From someplace in the back another woman came out, this one dressed like a nurse. She warn't Chinese either.

"I don't understand," the woman behind the desk said. From her accent she warn't from around here—like I didn't already know that. "Are you sick?"

"No, ma'am."

"Then how can I—"

Carrie waddled into the door, the baby balanced on her belly. Now my visit would be table-talk everywhere. All at once I just wanted to get it over with.

"I'm not sick," I said, too loud. "I just want to see a doctor." I took a deep breath. "My name is Ludmilla Connors."

The nurse stopped walking toward Carrie. The woman behind the counter half stood up, then sat down again. She tried to pretend like she hadn't done it, like she warn't pleased. If Bobby were that bad a liar, he'd a been in jail even more than he was.

"Certainly," the woman said. I didn't see her do nothing, but a man came out from the back, and he *was* Chinese. So was the woman who followed him.

"I'm Ludmilla Connors," I told him, and I clenched my ass together real hard to keep my legs steady. "And I want to volunteer for the experiment. But only if it pays what I heard. Only if."

The woman behind the desk took me back to a room with a table and some chairs and a whole lot of filing cabinets, and she left me there with the Chinese people. I looked at their smooth faces with those slanted, mostly closed eyes, and I wished I hadn't come. I guess these two were the reason everybody hereabouts called it the "Chinese clinic," even if everybody else there looked like regular Americans.

"Hello, Ms. Connors," the man said and he spoke English real good, even if it was hard to understand some words. "We are glad you are here. I am Dr. Dan Chung and this is my chief technician Jenny."

"Uh huh." He didn't look like no "Dan," and if she was "Jenny," I was a fish.

"Your mother is Courtney Connors and your father was Robert Connors?"

"How'd you know that?"

"We have family trees for everyone on the mountain. It's part of our work, you know. You said you want to aid us in this research?"

"I said I want to get paid."

"Of course. You will be. You are nineteen."

"Yeah." It warn't a question, and I didn't like that they knew so much about me. "How much money?"

He told me. It warn't as much as the rumors said, but it was enough. Unless they actually killed me, it was enough. And I didn't think they'd do that. The government wouldn't let them do that—not even this stinking government.

"Okay," I said. "Start the experiment."

Jenny smiled. I knew that kind of smile, like she was so much better than me. My fists clenched. Dr. Chung said, "Jenny, you may leave. Send in Mrs. Cully, please."

I liked the surprised look on Jenny's face, and then the angry look she tried to hide. Bitch.

Mrs. Cully didn't act like Jenny. She brought in a tray with coffee and cookies: just regular store-bought Pepperidge Farm, not Chinese. Under the tray was a bunch of papers. Mrs. Cully sat down at the table with us.

"These are legal papers, Ms. Connors," Dr. Chung said. "Before we begin, you must sign them. If you wish, you can take them home to read, or to a lawyer. Or you can sign them here, now. They give us permission to conduct the research, including the surgery. They say that you understand this procedure is experimental. They give the university, myself, and Dr. Liu all rights to information gained from your participation. They say that we do not guarantee any cure, or even any alleviation, of any medical disorder you may have. Do you want to ask questions?"

I did, but not just yet. Half of me was grateful that he didn't ask if I can read, the way tourists and social workers sometimes do. I can, but I didn't understand all the words on this page: *indemnify*, *liability*, *patent rights*. The other half of me resented that he was rushing me so.

I said something I warn't intending: "If Ratface Rollins warn't president, this clinic wouldn't be here at all!"

"I agree," Dr. Chung said. "But you Americans elected a Libertarian."

"Us Americans? Aren't you one?"

"No. I am a Chinese national, working in the United States on a visa arranged by my university."

I didn't know what to say to that, so I grabbed the pen and signed everything. "Let's get it over with, then."

Both Dr. Chung and Mrs. Cully looked startled. She said, "But.... Ludmilla, didn't you understand that this will take several visits, spread out over months?"

"Yeah, I know. And that you're going to pay me over several months, too, but the first bit today."

"Yes. After your interview."

She had one of those little recording cubes that I only seen on TV. They can play back an interview like a movie, or they can send the words to a computer to get put on screen. Maybe today would be just talking. That would be fine with me. I took a cookie.

"Initial interview with experimental subject Ludmilla Connors," Dr. Chung said, and gave the date and time. "Ms. Connors, you are here of your own free will?"

"Yeah."

"And you are a member of the Connors family, daughter of Courtney Ames Connors and the late Robert Connors?"

"Did you know my dad at the hospital? Were you one of his doctors?"

"No. But I am familiar with his symptoms and his early death. I am sorry."

I warn't sorry. Dad was a son-of-a-bitch even afore he got sick. Maybe knowing it was coming, that it was in his genes, made him that way, but a little girl don't care about that. I only cared that he hit me and screamed at me—hit and screamed at everybody until the night he took after Dinah so bad that Bobby shot him. Now Bobby, just four months from finishing doing his time at Luther Luckett, was getting sick, too. I knew I had to tell this foreigner all that, but it was hard. My family don't ask for help. "We don't got much," Granmama always said, "but we got our pride."

That, and the Connors curse. Fatal Familial Insomnia.

It turned out that Dr. Chung already knew a lot of my story. He knew about Dad, and Bobby, and Mama, and Aunt Carol Ames. He even knew which of the kids got the gene—it's a 50-50 chance—and which didn't. The safe ones: Cody, Patty, Arianna, Timothy. The losers: Shawn, Bonnie Jean, and Lewis. And me.

So I talked and talked, and the little light on the recording cube glowed green to show it was on, and Mrs. Cully nodded and looked sympathetic so damn much that I started wishing for Jenny back. Dr. Chung at least sat quiet, with no expression on that strange ugly face.

"Are you showing any symptoms at all, Ms. Connors?"

"I have some trouble sleeping at night."

"Describe it for me, in as much detail as you can."

I did. I knew I was young to start the troubles; Mama was forty-six and Bobby twenty-nine.

"And the others with the FFI gene? Your mother and Robert, Jr. and" —he looked at a paper "—Shawn Edmond and—"

"Look," I said, and it came out harsher than I meant, "I know I got to tell you everything. But I'm not going to talk none about any of my kin, not what they are or aren't doing. Especially not to a Chinaman."

Silence.

Then Dr. Chung said quietly, "I think, Ms. Connors, that you must not know how offensive that term is. Like 'spic' or 'nigger.'"

I didn't know. I felt my face grow warm.

He said, "I think it's like 'hillbilly' is to mountain people."

My face got even warmer. "I...I'm sorry."

"It's okay."

But it warn't. I'm not the kind to insult people, even Chinese people. I covered my embarrassment with bluster. "Can *I* ask some questions for a change?"

"Of course."

"Is this Chi—did this clinic come to Blaine and start treating people for what ails them, just to get my family's trust so you all can do these experiments on our brains?"

That was the scuttlebutt in town and I expected him to deny it, but instead he said, "Yes."

Mrs. Cully frowned.

I said, "Why? Because there are only forty-one families in the whole world with our sickness? Then why build a whole clinic just to get at us? We're just a handful of folk."

He said gently, "You know a lot about fatal familial insomnia."

"I'm not stupid!"

"I would never think that for even a moment." He shifted in his chair and turned off the recorder. "Listen, Ms. Connors. It's true that sufferers from FFI are a very small group. But the condition causes changes in the brain that involve neural pathways which everybody has. Memory is involved, and sleep regulation, and a portion of the brain called the thalamus that processes incoming sensory signals. Our research here is the best single chance to gain information beyond price about those pathways. And since we also hope to arrest FFI, we were able to get funding as a medical clinical trial. Your contribution to this science will be invaluable."

"That's not why I'm doing it."

"Whatever your reasons, the data will be just as valuable."

"And you know you got to do it to me fast. Afore the Libertarians lose power."

Mrs. Cully looked surprised. Why was she still sitting with us? Then I realized: Dr. Chung warn't supposed to be alone with a young woman. Well, fine by me. But at least *he* didn't seem surprised that I sometimes watch the news.

"That's true," he said. "If Rafe Bannerman wins this presidential election, and it certainly looks as if he will, then all the deregulations of the present administration may be reversed."

"So you got to cut into my skull afore then. And afore I get too sick." I said it nasty, goading him. I don't know why.

But he didn't push back. "Yes, we must install the optogenetic cable as soon as possible. You are a very bright young woman, Ms. Connors."

"Don't try to butter me up none," I said.

But after he took blood samples and all the rest of it, after we set up a whole series of appointments, after I answered ten million more questions, the Chinaman's—no, *Chinese man's*—words stayed in my head all the long trudge back up the mountain. Not as bright, those words, as the autumn leaves turning the woods to glory, but it was more praise than I'd gotten since I left school. That was something, anyway.

When I got back to the trailer, about noon, nobody wouldn't speak to me. Carrie must of dropped by. Bobby's wife, Dinah, sewed on her quilt for the women's co-op: the Rail Fence pattern in blue and yellow, real pretty. Mama sat smoking and drinking Mountain Dew. Granmama was asleep in her chair by the stove, which barely heated the trailer. It was cold for October and Bobby didn't dig no highway coal again. The kids were outside playing, Shawn warn't around, and inside it was silent as the grave.

I hung my coat on a door hook. "That quilt's coming nice, Dinah."

Nothing.

"You need some help, Mama?"

Nothing.

"The hell with you all!" I said.

Mama finally spoke. At least today she was making sense. "You better not let Bobby hear where you been."

"I'm doing it for you all!" I said, but they all went back to pretending I didn't exist. I grabbed my coat, and stomped back outside.

Not that I had any place to go. And it didn't matter if I was inside or out; Mama's words were the last ones anyone spoke to me for two mortal days. They hardly even looked at me, except for scared peeps from the littlest kids and a glare from Bonnie Jean, like nobody except a ten-year-old can glare. It was like I was dead.

But half the reason I was doing this was the hope—not strong, but there—that maybe I wouldn't end up dead, after first raving and thrashing and trying to hurt people and seeing things that warn't there. Like Dad, like Aunt Carol Ames, like Cousin Jess. And the other half of the reason was to put some decent food on the table for the kids that wouldn't look at me or speak to me from fear that Bobby would switch them hard. I had hopes of Shawn, who hadn't been home in a couple of days, out deer hunting with his buddies. Shawn and I always been close, and he was sweeter than Bobby even afore Bobby started showing our sickness. I hoped Shawn would be on my side. I needed somebody.

But that night in bed, with Patty on my other side as far away as she could get without actually becoming part of the wall, Bonnie Jean spooned into me. She smelled of apples and little kid. I hugged onto her like I warn't never going to let go, and I stayed that way all through the long cold night.

"We have good news," Dr. Chung said. "Your optogenetic vectors came out beautifully."

"Yeah? What does that mean?" I didn't really care, but my nerves were all standing on end and if I kept him talking, maybe it would distract me some. Or not.

We sat in his lab at the Chinese clinic, a squinchy little room all cluttered with computers and papers. No smoking bottles or bubbling tubes like in the movies, though. Maybe those were in another room. There was another Chinese doctor, too, Dr. Liu. Also Jenny, worse luck, but if she was the "chief technician" I guess she had to be around. I kept my back to her. She wore a pretty red shirt that I couldn't never afford to buy for Patty or Bonnie Jean.

"What does that mean?" I said, realized I'd said it afore, and twisted my hands together.

"It means we have constructed the bio-organism to go into your brain, from a light-sensitive opsin, a promoter, and a harmless virus. The opsin will be expressed in only those cells that activate the promoter. When light of a specific wavelength hits those cells, they will activate or silence, and we can control that by—Ms. Connors, you can still change your mind."

"*What?*" Jenny said, and Dr. Chung shot her a look that could wither skunkweed. I wouldn't of thought he could look like that.

"My mind is changed," I said. His talking warn't distracting me, it was just making it all worse. "I don't want to do it."

"All right."

"She signed the contracts!" Jenny said.

I whirled around on my chair to face her. "You shut up! Nobody warn't talking to you!"

Jenny got up and stalked out. Dr. Liu made like he would say something, then didn't. Over her shoulder Jenny said, "I'll call Dr. Morton. Although too bad she didn't decide that before the operating room was reserved at Johnson Memorial."

"I'm sorry," I said, and fled.

I got home, bone-weary from the walk plus my worst night yet, just as Jimmy Barton's truck pulled up at the trailer. Jimmy got out, looking grim, then two more boys, carrying Shawn.

I rushed up. "What happened? Did you shoot him?" Everybody knew that Jimmy was the most reckless hunter on the mountain.

"Naw. We never even got no hunting. He went crazy, is what. So we brought him back."

"Crazy how?"

"You know how, Ludie," Jimmy said, looking at me steady. "Like your family does."

"But he's only seventeen!"

Jimmy didn't say nothing to that, and the other two started for the trailer with Shawn. He had a purpled jaw where somebody slugged him, and he was out cold on whatever downers they made him take. My gut twisted so hard I almost bent over. *Shawn.* Seventeen.

Dinah and Patty came rushing out, streaming kids behind them. Dinah was shrieking enough to wake the dead. I looked at Shawn and thought about how it must of been in the hunting camp, him going off the rails and "expressing" that gene all over the place: shouting from the panic, grabbing his rifle and waving it around, heart pounding like mad, hitting out at anyone who talked sense. Like Bobby had been a few months ago, afore he got even worse. Nobody in my family ever lasted more than seven months after the first panic attack.

Shawn.

I didn't even wait to see if Mama was coming out of the trailer, if this was one of the days she could. I went back down the mountain, running as much as I could, gasping and panting, until I got to the Chinese clinic and the only hope I had for Shawn, for me, for all of us.

Dr. Morton turned out to be a woman. While they got the operating room ready at Johnson Memorial in Jackson, I sat with Dr. Chung in a room that was supposed to look cheerful and didn't. Yellow walls, a view of the parking lot. A nurse had shaved off a square patch on my hair. I stared out at a red Chevy, trying not to think. Dr. Chung said gently, "It isn't a complicated procedure, Ms. Connors. Really."

"Drilling a hole into my skull isn't complicated?"

"No. Humans have known how to do that part for thousands of years."

News to me. I said, "I forgot a hat."

"A hat?"

"To cover this bare spot in my hair."

"The first person from your family to visit, I will tell them."

"Nobody's going to visit."

"I see. Then I will get you a hat."

"Thanks." And then, surprising myself, "They don't want me to do none of this."

"No," he said quietly, and without asking what I meant, "I imagine they do not."

"They think you conduct experiments on us like we're lab animals. Like with the Nazis. Or Frankenstein."

"And what do you think?"

"I think they are…unknowing." It felt like a huge betrayal. Still, I kept on. "Especially my Granmama."

"Grandmothers are often fierce. Mine is." He made some notes on a tablet, typing and swiping without looking at it.

I hadn't thought of him—of any of them—as having a grandmother. I demanded, like that would make this grandmother more solid, "What's her name?"

"Chunhua. What is the name of your grandmother?"

"Ludmilla. Like me." I thought a minute. "'Fierce' is the right word."

"Then we have this in common, yes?"

But I warn't yet ready to give him that much. "I bet my granmama is more fierce than any of your kin."

He smiled, a crinkling of his strange bald face, eyes almost disappearing in folds of smooth skin. "I would—what is it you say, in poker?—'see that bet' if I could."

"Why can't you?"

He didn't answer, and his smile disappeared. I said, "What did your granmama do that was so fierce?"

"She made me study. Hours every day, hours every night. All spring, all summer, all winter. When I refused, she beat me. What does yours do?"

All at once I didn't want to answer. Was beating better or worse? Granmama never touched me, nor any of us. Dr. Chung waited. Finally I said, "She freezes me. Looks at me like…like she wants to make a icy wind in my mind. And then that wind blows, and I can't get away from it nohow, and then she turns her back on me."

"That is worse."

"Really? You think so?"

"I think so."

A long breath went out of me, clearing out my chest. I said, "Bobby warn't always like he is now. He taught me to fish."

"Do you like fishing?"

"No." But I liked Bobby teaching me, just the two of us laughing down by the creek, eating the picnic lunch Mama put up for us.

A nurse, masked and gowned like on TV, came in and said, "We're ready."

The last thing I remember was lying on the table, breathing in the knock-out gas, and thinking, *Now at least I'm going to get a long deep sleep.* Only at the very last minute I panicked some and my hand, strapped to the table, flapped around a bit. Another hand held it, strong and steady. Dr. Chung. I went under.

When I woke, it was in a different hospital room but Dr. Chung was still there, sitting in a chair and working a tablet. He put it down.

"Welcome back, Ms. Connors. How do you feel?"

I put my hand to my head. A thick bandage covered part of it. Nothing hurt, but my mouth was dry, my throat was scratchy, and I had a floaty feeling. "What do you got me on? Oxycontin?"

"No. Steroids to control swelling and a mild pain med. There are only a few nerve receptors in the skull. Tomorrow we will take you back to Blaine. Here."

He handed me a red knit hat.

All at once I started to cry. I never cry, but this was so weird—waking up with something foreign in my skull, and feeling rested instead of skitterish and tired, and then this *hat* from this strange-looking man.... I sobbed like I was Cody, three years old with a skinned knee. I couldn't stop sobbing. It was awful.

Dr. Chung didn't high-tail it out of there. He didn't try to there-there me, or take my hand, or even look embarrassed and angry mixed together, like every other man I ever knowed when women cry. He just sat and waited, and when I finally got myself to stop, he said, "I wish you would call me 'Dan.'"

"No." Crying had left *me* embarrassed, if not him. "It isn't your name. Is it?"

"No. It just seems more comfortable for Westerners."

"What is your damned name?"

"It is Hai. It means 'the ocean.'"

"You're nothing like any ocean."

"I know." He grinned.

"Do all Chinese names mean something?"

"Yes. I was astonished when I found out American names do not."

"When was that?"

"When I came here for graduate school."

I was talking too much. I never rattled on like this, especially not to Chinese men who had me cut open. It was the damn drugs they gave me, that thing for swelling or the "mild pain med." I'd always stayed strictly away from even aspirin, 'cause of watching Mama and Bobby. Afore I could say anything, Dr. Chung said, "Your meds might induce a little 'high,' Ludmilla. It will pass soon. Meanwhile, you are safe here."

"Like hell I am!"

"You are. And I apologize for calling you 'Ludmilla.' I have not received permission."

"Oh, go the fuck ahead. Only it's 'Ludie.'" I felt my skull again. I wanted to rip off the bandage. I wanted to run out of the hospital. I wanted to stay in this bed forever, talking, not having to deal with my family. I didn't know what I wanted.

Maybe Dr. Chung did, because he went on talking, a steadying stream of nothing: graduate school in California and riding busses in China and his wife's and daughters' names. They were named after flowers, at least in English: Lotus and Jasmine and Plum Blossom. I liked that. I listened, and grew sleepy, and drifted into dreams of girls with faces like flowers.

I was two days in Johnson Memorial and two more in a bed at the clinic, and every single one of them I worried about Shawn. Nobody came to see me. I thought Patty might, or maybe even Dinah if Bobby'd a let her, but they didn't. Well, Patty was only twelve, still pretty young to come alone. So I watched TV and I talked with Dr. Chung, who didn't seem to have a whole lot to do.

"Don't you got to see patients?"

"I'm not an M.D., Ludie. Dr. Liu mostly sees the patients."

"How come Blaine got so many Chinese doctors? Aren't Americans working on optogenetics?"

"Of course they are. Liu Bo and I became friends at the university and so applied for this grant together."

"And you brought Jenny."

"She is Bo's fiancé."

"Oh. She warn't—there he is, the bastard!"

President Rollins was on TV, giving a campaign speech. Red and blue balloons sailed up behind him. My hands curled into fists. Dr. Chung watched me, and I realized—stupid me!—that of course he *was* working. He was observing me, the lab rat.

He said, "Why do you hate the president so?"

"He stopped the government checks and the food stamps. It's 'cause of him and his Libbies that most of Blaine is back to eating squirrels."

Dr. Chung looked at the TV like it was the most fascinating thing in the world, but I knew his attention was really on me. "But under the Libertarians, aren't your taxes lower?"

I snorted. "Five percent of nothing isn't less to pay than fifteen percent of nothing."

"I thought the number of jobs in the coal mines had increased."

"If you can get one. My kin can't."

"Why not?"

I didn't tell him why not. Bobby and Uncle Ted and maybe even now Shawn—they can't none of them pass a drug screen. So I snapped, "You defending Ratface Rollins?"

"Certainly not. He has drastically and tragically cut funding for basic research."

"But here you all are." I waved my arm to take in the room and the machines hooked up to me and the desk in the lobby where Mrs. Cully was doing something on a computer. I was still floating.

"Barely," Dr. Chung said. "This study is funded as part of a grant now four years old and up for renewal. If—" He stopped and looked—for just a minute, and the first time ever—a little confused. He didn't know why he was telling me so much. I didn't know, either. *My* excuse was the pain drugs.

I said, "If Ratface wins, you lose the money for this clinic?"

"Yes."

"Why? I mean, why this one specially?"

He chewed on his bottom lip, something else I didn't see him do afore. I thought he warn't going to say any more, but then he did. "The study so far has produced no publishable results. The population affected is small. We obtained the current grant just before President Rollins came into office and all but abolished both the FDA and research money. If the Libertarians are re-elected, it's unlikely our grant will be renewed."

"Isn't there someplace else to get the money?"

"Not that we have found so far."

Mrs. Cully called to him then and he left. I sat thinking about what he said. It was like a curtain lifted on one corner, and behind that curtain was a place just as dog-eat-dog as Blaine. Bobby scrambled to dig coal from the side of the highway, and these doctors scrambled to dig money out of the government. Dinah worked hard to make it okay that Bobby hit her ("It ain't him, it's the fucking sickness!"), and Dr. Chung worked hard to convince the government it was a good idea to put a bunch of algae and a light switch in my skull. Then I thought about how much I liked him telling me all that, and about the bandages coming off and the real experiment starting tomorrow, and about lunch coming soon. And then I didn't think about nothing because Bobby burst into the clinic with his .22.

"Where is she? Where's my fucking sister?"

"Bobby!"

He didn't hear me, or he couldn't. I scrambled out of bed but I was still hooked up to a bunch of machines. I yanked the wires. Soothing voices in the lobby but I couldn't make out no words.

The .22 fired, sounding like a mine explosion.

"Bobby!"

Oh sweet Jesus, no—

But he hadn't hit nobody. Mrs. Cully crouched on the floor behind her counter. The bullet hole in the wall warn't anywhere near her or Dr. Chung, who stood facing Bobby and talking some soothers that there was no way Bobby was going to hear. He was wild-eyed like Dad had been near the end, and I knew he hadn't slept in days and he was seeing things that warn't there. "Bobby—"

"You whore!" He fired again and this time the bullet whizzed past Dr. Chung's ear and hit the backside of Mrs. Cully's computer. Bobby swung the rifle toward me. I stood stock still, but Dr. Chung started forward to grab the barrel. That would get Bobby's attention and he would—God no *no*...

But afore I could yell again, the clinic door burst open and Shawn grabbed Bobby from behind. Bobby shouted something, I couldn't tell what, and they fought. Shawn didn't have his whole manhood growth yet, but he didn't have Bobby's way-gone sickness yet, neither. Shawn got the rifle away from Bobby and Bobby on the ground. Shawn kicked him in the head and Bobby started to sob.

I picked up the rifle and held it behind me. Dr. Chung bent over Bobby. By this time the lobby was jammed with people, two nurses and Dr. Liu and Jenny and Pete Lawler, who must a been in a examining room. All this happened so fast that Shawn was just preparing to kick Bobby again when I grabbed his arm. "Don't!"

Shawn scowled at the bandage on my head. "He's going to get us all put behind bars. Just the same, he ain't wrong. You're coming home with me."

The breath went out of me. I warn't ready for this. "No, Shawn. I'm not."

"You come home with me or you don't never come home again. Granmama says."

"I'm not going. They're going to help me here, and they can help you, too! You don't need to get like Bobby, like Dad was—"

He shook off my arm. And just like that, I lost him. The Connors men don't hardly never change their minds once they make them up. And soon Shawn wouldn't even have a mind. Seven months from the first sleeplessness to death.

Shawn yanked Bobby to his feet. Bobby was quiet now, bleeding from his head where Shawn kicked him. Dr. Liu started to say, "We must—" but Dr. Chung put a hand on his arm and he shut up. Shawn held out his other hand to me, his face like stone, and I handed him Bobby's gun. Then they were gone, the truck Shawn borrowed or stole roaring away up the mountain.

Dr. Chung knew better than to say anything to me. I looked at the busted computer and wondered how much it cost, and if they would take it out of my pay. Then I went back into my room, closed the door, and got into bed. I would a given anything, right up to my own life, if I could a slept then. But I knew I wouldn't. Not now, not tonight, not—it felt like at that minute—ever again. And by spring, Shawn would be like Bobby. And so would I.

"You need a pass-out," I said to Dr. Chung.

He paused in his poking at my head. "A what?"

"When Bonnie Jean got a fish at a pet store once, they gave her a pass-out paper, TAKING CARE OF YOUR GOLDFISH. To tell her how to do for the fish—not that she done it. You need a pass-out, TAKING CARE OF YOUR BRAIN ALGAE."

Dr. Chung laughed. When he did that, his eyes almost disappeared, but by now I liked that. Nobody else never thought I was funny, even if my funning now was just a cover for nerves. Dr. Liu, at the computer, didn't laugh, and neither did Jenny. I still didn't like *her* eyes.

I sat on a chair, just a regular chair, with my head bandage off and the shaved patch on my head feeling too bare. All my fingers could feel was a tiny bit of something hard poking above my skull: the end of the fiber-optic implant. Truth was, I didn't need a pass-out paper. I knew what was going to happen because Dr. Chung explained it, as many times as I wanted, till I really understood. The punchpad in his hand controlled what my "optrode" did. He could send blue or yellow laser light down it, which would make my new algae release tiny particles that turned on and off some cells in my brain. I'd seen the videos of mice, with long cables coming from their skulls, made to run in circles, or stop staggering around drunk-like, or even remember mazes quicker.

Last night I asked Dr. Chung, "You can control me now, can't you?"

"I have no wish to control you."

"But you *could*."

"No one will control you."

I'd laughed then, too, but it tasted like lemons in my mouth.

"Ready?" Dr. Liu said.

"Ready." I braced myself, but nothing happened. I didn't feel nothing at all. But at the screen Jenny went, "Aaaaaaaahhh."

"What?" I said.

"It works," Dr. Chung said quietly. "We are getting a good picture of optrode response."

On the screen was a bunch of wavy lines, with a lot of clicking noises.

That went on for a long bit: me sitting in the chair feeling nothing, Dr. Chung turning lights on and off in my head that I didn't see, lines and numbers on the computer, and lots of long discussions with words I didn't understand. Maybe some of them were Chinese. And then, just when I was getting antsy and bored both at the same time, something happened. Another press of the punchpad and all at once I saw the room. Not like I saw it afore—I mean I really *saw* it. Every little thing was clear and bright and separate and itself: the hard edge of the computer screen, the way the overhead light made a shadow in the corner, a tiny brown stain on the hem of Jenny's white coat—*everything.* The room was like Reverend Baxter said the world looked right when God created it: fresh and new and shining. I could feel my mouth drop open and my eyes get wide.

"What?" Dr. Chung said. "What is it, Ludie?"

I told him. He did something with the switch in his hand and all the fresh clearness went away. "Oh! Bring it back!"

"Hyperawareness," Dr. Liu said. "The opsins could be over-expressing?"

"Not that quickly," Dr. Chung said. "But—"

"Bring it back!" I almost shouted it.

He did. But after a minute it was almost too much. Too bright, too clear, too strange. And then it got clearer and brighter, so that it almost blinded me and I couldn't see and everything was wrong and—

It all stopped. Dr. Chung had pressed some switch. And then I wanted it back.

"Not yet, Ludie," he said. He sounded worried. "You were injected with multiple opsins, you know, each responding to a different wavelength of light. We're going to try a different one. Would you stand up, please? Good...now walk toward me."

I did, and he did something with his switch, and all at once I couldn't move. I was frozen. The computer started clicking loud as a plague of locusts.

Jenny said, "Pronounced inhibitory motor response."

I said, "Stop!"

Then I could move again and I was pounding on Dr. Chung with my fists. "You said you warn't going to control me! You said!"

He grabbed my wrists and held them; he was stronger than he looked. "I didn't know that would happen, Ludie. This is all new, you know. Nobody wants to control you."

"You just did, you bastard!"

"I did not know the inhibitory neurons would fire that strongly. Truly, I did not."

Jenny said something in Chinese.

"No," Dr. Chung said sharply to her.

"I'm done here," I said.

"Yes, that's enough for a first session," Dr. Liu said. Which warn't what I meant. I meant I was going home.

But I didn't. Instead I went to my room in the clinic, got into bed, and slept a little. Not long, not real hard, but enough to calm me down. Then I got up and found Dr. Chung in his office.

If he was glad to see me, he didn't let on. Instead he handed me an envelope. "This came for you in the mail."

Inside was a single page torn from the Sears catalogue, a page with kids' coats on the top and enough white space at the bottom for Dinah to print THANK U. So she got the money I been sending her from my pay. Where did she tell Bobby the warm clothes come from, the coats and stuff for Lewis, Arianna, Timmy, Cody, Bonnie Jean? No, that was stupid—Bobby was too far gone to notice even if the kids ran around buck naked.

I turned on Dr. Chung. "Did you give me this right now so's I'd stay?"

"Ludie, how could I know what was in your envelope? I still don't know."

"You know sure enough what's in my head!"

"I know there are abnormal FFI prions, which we hope to arrest. I know, too, that there is valuable information about how the brain works."

"You told me afore that you can't get them prions out of my head!"

"We cannot, no. What we hope is to disrupt the formation of any more. For your sake, as much as ours."

"I don't believe that crap!"

Only I wanted to believe it.

"Okay," I said, "here's the deal. I stay and you do your experiments, but the minute I tell you to stop something, you do it." It was lame bluster, and he knew it.

"Yes. I already did so, you know. You told me to stop the inhibition of motor activity, and I did."

"And another thing. I want a pass-out, after all."

He blinked. "You want—"

"I want you to write out in words I can understand just what you're doing to me. So's I can study on it afore we do it again."

Dr. Chung smiled. "I will be glad to do that, Ludie."

I flounced out of there, knowing I hadn't told him the whole truth. I wanted to keep sending money to Dinah, yes. I wanted him to not freeze me no more, yes. I wanted a pass-out paper, yes. But I also wanted that shining clearness back, that thing Jenny had called hyper-awareness. I wanted it enough to go on risking my brain.

If that's really what I was doing.

Ludie—you have Fatal Familial Insomnia. Inside a part of your brain called the thalamus, some proteins called prions are folding up wrong. The wrongly folded proteins are making other proteins also fold wrong. These are sticking together in clumps and interfering with what cells are supposed to do. The main thing thalamus cells are supposed to do is process communications among different parts of the brain. The thalamus is like a switchboard, except that it also changes the communications in ways we are trying to learn about. Things which the thalamus communicates with the rest of the brain about include: moving the body, thinking, seeing, making decisions, memory formation and retrieval, and sleeping. When you get a lot of sticky, misfolded proteins in the thalamus, you can't go into deep sleep, or move properly, or think clearly. You get hallucinations and insomnia and sometimes seizures.

We are trying to do three things: (1) Stop your brain making more misfolded prions, even if we can't get rid of the ones that are already there. We are trying to do this by interfering with the making of a protein that the prions use to fold wrong. Unhappily, the only way we will know if this happens is if your symptoms do not get worse. (2) Your brain works partly by sending electrical signals between cells. We are trying to map how these go, called "neural pathways." (3) We want to find out more about what the

special algae (opsins) we put in your brain can do. They release different chemicals when we put different laser lights down the cable. We want to know the results of each different thing we do, to aid science.

Well, Dr. Chung wrote good, even though I didn't know what a "switchboard" might be.

I thought of Mama, her brain full of these misfolded proteins, gummed up like a drain full of grease and hair. And Bobby's brain, even worse. Mine, too, soon?

It was dark outside by the time I finished reading that damn paper over and over and over. Everybody'd gone home from the clinic except the night nurse, a skinny rabbitty-looking girl named Susannah. I knowed that she was mountain-born the minute I laid eyes on her, and that somehow she'd got out, and I'd tried not to have nothing to do with her. But now I marched out to where she was reading a magazine in the lobby and said, "Call Dr. Chung. Now."

"What's wrong?"

"Never you mind. Just call him."

"It's ten o'clock at—"

"I know what time it is. Call him."

She did, and he came. I said, "We're going to work now. Now, not in the morning. Them proteins are folding in me right this second, aren't they? You call Jenny and Dr. Liu if you really need them. We're going to work all night. Afore I change my mind."

He looked at me hard. Funny how when you know a person long enough, even a strange and ugly person, they don't look so bad no more.

"Okay," he said. "Let's work."

We worked all night. We worked all week. We worked another week, then another. And I didn't get no worse. No better, but no worse. What I got was scared.

Nobody ought to be able to do those things to somebody else's brain, using nothing except little bits of light.

Dr. Chung froze me again while I was walking around.

Dr. Liu said, "Filtering signals is an important thalamic function, and any change in filtering may give rise to physiological effects."

Dr. Chung made the "hyperawareness" come back, even stronger.

Jenny said, "Interfering with action potentials on cell membranes changes the way cells process information."

Dr. Chung made me remember things from when I was really little—Mama singing to me. Shawn and me wrestling. Granmama telling me troll stories while I sat on her knee. Bobby teaching me to fish. The memories were so sharp, they felt like they was slicing into my brain. Good memories but too razored, making my mind bleed.

Dr. Liu said, "Are the opsins in the anterior nuclei over-expressing? That could cause problems."

Dr. Chung did something that made me stutter so's I couldn't get a word out whole no matter how much I tried.

Jenny said, "Neural timing—even the shift of a few milliseconds can reverse the effect of the signal on the rest of the nervous system. Not good."

I didn't think any of it was good. But I warn't going to say anything in front of that Jenny; I waited until I got Dr. Chung alone.

"I got to ask you something."

"Of course, Ludie." He had just finished checking on my heart and blood pressure and all that. "Are you pleased by the way the study is going? You say your FFI symptoms aren't any worse, and with the usual rapid progression of the disease in your family, that may mean genuine progress."

"I'm happy about that, yeah, if it goes on like now. But I got a different question. I been reading in that book you gave me, how the brain is and isn't like a computer." The book was hard going, but interesting.

"Yes?" He looked really caught on what I was saying. For the first time, I wondered what his wife was like. Was she pretty?

"A computer works on teeny switches that have two settings, on and off, and that's how it knows things."

"A binary code, yes."

"Well, those laser switches on the bundle of optic cables you put in my head—they're off and on, too. Could you make my head into a computer? And put information into it, like into a computer—information that warn't there afore?"

Dr. Chung stood. He breathed deep. I saw the second he decided not to lie to me. "Not now, not with what we know at present, which isn't nearly enough. But potentially, far down the road and with the right connections to the cortex, it's not inconceivable."

Which was a fancy way of saying yes.

"Good night," I said abruptly and went into my room.

"Ludie—"

But I didn't have nothing more to say to him. In bed, though, I used the tablet he loaned me—that's what I been reading the book on—to get the Internet and find Dr. Chung. I got a lot of hits. One place I found a picture of him with his wife. She was pretty, all right, and refined-looking. Smart. He had his arm around her.

Sleep was even harder that night than usual. Then, the next day, it all happened.

We were in the testing room, and my hyperawareness was back. Everything was clear as mountain spring water, as sharp as a skinning knife. I kept rising up on my tip-toes, just from sheer energy. It didn't feel bad. Dr. Chung watched me real hard, with a little frown.

"Do you want a break, Ludie?"

"No. Bring it on."

"Hippocampal connection test 48," Jenny said, and Dr. Chung's hand moved on his punchpad. The computer started clicking louder and louder. The door burst open and Bobby charged in, waving a knife and screaming.

"Whore! Whore!" He plunged the knife into Jenny and blood spurted out of her in huge, foaming gushes. I shouted and tried to throw myself in front of Dr. Chung, but Bobby got him next. Dr. Liu had vanished. Bobby turned on me and he warn't Bobby no more but a troll from Granmama's stories, a troll with Bobby's face, and Bonnie Jean hung mangled and bloody from his teeth. I hit out at the troll and his red eyes bored into me and his knife raised and—

I lay on the floor, Dr. Chung holding me down, Jenny doubled over in pain, and the computer screen laying beside me.

"Ludie—"

"What did you do?" I screamed. "What did you do to me? What did I do?" I broke free of him, or he let me up. "*What?*"

"You had a delusional episode," Dr. Chung said, steady but pale, watching me like I was the Bobby-troll. And I was. I had hit Jenny and knocked over the computer, only it was—

"Don't you touch me!"

"All right," Dr. Chung said quietly, "I won't." Dr. Liu was picking up the computer, which was still clicking like a crazy thing. Mrs. Cully and a nurse stood in the doorway. Jenny gasped and wheezed. "You had a delusional episode, Ludie. Perhaps because of the FFI, perhaps—"

"It was you, and you know it was you! You done it to me! You said you wouldn't control my brain and now you—" I pulled at the optrode sticking up from my skull, but of course it didn't budge. "You can't do that to me! You can't!"

"We don't know what the—"

"You don't know nothing! And I'm done with the lot of you!" It all came together in me then, all the strangeness of what they was doing and the fear for my family and them throwing me out and the lovely hyperawareness gone when the switch went off and Dr. Chung's pretty wife—*all of it*.

I didn't listen to nothing else they said. I walked straight out of that clinic, my legs shaking, without even grabbing my coat. And there was Shawn pulling up in Jimmy Barton's truck, getting out and looking at me with winter in his face. "Bobby's dead," he said. "He killed himself."

I said, "I know."

The funeral was a week later—it took that long for the coroner to get done fussing with Bobby's body. It was election day, and Ratface Rollins lost, along with the whole Libertarian party.

The November wind blew cold and raw. Mama was too bad off to go to the graveyard. But Shawn brought her to the service where she sat muttering, even through the church choir singing her favorite, "In the Sweet Bye and Bye." I don't know if she even knew what was going on; for sure she didn't recognize me. It warn't be long afore she'd be as bad as Bobby, or in a coma like Aunt Carol Ames. Granmama recognized me, of course, but she didn't say nothing when I came into the trailer, or when I stayed there, sleeping in my old bed with Patty and Bonnie Jean, or when I cleaned up the place a bit and cooked a stew with groceries from my clinic money. Granmama didn't thank me, but I didn't expect that. She was grieving Bobby. And she was Granmama.

Dinah kept to her room, her kids pretty much in there with her day and night.

I kept a hat on, over my part-shaved head. Not the red knit hat Dr. Chung gave me, which I wadded up and threw in the creek. In the trailer I wore Bobby's old baseball cap, and at the funeral I wore a black straw hat that Mama had when I was little.

"'The Lord is my Shepherd; I shall not want. He maketh me to lie down in green pastures...'" Reverend Baxter did funerals old-fashioned.

Bobby's casket was lowered into the hole in the churchyard. The last of the maple leaves blew down and skittered across the grass.

Dinah came forward, hanging onto Shawn, and tossed her flower into the grave. Then Granmama, then me, then Patty. The littlest kids, Lewis and Arianna and Timothy and Cody, were in relatives' arms. The last to throw her flower was Bonnie Jean, and that's when I saw it.

Bonnie Jean wore an old coat of Patty's, too big for her, so's the hem brushed the ground. When she stood by the grave that hem was shaking like aspen leaves. Her face had froze, and the pupils of her eyes were so wide it looked like she was on something. She warn't. And it warn't just the fear and grief of a ten-year-old at a funeral, neither.

"Ashes to ashes, dust to dust...."

Neighbors brought cakes and covered dishes to the trailer. Nobody didn't stay long 'cause they knew we didn't want them to. Dinah went back into her room with her two kids, Mama was muttering beside the stove, Shawn sat smoking and drinking Bud. I told Patty to watch Timmy and Cody and I took Bonnie Jean into our bedroom.

"How long since you slept through the whole night?"

She was scared enough to give me lip. "I sleep. You been right there next to me!"

"How long, Bonnie Jean?"

"I don't got to tell you nothing! You're a whore, sleeping with them Chinese and letting them do bad things to you—Bobby said!"

"How long?"

She looked like she was going to cry, but instead she snatched Bobby's baseball hat off my head. It seemed to me that my optrode burned like a forest fire, though of course it didn't. Bonnie Jean stared at it and spat, "Chink Frankenstein!"

Probably she didn't even know what the words meant, just heard them at school. Or at home.

Then she started to cry, and I picked her up in my arms and sat with her on the edge of the bed, and she let me. All at once I saw that the bed was covered with the Fence Rail quilt Dinah had been making for the women's co-op. She'd put it on my bed instead.

I held Bonnie Jean while she cried. She told me it had been two weeks since she couldn't sleep right and at the graveyard was her second panic attack—what she called "the scared shakes." She was ten years old, and she carried the gene Granmama and God-knows-who-else had passed on without being affected themselves. Insomnia and panic attacks and phobias. Then hallucinations and more panic attacks and shrinking away to hardly no weight at all. Then dementia or coma or Bobby's way out. Ten years old. While I was nineteen and I hadn't even felt her restless beside me in the long cold night.

I knowed, then, what I had to do.

The Chinese clinic was almost empty.

A sign outside said CLOSED. Through the window I could see the lobby stripped of its chairs and pictures and clothes basket of toys. But a light shone in a back room, bright in the drizzly gray rain. I rattled the lock on the door and shouted "Hey!" and pretty soon Mrs. Cully opened it.

She wore jeans and a sweatshirt instead of her usual dress, and her hair was wrapped in a big scarf. In one hand was a roll of packing tape. She didn't look surprised to see me. She looked something, but I couldn't read it.

"Ludie. Come in."

"You all leaving Blaine?"

"Our grant won't be renewed. Dr. Chung found out the day after the election from a man he knows in Washington."

"But Rollins lost!"

"Yes, but the new president made campaign promises to reinstate the FDA with tight regulations on studies with human subjects. Under Rollins there was too much abuse. So Doctors Chung and Liu are using their remaining money for data analysis, back at the university—*especially* since we have no research subjects here. I'm packing files and equipment."

The rooms behind her, all their doors open, were full of boxes, some sealed, some still open. A feeling washed over me that matched the weather outside. The clinic never had no chance no matter who won the election.

Mrs. Cully said, "But Dr. Chung left something for you, in case you came back." She plucked a brown envelope off the counter, and then she went back to her packing while I opened it. Tact—Mrs. Cully always had tact.

Inside the envelope was a cell phone, a pack of money with a rubber band around it, and a letter.

Ludie—

This is the rest of what the clinic owes you. Along with it, accept my deepest gratitude for your help with this study. Even though

not finished, it—and you—have made a genuine contribution to science. You are an exceptional young woman, with exceptional intelligence and courage.

This cell phone holds the phone number for Dr. Morton, who implanted your optrode, and who will remove it. Call her to schedule the operation. There will of course be no charge. The phone also holds my number. Please call me. If you don't, I will call this number every day at 11:00 a.m. until I reach you. I want only to know that you are all right.

Your friend,

Hai Chung

The phone said it was 9:30 a.m. Mrs. Cully said, "Is that your suitcase?"

"Yeah. It is. I need Dr. Chung's address, ma'am."

She looked at me hard. "Call him first."

"Okay." But I wouldn't. By the time the phone rang, I would be on the 10:17 Greyhound to Lexington.

She gave me his university address but wouldn't give out his home. It didn't really matter. I knew he would give it to me, plus whatever else I needed. And not just for the study, neither.

Dr. Chung told me, one time, about a scientist called Daniel Zagury He was studying on AIDS, and he shot himself up with a vaccine he was trying to make, to test it. Dr. Chung didn't do no experiments on himself; he used me instead, just like I was using him for the money. Only that warn't the whole story, no more than Bobby's terrible behavior when he got really sick was the whole story of Bobby. The Chinese clinic warn't Chinese, and I'm not no Frankenstein. I'm not all that "courageous," neither, though I sure liked Dr. Chung saying it. What I *am* is connected to my kin, no matter how much I used to wish I warn't. Right now, connected don't mean staying in Blaine to help Dinah with her grief and Shawn with his sickness and the kids with their schooling. It don't mean waiting for Mama's funeral, or living with Granmama's sour anger at what her genes did to her family. Right now, being connected means getting on a Greyhound to Lexington.

It means going on with Dr. Chung's study.

It means convincing him, and everybody else, to put a optrode in Bonnie Jean's head, and Shawn's, and maybe even Lewis's, so laser light can "disrupt their neural pathways" and they don't get no more misfolded prions than they already got.

It means paying for this with whatever work I get.

And maybe it even means going to Washington, D.C. and talking to my congressman—whoever he is—about why this study is a good thing. I read on Dr. Chung's tablet that other scientists sometimes do that. Maybe I could take Bonnie Jean with me. She's real pretty, and I can teach her to look pathetic. Maybe.

I never had no thoughts like this afore, and maybe that's the opsins, too. But maybe not. I don't know. I only know that this is my path and I'm going to walk it.

I hike to the highway, suitcase in one hand and cell phone in the other, and I flag down the bus.

Afterword to "Pathways"

In 2013 Stephen Cass, editor of *MIT Tech Review*, contacted me about writing a hard-SF, near-future story for the *Review*. I jumped at the chance. Untrained in any of the sciences, I am nonetheless a science groupie who haloes physics and biology and chemistry in a golden glow. Stephen gave me a possible list of breakthrough fields to choose from. Optogenetics intrigued me the most, at least in part because its consequences seemed the most scary.

Since this story was written, research in optogenetics has gotten even scarier. MIT researchers have succeeded in altering the ways that mice remember bad or good experiences. The memory itself is not altered, but the emotions around it can be changed so that bad memories evoke less stress in mice, and good ones less pleasure—all through directing pulses of light into genemod neurons. This could have positive outcomes for treatment of psychological disorders. It could also lead to exactly what Ludmilla fears.

As always, science is a tool, and we decide what to do with it.

DANCING ON AIR

"When a man has been guilty of a mistake, either in ordering his own affairs, or in directing those of State, or in commanding an army, do we not always say, So-and-so has made a false step in this affair? And can making a false step derive from anything but lack of skill in dancing?"

— Molière

1.

Sometimes I understand the words. Sometimes I do not understand the words.

Eric brings me to the exercise yard. A man and a woman stand there. The man is tall. The woman is short. She has long black fur on her head. She smells angry.

Eric says, "This is Angel. Angel, this is John Cole and Caroline Olson."

"Hello," I say.

"I'm supposed to understand that growl?" the woman says. "Might as well be Russian!"

"Caroline," the man says, "you promised..."

"I know what I promised." She walks away. She smells very angry. I don't understand. My word was *hello. Hello* is one of the easy words.

The man says, "Hello, Angel." He smiles. I sniff his shoes and bark. He smells friendly. I smell two cats and a hot dog and street tar and a car. I feel happy. I like cars.

The woman comes back. "If we have to do this, then let's just do it, for Chrissake. Let's sign the papers and get out of this hole."

John Cole says, "The lawyers are all waiting in Eric's office."

Eric's office smells of many people. I go to my place beside the door. I lie down. Maybe later somebody takes me in the car.

A woman looks at many papers and talks. "A contract between Biomod Canine Protection Agency, herein referred to as the party of the first part, and the New York City Ballet, herein referred to as the party of the second part, in fulfillment of the requirements of Columbia Insurance Company, herein referred to as the party of the third part, as those requirements are set forth in Policy 438-69, Section 17, respecting prima ballerina Caroline Olson. The party of the first part shall furnish genetically-modified canine protection to Caroline Olson under, and not limited to, the following conditions..."

The words are hard.

I think words I can understand.

My name is Angel. I am a dog. I protect. Eric tells me to protect. No people can touch the one I protect except safe people. I love people I protect. I sleep now.

"Angel," Eric says from his chair, "Wake up now. You must protect."

I wake up. Eric walks to me. He sits next to me. He puts his voice in my ear.

"This is Caroline. You must protect Caroline. No one must hurt Caroline. No one must touch Caroline except safe people. Angel—*protect Caroline*."

I smell Caroline. I am very happy. I protect Caroline.

"Jesus H. Christ," Caroline says. She walks away.

I love Caroline.

We go in the car. We go very far. Many people. Many smells. John drives the car. John is safe. He may touch Caroline. John stops the car. We get out. There are many tall buildings and many cars.

"You sure you're going to be okay?" John Cole says.

"You've protected your investment, haven't you?" Caroline snarls. John drives away.

A man stands by the door. The man says, "Evening, Miss Olson."

"Evening, Sam. This is my new guard dog. The company insists I have one, after...what's been happening. They say the insurance company is paranoid. Yeah, sure. I need a dog like I need a knee injury."

"Yes, ma'am. Doberman, isn't he? He looks like a goooood ol' dog. Hey, big fella, what's your name?"

"Angel," I say.

The man jumps and makes a noise. Caroline laughs.

"Bioenhanced. Great for my privacy, right? Rover, Sam is safe. Do you hear me? Sam is *safe*."

I say, "My name is Angel."

Caroline says, "Sam, you can relax. Really. He only attacks on command, or if I scream, or if he hasn't been told a person is safe and that person touches me."

"Yes, Ma'am." Sam smells afraid. He looks at me hard. I bark and my tail moves.

Caroline says, "Come on, Fido. Your spy career is about to begin."

I say, "My name is Angel."

"Right," Caroline says.

We go in the building. We go in the elevator. I say, "Sam has a cat. I smell Sam's cat."

"Who the fuck cares," Caroline says.

I am a dog.

I must love Caroline.

2.

Two days after the second ballerina was murdered, Michael Chow, senior editor of *New York Now* and my boss, called me into his office. I already knew what he wanted, and I already knew I didn't want to do it. He knew that, too. We both knew it wouldn't make any difference.

"You're the logical reporter, Susan," Michael said. He sat behind his desk, always a bad sign. When he thought I'd want an assignment, he leaned casually against the front of the desk. Its top was cluttered with print-outs; with disposable research cartridges, some with their screens alight; with pictures of Michael's six children. *Six*. They all looked like Michael: straight black hair and a smooth face like a peeled egg. At the apex of the mess sat a hardcopy of the *Times* 3:00 p.m. on-line lead: AUTOPSY DISCOVERS BIOENHANCERS IN CITY BALLET DANCER. "You have an in. Even Anton Privitera will talk to you."

"Not about this. He already gave his press conference. Such as it was."

"So? You can get to him as a parent and leverage from there."

My daughter Deborah was a student in the School of American Ballet, the juvenile province of Anton Privitera's kingdom. For thirty years he had ruled the New York City Ballet like an anointed tyrant. Sometimes it seemed he could even levy taxes and raise armies, so exalted was his reputation in the dance world, and so good was his business manager John Cole at raising funds and enlisting corporate patrons. Dancers had flocked to the City Ballet from Europe, from Asia, from South America, from the serious ballet schools in the patrolled zones of America's dying cities. Until biohancers, the New York City Ballet had been the undisputed grail of the international dance world.

Now, of course, that was changing.

Privitera was dynamic with the press as long as we were content with what he wished us to know. He wasn't going to want to discuss the murder of two dancers, one of them his own.

A month ago Nicole Heyer, a principal dancer with the American Ballet Theater, had been found strangled in Central Park. Three days ago the body of Jennifer Lang had been found in her modest apartment. Heyer had been a bioenhanced dancer who had come to the ABT from the Stuttgart Ballet. Lang, a minor soloist with the City Ballet, had of course been natural. Or so everybody thought until the autopsy. The entire company had been bioscanned only three weeks ago, Artistic Director Privitera had told the press, but apparently these particular viro-enhancers were so new and so different that they hadn't even shown up on the scan.

I wondered how to make Michael understand the depth of my dislike for all this.

"Don't cover the usual police stuff," Michael said, "nor the scientific stuff on bioenhancement. Concentrate on the human angle you do so well. What's the effect of these murders on the other dancers? Has it affected their dancing? Does Privitera seemed more confirmed in his company policy now, or has this shaken him enough to consider a change? What's he doing to protect his dancers? How do the parents feel about the youngsters in the ballet school? Are they withdrawing them until the killer is caught?"

I said, "You don't have any sensitivity at all, do you, Michael?"

He said quietly, "Your girl's seventeen, Susan. If you couldn't get her to leave dancing before, you're not going to get her to leave now. Will you do the story?"

I looked again at the scattered pictures of Michael's children. His oldest was at Harvard Law. His second son was a happily married house-husband, raising three kids. His third child, a daughter, was doing six-to-ten in Rock Mountain Maximum Security State Prison for armed robbery. There was no figuring it out. I said, "I'll do the story."

"Good," he said, not looking at me. "Just hold down the metaphors, Susan. You're still too given to metaphors."

"*New York Now* could use a few metaphors. A feature magazine isn't supposed to be a TV holo bite."

"A feature magazine isn't art, either," Michael retorted. "Let's all keep that in mind."

"You're in luck," I said. "As it happens, I'm not a great lover of art."

I couldn't decide whether to tell Deborah I had agreed to write about ballet. She would hate my writing about her world under threat.

Which was a reason both for and against.

September heat and long, cool shadows fought it out over the wide plaza of Lincoln Center. The fountain splashed, surrounded by tourists and students and strollers and derelicts. I thought Lincoln Center was ugly, shoe-box architecture stuck around a charmless expanse of stone unredeemed by a little splashing water. Michael said I only felt that way because I hated New York. If Lincoln Center had been built in Kentucky, he said, I would have admired it.

I had remembered to get the electronic password from Deborah. Since the first murder, the New York State Theater changed it weekly. Late afternoon was heavy rehearsal time; the company was using the stage as well as the studios. I heard the Spanish bolero from the second act of *Coppelia*. Deborah had been trying to learn it for weeks. The role of Swanilda, the girl who pretends to be a doll, had first made the brilliant Caroline Olson a superstar.

Privitera's office was a jumble of dance programs, costume swatches, and computers. He made me wait for him twenty minutes. I sat and thought about what I knew about bioenhanced dancers, besides the fact that there weren't supposed to have been any at City Ballet.

There were several kinds of bioenhancement. All of them were experimental, all of them were illegal in The United States, all of them were constantly in flux as new discoveries were made and rushed onto the European, South American, and Japanese markets. It was a new science, chaotic and contradictory, like physics at the start of the last century, or cancer cures at the start of this one. No bioenhancements had been developed specifically for ballet dancers, who were an insignificant portion of the population. But European dancers submitted to experimental versions, as did American dancers who could travel to Berlin or Copenhagen or Rio for the very expensive privilege of injecting their bodies with tiny, unproven biological "machines."

Some nanomachines carried programming that searched out deviations in the body and repaired them to match surrounding tissue. This speeded the healing of some injuries some of the time, or only erratically, or not at all, depending on whom you believed. Jennifer Lang had been receiving these treatments, trying desperately to lessen the injury rate that went hand-in-hand with ballet. The nanomachines were highly experimental, and nobody was sure what long-term effect they might have, reproducing themselves in the human body, interacting with human DNA.

Bone builders were both simpler and more dangerous. They were altered viruses, reprogrammed to change the shape or density of bones. Most of the experimental work had been done on old women with advanced osteoporosis. Some grew denser bones after treatment. The rest didn't. In ballet, the legs are required to rotate 180 degrees in the hip sockets—the famous "turnout" that had destroyed so many dancers' hips and knees. If bones could be altered to swivel 180 degrees *naturally* in their sockets, turnout would cause far less strain and disintegration. Extension could also be higher, making easier the spectacular *arabesques* and *grand battement* kicks.

If the bones of the foot were reshaped, foot injuries could be lessened in the unnatural act of dancing on toe.

Bioenhanced leg muscles could be stronger, for higher jumps, greater speed, more stamina.

Anything that helped metabolic efficiency or lung capacity could help a dancer sustain movements. They could also help her keep down her weight without anorexia, the secret vice of the ballet world.

Dancers in Europe began to experiment with bioenhancement. First cautiously, clandestinely. Then scandalously. Now openly, as a mark of pride. A dancer with the Royal Ballet or the Bolshoi or the Nederlands Dans Theater who didn't have his or her body enhanced was considered undevoted to movement. A dancer at the New York City Ballet who did have his or her body enhanced was considered undevoted to art.

Privitera swept into his office without apology for being late. "Ah, there you are. What can I do for you?" His accent was very light, but still the musical tones of his native Tuscany were there. It gave his words a deceptive intimacy.

"I've come about my daughter, Deborah Anders. She's in D level at SAB. She's the one who—"

"Yes, yes, yes, I know who she is. I know all my dancers, even the very young ones. Of course. But shouldn't you be talking with Madame Alois? She is the director of our School."

"But you make all the important decisions," I say, trying to smile winningly.

Privitera sat on a wing chair. He must have been in his seventies, yet he moved like a young man: straight strong back, light movements. The famous bright blue eyes met mine shrewdly. His vitality and physical presence on stage had made him a legendary dancer; now he was simply a legend. Whatever he decided the New York City Ballet should be, it became. I didn't like him. That absolute power bothered me—even though it was merely power over an art form seen by only a fraction of the people who watched soccer or football.

"I have three questions about Deborah, Mr. Privitera. First—and I'm sure you hear this all the time—can you give me some idea of her chances as a professional dancer? She'll have to apply to college this fall, if she's going to go, and although what she really wants is to dance professionally, if that's not going to happen then we need to think about other—"

"Yes, yes," Privitera said, swatting away this question like the irrelevancy he considered it to be. "But dance is never a second choice, Ms. Anders."

"Matthews," I said. "Susan Matthews. Anders is Deborah's name."

"If Deborah has it in her to be a dancer, that's what she will be. If not—" He shrugged. People who were not dancers ceased to exist for Anton Privitera.

"That's what I want to know. Does she have it in her to be a professional dancer? Her teachers say she has good musicality and rhythm, but..."

My hands gripped together so tightly the skin was gray.

"Perhaps. Perhaps. You must leave it to me to judge when the time comes."

"But that's what I'm saying," I said, as agreeably as I could. "The time *has* come. College—"

"You cannot hurry art. If Deborah is meant to be a dancer, she will become one. Leave it to me, dear."

Dear. It was what he called all his dancers. I saw that it had just slipped out. *Leave it to me, dear. I know best.* How often did he say that in class, in rehearsal, during a choreography session, before a performance?

The muted strains of *Coppelia* drifted through the walls. I said, "Then let me ask my second question. As a parent, I'm naturally concerned about Deborah's safety since these awful murders. What steps has City Ballet taken to ensure the safety of the students and dancers?"

The intense eyes contracted to blue shards. But I could see the moment he decided the question was within a parent's right to ask. "The police do not think there is danger to the students. This…madman, this *bestia*, apparently attacks only full-fledged dancers, soloists and principals who have tried to reach art through medicine and not through dancing. No dancer in my company or my school is bioenhanced. My dancers believe as I do: You can achieve art only through talent and work, through opening yourself to the dance, not through mechanical aids. What they do at the ABT—that is *not art*! Besides," he added, with an abrupt descent to the practical, "students cannot afford bioenhancing operations."

Idealism enforced by realism—I saw the combination that kept the City Ballet a success, despite the technically superior performances of bio-enhanced dancers. I could almost hear dancers and patrons alike: *'The only real ballet.' 'Dance that preserves the necessary illusion that the performers' bodies and the audience's are fundamentally the same.' 'My dear, he's simply the most wonderful man, saving the precious traditions that made dance great in the first place. We've pledged $20,000—'*

I decided to push. "But Jennifer Lang apparently found a way to afford illegal bioenhancements that—"

"That has nothing to do with your Deborah," Privitera said, standing in one fluid movement. His blue eyes were arctic. "Now if you will excuse me, many things call me."

"But you haven't said what you *are* doing for the students' safety," I said, not rising from my chair, trying to sound as if my only interest were parental. "Please, I need to know. Deborah…"

He barely repressed a sigh. "We have increased security, Ms. Anders. Electronic surveillance both at SAB and Lincoln Center has been added to, with specifics that I cannot discuss. We have hired additional escorts for those students performing small professional roles who must leave Lincoln Center after ten at night. We have created new emphasis on teaching our young dancers the importance, the complete *necessity*, of training their bodies for dance, not relying on drugs and operations that can only offer tawdry imitations of the genuine experience of art."

I doubted City Ballet had actually done all that: it had only been three days since Jennifer Lang's murder. But Privitera's rhetoric helped me ask my last questions.

"Have any other parents withdrawn their sons and daughters from SAB? For that matter, have any of your dancers altered their performance schedules? How has the company as a whole been affected?"

Privitera looked at me with utter scorn. "If a dancer—even a student dancer—leaves me because some *bestia* is killing performers who do what I have insisted my dancers *not* do—such a so-called dancer should leave. There is no place for such a dancer in my school or my company. Don't you understand, Ms. Anders—this is the *New York City Ballet*."

He left. Through the open door the music was clear: still the Spanish dance from *Coppelia*. The girl who turned herself into a beautiful doll.

Michael was right. I was definitely too given to metaphors.

As I walked down the hall, it occurred to me that Privitera hadn't mentioned increased bioscanning. Surely that would make the most sense—discover which dancers were attaining their high jumps and strong *développés* through bioenhancement, and then eliminate those dancers from the purity of the company? Before some *bestia* did it first.

Deborah, I knew, was taking an extra class in Studio 3. I shouldn't go. If I went, we would only fight again. I pushed open the door to Studio 3.

I sat on a hard small chair with the ballet mothers waiting for the class to end. I knew better than to talk to any of them. They all wanted their daughters to succeed in ballet.

Barre warm-ups were over. The warm air smelled of rosin on wood. Dancers worked in the center of the floor, sweat dripping off their twirling and leaping bodies. *Bourees, pirouettes, entrechats.* "Non, non!" the teacher called, a retired French dancer whom I had never seen smile. "When you jump, your arms must help. They must pull you through from left to right. Like this."

Deborah did the step wrong. "Non, non!" the teacher called. "Like this!"

Deborah still did it wrong. She grimaced. I felt my stomach tighten.

Deborah tried again. It was still wrong. The teacher gestured toward the back of the room. Deborah walked to the *barre* and practiced the step alone while the rest of the class went on leaping. *Plié, relevé,* then...I didn't know the names of the rest of these steps. Whatever they were, she was still doing them wrong. Deborah tried over and over again, her face clenched. I couldn't watch.

When Deborah was fourteen, she ran away from home in St. Louis to her father's hovel in New York, the same father she had not seen since she was three. She wanted to dance for Anton Privitera, she said. I demanded that Pers, whom I had divorced for desertion, send her back. He refused. Deborah moved into his rat-trap on West 110th, way outside Manhattan's patrolled zone. The lack of police protection didn't deter her, the filthy toilet down the hall didn't deter her, the nine-year-old who was shot dealing sunshine on the stoop next door didn't deter her. When I flew to New York, she cried but refused to go home. She wanted to dance for Anton Privitera.

You can't physically wrestle a fourteen-year-old onto a plane. You can argue, and scream, and threaten, and plead, and cry, but you cannot physically move her. Not without a court order. I filed for breach of custody.

Pers did the most effective thing you can do in the New York judicial system: nothing. Since Pers was an indigent periodically on public assistance, the court appointed a public defender for him. The public defender had 154 cases. He asked for three continuances in a row. The judge had a docket full six months ahead. In less than a year and a half Deborah would be sixteen, legally entitled to leave home. She auditioned for Privitera, and the School of American Ballet accepted her.

Another kid was shot, this one on the subway just before Pers's stop. She was twelve. A boy was knifed, a young mother was raped, houses were torched. Pers's lawyer resigned. Another was appointed, who immediately filed for a continuance.

I quit my job with *St. Louis On-Line* and moved to New York. I left behind a new promotion, a house I loved, and a man I had just started to care about. I found work on Michael's magazine, for half the prestige and two-thirds the salary, in a city twice as expensive and three times as dangerous. I took a two-room apartment on West Seventy-fifth, shabby but decent, just inside the patrolled zone. From my living room window I could see the shimmer of the electronic fence marking the zone. The shimmer bent to exclude all of Central Park south of Seventieth. I bought a gun.

After a few tense weeks, Deborah moved in with me. We lived with piles of toe shoes and surgical tape, with leotards and tights drying on a line strung across the living room, with *Dance* magazine in tattered third-hand copies that would go on to be somebody else's fourth-hand copies, with bunions and inflamed tendons and pulled ligaments. We lived with Deborah's guilt and my anger. At night I lay awake on the pull-out sofa, staring at the ceiling, remembering the day Deborah had started kindergarten and I had opened a college fund for her. She refused now to consider college. She wanted to dance for Anton Privitera.

Privitera had not yet invited her to join the company. She had just turned seventeen. This was her last year with the School. If she weren't invited into the corps de ballet this year, she could forget about dancing for the New York City Ballet.

I sat with the ballet mothers and watched. Deborah's extension was not as high as some of the other girls', her strength not always enough to sustain a slow, difficult move.

So glamorous! the ballet mothers screeched. So beautiful! So wonderful for a girl to know so young what she wants to do with her life! The ballet mothers apparently never saw the constant injuries, the fatigue, the competition that made every friend a deadly rival, the narrowing down of a young world until there is only one definition of success: Do I get to dance for Privitera? Everything else is failure. Life and death, determined at seventeen. "I don't know what I'll do if Jeannie isn't asked to join the company," Jeannie's mother told me. "It would be like we both died. Maybe we would."

"You're so unfair, Mom!" Deborah shouted at me periodically in the tiny, jammed apartment. "You never see the good side of dancing! You're so against me!"

Is it so unfair to hope that your child will be forced out of a life that can only break her body and her heart? A life whose future will belong only to those willing to become human test tubes for inhuman biological experiments?

Nicole Heyer, the dead ABT dancer, had apparently come to the United States from Germany because she could not compete with the dazzlingly bioenhanced dancers in her own country. Jennifer Lang, an ordinary girl from an ordinary Houston family, had lacked the money for major experimentation. To finance her bioenhancements in European labs, she had rented herself out as a glamorous and expensive call girl. Fuck a ballerina! That was how her killer had gotten into her apartment.

In her corner of Studio 3, Deborah finally got the sequence of steps straight, although I could see she was wobbly. She rejoined the class. The room had become as steamy as a Turkish bath. Students ran and leapt the whole length of the hall, corner to corner, in groups of six. "*Grand jeté* in third *arabesque*," Madame called. "Non, non, more extension, Lisa. Victoria, more quick—*vite*! *vite*!. One, two...next group."

Deborah ran, jumped, and crashed to the ground.

I stood. Jeannie's mother put a hand on my arm. "You can't go to her," she said matter-of-factly. "You'll interfere with her discipline."

Madame ran gnarled hands over Deborah's ankle. "Lisa, help her to the side. Ninette, go tell the office to send the doctor. Alors, next group, *grand jeté* in third *arabesque*..."

I shook off Jeannie's mother's hand and walked slowly to where Deborah sat, her face twisted in pain.

"It's nothing, Mom."

"Don't move it until the doctor gets here."

"I said it's nothing!"

It was a sprain. The doctor taped it and said Deborah shouldn't dance for a week.

At home she limped to her room. An hour later I found her at the barre.

"Deborah! You heard what the doctor said!"

Her eyes were luminous with tears: Odette as the dying swan, Giselle in the mad scene. "I have to, Mom! You don't understand! They're casting *Nutcracker* in two weeks! I have to be there, dancing!"

"Deborah—"

"I can dance through the injury! Leave me alone!"

Deborah had never yet been cast in Privitera's *Nutcracker*. I watched her transfer her weight gingerly to the injured ankle, wince, and *plié*. She wouldn't meet my eyes in the mirror.

Slowly I closed the door.

That night we had tickets to see *Coppelia*. Caroline Olson skimmed across the stage, barely seeming to touch ground. Her *grand jetés* brought gasps from the sophisticated New York ballet audience. In the final act, when Swanilda danced a tender *pas de deux* with her lover Franz, I could see heads motionless all over the theater, lips slightly parted, barely breathing. Franz turned her slowly in a liquid *arabesque*, her leg impossibly high, followed by *pirouettes*. Swanilda melted from one pose to another, her long silken legs forming a perfect line with her body, flesh made light and strong and elegant as the music itself.

Beside me, I felt Deborah's despair.

3.

Caroline jumps. She jumps with her hind legs out straight, one in front and one in back. She runs in circles and jumps again. Dmitri catches her.

"No, no," Mr. Privitera says. "Not like that. *Promenade en couronne, attitude, arabesque efface.* Now the lift. Dimitri, you are handling her like a sack of grain. Like this."

Mr. Privitera picks up Caroline. My ears raise. But Mr. Privitera is safe. Mr. Privitera can touch Caroline. Dmitri can touch Caroline. Carlos can touch Caroline.

Dmitri says, "It's the damn *dog.* How am I supposed to learn the part with him staring at me, ready to tear me from limb to limb? How the hell am I supposed to concentrate?"

John Cole sits next to me. John says, "Dmitri, there's no chance Angel will attack you. His biochip is state-of-the-art programming. I told you. If you're in his 'safe' directory, you'd have to actually attack Caroline yourself before Angel would act, unless Caroline told you otherwise. There's no real danger to break your concentration."

Dmitri says, "And what if I drop her accidentally? How do I know that won't look like an attack to that dog?"

Caroline sits down. She looks at John. She looks at Dmitri. She does not look at me. She smiles.

John says, "A drop is not an attack. Unless Caroline screams—and we all know she never does, no matter what the injury—there's no danger. Believe me."

"I don't," Dmitri says.

Everybody stands quiet.

Mr. Privitera says, "Caroline, dear, let me drop you. Stand up. Ready—lift."

Caroline smells surprised. She stands. Mr. Privitera picks up Caroline. She jumps a little. He picks her up over his head. She falls down hard. My ears raise. Caroline does not scream. She is not hurt. Mr. Privitera is safe. Caroline said Mr. Privitera is safe.

"See?" Mr. Privitera says. He breathes hard. "No danger. Positions, please. *Promenade en couronne, attitude, arabesque efface*, lift."

Dmitri picks up Caroline. The music gets loud. John says in my ear, "Angel—did Caroline go away from her house last night?"

"Yes," I say.

"Where did Caroline go?"

"Left four blocks, right one block. Caroline gave money."

"The bakery," John says. "Did she go away to any more places, or did she go home?"

"Caroline goes home last night."

"Did anyone come to Caroline's house last night?"

"No people come to Caroline's house last night."

"Thank you," John says. He pats me. I feel happy.

Caroline looks at us. A woman ties a long cloth on Caroline's waist. The woman gives Caroline a piece of wood. Yesterday I ask John what the wood is. Yesterday John says it is a fan. The music starts, faster. Caroline does not jump. Yesterday Caroline jumps with the fan.

"Caroline?" Mr. Privitera says. "Start here, dear."

Caroline jumps. She still looks at John. He looks at me.

Some woman here smells of yogurt and a bitch collie in heat.

Caroline opens the bedroom door. She comes out. She wears jeans on her hind legs. She wears a hat on her head. It covers all her fur. She walks to the door. She says to me, "Stay, you old fleabag. You hear me? Stay!"

I walk to the door.

"Christ." Caroline opens the door a little way. She pushes her body through the door. She closes the door. I push through the door hard with her.

"I said stay!" Caroline opens the door again. She pushes me. I do not go inside. Caroline goes inside. I follow Caroline.

"Take two," Caroline says. She opens the door. She walks away. She goes back. She closes the door. She opens the door. She closes the door. She turns around. She goes through the door and closes it hard. She is very fast. I am inside alone.

"Gotcha, Fido!" Caroline says through the door.

I howl. I throw me against the door. I bark and howl. The light goes on in my head. I howl and howl.

Soon Caroline comes through the door. A man holds her arm. He smells of iron. He talks to a box.

"Subject elected to return to her apartment, sir, rather than have me accompany her to her destination. We're in here now."

Caroline grabs the box. "John, you shit, how *dare* you! You had the dog bio-wired! That's an invasion of privacy, I'll sue your ass off, I'll quit the company, I'll—"

"Caroline," John's voice said. I look. There is no John smell. John is not here. Only John's voice is here. "You have no legal grounds. This man is allowed to accompany you, according to the protection contract you signed. *You* signed it, my dear. As for quitting the City Ballet…That's up to you. But while you dance for us, Angel goes where you do. If he gets too excited over not seeing you, the biosignal triggers. Just where were you going that you didn't want Angel with you?"

"To turn tricks on street corners!" Caroline yells. "And I bet he has a homing device embedded in him, too, doesn't he?"

She smells very angry. She is angry at me. I lie on the floor. I put my paws on my head. It is not happy here.

The man says, "Departing the apartment now, sir." He leaves. He takes the small box.

Caroline sits on the floor. Her back is against the door. She looks at me. My paws are on my head. Caroline smells angry.

Nothing happens.

A little later Caroline says, "I guess it's you and me, then. They set it up that way. I'm stuck with you."

I do not move my paws. She still smells angry.

"All right, let's try another approach. Disarm the enemy from within. Psychological sabotage. You don't have any idea what I'm talking about, do you? What did they give you, a five-year-old's IQ? Angel…"

I look at Caroline. She says my right name.

"…tell me about Sam's cat."

"What?"

"Sam's cat. You said that first day you came home with me that you smelled a cat on Sam, the day doorman. Do you still smell it? Can you tell what kind of cat it is?"

I am confused. Caroline says nice words. Caroline smells angry. Her back is too straight. Her fur is wrong.

"Is it a male cat or a female cat? Can you tell that?"

"A female cat," I say. I remember the cat smell. My muscles itch.

"Did you want to chase it?"

"I must never chase cats. I must protect Caroline."

Caroline's smell changes. She leans close to my ear.

"But did you *want* to chase it, Angel? Did you want to get to behave like a dog?"

"I want to protect Caroline."

"Hoo boy. They did a job on you, didn't they, boy?"

The words are too hard. Caroline still smells a little angry. I do not understand.

"It's nothing compared to what they're doing in South America and Europe," she says. Her body shakes.

"Are you hurt?" I say.

Caroline puts a hand on my back. The hand is very soft. She says no words.

I am happy. Caroline talks to me. She tells me about dancing. Caroline is a dancer. She jumps and runs in circles. She stands high on her hind legs. People come in cars to watch her. The people are happy when Caroline dances.

We walk outside. I protect Caroline. We go many places. Caroline gives me cake and hot dogs. There are many smells. Sometimes Caroline and I follow the smells. We see many dogs and many cats. The man with the small box comes with us sometimes. John says the man is safe.

"What if I tell Angel you're not 'safe'?" Caroline says to the man. He follows us on a long walk. "What if I order him to tear you limb to limb?" She smells angry again.

"You don't have programming override capacity. The biochip augmenting his bioenhancement is very specific, Ms. Olson. I'm hardwired in."

"I'll bet," Caroline says. "Did anybody ask Angel if he wants this life?"

The man smiles.

We go to Lincoln Center every day. Caroline dances there. She dances in the day. She dances at night. More people watch at night.

John asks me where Caroline and I go. Every day I tell him.

Nobody tries to touch Caroline. I protect her.

"I can't do it," Caroline tells a man on the street corner. The man stands very close to Caroline. I growl soft. "For God's sake, Stan, don't touch me. The dog. And I'm probably being watched."

"Do they care *that* much?"

"I could blow the whistle on the whole unofficial charade," Caroline says. She smells tired. "No matter what Privitera's delusions are. But then we'd lose our chance, wouldn't we?"

"Thanks for the time," the man says, loud. He smiles. He walks away.

Later John says, "Who did Caroline talk to?"

"A man," I say. "He wants the time."

Later Caroline says, "Angel, we're going tonight to see my mother."

4.

Demonstrators dyed the fountain at Lincoln Center blood red.

They marched around the gruesome jets of water, shouting and resisting arrest. I sprinted across the plaza, trying to get there to see which side they were on before the police carted all of them away. Even from this distance I could tell they weren't dancers, not with those thick bodies. The electronic placards dissolved from HOW MANY MUST DIE FROM DENYING EVOLUTION! to FREE MEDICAL RESEARCH FROM GOVERNMENT STRAIGHTJACKETS! to MY BODY BELONGS TO ME! Pro-human bioenhancement, then. A holograph projector, which a cop was shutting down, spewed out a ten-foot high holo of Jane and June Welsh, Siamese twins who had been successfully separated only after German scientists had bioenhanced their bodies to force alterations in major organs. The holo loop showed the attached twins dragging each other around, followed by the successfully separated twins waving gaily. The cop did something and Jane and June disappeared.

"They died," I said to a demonstrator, a slim boy wearing a FREE MY BODY! button. "Ultimately, neither of their hearts could stand the stress of bioenhancement."

He glared at me. "That was their risk to take, wasn't it?"

"Their combined IQ didn't equal your weight. How could they evaluate risk?"

"This is a *revolution*, lady. In any revolution you have casualties that—" A cop grabbed his arm. The boy took a wild swing at him and the cop pressed his nerve gun to the boy's neck. He dropped peacefully, smiling.

Abruptly more people gathered, some of them wilier than the boy. Demonstrators stood with their hands on their heads, singing slogans. Media robocams zoomed in from the sky; the live crews would be here in minutes. A group of counter-demonstrators formed across the plaza, in front of the Met. I backed away slowly, hands on my head, not singing—and stopped abruptly halfway across the chaotic plaza.

An old woman in a powerchair was watching the demonstration with the most intense expression I had ever seen. It was as if she were watching a horrifying execution, judging it judiciously as art. Bodyguards flanked the chair. She wore an expensive, pale blue suit and large, perfectly-matched pearls. Her wrinkled, cold face was completely familiar. This was how Caroline Olson would look in forty years, if she refused all cosmetic treatment.

She caught me watching her. Her expression didn't change. It passed over me as if I didn't exist.

I took the chance. "Ms. Olson?"

She didn't deny the name. "Yes?"

"I'm a reporter with *New York Now*, doing an article on the New York City Ballet. I'd like to ask you a few questions about your daughter Caroline, if that's all right."

"I never give interviews."

"Yes, ma'am. Just a few informal questions—you must be so proud of Caroline. But are you worried about her safety in light of the recent so-called ballerina murders?"

She shocked me. She smiled. "No, not at all."

"You're *not*?"

She gazed at the break-up of the demonstration. "Do you know the work on dancers' bodies they're doing in Berlin?"

"No, I—"

"Then you have no business interviewing anyone on the subject." She watched the last of the demonstrators being dragged away by the cops. "The New York City ballet is finished. The future of the art lies with bioenhancement."

I must have looked like a fish, staring at her with my mouth working. "But Caroline is the prima ballerina, she's only twenty-six—"

"Caroline had a good run. For a dancer." She made a signal, an imperious movement of her hand, and one of the bodyguards turned her chair and wheeled it away.

I trotted after it. "But, Ms. Olson, are you saying you think your daughter and her whole company *should* be replaced by bioenhanced dancers because they can achieve higher lifts, fewer injuries, more spectacular turnout—"

"I never give interviews," she said, and the other bodyguard moved between us.

I gazed after her. She had spoken about Caroline as if her daughter were an obsolete Buick. It took me a moment to remember to pull out a notebook and tell it what she had said.

Someone dumped something into the fountain. Immediately the red disappeared and the water spouted clear once more. A bioenhanced dog trotted over and lapped at the water, the dog's owner patiently holding the leash while his pink-furred, huge-eyed poodle drank its fill.

After an hour at a library terminal at *New York Now*, I knew that Anna Olson was a major contributor to the American Ballet Theater but not to the New York City Ballet, where her daughter had chosen to dance. Caroline's father was dead. He had left his widow an East Side mansion, three Renoirs, and a fortune invested in Peruvian sugar, Japanese weather-control equipment, and German pharmaceuticals. According to *Ballet News*, mother and daughter were estranged. To find out more than that, I'd need professional help.

Michael didn't want to do it. "There's no money for that kind of research, Susan. Not to even mention the ethics involved."

"Oh, come on, Michael. It's no worse than using criminal informers for any other story."

"This isn't your old newspaper job, Susie. We're a feature magazine, remember? We don't use informants, and we don't do investigative reporting." He leaned against his desk, his peeled-egg face troubled.

"The magazine doesn't have to do any investigating at all. Just give me the number. I know you know it. If I'd been doing the job I should have for the last two years instead of sulking because I hate New York, I'd know it, too. Just the number, Michael. That's all. Neither you nor the magazine will even be mentioned."

He ran his hand through his hair. For the first time, I noticed that it was thinning. "All right. But Susan—don't get obsessed. For your own sake." He looked at the picture of his daughter doing time in Rock Mountain.

I called the Robin Hood and arranged to see him. He was young—they all are—maybe as young as twenty, operating out of a dingy apartment in Tribeca. I couldn't judge his equipment: beyond basic literacy, computers are as alien to me as dancers. Like dancers, they concentrate on one aspect of the world, dismissing the rest.

The Robin Hood furnished the usual proofs that he could tap into private databanks, that he could access government records, and that his translation programs could handle international airline d-bases. He promised a two-day turn around. The price was astronomical by my standards, although probably negligible by his. I transferred the credits from my savings account, emptying it.

I said, "You do know that the original Robin Hood transferred goods for free?"

He said, not missing a beat, "The original Robin Hood didn't have to pay for a Seidman-Nuwer encrypter."

I really hadn't expected him to know who the original Robin Hood was.

When I got home, Deborah had fallen asleep across her bed, still dressed in practice clothes. The toes of her tights were bloody. A new pair of toe shoes were shoved between the bedroom door and the door jamb; she softened the stiff boxes by slamming the door on them. There were three E-mail messages for her from SAB, but I erased them all. I covered her, closed her door, and let her sleep.

I met with the Robin Hood two days later. He handed me a sheaf of hardcopy. "The City Ballet injury records show two injuries for Caroline Olson in the last four years, which is as far back as the files are kept. One shin splint, one pulled ligament. Of course, if she had other injuries and saw a private doctor, that wouldn't show up on their records, but if she did see one it wasn't anybody on the City Ballet Recommended Physician List. I checked that."

"Two injuries? In four *years*?"

"That's what the record shows. These here are four-year records of City Ballet bioscans. All negative. Nobody shows any bioenhancement, not even Jennifer Lang. These are the City Ballet attendance figures over ten years, broken down by subscription and single-event tickets."

I was startled; the drop in attendance over the last two years was more dramatic than the press had ever indicated.

"This one is Mrs. Anna Olson's tax return for last year. All that income—all of it—is from investments and interests, and none of it is tied up in trusts or entails. She controls it all, and she can waste the whole thing if she wants to. You asked about unusual liquidation of stock in the last ten years: There wasn't any. There's no trust fund for Caroline Olson. This is Caroline's tax return—only her salary with City Ballet, plus guest appearance fees. Hefty, but nothing like what the old lady controls.

"This last is the air flight stuff you wanted: No flights on major commercial airlines out of the country for Caroline in the last six years, except when the City Ballet did its three international tours, and then Caroline flew pretty much with everybody else in the group. Of course if she did go to Rio or Copenhagen or Berlin, she could have gone by chartered plane or private jet. My guess is private jet. Those aren't required to file passenger lists."

It wasn't what I'd hoped to find. Or rather, it was half of what I'd hoped. No dancer is injured that seldom. It just doesn't happen. I pictured Caroline Olson's amazing extension, her breathtaking leaps; she reached almost the height expected of male superstars. And her crippled horror of a mother had huge amounts of money. *"Caroline had a good run."*

I would bet my few remaining dollars that Caroline Olson was bioenhanced, no matter what her bioscans said. Jennifer Lang's had been negative, too. Apparently the DNA hackers were staying one step ahead of the DNA security checkers. Although it was odd that the records didn't show a single dancer trying to get away with bioenhancement, not even once, even in the face of Privitera's fervency. There are always some people who value their own career advancement over the received faith.

But I had assumed that Caroline would have needed to leave the country. Bioenhancement labs are large, full of sensitive and costly and nonportable equipment, and dozens of technicians. Not easy to hide. Police investigators had traced both Jennifer Lang and Nicole Heyer to Danish labs. I didn't think one could exist illegally in New York.

Maybe I was wrong.

The Robin Hood watched me keenly. In the morning light from the window he looked no older than Deborah. He had thick brown hair, nice shoulders. I wondered if he had a life outside his lab. So many of them didn't.

"Thanks," I said.

"Susan—"

"What?"

He hesitated. "I don't know what you're after with this data. But I've worked with friends of Michael's before. If you're thinking about trying to leverage anything to do with human bioenhancement…"

"Yeah?"

"Don't." He looked intently at his console. "That's out of both our leagues. Magazine reporters are very small against the kind of high-stakes shit those guys are into."

"Thanks for the advice," I said. And then, on impulse, "Would you by any chance like a home-cooked meal? I have a daughter about your age, seventeen, she's a dancer…"

He stared at me in disbelief. He shook his head. "You're a *client*, Susan. And anyway, I'm twenty-six. And I'm married." He shook his head again. "And if you don't know enough not to ask a Robin Hood to dinner, you really don't know enough to mess around with bioenhancement. That stuff's life or death."

Life or death. Enough for a bioenhancement corporation to murder two dancers?

But I rejected that idea. It was always too easy to label the corporations the automatic bad guys. That was the stuff of cheap holovids. Most corporate types I knew just tried to keep ahead of the IRS.

I said, "Most life-and-death stuff originates at home."

I could feel him shaking his head as I left, but I didn't turn around.

5.

Caroline and I ride in a taxi. It is late at night. We ride across the park. Then we ride more. Caroline says words to a gate. A man opens the door to a very big house. He smells surprised. He wears pajamas. "Miss Caroline!"

"Hello, Seacomb. Is my mother in?"

"She's asleep, of course. If there's an emergency—"

"No emergency. But my apartment pipes sprung a leak and I'll be spending the night here. This is my dog, Angel. Angel, Seacomb is safe."

"Of course, Miss," Seacomb says. He smells very unhappy. "It's just—"

"Just that you have orders not to let me use this house?"

"No, Miss," the man says. "My orders are to let you use the house as you choose. Only—"

"Of course they are," Caroline says. "My mother wants me to grovel back here. She's been panting for that. Well, here I am. Only she's taken a sleeping pill and is out cold until morning, right?"

"Yes, Miss," the man says. He smells very unhappy. There are no cats or dogs in this place, but there are mice. The mice droppings smell interesting.

"I'll sleep in the downstairs study. And, oh, Seacomb, I'm expecting guests. Please disable the electric gate. They'll use the back entrance, and I'll let them in myself. You needn't take any trouble about it."

"It's no trouble to—"

"I said I'll let them in myself."

"Yes, Miss," Seacomb says. He smells very very unhappy.

He leaves. Caroline and I go down stairs. Caroline drinks. She gives me water. I smell a mouse in a cupboard. My ears raise. There are interesting things here.

"Well, Angel, here we are at my mother's house. Do you remember your mother, boy?"

"No," I say. I am confused. The words are a little hard.

"There are some people coming for a party. Some dancers. Kristine Meyers is coming. You remember Kristine Meyers?"

"Yes," I say. Kristine Meyers dances with Caroline. They run in circles and jump high. Caroline jumps higher.

"We're going to talk about dancing, Angel. This is a prettier house than mine to talk about dancing. This is a good house for a party, which is what we're going to have. My mother lets me use her house for parties. Remember that, boy."

Later Caroline opens the door. Some people stand there. We go into the basement. Kristine Meyers is there. She smells frightened. Some men are with her. They carry papers. They talk a long time.

"Here, Angel, have a pretzel," a man says. "It's a party."

Some people dance to a radio. Kristine smells angry and confused. Her fur stands up. Caroline says words to her. The words are hard. The words are long. I have a pretzel. Nobody touches Caroline.

We are there all night. Kristine cries.

"Her boyfriend is gone," Caroline says to me.

In early morning we go home. We go in a taxi. Somebody is sick in the taxi yesterday. It smells bad. Caroline sleeps. I sleep. Caroline does not go to class.

In the afternoon we go to Lincoln Center. Kristine is there. She sleeps on a couch in the lounge. Caroline dances with Dmitri.

John Cole bends close to my ear. "You went out with Caroline all last night."

"Yes," I say.

"Where did you go?"

"We go to Caroline's mother's house. We go to a party. Caroline's mother lets Caroline use her house for parties."

"Who was at this party?"

"Dancers. Kristine is at the party. Kristine is safe."

John looks at Kristine. She still sleeps on the couch.

"Who else was at the party? What did they do?"

I remember hard. "Dancers are at the party. We eat pretzels. We talk about dancing. People dance to the radio. Nobody touches Caroline. There is music."

John's body relaxes. "Good," he says. "Okay."

"I like pretzels," I say. But John does not give me a pretzel today.

Caroline and I walk in the park. There are many good smells. Caroline sits under a tree. The long fur on her head falls down. She pats my head. She gives me a cookie.

"It's easy for you, isn't it, Angel?" Caroline says.

I say, "The words are hard."

"You like being a dog? A bioenhanced servant dog?"

"The words are hard."

"Are you happy, Angel?"

"I am happy. I love Caroline."

She pats my head again. The sun is warm. The smells are good. I close my eyes.

"I love to dance," Caroline says. "And I hate that I love it."

I open my eyes. Caroline smells unhappy.

"Goddamn it, I love it anyway. I do. Even though it wasn't my choice. You didn't choose what you are, either, did you, Angel? They goddamn made you what they needed you to be. Yet you love it. And for you there's no account due."

The words are too hard. I put my nose into Caroline's front legs. She puts her front legs around me. She holds me tight.

"It's not *fair*," Caroline whispers into my fur.

Caroline does not hold me yesterday. She holds me today. I am happy. But Caroline smells unhappy.

Where is my happy if Caroline smells unhappy?

I do not understand.

6.

Deborah didn't get cast in *Nutcracker*. An SAB teacher told her she might want to consider auditioning for one of the regional companies rather than City Ballet—a death sentence, from her point of view. She told me this quietly, without histrionics, sitting cross-legged on the floor sewing ribbons onto a pair of toe shoes. Not wanting to say the wrong thing, I said nothing, contenting myself with touching her hair, coiled at the nape of her neck into the ballerina bun. Two days later she told me she was dropping out of high school.

"I need the time to dance," she said. "You just don't understand, Mom."

The worst thing I could do was let her make me into the enemy. "I do understand, honey. But there will be lots of time to dance after you finish school. And if you don't—"

"Finishing is a year away! I can't afford the time. I have to take more classes, work harder, get asked into the company. *This year.* I'm sorry, Mom, but I just can't waste my time on all that useless junk in school."

I locked my hands firmly on my lap. "Well, let's look at this reasonably. Suppose after all you do get asked to join the company—"

"I *will* be asked! I'll work so hard they'll have to ask me!"

"All right. Then you dance with them until, say, you're thirty-five. At thirty-five you have over half your life left. You saw what happened to Carla Cameri and Maura Jones." Carla's hip had disintegrated; Maura's Achilles tendon had forced her into retirement at thirty-two. Both of them worked in a clothing store, for pitifully small salaries. Dancers didn't get pensions unless they'd been with the same company for ten years, a rarity in the volatile world of artistic directors with absolute power, who often fired dancers because they were remaking a company into a different "look."

I pressed my point. "What will you do at thirty or thirty-five with your body debilitated and without even a high school education?"

"I'll teach. I'll coach. I'll go back to school. Oh, Mom, how do I know? That's decades away! I have to think about what I need to do for my career now!"

No mother love is luminous enough to make a sixteen-year-old see herself at thirty-five.

I said, "No, Deborah. You can't quit school. I'd have to sign for you, and I won't."

"Daddy already did."

We looked at each other. It was too late; she'd already made me into the enemy. Because she needed one.

She said, in a sudden burst of passion, "You don't understand! You never felt about your job the way I feel about ballet! You never loved anything enough to give up everything else for it!" She rushed to her room and slammed the door. I put my head in my hands.

After a while, I started to laugh. I couldn't help it. *Never loved anything enough to give up everything else for it.*

Right.

Pers wasn't available to yell at. I phoned six times. I left messages on E-mail, even though I had no idea whether he had a terminal. I made the trip out of the protected zone to his apartment. The area was worse than I remembered: glass, broken machinery, shit, drug paraphernalia. The cab driver was clearly eager to leave, but I made him wait while I questioned a kid who came out of Pers's building. The boy, about eight, had a long pus-encrusted cut down one cheek.

"Do you know when Pers Anders usually comes home? He lives in 2C."

The kid stared at me, expressionless. The cab driver leaned out and said, "One more minute and I'm leaving, lady."

I pulled out a twenty-dollar bill and held it close to me. "When does Pers Anders usually come home?"

"He moved."

"Moved?"

"Left his stuff. He say he go someplace better than this shithole. I hear him say it. Don't you try to prong me, lady. You give me that money."

"Do you know the address?"

He greeted this with the scorn it deserved. I gave him the money.

Deborah left school and started spending all day and much of the night at Lincoln Center. Finally I walked over to SAB and caught her just before a partnering class. She had twisted a bright scarf around her waist, over her leotard, and her sweaty hair curled in tendrils where it had escaped her bun.

"Deborah, why didn't you tell me your father had moved?"

She looked wary, wiping her face with a towel to gain time. "I didn't think you'd care. You hate him."

"As long as you still visit him, I need to know where he is."

She considered this. Finally she gave me the address. It was a good one, in the new luxury condos where the old main library had been.

"How can Pers afford *that*?"

"He didn't say. Maybe he's got a job. Mom, I have class."

"Pers is allergic to jobs."

"Mom, Mr. Privitera is teaching this class *himself*!"

I didn't stay to watch class. On the way out, I passed Privitera, humming to himself on his way to elate or cast down his temple virgins.

The police had released no new information on the ballerina murders.

I turned in the article on the New York City Ballet. It seemed to me neither good nor bad; everything important about the subject didn't fit the magazine's focus. There weren't too many metaphors. Michael read it without comment. I worked on an article about computerized gambling, and another about holographic TV. I voted in the Presidential election. I bought Christmas presents.

But every free minute, all autumn and early winter, I spent at the magazine library terminals, reading about human bioenhancement, trying to guess what Caroline Olson was having done to herself. What might someday lie in Deborah's future, if she were as big a fool then as she was being now.

"Don't get obsessed," Michael had said.

The literature was hard to interpret. I wasn't trained in biology, and as far as I could see, the cutting-edge research was chaotic, with various discoveries being reported one month, contradicted the next. All the experiments were carried out in other countries, which meant they were reported in other languages, and I didn't know how far to trust the biases of the translators. Most of them seemed to be other scientists in the same field. This whole field seemed to me like a canoe rushing toward the falls: nobody in charge, both oars gone, control impossible.

I read about splendid, "revolutionary" advances in biological nanotechnology that always seemed under development, or not quite practical yet, or hotly disputed by people practicing other kinds of revolutionary advances. I read about gene-splicing retroviruses and setting them loose in human organs to accomplish potentially wonderful things. Elimination of disease. Perfect metabolic functioning. Immortality. The studies were always concerned with one small, esoteric facet of scientific work, but the "Conclusions" sections were often grandiose, speculating wildly.

I even picked up hints of experimental work on altering genetic makeup *in vitro*, instead of trying to reshape adult bodies. Some scientists seemed to think this might actually be easier to accomplish. But nowhere in the world was it legal to experiment on an embryo not destined for abortion, an embryo that would go on to become a human being stuck with the results of arbitrary and untested messing around with his basic cellular blueprints. Babies were not tinker toys—or dogs. The Copenhagen Accord, signed twenty-seven years by most technologically civilized countries, had seen to that. The articles on genetic modification *in vitro* were carefully speculative.

But then so was nearly everything else I read. The proof was walking around in inaccessible foreign hospitals, or living anonymously in inaccessible foreign cities—the anonymity of the experimental subjects seemed to be a given, which also made me wonder how many of them were experimental casualties. And if so, of what kind.

Michael wasn't going to want any article built on this tentative speculation. Lawsuits would loom. But I was beyond caring what Michael wanted.

I learned that the Fifth International Conference on Human Bioenhancement was going to be held in Paris in late April. After paying the Robin Hood, I had no money left for a trip to Paris. Michael would have to pay for it. I would have to give him a reason.

One night in January I did a stupid thing. I went alone to Lincoln Center and waited by the stage door of the New York State Theater. Caroline Olson came out at 11:30, dressed in jeans and parka, accompanied only by a huge black Doberman on the most nominal of leashes. They walked south on Broadway, to an all-night restaurant. I sat myself at the next table.

For the last few months, her reviews had not been good. "A puzzling and disappointing degeneration," said *The New Yorker.* "Technical sloppiness not associated with either Olson or Privitera," said *Dance Magazine.* "This girl is in trouble, and Anton Privitera had better find out what kind of trouble and move to correct it," said the *Times On-Line.*

Caroline ate abstractly, feeding bits to the dog, oblivious to the frowns of a fastidious waiter who was undoubtedly an out-of-work actor. Up close, the illusion of power and beauty I remembered from *Coppelia* evaporated. She looked like just another mildly pretty, self-absorbed, overly thin young woman. Except for the dog, the waiter/actor didn't give her a second glance.

"We go now?" the dog said.

I choked on my sandwich. Caroline glanced at me absently. "Soon, Angel."

She went on eating. I left, waited for her, and followed her home. She and the dog lived on Central Park South, a luxury building where the late-night electronic surveillance system greeted them both by name.

I took a cab home. Deborah had never mentioned that the City Ballet prima ballerina was protected by a bioenhanced Doberman. She knew I'd written the story about the ballerina murders. Anton Privitera hadn't mentioned it, either, in his press conference about dancer safety. I wondered why not. While I was parceling out wonder, I devoted some to the question of City Ballet's infrequent, superficial, and always-positive bioscans. Shouldn't a company devoted to the religion of "natural art" be more zealous about ferreting out heretics?

Unless, of course, somebody didn't really want to know.

Privitera? But that was hard to reconcile with his blazing, intolerant sincerity.

It occurred to me that I had never seen an admittedly bioenhanced dancer perform. Until tonight, I'd gone to finished performances rarely and only with Deborah, who of course scorned such perverts and believed that they had nothing to teach her.

She was out when I got back to our apartment. Each week, it seemed, she was gone more. I fell asleep, waiting for her to come home.

7.

Snow falls. It is cold. Caroline and I walk to Lincoln Center. A man takes Caroline's purse. He runs. Caroline says "Shit!" Then she says, "Angel? Go stop him!" She drops my leash.

I run and jump on the man. He screams. I do not hurt him. Caroline says *stop him*. She does not say *attack him*. So I stand on the man's chest and growl and nip at his foreleg. He brings out a knife. Then I bite him. He drops the knife and screams again. The police come.

"Holy shit," Caroline says to me. "You really do that. You really do."

"I protect Caroline," I say.

Caroline talks to police. Caroline talks to reporters. I get a steak to eat.

I am happy.

The snow goes away. The snow is there many many days, but it goes away. We visit Caroline's mother's house for two more parties in the basement. It gets warm in the park. Ducks live in the water again. Flowers grow. Caroline says not to dig up flowers.

I lie backstage. Caroline dances on stage. John and Mr. Privitera stand beside me. They smell unhappy. John's shoes smell of tar and food and leaves and cats and other good things. I sniff John's shoes.

"She looks exhausted," John says. "She's giving it everything she's got, but it's just not there, Anton."

Mr. Privitera says no words. He watches Caroline dance.

"William Scholes attacked again in the *Times*. He said that watching her had become painful—'like watching a reed grown stiff and brittle.'"

"I will talk to her again," Mr. Privitera says.

"Scholes called the performance 'a travesty,'" John says.

Caroline comes backstage. She limps. She wipes her face with a towel. She smells afraid.

"Dear, I'd like to see you," Mr. Privitera says.

We go to Caroline's dressing room. Caroline sits down. She trembles. Her body smells sick. I growl. Caroline puts a hand on my head.

Mr. Privitera says, "First of all, dear, I have good news for all of us. The police have caught that unspeakable murderer who killed Jennifer Lang and the ABT dancer."

Caroline sits up a little straighter. Her smell changes. "They did! How?"

"They caught him breaking into the Plaza Hotel room where Marie D'Arbois is staying while she guests with ABT."

"Is Marie—"

"She's fine. She wasn't alone, she had a lover or something with her. The madman just got careless. The police are holding back the details. Marie, of course, is another of those bioenhanced dancers. I don't know if you ever saw her dance."

"I did," Caroline says. "I thought she was wonderful."

Caroline and Mr. Privitera look hard at each other. They smell ready to attack. But they do not attack. I am confused. Mr. Privitera is safe. He may touch Caroline.

Mr. Privitera says, "We must all be grateful to the police. Now there's something else I need to discuss with you, dear."

Caroline closes her hand on my fur. She says, "Yes?"

"I want you to take a good long rest, dear. You know your dancing has deteriorated. You tell me you're not doing drugs or working sketchily, and I believe you. Sometimes it helps a dancer to take a rest from performing. Take class, eat right, get strong. In the fall we'll see."

"You're telling me you're cutting me from the summer season at Saratoga."

"Yes, dear."

Caroline is quiet. Then she says, "There's nothing wrong with me. My timing has just been a little off, that's all."

"Then take the summer to work on your timing. And everything else."

Mr. Privitera and Caroline look hard at each other again. Caroline's hand still pulls my fur. It hurts a little. I do not move.

Mr. Privitera leans close to Caroline. "Listen, dear. *Jewels* was one of your best roles. But tonight...And not just *Jewels*. You wobbled and wavered through *Starscape*. Your Nikiya in the 'Shades' section of *La Bayadere* was...embarrassing. There is no other word. You danced as if you had never learned the steps. And you couldn't even complete the *Don Quixote pas de deux* at the gala."

"I fell! Dancers get injured all the time! My injury rate compared to—"

"You've missed rehearsals and even performances," Mr. Privitera said. He stands up. "I'm sorry, dear. Take the summer. Rest. Work. In the fall, we'll see."

Caroline says, "What about the last two weeks of the season?"

Mr. Privitera says, "I'm sorry, dear."

He walks to the door. He puts his hand on the door. He says, "Oh, at least you won't have to be burdened with that dog anymore. Now that the madman's been caught, I'll have John notify the protection agency to come pick it up."

Caroline raises her head. Her fur all stands up. She smells angry. Soon she runs out the door. Mr. Privitera is gone. She runs to the offices. "John! John, you bastard!"

The office hall is dark. The doors do not open. John is not here.

Caroline runs up steps to the offices. She falls. She falls down some of the steps and hits the wall. She lies on the floor. She holds her hind foot and smells hurt.

"Angel," she says. "Go get somebody to help me."

I go to the lounge. One dancer is there. She says, "Oh! I'm sorry, I didn't know that anybody—Angel?"

"Caroline is hurt," I say. "Come. Come fast."

She comes. Caroline says, "Who are you? No, wait—Deborah, right? From the corps?"

"No, I'm not...I haven't been invited to join the corps yet. I'm a student at SAB. I'm just here a lot...Are you hurt? Can you stand?"

"Help me up," Caroline says. "Angel, Deborah is safe."

Deborah tries to pick up Caroline. Caroline makes a little noise. She cannot stand. Deborah gets John. He picks up Caroline.

"It's nothing," she says. "No doctor. Just get me a cab…dammit, John, don't fuss, it's nothing!" She looks at John hard. "You want to take Angel away from me."

John smells surprised. He says, "Who told you that?"

"His Majesty himself. But now you've decided whatever you thought I was doing so privately doesn't matter anymore, is that right?"

"It's a mistake. Of course you can keep the dog. Anton doesn't understand," John says. He smells angry.

"No, I'll just bet he doesn't," Caroline says. "You might have picked a kinder way to tell me I'm through at City Ballet."

"You're not through, Caroline," John says. Now he smells bad. His words are not right. He smells like the man who takes Caroline's purse.

"Right," Caroline says. She sits in the cab.

Deborah steps back. She smells surprised.

"I'm keeping the dog," Caroline says. "So we're in agreement, aren't we, John? Come on, Angel. Let's go home."

We go to class. Caroline cannot dance. She tries and then stops. She sits in a corner. Mr. Privitera sits in another corner. Caroline watches Deborah. The dancers raise one hind leg. They spin and jump.

Madame holds up her hand. The music stops. "Deborah, let us see that again, *s'il vous plais*. Alone."

The other dancers move away. They look at each other. They smell surprised. The music starts again and Deborah raises one hind leg very high. She spins and jumps.

Mr. Privitera says, "Let me see the bolero from *Coppelia*. Madame says you know it."

"Y-yes," Deborah says. She dances alone.

"Very nice, dear," Mr. Privitera says. "You are much improved."

The other dancers look at each other again.

Everybody dances.

Caroline watches Deborah hard.

8.

Deborah's face looked like every Christmas morning in the entire world. She grabbed both my hands. "They invited me to join the company!"

My suitcase lay open on the bed, surrounded by discarded clothes I wasn't taking to the bioenhancement conference in Paris. My daughter picked up a pile of spidersilk blouses and hurled them into the air. In the soft April air from the open window the filmy, artificial material drifted and danced. "I can't believe it! They asked me to join the company! I'm in!"

She whirled around the tiny room, rising on toe in her street shoes, laughing and exclaiming. My silence went unnoticed. Deborah did an *arabesque* to the bedpost, then plopped herself down on my best dress. "Don't you want to know what happened, Mom?"

"What happened, Deborah?"

"Well, Mr. Privitera came to watch class, and Madame asked me to repeat the variation alone. God, I thought I'd die. Then *Mr. Privitera*—not Madame—asked me to do the bolero from *Coppelia*. For an awful minute I couldn't remember a single step. Then I did, and he said it was very nice! He said I was much improved!"

Accolades from the king. But even in my numbness I could see there was something she wasn't telling me.

"I thought you told me the company doesn't choose any new dancers this close to the end of the season?"

She sobered immediately. "Not usually. But Caroline Olson was fired. She missed rehearsals and performances, and she wasn't even taking the trouble to prepare her roles. Her reviews have been awful."

"I saw them," I said.

Deborah looked at me sharply. "Ego, I guess. Caroline's always been sort of a bitch. So apparently they're not letting her go to Saratoga, because Tina Patrochov and a guest artist are dividing her roles, and Mr. Privitera told Jill Kerrigan to learn Tina's solo from *Sleeping Beauty*. So that left a place in the corps de ballet, and they chose me!"

I had had enough time to bring myself to say it.

"Congratulations, sweetheart."

"When does your plane for Paris leave?"

This non-sequitur—if it was that—turned me back to my packing. "Seven tonight."

"And you'll be gone ten days. You'll have a great time in Paris. Maybe the next time the company goes on tour, I'll go with them!"

She whirled out of the room.

I sat at the end of the bed, holding onto the bedpost. When Deborah was three, she'd wanted a ride on a camel. Somehow it had become an obsession. She talked about camels in daycare, at dinnertime, at bedtime. She drew pictures of camels, misshapen things with one huge hump. Camels were in short supply in St. Louis. Ignore it, everyone said, kids forget these things, she'll get over it. Deborah never forgot. She didn't get over it. Pers had just left us, and I was consumed with the anxiety of a single parent. Finally I paid a friend to tie a large wad of hay under a blanket on his very old, very swaybacked horse. A Peruvian camel, I told my three-year-old. A very special kind. You can have a ride.

"That's not a camel," Deborah had said, with nostril-lifted disdain. "That's a heffalunt!"

I read last week in *World* that the animal-biotech scientists have built a camel with the flexible trunk of an elephant. The trunk can lift up to forty-five pounds. It was expected to be a useful beast of burden in the Sahara.

I finished packing for Paris.

Paris in April was an unending gray drizzle. The book and software stalls along the Seine kept up their electronic weather shields, giving them the hazy, streaming-gutter look of abandoned outhouses. The gargoyles on Notre Dame looked insubstantial in the rain, irrelevant in the face of camels with trunks. The French, as usual, conspired to make Americans—especially Americans who speak only rudimentary French—feel crass and barbaric. My clothes were wrong. My desire for a large breakfast was wrong. The Fifth International Conference on Human Bioenhancement had lost my press credentials.

The conference was held in one of the huge new hotels in Neuilly, near the Eurodisney Gene Zoo. I couldn't decide if this was an attempt to provide entertainment or irony. Three hundred scientists and doctors, a hundred press, and at least that many industrial representatives, plus groupies, thronged the hotel. The scientists presented papers; the industrial reps, mostly from biotech or pharmaceutical firms, presented "infoforums." The moment I walked in, carrying provisional credentials, I felt the tension, a peculiar kind of tension instantly recognizable to reporters. Something big was going on. Big and unpleasant.

From the press talk in the bar I learned that the presentation to not miss was Thursday night by Dr. Gerard Taillebois of the Pasteur Research Institute, in conjunction with Dr. Greta Erbland of Steckel und Osterhoff. This pairing of a major research facility with a commercial biotech firm was common in Europe. Sometimes the addition of a hospital made it a triumvirate. A hand-written addendum on the program showed that the presentation had been moved from the Napoleon Room to the Grand Ballroom. I checked out the room; it was approximately the size of an airplane hangar. Hotel employees were setting up acres of chairs.

I asked a garçon to point out Dr. Taillebois to me. He was a tall, bald man in his sixties or seventies who looked like he hadn't slept or eaten in days.

Wednesday night I went to the Paris Opera Ballet. The wet pavement in front of the Opera House gleamed like black patent leather. Patrons dripped jewels and fur. This gala was why Michael had funded my trip; my first ballet article for *New York Now* had proved popular, despite its vapidity. Or maybe because of it. Tonight the famous French company was dancing an eclectic program, with guest artists from the Royal Ballet and the Kirov. Michael wanted 5,000 words on the oldest ballet company in the world.

I watched bioenhanced British dancers perform the wedding *pas de deux* from *Sleeping Beauty*, with its famous fish dives; Danish soloists in twentieth-century dances by Georges Balanchine; French ballerinas in contemporary works by their brilliant choreographer Louis Dufort. All of them were breathtaking. In the new ballets, especially choreographed for these bioenhanced bodies, the dancers executed sustained movements no natural body would have been capable of making at all, at a speed that never looked machine-like. Instead the dancers were flashes of light: lasers, optic signals, nerve impulses surging across the stage and triggering pleasure centers in the brains of the delighted audience.

I gaped at one *pas de trois* in which the male dancer lifted two women at once, holding them aloft in swallow lifts over his head, one on each palm, then turning them slowly for a full ninety seconds. It wasn't a bench-pressing stunt. It was the culmination of a yearning, lyrical dance, as tender as any in the great nineteenth-century ballets. The female dancers were lowered slowly to the floor, and they both flowed through a *fouette of adage* as if they hadn't any bones.

Not one dancer had been replaced in the evening's program due to injury. I tried to remember the last time I'd seen a performance of the New York City Ballet without a last-minute substitution.

During intermission, profoundly depressed, I bought a glass of wine in the lobby. The eddying crowd receded for a moment, and I was face to face with Anna Olson, seated regally in her powerchair and flanked by her bodyguards. Holding tight to her hand was a little girl of five or six, dressed in a pink party dress and pink tights, with wide blue eyes, black hair, and a long slim neck. She might have been Caroline Olson twenty years ago.

"Ms. Olson," I said.

She looked at me coldly, without recognition.

"I'm Susan Matthews. We met at the private reception for Anton Privitera at Georgette Allen's," I lied.

"Yes?" she said, but her eyes raked me. My dress wasn't the sort that turned up at the private fundraisers of New York billionaires. I didn't give her a chance to cut me.

"This must be your—" granddaughter? Caroline, an only child, had never interrupted her dancing career for pregnancy. Niece? Grandniece? "—your ward."

"Je m'appelle Marguerite," the child said eagerly. "Nous regardons le ballet."

"Do you study ballet, Marguerite?"

"Mais oui!" she said scornfully, but Anna Olson made a sign and the bodyguards deftly cut me off from both of them. By maneuvering around the edge of the hall, I caught a last, distant glimpse of Marguerite. She waited patiently in line to go back to her seat. Her small feet in pink ballet slippers turned out in a perfect fifth position.

Thursday afternoon I drove into Paris to rent an electronic translator for the presentation by Taillebois and Erbland. The translators furnished by the conference were long since claimed. People who had rented them for the opening talks simply hung onto them, afraid to miss anything. The Taillebois/Erbland presentation would include written handouts in French, English, German, Spanish, Russian, and Japanese, but not until the session was over. I was afraid to miss anything, either.

I couldn't find an electronic translator with a brand name I trusted. I settled for a human named Jean-Paul, from a highly recommended commercial agency. He was about four feet ten, with sad brown eyes and a face wrinkled into fantastic crevasses. He told me he had translated for Charles de Gaulle during the crisis in Algeria. I believed him. He looked older than God.

We drove back to Neuilly in the rain. I said, "Jean-Paul, do you like ballet?"

"Non," he said immediately. "It is too slippery an art for me."

"Slippery?"

"Nothing is real. Girls are spirits of the dead, or joyous peasants, or other silly things. Have you ever seen any real peasants, Mademoiselle? They are not joyous. And girls lighter than air land on stage with a thump!" He illustrated by smacking the dashboard with his palm. "Men die of love for those women. Nobody dies for love. They die for money, or hate, but not love. Non."

"But isn't all art no more than illusion?"

He shrugged. "Not all illusion is worth creating. Not silly illusions. Dancers wobbling on tippy toes…non, non."

I said carefully, "French dancers can be openly bioenhanced. Not like in the United States. To some of us, that gives the art a whole new excitement. Technical, if not artistic."

Jean-Paul shrugged again. "Anybody can be bioenhanced, if they have the money. Bioenhancement, by itself it does not impress me. My grandson is bioenhanced."

"What does he do?"

Jean-Paul twisted his body toward me in the seat of the car. "He is a soccer player! One of the best in the world! If you followed the sport, you would know his name. Claude Despreaux. Soccer—now *there* is illusion worth creating!"

His tone was exactly Anton Privitera's, talking about ballet.

Thursday evening, just before the presentation, I finally caught Deborah at home. Her face on the phonevid was drawn and strained. "What's wrong?"

"Nothing, Mom. How's Paris?"

"Wet. Deborah, you're not telling me the truth."

"Everything's fine! I just…just had a complicated rehearsal today."

The corps de ballet does not usually demand complicated rehearsals. The function of the corps is to move gracefully behind the soloists and principal dancers; it's seldom allowed to do anything that will distract from their virtuosity. I said carefully, "Are you injured?"

"No, of course not. Look, I have to go."

"Deborah…"

"They're waiting for me!" The screen went blank.

Who was waiting for her?

When I called back, there was no answer.

I went to the Grand Ballroom. Jean-Paul had been holding both our seats, lousy ones, since noon. An hour later, the presentation still had not started.

The audience fidgeted, tense and muttering. Finally a woman dressed in a severe suit entered. She spoke German. Jean-Paul translated into my ear.

"Good evening. I am Katya Waggenschauser. I have an announcement before we begin. I regret to inform you that Dr. Taillebois will not appear. Dr. Taillebois...He..." Abruptly she ran off the stage.

The muttering rose to an astonished roar.

A man walked on stage. The crowd quieted immediately. Jean-Paul translated from the French, "I am Dr. Valois of the Pasteur Institute. Shortly Dr. Erbland will begin the presentation. But I regret to inform you that Dr. Taillebois will not appear. There has been an unfortunate accident. Dr. Taillebois is dead."

The murmuring rose, fell again. I heard reporters whispering into camphones in six languages.

"In a few moments Dr. Erbland will make her and Dr. Taillebois's presentation. Please be patient just a few moments longer."

Eventually someone introduced Dr. Erbland, a long and fulsome introduction, and she walked onto the stage. A thin, tall woman in her sixties, she looked shaken and pale. She opened by speaking about how various kinds of bioenhancement differed from each other in intent, procedure, and biological mechanism. Most bioenhancements were introduced into an adult body that had already finished growing. A few, usually aimed at correcting hereditary problems, were carried out on infants. Those procedures were somewhat closer to the kinds of genetic re-engineering—it was not referred to merely as "bioenhancement"—that produced new strains of animals. And as with animals, science had long known that it was possible to manipulate pre-embryonic human genes in the same way, *in vitro.*

The audience grew completely quiet.

In vitro work, Dr. Erbland said, offered by its nature fewer guides and guarantees. There were much coded redundancies in genetic information, and that made it difficult to determine long-term happenings. The human genome map, the basis of all embryonic re-engineering, had been complete for forty years, but "complete" was not the same as "understood." The body had many genetic behaviors that researchers were only just beginning to understand. No one could have expected that when embryonic re-engineering first began, as a highly experimental undertaking, that genetic identity would be so stubborn.

Stubborn? I didn't know what she meant. Apparently, neither did anybody else in the audience. People scarcely breathed.

This experimental nature of embryonic manipulation in humans did not, of course, stop experimentation, Dr. Erbland continued. Before such experimentation was declared illegal by the Copenhagen Accord, many laboratories around the world had advanced science with the cooperation of voluntary subjects. Completely voluntary, she said. She said it three times.

I wondered how an embryo volunteered.

These voluntary subjects had been re-engineered using variants of the same techniques that produced *in vitro* bioenhancements in other mammals. Her company, in conjunction with the Pasteur Research Institute, had been pioneers in the new techniques. For over thirty years.

Thirty years. My search of the literature had found nothing going back that far. At least not those available on the standard scientific nets. If such "re-engineered" embryos had been allowed to fully gestate, and had survived, they were just barely within the cut-off date for legal existence. Were we talking about embryos or people here?

Dr. Erblans made a curious gesture: raising both arms from the elbow, then letting them fall. It looked almost like a plea. Was she making a public confession of breaking international law? Why would she do that?

Over such a long time, Dr. Erblans continued, the human genetic identity, encoded in "jumping genes" in many unsuspected redundant ways, reasserted itself. This was the subject of her and Dr. Taillebois's work. Unfortunately, the effect on the organism—completely unanticipated by anyone—could be biologically devastating. This first graphic showed basal DNA changes in a re-engineered embryo created twenty-five years ago. The subject, a male, was —

A holograph projected a complicated, three-dimensional genemap. The scientists in the audience leaned forward intently. The non-scientists looked at each other.

As the presentation progressed, anchored in graphs and formulas and genemap holos, it became clear even to me what Dr. Erbland was actually saying.

European geneticists had been experimenting on embryos as long as thirty years ago, and never stopped. They'd allowed some of those embryos to become people. Against international law, and without knowing the long-term effects. And now the long-term effects, like old bills, were coming due, and those people's bodies were destroying themselves at the genetic level.

We had engineered a bioenhanced cancer to replace the natural one we had conquered.

It was a few moments before I noticed that Jean-Paul had stopped translating. He sat like stone, his wrinkled face lengthened in sorrow.

The audience forgot this was a scientific conference. "How many people have been re-engineered at an embryonic level?" someone shouted in English. "Total number worldwide!"

Someone else shouted, "Y todos van a morir?"

"Les lois internationales—"

"Der sagt—"

Dr. Erbland broke into a long, passionate speech, clearly not part of the prepared presentation. I caught the word "sagt" several times: *law.* I remembered that Dr. Erblans worked for a commercial biotech firm wholly owned by a pharmaceutical company.

The same company in which Anna Olson owned a fortune in stock.

Jean-Paul said quietly, "My grandson. Claude. He was one of those embryos. They told us it was safe..."

I looked at the old man, slumped forward, and I couldn't find any sympathy for him. That appalled me. A cherished grandson...But they had agreed, Claude's parents, to roulette with a child's life. In order to produce a superior soccer player. *"Soccer—now there is an illusion worth creating."*

I remembered Anna Olson at the demonstration by the Lincoln Center fountain: *"Caroline had a good run. For a dancer."* Caroline Olson, Deborah said, had been fired because she missed rehearsals and performances. The *Times* had called her last performance "a travesty." Because her body was eating itself at a genetic level, undetectable by the City Ballet bioscans that assumed you could compare new DNA patterns to the body's original, which no procedure completely erased. But for Caroline, the original itself had carried the hidden blueprint for destruction. For twenty-six years.

The ultimate ballet mother had made Caroline into what Anna Olson needed her to be. For as long as Caroline might last.

And then I remembered little Marguerite, standing with her perfect turnout in fifth position.

I stood and pushed my way to the exit. I had to get out of that room. Nobody else left. Dr. Erbland, rattled and afraid, tried to answer questions shouted in six languages. I shoved past a woman who was punching her neighbor. Gendarmes appeared as if conjured from the floorboards. Maybe that would be next.

The hardcopies of Dr. Taillebois's original presentation were stacked neatly on tables in the lobby. I took one in English. As I went out the door, I heard a gendarme say clearly to somebody, "Oui, il s'a suicide, Dr. Taillebois."

I didn't want to stay an hour longer in Paris. I packed at the hotel and changed my ticket at Orly. On the plane home I made myself read the Taillebois/Erbland paper. Most of it was incomprehensible to me; what I understood was obscene. I kept seeing Marguerite in her pink ballet slippers, Caroline staggering on stage. If my lack of sympathy for Taillebois and Erbland was a lack in me, then so be it.

For the first time since Deborah had entered the School of American Ballet, and despite the dazzling performances at the Paris Opera, I found myself respecting Anton Privitera.

When I landed at Kennedy, at almost midnight, there was a message from the electronic gate keeper, "Call this number immediately. Urgent and crucial." I didn't recognize the number.

Deborah. An accident. I raced to the nearest public phone. But it wasn't a hospital; it was an attorney's office.

"Ms. Susan Matthews? Hold, please."

A man's face came on the screen. "This is James Beecher, Ms. Matthews. I'm attorney for Pers Anders. He's being held without bail, pending trial. He left a message for you, most urgent. The message is—"

"Trial? On what charges?" But I think I already knew. The well-cut suit on the lawyer. The move to an expensive neighborhood. Pers was working for somebody, and there weren't very many things he knew how to do.

"The charges are dealing in narcotics. First-degree felony. The message is—"

"Sunshine, right? No, that wouldn't have been expensive enough for Pers," I said bitterly. "Designer viruses? Pleasure center beanos?"

"The message is, 'Don't look in the caverns of the moon.' That's all." The screen went blank.

I stared at it anyway. When Deborah was tiny, in the brief period a million years ago when Pers and I were still together and raising her, she had a game she loved. She'd hide a favorite toy somewhere and call out, "Don't look in the closet! Don't look under the bed! Don't look in the sock drawer!" The toy was always wherever she said not to look. The caverns of the moon was what she called her bedroom, but that was much later, long after Pers had deserted us both but before she tracked him down in New York. I didn't know that he even knew about it.

Don't look in the caverns of the moon.

I took a helio right to the Central Park landing stage, charging it to the magazine. The last five blocks I ran, past the automated stores that never sleep and the night people who had just gotten up. Deborah wasn't home; she didn't expect me back from Paris until tomorrow. I tore apart her bedroom, and in an old dance bag I found it, flattened between the mattress and box spring. No practiced criminal, my Deborah.

The powder was pinkish, with no particular odor. There was a lot of it. I had no idea what it was; probably it had a unique name to go with a unique formula matched to some brain function. What kind of father would use his own daughter as a courier for this designer-gene abyss? Would the cops have already been here if I'd come home a day later? An hour later?

I flushed it all down the toilet, including the dance bag, which I first cut into tiny pieces. Then I searched the rest of the apartment, and then I searched it again. There were no more drugs. There was no money.

She wasn't running stuff for Pers for free. Not Deborah. She had spent the money somewhere.

"They asked me to join the company! He said it was very nice! He said I was much improved!"

I made myself sit and think. It was one o'clock in the morning. Lincoln Center would be locked and dark. She might be at a restaurant with other dancers; she might be staying the night with a friend. I called other SAB students. Each answered sleepily. Deborah wasn't there. Ninette told me that after the evening performance Deborah had said she was going home.

"Well, yes, Ms. Matthews, she did seem a little tense," Ninette said, stifling a yawn, her long hair tousled on the shoulders of her nightgown. "But it was only her second night in actual performance, so I thought..." The young voice trailed off. I wasn't going to be told whatever this girl thought. Clearly I was an interfering mother.

You bet I was.

I waited another hour. Deborah didn't come home. I called a cab and went to Caroline Olson's apartment on Central Park South.

It had to be Caroline. She must have known she herself was bioenhanced, and I had seen her dance before her downfall: the complete abandon to ballet, the joy. Maybe she thought that helping other dancers to illegal bioenhancement was a favor to them, a benefit. She might be making a distinction—the same one Dr. Erbland had made—between the ultimately destructive re-engineering done to her *in vitro* and the bioenhancements done to European dancers. Or maybe she didn't connect her own sudden deterioration with how her mother had genetically consecrated her to ballet.

Or maybe she did. Maybe she knew that her meteoric success was what was now killing her. Maybe she was so sick and so enraged that she *wanted* to destroy other dancers along with her. If she couldn't dance out her full career, then neither would they.

Or maybe she thought it was worth it. A short life but a brilliant one. Anything for art. Most dancers ended up crippling their bodies anyway, although more slowly. The great Suzanne Farrell had ended up with a plastic hip, her pelvis destroyed by constant turnout. Mikhail Baryshnikov ruined his knees. Miranda Mains was unable to walk by the time she was twenty-eight. Maybe Caroline Olson thought no sacrifice was too great for ballet, even a life.

But not my Deborah's.

I buzzed the security system of Caroline's apartment for five solid minutes. There was no answer. Finally the system said politely, "Your party does not answer. Further buzzing may constitute legal harassment. You should leave now."

I got back in the cab, chewing on my thumb. I felt that kind of desperation you think you can't live through; it consumes your belly, chokes your breath. The driver waited indifferently. *Where?* God, in New York they could be anywhere.

Anywhere nobody would think to look for illegal medical operations. Anywhere safe, and protected, and easily accessible by dancers, without suspicion.

I gave the driver Anna Olson's address, remembered from the tax return pirated by the Robin Hood. Then I transferred the gun from my purse to my pocket.

I think I wasn't quite sane.

9.

Caroline and I ride in a taxi. I like taxis. I put my head out the window. The taxi has many smells. We stop at Deborah's house. Caroline and I go get Deborah.

"I've changed my mind," Deborah says. Her door is open only a little. She stands behind her door. "I'm not going."

"Yes, you are," Caroline says.

Deborah says, "You're not my mother!"

Caroline changes her smell. She has a cane to walk. She leans on her cane. Her voice gets soft. "No, I'm not your mother. And I'm not going to push you like a mother. Believe me, Deborah, I know what that's like. But as a senior dancer, I'm going to ask you to come with me. I'm willing to beg you to come. It's that important. Not just to you, but to me."

Deborah looks at the floor.

"Don't be embarrassed. Just understand that I mean it. I'll beg, I'll grovel. But first I'm asking, as a senior member of the company."

Deborah looks up. She smells angry. "Why do you care? It's my life!"

"Yes. Yours and Privitera's." Caroline closes her eyes. "You owe him something, too. No, don't consider that. Just come because I'm asking you."

Deborah still smells angry. But she comes.

We ride in the taxi to Caroline's mother's house. I say, "Is there a party tonight?"

Deborah laughs. It sounds funny. Caroline says, "Yes, Angel. Another party. With music and dancers and talking. And you can have some pretzels."

"I like pretzels," I say. "Does Deborah like pretzels?"

"No," Deborah says, and now she smells scared.

We go in the back way. Caroline has a key. People come to the basement. Someone starts music. "Not so loud!" a man says.

"No, it's all right," Caroline says. "My mother's still in Europe and the staff is on vacation while she's gone. We have the place to ourselves."

A woman brings me a pretzel. People talk. Caroline and Deborah and two men talk in the corner. I don't hear the words. The words at parties are very hard. I watch Caroline, and eat pretzels, and watch two people dance to the radio.

"Christ," the man dancer says, "is this fake revelry really necessary?"

"Yes," the woman says. She looks at me. "Caroline says yes."

In the corner, two men show Deborah some papers. Caroline sits with them. Deborah starts to cry.

I watch Caroline. Deborah may touch Caroline. The two men may touch Caroline. But Caroline says parties are happy. No people smell happy. I do not understand.

The buzzer rings.

Nobody moves. People look at each other. Caroline says, "Is the gate still open? Let it go. It's probably kids. There's nobody home but us."

The buzzer rings and rings. Then it stops. Caroline talks to Deborah. The door opens at the top of the stairs.

A man with Caroline takes a bottle from his pocket very fast. He puts the papers on the floor and pours the bottle on it. The papers disappear. "All right, everybody, this is a party," he says.

Steps run down the stairs. A voice calls, "Wait! You can't go down there! Young woman! You can't go down there!" The voice is angry. It is Caroline's mother.

I walk to Caroline. She smells surprised.

A woman comes into the basement. She holds a gun. My ears raise. I stand next to Caroline.

"Nobody move," the woman says. Deborah says, "Mom!"

Caroline looks at the woman, then at Deborah, then at the woman. She walks with her cane to the woman.

"Stay right there," the woman says. She smells angry and scared. I move with Caroline.

"Christ, you sound like a bad holovid," Caroline says. "You're Deborah's mother? What the hell do you think you're doing here?"

From the top of the stairs Caroline's mother calls, "Caroline! What is the meaning of this?"

The woman says very fast, "Deborah, you're making a terrible mistake. Bioenhancement may help your dancing for a while, but it could also kill you. The conference on genetics in Paris—they presented scientific proof that one kind of bioenhancement kills, and if they're just finding that out now about enhancements done twenty-five years ago—then who knows what kind of insane risk you're running with these other kinds? Don't take my word for it, it's on-line this morning. Pers was arrested, damn him, and I found your drug stash just before the police did. That's how you're paying for this, isn't it? Debbie—how could you be such a damn *fool*?"

"Wait a minute," Caroline says. She leans on her cane. "You thought we brought Deborah here *to bioenhance her*?" Caroline starts to laugh. She puts her hand on her face. "Oh my God!"

Caroline's mother calls from the top of the stairs, "I'm phoning the police."

Caroline says, very fast, "Go bring her down here, James. You'll have to lift her out of her chair and carry her. Keith, get her chair." The two men run up the stairs.

Caroline is shaking. I stand beside her. I growl. The woman still has the gun. She points the gun at Caroline. I wait for Caroline to tell me *Attack*.

The woman says, "Don't try to deny it. You'd do anything for ballet, wouldn't you? All of you. You're sick—but you're not murdering my daughter!"

Caroline's face changes. Her smell changes. I feel her hand on my head. Her hand shakes. Her body shakes. I smell anger bigger than other angers. I wait for *Attack*.

Deborah says, "You're all wrong, Mom! Just like you always are! Does this look like a bioenhancement lab? *Does it?* These people aren't enhancing me—they're trying to talk me out of it! These two guys are doctors and they're trying to 'deprogram' me—just like you tried to program me all my life! You never wanted me to dance, you always tried to make me into this cute little college-bound student that *you* needed me to be. Never what *I* needed!"

The men carry Caroline's mother and Caroline's mother's chair down the steps. They put Caroline's mother in the chair. Caroline's mother also smells angry. But Caroline smells more angry than everybody.

Caroline says, "Sound familiar, Mother dear? What Deborah's saying? What did *you* learn at the genetic conference? What I've been telling you for months, right? Your gift to dance is dying. Because you wanted a prima ballerina at any price. Even if I'm the one to pay it."

Caroline's mother says, "You love dance. You wanted it as much as I did. You were a star."

"I never got to find out if I would have been one anyway! That isn't so inconceivable, is it? And then I might have still been dancing! But instead I was...*made*. Molded, sewed, carpentered. Into what you needed me to be."

Deborah's mother lowers her gun. Her eyes are big. Caroline's mother says, "You were a star. You had a good run. Without me, you might have been nothing. Worthless."

A man says, very soft, "Jesus H. Christ."

Caroline is shaking hard. I am afraid she will fall again. Her hand is on her cane. The cane shakes. Her other hand is on me.

Caroline says, "You cold, self-centered bitch—"

A little girl runs down the stairs.

The little girl says, "Tante Anna! Tante Anna! Ou etes-vous?" She stops at the bottom of the steps. She smells afraid. "Qui sont tout ces gens?"

Caroline looks at the little girl. The little girl has no shoes. She has long black fur on her head. Her hind feet go out like Caroline's feet when Caroline dances. The toes look strange. I don't understand the little girl's feet.

Caroline says again, "You cold, self-centered bitch." Her voice is soft now. She stops shaking. "When did you have her made? Five years ago? Six? A new model with improved features? Who will decay all the sooner?"

Caroline's mother says, "You are a hysterical fool."

Caroline says, "Angel—attack. Now."

I attack Caroline's mother. I knock over the chair. I bite her foreleg. Someone screams, "Caroline! For God's sake! Caroline!" I bite Caroline's mother's head. I must protect Caroline. This person hurts Caroline. I must protect Caroline.

A gun fires and I hurt and hurt and hurt—

I love Caroline.

10.

The town of Saratoga, where the American Ballet Theater is dancing its summer season, is itself a brightly-colored stage. Visitors throng the racetrack, the brand-new Electronics Museum, the historical battle sites. In 1777, right here, Benedict Arnold and his half-trained revolutionaries stopped British forces under General John Burgoyne. It was the first great victory of freedom over the old order.

Until this year, the New York City Ballet danced here every summer. But the Performing Arts Center chose not to renew the City Ballet contract. In New York, too, City Ballet attendance is half of what it was only a few years ago.

The Saratoga pavilion is open to the countryside. Ballet lovers fill the seats, spread blankets up the sloping lawn, watch dancers accompanied not only by Tchaikovsky or Chopin but also by crickets and robins. In Saratoga, the ballet smells of freshly mown grass. The classic "white ballets"—*Swan Lake, Les Sylphides*—are remembered green. Small girls whose first taste of dance is at Saratoga will dream, for the rest of their life, of toe shoes skimming over wildflowers.

I take my seat, in the back of the regular seating, as the small orchestra finishes tuning up. The conductor enters to the usual thunderous applause, even though nobody here knows his name and very few care. They have come to see the dancers.

Debussy floats out over the countryside. *Afternoon of a Faun*: slow, melting. On the nearly bare stage, furnished only with barre and mirrors, a male dancer in practice clothes wakes up, stretches, warms up his muscles in a series of low, languorous moves.

A girl appears in the mirror, which isn't really a mirror but an empty place in the backdrop. A void. She, too, stretches, poses, plies. Both dancers watch the mirrors. They are so absorbed in their own reflections that they only gradually become aware of each other's presence. Even then, they exist for each other only as foils, presences to dance to. In the end the girl will step back through the mirror. There is the feeling that for the boy, she may not really have existed at all, except as a dream.

It is Deborah's first lead in a one-act ballet. Her extension is high, her turnout perfect, her movements sure and strong and sustained, filled with the joy of dancing. I can barely stand to look at her. This is her reward, her grail, for continuing her bioenhancement. She isn't dancing for Anton Privitera, but she is dancing. A year and a half of bioenhancement, bought legally now in Copenhagen and paid for by selling her story to an eager press, has given her the physical possibilities to match her musicality, and her rhythm, and her drive.

The faun finally touches the girl, turning her slowly *en attitude*. Deborah smiles. This is her afternoon. She's willing to pay whatever price the night demands, even though science has no idea yet what, for her kind of treatments, it might be.

Privitera must have known that some of his dancers were bioenhanced. The completely inadequate bioscans at City Ballet, the phenomenally low injury rate of his prima ballerinas—Privitera must have known. Or maybe his staff let him remain in official ignorance, keeping from him any knowledge of heresy in the ranks. There was a rumor that Privitera's business manager John Coles even tried to keep Caroline from "deprogramming" dancers who wanted bioenhancement. The rumor about Coles was never substantiated. But in the last year, City Ballet has been struggling to survive. Too many patrons have withdrawn their favor. The mystique of natural art, like other mystiques, didn't last forever. It had a good run.

"If you could have chosen, and that was the *only* way you could have had the career, would you have chosen the embryonic engineering anyway?" was the sole thing Deborah had asked Caroline in jail, through bullet-proof plastic glass and electronic speaking systems, under the hard eyes of matrons. Caroline, awaiting trial for second-degree murder, didn't seem to mind Deborah's brusqueness, her self-absorption. Caroline was silent a long time, her gaunt face lengthened from the girlish roundness I remembered. Then she said to Deborah, "No."

"I would," Deborah said.

Caroline only looked at her.

They're here, Caroline and her dog. Somewhere up on the grass, Caroline in a powerchair, Angel hobbling on the three legs my bullet left him. Caroline was acquitted by reason of temporary insanity. They didn't let Angel stay with her during the trial. Nor did they let him testify, which would have been abnormal but not impossible. Five-year-olds can testify under some circumstances, and Angel has the biochip-and-reengineered intelligence of a five-year-old. Maybe it wouldn't have been so abnormal. Or maybe all of us, not just Anton Privitera, will have to change our definition of abnormal.

Five-year-olds know a lot. It was Marguerite who cried out, "Vous avez assassiné ma tante Anna!" She knew whom I was aiming at, even if the police did not. But Marguerite couldn't know how much I loathed the old woman who had made her daughter into what the mother needed her to be—just as I, out of love, had tried to do to mine.

On stage Deborah *pirouettes*. Maybe her types of bioenhancement will be all right, despite the growing body of doubts collected by Caroline's doctor allies. When the first cures for cancer were developed from reengineered retroviruses, dying and desperate patients demanded they be administered without long, drawn-out FDA testing. Some of the patients died even sooner, possibly from the cures. Some lived until 90. The edge of anything is a lottery, and protection doesn't help—not against change, or madmen, or errors of judgement. *I protect Caroline*, Angel kept saying after I shot him, yelping in pain between sentences. *I protect Caroline.*

Deborah flows into a *retiré*, one leg bent at the knee, and rises on toe. Her face glows. Her partner lifts her above his head and turns her slowly, her feet perfectly arched in their toe shoes, dancing on air.

Afterword to "Dancing on Air"

I love ballet. I had lessons as a child, which proved to be a disaster. My ballet teacher told my mother, "She lacks coordination, rhythm, flexibility, musicality, and stamina, and she's too tall." There went that career.

Eventually, however, I learned to write about ballet, both its beauty and the bodily torture it takes to create that beauty. "Dancing on Air" also includes another major theme of mine: families. From much science fiction, you'd get the impression that nobody whizzing around space and time has any familial ties. Yet all of us started life in some sort of families, many of us have children, and such ties exert powerful claims on the choices we make. I wanted to write about that.

"Dancing on Air" was a nominee for both the Nebula and the Hugo. I lost the latter by three votes, to Charles Sheffield, whom a few years later I would marry. You just never know.

UNTO THE DAUGHTERS

This is not the way you heard the story.

In the beginning, the tree was young. White blossoms scenting the air for a quarter mile. Shiny succulent fruit, bending the same boughs that held blossoms. Leaves of that delicate yellow-green that cannot, will not, last. Yet it did. He always did have gaudy taste. No restraint. Just look at the Himalayas. Or blowfish. I mean really!

The woman was young, too. Pink curling toes, breasts as barely budded as the apple blossoms. And the man! My dear, those long, firm flanks alone could make you ache inside for hours. He could run five miles and not even be winded. He could make love to the woman five times a day. And did.

The flowers were young. The animals, tumbling and cavorting on the grass, were young. The fucking beach sand was young, clean evenly shaped grains that only yesterday had been igneous rock. There was virgin rain.

Only I was old.

But it wasn't that. That was the first thing that came to your mind, wasn't it? Jealousy of glorious youth, revenge by the dried-up and jaded. Oh, you don't know, you sitting there so many centuries ahead. It wasn't that at all. I mean, I loved them both.

Looking at them, how could one not?

"Go away," Eve says. "I'm not going to eat one."

She sits cross-legged, braiding flowers into a crown. The flowers are about what you'd expect from Him, garish scarlet petals and a vulva-shaped pistil like a bad joke. Braiding them, her fingers are deft and competent. Some lion cubs tumble tiresomely on the grass.

"I want to give you a reason why you should eat one," I say, not gently.

"I've heard all your reasons."

"Not this one, Eve. This is a *new* reason."

She isn't interested. She knots the crown of flowers, puts it on her head, giggles, tosses it at the lions. It settles lopsided over one cub's left ear. The cub looks up with comic surprise, and Eve explodes into laughter.

Really, sometimes I wonder why I bother. She's so stupid, compared to the man.

I bother because she's so stupid compared to the man.

"Listen, Eve. He withholds knowledge from you two because He's selfish. What else would you call it to keep knowledge to yourself when you could just as well share it?"

"I don't need knowledge," Eve says airily. "What do I need knowledge for? And anyway, that's not a new reason. You've said that before."

"A tree, Eve. A fucking *tree*. To invest knowledge in. Doesn't that strike you as just a teeny bit warped? Mathematics in xylem, morality in fruit pulp? Astronomy rotting on the ground every time an apple falls. Don't you wonder what kind of a mind would do that?"

She only stares at me blankly. Oh, she's dumb. I mean!

I shout, in the temper of perfect despair, "Without knowledge, nothing will change!"

"Are you here again?" Adam says. I hadn't heard him climb over the rock behind us. He has a very quiet footstep for someone whose toenails have never ever been cut. Also a quiet, penetrating voice. Eve jumps up as if she's been shot.

"I thought I told you not to talk to this...thing ever again," Adam says. "Didn't I tell you that?"

Eve hangs her pretty head. "Yes, Adam. You did. I forgot."

He looks at her and his face softens. That blooming skin, those sweet lips. Her hair falls forward, lustrous as night. I don't think my despair can go any deeper, but it does. She is so pretty. He will always forgive her. And she will always forget everything he says two minutes after he says it.

"Be gone! You don't belong here!" Adam shouts, and throws a rock at me. It hits just behind my head. It hurts like hell. One of the lion cubs happily fetches it back, wagging a golden tail. The other one is still wearing the lopsided crown of flowers.

As I slither away, half blind with pain, Eve calls after me. "I don't want anything to change! I really don't!"

The hell with her.

"Just listen," I say. "Just put your entire tiny mind on one thing for once and listen to me."

Eve sits sewing leaves into a blanket. Not cross-legged anymore: She is six months pregnant. The leaves are wide and soft, with a sort of furry nap on their underside. They appeared in the garden right after she got pregnant, along with tough spider webs that make splendid thread. Why not a bush that grows little caps? Or tiny diapers with plastic fastening tabs? Really, He has such a banal imagination.

Eve hums as she sews. Beside her is the cradle Adam made. It's carved with moons and numbers and stars and other cabalistic signs: a lovely piece of work. *Adam* has imagination.

"You have to listen, Eve. Not just hear—listen. Stop that humming. I know the future—how could I know the future unless I am exactly what I say I am? I know everything that's going to happen. I told you when you'd conceive, didn't I? That alone should have convinced you. And now I'm telling you that your baby will be a boy, and you'll call him Cain, and he—"

"No, I'm going to call him Silas," Eve says. She knots the end of her spider-thread and bites it off. "I love the name Silas."

"You're going to call him Cain, and he—"

"Do you think it would be prettier to embroider roses on this blanket, or daisies?"

"Eve, listen, if I can foretell the future then isn't it logical, isn't it reasonable for you to think—"

"I don't have to think," Eve says. "Adam does that for both of us, plus all the forest-dressing and fruit-tending. He works so hard, poor dear."

"Eve—"

"Roses, I think. In blue."

I can't stand it anymore. I go out into the constant, perpetual, monotonous sunshine, which smells like roses, like wisteria, like gardenia, like wood smoke, like new-mown hay. Like heaven.

Eve has the baby at nine months, thirty-two seconds. She laughs as the small head slides out, which takes two painless minutes. The child is perfect.

"We'll call him Cain," Adam says.

"I thought we might call him Silas. I love the na—"

"Cain," Adam says firmly.

"All right, Adam."

He will never know she was disappointed.

"Eve," I say. "Listen."

She is bathing the two boys in the river, in the shallows just before the river splits into four parts and leaves the garden. Cain is diligently scrubbing his small penis, but Abel has caught at some seaweed and is examining how it hangs over his chubby fists. He turns it this way and that, bending his head close. He is much more intelligent than his brother.

"Eve, Adam will be back soon. If you'd just listen..."

"Daddy," Abel says, raising his head. He has a level gaze, friendly but evaluative, even at his age. He spends a lot of time with his father. "Daddy gone."

"Oh, yes, Daddy's gone to pick breadfruit in the west!" Eve cries, in a perfect ecstasy of maternal pride. "He'll be back tonight, my little poppets. He'll be home with his precious little boys!"

Cain looks up. He has succeeded in giving his penis the most innocent of erections. He smiles beatifically at Abel, at his mother, who does not see him because she is scrubbing Abel's back, careful not to drip soapstone onto his seaweed.

"Daddy pick breadfruit," Abel repeats. "Mommy not."

"Mommy doesn't want to go pick breadfruit," Eve says. "Mommy is happy right here with her little poppets."

"Mommy not," Abel repeats, thoughtfully.

"Eve," I say, "only with knowledge can you make choices. Only with truth can you be free. Four thousand years from now—"

"I am free," Eve says, momentarily startled. She looks at me. Her eyes are as fresh, as innocent, as when she was created. They open very wide. "How could anyone not think I'm perfectly free?"

"If you'd just listen—"

"Daddy gone," Abel says a third time. "Mommy not."

"Even thirty seconds of careful listening—"

"Mommy never gone."

"Tell that brat to shut up while I'm trying to talk to you!"

Wrong, wrong. Fury leaps into Eve's eyes. She scoops up both children as if I were trying to stone them, the silly bitch. She hugs them tight to her chest, breathing something from those perfect lips that might have been "Well!" or "Ugly!" or even "Help!" Then she staggers off with both boys in her arms, dripping water, Abel dripping seaweed.

"Put Abel down," Abel says dramatically. "Abel walk."

She does. The child looks at her. "Mommy do what Abel say!"

I go eat worms.

The third child is a girl, whom they name Sheitha.

Cain and Abel are almost grown. They help Adam with the garden dressing, the animal naming, whatever comes up. I don't know. I'm getting pretty sick of the whole lot of them. The tree still has both blossoms and fruit on the same branch. The river still flows into four exactly equal branches just beyond the garden: Pison, Gihon, Hiddekel, Euphrates. Exactly the same number of water molecules in each. I stop thinking He's theatrical and decide instead that He's compulsive. I mean—really. Fish lay the exact same number of eggs in each river.

Eve hasn't seen Him in decades. Adam, of course, walks with Him in the cool of every evening. Now the two boys go, too. Heaven knows what they talk about; I stay away. Often it's my one chance at Eve, who spends every day sewing and changing diapers and sweeping bowers and slicing breadfruit. Her toes are still pink curling delicacies.

"Eve, listen—"

Sheitha giggles at a bluebird perched on her dimpled knee.

"Adam makes all the decisions, decides all the rules, thinks up all the names, does all the thinking—"

"So?" Eve says. "Sheitha—you precious little angel!" She catches the baby in her arms and covers her with kisses. Sheitha crows in delight.

"Eve, listen—" Miraculously, she does. She sets the baby on the grass and says seriously, "Adam says you aren't capable of telling the truth."

"Not *his* truth," I say. "Or His." But of course this subtlety of pronoun goes right over her head.

"Look, snake, I don't want to be rude. You've been very kind to me, keeping me company while I do my housework, and I appreciate—"

"I'm not being kind," I say desperately. Kind! Oh, my Eve... "I'm too old and tired for kindness. I'm just trying to show you, to get you to listen—"

"Adam's back," Eve says quickly. I hear him then, with the two boys. There is just time enough to slither under a bush. I lie there very still. Lately Adam has turned murderous toward me; I think he must have a special dispensation for it. *He* must have told Adam violence toward me doesn't count, because I have stepped out of my place. Which, of course, I have.

But this time Adam doesn't see me. The boys fall into some game with thread and polished stones. Sheitha toddles toward her daddy, grinning.

"We're just here to get something to eat," Adam says. "Ten minutes, is all—what, Eve, isn't there anything ready? What have you been doing all morning?"

Eve's face doesn't fall. But her eyes deepen in color a little, like skin that has been momentarily bruised. Of course, skin doesn't stay bruised here. Not here.

"I'm sorry, dear! I'll get something ready right away!"

"Please," Adam says. "Some of us have to work for a living."

She bustles quickly around. The slim pretty fingers are deft as ever. Adam throws himself prone into a bower. Sheitha climbs into his lap. She is as precocious as the boys were.

"Daddy go back?"

"Yes, my little sweetie. Daddy has to go cut more sugar cane. And name some new animals."

"Animals," Sheitha says happily. She loves animals. "Sheitha go."

Adam smiles. "No, precious, Sheitha can't go. Little girls can't go."

"Sheitha go!"

"No," Adam says. He is still smiling, but he stands up and she tumbles off his lap. The food is ready. Eve turns with a coconut shell of salad just as Sheitha is picking herself up. The baby stands looking up at her father. Her small face is crumpled in disappointment, in disbelief, in anguish. Eve stops her turning motion and looks, her full attention on Sheitha's face.

I draw a deep breath.

The moment spins itself out, tough as spider-thread.

Eve breaks it. "Adam—can't you take her?"

He doesn't answer. Actually, he hasn't even heard her. He can't, in exactly the same way Eve cannot hear Him in the cool of the evening.

You could argue that this exempts him from fault.

Eve picks up the baby and stands beside the bower. Fragrance rises from the newly crushed flower petals where Adam was lying. When he and the boys have left again, I slither forward. Eve, the baby in her arms, has still not moved. Her head is bent. Sheitha is weeping, soft tears of vexation that will not, of course, last very long. Not here. I don't have much time.

"Eve," I say. "Listen—"

I tell her how it will be for Sheitha after she marries Cain, who is not as sweet-tempered as his father. I tell her how it will be for Sheitha's daughter's daughter. I spare her nothing: not the expansion of the garden until the home bowers are insignificant. Not the debate over whether women have souls. Not foot-binding nor clitorectomy nor suttee nor the word "chattel." Sheitha, I say. Sheitha and Sheitha's daughter and Sheitha's daughter's daughter...I am hoarse before I'm done talking. Finally, I finish, saying for perhaps the fortieth or fiftieth time, "Knowledge is the only way to change it. Knowledge, and truth. Eve, listen—"

She goes with me to the tree. Her baby daughter in her arms, she goes with me. She chooses a bright red apple, and she chews her mouthful so completely that when she transfers it to Sheitha's lips there is no chance the baby could choke on it. Together, they eat the whole thing.

I am tired. I don't wait around for the rest: Adam's return, and his outrage that she has acted without him, his fear that now she knows things he does not. His arrival. I don't wait. I am too tired, and my gut twists as if I had swallowed something foul, or bitter. That happens sometimes, without my intending it. Sometimes I eat something with a vitamin I know I need, and it lies hard in my belly like pain.

This is not the way you heard the story.

But consider who eventually wrote that story down. Consider, too, who wiped up the ink or scrubbed the chisel or cleaned the printing office after the writing down was done. For centuries and centuries.

But not forever.

So this may not be the way you heard the story, but you, centuries and centuries hence, my sisters, know better. Finally you know, yes, about Eve's screams on her childbed, and Sheitha's murder at the hands of her husband, and Sheitha's daughter's cursing of her rebellious mother as the girl climbed willingly onto her husband's funeral pyre, and her daughter's harlotry, and her daughter's forced marriage at age nine to a man who gained control of all her camels and oases. You know all that, all the things I didn't tell poor Eve would happen anyway. But you know, too—as Eve would not have, had it not been for me—that knowledge can bring change. You sit cross-legged at your holodecks or in your pilot chairs or on your Councils, humming, and you finally know. Finally—it took you so fucking long to digest the fruit of knowledge and shit it out where it could fertilize anything. But you did. You are not stupid. More—you know that stupidity is only the soul asleep. The awakened sleeper may stumble a long time in the dark, but eventually the light comes. Even here.

I woke Eve up.

I, the mother.

So that may not be the way you heard the story, but it is the way it happened. And now—finally, finally—you know.

And can forgive me.

Afterword to "Unto the Daughters"

So a spaceship crashes on Earth and only two people survive, and at the end of the story we learn that their names are Adam and Eve.... No, wait. That's the SF story you're *not* supposed to write, the cliché of clichés.

But I wanted to write an Adam and Eve story (who knows why). Furthermore, I wanted it to be a feminist Eve story. It always seemed to me that Adam was a wimp, blaming Eve for his own choice to eat the apple she offered him. But Eve, misled so easily by the snake, wasn't very promising as a strong heroine. That left...

Yes. After all, Genesis is vague about the gender of the snake. Perhaps whoever wrote down the story didn't think gender mattered much. But it does. Throughout history, it always has.

The thing I enjoyed most about writing "Unto the Daughters" was the voice. In creating characters, I try to become that character. With the snake, it was alarmingly easy.

Hmmmm...

LAWS OF SURVIVAL

My name is Jill. I am somewhere you can't imagine, going somewhere even more unimaginable. If you think I like what I did to get here, you're crazy.

Actually, I'm the one who's crazy. You—any "you"—will never read this. But I have paper now, and a sort of pencil, and time. Lots and lots of time. So I will write what happened, all of it, as carefully as I can.

After all—why the hell not?

I went out very early one morning to look for food. Before dawn was safest for a woman alone. The boy-gangs had gone to bed, tired of attacking each other. The trucks from the city hadn't arrived yet. That meant the garbage was pretty picked over, but it also meant most of the refugee camp wasn't out scavenging. Most days I could find enough: a carrot stolen from somebody's garden patch, my arm bloody from reaching through the barbed wire. Overlooked potato peelings under a pile of rags and glass. A can of stew thrown away by one of the soldiers on the base, but still half full. Soldiers on duty by the Dome were often careless. They got bored, with nothing to do.

That morning was cool but fair, with a pearly haze that the sun would burn off later. I wore all my clothing, for warmth, and my boots. Yesterday's garbage load, I'd heard somebody say, was huge, so I had hopes. I hiked to my favorite spot, where garbage spills almost to the Dome wall. Maybe I'd find bread, or even fruit that wasn't too rotten.

Instead I found the puppy.

Its eyes weren't open yet and it squirmed along the bare ground, a scrawny brown-and-white mass with a tiny fluffy tail. Nearby was a fluid-soaked towel. Some sentimental fool had left the puppy there, hoping... what? It didn't matter. Scrawny or not, there was some meat on the thing. I scooped it up.

The sun pushed above the horizon, flooding the haze with golden light.

I hate it when grief seizes me. I hate it and it's dangerous, a violation of one of Jill's Laws of Survival. I can go for weeks, months without thinking of my life before the War. Without remembering or feeling. Then something will strike me—a flower growing in the dump, a burst of birdsong, the stars on a clear night—and grief will hit me like the maglevs that no longer exist, a grief all the sharper because it contains the memory of joy. I can't afford joy, which always comes with an astronomical price tag. I can't even afford the grief that comes from the memory of living things, which is why it is only the flower, the birdsong, the morning sunlight that starts it. My grief was not for that puppy. I still intended to eat it.

But I heard a noise behind me and turned. The Dome wall was opening.

Who knew why the aliens put their Domes by garbage dumps, by waste pits, by radioactive cities? Who knew why aliens did anything?

There was a widespread belief in the camp that the aliens started the War. I'm old enough to know better. That was us, just like the global warming and the bio-crobes were us. The aliens didn't even show up until the War was over and Raleigh was the northernmost city left on the East Coast and refugees poured south like mudslides. Including me. That's when the ships landed and then turned into the huge gray Domes like upended bowls. I heard there were many Domes, some in other countries. The Army, what was left of it, threw tanks and bombs at ours. When they gave up, the refugees threw bullets and Molotov cocktails and prayers and graffiti and candle-light vigils and rain dances. Everything slid off and the Domes just sat there. And sat. And sat. Three years later, they were still sitting, silent and closed, although of course there were rumors to the contrary. There are always rumors. Personally, I'd never gotten over a slight disbelief that the Dome was there at all. Who would want to visit us?

The opening was small, no larger than a porthole, and about six feet above the ground. All I could see inside was a fog the same color as the Dome. Something came out, gliding quickly toward me. It took me a moment to realize it was a robot, a blue metal sphere above a hanging basket. It stopped a foot from my face and said, "This food for this dog."

I could have run, or screamed, or at the least—the very least—looked around for a witness. I didn't. The basket held a pile of fresh produce, green lettuce and deep purple eggplant and apples so shiny red they looked lacquered. And *peaches*...My mouth filled with sweet water. I couldn't move.

The puppy whimpered.

My mother used to make fresh peach pie.

I scooped the food into my scavenger bag, laid the puppy in the basket, and backed away. The robot floated back into the Dome, which closed immediately. I sped back to my corrugated-tin and windowless hut and ate until I couldn't hold any more. I slept, woke, and ate the rest, crouching in the dark so nobody else would see. All that fruit and vegetables gave me the runs, but it was worth it.

Peaches.

Two weeks later, I brought another puppy to the Dome, the only survivor of a litter deep in the dump. I never knew what happened to the mother. I had to wait a long time outside the Dome before the blue sphere took the puppy in exchange for produce. Apparently the Dome would only open when there was no one else around to see. What were they afraid of? It's not like PETA was going to show up.

The next day I traded three of the peaches to an old man in exchange for a small, mangy poodle. We didn't look each other in the eye, but I nonetheless knew that his held tears. He limped hurriedly away. I kept the dog, which clearly wanted nothing to do with me, in my shack until very early morning and then took it to the Dome. It tried to escape but I'd tied a bit of rope onto its frayed collar. We sat outside the Dome in mutual dislike, waiting, as the sky paled slightly in the east. Gunshots sounded in the distance.

I have never owned a dog.

When the Dome finally opened, I gripped the dog's rope and spoke to the robot. "Not fruit. Not vegetables. I want eggs and bread."

The robot floated back inside.

Instantly I cursed myself. Eggs? Bread? I was crazy not to take what I could get. That was Law of Survival #1. Now there would be nothing.

Eggs, bread...*crazy*. I glared at the dog and kicked it. It yelped, looked indignant, and tried to bite my boot.

The Dome opened again and the robot glided toward me. In the gloom I couldn't see what was in the basket. In fact, I couldn't see the basket. It wasn't there. Mechanical tentacles shot out from the sphere and seized both me and the poodle. I cried out and the tentacles squeezed harder. Then I was flying through the air, the stupid dog suddenly howling beneath me, and we were carried through the Dome wall and inside.

Then nothing.

A nightmare room made of nightmare sound: barking, yelping, whimpering, snapping. I jerked awake, sat up, and discovered myself on a floating platform above a mass of dogs. Big dogs, small dogs, old dogs, puppies, sick dogs, dogs that looked all too healthy, flashing their forty-two teeth at me—why did I remember that number? From where? The largest and strongest dogs couldn't quite reach me with their snaps, but they were trying.

"You are operative," the blue metal sphere said, floating beside me. "Now we must begin. Here."

Its basket held eggs and bread.

"Get them away!"

Obediently it floated off.

"Not the food! The dogs!"

"What to do with these dogs?"

"Put them in cages!" A large black animal—German shepherd or Boxer or something—had nearly closed its jaws on my ankle. The next bite might do it.

"Cages," the metal sphere said in its uninflected mechanical voice. "Yes."

"Son of a bitch!" The shepherd leaping high, had grazed my thigh; its spittle slimed my pants. "Raise the goddamn platform!"

"Yes."

The platform floated so high, so that I had to duck my head to avoid hitting the ceiling. I peered over the edge and...no, that wasn't possible. But it was happening. The floor was growing upright sticks, and the sticks were growing cross bars, and the crossbars were extending themselves into mesh tops...Within minutes, each dog was encased in a cage just large enough to hold its protesting body.

"What to do now?" the metal sphere asked.

I stared at it. I was, as far as I knew, the first human being to ever enter an alien Dome, I was trapped in a small room with feral caged dogs and a robot...*what to do now*?

"Why...why am I here?" I hated myself for the brief stammer and vowed it would not happen again. Law of Survival #2: Show no fear.

Would a metal sphere even recognize fear?

It said, "These dogs do not behave correctly."

"Not behave correctly?"

"No."

I looked down again at the slavering and snarling mass of dogs; how strong was that mesh on the cage tops? "What do you want them to do?"

"Do you want to see the presentation?"

"Not yet." Law #3: Never volunteer for anything.

"What to do now?"

How the hell should I know? But the smell of the bread reached me and my stomach flopped. "Now to eat," I said. "Give me the things in your basket."

It did, and I tore into the bread like a wolf into deer. The real wolves below me increased their howling. When I'd eaten an entire loaf, I looked back at the metal sphere. "Have those dogs eaten?"

"Yes."

"What did you give them?"

"Garbage."

"*Garbage?* Why?"

"In hell they eat garbage."

So even the robot thought this was Hell. Panic surged through me; I pushed it back. Surviving this would depend on staying steady. "Show me what you fed the dogs."

"Yes." A section of wall melted and garbage cascaded into the room, flowing greasily between the cages. I recognized it: It was exactly like the garbage I picked through every day, trucked out from a city I could no longer imagine and from the Army base I could not approach without being shot. Bloody rags, tin cans from before the War, shit, plastic bags, dead flowers, dead animals, dead electronics, cardboard, eggshells, paper, hair, bone, scraps of decaying food, glass shards, potato peelings, foam rubber, roaches, sneakers with holes, sagging furniture, corn cobs. The smell hit my stomach, newly distended with bread.

"You fed the dogs *that*?"

"Yes. They eat it in hell."

Outside. Hell was outside, and of course that's what the feral dogs ate, that's all there was. But the metal sphere had produced fruit and lettuce and bread for me.

"You must give them better food. They eat that in…in hell because they can't get anything else."

"What to do now?"

It finally dawned on me—slow, I was too slow for this, only the quick survive—that the metal sphere had limited initiative along with its limited vocabulary. But it had made cages, made bread, made fruit—hadn't it? Or was this stuff grown in some imaginable secret garden inside the Dome? "You must give the dogs meat."

"Flesh?"

"Yes."

"No."

No change in that mechanical voice, but the "no" was definite and quick. Law of Survival #4: Notice everything. So—no flesh-eating allowed here. Also no time to ask why not; I had to keep issuing orders so that the robot didn't start issuing them. "Give them bread mixed with… with soy protein."

"Yes."

"And take away the garbage."

"Yes."

The garbage began to dissolve. I saw nothing poured on it, nothing rise from the floor. But all that stinking mass fell into powder and vanished. Nothing replaced it.

I said, "Are you getting bread mixed with soy powder?" *Getting* seemed the safest verb I could think of.

"Yes."

The stuff came then, tumbling through the same melted hole in the wall, loaves of bread with, presumably, soy powder in them. The dogs, barking insanely, reached paws and snouts and tongues through the bars of their cages. They couldn't get at the food.

"Metal sphere—do you have a name?"

No answer.

"Okay. Blue, how strong are those cages? Can the dogs break them? Any of the dogs?"

"No."

"Lower the platform to the floor."

My safe perch floated down. The aisles between the cages were irregular, some wide and some so narrow the dogs could reach through to touch each other, since each cage had "grown" wherever the dog was at the time. Gingerly I picked my way to a clearing and sat down. Tearing a loaf of bread into chunks, I pushed the pieces through the bars of the least dangerous-looking dogs, which made the bruisers howl even more. For them, I put chunks at a distance they could just reach with a paw through the front bars of their prisons.

The puppy I had first brought to the Dome lay in a tiny cage. Dead.

The second one was alive but just barely.

The old man's mangy poodle looked more mangy than ever, but otherwise alert. It tried to bite me when I fed it.

"What to do now?"

"They need water."

"Yes."

Water flowed through the wall. When it had reached an inch or so, it stopped. The dogs lapped whatever came into their cages. I stood with wet feet—a hole in my boot after all, I hadn't known—and a stomach roiling from the stench of the dogs, which only worsened as they got wet. The dead puppy smelled especially horrible. I climbed back onto my platform.

"What to do now?"

"You tell me," I said.

"These dogs do not behave correctly."

"Not behave correctly?"

"No."

"What do you want them to do?"

"Do you want to see the presentation?"

We had been here before. On second thought, a "presentation" sounded more like acquiring information ("Notice everything") than like undertaking action ("Never volunteer"). So I sat cross-legged on the platform, which was easier on my uncushioned bones, breathed through my mouth instead of my nose, and said "Why the hell not?"

Blue repeated, "Do you want to see the presentation?"

"Yes." A one-syllable answer.

I didn't know what to expect. Aliens, spaceships, war, strange places barely comprehensible to humans. What I got was scenes from the dump.

A beam of light shot out from Blue and resolved into a three-dimensional holo, not too different from one I'd seen in a science museum on a school field trip once (*no, push memory away*), only this was far sharper and detailed. A ragged and unsmiling toddler, one of thousands, staggered toward a cesspool. A big dog with patchy coat dashed up, seized the kid's dress, and pulled her back just before she fell into the waste.

A medium-sized brown dog in a guide-dog harness led around someone tapping a white-headed cane.

An Army dog, this one sleek and well-fed, sniffed at a pile of garbage, found something, pointed stiffly at attention.

A group of teenagers tortured a puppy. It writhed in pain, but in a long lingering close-up, tried to lick the torturer's hand.

A thin, small dog dodged rocks, dashed inside a corrugated tin hut, and laid a piece of carrion beside an old lady lying on the ground.

The holo went on and on like that, but the strange thing was that the people were barely seen. The toddler's bare and filthy feet and chubby knees, the old lady's withered cheek, a flash of a camouflage uniform above a brown boot, the hands of the torturers. Never a whole person, never a focus on people. Just on the dogs.

The "presentation" ended.

"These dogs do not behave correctly," Blue said.

"These dogs? In the presentation?"

"These dogs here do not behave correctly."

"These dogs *here*." I pointed to the wet, stinking dogs in their cages. Some, fed now, had quieted. Others still snarled and barked, trying their hellish best to get out and kill me.

"These dogs here. Yes. What to do now?"

"You want these dogs to behave like the dogs in the presentation."

"These dogs here must behave correctly. Yes."

"You want them to...do what? Rescue people? Sniff out ammunition dumps? Guide the blind and feed the hungry and love their torturers?"

Blue said nothing. Again I had the impression I had exceeded its thought processes, or its vocabulary, or its something. A strange feeling gathered in my gut.

"Blue, you yourself didn't build this Dome, or the starship that it was before, did you? You're just a...a computer."

Nothing.

"Blue, who tells you what to do?"

"What to do now? These dogs do not behave correctly."

"Who wants these dogs to behave correctly?" I said, and found I was holding my breath.

"The masters."

The masters. I knew all about them. Masters were the people who started wars, ran the corporations that ruined the Earth, manufactured the bioweapons that killed billions, and now holed up in the cities to send their garbage out to us in the refugee camps. Masters were something else I didn't think about, but not because grief would take me. Rage would.

Law of Survival #5: Feel nothing that doesn't aid survival.

"Are the masters here? In this...inside here?"

"No."

"Who is here inside?"

"These dogs here are inside."

Clearly. "The masters want these dogs here to behave like the dogs in the presentation."

"Yes."

"The masters want these dogs here to provide them with loyalty and protection and service."

No response.

"The masters aren't interested in human beings, are they? That's why they haven't communicated at all with any government."

Nothing. But I didn't need a response; the masters' thinking was already clear to me. Humans were unimportant—maybe because we had, after all, destroyed each other and our own world. We weren't worth contact. But dogs: companion animals capable of selfless service and great unconditional love, even in the face of abuse. For all I knew, dogs were unique in the universe. For all I knew.

Blue said, "What to do now?"

I stared at the mangy, reeking, howling mass of animals. Some feral, some tamed once, some sick, at least one dead. I chose my words to be as simple as possible, relying on phrases Blue knew. "The masters want these dogs here to behave correctly."

"Yes."

"The masters want *me* to make these dogs behave correctly."

"Yes."

"The masters will make me food, and keep me inside, to make these dogs behave correctly."

Long pause; my sentence had a lot of grammatical elements. But finally Blue said, "Yes."

"If these dogs do not behave correctly, the masters—what to do then?"

Another long pause. "Find another human."

"And *this* human here?"

"Kill it."

I gripped the edges of my floating platform hard. My hands still trembled. "Put me outside now."

"No."

"I must stay inside."

"These dogs do not behave correctly."

"I must make these dogs behave correctly."

"Yes."

"And the masters want these dogs to display..." I had stopped talking to Blue. I was talking to myself, to steady myself, but even that I couldn't manage. The words caromed around in my mind—loyalty, service, protection—but none came out of my mouth. I couldn't do this. I was going to die. The aliens had come from God-knew-where to treat the dying Earth like a giant pet store, intrigued only by a canine domestication that had happened ten thousand years ago and by nothing else on the planet, nothing else humanity had or might accomplish. Only dogs. *The masters want these dogs to display—*

Blue surprised me with a new word. "Love," it said.

Law #4: Notice everything. I needed to learn all I could, starting with Blue. He'd made garbage appear, and food and water and cages. What else could he do?

"Blue, make the water go away." And it did, just sank into the floor, which dried instantly. I was fucking Moses, commanding the Red Sea. I climbed off the platform, inched among the dog cages, and studied them individually.

"You called the refugee camp and the dump 'hell.' Where did you get that word?"

Nothing.

"Who said 'hell'?"

"Humans."

Blue had cameras outside the Dome. Of course he did; he'd seen me find that first puppy in the garbage. Maybe Blue had been waiting for someone like me, alone and non-threatening, to come close with a dog. But it had watched before that, and it had learned the word "hell," and maybe it had recorded the incidents in the "presentation." I filed this information for future use.

"This dog is dead." The first puppy, decaying into stinking pulp. "It is killed. Non-operative."

"What to do now?"

"Make the dead dog go away."

A long pause: thinking it over? Accessing data banks? Communicating with aliens? And what kind of moron couldn't figure out by itself that a dead dog was never going to behave correctly? So much for artificial intelligence.

"Yes," Blue finally said, and the little corpse dissolved as if it had never been.

I found one more dead dog and one close to death. Blue disappeared the first, said no to the second. Apparently we had to just let it suffer until it died. I wondered how much the idea of "death" even meant to a robot. There were twenty-three live dogs, of which I had delivered only three to the Dome.

"Blue—did another human, before you brought me here, try to train the dogs?"

"These dogs do not behave correctly."

"Yes. But did a human *not me* be inside? To make these dogs behave correctly?"

"Yes."

"What happened to him or her?"

No response.

"What to do now with the other human?"

"Kill it."

I put a hand against the wall and leaned on it. The wall felt smooth and slick, with a faint and unpleasant tingle. I removed my hand.

All computers could count. "How many humans did you kill?"

"Two."

Three's the charm. But there were no charms. No spells, no magic wards, no cavalry coming over the hill to ride to the rescue; I'd known that ever since the War. There was just survival. And, now, dogs.

I chose the mangy little poodle. It hadn't bit me when the old man had surrendered it, or when I'd kept it overnight. That was at least a start. "Blue, make this dog's cage go away. But *only* this one cage!"

The cage dissolved. The poodle stared at me distrustfully. Was I supposed to stare back, or would that get us into some kind of canine pissing contest? The thing was small but it had teeth.

I had a sudden idea. "Blue, show me how this dog does not behave correctly." If I could see what it wasn't doing, that would at least be a start.

Blue floated to within a foot of the dog's face. The dog growled and backed away. Blue floated away and the dog quieted but it still stood in what would be a menacing stance if it weighed more than nine or ten pounds: ears raised, legs braced, neck hair bristling. Blue said, "Come." The dog did nothing. Blue repeated the entire sequence and so did Mangy.

I said, "You want the dog to follow you. Like the dogs in the presentation."

"Yes."

"You want the dog to come when you say 'Come.'"

"Love," Blue said.

"What is 'love,' Blue?"

No response.

The robot didn't know. Its masters must have had some concept of "love," but fuck-all knew what it was. And I wasn't sure I knew any more, either. That left Mangy, who would never "love" Blue or follow him or lick his hand because dogs operated on smell—even I knew that about them—and Blue, a machine, didn't smell like either a person or another dog. Couldn't the aliens who sent him here figure that out? Were they watching this whole farce, or had they just dropped a half-sentient computer under an upturned bowl on Earth and told it, "Bring us some loving dogs"? Who knew how aliens thought?

I didn't even know how dogs thought. There were much better people for this job—professional trainers, or that guy on TV who made tigers jump through burning hoops. But they weren't here, and I was. I squatted on my haunches a respectful distance from Mangy and said, "Come."

It growled at me.

"Blue, raise the platform this high." I held my hand at shoulder height. The platform rose.

"Now make some cookies on the platform."

Nothing.

"Make some…cheese on the platform."

Nothing. You don't see much cheese in a dump.

"Make some bread on the platform."

Nothing. Maybe the platform wasn't user-friendly.

"Make some bread."

After a moment, loaves tumbled out of the wall. "Enough! Stop!"

Mangy had rushed over to the bread, tearing at it, and the other dogs were going wild. I picked up one loaf, put it on the platform, and said, "Make the rest of the bread go away."

It all dissolved. No wonder the dogs were wary; I felt a little dizzy myself. A sentence from some long-ago child's book rose in my mind: *Things come and go so quickly here!*

I had no idea how much Blue could, or would, do on my orders. "Blue, make another room for me and this one dog. Away from the other dogs."

"No."

"Make this room bigger."

The room expanded evenly on all sides. "Stop." It did. "Make only this end of the room bigger."

Nothing.

"Okay, make the whole room bigger."

When the room stopped expanding, I had a space about forty feet square, with the dog cages huddled in the middle. After half an hour of experimenting, I got the platform moved to one corner, not far enough to escape the dog stench but better than nothing. (Law #1: Take what you can get.) I got a depression in the floor filled with warm water. I got food, drinking water, soap, and some clean cloth, and a lot of rope. By distracting Mangy with bits of bread, I got rope onto her frayed collar. After I got into the warm water and scrubbed myself, I pulled the poodle in. She bit me. But somehow I got her washed, too. Afterwards she shook herself, glared at me, and went to sleep on the hard floor. I asked Blue for a soft rug.

He said, "The other humans did this."

And Blue killed them anyway.

"Shut up," I said.

The big windowless room had no day, no night, no sanity. I slept and ate when I needed to, and otherwise I worked. Blue never left. He was an oversized, all-seeing eye in the corner. Big Brother, or God.

Within a few weeks—maybe—I had Mangy trained to come when called, to sit, and to follow me on command. I did this by dispensing bits of bread and other goodies. Mangy got fatter. I didn't care if she ended up the Fat Fiona of dogs. Her mange didn't improve, since I couldn't get

Blue to wrap his digital mind around the concept of medicines, and even if he had I wouldn't have known what to ask for. The sick puppy died in its cage.

I kept the others fed and watered and flooded the shit out of their cages every day, but that was all. Mangy took all my time. She still regarded me warily, never curled up next to me, and occasionally growled. Love was not happening here.

Nonetheless, Blue left his corner and spoke for the first time in a week, scaring the hell out of me. "This dog behaves correctly."

"Well, thanks. I tried to...no, Blue..."

Blue floated to within a foot of Mangy's face, said, "Follow," and floated away. Mangy sat down and began to lick one paw. Blue rose and floated toward me.

"This dog does not behave correctly."

I was going to die.

"No, listen to me—listen! The dog can't smell you! It behaves for humans because of humans' smell! Do you understand?"

"No. This dog does not behave correctly."

"Listen! How the hell can you learn anything if you don't listen? You have to have a smell! Then the dog will follow you!"

Blue stopped. We stood frozen, a bizarre tableau, while the robot considered. Even Mangy stopped licking her paw and watched, still. They say dogs can smell fear.

Finally Blue said, "What is smell?"

It isn't possible to explain smell. Can't be done. Instead I pulled down my pants, tore the cloth I was using as underwear from between my legs, and rubbed it all over Blue, who did not react. I hoped he wasn't made of the same stuff as the Dome, which even spray paint had just slid off of. But, of course, he was. So I tied the strip of cloth around him with a piece of rope, my fingers trembling. "Now try the dog, Blue."

"Follow," Blue said, and floated away from Mangy.

She looked at him, then at me, then back at the floating metal sphere. I held my breath from some insane idea that I would thereby diminish my own smell. Mangy didn't move.

"This dog does not be—"

"She will if I'm gone!" I said desperately. "She smells me *and* you... and we smell the same so it's confusing her! But she'll follow you fine if I'm gone, do you understand?"

"No."

"Blue...I'm going to get on the platform. See, I'm doing it. Raise the platform *very high*, Blue. Very high."

A moment later my head and ass both pushed against the ceiling, squishing me. I couldn't see what was happening below. I heard Blue say, "Follow," and I squeezed my eyes shut, waiting. My life depended on a scrofulous poodle with a gloomy disposition.

Blue said, "This dog behaves correctly."

He lowered my platform to a few yards above the floor, and I swear that—eyeless as he is and with part of his sphere obscured by my underwear—he looked right at me.

"This dog does behave correctly. This dog is ready."

"Ready? For...for what?"

Blue didn't answer. The next minute the floor opened and Mangy, yelping, tumbled into it. The floor closed. At the same time, one of the cages across the room dissolved and a German shepherd hurtled towards me. I shrieked and yelled, "Raise the platform!" It rose just before the monster grabbed me.

Blue said, "What to do now? This dog does not behave correctly."

"For God's sakes, Blue—"

"This dog must love."

The shepherd leapt and snarled, teeth bared.

I couldn't talk Blue out of the shepherd, which was as feral and vicious and unrelenting as anything in a horror movie. Or as Blue himself, in his own mechanical way. So I followed the First Law: Take what you can get.

"Blue, make garbage again. A lot of garbage, right here." I pointed to the wall beside my platform.

"No."

Garbage, like everything else, apparently was made—or released, or whatever—from the opposite wall. I resigned myself to this. "Make a lot of garbage, Blue."

Mountains of stinking debris cascaded from the wall, spilling over until it reached the dog cages.

"Now stop. Move my platform above the garbage."

The platform moved. The caged dogs howled. Uncaged, the shepherd poked eagerly in the refuse, too distracted to pay much attention to me. I had Blue lower the platform and I poked among it, too, keeping one eye on Vicious. If Blue was creating the garbage and not just trucking it in, he was doing a damn fine job of duplication. Xerox should have made such good copies.

I got smeared with shit and rot, but I found what I was looking for. The box was nearly a quarter full. I stuffed bread into it, coated the bread thoroughly, and discarded the box back onto the pile.

"Blue, make the garbage go away."

It did. Vicious glared at me and snarled. "Nice doggie," I said, "have some bread." I threw pieces and Vicious gobbled them.

Listening to the results was terrible. Not, however, as terrible as having Vicious tear me apart or Blue vaporize me. The rat poison took all "night" to kill the dog, which thrashed and howled. Throughout, Blue stayed silent. He had picked up some words from me, but he apparently didn't have enough brain power to connect what I'd done with Vicious's death. Or maybe he just didn't have enough experience with humans. What does a machine know about survival?

"This dog is dead," Blue said in the "morning."

"Yes. Make it go away." And then, before Blue could get there first, I jumped off my platform and pointed to a cage. "This dog will behave correctly next."

"No."

"Why not this dog?"

"Not big."

"Big. You want big." Frantically I scanned the cages, before Blue could choose another one like Vicious. "This one, then."

"Why the hell not?" Blue said.

It was young. Not a puppy but still frisky, a mongrel of some sort with short hair of dirty white speckled with dirty brown. The dog looked liked something I could handle: big but not too big, not too aggressive, not too old, not too male. "Hey, Not-Too," I said, without enthusiasm, as Blue dissolved her cage. The mutt dashed over to me and tried to lick my boot.

A natural-born slave.

I had found a piece of rotten, moldy cheese in the garbage, so Blue could now make cheese, which Not-Too went crazy for. Not-Too and I stuck with the same routine I used with Mangy, and it worked pretty well. Or the cheese did. Within a few "days" the dog could sit, stay, and follow on command.

Then Blue threw me a curve. "What to do now? The presentation."

"We had the presentation," I said. "I don't need to see it again."

"What to do now? The presentation."

"Fine," I said, because it was clear I had no choice. "Let's have the presentation. Roll 'em."

I was sitting on my elevated platform, combing my hair. A lot of it had fallen out during the malnourished years in the camp, but now it was growing again. Not-Too had given up trying to jump up there with me and gone to sleep on her pillow below. Blue shot the beam out of his sphere and the holo played in front of me.

Only not the whole thing. This time he played only the brief scene where the big, patchy dog pulled the toddler back from falling into the cesspool. Blue played it once, twice, three times. Cold slid along my spine.

"You want Not-Too...you want this dog here to be trained to save children."

"This dog here does not behave correctly."

"Blue...How can I train a dog to save a child?"

"This dog here does not behave correctly."

"Maybe you haven't noticed, but we haven't got any fucking children for the dog to practice on!"

Long pause. "Do you want a child?"

"No!" Christ, he would kidnap one or buy one from the camp and I would be responsible for a kid along with nineteen semi-feral dogs. No.

"This dog here does not behave correctly. What to do now? The presentation."

"No, not the presentation. I saw it, *I saw it*. Blue...the other two humans who did not make the dogs behave correctly..."

"Killed."

"Yes. So you said. But they did get one dog to behave correctly, didn't they? Or maybe more than one. And then you just kept raising the bar higher. Water rescues, guiding the blind, finding lost people. Higher and higher."

But to all this, of course, Blue made no answer.

I wracked my brains to remember what I had ever heard, read, or seen about dog training. Not much. However, there's a problem with opening the door to memory: you can't control what strolls through. For the first time in years, my sleep was shattered by dreams.

I walked through a tiny garden, picking zinnias. From an open window came music, full and strong, an orchestra on CD. A cat paced beside me, purring. And there was someone else in the window, someone who called my name and I turned and—

I screamed. Clawed my way upright. The dogs started barking and howling. Blue floated from his corner, saying something. And Not-Too made a mighty leap, landed on my platform, and began licking my face.

"Stop it! Don't do that! I won't remember!" I shoved her so hard she fell off the platform onto the floor and began yelping. I put my head in my hands.

Blue said, "Are you not operative?"

"Leave me the fuck alone!"

Not-Too still yelped, shrill cries of pain. When I stopped shaking, I crawled off the platform and picked her up. Nothing seemed to be broken—although how would I know? Gradually she quieted. I gave her some cheese and put her back on her pillow. She wanted to stay with me but I wouldn't let her.

I would not remember. *I would not.* Law #5: Feel nothing.

We made a cesspool, or at least a pool. Blue depressed part of the floor to a depth of three feet and filled it with water. Not-Too considered this a swimming pool and loved to be in it, which was not what Blue wanted ("This water does not behave correctly"). I tried having the robot dump various substances into it until I found one that she disliked and I could tolerate: light-grade motor oil. A few small cans of oil like those in the dump created a polluted pool, not unlike Charleston Harbor. After every practice session I needed a bath.

But not Not-Too, because she wouldn't go into the "cesspool." I curled myself as small as possible, crouched at the side of the pool, and thrashed. After a few days, the dog would pull me back by my shirt. I moved into the pool. As long as she could reach me without getting any liquid on her, Not-Too happily played that game. As soon as I moved far enough out that I might actually need saving, she sat on her skinny haunches and looked away.

"This dog does not behave correctly."

I increased the cheese. I withheld the cheese. I pleaded and ordered and shunned and petted and yelled. Nothing worked. Meanwhile, the dream continued. The same dream, each time not greater in length but increasing in intensity. *I walked through a tiny garden, picking zinnias. From an open window came music, full and strong, an orchestra on CD. A cat paced beside me, purring. And there was someone else in the window, someone who called my name and I turned and—*

And woke screaming.

A cat. I had had a cat, before the War. Before everything. I had always had cats, my whole life. Independent cats, aloof and self-sufficient, admirably disdainful. Cats—

The dog below me whimpered, trying to get onto my platform to offer comfort I did not want.

I would not remember.

"This dog does not behave correctly," day after day.

I had Blue remove the oil from the pool. But by now Not-Too had been conditioned. She wouldn't go into even the clear water that she'd reveled in before.

"This dog does not behave correctly."

Then one day Blue stopped his annoying mantra, which scared me even more. Would I have any warning that I'd failed, or would I just die?

The only thing I could think of was to kill Blue first.

Blue was a computer. You disabled computers by turning them off, or cutting the power supply, or melting them in a fire, or dumping acid on them, or crushing them. But a careful search of the whole room revealed no switches or wires or anything that looked like a wireless control. A fire in this closed room, assuming I could start one, would kill me, too. Every kind of liquid or solid slid off Blue. And what would I crush him with, if that was even possible? A piece of cheese?

Blue was also—sort of—an intelligence. You could kill those by trapping them somewhere. My prison-or-sanctuary (depending on my mood) had no real "somewheres." And Blue would just dissolve any structure he found himself in.

What to do now?

I lay awake, thinking, all night, which at least kept me from dreaming. I came up with two ideas, both bad. Plan A depended on discussion, never Blue's strong suit.

"Blue, this dog does not behave correctly."

"No."

"This dog is not operative. I must make another dog behave correctly. Not this dog."

Blue floated close to Not-Too. She tried to bat at him. He circled her slowly, then returned to his position three feet above the ground. "This dog is operative."

"No. This dog *looks* operative. But this dog is not operative inside its head. I cannot make this dog behave correctly. I need a different dog."

A very long pause. "This dog is not operative inside its head."

"Yes."

"You can make another dog behave correctly. Like the presentation."

"Yes." It would at least buy me time. Blue must have seen "not operative" dogs and humans in the dump; God knows there were enough of them out there. Madmen, rabid animals, druggies raving just before they died, or were shot. And next time I would add something besides oil to the pool; there must be something that Blue would consider noxious enough to simulate a cesspool but that a dog would enter. If I had to, I'd use my own shit.

"This dog is not operative inside its head," Blue repeated, getting used to the idea. "You will make a different dog behave correctly."

"Yes!"

"Why the hell not?" And then, "I kill this dog."

"No!" The word was torn from me before I knew I was going to say anything. My hand, of its own volition, clutched at Not-Too. She jumped but didn't bite. Instead, maybe sensing my fear, she cowered behind me, and I started to yell.

"You can't just kill everything that doesn't behave like you want! People, dogs...you can't just kill everything! You can't just...I had a cat...I never wanted a dog but this dog...she's behaving correctly for her! For a fucking traumatized dog and you can't just—I had a dog I mean a cat I had....I had...."

—from an open window came music, full and strong, an orchestra on CD. A cat paced beside me, purring. And there was someone else in the window, someone who called my name and I turned and—

"I had a child!"

Oh, God no no no...It all came out then, the memories and the grief and the pain I had pushed away for three solid years in order to survive...*Feel nothing*...Zack Zack *Zack* shot down by soldiers like a dog *Look, Mommy, here I am Mommy look...*

I curled in a ball on the floor and screamed and wanted to die. Grief had been postponed so long that it was a tsunami. I sobbed and screamed;

I don't know for how long. I think I wasn't quite sane. No human should ever have to experience that much pain. But of course they do.

However, it can't last too long, that height of pain, and when the flood passed and my head was bruised from banging it on the hard floor, I was still alive, still inside the Dome, still surrounded by barking dogs. Zack was still dead. Blue floated nearby, unchanged, a casually murderous robot who would not supply flesh to dogs as food but who would kill anything he was programmed destroy. And he had no reason not to murder me.

Not-Too sat on her haunches, regarding me from sad brown eyes, and I did the one thing I told myself I never would do again. I reached for her warmth. I put my arms around her and hung on. She let me.

Maybe that was the decision point. I don't know.

When I could manage it, I staggered to my feet. Taking hold of the rope that was Not-Too's leash, I wrapped it firmly around my hand. "Blue," I said, forcing the words past the grief clogging my throat, "make garbage."

He did. That was the basis of Plan B; that Blue made most things I asked of him. Not release, or mercy, but at least rooms and platforms and pools and garbage. I walked toward the garbage spilling from the usual place in the wall.

"More garbage! Bigger garbage! I need garbage to make this dog behave correctly!"

The reeking flow increased. Tires, appliances, diapers, rags, cans, furniture. The dogs' howling rose to an insane, deafening pitch. Not-Too pressed close to me.

"Bigger garbage!"

The chassis of a motorcycle, twisted beyond repair in some unimaginable accident, crashed into the room. The place on the wall from which the garbage spewed was misty gray, the same fog that the Dome had become when I had been taken inside it. Half a sofa clattered through. I grabbed Not-Too, dodged behind the sofa, and hurled both of us through the onrushing garbage and into the wall.

A broken keyboard struck me in the head, and the gray went black.

Chill. Cold with a spot of heat, which turned out to be Not-Too lying on top of me. I pushed her off and tried to sit up. Pain lanced through my head and when I put a hand to my forehead, it came away covered with blood. The same blood streamed into my eyes, making it hard to see. I wiped the blood away with the front of my shirt, pressed my hand hard on my forehead, and looked around.

Not that there was much to see. The dog and I sat at the end of what appeared to be a corridor. Above me loomed a large machine of some type, with a chute pointed at the now-solid wall. The machine was silent. Not-Too quivered and pressed her furry side into mine, but she, too, stayed silent. I couldn't hear the nineteen dogs on the other side of the wall, couldn't see Blue, couldn't smell anything except Not-Too, who had made a small yellow puddle on the floor.

There was no room to stand upright under the machine, so I moved away from it. Strips ripped from the bottom of my shirt made a bandage that at least kept blood out of my eyes. Slowly Not-Too and I walked along the corridor.

No doors. No openings or alcoves or machinery. Nothing until we reached the end, which was the same uniform material as everything else. Gray, glossy, hard. Dead.

Blue did not appear. Nothing appeared, or disappeared, or lived. We walked back and studied the overhead bulk of the machine. It had no dials or keys or features of any kind.

I sat on the floor, largely because I couldn't think what else to do, and Not-Too climbed into my lap. She was too big for this and I pushed her away. She pressed against me, trembling.

"Hey," I said, but not to her. Zack in the window *Look, Mommy, here I am Mommy look*.... But if I started down that mental road, I would be lost. Anger was better than memory. Anything was better than memory. "Hey!" I screamed. "Hey, you bastard Blue, what to do now? What to do now, you Dome shits, whoever you are?"

Nothing except, very faint, an echo of my own useless words.

I lurched to my feet, reaching for the anger, cloaking myself in it. Not-Too sprang to her feet and backed away from me.

"What to do now? What bloody fucking hell to do *now*?"

Still nothing, but Not-Too started back down the empty corridor. I was glad to transfer my anger to something visible, real, living. "There's nothing there, Not-Too. *Nothing*, you stupid dog!"

She stopped halfway down the corridor and began to scratch at the wall.

I stumbled along behind her, one hand clamped to my head. What the hell was she doing? This piece of wall was identical to every other piece of wall. Kneeling slowly—it hurt my head to move fast—I studied

Not-Too. Her scratching increased in frenzy and her nose twitched, as if she smelled something. The wall, of course, didn't respond; nothing in this place responded to anything. Except—

Blue had learned words from me, had followed my commands. Or had he just transferred my command to the Dome's unimaginable machinery, instructing it to do anything I said that fell within permissible limits? Feeling like an idiot, I said to the wall, "Make garbage." Maybe if it complied and the garbage contained food...

The wall made no garbage. Instead it dissolved into the familiar gray fog, and Not-Too immediately jumped through, barking frantically.

Every time I had gone through a Dome wall, my situation had gotten worse. But what other choices were there? Wait for Blue to find and kill me, starve to death, curl up and die in the heart of a mechanical alien mini-world I didn't understand. Not-Too's barking increased in pitch and volume. She was terrified or excited or thrilled...How would I know? I pushed through the gray fog.

Another gray metal room, smaller than Blue had made my prison but with the same kind of cages against the far wall. Not-Too saw me and raced from the cages to me. Blue floated toward me...No, not Blue. This metal sphere was dull green, the color of shady moss. It said, "No human comes into this area."

"Guess again," I said and grabbed the trailing end of Not-Too's rope. She'd jumped up on me once and then had turned to dash back to the cages.

"No human comes into this area," Green repeated. I waited to see what the robot would do about it. Nothing.

Not-Too tugged on her rope, yowling. From across the room came answering barks, weirdly off. Too uneven in pitch, with a strange undertone. Blood, having saturated my makeshift bandage, once again streamed into my eyes. I swiped at it with one hand, turned to keep my gaze on Green, and let Not-Too pull me across the floor. Only when she stopped did I turn to look at the mesh-topped cages. Vertigo swooped over me.

Mangy was the source of the weird barks, a Mangy altered not beyond recognition but certainly beyond anything I could have imagined. Her mange was gone, along with all her fur. The skin beneath was now gray, the same gunmetal gray as everything else in the Dome. Her ears, the floppy poodle ears, were so long they trailed on the floor of her cage, and so was her tail. Holding on to the tail was a gray grub.

Not a grub. Not anything Earthly. Smooth and pulpy, it was about the size of a human head and vaguely oval. I saw no openings on the thing but

Mangy's elongated tail disappeared into the doughy mass. and so there must have been at least one orifice. As Mangy jumped at the bars, trying to get at Not-Too, the grub was whipped back and forth across the cage floor. It left a slimy trail. The dog seemed oblivious.

"This dog is ready," Blue had said.

Behind me Green said, "No human comes into this area."

"Up yours."

"The human does not behave correctly."

That got my attention. I whirled around to face Green, expecting to be vaporized like the dead puppy, the dead Vicious. I thought I was already dead—and then I welcomed the thought. *Look, Mommy, here I am Mommy look*... The laws of survival that had protected me for so long couldn't protect me against memory, not any more. I was ready to die.

Instead Mangy's cage dissolved, she bounded out, and she launched herself at me.

Poodles are not natural killers, and this one was small. However, Mangy was doing her level best to destroy me. Her teeth closed on my arm. I screamed and shook her off, but the next moment she was biting my leg above my boot, darting hysterically toward and away from me, biting my legs at each lunge. The grub, or whatever it was, lashed around at the end of her new tail. As I flailed at the dog with both hands, my bandage fell off. Fresh blood from my head wound blinded me. I stumbled and fell and she was at my face.

Then she was pulled off, yelping and snapping and howling.

Not-Too had Mangy in her jaws. Twice as big as the poodle, she shook Mangy violently and then dropped her. Mangy whimpered and rolled over on her belly. Not-Too sprinted over to me and stood in front of me, skinny legs braced and scrawny hackles raised, growling protectively.

Dazed, I got to my feet. Blood, mine and the dogs', slimed the everything. The floor wasn't trying to reabsorb it. Mangy, who'd never really liked me, stayed down with her belly exposed in submission, but she didn't seem to be badly hurt. The grub still latched onto the end of her tail like a gray tumor. After a moment she rolled onto her feet and began to nuzzle the grub, one baleful eye on Not-Too: *Don't you come near this thing!* Not-Too stayed in position, guarding me.

Green said—and I swear its mechanical voice held satisfaction, no one will ever be able to tell me any different—"These dogs behave correctly."

The other cages held grubs, one per cage. I reached through the front bars and gingerly touched one. Moist, firm, repulsive. It didn't respond to my touch, but Green did. He was beside me in a flash. "No!"

"Sorry." His tone was dog-disciplining. "Are these the masters?"

No answer.

"What to do now? One dog for one…" I waved at the cages.

"Yes. When these dogs are ready."

This dog is ready, Blue had said of Mangy just before she was tumbled into the floor.

Ready to be a pet, a guardian, a companion, a service animal to alien… what? The most logical answer was "children." Lassie, Rin Tin Tin, Benji, Little Guy. A boy and his dog. The aliens found humans dangerous or repulsive or uncaring or whatever, but dogs…You could count on dogs for your kids. Almost, and for the first time, I could see the point of the Domes.

"Are the big masters here? The adults?"

No answer.

"The masters are not here," I said. "They just set up the Domes as… as nurseries-slash-obedience schools." And to that statement I didn't even expect an answer. If the adults had been present, surely one or more would have come running when an alien blew into its nursery wing via a garbage delivery. There would have been alarms or something. Instead there was only Blue and Green and whatever 'bots inhabited whatever place held the operating room. Mangy's skin and ears and tail had been altered to fit the needs of these grubs. And maybe her voice-box, too, since her barks now had that weird undertone, like the scrape of metal across rock. Somewhere there was an OR.

I didn't want to be in that somewhere.

Green seemed to have no orders to kill me, which made sense because he wasn't programmed to have me here. I wasn't on his radar, which raised other problems.

"Green, make bread."

Nothing.

"Make water."

Nothing.

But two indentations in a corner of the floor, close to a section of wall, held water and dog-food pellets. I tasted both, to the interest of Not-Too and the growling of Mangy. Not too bad. I scooped all the rest of the dog food out of the trough. As soon as the last piece was out, the wall filled it up again. If I died, it wasn't going to be of starvation.

A few minutes ago, I had wanted to die. *Zack...*

No. Push the memory away. Life was shit, but I didn't want death, either. The realization was visceral, gripping my stomach as if that organ had been laid in a vise, or...There is no way to describe it. The feeling just was, its own justification. I wanted to live.

Not-Too lay a short distance away, watching me. Mangy was back in her cage with the grub on her tail. I sat up and looked around. "Green, this dog is not ready."

"No. What to do now?"

Well, that answered one question. Green was programmed to deal with dogs, and you didn't ask dogs "what to do now." So Green must be in some sort of communication with Blue, but the communication didn't seem to include orders about me. For a star-faring advanced race, the aliens certainly weren't very good at LANs. Or maybe they just didn't care—how would I know how an alien thinks?

I said, "I make this dog behave correctly." The all-purpose answer.

"Yes."

Did Green know details—that Not-Too refused to pull me from oily pools and thus was an obedience-school failure? It didn't seem like it. I could pretend to train Not-Too—I could actually train her, only not for water rescue—and stay here, away from the killer Blue, until...until what? As a survival plan, this one was shit. Still, it followed Laws #1 and #3: Take what you can get and never volunteer. And I couldn't think of anything else.

"Not-Too," I said wearily, still shaky from my crying jag, "Sit."

"Days" went by, then weeks. Not-Too learned to beg, roll over, bring me a piece of dog food, retrieve my thrown boot, lie down, and balance a pellet of dog food on her nose. I had no idea if any of these activities would be useful to an alien, but as long as Not-Too and I were "working," Green left us alone. No threats, no presentations, no objections. We were behaving correctly. I still hadn't thought of any additional plan. At night I dreamed of Zack and woke in tears, but not with the raging insanity of my first day of memory. Maybe you can only go through that once.

Mangy's grub continued to grow, still fastened onto her tail. The other grubs looked exactly the same as before. Mangy growled if I came too close to her, so I didn't. Her grub seemed to be drying out as it got bigger. Mangy licked it and slept curled around it and generally acted like some mythical dragon guarding a treasure box. Had the aliens bonded those two with some kind of pheromones I couldn't detect? I had no way of knowing.

Mangy and her grub emerged from their cage only to eat, drink, or shit, which she did in a far corner. Not-Too and I used the same corner, and all of our shit and piss dissolved odorlessly into the floor. Eat your heart out, Thomas Crapper.

As days turned into weeks, flesh returned to my bones. Not-Too also lost her starved look. I talked to her more and more, her watchful silence preferable to Green's silence or, worse, his inane and limited repertoires of answers. *"Green, I had a child named Zack. He was shot in the war. He was five." "This dog is not ready."*

Well, none of us ever are.

Not-Too started to sleep curled against my left side. This was a problem because I thrashed in my sleep, which woke her, so she growled, which woke me. Both of us became sleep-deprived and irritable. In the camp, I had slept twelve hours a day. Not much else to do, and sleep both conserved energy and kept me out of sight. But the camp was becoming distant in my mind. Zack was shatteringly vivid, with my life before the war, and the Dome was vivid, with Mangy and Not-Too and a bunch of alien grubs. Everything in between was fading.

Then one "day"—after how much time? I had no idea—Green said, "This dog is ready."

My heart stopped. Green was going to take Not-Too to the hidden OR, was going to— "No!"

Green ignored me. But he also ignored Not-Too. The robot floated over to Mangy's cage and dissolved it. I stood and craned my neck for a better look.

The grub was hatching.

Its "skin" had become very dry, a papery gray shell. Now it cracked along the top, parallel to Mangy's tail. She turned and regarded it quizzically, this thing wriggling at the end of her very long tail, but didn't attack or even growl. Those must have been some pheromones.

Was I really going to be the first and only human to see a Dome alien?

I was not. The papery covering cracked more and dropped free of the dog's tail. The thing inside wiggled forward, crawling out like a snake shedding its skin. It wasn't a grub but it clearly wasn't a sentient being, either. A larva? I'm no zoologist. This creature was as gray as everything else in the Dome but it had legs, six, and heads, two. At least, they might have been heads. Both had various indentations. One "head" crept forward, opened an orifice, and fastened itself back onto Mangy's tail. She continued to gaze at it. Beside me, Not-Too growled.

I whirled to grab frantically for her rope. Not-Too had no alterations to make her accept this…thing as anything other than a small animal to attack. If she did—

I turned just in time to see the floor open and swallow Not-Too. Green said again, "This dog is ready," and the floor closed.

"No! Bring her back!" I tried to pound on Green with my fists. He bobbed in the air under my blows. "Bring her back! Don't hurt her! Don't…" do what?

Don't turn her into a nursemaid for a grub, oblivious to me.

Green moved off. I followed, yelling and pounding. Neither one, of course, did the slightest good. Finally I got it together enough to say, "When will Not-Too come back?"

"This human does not behave correctly."

I looked despairingly at Mangy. She lay curled on her side, like a mother dog nursing puppies. The larva wasn't nursing, however. A shallow trough had appeared in the floor and filled with some viscous glop, which the larva was scarfing up with its other head. It looked repulsive.

Law #4: Notice everything.

"Green…okay. Just…okay. When will Not-Too come back here?"

No answer; what does time mean to a machine?

"Does the other dog return here?"

"Yes."

"Does the other dog get a…" A what? I pointed at Mangy's larva.

No response. I would have to wait.

But not, apparently, alone. Across the room another dog tumbled, snarling, from the same section of wall I had once come through. I recognized it as one of the nineteen left in the other room, a big black beast with powerful looking jaws. It righted itself and charged at me. There was no platform, no place to hide.

"No! Green, no, it will hurt me! This dog does not behave—"

Green didn't seem to do anything. But even as the black dog leapt toward me, it faltered in mid-air. The next moment, it lay dead on the floor.

The moment after that, the body disappeared, vaporized.

My legs collapsed under me. That was what would happen to me if I failed in my training task, was what had presumably happened to the previous two human failures. And yet it wasn't fear that made me sit so abruptly on the gray floor. It was relief, and a weird kind of gratitude. Green had protected me, which was more than Blue had ever done. Maybe

Green was brighter, or I had proved my worth more, or in this room as opposed to the other room, all dog-training equipment was protected. I was dog-training equipment. It was stupid to feel grateful.

I felt grateful.

Green said, "This dog does not—"

"I know, *I know.* Listen, Green, what to do now? Bring another dog here?"

"Yes."

"*I* choose the dog. I am the…the dog leader. Some dogs behave correctly, some dogs do not behave correctly. I choose. Me."

I held my breath. Green considered, or conferred with Blue, or consulted its alien and inadequate programming. Who the hell knows? The robot had been created by a race that preferred Earth dogs to whatever species usually nurtured their young, if any did. Maybe Mangy and Not-Too would replace parental care on the home planet, thus introducing the idea of babysitters. All I wanted was to not be eaten by some canine nanny-trainee.

"Yes," Green said finally, and I let out my breath.

A few minutes later, eighteen dog cages tumbled through the wall like so much garbage, the dogs within bouncing off their bars and mesh tops, furious and noisy. Mangy jumped, curled more protectively around her oblivious larva, and added her weird, rock-scraping bark to the din. A cage grew up around her. When the cages had stopped bouncing, I walked among them like some kind of tattered lord, choosing.

"This dog, Green." It wasn't the smallest dog but it had stopped barking the soonest. I hoped that meant it wasn't a grudge holder. When I put one hand into its cage, it didn't bite me, also a good sign. The dog was phenomenally ugly, the jowls on its face drooping from small, rheumy eyes into a sort of folded ruff around its short neck. Its body seemed to be all front, with stunted and short back legs. When it stood, I saw it was male.

"This dog? What to do now?"

"Send all the other dogs back."

The cages sank into the floor. I walked over to the feeding trough, scooped up handfuls of dog food, and put the pellets into my only pocket that didn't have holes. "Make all the rest of the dog food go away."

It vaporized.

"Make this dog's cage go away."

I braced myself as the cage dissolved. The dog stood uncertainly on the floor, gazing toward Mangy, who snarled at him. I said, as commandingly as possible, "Ruff!"

He looked at me.

"Ruff, come."

To my surprise, he did. Someone had trained this animal before. I gave him a pellet of dog food.

Green said, "This dog behaves correctly."

"Well, I'm really good," I told him, stupidly, while my chest tightened as I thought of Not-Too. The aliens, or their machines, did understand about anesthetic, didn't they? They wouldn't let her suffer too much? I would never know.

But now I *did* know something momentous. I had choices. I had chosen which room to train dogs in. I had chosen which dog to train. I had some control.

"Sit," I said to Ruff, who didn't, and I set to work.

Not-Too was returned to me three or four "days" later. She was gray and hairless, with an altered bark. A grub hung onto her elongated tail, undoubtedly the same one that had vanished from its cage while I was asleep. But unlike Mangy, who'd never liked either of us, Not-Too was ecstatic to see me. She wouldn't stay in her grub-cage against the wall but insisted on sleeping curled up next to me, grub and all. Green permitted this. I had become the alpha dog.

Not-Too liked Ruff, too. I caught him mounting her, her very long tail conveniently keeping her grub out of the way. Did Green understand the significance of this behavior? No way to tell.

We settled into a routine of training, sleeping, playing, eating. Ruff turned out to be sweet and playful but not very intelligent, and training took a long time. Mangy's grub grew very slowly, considering the large amount of glop it consumed. I grew, too; the waistband of my ragged pants got too tight and I discarded them, settling for a loin cloth, shirt, and my decaying boots. I talked to the dogs, who were much better conversationalists than Green since two of them at least pricked up their ears, made noises back at me, and wriggled joyfully at attention. Green would have been a dud at a cocktail party.

I don't know how long this all went on. Time began to lose meaning. I still dreamed of Zack and still woke in tears, but the dreams grew gentler and farther apart. When I cried, Not-Too crawled onto my lap, dragging her grub, and licked my chin. Her brown eyes shared my sorrow. I wondered how I had ever preferred the disdain of cats.

Not-Too got pregnant. I could feel the puppies growing inside her distended belly.

"Puppies will be easy to make behave correctly," I told Green, who said nothing. Probably he didn't understand. Some people need concrete visuals in order to learn.

Eventually, it seemed to me that Ruff was almost ready for his own grub. I mulled over how to mention this to Green but before I did, everything came to an end.

Clang! Clang! Clang!

I jerked awake and bolted upright. The alarm—a very human-sounding alarm—sounded all around me. Dogs barked and howled. Then I realized that it was a human alarm, coming from the Army camp outside the Dome, on the opposite side to garbage dump. I could *see* the camp—in outline and faintly, as if through heavy gray fog. The Dome was dissolving.

"Green—what—no!"

Above me, transforming the whole top half of what had been the Dome, was the bottom of a solid saucer. Mangy, in her cage, floated upwards and disappeared into a gap in the saucer's underside. The other grub cages had already disappeared. I glimpsed a flash of metallic color through the gap: Blue. Green was halfway to the opening, drifting lazily upward. Beside me, both Not-Too and Ruff began to rise.

"No! No!"

I hung onto Not-Too, who howled and barked. But then my body froze. I couldn't move anything. My hands opened and Not-Too rose, yowling piteously.

"No! No!" And then, before I knew I was going to say it, "Take me, too!" Green paused in mid-air. I began babbling.

"Take me! Take me! I can make the dogs behave correctly—I can—you need me! Why are you going? Take me!"

"Take this human?"

Not Green but Blue, emerging from the gap. Around me the Dome walls thinned more. Soldiers rushed toward us. Guns fired.

"Yes! What to do? Take this human! The dogs want this human!"

Time stood still. Not-Too howled and tried to reach me. Maybe that's what did it. I rose into the air just as Blue said, "Why the hell not?"

Inside—inside *what*?—I was too stunned to do more than grab Not-Too, hang on, and gasp. The gap closed. The saucer rose.

After a few minutes, I sat up and looked around. Gray room, filled with dogs in their cages, with grubs in theirs, with noise and confusion and the two robots. The sensation of motion ceased. I gasped, "Where... where are we going?"

Blue answered. "Home."

"*Why?*"

"The humans do not behave correctly." And then, "What to do now?"

We were leaving Earth in a flying saucer, and it was asking *me*?

Over time—I have no idea how much time—I actually got some answers from Blue. The humans not behaving correctly had apparently succeeding in breaching one of the Domes somewhere. They must have used a nuclear bomb, but that I couldn't verify. Grubs and dogs had both died, and so the aliens had packed up and left Earth. Without, as far as I could tell, retaliating. Maybe.

If I had stayed, I told myself, the soldiers would have shot me. Or I would have returned to life in the camp, where I would have died of dysentery or violence or cholera or starvation. Or I would have been locked away by whatever government still existed in the cities, a freak who had lived with aliens, none of my story believed. I barely believed it myself.

I *am* a freak who lives with aliens. Furthermore, I live knowing that at any moment Blue or Green or their "masters" might decide to vaporize me. But that's really not much different from the uncertainty of life in the camp, and here I actually have some status. Blue produces whatever I ask for, once I get him to understand what that is. I have new clothes, good food, a bed, paper, a sort of pencil.

And I have the dogs. Mangy still doesn't like me. Her larva hasn't as yet done whatever it will do next. Not-Too's grub grows slowly, and now Ruff has one, too. Their three puppies are adorable and very trainable. I'm not so sure about the other seventeen dogs, some of whom look wilder than ever after their long confinement in small cages. Aliens are not, by definition, humane.

I don't know what it will take to survive when, and if, we reach "home" and I meet the alien adults. All I can do is rely on Jill's Five Laws of Survival:

#1: Take what you can get.

#2: Show no fear.

#3: Never volunteer.

#4: Notice everything.

But the Fifth Law has changed. As I lie beside Not-Too and Ruff, their sweet warmth and doggie-odor, I know that my first formulation was wrong. “Feel nothing”—that can take you some ways toward survival, but not very far. Not really.

Law #5: Take the risk. Love something.

The dogs whuff contentedly and we speed toward the stars.

Afterword to "Laws of Survival"

In 2002 I acquired a dog (Cosette, the world's most spoiled toy poodle) and since then, my fiction has been full of dogs. A novel, titled *Dogs* ("Tell it like it is, baby") was rejected by several publishers who said they loved the writing, the characters, the plot—"but you kill dogs!" Apparently you can wipe out entire star systems of humans, but don't touch a canine.

"Laws of Survival" kills a few, from necessity. Jill doesn't have much, but she has a strong will to keep on living. She also has resourcefulness, plus adaptability to genuinely bizarre circumstances. What more do any of us need?

Maybe a dog.

SOMEONE TO WATCH OVER ME

"I still hate this," Trevor said. "That you're doing this to Becky."

"So you've told me," I said wearily. "Many times."

We sat in the clinic waiting room, done in Martian rust reds, very trendy for such an illegal operation. But, then, this was very upscale illegality. Trevor, who had so much money he never thought about it, hadn't asked how I was paying for Becky's surgery, and I hadn't volunteered that I'd cashed in my retirement fund at Payne, Jeffers. We'd been waiting on the rust-red conformachairs, which were not as comfortable as advertised, for nearly an hour.

Trevor scowled at me. "Amanda, as a tactic this lacks—"

"Sweetness," I said. "I know. I'm not a sweet person, Trevor. This is a surprise? You've known this about me since we were nine. We didn't become friends because you value sweetness."

"I didn't—"

But I was, all at once, beyond restraint. I turned on him. "And Jake didn't marry me for sweetness, either. Who wants to go to bed with a lump of marzipan—he used to say that to me! And he didn't leave me for lack of sweetness, either, or he wouldn't have chosen…what does she have that I don't?"

My voice had risen to a shout. The three other people in the waiting room, two of whom were holo-masked, stared. I twisted my hands together and spoke more softly. "He's just erased me from his life. That's what I really can't stand—that he acts like I never existed at all."

Trevor put his arms around me. I collapsed against his thin chest and narrow shoulders—delicate frames were hot just now with gays—and sobbed quietly. The man sitting two chairs away moved to four chairs away.

After I finally blew my nose, I said, "Trevvy, I have to know. Jake was the love of my life."

"Jake is a cheating and lying bastard, and anyway, I'm the love of your life."

"Not carnally."

"Overrated."

"You don't believe that."

"Well, no." He held me at arm's length. "You look like a dead spot in the ocean. Go put on some makeup. Obsession is not a good look for you. Anyway, Becky should be the love of your life."

His expression stopped my remaining sniffles. Trevor always smiles and he is never, ever critical of me. Not seriously. I said, "She is."

He didn't bother to correct the lie. But he looked away from me, and something in my neck went cold. I'd lost my soon-to-be-ex husband. If I lost Trevor, too....

"I'm here, Amanda. Always. And no, I don't need sweetness from you. I just need—"

My wristband brightened and said, "Ms. Rydder, the surgery went fine, and you can see Rebecca now. First door to your left."

I charged through the door. Becky lay in a smartcrib, watching a holo-mobile two feet above her. Bright, nonexistent shapes twisted and flowed in the air. Becky's plump little hands reached for them until she saw me. She crowed with delight, and I picked her up and cuddled her, studying her right eye.

It was clear, stained-glass green with thick, dark lashes. Just like Jake's eyes.

No scars on the smooth baby skin.

No grogginess from the anesthesia, no pain, no cloudiness in her iris.

You couldn't tell that anything had been done to her at all.

Using the software was as uncomplicated as the implant itself. What was hard was setting it up. The manufacturer doesn't do that for you, understanding more than anyone the absolute necessity of customized, unhackable encryption on dedicated and shielded computers. Most wearers of Opti-Cam implants are not six-month-old infants. Last month alone, six major mobsters were indicted and an Asian dictator assassinated using information from Opti-Cams.

Trevor set up my system. It was pretty minimal: receiver, screen, retransmitter, basic encryption. He protested the retransmitter. "This data isn't something you should view on anything but this one screen here in your bedroom, off-line for all the Internets. Don't retransmit to your wrister or, *quod di prohibeant*, to any screen anywhere at your job. Do I have to remind you that this whole setup is illegal?"

"Just get it working. And drop the Latin—it's pretentious."

"You never did have any sense of verbal fashion, Mandy. No, don't touch that...wait a minute...there."

The screen brightened to an expanse of white. I was about to protest that the system didn't work when I realized: Becky was staring at the ceiling.

She lay in her crib across the room, drowsy and blinking. The white expanse disappeared, reappeared, disappeared again. I said, too shrilly, "Mobile on," and her smartcrib activated it. Becky's eyes opened wide and she cooed. My screen showed somersaulting kittens made of light, seen from Becky's perspective as the camera behind her cornea sent its images to the receiver.

"Mobile off." The kittens disappeared. I crossed the room and loomed over Becky, looking back over my shoulder. On-screen was her view of me, head turned away.

Trevor said, "I still don't think you've thought this through. And I still hate it. Becky—"

"Won't know a thing. She doesn't feel the implant, and the images don't get stored in her brain, at least not any more than they would from her own vision. Nothing connects to her memory. There are dozens of studies proving that."

"With adult subjects. Not infants."

"Infants remember even less than we do."

"I wish you remembered less," Trevor said. "Remembered less, felt less, schemed less—"

I'd stopped listening to him. I watched Becky watch me until her lids fell into sleep and the screen went blank.

This was Wednesday. On Friday Jake would pick up Becky for his weekend of shared custody.

"What's with you?" Felicity said to me in the ladies' room nearest our cubicles. "You're jumpy as a cat."

"Cats aren't particularly jumpy. Neither am I. Just stressed about the GloBiz account."

Felicity frowned, but before she could point out that GloBiz was consistently thrilled with our campaign for them, I was out of the ladies' room, out of the building, in a cab home. Only 4:00 p.m., but so what? Even a copywriter deserves a dangerous, illegal, utterly stupid hobby.

In my bedroom I turned on the dedicated computer. Becky gazed at the back of a head in a moving car. One head, not two. Jake, alone, had picked her up at day care.

Then his apartment, not Pam's. I had never been inside either one, but I recognized his half of what had once been our furniture. He put Becky on the floor to crawl, and whenever she glanced over at him, I glimpsed the slippers I'd given him for his last birthday.

In college, I'd been a film major. No Fellini retrospective, no Welles film work, had ever enthralled me like the images on my screen that Friday evening. Jake's slippers, Becky's toys, a rubber ducky floating in the bathtub. Quick shots of Jake's face, laughing or talking to her—why didn't the implant have audio! Pam did not appear. When Becky finally fell asleep, I turned off the computer and then sat for a long time in the dark, tears running down my face, rage in my heart.

He had no right to do this to me. To Becky. To live his life as if I'd never occupied the center of it.

At midnight I gave in and keyed his number into my cell. He answered sleepily. "Hello?"

Not breathing, I clutched the phone.

More sharply: "Hello?" And then, "Amanda, if this is you, you're violating the restraining order. Please stop. I mean it this time. I'll go back to court if I have to."

I said nothing. Tears and rage, tears and rage. Long after he hung up, I clutched the phone as if I could crush it.

On Saturday, Pam appeared in Becky's field of vision.

At first I got only flashes of her; Becky was not interested in focusing on this unknown person. It was eerie to glimpse a red-shirted elbow, the toe of a black boot, the back of a blond head. It disassembled her, made her less than real. Eventually, however, she sat down in front of Becky and fed the baby strained applesauce.

Instantly, I wanted to leap through the lens and shove her away from my baby. Leave her alone, you bitch, she's mine! Pam was pretty but not gorgeous, a girl-next-door type if the door happened to open on a Hamptons beach house. Sun-streaked hair, fine sun lines around brown eyes, no makeup, vintage lululemon workout clothes. On the street I'd never have noticed her. Her body looked nicely curved but neither buxom nor model-elegant. What did she have that I didn't?

Becky spat applesauce at her and the view vibrated—she must have been giggling. Pam giggled back.

Stop. Leave her alone! She's mine!

He's mine.

By Sunday afternoon, when Jake brought Becky back, I had slept a total of three hours. All weekend I'd sat by the screen, seldom eating, scarcely going to the bathroom. Becky might wake in the night; there might be something to see. It was, as I'd discovered online, a one-bedroom apartment. Did Jake wheel her crib out into the living room so he and Pam could have sex in the bedroom? Or did they do it with Becky asleep beside them?

By order of the court, ever since that stupid misunderstanding two months ago, Jake and I had no contact when Becky was returned on Sunday. Jake brought his sister with him every single week. Linda brought Becky into my building, and the two of us did not exchange a word.

I unwrapped Becky and studied every inch of her, looking for—what? Anything amiss, a bruise or a dirty diaper or ripped pj's. There was nothing, of course. Jake had always been a terrific father.

The baby was asleep by seven o'clock. I called Trevor to come over; my call went straight to voice mail. Felicity had a date. TV was boring. I roamed the house, unable to sit for even a moment.

Until I stopped cold, feeling my own mouth open into an O. After checking on Becky one last time, I brought the small, dedicated computer into the living room and connected it to my wall system.

Trevor had made his fortune with Holo-Shop. He invented it, patented it, and sold it for an exorbitant sum plus royalties to Microsoft.

There had been other holographic conversion programs on the market, but they were quirky, experimental, difficult to use. Holo-Shop was none of those, and the results were sharper than anything before it. You brought up a flat image on a screen, set the parameters you wanted, and touched the H-S icon. The image sprang from the screen in holographic three dimensions. It could be small or large, although the larger you made it, and the farther away the hologram from the screen, the lower the resolution. A three-inch rose was a miracle of dense perfection; a room-sized puppy was insubstantial vapor.

Holo-Shop could not evoke moving images, not yet, although Microsoft was reportedly working on it. Meanwhile, advertisers and artists and retail outlets manipulated holograms to sometimes powerful effect, sometimes laughable kitsch. Ditto the millions of users who wanted the pyramids to decorate their trendy Egyptian-themed living room but to disappear when they needed to set up a card table for poker.

I ran the camera images of Jake as Becky saw him until I found a good one: Jake crouching on the floor, smiling, green eyes alight, arms extended for the baby to crawl into them. I froze the image, projected it with H-S, and fooled with it for a while. When it was done, Jake sat life-size on my bedroom floor, ghostly enough to see the dresser behind him, arms outstretched. The dresser didn't matter. I got down on the floor and moved to sit in the circle of his arms.

The second weekend that Jake had Becky, Pam was there all weekend. I watched them every minute that Becky was awake. They kissed in the kitchen, took Becky to the park, watched something on TV while she crawled around the floor. Pam wore Carson Davies boots in calfskin, $800. When Trevor called with tickets to the hottest play in town, I told him I had the flu. By Sunday afternoon, when Linda handed Becky back to me, I was groggy from sleeplessness, reeking from not bathing. I didn't look at Linda looking at me.

I once saw a show about toxoplasmosis, a parasitic disease. When mice contract it, they lose their natural fear of cats, making it easier for cats to eat them and the parasite to get into the cat. There was some evidence from brain scans that the mice realized this lack of fear was stupid, but they couldn't help themselves. They were compelled to let the cats see them.

At work I accomplished nothing. I'd set the retransmitter to send the images of Jake and Pam to my wrister; the hell with what Trevor said. Whenever I could, I ducked into the ladies' room and brought up images to study. Felicity went from warmly supportive ("You don't feel well? Oh, I can finish that copy, Amanda") to faintly resentful ("You haven't even started on the McMahon account stuff? But we got it over a week ago").

On Thursday night, Trevor called. I told him I had the flu. On Friday night, he let himself into my apartment with his emergency key. I barely had time to dart out of the bedroom and close the door.

"Trevor! I told you I'm sick!"

"It's not flu season, Mandy." His handsome face looked strange without its habitual smile.

"If I say I have the flu, then I have the flu!"

"I don't think you do. You're doing it again, aren't you? Two restraining orders and a court fine weren't enough?"

"I'm not. I'm not stalking Jake."

"Swear on pussy willows' pussies?" Our childhood oath; at ten years old it had seemed hilarious.

"Swear on pussy willows' pussies."

"Then you're obsessing over the Opti-Cam images."

"Isn't that my business?"

Trevor lost his temper, something even rarer than losing his smile. "Oh, Christ, Mandy, you're my business! Don't you know that if I were straight, you and I would have married and had three Beckys of our own? Don't you know how much better I'd have been for you than Jake? I can handle your intensity, he couldn't. And I know when you're lying to me."

"Please go, Trevor. I'm not up to this right now, really I'm not—"

He left, slamming the door behind him. Once, nothing in the world would have kept me from following him. Trevor, my best friend, my support and confidant....

On the screen in the bedroom, Becky lay in her infant seat, studying her bare toes. She must have just woken up. On the rug, barely within the circle of her unknowing vision, Jake and Pam made love.

Frantically I keyed in his cell number. Anything to disrupt them, anything! The call went to voice mail. "Stop!" I screamed. "Stop, stop, stop!" The cell must have been on silent; they didn't stop.

I am not sane, I thought, which was my last sane thought.

I called in sick to work on Monday, Tuesday, Wednesday. I never left my bedroom. It began to smell: of Becky's diapers, piled in the corner whenever I changed her. Of a pizza molding on the dresser. Of me.

On Thursday morning, Trevor returned.

"Mandy?"

"Go away! Go away!" I'd waited all week for 10:00 a.m. on Thursday! Trevor was not going to spoil this!

"Mandy…oh my God." He stood in the door to my bedroom. Becky gurgled in her swing. She was dressed in her snowsuit; the window stood open to help with the stench.

"Go away!" I barely glanced at him—it was 9:57!

"Mandy, darling, whatever you're going to do…don't."

9:58.

"Let me help you. You know we've always helped each other."

"Don't touch me!"

"I won't. You know I won't if you don't want me to. I'm just going to pick up Becky, okay? Here we go, sweetheart, come to Uncle Trevor…."

9:59.

Jake's law office was superefficient. The partners would be gathering in his spacious office for the regular Thursday morning meeting. His wall screen would be on, ready to bring up the week's data. He didn't know I had his office password; I'd stolen it right after he told me he was leaving me, but despite everything that had led to the restraining order I'd never used it. Until now.

Trevor said, "Mandy, what are you doing? Put down your cell if you're calling the cops. I'm not here to force you to do anything you don't want to do, I promise. Put down the cell."

10:00.

I pushed both buttons simultaneously, my cell and the "Send" button on the computer. The phone number bypassed Jake's office answering system—a direct line for privileged clients who needed to reach their lawyer instantly for some legal emergency. Jake would not recognize the number of my new, throwaway cell. His voice said, "Hello?"

Now it would happen. Now I would get what I had been trying for so long, what I needed more than food or water or even Becky: I would get a reaction from Jake. The image of him and Pam naked on the rug would burst from the wall screen in his office in all its color-saturated, three-dimensional luridness, and Jake would know I had done it. That he could not erase me.

"Hello? Who is this?" Jake said, still calm. "Can I help you?"

I waited.

Nothing happened.

No one in the background gasped or laughed or said, "What the hell—?" Nothing.

Jake tried one last "Can I help you?" and then cut the connection.

Trevor, patting Becky's back, said softly, "Mandy. . . ."

I cried, "Why didn't it work?"

Trevor's face changed. His gaze moved to the computer. He knew, then; he was always smarter than anybody else I knew. He said, "Because Jake knew you'd do something like that. He put a detailed blocker on his system."

"I just wanted him to acknowledge I exist!"

"Oh, he acknowledges it," Trevor said. "How do you think he knew what you'd do?"

He held Becky, now squirming in her snowsuit, away from him and stared into her eyes, first the right and then the left, again the right, again the left. "The technology's available to everyone. Including Jake."

I don't like to lie to Trevor. Sometimes, however, you have to do certain things you might not want to do. He went with me to the clinic, but of course he couldn't sign any papers; he is not related to Becky. I told him I'd had both Opti-Cams removed. I swore on pussy willows.

Now I stand in my bedroom, which sparkles with cleanliness. Becky sits in her swing, gurgling at me. I lean closer to her. My hair, clean and shining, swings toward her. My makeup has been professionally done. My cleavage gets help from a $200 bra. I smile at my baby.

Jake is watching.

Afterword to "Someone To Watch Over Me"

This is the newest story in this volume, written at the request of the editor of *IEEE Spectrum*. The Institute for Electrical and Electronics Engineers, the world's largest professional organization for the advancement of technology, does not usually deal in fiction. In 2014, however, the publication decided to solicit six stories featuring plausible, near-future technology.

I do not do well with cameras. I end up with pictures of my thumb, or the top of someone's head, or a blurry tree. Recently I didn't realize I had my camera set on "video" and ended up with a film of Mt. Ranier instead of a series of stills. Mountains don't change much in 3 ½ minutes. So a camera that photographed continuously, sharply, and in focus, would be great. However, I would never put it where Amanda did, or for the purpose she chose.

Is this tech possible? My sources say yes, it is. Not now, but maybe soon—a genuinely creepy possibility.

THE FLOWERS OF AULIT PRISON

My sister lies sweetly on the bed across the room from mine. She lies on her back, fingers lightly curled, her legs stretched straight as elindel trees. Her pert little nose, much prettier than my own, pokes delicately into the air. Her skin glows like a fresh flower. But not with health. She is, of course, dead.

I slip out of my bed and stand swaying a moment, with morning dizziness. A Terran healer once told me my blood pressure was too low, which is the sort of nonsensical thing Terrans will sometimes say—like announcing the air is too moist. The air is what it is, and so am I.

What I am is a murderer.

I kneel in front of my sister's glass coffin. My mouth has that awful morning taste, even though last night I drank nothing stronger than water. Almost I yawn, but at the last moment I turn it into a narrow-lipped ringing in my ears that somehow leaves my mouth tasting worse than ever. But at least I haven't disrespected Ano. She was my only sibling and closest friend, until I replaced her with illusion.

"Two more years, Ano," I say, "less forty-two days. Then you will be free. And so will I."

Ano, of course, says nothing. There is no need. She knows as well as I the time until her burial, when she can be released from the chemicals and glass that bind her dead body and can rejoin our ancestors. Others I have known whose relatives were under atonement bondage said the bodies complained and recriminated, especially in dreams, making the house a misery. Ano is more considerate. Her corpse never troubles me at all. I do that to myself.

I finish the morning prayers, leap up, and stagger dizzily to the piss closet. I may not have drunk pel last night, but my bladder is nonetheless bursting.

At noon a messenger rides into my yard on a Terran bicycle. The bicycle is an attractive design, sloping, with interesting curves. Adapted for our market, undoubtedly. The messenger is less attractive, a surly boy probably in his first year of government service. When I smile at him, he looks away. He would rather be someplace else. Well, if he doesn't perform his messenger duties with more courteous cheer, he will be.

"Letter for Uli Pek Bengarin."

"I am Uli Pek Bengarin."

Scowling, he hands me the letter and pedals away. I don't take the scowl personally. The boy does not, of course, know what I am, any more than my neighbors do. That would defeat the whole point. I am supposed to pass as fully real, until I can earn the right to resume being so.

The letter is shaped into a utilitarian circle, very business-like, with a generic government seal. It could have come from the Tax Section, or Community Relief, or Processions and Rituals. But of course it hasn't; none of those sections would write to me until I am real again. The sealed letter is from Reality and Atonement. It's a summons; they have a job for me.

And about time. I have been home nearly six weeks since the last job, shaping my flowerbeds and polishing dishes and trying to paint a skyscape of last month's synchrony, when all six moons were visible at once. I paint badly. It is time for another job.

I pack my shoulder sack, kiss the glass of my sister's coffin, and lock the house. Then I wheel my bicycle—not, alas, as interestingly curved as the messenger's—out of its shed and pedal down the dusty road toward the city.

Frablit Pek Brimmidin is nervous. This interests me; Pek Brimmidin is usually a calm, controlled man, the sort who never replaces reality with illusion. He's given me my previous jobs with no fuss. But now he actually can't sit still; he fidgets back and forth across his small office, which is cluttered with papers, stone sculptures in an exaggerated style I don't like at all, and plates of half-eaten food. I don't comment on either the food or the pacing. I am fond of Pek Brimmidin, quite apart from my gratitude to him, which is profound. He was the official in R&A who voted to give me a chance to become real again. The other two judges voted for perpetual death, no chance of atonement. I'm not supposed to know this much detail about my own case, but I do. Pek Brimmidin is middle-aged, a stocky man whose neck fur has just begun to yellow. His eyes are gray, and kind.

"Pek Bengarin," he says, finally, and then stops.

"I stand ready to serve," I say softly, so as not to make him even more nervous. But something is growing heavy in my stomach. This does not look good.

"Pek Bengarin." Another pause. "You are an informer."

"I stand ready to serve our shared reality," I repeat, despite my astonishment. Of course I'm an informer. I've been an informer for two years and eighty-two days. I killed my sister, and I will be an informer until my atonement is over, I can be fully real again, and Ano can be released from death to join our ancestors. Pek Brimmidin knows this. He's assigned me every one of my previous informing jobs, from the first easy one in currency counterfeiting right through the last one, in baby stealing. I'm a very good informer, as Pek Brimmidin also knows. What's wrong with the man?

Suddenly Pek Brimmidin straightens. But he doesn't look me in the eye. "You are an informer, and the Section for Reality and Atonement has an informing job for you. In Aulit Prison."

So that's it. I go still. Aulit Prison holds criminals. Not just those who have tried to get away with stealing or cheating or child-snatching, which are, after all, normal. Aulit Prison holds those who are unreal, who have succumbed to the illusion that they are not part of shared common reality and so may do violence to the most concrete reality of others: their physical bodies. Maimers. Rapists. Murderers.

Like me.

I feel my left hand tremble, and I strive to control it and to not show how hurt I am. I thought Pek Brimmidin thought better of me. There is of course no such thing as partial atonement—one is either real or one is not—but a part of my mind nonetheless thought that Pek Brimmidin had recognized two years and eighty-two days of effort in regaining my reality. I have worked so hard.

He must see some of this on my face because he says quickly, "I am sorry to assign this job to you, Pek. I wish I had a better one. But you've been requested specifically by Rafkit Sarloe." Requested by the capital; my spirits lift slightly. "They've added a note to the request. I am authorized to tell you the informant job carries additional compensation. If you succeed, your debt will be considered immediately paid, and you can be restored at once to reality."

Restored at once to reality. I would again be a full member of World, without shame. Entitled to live in the real world of shared humanity, and to hold my head up with pride. And Ano could be buried, the artificial chemicals washed from her body, so that it could return to World and her sweet spirit could join our ancestors. Ano, too, would be restored to reality.

"I'll do it," I tell Pek Brimmidin. And then, formally, "I stand ready to serve our shared reality."

"One more thing, before you agree, Pek Bengarin." Pek Brimmidin is figeting again. "The suspect is a Terran."

I have never before informed on a Terran. Aulit Prison, of course, holds those aliens who have been judged unreal: Terrans, Fallers, the weird little Huhuhubs. The problem is that even after thirty years of ships coming to World, there is still considerable debate about whether any aliens are real at all. Clearly their bodies exist; after all, here they are. But their thinking is so disordered they might almost qualify as all being unable to recognize shared social reality, and so just as unreal as those poor empty children who never attain reason and must be destroyed.

Usually we on World just leave the aliens alone, except of course for trading with them. The Terrans in particular offer interesting objects, such as bicycles, and ask in return worthless items, mostly perfectly obvious information. But do any of the aliens have souls, capable of recognizing and honoring a shared reality with the souls of others? At the universities, the argument goes on. Also in market squares and pel shops, which is where I hear it. Personally, I think aliens may well be real. I try not to be a bigot.

I say to Pek Brimmidin, "I am willing to inform on a Terran."

He wiggles his hand in pleasure. "Good, good. You will enter Aulit Prison a Capmonth before the suspect is brought there. You will use your primary cover, please."

I nod, although Pek Brimmidin knows this is not easy for me. My primary cover is the truth: I killed my sister Ano Pek Bengarin two years and eighty-two days ago and was judged unreal enough for perpetual death, never able to join my ancestors. The only untrue part of the cover is that I escaped and have been hiding from the Section police ever since.

"You have just been captured," Pek Brimmidin continues, "and assigned to the first part of your death in Aulit. The Section records will show this."

Again I nod, not looking at him. The first part of my death in Aulit; the second, when the time came, in the kind of chemical bondage that holds Ano. And never ever to be freed—ever. What if it were true? I should go mad. Many do.

"The suspect is named 'Carryl Walters.' He is a Terran healer. He murdered a World child, in an experiment to discover how real people's brains function. His sentence is perpetual death. But the Section believes that Carryl Walters was working with a group of World people in these experiments. That somewhere on World there is a group that's so lost its hold on reality that it would murder children to investigate science."

For a moment the room wavers, including the exaggerated swooping curves of Pek Brimmidin's ugly sculptures. But then I get hold of myself. I am an informer, and a good one. I can do this. I am redeeming myself, and releasing Ano. I am an informer.

"I'll find out who this group is," I say. "And what they're doing, and where they are."

Pek Brimmidin smiles at me. "Good." His trust is a dose of shared reality: two people acknowledging their common perceptions together, without lies or violence. I need this dose. It is probably the last one I will have for a long time.

How do people manage in perpetual death, fed on only solitary illusion? Aulit Prison must be full of the mad.

Traveling to Aulit takes two days of hard riding. Somewhere my bicycle loses a bolt and I wheel it to the next village. The woman who runs the bicycle shop is competent but mean, the sort who gazes at shared reality mostly to pick out the ugly parts.

"At least it's not a Terran bicycle."

"At least," I say, but she is incapable of recognizing sarcasm.

"Sneaky soulless criminals, taking us over bit by bit. We should never have allowed them in. And the government is supposed to protect us from unreal slime, ha, what a joke. Your bolt is a nonstandard size."

"Is it?" I say.

"Yes. Costs you extra."

I nod. Behind the open rear door of the shop, two little girls play in a thick stand of moonweed.

"We should kill all the aliens," the repairer says. "No shame in destroying them before they corrupt us."

"Eurummmn," I say. Informers are not supposed to make themselves conspicuous with political debate. Above the two children's heads, the moonweed bends gracefully in the wind. One of the little girls has long brown neck fur, very pretty. The other does not.

"There, that bolt will hold fine. Where you from?"

"Rakfit Sarloe." Informers never name their villages.

She gives an exaggerated shudder. "I would never visit the capital. Too many aliens. They destroy our participation in shared reality without a moment's thought! Three and eight, please."

I want to say *No one but you can destroy your own participation in shared reality*, but I don't. Silently I pay her the money.

She glares at me, at the world. "You don't believe me about the Terrans. But I know what I know!"

I ride away, through the flowered countryside. In the sky, only Cap is visible, rising on the horizon opposite the sun. Cap glows with a clear white smoothness, like Ano's skin.

The Terrans, I am told, have only one moon. Shared reality on their world is, perhaps, skimpier than ours: less curved, less rich, less warm.

Are they ever jealous?

Aulit prison sits on a flat plain inland from the South Coast. I know that other islands on World have their own prisons, just as they have their own governments, but only Aulit is used for the alien unreal, as well as our own. A special agreement among the governments of World makes this possible. The alien governments protest, but of course it does them no good. The unreal is the unreal, and far too painful and dangerous to have running around loose. Besides, the alien governments are far away on other stars.

Aulit is huge and ugly, a straight-lined monolith of dull red stone, with no curves anywhere. An official from R&A meets me and turns me over to two prison guards. We enter through a barred gate, my bicycle chained to the guards', and I to my bicycle. I am led across a wide dusty yard toward a stone wall. The guards of course don't speak to me; I am unreal.

My cell is square, twice my length on a side. There is a bed, a piss pot, a table, and a single chair. The door is without a window, and all the other doors in the row of cells are closed.

"When will the prisoners be allowed to be all together?" I ask, but of course the guard doesn't answer me. I am not real.

I sit in my chair and wait. Without a clock, it's difficult to judge time, but I think a few hours pass totally without event. Then a gong sounds and my door slides up into the ceiling. Ropes and pulleys, controlled from above, inaccessible from inside the cell.

The corridor fills with illusionary people. Men and women, some with yellowed neck fur and sunken eyes, walking with the shuffle of old age. Some young, striding along with that dangerous mixture of anger and desperation. And the aliens.

I have seen aliens before, but not so many together. Fallers, about our size but very dark, as if burned crisp by their distant star. They wear their neck fur very long and dye it strange bright colors, although not in prison. Terrans, who don't even have neck fur but instead fur on their heads, which they sometimes cut into fanciful curves—rather pretty. Terrans are a little intimidating because of their size. They move slowly. Ano, who had one year at the university before I killed her, once told me that the Terran's world makes them feel lighter than ours does. I don't understand this, but Ano was very intelligent and so it's probably true. She also explained that Fallers, Terrans, and World people are somehow related far back in time, but this is harder to believe. Perhaps Ano was mistaken.

Nobody ever thinks Huhuhubs could be related to us. Tiny, scuttling, ugly, dangerous, they walk on all fours. They're covered with warts. They smell bad. I was glad to see only a few of them, sticking close together, in the corridor at Aulit.

We all move toward a large room filled with rough tables and chairs and, in the corner, a trough for the Huhuhubs. The food is already on the tables. Cereal, flatbread, elindel fruit—very basic, but nutritious. What surprises me most is the total absence of guards. Apparently prisoners are allowed to do whatever they wish to the food, the room, or each other, without interference. Well, why not? We aren't real.

I need protection, quickly.

I choose a group of two women and three men. They sit at a table with their backs to the wall, and others have left a respectful distance around them. From the way they group themselves, the oldest woman is the leader. I plant myself in front of her and look directly into her face. A long scar ridges her left cheek to disappear into grizzled neck fur.

"I am Uli Pek Bengarin," I say, my voice even but too low to be heard beyond this group. "In Aulit for the murder of my sister. I can be useful to you."

She doesn't speak, and her flat dark eyes don't waver, but I have her attention. Other prisoners watch furtively.

"I know an informer among the guards. He knows I know. He brings things into Aulit for me, in return for not sharing his name."

Still her eyes don't waver. But I see she believes me; the sheer outrage of my statement has convinced her. A guard who had already forfeited reality by informing—by violating shared reality—might easily turn it to less pernicious material advantage. Once reality is torn, the rents grow. For the same reason, she easily believes that I might violate my supposed agreement with the guard.

"What sort of things?" she says, carelessly. Her voice is raspy and thick, like some hairy root.

"Letters. Candy. Pel." Intoxicants are forbidden in prison; they promote shared conviviality, to which the unreal have no right.

"Weapons?"

"Perhaps," I say.

"And why shouldn't I beat this guard's name out of you and set up my own arrangement with him?"

"He will not. He is my cousin." This is the trickiest part of the cover provided to me by R&A Section; it requires that my would-be protector believe in a person who has kept enough sense of reality to honor family ties but will nonetheless violate a larger shared reality. I told Pek Brimmidin that I doubted that such a twisted state of mind would be very stable, and so a seasoned prisoner would not believe in it. But Pek Brimmidin was right and I was wrong. The woman nods.

"All right. Sit down."

She does not ask what I wish in return for the favors of my supposed cousin. She knows. I sit beside her, and from now on I am physically safe in Aulit Prison from all but her.

Next, I must somehow befriend a Terran.

This proves harder than I expect. The Terrans keep to themselves, and so do we. They are just as violent toward their own as all the mad doomed souls in Aulit; the place is every horror whispered by children trying to shock each other. Within a tenday I see two World men hold down and rape a woman. No one interferes. I see a Terran gang beat a Faller. I see a World woman knife another woman, who bleeds to death on the stone floor. This is the only time guards appear, heavily armored. A priest is with them. He wheels in a coffin of chemicals and immediately immerses the body so that it cannot decay to release the prisoner from her sentence of perpetual death.

At night, isolated in my cell, I dream that Frablit Pek Brimmidin appears and rescinds my provisional reality. The knifed, doomed corpse becomes Ano; her attacker becomes me. I wake from the dream moaning and weeping. The tears are not grief but terror. My life, and Ano's, hang from the splintery branch of a criminal alien I have not yet even met.

I know who he is, though. I skulk as close as I dare to the Terran groups, listening. I don't speak their language, of course, but Pek Brimmidin taught me to recognize the cadences of "Carryl Walters" in several of their dialects. Carryl Walters is an old Terran, with gray head fur cut in boring straight lines, wrinkled brownish skin, and sunken eyes. But his ten fingers—how do they keep the extra ones from tangling them up?—are long and quick.

It takes me only a day to realize that Carryl Walters's own people leave him alone, surrounding him with the same nonviolent respect that my protector gets. It takes me much longer to figure out why. Carryl Walters is not dangerous, neither a protector nor a punisher. I don't think he has any private shared realities with the guards. I don't understand until the World woman is knifed.

It happens in the courtyard, on a cool day in which I am gazing hungrily at the one patch of bright sky overhead. The knifed woman screams. The murderer pulls the knife from her belly and blood shoots out. In seconds the ground is drenched. The woman doubles over. Everyone looks the other way except me. And Carryl Walters runs over with his old-man stagger and kneels over the body, trying uselessly to save the life of a woman already dead anyway.

Of course. He is a healer. The Terrans don't bother him because they know that, next time, it might be they who have need of him.

I feel stupid for not realizing this right away. I am supposed to be good at informing. Now I'll have to make it up by immediate action.

The problem, of course, is that no one will attack me while I'm under Afa Pek Fakar's protection, and provoking Pek Fakar herself is far too dangerous.

I can see only one way to do this.

I wait a few days. Outside in the courtyard, I sit quietly against the prison wall and breathe shallowly. After a few minutes I leap up. The dizziness takes me; I worsen it by holding my breath. Then I ram as hard as I can into the rough stone wall and slide down it. Pain tears through my arm and forehead. One of Pek Fakar's men shouts something.

Pek Fakar is there in a minute. I hear her—hear all of them—through a curtain of dizziness and pain.

"—just ran into the wall, I saw it—"

"—told me she gets these dizzy attacks—"

"—head broken in—"

I gasp, through sudden real nausea, "The healer. The Terran—"

"The Terran?" Pek Fakar's voice, hard with sudden suspicion. But I gasp out more words, "...disease...a Terran told me...since childhood... without help I..." My vomit, unplanned but useful, spews over her boots.

"Get the Terran," Pek Fakar rasps to somebody. "And a towel!"

Then Carryl Walters bends over me. I clutch his arm, try to smile, and pass out.

When I come to, I am lying inside, on the floor of the eating hall, the Terran cross-legged beside me. A few World people hover near the far wall, scowling. Carryl Walters says, "How many fingers you see?"

"Four. Aren't you supposed to have five?"

He unbends the fifth from behind his palm and says, "You fine."

"No, I'm not," I say. He speaks childishly, and with an odd accent, but he's understandable. "I have a disease. Another Terran healer told me so."

"Who?"

"Her name was Anna Pek Rakov."

"What disease?"

"I don't remember. Something in the head. I get spells."

"What spells? You fall, flop on floor?"

"No. Yes. Sometimes. Sometimes it takes me differently." I look directly into his eyes. Strange eyes, smaller than mine, and that improbable blue. "Pek Rakov told me I could die during a spell, without help."

He does not react to the lie. Or maybe he does, and I don't know how to read it. I have never informed on a Terran before. Instead he says something grossly obscene, even for Aulit Prison: "Why you unreal? What you do?"

I move my gaze from his. "I murdered my sister." If he asks for details, I will cry. My head aches too hard.

He says, "I sorry."

Is he sorry that he asked, or that I killed Ano? Pek Rakov was not like this; she had some manners. I say, "The other Terran healer said I should be watched carefully by someone who knows what to do if I get a spell. Do you know what to do, Pek Walters?"

"Yes."

"Will you watch me?"

"Yes." He is, in fact, watching me closely now. I touch my head; there is a cloth tied around it where I bashed myself. The headache is worse. My hand comes away sticky with blood.

I say, "In return for what?"

"What you give Pek Fakar for protection?"

He is smarter than I thought. "Nothing I can also share with you." She would punish me hard.

"Then I watch you, you give me information about World."

I nod; this is what Terrans usually request. And where information is given, it can also be extracted. "I will explain your presence to Pek Fakar," I say, before the pain in my head swamps me without warning, and everything in the dining hall blurs and sears together.

Pek Fakar doesn't like it. But I have just given her a gun, smuggled in by my "cousin." I leave notes for the prison administration in my cell, under my bed. While the prisoners are in the courtyard—which we are every day, no matter what the weather—the notes are replaced by whatever I ask for. Pek Fakar had demanded a "weapon;" neither of us expected a Terran gun. She is the only person in the prison to have such a thing. It is to me a stark reminder that no one would care if all we unreal killed each other off completely. There is no one else to shoot; we never see anyone not already in perpetual death.

"Without Pek Walters, I might have another spell and die," I say to the scowling Pek Fakar. "He knows a special Terran method of flexing the brain to bring me out of a spell."

"He can teach this special method to me."

"So far, no World person has been able to learn it. Their brains are different from ours."

She glares at me. But no one, even those lost to reality, can deny that alien brains are weird. And my injuries are certainly real: bloody head cloth, left eye closed from swelling, skin scraped raw the length of my left cheek, bruised arm. She strokes the Terran gun, a boringly straight-lined cylinder of dull metal. "All right. You may keep the Terran near you—if he agrees. Why should he?"

I smile at her slowly. Pek Fakar never shows a response to flattery; to do so would be to show weakness. But she understands. Or thinks she does. I have threatened the Terran with her power, and the whole prison now knows that her power extends among the aliens as well as her own people. She goes on glaring, but she is not displeased. In her hand the gun gleams.

And so begin my conversations with a Terran.

Talking with Carryl Pek Walters is embarrassing and frustrating. He sits beside me in the eating hall or the courtyard and publicly scratches his head. When he is cheerful, he makes shrill horrible whistling noises between his teeth. He mentions topics that belong only among kin: the state of his skin (which has odd brown lumps on it) and his lungs (clogged with fluid, apparently). He does not know enough to begin conversations with ritual comments on flowers. It is like talking to a child, but a child who suddenly begins discussing bicycle engineering or university law.

"You think individual means very little, group means everything," he says.

We are sitting in the courtyard, against a stone wall, a little apart from the other prisoners. Some watch us furtively, some openly. I am angry. I am often angry with Pek Walters. This is not going as I'd planned.

"How can you say that? The individual is very important on World! We care for each other so that no individual is left out of our common reality, except by his own acts!"

"Exactly," Pek Walters says. He has just learned this word from me. "You care for others so no one left alone. Alone is bad. Act alone is bad. Only together is real."

"Of course," I say. Could he be stupid after all? "Reality is always shared. Is a star really there if only one eye can perceive its light?"

He smiles and says something in his own language, which makes no sense to me. He repeats it in real words. "When tree falls in forest, is sound if no person hears?"

"But—do you mean to say that on your star, people believe they..." What? I can't find the words.

He says, "People believe they always real, alone or together. Real even when other people say they dead. Real even when they do something very bad. Even when they murder."

"But they're not real! How could they be? They've violated shared reality! If I don't acknowledge you, the reality of your soul, if I send you to your ancestors without your consent, that is proof that I don't understand reality and so am not seeing it! Only the unreal could do that!"

"Baby not see shared reality. Is baby unreal?"

"Of course. Until the age when children attain reason, they are unreal."

"Then when I kill baby, is all right, because I not kill real person?"

"Of course it's not all right! When one kills a baby, one kills its chance to become real, before it could even join its ancestors! And also all the chances of the babies to which it might become ancestor. No one would kill a baby on World, not even these dead souls in Aulit! Are you saying that on Terra, people would kill babies?"

He looks at something I cannot see. "Yes."

My chance has arrived, although not in a form I relish. Still, I have a job to do. I say, "I have heard that Terrans will kill people for science. Even babies. To find out the kinds of things that Anna Pek Rakov knew about my brain. Is that true?"

"Yes and no."

"How can it be yes and no? Are children ever used for science experiments?"

"Yes."

"What kinds of experiments?"

"You should ask, what kind children? Dying children. Children not born yet. Children born...wrong. With no brain, or broken brain."

I struggle with all this. Dying children...he must mean not children who are really dead, but those in the transition to join their ancestors. Well, that would not be so bad, provided the bodies were then allowed to decay properly and release the souls. Children without brains or with broken brains...not bad, either. Such poor unreal things would be destroyed anyway. But children not born yet…in or out of the mother's womb? I push this away, to discuss another time. I am on a different path.

"And you never use living, real children for science?"

He gives me a look I cannot read. So much of Terran expression is still strange. "Yes. We use. In some experiments. Experiments who not hurt children."

"Like what?" I say. We are staring directly at each other now. Suddenly I wonder if this old Terran suspects that I am an informer seeking information, and that is why he accepted my skimpy story about having spells. That would not necessarily be bad. There are ways to bargain with the unreal once everyone admits that bargaining is what is taking place. But I'm not sure whether Pek Walters knows that.

He says, "Experiments who study how brain work. Such as, how memory work. Including shared memory."

"Memory? Memory doesn't 'work.' It just is."

"No. Memory work. By memory-building pro-teenz." He uses a Terran word, then adds, "Tiny little pieces of food," which makes no sense. What does food have to do with memory? You don't eat memories, or obtain them from food. But I am further down the path, and I use his words to go further still.

"Does memory in World people work with the same…'pro-teenz' as Terran memory?"

"Yes and no. Some same or almost same. Some different." He is watching me very closely.

"How do you know that memory works the same or different in World people? Have Terrans done brain experiments on World?"

"Yes."

"With World children?"

"Yes."

I watch a group of Huhuhubs across the courtyard. The smelly little aliens are clustered together in some kind of ritual or game. "And have you, personally, participated in these science experiments on children, Pek Walters?"

He doesn't answer me. Instead he smiles, and if I didn't know better, I'd swear the smile was sad. He says, "Pek Bengarin, why you kill your sister?"

The unexpectedness of it—now, so close to almost learning something useful—outrages me. Not even Pek Fakar has asked me that. I stare at him angrily. He says, "I know, I not should ask. Wrong for ask. But I tell you much, and answer is important—"

"But the question is obscene. You should not ask. World people are not so cruel to each other."

"Even people damned in Aulit Prison?" he says, and even though I don't know one of the words he uses, I see that yes, he recognizes that I am an informer. And that I have been seeking information. All right, so much the better. But I need time to set my questions on a different path.

To gain time, I repeat my previous point. "World people are not so cruel."

"Then you—"

The air suddenly sizzles, smelling of burning. People shout. I look up. Aka Pek Fakar stands in the middle of the courtyard with the Terran gun, firing it at the Huhuhubs. One by one they drop as the beam of light hits them and makes a sizzling hole. The aliens pass into the second stage of their perpetual death.

I stand and tug on Pek Walters's arm. "Come on. We must clear the area immediately or the guards will release poison gas."

"Why?"

"So they can get the bodies into bondage chemicals, of course!" Does this alien think the prison officials would let the unreal get even a little bit decayed? I thought that after our several conversations, Pek Walters understood more than that.

He rises slowly, haltingly, to his feet. Pek Fakar, laughing, strolls toward the door, the gun still in her hand.

Pek Walters says, "World people not cruel?"

Behind us, the bodies of the Huhuhubs lie sprawled across each other, smoking.

The next time we are herded from our cells into the dining hall and then the courtyard, the Huhuhub corpses are of course gone. Pek Walters has developed a cough. He walks more slowly, and once, on the way to our usual spot against the far wall, he puts a hand on my arm to steady himself.

"Are you sick, Pek?"

"Exactly," he says.

"But you are a healer. Make the cough disappear."

He smiles, and sinks gratefully against the wall. "'Healer, heal own self.'"

"What?"

"Nothing. So you are informer, Pek Bengarin, and you hope I tell you something about science experiments on children on World."

I take a deep breath. Pek Fakar passes us, carrying her gun. Two of her own people now stay close beside her at all times, in case another prisoner tries to take the gun away from her. I cannot believe anyone would try, but maybe I'm wrong. There's no telling what the unreal will do. Pek Walters watches her pass, and his smile is gone. Yesterday Pek Fakar shot another person, this time not even an alien. There is a note under my bed requesting more guns.

I say, "You say I am an informer. I do not say it."

"Exactly," Pek Walters says. He has another coughing spell, then closes his eyes wearily. "I have not an-tee-by-otics."

Another Terran word. Carefully I repeat it. "'An-tee-by-otics'?"

"Pro-teenz for heal."

Again that word for very small bits of food. I make use of it. "Tell me about the pro-teenz in the science experiments."

"I tell you everything about experiments. But only if you answer questions first."

He will ask about my sister. For no reason other than rudeness and cruelty. I feel my face turn to stone.

He says, "Tell me why steal baby not so bad for make person unreal always."

I blink. Isn't this obvious? "To steal a baby doesn't damage the baby's reality. It just grows up somewhere else, with some other people. But all real people of World share the same reality, and anyway after the transition, the child will rejoin its blood ancestors. Baby stealing is wrong, of course, but it isn't a really serious crime."

"And make false coins?"

"The same. False, true—coins are still shared."

He coughs again, this time much harder. I wait. Finally he says, "So when I steal your bicycle, I not violate shared reality too much, because bicycle still somewhere with people of World."

"Of course."

"But when I steal bicycle, I violate shared reality a little?"

"Yes." After a minute I add, "Because the bicycle is, after all, mine. You...made my reality shift a little without sharing the decision with me." I peer at him; how can all this not be obvious to such an intelligent man?

He says, "You are too trusting for be informer, Pek Bengarin."

I feel my throat swell with indignation. I am a very good informer. Haven't I just bound this Terran to me with a private shared reality in order to create an exchange of information? I am about to demand his share of the bargain when he says abruptly, "So why you kill your sister?"

Two of Pek Fakar's people swagger past. They carry the new guns. Across the courtyard a Faller turns slowly to look at them, and even I can read fear on that alien face.

I say, as evenly as I can manage, "I fell prey to an illusion. I thought that Ano was copulating with my lover. She was younger, more intelligent, prettier. I am not very pretty, as you can see. I didn't share the reality with her, or him, and my illusion grew. Finally it exploded in my head, and I... did it." I am breathing hard, and Pek Fakar's people look blurry.

"You remember clear Ano's murder?"

I turn to him in astonishment. "How could I forget it?"

"You cannot. You cannot because memory-building pro-teenz. Memory is strong in your brain. Memory-building pro-teenz are strong in your brain. Scientific research on World children for discover what is structure of pro-teenz, where is pro-teenz, how pro-teenz work. But we discover different thing instead."

"What different thing?" I say, but Pek Walters only shakes his head and begins coughing again. I wonder if the coughing spell is an excuse to violate our bargain. He is, after all, unreal.

Pek Fakar's people have gone inside the prison. The Faller slumps against the far wall. They have not shot him. For this moment, at least, he is not entering the second stage of his perpetual death.

But beside me, Pek Walters coughs blood.

He is dying. I am sure of it, although of course no World healer comes to him. He is dead anyway. Also, his fellow Terrans keep away, looking fearful, which makes me wonder if his disease is catching. This leaves only me. I walk him to his cell, and then wonder why I can't just stay when the door closes. No one will check. Or, if they do, will care. And this may be my last chance to gain the needed information, before either Pek Walters is coffined or Pek Fakar orders me away from him because he is too weak to watch over my supposed blood sickness.

His body has become very hot. During the long night he tosses on his bunk, muttering in his own language, and sometimes those strange alien eyes roll in their sockets. But other times he is clearer, and he looks at me as if he recognizes who I am. Those times, I question him. But the lucid times and unlucid ones blur together. His mind is no longer his own.

"Pek Walters. Where are the memory experiments being conducted? In what place?"

"Memory...memories..." More in his own language. It has the cadences of poetry.

"Pek Walters. In what place are the memory experiments being done?"

"At Rafkit Sarloe," he says, which makes no sense. Rafkit Sarloe is the government center, where no one lives. It is not large. People flow in every day, running the Sections, and out to their villages again at night. There is no square measure of Rafkit Sarloe that is not constantly shared physical reality.

He coughs, more bloody spume, and his eyes roll in his head. I make him sip some water. "Pek Walters. In what place are the memory experiments being done?"

"At Rafkit Sarloe. In the Cloud. At Aulit Prison."

It goes on and on like that. And in the early morning, Pek Walters dies.

There is one moment of greater clarity, somewhere near the end. He looks at me, out of his old, ravaged face gone gaunt with his transition. The disturbing look is back in his eyes, sad and kind, not a look for the unreal to wear. It is too much sharing. He says, so low I must bend over him to hear, "Sick brain talks to itself. You not kill your sister."

"Hush, don't try to talk..."

"Find...Brifjis. Maldon Pek Brifjis, in Rafkit Haddon. Find..." He relapses again into fever.

A few moments after he dies, the armored guards enter the cell, wheeling the coffin full of bondage chemicals. With them is the priest. I want to say: Wait, he is a good man, he doesn't deserve perpetual death—but of course I do not. I am astonished at myself for even thinking it. A guard edges me into the corridor and the door closes.

That same day, I am sent away from Aulit Prison.

"Tell me again. Everything," Pek Brimmidin says.

Pek Brimmidin is just the same: stocky, yellowing, slightly stooped. His cluttered office is just the same. Food dishes, papers, overelaborated sculptures. I stare hungrily at the ugly things. I hadn't realized how much

I'd longed, in prison, for the natural sight of curves. I keep my eyes on the sculptures, partly to hold back my question until the proper time to ask it.

"Pek Walters said he would tell me everything about the experiments that are, yes, going on with World children. In the name of science. But all he had time to tell me was that the experiments involve 'memory-building pro-teenz,' which are tiny pieces of food from which the brain constructs memory. He also said the experiments were going on in Rafkit Sarloe and Aulit Prison."

"And that is all, Pek Bengarin?"

"That is all."

Pek Brimmidin nods curtly. He is trying to appear dangerous, to scare out of me any piece of information I might have forgotten. But Frablit Pek Brimmidin can't appear dangerous to me. I have seen the real thing.

Pek Brimmidin has not changed. But I have.

I ask my question. "I have brought to you all the information I could obtain before the Terran died. Is it sufficient to release me and Ano?"

He runs a hand through his neck fur. "I'm sorry I can't answer that, Pek. I will need to consult my superiors. But I promise to send you word as soon as I can."

"Thank you," I say, and lower my eyes. *You are too trusting for be informer, Pek Bengarin.*

Why didn't I tell Frablit Pek Brimmidin the rest of it, about 'Maldon Pek Brifjis' and 'Rafkit Haddon' and not really killing my sister? Because it is most likely nonsense, the ravings of a fevered brain. Because this 'Maldon Pek Brifjis' might be an innocent World man, who does not deserve trouble brought to him by an unreal alien. Because Pek Walters's words were personal, addressed to me alone, on his deathbed. Because I do not want to discuss Ano with Pek Brimmidin's superiors one more useless painful time.

Because, despite myself, I trust Carryl Pek Walters.

"You may go," Pek Brimmidin says, and I ride my bicycle along the dusty road home.

I make a bargain with Ano's corpse, still lying in curled-finger grace on the bed across from mine. Her beautiful brown hair floats in the chemicals of the coffin. I used to covet that hair desperately, when we were very young. Once I even cut it all off while she slept. But other times I would weave it for her, or braid it with flowers. She was so pretty. At one point, when she was still a child, she wore eight bid rings, one on each finger. Two of the bids were in negotiation between the boys' fathers and ours. Although older, I have never had a single bid.

Did I murder her?

My bargain with her corpse is this: If the Reality & Atonement Section releases me and Ano because of my work in Aulit Prison, I will seek no further. Ano will be free to join our ancestors; I will be fully real. It will no longer matter whether or not I killed my sister, because both of us will again be sharing in the same reality as if I had not. But if Reality & Atonement holds me unreal still longer, after all I have given them, I will try to find this 'Maldon Pek Brifjis.'

I say none of this aloud. The guards at Aulit Prison knew immediately when Pek Walters died, inside a closed and windowless room. They could be watching me here, now. World has no devices to do this, but how did Pek Walters know so much about a World man working with a Terran science experiment? Somewhere there are World people and Terrans in partnership. Terrans, as everyone knows, have all sorts of listening devices we do not.

I kiss Ano's coffin. I don't say it aloud, but I hope desperately that Reality & Atonement releases us. I want to return to shared reality, to the daily warmth and sweetness of belonging, now and forever, to the living and dead of World. I do not want to be an informer any more.

Not for anyone, even myself.

The message comes three days later. The afternoon is warm and I sit outside on my stone bench, watching my neighbor's milkbeasts eye her sturdily fenced flowerbeds. She has new flowers that I don't recognize, with blooms that are entrancing but somehow foreign—could they be Terran? It doesn't seem likely. During my time in Aulit Prison, more people seem to have made up their minds that the Terrans are unreal. I have heard more mutterings, more anger against those who buy from alien traders.

Frablit Pek Brimmidin himself brings the letter from Reality and Atonement, laboring up the road on his ancient bicycle. He has removed his uniform, so as not to embarrass me in front of my neighbors. I watch him ride up, his neck fur damp with unaccustomed exertion, his gray eyes abashed, and I know already what the sealed message must say. Pek

Brimmidin is too kind for his job. That is why he is only a low-level messenger boy all the time, not just today.

These are things I never saw before.

You are too trusting for be informer, Pek Bengarin.

"Thank you, Pek Brimmidin," I say. "Would you like a glass of water? Or pel?"

"No, thank you, Pek," he says. He does not meet my eyes. He waves to my other neighbor, fetching water from the village well, and fumbles meaninglessly with the handle of his bicycle. "I can't stay."

"Then ride safely," I say, and go back in my house. I stand beside Ano and break the seal on the government letter. After I read it, I gaze at her a long time. So beautiful, so sweet-natured. So loved.

Then I start to clean. I scrub every inch of my house, for hours and hours, climbing on a ladder to wash the ceiling, sloshing thick soapsuds in the cracks, scrubbing every surface of every object and carrying the more intricately-shaped outside into the sun to dry. Despite my most intense scrutiny, I find nothing that I can imagine being a listening device. Nothing that looks alien, nothing unreal.

But I no longer know what is real.

Only Bata is up; the other moons have not risen. The sky is clear and starry, the air cool. I wheel my bicycle inside and try to remember everything I need.

Whatever kind of glass Ano's coffin is made of, it is very tough. I have to swing my garden shovel three times, each time with all my strength, before I can break it. On the third blow the glass cracks, then falls leisurely apart into large pieces that bounce slightly when they hit the floor. Chemicals cascade off the bed, a waterfall of clear liquid that smells only slightly acrid.

In my high boots I wade close to the bed and throw containers of water over Ano to wash off chemical residue. The containers are waiting in a neat row by the wall, everything from my largest wash basin to the kitchen bowls. Ano smiles sweetly.

I reach onto the soggy bed and lift her clear.

In the kitchen, I lay her body—limp, soft-limbed—on the floor and strip off her chemical-soaked clothing. I dry her, move her to the waiting blanket, take a last look, and wrap her tightly. The bundle of her and the shovel balances across the handles of my bicycle. I pull off my boots and open the door.

The night smells of my neighbor's foreign flowers. Ano seems weightless. I feel as if I can ride for hours. And I do.

I bury her, weighted with stones, in marshy ground well off a deserted road. The wet dirt will speed the decay, and it is easy to cover the grave with reeds and toglif branches. When I've finished, I bury my clothes and dress in clean ones in my pack. Another few hours of riding and I can find an inn to sleep in. Or a field, if need be.

The morning dawns pearly, with three moons in the sky. Everywhere I ride are flowers, first wild and then cultivated. Although exhausted, I sing softly to the curving blooms, to the sky, to the pale moonlit road. Ano is real, and free.

Go sweetly, sweet sister, to our waiting ancestors.

Two days later I reach Rafkit Haddon.

It is an old city, sloping down the side of a mountain to the sea. The homes of the rich either stand on the shore or perch on the mountain, looking in both cases like rounded great white birds. In between lie a jumble of houses, market squares, government buildings, inns, pel shops, slums and parks, the latter with magnificent old trees and shabby old shrines. The manufacturing shops and warehouses lie to the north, with the docks.

I have experience in finding people. I start with Rituals & Processions. The clerk behind the counter, a pre-initiate of the priesthood, is young and eager to help. "Yes?"

"I am Ajma Pek Goranalit, attached to the household of Menanlin. I have been sent to inquire about the ritual activity of a citizen, Maldon Pek Brifjis. Can you help me?"

"Of course," she beams. An inquiry about ritual activity is never written; discretion is necessary when a great house is considering honoring a citizen by allowing him to honor their ancestors. A person so chosen gains great prestige—and considerable material wealth. I picked the name "Menanlin" after an hour's judicious listening in a crowded pel shop. The family is old, numerous, and discreet.

"Let me see," she says, browsing among her public records. "Brifjis... Brifjis...it's a common name, of course...which citizen, Pek?"

"Maldon."

"Oh, yes…here. He paid for two musical tributes to his ancestors last year, made a donation to the Rafkit Haddon Priest House…Oh! And he was chosen to honor the ancestors of the house of Choulalait!"

She sounds awe-struck. I nod. "We know about that, of course. But is there anything else?"

"No, I don't think so…wait. He paid for a charity tribute for the ancestors of his clu merchant, Lam Pek Flanoe, a poor man. Quite a lavish tribute, too. Music, and three priests."

"Kind," I said.

"Very! Three priests!" Her young eyes shine. "Isn't it wonderful how many truly kind people share reality?"

"Yes," I say. "It is."

I find the clu merchant by the simple method of asking for him in several market squares. Sales of all fuels are of course slow in the summer; the young relatives left in charge of the clu stalls are happy to chat with strangers. Lam Pek Flanoe lives in a run-down neighborhood just behind the great houses by the sea. The neighborhood is home to servants and merchants who provide for the rich. Four more glasses of pel in three more pel shops, and I know that Maldon Pek Brifjis is currently a guest in the home of a rich widow. I know the widow's address. I know that Pek Brifjis is a healer.

A healer.

Sick brain talks to itself. You not kill your sister.

I am dizzy from four glasses of pel. Enough. I find an inn, the kind where no one asks questions, and sleep without the shared reality of dreams.

It takes me a day, disguised as a street cleaner, to decide which of the men coming and going from the rich widow's house is Pek Brifjis. Then I spend three days following him, in various guises. He goes a lot of places and talks to a lot of people, but none of them seems unusual for a rich healer with a personal pleasure in collecting antique water carafes. On the fourth day I look for a good opportunity to approach him, but this turns out to be unnecessary.

"Pek," a man says to me as I loiter, dressed as a vendor of sweet flatbreads, outside the baths on Elindel Street. I have stolen the sweets before dawn from the open kitchen of a bake shop. I know at once that the man approaching me is a bodyguard, and that he is very good. It's in the way he walks, looks at me, places his hand on my arm. He is also very handsome, but that thought barely registers. Handsome men are never for such as me. They are for Ano.

Were for Ano.

"Come with me, please," the bodyguard says, and I don't argue. He leads me to the back of the baths, through a private entrance, to a small room apparently used for private grooming of some sort. The only furniture is two small stone tables. He checks me, expertly but gently, for weapons, looking even in my mouth. Satisfied, he indicates where I am to stand, and opens a second door.

Maldon Pek Brifjis enters, wrapped in a bathing robe of rich imported cloth. He is younger than Carryl Walters, a vigorous man in vigorous prime. His eyes are striking, a deep purple with long gold lines radiating from their centers. He says immediately, "Why have you been following me for three days?"

"Someone told me to," I say. I have nothing to lose by an honest shared reality, although I still don't fully believe I have anything to gain.

"Who? You may say anything in front of my guard."

"Carryl Pek Walters."

The purple eyes deepen even more. "Pek Walters is dead."

"Yes," I say. "Perpetually. I was with him when he entered the second stage of death."

"And where was that?" He is testing me.

"In Aulit Prison. His last words instructed me to find you. To...ask you something."

"What do you wish to ask me?"

"Not what I thought I would ask," I say, and realize that I have made the decision to tell him everything. Until I saw him up close, I wasn't completely sure what I would do. I can no longer share reality with World, not even if I went to Frablit Pek Brimmidin with exactly the knowledge he wants about the scientific experiments on children. That would not atone for releasing Ano before the Section agreed. And Pek Brimmidin is only a messenger, anyway. No, less than a messenger: a tool, like a garden shovel, or a bicycle. He does not share the reality of his users. He only thinks he does.

As I had thought I did.

I say, "I want to know if I killed my sister. Pek Walters said I did not. He said 'sick brain talks to itself,' and that I had not killed Ano. And to ask you. Did I kill my sister?"

Pek Brifjis sits down on one of the stone tables. "I don't know," he says, and I see his neck fur quiver. "Perhaps you did. Perhaps you did not."

"How can I discover which?"

"You cannot."

"Ever?"

"Ever." And then, "I am sorry."

Dizziness takes me. The "low blood pressure." The next thing I know, I lie on the floor of the small room, with Pek Brifjis's fingers on my elbow pulse. I struggle to sit up.

"No, wait," he says. "Wait a moment. Have you eaten today?"

"Yes."

"Well, wait a moment anyway. I need to think."

He does, the purple eyes turning inward, his fingers absently pressing the inside of my elbow. Finally he says, "You are an informer. That's why you were released from Aulit Prison after Pek Walters died. You inform for the government."

I don't answer. It no longer matters.

"But you have left informing. Because of what Pek Walters told you. Because he told you that the skits-oh-free-nia experiments might have… No. It can't be."

He too has used a word I don't know. It sounds Terran. Again I struggle to sit up, to leave. There is no hope for me here. This healer can tell me nothing.

He pushes me back down on the floor and says swiftly, "When did your sister die?" His eyes have changed once again; the long golden flecks are brighter, radiating from the center like glowing spokes. "Please, Pek, this is immensely important. To both of us."

"Two years ago, and 152 days."

"Where? In what city?"

"Village. Our village. Gofkit Ilo."

"Yes," he says. "Yes. Tell me everything you remember of her death. Everything."

This time I push him aside and sit up. Blood rushes from my head, but anger overcomes the dizziness. "I will tell you nothing. Who do you people think you are, ancestors? To tell me I killed Ano, then tell me I didn't, then say you don't know—to destroy the hope of atonement I had as an informer, then to tell me there is no other hope—no, there might be hope—no, there's not—how can you live with yourself? How can you twist people's brains away from shared reality and offer nothing to replace it!" I am screaming. The bodyguard glances at the door. I don't care; I go on screaming.

"You are doing experiments on children, wrecking their reality as you have wrecked mine! You are a murderer—" But I don't get to scream all that. Maybe I don't get to scream any of it. For a needle slides into my elbow, at the inner pulse where Maldon Brifjis has been holding it, and the room slides away as easily as Ano into her grave.

A bed, soft and silky, beneath me. Rich wall hangings. The room is very warm. A scented breeze whispers across my bare stomach. Bare? I sit up and discover I am dressed in the gauzy skirt, skimpy bandeau, and flirting veil of a prostitute.

At my first movement, Pek Brifjis crosses from the fireplace to my bed. "Pek. This room does not allow sound to escape. Do not resume screaming. Do you understand?"

I nod. His bodyguard stands across the room. I pull the flirting veil from my face.

"I am sorry about that," Pek Brifjis says. "It was necessary to dress you in a way that accounts for a bodyguard carrying a drugged woman into a private home without raising questions."

A private home. I guess that this is the rich widow's house by the sea. A room that does not allow sound to escape. A needle unlike ours: sharp and sure. Brain experiments. "Skits-oh-fren-ia."

I say, "You work with the Terrans."

"No," he says. "I do not."

"But Pek Walters..." It doesn't matter. "What are you going to do with me?"

He says, "I am going to offer you a trade."

"What sort of trade?"

"Information in return for your freedom."

And he says he does not work with Terrans. I say, "What use is freedom to me?" although of course I don't expect him to understand that. I can never be free.

"Not that kind of freedom," he says. "I won't just let you go from this room. I will let you rejoin your ancestors, and Ano."

I gape at him.

"Yes, Pek. I will kill you and bury you myself, where your body can decay."

"You would violate shared reality like that? For me?"

His purple eyes deepen again. For a moment, something in those eyes looks almost like Pek Walters's blue ones. "Please understand. I think there is a strong chance you did not kill Ano. Your village was one where…subjects were used for experimentation. I think that is the true shared reality here."

I say nothing. A little of his assurance disappears. "Or so I believe. Will you agree to the trade?"

"Perhaps," I say. Will he actually do what he promises? I can't be sure. But there is no other way for me. I cannot hide from the government all the years until I die. I am too young. And when they find me, they will send me back to Aulit, and when I die there they will put me in a coffin of preservative chemicals…

I would never see Ano again.

The healer watches me closely. Again I see the Pek Walters look in his eyes: sadness and pity.

"Perhaps I will agree to the trade," I say, and wait for him to speak again about the night Ano died. But instead he says, "I want to show you something."

He nods at the bodyguard who leaves the room, returning a few moments later. By the hand he leads a child, a little girl, clean and well-dressed. One look makes my neck fur bristle. The girl's eyes are flat and unseeing. She mutters to herself. I offer a quick appeal for protection to my ancestors. The girl is unreal, without the capacity to perceive shared reality, even though she is well over the age of reason. She is not human. She should have been destroyed.

"This is Ori," Pek Brifjis says. The girl suddenly laughs, a wild demented laugh, and peers at something only she can see.

"Why is it here?" I listen to the harshness in my own voice.

"Ori was born real. She was made this way by the scientific brain experiments of the government."

"Of the government! That is a lie!"

"Is it? Do you still, Pek, have such trust in your government?"

"No, but…" To make me continue to earn Ano's freedom, even after I had met their terms…to lie to Pek Brimmidin…those offenses against shared reality are one thing. The destruction of a real person's physical body, as I had done with Ano's (had I?) is another, far far worse.

To destroy a mind, the instrument of perceiving shared reality...Pek Brifjis lies.

He says, "Pek, tell me about the night Ano died."

"Tell me about this...thing!"

"All right." He sits down in a chair beside my luxurious bed. The thing wanders around the room, muttering. It seems unable to stay still.

"She was born Ori Malfisit, in a small village in the far north—"

"What village?" I need desperately to see if he falters on details.

He does not. "Gofkit Ramloe. Of real parents, simple people, an old and established family. At six years old, Ori was playing in the forest with some other children when she disappeared. The other children said they heard something thrashing toward the marshes. The family decided she had been carried off by a wild kilfreit—there are still some left, you know, that far north—and held a procession in honor of Ori's joining their ancestors.

"But that's not what happened to Ori. She was stolen by two men, unreal prisoners promised atonement and restoration to full reality, just as you were. Ori was carried off to Rafkit Sarloe, with eight other children from all over World. There they were given to the Terrans, who were told that they were orphans who could be used for experiment. The experiments were ones that would not hurt or damage the children in any way."

I look at Ori, now tearing a table scarf into shreds and muttering. Her empty eyes turn to mine, and I have to look away.

"This part is difficult," Pek Brifjis says. "Listen hard, Pek. The Terrans truly did not hurt the children. They put ee-lek-trodes on their heads... you don't know what that means. They found ways to see which parts of their brains worked the same as Terran brains and which did not. They used a number of tests and machines and drugs. None of it hurt the children, who lived at the Terran scientific compound and were cared for by World childwatchers. At first the children missed their parents, but they were young, and after a while they were happy."

I glance again at Ori. The unreal, not sharing in common reality, are isolated and therefore dangerous. A person with no world in common with others will violate those others as easily as cutting flowers. Under such conditions, pleasure is possible, but not happiness.

Pek Brifjis runs his hand through his neck fur. "The Terrans worked with World healers, of course, teaching them. It was the usual trade, only this time we received the information and they the physical reality:

children and watchers. There was no other way World could permit Terrans to handle our children. Our healers were there every moment."

He looks at me. I say, "Yes," just because something must be said.

"Do you know, Pek, what it is like to realize you have lived your whole life according to beliefs that are not true?"

"No!" I say, so loudly that Ori looks up with her mad, unreal gaze. She smiles. I don't know why I spoke so loud. What Pek Brifjis said has nothing to do with me. Nothing at all.

"Well, Pek Walters knew. He realized that the experiments he participated in, harmless to the subjects and in aid of biological understanding of species differences, were being used for something else. The roots of skits-oh-free-nia, misfiring brain sir-kits—" He is off on a long explanation that means nothing to me. Too many Terran words, too much strangeness. Pek Brifjis is no longer talking to me. He is talking to himself, in some sort of pain I don't understand.

Suddenly the purple eyes snap back to mine. "What all that means, Pek, is that a few of the healers—our own healers, from World—found out how to manipulate the Terran science. They took it and used it to put into minds memories that did not happen."

"Not possible!"

"It is possible. The brain is made very excited, with Terran devices, while the false memory is recited over and over. Then different parts of the brain are made to…to recirculate memories and emotions over and over. Like water recirculated through mill races. The water gets all scrambled together…No. Think of it this way: different parts of the brain send signals to each other. The signals are forced to loop together, and every loop makes the unreal memories stronger. It is apparently in common use on Terra, although tightly controlled."

Sick brain talks to itself.

"But—"

"There are no objections possible, Pek. It is real. It happened. It happened to Ori. The World scientists made her brain remember things that had not happened. Small things, at first. That worked. When they tried larger memories, something went wrong. It left her like this. They were still learning; that was five years ago. They got better, much better. Good enough to experiment on adult subjects who could then be returned to shared reality."

"One can't plant memories like flowers, or uproot them like weeds!"

"These people could. And did."

"But—why?"

"Because the World healers who did this—and they were only a few—saw a different reality."

"I don't—"

"They saw the Terrans able to do everything. Make better machines than we can, from windmills to bicycles. Fly to the stars. Cure disease. Control nature. Many World people are afraid of Terrans, Pek. And of Fallers and Huhuhubs. Because their reality is superior to ours."

"There is only one comon reality," I said. "The Terrans just know more about it than we do!"

"Perhaps. But Terran knowledge makes people uneasy. And afraid. And jealous."

Jealous. Ano saying to me in the kitchen, with Bata and Cap bright at the window, "I will too go out tonight to see him! You can't stop me! You're just jealous, a jealous ugly shriveled thing that not even your lover wants, so you don't wish me to have any—" And the red flood swamping my brain, the kitchen knife, the blood—

"Pek?" the healer says. "Pek?"

"I'm…all right. The jealous healers, they hurt their own people, World people, for revenge on the Terrans—that makes no sense!"

"The healers acted with great sorrow. They knew what they were doing to people. But they needed to perfect the technique of inducing controlled skits-oh-free-nia…they needed to do it. To make people angry at Terrans. Angry enough to forget the attractive trade goods and rise up against the aliens. To cause war. The healers are mistaken, Pek. We have not had a war on World in a thousand years; our people cannot understand how hard the Terrans would strike back. But you must understand: the outlaw scientists thought they were doing the right thing. They thought they were creating anger in order to save World.

"And another thing—with the help of the government, they were careful not to make any World man or woman permanently unreal. The adults manipulated into murder were all offered atonement as informers. The children are all cared for. The mistakes, like Ori, will be allowed to decay someday, to return to her ancestors. I will see to that myself."

Ori tears the last of the scarf into pieces, smiling horribly, her flat eyes empty. What unreal memories fill her head?

I say bitterly, "Doing the right thing…letting me believe I killed my sister!"

"When you rejoin your ancestors, you will find it isn't so. And the means of rejoining them was made available to you: the completion of your informing atonement."

But now that atonement never will be completed. I stole Ano and buried her without Section consent. Maldon Brifjis, of course, does not know this.

Through my pain and anger I blurt, "And what of you, Pek Brifjis? You work with these criminal healers, aiding them in emptying children like Ori of reality—"

"I don't work with them. I thought you smarter, Pek. I work against them. And so did Carryl Walters, which is why he died in Aulit Prison."

"Against them?"

"Many of us do. Carryl Walters among them. He was an informer. And my friend."

Neither of us says anything. Pek Brifjis stares into the fire. I stare at Ori, who has begun to grimace horribly. She squats on an intricately woven curved rug which looks very old. A reek suddenly fills the room. Ori does not share with the rest of us the reality of piss closets. She throws back her head and laughs, a horrible sound like splintering metal.

"Take her away," Pek Brifjis says wearily to the guard, who looks unhappy. "I'll clean up here." To me he adds, "We can't allow any servants in here with you."

The guard leads away the grimacing child. Pek Brifjis kneels and scrubs at the rug with chimney rags dipped in water from my carafe. I remember that he collects antique water carafes. What a long way that must seem from scrubbing shit: from Ori, from Carryl Walters coughing out his lungs in Aulit Prison, among aliens.

"Pek Brifjis—did I kill my sister?"

He looks up. There is shit on his hands. "There is no way to be absolutely sure. It is possible you were one of the experiment subjects from your village. You would have been drugged in your house, to awake with your sister murdered and your mind altered."

I say, more quietly than I have said anything else in this room, "You will really kill me, let me decay, and enable me to rejoin my ancestors?"

Pek Brifjis stands and wipes the shit from his hands. "I will."

"But what will you do if I refuse? If instead I ask to return home?"

"If you do that, the government will arrest you and once more promise you atonement—if you inform on those of us working to oppose them."

"Not if I go first to whatever part of the government is truly working to end the experiments. Surely you aren't saying the entire government is doing this...thing."

"Of course not. But do you know for certain which Sections, and which officials in those Sections, wish for war with the Terrans, and which do not? We can't be sure. How can you?"

Frablit Pek Brimmidin is innocent, I think. But the thought is useless. Pek Brimmidin is innocent, but powerless.

It tears my soul to think that the two might be the same thing.

Pek Brifjis rubs at the damp carpet with the toe of his boot. He puts the rags in a lidded jar and washes his hands at the washstand. A faint stench still hangs in the air. He comes to stand beside my bed.

"Is that what you want, Uli Pek Bengarin? That I let you leave this house, not knowing what you will do, whom you will inform on? That I endanger everything we have done in order to convince you of its truth?"

"Or you can kill me and let me rejoin my ancestors. Which is what you think I will choose, isn't it? That choice would let you keep faith with the reality you have decided is true, and still keep yourself secret from the criminals. Killing me would be easiest for you. But only if I consent to my murder. Otherwise, you will violate even the reality you have decided to perceive."

He stares down at me, a muscular man with beautiful purple eyes. A healer who would kill. A patriot defying his government to prevent a violent war. A sinner who does all he can to minimize his sin and keep it from denying him the chance to rejoin his own ancestors. A believer in shared reality who is trying to bend the reality without breaking the belief.

I keep quiet. The silence stretches on. Finally it is Pek Brifjis that breaks it. "I wish Carryl Walters had never sent you to me."

"But he did. And I choose to return to my village. Will you let me go, or keep me prisoner here, or murder me without my consent?"

"Damn you," he says, and I recognize the word as one Carryl Walters used, about the unreal souls in Aulit Prison.

"Exactly," I say. "What will you do, Pek? Which of your supposed multiple realities will you choose now?"

It is a hot night, and I cannot sleep.

I lie in my tent on the wide empty plain and listen to the night noises. Rude laughter from the pel tent, where a group of miners drinks far too late at night for men who must bore into hard rock at dawn. Snoring from the tent to my right. Muffled lovemaking from a tent farther down the row, I'm not sure whose. The woman giggles, high and sweet.

I have been a miner for half a year now. After I left the northern village of Gofkit Ramloe, Ori's village, I just kept heading north. Here on the equator, where World harvests its tin and diamonds and pel berries and salt, life is both simpler and less organized. Papers are not necessary. Many of the miners are young, evading their government service for one reason or another. Reasons that must seem valid to them. Here government sections rule weakly, compared to the rule of the mining and farming companies. There are no messengers on Terran bicycles. There is no Terran science. There are no Terrans.

There are shrines, of course, and rituals and processions, and tributes to one's ancestors. But these things actually receive less attention than in the cities, because they are more taken for granted. Do you pay attention to air?

The woman giggles again, and this time I recognize the sound. Awi Pek Crafmal, the young runaway from another island. She is a pretty thing, and a hard worker. Sometimes she reminds me of Ano.

I asked a great many questions in Gofkit Ramloe. Ori Malfisit, Pek Brifjis said her name was. An old and established family. But I asked and asked, and no such family had ever lived in Gofkit Ramloe. Wherever Ori came from, and however she had been made into that unreal and empty vessel shitting on a rich carpet, she had not started her poor little life in Gofkit Ramloe.

Did Maldon Brifjis know I would discover that, when he released me from the rich widow's house overlooking the sea? He must have. Or maybe, despite knowing I was an informer, he didn't understand that I would actually go to Gofkit Ramloe and check. You can't understand everything.

Sometimes, in the darkest part of the night, I wish I had taken Pek Brifjis's offer to return me to my ancestors.

I work on the rock piles of the mine during the day, among miners who lift sledges and shatter solid stone. They talk, and curse, and revile the Terrans, although few miners have as much as seen one. After work the miners sit in camp and drink pel, lifting huge mugs with dirty hands, and laugh at obscene jokes. They all share the same reality, and it binds them together, in simple and happy strength.

I have strength, too. I have the strength to swing my sledge with the other women, many of whom have the same rough plain looks as I, and who are happy to accept me as one of them. I had the strength to shatter Ano's coffin, and to bury her even when I thought the price to me was perpetual death. I had the strength to follow Carryl Walters's words about the brain experiments and seek Maldon Brifjis. I had the strength to twist Pek Brifjis's divided mind to make him let me go.

But do I have the strength to go where all of that leads me? Do I have the strength to look at Frablit Brimmidin's reality, and Carryl Walters's reality, and Ano's, and Maldon Brifjis's, and Ori's—and try to find the places that match and the places that don't? Do I have the strength to live on, never knowing if I killed my sister, or if I did not? Do I have the strength to doubt everything, and live with doubt, and sort through the millions of separate realities on World, searching for the true pieces of each—assuming that I can even recognize them?

Should anyone have to live like that? In uncertainty, in doubt, in loneliness. Alone in one's mind, in an isolated and unshared reality.

I would like to return to the days when Ano was alive. Or even to the days when I was an informer. To the days when I shared in World's reality, and knew it to be solid beneath me, like the ground itself. To the days when I knew what to think, and so did not have to.

To the days before I became—unwillingly—as terrifyingly real as I am now.

Afterword to "The Flowers of Aulit Prison"

What is reality? This is one of the two great questions that have preoccupied philosophers throughout the ages (the other is, How can I get more sex?) Is reality "objective," outside of ourselves whether we are here or not, or do we create it through our limited perceptions, limited mental capacities, limited knowledge of large and unseen truths?

I first explored these ideas in "Trinity," where the search was for an unseen God. In "The Flowers of Aulit Prison" I was after something else: the creation of an alien perception of reality, from the alien's point of view. And yet despite her consensus reality, Uli Pek Bengarin has many human traits: resentment, guilt, cunning, the desires for both revenge and atonement. Even when we try to create the alien, we are still bound to what is comprehensible to us as both writers and readers, to reality as we know it.

"The Flowers of Aulit Prison," due to vagaries of award qualifications, won the 1997 Sturgeon Award and the 1998 Nebula.

THE PRICE OF ORANGES

"I'm worried about my granddaughter," Harry Kramer said, passing half of his sandwich to Manny Feldman. Manny took it eagerly. The sandwich was huge, thick slices of beef and horseradish between fresh slabs of crusty bread. Pigeons watched the park bench hopefully.

"Jackie. The granddaughter who writes books," Manny said. Harry watched to see that Manny ate. You couldn't trust Manny to eat enough; he stayed too skinny. At least in Harry's opinion. Manny, Jackie—the world, Harry sometimes thought, had all grown too skinny when he somehow hadn't been looking. Skimpy. Stretched feeling. Harry nodded to see horseradish spurt in a satisfying stream down Manny's scraggly beard.

"Jackie. Yes," Harry said.

"So what's wrong with her? She's sick?" Manny eyed Harry's strudel, cherry with real yeast bread. Harry passed it to him. "Harry, the whole thing? I couldn't."

"Take it, take it, I don't want it. You should eat. No, she's not sick. She's miserable." When Manny, his mouth full of strudel, didn't answer, Harry put a hand on Manny's arm. *"Miserable."*

Manny swallowed hastily. "How do you know? You saw her this week?"

"No. Next Tuesday. She's bringing me a book by a friend of hers. I know from this." He drew a magazine from an inner pocket of his coat. The coat was thick tweed, almost new, with wooden buttons. On the cover of the glossy magazine a woman smiled contemptuously. A woman with hollow, starved-looking cheeks who obviously didn't get enough to eat either.

"That's not a book," Manny pointed out.

"So she writes stories, too. Listen to this, just listen. 'I stood in my backyard, surrounded by the false bright toxin-fed green, and realized that the earth was dead. What else could it be, since we humans swarmed upon it like maggots on carrion, growing our hectic gleaming molds, leaving our slime trails across the senseless surface?' Does that sound like a happy woman?"

"Hoo boy," Manny said.

"It's all like that. 'Don't read my things, Popsy,' she says. 'You're not in the audience for my things.' Then she smiles without ever once showing her teeth." Harry flung both arms wide. "Who else should be in the audience but her own grandfather?"

Manny swallowed the last of the strudel. Pigeons fluttered angrily. "She never shows her teeth when she smiles? Never?"

"Never."

"Hoo boy," Manny said. "Did you want all of that orange?"

"No, I brought it for you, to take home. But did you finish that whole half a sandwich already?"

"I thought I'd take it home," Manny said humbly. He showed Harry the tip of the sandwich, wrapped in the thick brown butcher paper, protruding from the pocket of his old coat.

Harry nodded approvingly. "Good, good. Take the orange, too. I brought it for you."

Manny took the orange. Three teenagers carrying huge shrieking radios sauntered past. Manny started to put his hands over his ears, received a look of dangerous contempt from the teenager with green hair, and put his hands on his lap. The kid tossed an empty beer bottle onto the pavement before their feet. It shattered. Harry scowled fiercely but Manny stared straight ahead. When the cacophony had passed, Manny said, "Thank you for the orange. Fruit, it costs so much this time of year."

Harry still scowled. "Not in 1937."

"Don't start that again, Harry."

Harry said sadly, "Why won't you ever believe me? Could I afford to bring all this food if I got it at 1989 prices? Could I afford this coat? Have you seen buttons like this in 1989, on a new coat? Have you seen sandwiches wrapped in that kind of paper since we were young? Have you? Why won't you believe me?"

Manny slowly peeled his orange. The rind was pale, and the orange had seeds. "Harry. Don't start."

"But why won't you just come to my room and *see*?"

Manny sectioned the orange. "Your room. A cheap furnished room in a Social Security hotel. Why should I go? I know what will be there. What will be there is the same thing in my room. A bed, a chair, a table, a hot plate, some cans of food. Better I should meet you here in the park, get at least a little fresh air." He looked at Harry meekly, the orange clutched in one hand. "Don't misunderstand. It's not from a lack of friendship I say this. You're good to me, you're the best friend I have. You bring me things from a great deli, you talk to me, you share with me the family I don't have. It's enough, Harry. It's more than enough. I don't need to see where you live like I live."

Harry gave it up. There were moods, times, when it was just impossible to budge Manny. He dug in, and in he stayed. "Eat your orange."

"It's a good orange. So tell me more about Jackie."

"Jackie." Harry shook his head. Two kids on bikes tore along the path. One of them swerved towards Manny and snatched the orange from his hand. "Aw riggghhhtttt!"

Harry scowled after the child. It had been a girl. Manny just wiped the orange juice off his fingers onto the knee of his pants. "Is everything she writes so depressing?"

"Everything," Harry said. "Listen to this one." He drew out another magazine, smaller, bound in rough paper with a stylized line drawing of a woman's private parts on the cover. On the cover! Harry held the magazine with one palm spread wide over the drawing, which made it difficult to keep the pages open while he read. "'She looked at her mother in the only way possible: with contempt, contempt for all the betrayals and compromises that had been her mother's life, for the sad soft lines of defeat around her mother's mouth, for the bright artificial dress too young for her wasted years, for even the leather handbag, Gucci of course, filled with blood money for having sold her life to a man who had long ceased to want it.'"

"Hoo boy," Manny said. "About a *mother* she wrote that?"

"About everybody. All the time."

"And where is Barbara?"

"Reno again. Another divorce." How many had that been? After two, did anybody count? Harry didn't count. He imagined Barbara's life as a large roulette wheel like the ones on TV, little silver men bouncing in and out of red and black pockets. Why didn't she get dizzy?

Manny said slowly, "I always thought there was a lot of love in her."

"A lot of that she's got," Harry said dryly.

"Not Barbara—Jackie. A lot of...I don't know. Sweetness. Under the way she is."

"The way she is," Harry said gloomily. "Prickly. A cactus. But you're right, Manny, I know what you mean. She just needs someone to soften her up. Love her back, maybe. Although I love her."

The two old men looked at each other. Manny said, "Harry..."

"I know, I know. I'm only a grandfather, my love doesn't count, I'm just there. Like air. 'You're wonderful, Popsy,' she says, and still no teeth when she smiles. But you know, Manny—you are right!" Harry jumped up from the bench. "You are! What she needs is a young man to love her!"

Manny looked alarmed. "I didn't say—"

"I don't know why I didn't think of it before!"

"Harry—"

"And her stories, too! Full of ugly murders, ugly places, unhappy endings. What she needs is something to show her that writing could be about sweetness, too."

Manny was staring at him hard. Harry felt a rush of affection. That Manny should have the answer! Skinny wonderful Manny!

Manny said slowly, "Jackie said to me, 'I write about reality.' That's what she said, Harry."

"So there's no sweetness in reality? Put sweetness in her life, her writing will go sweet. She *needs* this, Manny. A really nice fellow!"

Two men in jogging suits ran past. One of their Reeboks came down on a shard of beer bottle. "Every fucking time!" he screamed, bending over to inspect his shoe. "Fucking park!"

"Well, what do you expect?" the other drawled, looking at Manny and Harry. "Although you'd think that if we could clean up Lake Erie..."

"Fucking derelicts!" the other snarled. They jogged away.

"Of course," Harry said, "it might not be easy to find the sort of guy to convince Jackie."

"Harry, I think you should maybe think—"

"Not here," Harry said suddenly. "Not here. *There*. In 1937."

"Harry..."

"Yeah," Harry said, nodding several times. Excitement filled him like light, like electricity. What an idea! "It was different then."

Manny said nothing. When he stood up, the sleeve of his coat exposed the number tattooed on his wrist. He said quietly, "It was no paradise in 1937 either, Harry."

Harry seized Manny's hand. "I'm going to do it, Manny. Find someone for her there. Bring him here."

Manny sighed. "Tomorrow at the chess club, Harry? At one o'clock? It's Tuesday."

"I'll tell you then how I'm coming with this."

"Fine, Harry. Fine. All my wishes go with you. You know that."

Harry stood up too, still holding Manny's hand. A middle-aged man staggered to the bench and slumped onto it. The smell of whiskey rose from him in waves. He eyed Manny and Harry with scorn. "Fucking fags."

"Good night, Harry."

"Manny—if you'd only come...money goes so much farther there..."

"Tomorrow at one. At the chess club."

Harry watched his friend walk away. Manny's foot dragged a little; the knee must be bothering him again. Harry wished Manny would see a doctor. Maybe a doctor would know why Manny stayed so skinny.

Harry walked back to his hotel. In the lobby, old men slumped in upholstery thin from wear, burned from cigarettes, shiny in the seat from long sitting. Sitting and sitting, Harry thought—life measured by the seat of the pants. And now it was getting dark. No one would go out from here until the next daylight. Harry shook his head.

The elevator wasn't working again. He climbed the stairs to the third floor. Halfway there, he stopped, felt in his pocket, counted five quarters, six dimes, two nickels, and eight pennies. He returned to the lobby. "Could I have two dollar bills for this change, please? Maybe old bills?"

The clerk looked at him suspiciously. "Your rent paid up?"

"Certainly," Harry said. The woman grudgingly gave him the money.

"Thank you. You look very lovely today, Mrs. Raduski." Mrs. Raduski snorted.

In his room, Harry looked for his hat. He finally found it under his bed—how had it gotten under his bed? He dusted it off and put it on. It had cost him $3.25. He opened the closet door, parted the clothes hanging from their metal pole—like Moses parting the sea, he always thought, a Moses come again—and stepped to the back of the closet, remembering with his body rather than his mind the sharp little twist to the right just past the far gray sleeve of his good wool suit.

He stepped out into the bare corner of a warehouse. Cobwebs brushed his hat; he had stepped a little too far right. Harry crossed the empty concrete space to where the lumber stacks started, and threaded his way through them. The lumber, too, was covered with cobwebs; not much building going on. On his way out the warehouse door, Harry passed the night watchman coming on duty.

"Quiet all day, Harry?"

"As a church, Rudy," Harry said. Rudy laughed. He laughed a lot. He was also indisposed to question very much. The first time he had seen Harry coming out of the warehouse in a bemused daze, he must have assumed that Harry had been hired to work there. Peering at Rudy's round, vacant face, Harry realized that he must hold this job because he was someone's uncle, someone's cousin, someone's something. Harry had felt a small glow of approval; families should take care of their own. He had told Rudy that he had lost his key and asked him for another.

Outside it was late afternoon. Harry began walking. Eventually there were people walking past him, beside him, across the street from him. Everybody wore hats. The women wore bits of velvet or wool with dotted veils across their noses and long, graceful dresses in small prints. The men wore fedoras with suits as baggy as Harry's. When he reached the park there were children, girls in long black tights and hard shoes, boys in buttoned shirts. Everyone looked like it was Sunday morning.

Pushcarts and shops lined the sidewalks. Harry bought a pair of socks, thick gray wool, for 89 cents. When the man took his dollar, Harry held his breath: each first time made a little pip in his stomach. But no one ever looked at the dates of old bills. He bought two oranges for five cents each, and then, thinking of Manny, bought a third. At a candy store he bought *G-8 and His Battle Aces* for fifteen cents. At The Collector's Cozy in the other time they would gladly give him thirty dollars for it. Finally, he bought a cherry Coke for a nickel and headed toward the park.

"Oh, excuse me," said a young man who bumped into Harry on the sidewalk. "I'm so sorry!" Harry looked at him hard: but, no. Too young. Jackie was twenty-eight.

Some children ran past, making for the movie theater. Spencer Tracy in *Captains Courageous*. Harry sat down on a green-painted wooden bench under a pair of magnificent Dutch elms. On the bench lay a newsmagazine. Harry glanced at it to see when in September this was: the 28th. The cover pictured a young blond Nazi soldier standing at stiff salute. Harry thought again of Manny, frowned, and turned the magazine cover down.

For the next hour, people walked past. Harry studied them carefully. When it got too dark to see, he walked back to the warehouse, on the way buying an apple kuchen at a bakery with a curtain behind the counter looped back to reveal a man in his shirt sleeves eating a plate of stew at a table bathed in soft yellow lamplight. The kuchen cost thirty-two cents.

At the warehouse, Harry let himself in with his key, slipped past Rudy nodding over *Paris Nights*, and walked to his cobwebby corner. He emerged from his third-floor closet into his room. Beyond the window, sirens wailed and wailed and would not stop.

✹

"So how's it going?" Manny asked. He dripped kuchen crumbs on the chessboard; Harry brushed them away. Manny had him down a knight.

"It's going to take some time to find somebody that's right," Harry said. "I'd like to have someone by next Tuesday when I meet Jackie for dinner, but I don't know. It's not easy. There are requirements. He has to be young enough to be attractive, but old enough to understand Jackie. He has to be sweet-natured enough to do her some good, but strong enough not to panic at jumping over fifty-two years. Somebody educated. An educated man—he might be more curious than upset by my closet. Don't you think?"

"Better watch your queen," Manny said, moving his rook. "So how are you going to find him?"

"It takes time," Harry said. "I'm working on it." Manny shook his head. "You have to get somebody here, you have to convince him he *is* here, you have to keep him from turning right around and running back in time through your shirts…I don't know, Harry. I don't know. I've been thinking. This thing is not simple. What if you did something wrong? Took somebody important out of 1937?"

"I won't pick anybody important."

"What if you made a mistake and brought your own grandfather? And something happened to him here?"

"My grandfather was already dead in 1937."

"What if you brought me? I'm already here."

"You didn't live here in 1937."

"What if you brought you?"

"I didn't live here either."

"What if you…"

"Manny," Harry said, 'I'm not bringing somebody important. I'm not bringing somebody we know. I'm not bringing somebody for permanent.

I'm just bringing a nice guy for Jackie to meet, go dancing, see a different kind of nature. A different view of what's possible. An innocence. I'm sure there are fellows here that would do it, but I don't know any, and I don't know how to bring any to her. From there I know. Is this so complicated? Is this so unpredictable?"

"Yes," Manny said. He had on his stubborn look again. How could somebody so skimpy look so stubborn? Harry sighed and moved his lone knight.

"I brought you some whole socks."

"Thank you. That knight, it's not going to help you much."

"Lectures. That's what there was there that there isn't here. Everybody went to lectures. No TV, movies cost money, they went to free lectures."

"I remember," Manny said. "I was a young man myself. Harry, this thing is not simple."

"Yes, it is," Harry said stubbornly.

"1937 was not simple."

"It will work, Manny."

"Check," Manny said.

That evening, Harry went back. This time it was the afternoon of September 16. On newsstands the *New York Times* announced that President Roosevelt and John L. Lewis had talked pleasantly at the White House. Cigarettes cost thirteen cents a pack. Women wore cotton stockings and clunky, high-heeled shoes. Schrafft's best chocolates were sixty cents a pound. Small boys addressed Harry as "sir."

He attended six lectures in two days. A Madame Trefania lectured on theosophy to a hall full of badly dressed women with thin, pursed lips. A union organizer roused an audience to a pitch that made Harry leave after the first thirty minutes. A skinny, nervous missionary showed slides of religious outposts in China. An archaeologist back from a Mexican dig gave a dry, impatient talk about temples to an audience of three people. A New Deal Democrat spoke passionately about aiding the poor, but afterwards addressed all the women present as "Sister." Finally, just when Harry was starting to feel discouraged, he found it.

A museum offered a series of lectures on "Science of Today—and Tomorrow." Harry heard a slim young man with a reddish beard speak with idealistic passion about travel to the moon, the planets, the stars. It seemed to Harry that compared to stars, 1989 might seem reasonably close. The young man had warm hazel eyes and a sense of humor. When he spoke about life in a spaceship, he mentioned in passing that women would be freed from much domestic drudgery they now endured.

Throughout the lecture, he smoked, lighting cigarettes with a masculine squinting of eyes and cupping of hands. He said that imagination was the human quality that would most help people adjust to the future. His shoes were polished.

But most of all, Harry thought, he had a glow. A fine golden Boy Scout glow that made Harry think of old covers for the *Saturday Evening Post*. Which here cost five cents.

After the lecture, Harry stayed in his chair in the front row, outwaiting even the girl with bright red lipstick who lingered around the lecturer, this Robert Gernshon. From time to time, Gernshon glanced over at Harry with quizzical interest. Finally the girl, red lips pouting, sashayed out of the hall.

"Hello," Harry said. "I'm Harry Kramer. I enjoyed your talk. I have something to show you that you would be very interested in."

The hazel eyes turned wary. "Oh, no, no," Harry said. "Something *scientific*. Here, look at this." He handed Gernshon a filtered Vantage Light.

"How long it is," Gernshon said. "What's this made of?"

"The filter? It's made of...a new filter material. Tastes milder and cuts down on the nicotine. Much better for you. Look at this." He gave Gernshon a styrofoam cup from McDonald's. "It's made of a new material, too. Very cheap. Disposable."

Gernshon fingered the cup. "Who are you?" he said quietly.

"A scientist. I'm interested in the science of tomorrow, too. Like you. I'd like to invite you to see my laboratory, which is in my home."

"In your home?"

"Yes. In a small way. Just dabbling, you know." Harry could feel himself getting rattled; the young hazel eyes stared at him so steadily. *Jackie*, he thought. Dead earths. Maggots and carrion. Contempt for mothers. What would Gernshon say? When would Gernshon say *anything*?

"Thank you," Gernshon finally said. "When would be convenient?"

"Now?" Harry said. He tried to remember what time of day it was now. All he could picture was lecture halls.

Gernshon came. It was nine-thirty in the evening of Friday, September 17. Harry walked Gernshon through the streets, trying to talk animatedly, trying to distract. He said that he himself was very interested in travel to the stars. He said it had always been his dream to stand on another planet and take in great gulps of completely unpolluted air. He said his great heroes were those biologists who made that twisty model of DNA. He said science had been his life. Gernshon walked more and more silently.

"Of course," Harry said hastily, "like most scientists, I'm mostly familiar with my own field. You know how it is."

"What is your field, Dr. Kramer?" Gernshon asked quietly.

"Electricity," Harry said, and hit him on the back of the head with a solid brass candlestick from the pocket of his coat. The candlestick had cost him three dollars at a pawn shop.

They had walked past the stores and pushcarts to a point where the locked business offices and warehouses began. There were no passersby, no muggers, no street dealers, no Guardian Angels, no punk gangs. Only him, hitting an unarmed man with a candlestick. He was no better than the punks. But what else could he do? Nothing but hit him softly, so softly that Gernshon was struggling again almost before Harry got his hands and feet tied, well before he got on the blindfold and gag. "I'm sorry, I'm sorry," he kept saying to Gernshon. Gernshon did not look as if the apology made any difference. Harry dragged him into the warehouse.

Rudy was asleep over *Spicy Stories*. Breathing very hard, Harry pulled the young man—not more than 150 pounds, it was good Harry had looked for slim—to the far corner, through the gate, and into his closet.

"Listen," he said urgently to Gernshon after removing the gag. "Listen. I can call the Medicare Emergency Hotline. If your head feels broken. Are you feeling faint? Do you think you maybe might go into shock?"

Gernshon lay on Harry's rug, glaring at him, saying nothing.

"Listen, I know this is maybe a little startling to you. But I'm not a pervert, not a cop, not anything but a grandfather with a problem. My granddaughter. I need your help to solve it, but I won't take much of your time. You're now somewhere besides where you gave your lecture. A pretty long ways away. But you don't have to stay here long, I promise. Just two weeks, tops, and I'll send you back. I promise, on my mother's grave. And I'll make it worth your while. I promise."

"Untie me."

"Yes. Of course. Right away. Only you have to not attack me, because I'm the only one who can get you back from here." He had a sudden inspiration. "I'm like a foreign consul. You've maybe traveled abroad?"

Gernshon looked around the dingy room. "Untie me."

"I will. In two minutes. Five, tops. I just want to explain a little first."

"Where am I?"

"1989."

Gernshon said nothing. Harry explained brokenly, talking as fast as he could, saying he could move from 1989 to September, 1937 when he wanted to, but he could take Gernshon back too, no problem. He said he made the trip often, it was perfectly safe. He pointed out how much farther a small Social Security check, no pension, could go at 1937 prices. He mentioned Manny's strudel. Only lightly did he touch on the problem of Jackie, figuring there would be a better time to share domestic difficulties, and his closet he didn't mention at all. It was hard to keep his eyes averted from the closet door. He did mention how bitter people could be in 1989, how lost, how weary from expecting so much that nothing was a delight, nothing a sweet surprise. He was just working up to a tirade on innocence when Gernshon said again, in a different tone, "Untie me."

"Of course," Harry said quickly, "I don't expect you to believe me. Why should you think you're in 1989? Go, see for yourself. Look at that light, it's still early morning. Just be careful out there, is all." He untied Gernshon and stood with his eyes squeezed shut, waiting.

When nothing hit him, Harry opened his eyes. Gernshon was at the door. "Wait!" Harry cried. "You'll need more money!" He dug into his pocket and pulled out a twenty-dollar bill, carefully saved for this, and all the change he had.

Gernshon examined the coins carefully, then looked up at Harry. He said nothing. He opened the door and Harry, still trembling, sat down in his chair to wait.

Gernshon came back three hours later, pale and sweating. "My God!"

"I know just what you mean," Harry said. "A zoo out there. Have a drink."

Gernshon took the mixture Harry had ready in his toothbrush glass and gulped it down. He caught sight of the bottle, which Harry had left on the dresser: Seagram's V.O., with the cluttered, tiny-print label. He threw the glass across the room and covered his face with his hands.

"I'm sorry," Harry said apologetically. "But back then it cost only $3.37 the fifth."

Gernshon didn't move.

"I'm really sorry," Harry said. He raised both hands, palms up, and dropped them helplessly. "Would you...would you maybe like an orange?"

Gernshon recovered faster than Harry had dared hope. Within an hour he was sitting in Harry's worn chair, asking questions about the space shuttle; within two hours taking notes; within three become again the intelligent and captivating young man of the lecture hall. Harry, answering as much as he could as patiently as he could, was impressed by the boy's resilience. It couldn't have been easy. What if he, Harry, suddenly had to skip fifty-two more years? What if he found himself in 2041? Harry shuddered.

"Do you know that a movie now costs six dollars?"

Gernshon blinked. "We were talking about the moon landing."

"Not any more, we're not. I want to ask *you* some questions, Robert. Do you think the earth is dead, with people sliming all over it like on carrion? Is this a thought that crosses your mind?"

"I...no."

Harry nodded. "Good, good. Do you look at your mother with contempt?"

"Of course not. Harry—"

"No, it's my turn. Do you think a woman who marries a man, and maybe the marriage doesn't work out perfect, whose does, but they raise at least one healthy child—say a daughter—that that woman's life has been a defeat and a failure?"

"No. I—"

"What would you think if you saw a drawing of a woman's private parts on the cover of a magazine?"

Gernshon blushed. He looked as if the blush annoyed him, but also as if he couldn't help it.

"Better and better," Harry said. "Now, think careful on this next one—take your time—no hurry. Does reality seem to you to have sweetness in it as well as ugliness? Take your time."

Gernshon peered at him. Harry realized they had talked right through lunch. "But not all the time in the world, Robert."

"Yes," Gernshon said. "I think reality has more sweetness than ugliness. And more strangeness than anything else. Very much more." He looked suddenly dazed. "I'm sorry, I just—all this has happened so—"

"Put your head between your knees," Harry suggested. "There—better now? Good. There's someone I want you to meet."

Manny sat in the park, on their late-afternoon bench. When he saw them coming, his face settled into long sorrowful ridges. "Harry. Where have you been for two days? I was worried, I went to your hotel—"

"Manny," Harry said, "this is Robert."

"So I see," Manny said. He didn't hold out his hand.

"Him," Harry said.

"Harry. Oh, Harry."

"How do you do, sir," Gernshon said. He held out his hand. "I'm afraid I didn't get your full name. I'm Robert Gernshon."

Manny looked at him—at the outstretched hand, the baggy suit with wide tie, the deferential smile, the golden Baden-Powell glow. Manny's lips mouthed a silent word: *sir*?

"I have a lot to tell you," Harry said.

"You can tell all of us, then," Manny said. "Here comes Jackie now."

Harry looked up. Across the park a woman in jeans strode purposefully toward them. "Manny! It's only Monday!"

"I called her to come," Manny said. "You've been gone from your room two days, Harry, nobody at your hotel could say where—"

"But *Manny*," Harry said, while Gernshon looked, frowning, from one to the other and Jackie spotted them and waved.

She had lost more weight, Harry saw. Only two weeks, yet her cheeks had hollowed out and new, tiny lines touched her eyes. Skinny lines. They filled him with sadness. Jackie wore a blue T-shirt that said LIFE IS A BITCH—THEN YOU DIE. She carried a magazine and a small can of mace disguised as hair spray.

"Popsy! You're here! Manny said—"

"Manny was wrong," Harry said. "Jackie, sweetheart, you look—it's good to see you. Jackie, I'd like you to meet somebody, darling. This is Robert. My friend. My friend Robert. Jackie Snyder."

"Hi," Jackie said. She gave Harry a hug, and then Manny one. Harry saw Gernshon gazing at her very tight jeans.

"Robert's a…a scientist," Harry said. It was the wrong thing to say; Harry knew the moment he said it that it was the wrong thing. Science—all science—was, for some reason not completely clear to him, a touchy subject with Jackie. She tossed her long hair back from her eyes. "Oh, yeah? Not *chemical*, I hope?"

"I'm not actually a scientist," Gernshon said winningly. "Just a dabbler. I popularize new scientific concepts, write about them to make them intelligible."

"Like what?" Jackie said.

Gernshon opened his mouth, closed it again. A boy suddenly flashed past on a skateboard, holding a boom box. Metallica blasted the air. Overhead, a jet droned. Gernshon smiled weakly. "It's hard to explain."

"I'm capable of understanding," Jackie said coldly. "Women *can* understand science, you know."

"Jackie, sweetheart," Harry said, "what have you got there? Is that your new book?"

"No," Jackie said, "this is the one I said I'd bring you, by my friend. It's brilliant. It's about a man whose business partner betrays him by selling out to organized crime and framing the man. In jail he meets a guy who has founded his own religion, the House of Divine Despair, and when they both get out they start a new business, Suicide Incorporated, that helps people kill themselves for a fee. The whole thing is just a brilliant denunciation of contemporary America."

Gernshon made a small sound.

"It's a comedy," Jackie added.

"It sounds…it sounds a little depressing," Gernshon said.

Jackie looked at him. Very distinctly, she said, "It's reality."

Harry saw Gernshon glance around the park. A man nodded on a bench, his hands slack on his knees. Newspapers and McDonald's wrappers stirred fitfully in the dirt. A trash container had been knocked over. From beside a scrawny tree, enclosed shoulder-height by black wrought iron, a child watched them with old eyes.

"I brought you something else, too, Popsy," Jackie said. Harry hoped that Gernshon noticed how much gentler her voice was when she spoke to her grandfather. "A scarf. See, it's llama wool. Very warm."

Gernshon said, "My mother has a scarf like that. No, I guess hers is some kind of fur."

Jackie's face changed. "What kind?"

"I—I'm not sure."

"Not an endangered species, I hope."

"No. Not that. I'm sure not…that."

Jackie stared at him a moment longer. The child who had been watching strolled toward them. Harry saw Gernshon look at the boy with relief. About eleven years old, he wore a perfectly tailored suit and Italian shoes. Manny shifted to put himself between the boy and Gernshon. "Jackie, darling, it's so good to see you…"

The boy brushed by Gernshon on the other side. He never looked up, and his voice stayed boyish and low, almost a whisper. "Crack…."

"Step on one and you break your mother's back," Gernshon said brightly. He smiled at Harry, a special conspiratorial smile to suggest that children, at least, didn't change in fifty years. The boy's head jerked up to look at Gernshon.

"You talking about my mama?"

Jackie groaned. "No," she said to the kid. "He doesn't mean anything. Beat it."

"I don't forget," the boy said. He backed away slowly.

Gernshon said, frowning, "I'm sorry. I'm not sure exactly what all that was, but I'm sorry."

"Are you for real?" Jackie said angrily. "What the fucking hell *was* all that? Don't you realize this park is the only place Manny and my grandfather can get some fresh air?"

"I didn't—"

"That punk runner meant it when he said he won't forget!"

"I don't like your tone," Gernshon said. "Or your language."

"My language!" The corners of Jackie's mouth tightened. Manny looked at Harry and put his hands over his face. The boy, twenty feet away, suddenly let out a noise like a strangled animal, so piercing all four of them spun around. Two burly teenagers were running toward him. The child's face crumpled; he looked suddenly much younger. He sprang away, stumbled, made the noise again, and hurled himself, all animal terror, toward the street behind the park bench.

"No!" Gernshon shouted. Harry turned towards the shout but Gernshon already wasn't there. Harry saw the twelve-wheeler bearing down, heard Jackie's scream, saw Gernshon's wiry body barrel into the boy's. The truck shrieked past, its air brakes deafening.

Gernshon and the boy rose in the street on the other side.

Car horns blared. The boy bawled, "Leggo my suit! You tore my suit!" A red light flashed and a squad car pulled up. The two burly teenagers melted away, and then the boy somehow vanished as well.

"Never find him," the disgruntled cop told them over the clipboard on which he had written nothing. "Probably just as well." He went away.

"Are you hurt?" Manny said. It was the first time he had spoken. His face was ashen. Harry put a hand across his shoulders.

"No," Gernshon said. He gave Manny his sweet smile. "Just a little dirty."

"That took *guts*," Jackie said. She was staring at Gernshon with a frown between her eyebrows. "Why did you do it?"

"Pardon?"

"Why? I mean, given what that kid is, given—oh, all of it—" she gestured around the park, a helpless little wave of her strong, young hands that tore at Harry's heart. "Why bother?"

Gernshon said gently, "What that kid is, is a kid."

Manny looked skeptical. Harry moved to stand in front of Manny's expression before anyone wanted to discuss it. "Listen, I've got a wonderful idea, you two seem to have so much to talk about, about... bothering, and...everything. Why don't you have dinner together, on me? My treat."

He pulled another twenty dollar bill from his pocket. Behind him he could feel Manny start.

"Oh, I couldn't," Gernshon said, at the same moment that Jackie said warningly, "Popsy...."

Harry put his palms on both sides of her face. "Please. Do this for me, Jackie. Without the questions, without the female protests. Just this once. For me."

Jackie was silent a long moment before she grimaced, nodded, and turned with half-humorous appeal to Gernshon.

Gernshon cleared his throat. "Well, actually, it would probably be better if all four of us came. I'm embarrassed to say that prices are higher in this city than in...that is, I'm not able to...but if we went somewhere less expensive, the Automat maybe, I'm sure all four of us could eat together."

"No, no," Harry said. "We already ate." Manny looked at him.

Jackie began, offended, "I certainly don't want...just what do you think is going on here, buddy? This is just to please my grandfather. Are you afraid I might try to jump your bones?"

Harry saw Gernshon's quick, involuntary glance at Jackie's tight jeans. He saw, too, that Gernshon fiercely regretted the glance the instant he had made it. He saw that Manny saw, and that Jackie saw, and that Gernshon saw that they saw.

Manny made a small noise. Jackie's face began to turn so black that Harry was astounded when Gernshon cut her off with a dignity no one had expected.

"No, of course not," he said quietly. "But *I* would prefer all of us to have dinner together for quite another reason. My wife is very dear to me, Miss Snyder, and I wouldn't do anything that might make her feel uncomfortable. That's probably irrational, but that's the way it is."

Harry stood arrested, his mouth open. Manny started to shake with what Harry thought savagely had better not be laughter. And Jackie, after staring at Gernshon a long while, broke into the most spontaneous smile Harry had seen from her in months.

"Hey," she said softly. "That's nice. That's really, genuinely, fucking nice."

The weather turned abruptly colder. Snow threatened but didn't fall. Each afternoon Harry and Manny took a quick walk in the park and then went inside, to the chess club or a coffee shop or the bus station or the library, where there was a table deep in the stacks on which they could eat lunch without detection. Harry brought Manny a poor boy with mayo, sixty-three cents, and a pair of imported wool gloves, one dollar on pre-season sale.

"So where are they today?" Manny asked on Saturday, removing the gloves to peek at the inside of the poor boy. He sniffed appreciatively. "Horseradish. You remembered, Harry."

"The museum, I think," Harry said miserably.

"What museum?"

"How should I know? He says, 'The museum today, Harry,' and he's gone by eight o'clock in the morning, no more details than that."

Manny stopped chewing. "What museum opens at eight o'clock in the morning?"

Harry put down his sandwich, pastrami on rye, thirty-nine cents. He had lost weight the past week.

"Probably," Manny said hastily, "they just talk. You know, like young people do, just talk...."

Harry eyed him balefully. "You mean like you and Leah did when you were young and left completely alone."

"You better talk to him soon, Harry. No, to her." He seemed to reconsider Jackie. "No, to *him*."

"Talk isn't going to do it," Harry said. He looked pale and determined. "Gernshon has to be sent back."

"Be sent?"

"He's *married*, Manny! I wanted to help Jackie, show her life can hold some sweetness, not be all struggle. What kind of sweetness is she going to find if she falls in love with a married man? You know how that goes! Jackie—" Harry groaned. How had all this happened? He had intended only the best for Jackie. Why didn't that count more? "He has to go back, Manny."

"How?" Manny said practically. "You can't hit him again, Harry. You were just lucky last time that you didn't hurt him. You don't want that on your conscience. And if you show him your, uh...your—"

"My closet. Manny, if you'd only come see, for a dollar you could get—"

"—then he could just come back any time he wants. So how?"

A sudden noise startled them both. Someone was coming through the stacks. "Librarians!" Manny hissed. Both of them frantically swept the sandwiches, beer (fifteen cents), and strudel into shopping bags. Manny, panicking, threw in the wool gloves. Harry swept the table free of crumbs. When the intruder rounded the nearest bookshelf, Harry was bent over *Making Paper Flowers* and Manny over *Porcelain of the Yung Cheng Dynasty.* It was Robert Gernshon.

The young man dropped into a chair. His face was ashen. In one hand he clutched a sheaf of paper, the handwriting on the last one trailing off into shaky squiggles.

After a moment of silence, Manny said diplomatically, "So where are you coming from, Robert?"

"Where's Jackie?" Harry demanded.

"Jackie?" Gernshon said. His voice was thick; Harry realized with a sudden shock that he had been crying. "I haven't seen her for a few days."

"A few *days*?" Harry said.

"No. I've been...I've been..."

Manny sat up straighter. He looked intently at Gernshon over *Porcelain of the Yung Cheng Dynasty* and then put the book down. He moved to the chair next to Gernshon's and gently took the papers from his hand. Gernshon leaned over the table and buried his head in his arms.

"I'm so awfully sorry, I'm being such a baby..." His shoulders trembled. Manny separated the papers and spread them out on the library table. Among the hand-copied notes were two slim books, one bound between black covers and the other a pamphlet. *A Memoir of Auschwitz. Countdown to Hiroshima*.

For a long moment nobody spoke. Then Harry said, to no one in particular, "I thought he was going to science museums."

Manny laid his arm, almost casually, across Gernshon's shoulders. "So now you'll know not to be at either place. More people should have only known." Harry didn't recognize the expression on his friend's face, nor the voice with which Manny said to Harry, "You're right. He has to go back."

"But Jackie..."

"Can do without this sweetness," Manny said harshly. "So what's so terrible in her life anyway that she needs so much help? Is she dying? Is she poor? Is she ugly? Is anyone knocking on her door in the middle of the night? Let Jackie find her own sweetness. She'll survive."

Harry made a helpless gesture. Manny's stubborn face, carved wood under the harsh fluorescent light, did not change. "Even *him*... Manny, the things he knows now—"

"You should have thought of that earlier."

Gernshon looked up. "Don't, I—I'm sorry. It's just coming across it, I never thought human beings—"

"No," Manny said. "But they can. You been here, every day, at the library, reading it all?"

"Yes. That and museums. I saw you two come in earlier. I've been reading, I wanted to know—"

"So now you know," Manny said in that same surprisingly casual, tough voice. "You'll survive, too."

Harry said, "Does Jackie know what's going on? Why you've been doing all this...learning?"

"No."

"And you—what will you do with what you now know?"

Harry held his breath. What if Gernshon just refused to go back? Gernshon said slowly, "At first, I wanted to not return. At all. How can I watch it, World War II and the camps—I have relatives in Poland. And then later the bomb and Korea and the gulags and Vietnam and Cambodia and the terrorists and AIDS—"

"Didn't miss anything," Harry muttered.

"And not be able to do anything, not be able to even hope, knowing that everything to come is already set into history—how could I watch all that without any hope that it isn't really as bad as it seems to be at the moment?"

"It all depends what you look at," Manny said, but Gernshon didn't seem to hear him.

"But neither can I stay, there's Susan and we're hoping for a baby...I need to think."

"No, you don't," Harry said. "You need to go back. This is all my mistake. I'm sorry. You need to go back, Gernshon."

"Lebanon," Gernshon said. "D.D.T. The Cultural Revolution. Nicaragua. Deforestation. Iran—"

"Penicillin," Manny said suddenly. His beard quivered. "Civil rights. Mahatma Gandhi. Polio vaccines. Washing machines." Harry stared at him, shocked. Could Manny once have worked in a hand laundry?

"Or," Manny said, more quietly, "Hitler. Auschwitz. Hoovervilles. The Dust Bowl. What you look at, Robert."

"I don't know," Gernshon said. "I need to think. There's so much… and then there's that girl."

Harry stiffened. "Jackie?"

"No, no. Someone she and I met a few days ago, at a coffee shop. She just walked in. I couldn't believe it. I looked at her and just went into shock—and maybe she did too, for all I know. The girl looked exactly like me. And she felt like—I don't know. It's hard to explain. She felt like *me*. I said hello but I didn't tell her my name; I didn't dare." His voice fell to a whisper. "I think she's my granddaughter."

"Hoo boy," Manny said.

Gernshon stood. He made a move to gather up his papers and booklets, stopped, left them there. Harry stood, too, so abruptly that Gernshon shot him a sudden, hard look across the library table. "Going to hit me again, Harry? Going to kill me?"

"Us?" Manny said. "Us, Robert?" His tone was gentle.

"In a way, you already have. I'm not who I was, certainly."

Manny shrugged. "So be somebody better."

"Damn it, I don't think you understand—"

"I don't think you do, Reuven, boychik. This is the way it is. That's all. Whatever you had back there, you have still. Tell me, in all that reading, did you find anything about yourself, anything personal? Are you in the history books, in the library papers?"

"The Office of Public Documents takes two weeks to do a search for birth and death certificates," Gernshon said, a little sulkily.

"So you lost nothing, because you really know nothing," Manny said. "Only history. History is cheap. Everybody gets some. You can have all the history you want. It's what you make of it that costs."

Gernshon didn't nod agreement. He looked a long time at Manny, and something moved behind the unhappy hazel eyes, something that made Harry finally let out a breath he didn't know he'd been holding. It suddenly seemed that Gernshon was the one that was old. And he was—with the fifty-two years he'd gained since last week, he was older than Harry had been in the 1937 of *Captains Courageous* and the wide-brimmed fedoras and clean city parks. But that was the good time, the one that Gernshon was going back to, the one Harry himself could choose, if it weren't for Jackie and Manny…still, he couldn't watch as Gernshon walked out of the book stacks, parting the musty air as heavily as if it were water.

Gernshon paused. Over his shoulder he said, "I'll go back. Tonight. I will."

After he had left, Harry said, "This is my fault."

"Yes," Manny agreed.

"Will you come to my room when he goes? To...to help?"

"Yes, Harry."

Somehow, that only made it worse.

Gernshon agreed to a blindfold. Harry led him through the closet, the warehouse, the street. Neither of them seemed very good at this; they stumbled into each other, hesitated, tripped over nothing. In the warehouse Gernshon nearly walked into a pile of lumber, and in the sharp jerk Harry gave Gernshon's arm to deflect him, something twisted and gave way in Harry's back. He waited, bent over, behind a corner of a building while Gernshon removed his blindfold, blinked in the morning light, and walked slowly away.

Despite his back, Harry found that he couldn't return right away. Why not? He just couldn't. He waited until Gernshon had a large head start and then hobbled towards the park. A carousel turned, playing bright organ music: September 24. Two children he had never noticed before stood just beyond the carousel, watching it with hungry, hopeless eyes. Flowers grew in immaculate flower beds. A black man walked by, his eyes fixed on the sidewalk, his head bent. Two small girls jumping rope were watched by a smiling woman in a blue-and-white uniform. On the sidewalk, just beyond the carousel, someone had chalked a swastika. The black man shuffled over it. A Lincoln Zephyr V-12 drove by, $1090. There was no way it would fit through a closet.

When Harry returned, Manny was curled up on the white chenille bedspread that Harry had bought for $3.28, fast asleep.

"What did I accomplish, Manny? What?" Harry said bitterly. The day had dawned glorious and warm, unexpected Indian summer. Trees in the park showed bare branches against a bright blue sky. Manny wore an old red sweater, Harry a flannel work shirt. Harry shifted gingerly, grimacing, on his bench. Sunday strollers dropped ice cream wrappers, cigarettes, newspapers, Diet Pepsi cans, used tissues, popcorn. Pigeons quarreled and children shrieked.

"Jackie's going to be just as hard as ever and why not?" Harry continued. "She finally meets a nice fellow, he never calls her again. Me, I leave a young man miserable on a sidewalk. Before I leave him, I ruin his life. While I leave him, I ruin my back. *After* I leave him, I sit here guilty. There's no answer, Manny."

Manny didn't answer. He squinted down the curving path.

"I don't know, Manny. I just don't know."

Manny said suddenly, "Here comes Jackie."

Harry looked up. He squinted, blinked, tried to jump up. His back made sharp protest. He stayed where he was, and his eyes grew wide.

"Popsy!" Jackie cried. "I've been looking for you!"

She looked radiant. All the lines were gone from around her eyes, all the sharpness from her face. Her very collar bones, Harry thought dazedly, looked softer. Happiness haloed her like light. She held the hand of a slim, red-haired woman with strong features and direct hazel eyes.

"This is Ann," Jackie said. "I've been looking for you, Popsy, because... well, because I need to tell you something." She slid onto the bench next to Harry, on the other side from Manny, and put one arm around Harry's shoulders. The other hand kept a close grip on Ann, who smiled encouragement. Manny stared at Ann as at a ghost.

"You see, Popsy, for a while now I've been struggling with something, something really important. I know I've been snappy and difficult, but it hasn't been—everybody needs somebody to love, you've often told me that, and I know how happy you and Grammy were all those years. And I thought there would never be anything like that for me, and certain people were making everything all so hard. But now...well, now there's Ann. And I wanted you to know that."

"Happy to meet you," Ann said. She had a low, rough voice and a sweet smile. Harry felt hurricanes, drought, sunshine.

Jackie said, "I know this is probably a little unexpected—"

Unexpected. "Well—" Harry said, and could say no more.

"It's just that it was time for me to come out of the closet."

Harry made a small noise. Manny managed to say, "So you live here, Ann?"

"Oh, yes. All my life. And my family, too, since forever."

"Has Jackie...has Jackie met any of them yet?"

"Not yet," Jackie said. "It might be a little...tricky, in the case of her parents." She smiled at Ann. "But we'll manage."

"I wish," Ann said to her, "that you could have met my grandfather. He would have been just as great as your Popsy here. He always was."

"Was?" Harry said faintly.

"He died a year ago. But he was just a wonderful man. Compassionate and intelligent."

"What…what did he do?"

"He taught history at the university. He was also active in lots of organizations—Amnesty International, the ACLU, things like that. During World War II he worked for the Jewish rescue leagues, getting people out of Germany."

Manny nodded. Harry watched Jackie's teeth.

"We'd like you both to come to dinner soon," Ann said. She smiled. "I'm a good cook."

Manny's eyes gleamed.

Jackie said, "I know this must be hard for you—" but Harry saw that she didn't really mean it. She didn't think it was hard. For her it was so real that it was natural weather, unexpected maybe, but not strange, not out of place, not out of time. In front of the bench, sunlight striped the pavement like bars.

Suddenly Jackie said, "Oh, Popsy, did I tell you that it was your friend Robert who introduced us? Did I tell you that already?"

"Yes, sweetheart," Harry said. "You did."

"He's kind of a nerd, but actually all right."

After Jackie and Ann left, the two old men sat silent a long time. Finally Manny said diplomatically, "You want to get a snack, Harry?"

"She's happy, Manny."

"Yes. You want to get a snack, Harry?"

"She didn't even recognize him."

"No. You want to get a snack?"

"Here, have this. I got it for you this morning." Harry held out an orange, a deep-colored navel with flawless rind: seedless, huge, guaranteed juicy, nurtured for flavor, perfect.

"Enjoy," Harry said. "It cost me ninety-two cents."

Afterword to "The Price of Oranges"

This is a time-travel story that is not really about time travel. Real stories in this subgenre, like Michael Swanwick's *Bones of the Earth*, tackle the paradoxes and complications inherent in the idea of going back in time. Often they feature characters who are either researchers or financial opportunists thrilled to know what the economy is going to do in the future. Or else, like Jeff in Ken Grimwood's excellent *Replay*, they are trapped in the past against their will.

Harry Kramer is not a researcher, not an opportunist, not trapped. He's a simple man with a simple goal: to raid 1937 for whatever will make 1989 easier for two elderly men on tiny budgets. To research this story, I spent a lot of time with issues of LIFE magazine from the 1930's. A much different world, as alien to me as is much of science fiction, and mostly unaware of the history about to come crashing down on the planet in the next decade. Sometimes ignorance is bliss—at least temporarily.

BY FOOLS LIKE ME

Hope creeps quietly into my bedroom without knocking, peering around the corner of the rough doorjamb. I'm awake; sleep eludes me so easily now. I know from the awful smell that she has been to the beach.

"Come in, child, I'm not asleep."

"Grandma, where's Mama and Papa?"

"Aren't they in the field?" The rains are late this year and water for the crops must be carried in ancient buckets from the spring in the dell.

"Maybe. I didn't see them. Grandma, I found something."

"What, child?"

She gazes at me and bites her lip. I see that this mysterious find bothers her. Such a sensitive child, though sturdy and healthy enough, God knows how.

"I went to the beach," she confesses in a rush. "Don't tell Mama! I wanted to dig you some trunter roots because you like them so much, but my shovel went clunk on something hard and I…I dug it up."

"Hope," I reprimand, because the beach is full of dangerous bits of metal and plastic, washed up through the miles of dead algae on the dead water. And if a soot cloud blows in from the west, it will hit the beach first.

"I'm sorry," she says, clearly lying, "but, Grandma, it was a metal box and the lock was all rusted and there was something inside and I brought it here."

"The box?"

"No, that was too heavy. The…just wait!"

No one can recognize most of the bits of rusted metal and twisted plastic from before the Crash. Anything found in a broken metal box should be decayed beyond recognition. I call "Hope! Don't touch anything slimy—" but she is already out of earshot, running from my tiny bedroom with its narrow cot, which is just blankets and pallet on a rope frame to keep me off the hard floor. It doesn't; the old ropes sag too much, just as the thick clay walls don't keep out the heat. But that's my fault. I close the window shutters only when I absolutely have to. Insects and heat are preferable to dark. But I have a door, made of precious and rotting wood, which is more than Hope or her parents have on their sleeping alcoves off the house's only other room. I expect to die in this room.

Hope returns, carrying a bubble of sleek white plastic that fills her bare arms. The bubble has no seams. No mold sticks to it, no sand. Carefully she lays the thing on my cot.

Despite myself, I say, "Bring me the big knife and be very careful, it's sharp."

She gets the knife, carrying it as gingerly as an offering for the altar. The plastic slits more readily than I expected. I peel it back, and we both gasp.

I am the oldest person on Island by two decades, and I have seen much. Not of the world my father told me about, from before the Crash, but in our world now. I have buried two husbands and five children, survived three great sandstorms and two years where the rains didn't come at all, planted and first-nursed a sacred tree, served six times at the altar. I have seen much, but I have never seen so much preserved sin in one place.

"What...Grandma...what is that?"

"A book, child. They're all books."

"Books?" Her voice holds titillated horror. "You mean...like they made before the Crash? Like they cut down *trees* to make?"

"Yes."

"Trees? Real *trees*?"

"Yes." I lift the top one from the white plastic bubble. Firm thick red cover, like...dear God, it's made from the skin of some animal. My gorge rises. Hope musn't know that. The edges of the sin are gold. My father told me about books, but not that they could look like this. I open it.

"Oh!" Hope cries. "Oh, Grandma!"

The first slate—no, first *page*, the word floating up from some childhood conversation—is a picture of trees, but nothing like the pictures children draw on their slates. This picture shows dozens of richly colored trees, crowded together, each with *hundreds* of healthy, beautifully detailed green leaves. The trees shade a path bordered with glorious flowers. Along the path runs a child wearing far too many wraps, following a large white animal dressed in a wrap and hat and carrying a small metal machine. At the top of the picture, words float on golden clouds: *Alice in Wonderland*.

"Grandma! Look at the—Mama's coming!"

Before I can say anything, Hope grabs the book, shoves it into the white bubble, and thrusts the whole thing under my cot. I feel it slide under my bony ass, past the sag that is my body, and hit the wall. Hope is standing up by the time Gloria crowds into my tiny room.

"Hope, have you fed the chickens yet?"

"No, Mama, I—"

Gloria reaches out and slaps her daughter. "Can't I trust you to do anything?"

"Please, Gloria, it's my fault. I sent her to see if there's any more mint growing in the dell."

Gloria scowls. My daughter-in-law is perpetually angry, perpetually exhausted. Before my legs gave out and I could still do a full day's work, I used to fight back. The Island is no more arid, the see-oh-too no higher, for Gloria than for anyone else. She has borne no more stillborn children than have other women, has endured no fewer soot clouds. But now that she and my son must feed my nearly useless body, I try to not anger her too much, to not be a burden. I weave all day. I twist rope, when there are enough vines to spare for rope. I pretend to be healthier than I am.

Gloria says, "We don't need mint, we need fed chickens. Go, Hope." She turns.

"Gloria—"

"What?" Her tone is unbearable. I wonder, for the thousandth time, why Bill married her, and for the thousandth time I answer my own question.

"Nothing," I say. I don't tell her about the sin under the bed. I could have, and ended it right there. But I do not.

God forgive me.

Gloria stands behind the altar, dressed in the tattered green robe we all wear during our year of service. I sit on a chair in front of the standing villagers; no one may miss services, no matter how old or sick or in need of help to hobble to the Grove. Bill half carried me here, afraid no doubt of being late and further angering his wife. It's hard to have so little respect for my son.

It is the brief time between the dying of the unholy wind that blows all day and the fall of night. Today the clouds are light gray, not too sooty, but not bearing rain, either.

The altar stands at the bottom of the dell, beside the spring that makes our village possible. A large flat slab of slate, it is supported by boulders painstakingly chiseled with the words of God. It took four generations to carve that tiny writing, and three generations of children have learned to read by copying the sacred texts onto their slates. I was among the first. The altar is shaded by the six trees of the Grove and from my uncomfortable seat, I can gaze up at their branches against the pale sky.

How beautiful they are! Ours are the tallest, straightest, healthiest trees of any village on Island. I planted and first-nursed one of them myself, the honor of my life. Even now I feel a thickness in my shriveled chest as I gaze up at the green leaves, each one wiped free of dust every day by those in service. Next year, Hope will be one of them. There is nothing on Earth lovelier than the shifting pattern of trees against the sky. Nothing.

Gloria raises her arms and intones, "'Then God said, "I give you every plant and every tree on the whole Earth. They will be food for you."'"

"Amen," call out two or three people.

"'Wail, oh pine tree,'" Gloria cries, "'for the cedar has fallen, the stately trees are ruined! Wail, oaks—'"

"Wail! Wail!"

I have never understood why people can't just worship in silence. This lot is sometimes as bad as a flock of starlings.

"'—oaks of Bashan, the—'"

Hope whispers, "Who's Bashan?"

Bill whispers back, "A person at the Crash."

"'—dense forest has been cut down! And they were told—told!—not to harm the grass of Earth or any plant or tree.'"

Revelation 9:4, I think automatically, although I never did find out what the words or numbers mean.

"'The vine is dried up!'" Gloria cries, "'The fig tree is withered! The pomegranate and the palm and the apple tree, all the trees of the field, are dried up! Surely the joy of mankind is withered away!'"

"Withered! Oh, amen, withered!"

Joel 1:12.

"'Offer sacrifices and burn incense on the high places, under any spreading tree!'"

Amy Martin, one of the wailers, comes forward with the first sacrifice, an unrecognizable piece of rusted metal dug up from the soil or washed up on the beach. She lays it on the altar. Beside me Hope leans forward, her mouth open and her eyes wide. I can read her young thoughts as easily as if they, too, are chiseled in stone: *That metal might have been part of a "car" that threw see-oh-two and soot into the air, might have been part of a "factory" that poisoned the air, might have even been part of a "saw" that cut down the forests!* Hope shudders, but I glance away from the intensity on her face. Sometimes she looks too much like Gloria.

Two more sacrifices are offered. Gloria takes an ember from the banked fire under the altar—the only fire allowed in the village—and touches it briefly to the sacrifices. "'Instead of the thornbush will grow the pine tree, and instead of briars the myrtle will grow. This will be for the Lord's glory, for an everlasting sign which—'"

I stop listening. Instead I watch the leaves move against the sky. What is "myrtle"—what did it look like, why was it such a desirable plant? The leaves blur. I have dozed off, but I realize this only when the whole Village shouts together, "We will never forget!" and services are over.

Bill carries me back through the quickening darkness without stars or moon. Without the longed-for rain. Without the candles I remember from my childhood on Island, or the dimly remembered (dreamed?) fireless lights from before that. There are no lights after dark on Island, nothing that might release soot into the air.

We will never forget.

It's just too bad that services are so boring.

Alice in Wonderland.
Pride and Prejudice
Birds of India and Asia
Moby Dick
Morning Light
Jane Eyre
The Sun Also Rises

I sit on my cot, slowly sounding out the strange words. Of course the sun rises—what else could it do? It's rising now outside my window, which lets in pale light, insects, and the everlasting hot wind.

"Can I see, Grandma?" Hope, naked in the doorway. I didn't hear the door open. She could have been Gloria. And is it right for a child to see this much sin?

But already she's snuggled beside me, smelling of sweat and grime and young life. Even her slight body makes the room hotter. All at once a memory comes to me, a voice from early childhood: *Here, Anna, put ice on that bruise. Listen, that's a—*

What bruise? What was I to listen to? The memory is gone.

"M—m—m—oh—bee—Grandma, what's a 'moby'?"

"I don't know, child."

She picks up a different one. "J—j—aye—n…Jane! That's Miss Anderson's name! Is this book about her?"

"No. Another Jane, I think." I open *Moby Dick*. Tiny, dense writing, page and pages of it, whole burned forests of it.

"Read the sin with the picture of trees!" She roots among the books until she finds *Alice in Wonderland* and opens it to that impossible vision of tens, maybe hundreds, of glorious trees. Hope studies the child blessed enough to walk that flower-bordered path.

"What's her name, Grandma?"

"Alice." I don't really know.

"Why is she wearing so many wraps? Isn't she *hot*? And how many days did her poor mother have to work to weave so many?"

I recognize Gloria's scolding tone. The pages of the book are crisp, bright and clear, as if the white plastic bubble had some magic to keep sin fresh. Turning the page, I begin to read aloud. "'Alice was beginning to get very tired of sitting by her sister on the bank—'"

"She has a *sister*," Hope breathes. Nearly no one does now; so few children are carried to term and born whole.

"'—and tired of having nothing to do: once—'"

"How could she have nothing to do? Why doesn't she carry water or weed crops or hunt trunter roots or—"

"Hope, are you going to let me read this to you or not?"

"Yes, Grandma. I'm sorry."

I shouldn't be reading to her at all. *Trees* were cut down to make this book; my father told me so. As a young man, not long after the Crash, he himself was in service as a book sacrificer, proudly. Unlike many of his generation, my father was a moral man.

"'—or twice she had peeped into the book her sister was reading, but it had no pictures or conversation in it, "and what is the use of a book," thought Alice, "without pictures or conversation?" So she was considering—'"

We read while the sun clears the horizon, a burning merciless ball, and our sweat drips onto the gold-edged page. Then Gloria and Bill stir in the next room and Hope is on the floor in a flash, shoving the books under my sagging cot, running out the door to feed the chickens and hunt for their rare, precious eggs.

The rains are very late this year. Every day Gloria, scowling, scans the sky. Every day at sunset she and Bill drag themselves home, bone-weary and smeared with dust, after carrying water from the spring to the crops. The spring is in the dell, and water will not flow uphill. Gloria is also in service this year and must nurse one of the trees, wiping the poisonous dust from her share of the leaves, checking for dangerous insects. More work, more time. Some places on Earth, I was told once, have too much water, too many plants from the see-oh-too. I can't imagine it. Island has heard from no other place since I was a young woman and the last radio failed. Now a radio would be sin.

I sit at the loom, weaving. I'm even clumsier than usual, my fingers stiff and eyes stinging. From too much secret reading, or from a high see-oh-too day? Oh, let it be from the reading!

"Grandma," Hope says, coming in from tending the chickens. "My throat hurts." Her voice is small; she knows.

Dear God, not *now*, not when the rains are already so late...But I look out the window and yes, I can see it on the western horizon, thick and brown.

"Bring in the chickens, Hope. Quick!"

She runs back outside while I hobble to the heavy shutters and wrestle them closed. Hope brings in the first protesting chicken, dumps it in her sleeping alcove, and fastens the rope fence. She races back for the next chicken as Bill and Gloria run over the fields toward the house.

Not *now*, when everything is so dry...

They get the chickens in, the food covered, as much water inside as can be carried. At the last moment Bill swings closed the final shutter, and we're plunged into darkness and even greater heat. We huddle against the west wall. The dust storm hits.

Despite the shutters, the holy protection of wood, dust drifts through cracks, under the door, maybe even through chinks in the walls. The dust clogs our throats, noses, eyes. The wind rages: *oooeeeeeeeoooeeeee.* Shrinking beside me, Hope gasps, "It's trying to get in!"

Gloria snaps, "Don't talk!" and slaps Hope. Gloria is right, of course; the soot carries poisons that Island can't name and doesn't remember. Only I remember my father saying, "Methane and bio-weapons..."

Here, Anna, put ice on that bruise. Listen, that's a—

A what? What was that memory?

Then Gloria, despite her slap, begins to talk. She has no choice; it's her service year and she must pray aloud. "'Wail, oh pine tree, for the cedar has fallen, the stately trees are ruined! Wail, oaks of Bashan, the dense forest has been cut down!'"

I want Gloria to recite a different scripture. I want, God forgive me, Gloria to shut up. Her anger burns worse than the dust, worse than the heat.

"'The vine is dried up and the fig is withered; the pomegranate—'"

I stop listening.

Listen, that's a—

Hope trembles beside me, a sweaty mass of fear.

The dust storm proves mercifully brief, but the see-oh-too cloud pulled behind it lasts for days. Everyone's breathing grows harsh. Gloria and Bill, carrying water, get fierce headaches. Gloria makes Hope stay inside, telling her to sit still. I see in Gloria's eyes the concern for her only living child, a concern that Hope is too young to see. Hope sees only her mother's anger.

Left alone, Hope and I sin.

All the long day, while her parents work frantically to keep us alive, we sit by the light of a cracked shutter and follow Alice down the rabbit hole, through the pool of tears, inside the White Rabbit's house, to the Duchess's peppery kitchen. Hope stops asking questions, since I know none of the answers. What is pepper, a crocodile, a caucus race, marmalade? We just read steadily on, wishing there were more pictures, until the book is done and Alice has woken. We begin *Jane Eyre*: "'There was no possibility of taking a walk that day....'"

Birds of India and Asia has gorgeous pictures, but the writing is so small and difficult that I can't read most of it. Nonetheless, this is the book I turn to when Hope is asleep. So many birds! And so many colors on wings and backs and breasts and rising from the tops of heads like fantastic feathered trees. I wish I knew if these birds were ever real, or if they are as imaginary as Alice, as the white Rabbit, as marmalade. I wish—

"Grandma!" Hope cries, suddenly awake. "It's raining outside!"

Joy, laughter, dancing. The whole village gathers at the altar under the trees. Bill carries me there, half running, and I smell his strong male sweat mingled with the sweet rain. Hope dances in her drenched wrap like some wild thing and chases after the other children.

Then Gloria strides into the Grove, grabs Hope, and throws her onto the altar. "You've sinned! My own daughter!"

Immediately everyone falls silent. The village, shocked, looks from Gloria to Hope, back to Gloria. Gloria's face is twisted with fury. From a fold of her wrap she pulls out *Alice in Wonderland*.

"This was in the chicken coop! This! A sin, trees *destroyed*...you had this in our very house!" Gloria's voice rises to a shriek.

Hope shrinks against the wide flat stone and she puts her hands over her face. Rain streams down on her, flattening her hair against her small skull. The book in Gloria's hand sheds droplets off its skin cover. Gloria tears out pages and throws them to the ground, where they go sodden and pulpy as maggots.

"Because of you, God might not have sent any rains at all this year! We're just lucky that in His infinite mercy—you risked—you—"

Gloria drops the mutilated book, pulls back her arm, and with all her force strikes Hope on the shoulder. Hope screams and draws into a ball, covering her head and neck. Gloria lashes out again, a sickening thud of hand on tender flesh. I cry, "Stop! No, Gloria, stop—Bill—let me go!"

He doesn't. No one else moves to help Hope, either. I can feel Bill's anguish, but he chokes out, "It's right, Mama." And then, invoking the most sacred scripture of all, he whispers, "We will never forget."

I cry out again, but nothing can keep Hope from justice, not even when I scream that it is my fault, my book, my sin. They know I couldn't have found this pre-Crash sin alone. They know that, but no one except me knows when Gloria passes beyond beating Hope for justice, for Godly retribution, into beating her from Gloria's own fury, her withered fig tree, her sin. No one sees but me. And I, an old woman, can do nothing.

Hope lies on her cot, moaning. I crouch beside her in her alcove, its small window unshuttered to the rain. Bill bound her broken arm with the unfinished cloth off my loom, then went into the storm in search of his wife.

"Hope...dear heart..."

She moans again.

If I could, I would kill Gloria with my own hands.

A sudden lone crack of lightning brightens the alcove. Already the skin on Hope's wet arms and swollen face has started to darken. One eye swells.

Here, Anna, put ice on that bruise. Listen, that's a—

"Grandma..."

"Don't talk, Hope."

"Water," Hope gasps and I hold the glass for her. Another flash of lightning and for a moment Gloria stands framed in the window. We stare at each other. With a kind of horror I feel my lips slide back, baring my teeth. Gloria sees, and cold slides down my spine.

Then the lightning is gone, and I lay my hand on Hope's battered body.

The rain lasts no more than a few hours. It's replaced by day after day of black clouds that thunder and roil but shed no water. Day after day. Gloria and Bill let half the field die in their attempt to save the other half. The rest of the village does much the same.

Hope heals quickly; the young are resilient. I sit beside her, weaving, until she can work again. Her bruises turn all the colors of the angry earth: black and dun and dead-algae green. Gloria never looks at or speaks to her daughter. My son smiles weakly at us all, and brings Hope her meal, and follows Gloria out the door to the fields.

"Grandma, we sinned."

Did we? I don't know any more. To cut down *trees* in order to make a book...my gorge rises at just the thought. Yes, that's wrong, as wrong as anything could ever be. Trees are the life of the Earth, are God's gift to us. Even my father's generation, still so selfish and sinful, said so. Trees absorb the see-oh-too, clean the air, hold the soil, cool the world. Yes.

But, against that, the look of rapture on Hope's face as Alice chased the White Rabbit, the pictures of *Birds of India and Asia*, Jane Eyre battling Mrs. Reed...Hope and I destroyed nothing ourselves. Is it so wrong, then, to enjoy another's sin?

"We sinned," Hope repeats, mourning, and it is her tone that hardens my heart.

"No, child. We didn't."

"We didn't?" Her eyes, one still swollen, grow wide.

"We didn't make the books. They already *were*. We just read them. Reading isn't sinful."

"Nooooo," she says reluctantly. "Not reading the altar scriptures. But Alice is—"

Gloria enters the house. She says to me, "Services tonight."

I say, "I'm not going."

Gloria stops dead halfway to the wash bucket, her field hat suspended in her hand. For the briefest moment I see something like panic on her face, before it vanishes into her usual anger. "Not going? To services?"

"No."

Hope, frightened, looks from her mother to me. Bill comes in.

Gloria snaps, with distinct emphasis, "*Your* mother says she's not going to services tonight."

Bill says, "Mama?"

"No," I say, and watch his face go from puzzlement to the dread of a weak man who will do anything to avoid argument. I hobble to my alcove and close the door. Later, from my window, I watch them leave for the Grove, Hope holding her father's hand.

Gloria must have given him silent permission to do that.

My son.

Painfully I lower myself to the floor, reach under my cot, and pull out the white plastic bubble. For a while I gaze at the pictures of the gorgeous birds of India and Asia. Then I read *Jane Eyre*. When my family returns at dusk, I keep reading as long as the light holds, not bothering to hide any of the books, knowing that no one will come in.

One heavy afternoon, when the clouds steadily darken and I can no longer see enough to make out words, a huge bolt of lightning shrieks through the sky—*crack!* For a long moment my head vibrates. Then silence, followed by a shout: "Fire!"

I haul myself to my knees and grasp the bottom of the window. The lightning hit one of the trees in the Grove. As I watch, numb, the fire leaps on the ceaseless wind to a second tree.

People scream and run, throwing buckets of muddy water from the spring. I can see that it will do no good—too much dry timber, too much wind. A third tree catches, a fourth, and then the grass too is on fire. Smoke and ash rise into the sky.

I sink back onto my cot. I planted one of those trees, nursed it as I'd once nursed Bill. But there is nothing I can do. Nothing.

By the light of the terrible flames I pick up *Jane Eyre* and, desperately, I read.

And then Hope bursts in, smeared with ash, sweat and tears on her face.

"Hope—no! Don't!"

"Give it to me!"

"No!"

We struggle, but she is stronger. Hope yanks *Jane Eyre* out of my hands and hurls it to the floor. She drops on top of it and crawls under my cot. Frantically I try to press down the sagging ropes so that she can't get past them, but I don't weigh enough. Hope backs out with the other books in their plastic bubble. She scrambles to her feet.

"We did this! You and me! Our sin made God burn the trees!"

"No! Hope—"

"Yes! We did this, just like the people before the Crash!"

We will never forget.

I reach for her, for the books, for everything I've lost or am about to lose. But Hope is already gone. From my window I see her silhouetted against the flames, running toward the grass. The village beats the grass with water-soaked cloths. I let go of the sill and fall back onto the cot before I can see Hope throw the books onto the fire.

Gloria beats Hope again, harder and longer this time. She and Bill might have put me out of the house, except that I have no place to go. So they settle for keeping me away from Hope, so that I cannot lead her further into sin.

Bill speaks to me only once about what happened. Bringing me my meal—meager, so meager—he averts his eyes from my face and says haltingly, "Mama…I…"

"Don't," I say.

"I have to…you…Gloria…" All at once he finds words. "A little bit of sin is just as bad a big sin. That's what *you* taught me. What all those people thought before the Crash—that their cars and machines and books each only destroyed a little air so it didn't matter. And look what happened! The Crash was—"

"Do you really think you're telling me something I don't know? Telling *me*?"

Bill turns away. But as he closes the door behind him, he mumbles over his shoulder, "A little bit of sin is as bad as a big sin."

I sit in my room, alone.

Bill is not right. Nor is Gloria, who told him what to say. Nor is Hope, who is after all a child, with a child's uncompromising, black-and-white faith. They are all wrong, but I can't find the arguments to tell them so. I'm too ignorant. The arguments must exist, they *must*—but I can't find them. And my family wouldn't listen anyway.

Listen, Anna, that's a—

A nightingale.

The whole memory flashes like lightning in my head: my father, bending over me in a walled garden, laughing, trying to distract me from some childish fall. *Here, Anna, put ice on that bruise. Listen, that's a nightingale!* A cube of frozen water pulled with strong fingers from his amber drink. Flowers everywhere, flowers of scarcely believable colors, crimson and gold and blue and emerald. And a burst of glorious unseen music, high and sweet. A bird, maybe one from *Birds of India and Asia*.

But I don't know, can't remember, what a nightingale looks like. And now I never will.

Afterword to "By Fools Like Me"

When I teach writing classes aimed at aspiring science fiction authors, one question I ask my students to consider is this: What is a crime in your invented society? Actions considered criminal, plus punishments considered appropriate, are dead give-aways to what a society values most. The rigid religiosity of the Inquisition made Protestantism a crime and burning at the stake its punishment. The low value put on peasants' lives made hunting them for sport not a crime in rural Czarist Russia. Adultery was once treason in a queen, punishable by death, because it violated beliefs about sacred royal bloodlines.

I wanted to write a society that is a plausible, if extreme, extension of our own, in which something normal to us is criminal to them. What better to choose than owning books? To us they represent pleasure, enlightenment, communication. To a society barely hanging onto a ruined ecology, they might well represent a wanton destruction of precious trees, the only hope for restoring the planet. We see the world as we are, not as it is—change the lens and you change the meaning.

I also wanted to write about an old person, as I later did in both "Fountain of Age" and "The Erdmann Nexus" (both, alas, too long to be included in this volume). Our society tends to consider old people largely irrelevant and uninteresting. So does Anna's. Both are wrong. The older I become—ahem!—the surer I am of that.

CASEY'S EMPIRE

This is the story of Jerry Casey, who lost a galactic empire. Oho, you sneer to yourself—one of those. You know, of course, from your vast reading, what a trivial and hackneyed idea a galactic empire is—even now. You know, of course, from your vast reading, about the convoluted, melodramatic machinations by which a hero loses an empire, and what that feels like. Go suck an egg; you wouldn't know a galactic empire if you tripped over it, which Casey did. Tripped over it and lost it. You think you know how that feels? You don't know. Unless it has happened to you, you don't know. You can't ever know.

He was born in the 1950's in Montana, but he didn't let it bother him. To his child's eyes, the big, lonely, empty plains were within the sound of the sea, within a hard day's climb of the Himalayas, within touch of the hibiscus-smelling rain forest. He walked on desert sands or ancient glaciers or the bottom of the Mariana Trench. At night the wide sky was impossibly full of stars, and he named them all and walked on their spangle-colored planets. Part of it, of course, was his reading, which he did so constantly that he failed the fifth grade. But not all of it. There was something else, something extra, something his own. His parents were puzzled but tolerant. They bought a new car every three years, new drapes every five, and saved up for yearly vacations in Las Vegas. Older people—he was a late, only child. Kind, decent, stupid people. Casey loved them.

His high school years were no more hellish than anyone else's; his college years were an anonymous marathon of beer blasts, rock concerts, and overdue term papers; his decision to enter graduate school was complicated by his advisor's doubt that any graduate school would enter him. But enrollment was falling, programs were being cut if too few live bodies registered for thesis seminar, and Casey found himself a teaching fellow in a small undistinguished college that was part of a large undistinguished state university system in the Northeast. He also found himself scorned. Politely, judiciously, even indulgently—he was in the Humanities, and indulgence was encouraged—but scorned is scorned.

"What's your area?" asked Paul Rizzo, the stocky, bearded teaching fellow with whom Casey shared an office. Rizzo was wearing a plaid flannel shirt, jeans, and Frye boots. All the male teaching fellows, Casey had noticed, wore plaid flannel shirts, jeans, and Frye boots. So did some of the females. Casey wore a sports jacket.

"Area?"

"For your thesis."

"I'm doing the option—the creative-writing thesis. A novel."

"A novel?"

"Yeah, you know," Casey said, "a fiction narrative over 40,000 words. You've heard of them."

Rizzo's eyes narrowed. "Have you started this, uh, novel?"

"Yes."

Rizzo seemed surprised. He stopped in the middle of changing his plaid flannel shirt for a football jersey, arms suspended in midair. Twice a week he scrimmaged to keep in shape, playing on a team limited to grad students and captained by a third-year fellow in the biology department who had his own grant from the federal government.

"What's it about?"

Casey smiled. "In twenty-five words or less?"

"All right, then, what's it like? Who would you say your writing was closest to, if you had to name an influence, a mentor? Barth? Hemingway? Dickens? Faulkner?"

Casey took a deep breath. "Burroughs."

"Naked Lunch?"

"No, not William."

"Then who—"

"Edgar."

"*Edgar Burroughs?* You write..."

"Yes. Yes, I do."

Rizzo finished sliding into his football jersey and picked up his helmet, rubbing a finger over a jagged nick. Then he smiled. Politely, judiciously.

"Well, chacun à sa gout, right?"

"Son gout," Casey said.

"My thesis is on Keats. The psycho-sexual relation of the 'Hyperion' fragment to his later work. You probably don't like Keats, though?"

"Why not?"

"If you write that...do you like Keats?"

Casey picked up Rizzo's football shoe and fingered the cleats. He tried each one in turn, pressing lightly with the end of his index finger. They were all dull. Rizzo waited. Indulgently.

"Well, I'll tell you, Paul. I really think Keats is some kind of poet. Not too commercial, you know, but a strong sensory receiver, quick on the end line. Some kind of poet. But, overall I guess I have to go with Edgar Guest. Enjambment-wise, that is."

Rizzo turned maroon. Casey smiled. Politely, judiciously, indulgently.

"Who you got for frosh comp?"

"Some flake in a striped sports jacket. Young. He talked about semicolons."

"Must be the new guy. Casey."

Casey, the new guy, ducked behind the gray bulk of the candy-and-pastries vending machine. The Styrofoam cup he was carrying sloshed coffee onto his striped sports jacket. The student on the other side of the vendor kicked it.

"Took my quarter again!"

"Here, have half my Babe Ruth."

"Effing machine. Any frat files on his assignments?"

"Not yet. He's new."

"Just my luck."

"It'll be all right. The new ones don't like to flunk anybody. Just go to class. The new ones take attendance."

"He wants us to write a paper for Friday."

"Get Sue to do it. She's an English major."

"Yeah. Jesus—*semicolons!*"

"Yeah."

✹

He got used to teaching freshmen. He made truce with Rizzo. What he couldn't get used to or make truce with, what led him to discover why a university was a bad place to write, was the faculty.

His professors spoke blithely of Shakespeare's "minor plays," Shaw's "failed efforts," Dickens' "unsuccessful pieces." Stories that Casey, stretched out on a flat rock under the blank Montana sky, had thrilled to and wondered at and anguished over, were assigned grades like so many frosh comp papers. B+ to Somerset Maugham and Jane Austen. B- to C.S. Lewis and *Timon of Athens*. His own half-finished stories, Casey figured, the stories sweated and bled and wept over in the $83-a-month hole above a barber shop, were about an H-. On a good day.

His thesis advisor was a Dreiser man. If you are a Dreiser man, Casey learned, if you champion Dreiser and the American realists for 25 years (including six articles in *PMLA*), if you dissect and evaluate and explore Dreiser, you can *be* Dreiser. You know what he wrote in the margins of his books, how he wore his hair and who cut it. You have his/your position in belles-lettres to defend, and you fight for it ferociously. When a prestigious Eastern university has a sudden unfortunate death among its existing faculty and so needs to acquire another American realist, you throw your hat into the academic ring and play politics with dead candidates. You win, and jolly well you should. Dreiser is a definite A. And then so, of course, are you.

Casey walked. He walked on village streets at noon, over snowy athletic fields before dawn, in night woods where one clumsy step could break his unwary neck. While he walked, he agonized. He agonized because he was not Tolstoy or Shakespeare or even Maugham. He agonized because he was honest enough to know that he never would be Tolstoy or Shakespeare or Maugham, complimented himself on being "at least" that honest with himself, and agonized that his self-compliments showed a lack of artistic passion. When he wasn't walking and agonizing, he wrote. It was all H-. When he wasn't writing, he read Dreiser. It was a definite A.

✹

"But I had my advisor's approval for the thesis before I began!" Casey said. He tried to sound indignant rather than desperate, and knew he failed. "Both Dr. Jensen and Dr. Schorer signed the approval form!"

"I know that," said Dr. Stine, Chairman of the Graduate Committee. He sat behind his book-cluttered desk in his book-lined office and looked distressed. Beyond the open window three students, exhilarated by the spring, were tossing a blue Frisbee; occasionally it hit the building with a soft clunk muffled by budding ivy.

"They both knew my novel was going to be s—"

"I know that, too, Mr. Casey." The chairman's distress was genuine. Casey didn't care. "We are not narrow in our academic outlook, Mr. Casey. There is room for many different types of writing in our creative thesis option. The graduate committee is perfectly aware that a lot of exciting research is being carried out right now in your field and that there is much literary merit in selected examples of sci-fi."

Casey winced. Dr. Stine didn't notice. The Frisbee hit the wall.

"We're also aware that Ph.D.'s are being granted by very prestigious universities for scholarly work in sci-fi. But both the writing and the research ends that are worthy of serious attention concern the best sci-fi, the work concerned with social insight and human verities. Hawthorne's 'truth of the human heart,' you know," the chairman said, and smiled, obviously pleased with this reference. The Frisbee hit the wall.

"Your novel, on the other hand, is just...just adventure. Escapist improbabilities. Surely you see—'galactic empire'!"

"It's a realistic interpretation of a possible technological—"

"Precisely. Technological, not humane. You don't deal with psychological or social themes at all. When your protagonist meets those aliens in the blue UFO—I'm sorry, Mr. Casey. It's not that your novel is badly written. In fact, it shows some commercial promise; it's colorful and fast-paced. But it doesn't measure up to the standards of serious literature. And serious literature is what a thesis-novel acceptable to the English department must at least try to be."

"It could very well happen just the way I—"

"I'm sorry, Mr. Casey. I wish you would believe that."

Casey did believe it. He uttered a short expletive that he hoped made the chairman even sorrier, and left the book-lined office just as the Frisbee missed the wall altogether and sailed through the window, a miniature blue UFO.

He resigned from the university, regretted it as pretentiously self-indulgent, and stayed resigned. To fill his time, he wrote, waited on tables at a local pizzeria, brooded over his rejection slips, and walked. The walking, he figured, was the best thing he did. He could walk for hours, could walk all night. After a while he no longer needed to look down at his own feet in even the darkest, most unfamiliar woods; his feet developed such sure sensing of the dead twigs and leaf-covered rabbit holes that he never stumbled. He could walk looking upward at the stars which, in some way, he couldn't say just exactly how, had betrayed him. He could walk on desert sands, on ancient glaciers, on the bottom of the Mariana Trench. His walking was a definite A.

"Hey, Casey!"

"Hello, Rizzo. What'll you have?"

"What do you want, Darlene?"

"Oh, I don't know—pepperoni, for sure. Mushrooms, green pepper, onions. And anchovies, if they're fresh. Are the anchovies fresh?"

"Are the anchovies fresh?" Rizzo asked Casey.

"No," Casey said.

"Well, then, no anchovies. OK, Darl?"

She said, "Are they good frozen anchovies?"

"Are they good frozen anchovies?" Rizzo asked Casey.

"No," Casey said.

"So what are you doing now?" Rizzo said, and added hastily, without glancing around the pizzeria, "What are you going to do? I mean your, uh, plans?"

"Bring you a pizza without anchovies," Casey said, saw that he was being a bastard again, and tried harder. "Guess what, Rizzo? I sold one."

Rizzo wrinkled his beefy forehead. "One what?"

"One story. I sold one."

"You did? Hey, that's great! Is it...is it one of those—"

"Yes. Yes, it is."

"Well, that's still great! Do you mind if I ask you what you got for it? No, never mind. None of my business."

"It wasn't much."

"I hear that market pays less. Comparatively."

"Generally, yes. There are exceptions."

"Of course—there always are. Speaking of exceptions, do you mind if *I* brag a little? I got a job. A real, tenure-track, full-time job. Starting as assistant professor."

"Congratulations. Where is it?"

"Lunell College. It's a small liberal arts college in Massachusetts. I really lucked out, you know what the market is, nobody wants humanities people. Only technology-gadget guys, computer specialists and all. But this is a bona fide good deal. Guess what the salary is."

"I couldn't."

"Go ahead, guess."

"I couldn't."

Rizzo told him. Casey smiled and underlined "no anchovies" on his order pad, thick and black. Twice. The pencil broke.

"I really did luck out," Rizzo said. "They just happened to need a Keats man."

He had not forgotten his childhood nomenclature for the stars, but now he learned everyone else's. This was easy because there seemed to be fewer stars than there had been in Montana. He wrote out a list of the more mellifluous ones, set the list to the melody of a sixteenth-century English madrigal, and chanted it while he walked:

Regulus Fomalhaut Betelguese
Ri-i-gel,
Arcturus Polaris Cano-o-pus
AL-TAIR.

The chant stayed in his head while he tried to write about galactic empires and interstellar battles; since he couldn't get the tune out, he learned to ignore it. After a while he found it rather soothing and came to depend upon it while he sweated and thrashed and fought, motionless at his Salvation Army desk.

The actual presence of real stars was less soothing. Nightly he glared upwards, weather permitting, with real anger, while summer dew soaked his sneakers and a crick developed at the back of his neck. He didn't try to understand his anger; it was more satisfying to revel in it. They had let him down, Regulus Fomalhaut Betelguese Ri-i-gel. They had all let him down. They had not delivered, somehow, what had been promised, promised to the Montana kids playing on the big flat rock in the middle of prosperous insignificance: Marty Hillek and Carl Nielsen and Billy DeTine and Jerry Casey, playing UFO and Sirian Invaders and Would-You-Go? They had deceived. They were not what he thought them. They had refused to let him go, as they had let Marty Hillek and Carl Nielsen and Billy DeTine go, but they had also refused to satisfy him. They were heartless, they were cold, they were shallow, and he himself was probably crazy to stand here thinking of them as anything but ongoing nuclear fusions. "Many thynges doth infect the ayre, as the influence of sondry sterres," he quoted aloud, enormously pleased to have remembered the quote from Renaissance Lit. He only quoted aloud when in deserted areas, however; his angry craziness demanded privacy to be fully wallowed in. It was a lovers' quarrel.

"Jerry! Happy birthday, dear!"

"Thanks, Mom."

"So how does it feel to be twenty-six, son?"

"Oh, I don't know, Dad. Not too different from twenty-five."

"Your presents are in the mail, dear. I'm sorry they didn't get East by your birthday, but I just couldn't get to town to the post office; the car was acting up, and your father couldn't figure out if it was the starter or that little black thing that goes from the—"

"Now, Mary, we don't need to tell him all that long distance."

"Guess not. How's everything going, dear?"

"Fine, just fine."

"Did you sell any more—"

"No. No, I haven't. It takes time, you know, Mom."

Fourteen hundred miles away, his father cleared his throat. Jerry held the receiver a little away from his ear and closed his eyes, waiting.

"Speaking of selling, son, I happened to talk to John Nielsen yesterday, and he still needs someone to help him and Carl at the Grain & Feed. Now I'm not pressuring you, you know that. Whatever you want to do is fine with your mother and me. That's what we've always said, and we mean it. But I just promised John I'd pass along the information to you, so I am."

"Okay," Casey said. "The information is passed." He could see his father holding the phone—the upstairs extension, it would be—lightly in his big hand, still wearing his Stetson with his boots and plaid flannel shirt.

"Just so's you know, son."

"I know," Casey said. There was a pause.

"Are you still seeing that girl, dear, that you wrote us about? The kindergarten teacher? Kara Phillips?"

"Yes. No. A little."

"I have an idea! Why don't you bring her with you when you come home for Christmas? You know we'd just love to have her!"

"Now, Mary, don't push," Casey's father said.

"I wasn't pushing, Calvin Casey! All I said was that we'd love to have Jerry's friend stay with us over Christmas, if he'd like to bring her. She could have the spare room, it was just freshly papered, it'd be no trouble at all."

"Thanks, Mom. Maybe I'll ask her."

"Of course, it's up to you. Write us when your presents arrive, so I know they fit, and tell us if Kara is coming for Christmas."

"Assistant manager," his father said. "Did I mention that it's assistant manager?"

"Well, bye, dear. Happy birthday!"

"Good starting salary, son."

"Love you," Casey's mother said.

"Love you, too," Casey said, and hung up the receiver carefully, with no sound.

He quit the pizzeria. One night in October he had waited on the Chairman of the Graduate Committee, Dr. Stine. The man had been so tactful, so diplomatic in chatting with Casey without once mentioning Casey's failed novel-thesis, Casey's inexpert self-haircut ($4.70 at the barber, and that without sideburns), Casey's tomato-and-mozzarella smeared apron, that Casey had been unable to stand it. He smiled at the chairman, said yes, fall was beautiful in this part of the country, said yes, it was interesting that the papers always reported an increase in UFO sightings in the fall, said no, he didn't think there was anything in it. Then he went into the kitchen and stuffed his apron into the pizza oven, where it turned the exact color of flabby frozen anchovies.

He found a job as part-time groundsman for an old, beautiful, tree-shaded cemetery. He wrote all morning and raked leaves all afternoon, avoiding funerals in progress. The metal rake prongs caught repeatedly at the bases of tombstones and then twanged back, a sound as monotonous and hypnotic as a pendulum. Sometimes he returned late at night and walked through the cemetery. The darkness was rich and velvety; it was the quick flashes of headlights beyond the iron gates that seemed like the ghosts. He read the oldest of the tombstones with a penlight, stooping to trace the letters with his finger when age had made them illegible:

ELIZABETH ANN CARMODY

1851-1862

Eleven years old, he thought. At eleven years old he had been playing Would-You-Go? on the big flat rock on the plains. Eleven years old.

JAMES ALLEN ROBERTS

1789-1812

DULCE ET DECORUM EST PRO PATRIA MORI

Ha, snorted Casey, child of draft card burnings and ping-pong detente.

CECILIA HARDWICK SMITH

1884-1940

BEYOND THIS NARROW VALE OF EARTH

WHERE BRIGHT CELESTIAL AGES ROLL

THE COUNTLESS STARS OF HEAVEN'S REALM

GUIDE AND LIGHT THE WAND'RING SOUL

Ha again, Casey told the stars, the lovers' quarrel having solidified into the cynical half-banter of an accepted marriage. So go ahead, guide and light. Send down knowledge. Send down enlightenment. Send down a publisher. Go ahead, I'm waiting, I'm a wandering soul, as duly specified, I'm ready. H- has arisen. Go ahead.

Clouds started to roll in from the west.

"And she said to tell you that it would be no trouble at all, you could have the spare room, and they'd love to have you."

Kara raised herself on one elbow in Casey's rumpled, un-spare bed. The neon barber pole just outside Casey's window striped her breasts with revolving red and blue.

"I don't think it's fair of you to change the subject in the middle of a discussion just because you're losing."

"I was losing?"

"You know you were. And then you just drop in this invitation to your parents' house for Christmas, and that really puts me at an emotional disadvantage, Jer. It's not fighting fair."

"So report me to the Geneva Convention."

"There you go, getting nasty again, de-railing the argument just because you haven't got a valid viewpoint that won't stand up to close scrutiny."

"I haven't got a valid viewpoint that will stand up to close scrutiny? And what is it you've got, an airtight case?"

"I didn't say that. I said—"

"More like a braintight case."

"—that not being able to prove that a thing exists isn't the same as being able to prove that it doesn't exist, and—"

"Absolutely impervious to the osmosis of facts."

"—just because the Navy doesn't choose to admit that a UFO—"

"Last month it was transactional analysis."

"That was different! If you'd just have an open mind—"

"With enough holes to fit the airtight case in?"

"That's enough!" Kara shouted. She bolted upright in bed and clutched Casey's grubby sheet around her. "You're so superior, aren't you, with your clever little wisecracks about my intelligence! Just because you've never seen one, they don't exist, right? If *Jerry Casey*, great unpublished novelist, hasn't personally seen and touched and goddamn tasted a UFO, then there's no such thing. Of course not! No matter that hundreds of sightings have been reported, no matter that a respected witness right here in town saw a ship streaking over the woods, no matter that there doesn't—if *Jerry Casey* didn't see it, it doesn't exist, because Jerry Casey is the great fictional expert on spaceships and galactic empires! If *Jerry Casey*, with three unpublished novels and the enormous authority of his sacred pile of rejection sl—"

Casey hit her. It wasn't a hard slap, he didn't know he was going to do it until he had, and instantly he regretted it more than he had ever regretted anything else in his life. Kara put her hand to her red cheek and turned away from him, the sheet twisting itself around her small striped breasts. Tears filled her eyes but did not fall. Casey put out one hand to touch her shoulder, but he couldn't make the hand quite connect and it hung there, suspended between them, useless.

"Kara...oh God, Kara, I'm *sorry*."

She didn't answer. The sheet humped up over her thin legs. Something broke in Casey, something so light and delicate he hadn't known himself that it was there, or what he would say when it wasn't.

"Kara, listen, I'm sorry I hit you, so fucking sorry I don't know how to say it. But, Kara, you don't know, you *can't* know, I've wanted there to be something out there since I was a kid, wanted it more desperately than anything else in my whole fucking life. I used to stand out there on the plains and squeeze my eyes shut and *will* them to be out there, to come down to me, because I was one of them. I knew it, so they had to know it, too. I made up whole stories, epics, about how I got left here by mistake and adopted by my parents, but they'd come back for me eventually. It was so real I could taste it, Kara, could shiver with it down to my bones, my marrow. It was like a religion, or an insanity. And I *still* would like to believe, would give fucking anything to believe, but I can't. The evidence against it is just too strong. Do you know what the odds are that intelligent life would behave like...so I started to convince myself that the stories were just made up. I started to make them up, to write them down. Kara, it's not 'superiority,' it's not wisecracks, it's...Kara, do you see what I'm talking about? Can you understand what I'm trying to mean? Kara?"

She didn't answer. After a while he touched her. She put her head on his shoulder. He wiped her tears. She let him. He stroked her hair and apologized all over again. She said it was all right, looking pensive and thoughtful. He pulled the blanket protectively up to her chin. She lay still in his arms. He kissed her. She smiled. A few days later she called and said they should have a long talk. He never saw her again.

Paul Rizzo was getting married, and he wrote to invite Casey to the wedding. His bride was a fellow faculty member at Lunell College—an *assistant professor*, Rizzo wrote, underlining the words twice. She was also "the only child of a wealthy shoe polish entrepreneur." Casey tried to figure out how you got really wealthy from shoe polish, couldn't, and knew that this proved nothing. He wouldn't have known how to become really wealthy if the process were detailed for him in heroic couplets. For all he knew, shoe polish was a rewarding and fulfilling way to make money enough to freshly wallpaper all the spare rooms in Montana. For all he knew, shoes and the right polish were what his life had been missing all along, the yin and yang of his universe's deficiencies. For all he knew.

With his letter Rizzo had enclosed a picture of his fiancée, cut from the local newspaper which had announced their engagement. She looked pretty, if a little blurry. The invitation was embossed with blue-and-white doves swooping around a quotation from Keats.

Tramping along over the hard Montana snows on Christmas night, Casey tried to picture the wedding. There would be champagne, and sexy-coy toasts, and good food. There would be women—bridesmaids in silky dresses, Lunell professors with good minds, college-student relatives giggly and flushed with wine. The wedding was in April, over Easter recess, so the bridesmaids and professors and gigglers would have on spring dresses, light and bare. They would smell of flowery perfumes. They would dance on strappy, high-heeled sandals. They would talk to Casey on the dance floor, at the bar, on the church steps. And they would all ask him, eventually, what it was that he "did." Or tried to do. Or was supposed to be doing.

Somewhere near the barns a cow lowed. Casey tramped up to his old flat rock, knocked the snow off it, and sat down. Overhead the stars blazed. He willed himself to concentrate on the stars, to forget the depressing mechanics of attending Rizzo's wedding, the self-kept score sheets. He just wouldn't think about it. Above him glittered Thekala, aka Aldebaran, aka The Red Terror. To the south and east shone Rigel, Sirius, Betelguese, Pollux, Procyon. The Orion Nebula, spawn ground of new stars. They used to pretend it was alive, like a queen bee. Only the southwest looked subdued, empty of all but the faint stars of Cetus. The sky there was a soft, even black, lustrous with reflected light, like....

Like shoe polish.

In January the ground froze so hard that no graves could be dug. People continued to die anyway, and their caskets were stacked, carefully labeled, in a brick vault to await a thaw. Casey was laid off. Nothing else seemed to be opening up in the cemetery line. So he took a job as a part-time janitor in a high school, nightly scrubbing anatomical impossibilities off lavatory walls with industrial-strength cleanser. He wrote.

In February, it snowed 52 inches, a century's record. During the entire month the sky remained cloudy; if the stars had all simultaneously winked out, their light spent like so many weary philanderers, Casey wouldn't have known it. He caught the flu and spent six days in bed, feverishly watching the barber pole revolve against the gray snow. He wrote.

In March, Dr. James Randall Stine, Chairman of the Graduate Committee and a widower for two years, announced his engagement to Miss Kara Phillips, a kindergarten teacher in the local public schools.

Casey's father called to just pass on the information that Marty Hillek's father was looking around for someone with business sense to help him run the Holiday Inn. He wrote.

In April, a week before Rizzo's wedding, Casey's third attempt at a novel sold to a major publisher. It was about a galactic empire.

He leaped through the dark April woods, the letter in his hand, the ground inches below his feet. He was Pan with scriptorial pipes, Orpheus with graphic lyre, Caesar of the literary space ways. He was the god-child of intergalactic muses. He was the first person in the universe to publish a novel. He was the Pied Piper with hordes at his singing back, Circe with spells to drive men mad. He was drunk, but only partly on California champagne.

Running wildly through springtime smells unseen in the darkness, he held the letter before him and a little to one side, like a spear, brandishing it upward.

"See! See!" he called up between the trees, drunkenly flaunting his own theatricality. "See! See what I did about you! Look! Look!"

The stars glittered.

Casey stopped running and stood panting beneath a sugar maple, holding his side. He was Shakespeare, he was Tolstoy, he was Dreiser, he was a definite A. He could walk on spangle-colored planets forever, just as soon as his stomach lay still.

The stars glittered.

Across the sky the branches of the sugar maple slanted like bars. Gemini sliced in half, Dubhe divided from Merak. Through the bars the Milky Way looked broken, fitful, about to sever and recede even more, and it was already so far away, so high…so high…they were all so high…. For a dizzy second Casey put his hand on the tree trunk, searching for a foothold. But the second passed and he stood on the ground, half-trampled fern shoots under his worn boots.

The stars glittered.

Okay, so the universe doesn't notice, hardly an original observation, Casey ol' boy, got to do better than that. What'd you expect—a supernova? No romantic despair; cosmic self-pity strictly forbidden in moments of drunken triumph, on pain of triviality. No brooding, no self-indulgent self-incrimination. "A man's reach should exceed…." so you've got a hell of a reach, kudos to you ol' Jer, good to have a hell of a reach. *Supposed* to have a hell of a reach. Reach for a star a star is born born to boogie...oh, hell. I am not Prufrock, nor was meant to be—

Meant to be what?

Abruptly, he saw that he was not alone. Under the sugar maple, at the edge of the wide circle of branches, stood a child. A skinny, grubby boy, ten years old, gazing upward. Casey lurched forward, but the boy ignored him. Motionless except for his eyes, he was conquering distant, spangle-colored planets, and in his shining look, Casey saw, there was no longing; no one longs for what he already possesses. He was still, complete, but as Casey grabbed wildly to throttle that unbearable wholeness in the rapt face that he knew perfectly well was not there, the champagne heaved and he threw up into the trampled fern shoots. When he could finally wipe his mouth on his shirt tail, the boy was gone.

The stars glittered.

Casey stumbled back through the woods. In one small clearing he smelled lilacs, barely budded but sweet in the dark, and he turned his head away. Somewhere he lost the path. Scratched by brambles, scuffing the decay of last year's leaves, he thrashed forward until the moon rose. It was easier, then, to walk, but the moonlit pattern of dark branches on the white letter made him squeeze his eyes shut, and it was thus that he tripped over the spaceship.

It wasn't really, of course. The ship itself was a hundred feet away, dully black in the moonlight, circled with birch branches that had been pushed aside by its landing and had snapped back. Casey, sprawled on the ground over a foot-long, log-shaped...whatever it was, could almost feel the crack of those returning birch limbs on his back and shoulders. He reached under himself to feel the Whatever; it was hard and smooth, faintly vibrating. Unlike the boy, it did not vanish.

Unsuspected additional champagne churned in his stomach.

The ship was small; it could hardly be more than some sort of shuttle. Curved into flowing lines and embraced by budding trees, it looked weirdly beautiful in the night woods, weirdly right. Moonlight slid off the black surface, a deep rich black the color of loam. Leaves and ferns grew right up to where the ship rested on the forest floor. There was no burned patch, no sign that the ship had not always been there, would not always be there, a part of the ferns and birches, surrounded by the usual night rustlings and scamperings. An owl hooted.

Under Casey's belly, the Whatever began to hum.

He rolled off it and scrambled to his feet. A section of the ship slid upward, sending a shaft of blue light over the ground. Slowly a ramp descended until it met the dead leaves, which sighed softly.

Casey closed his eyes. He was drunk, he told himself. He was drunk, he was emotionally exhausted, he was hallucinating in some bizarre, wish-fulfillment fantasy. He was insane, he was schizophrenic, he was dead. He was a grown man with a more-or-less job, aging parents, and his own copy of the ten-volume Oxford English Dictionary. He was afraid, but not of the ship.

When he opened his eyes, it was still there. The "door" was still open. Nothing was visible inside except the bright blue light. The log-shaped Whatever rose into the air as high as Casey's chest and floated towards the ship. Ten feet away it stopped, floated back to Casey's chest, then again toward the ship. When Casey didn't follow, it repeated the whole sequence. Casey took one step forward.

He was on the flat rock under the twilight sky. *Would You Go*? they asked each other, sprawled on concave stomachs. Nah, said Marty Hillek—too dangerous. Chicken! said Carl Nielsen, chicken! I'd go, said Billy DeTine, I wouldn't care, I'm not afraid, I'd go. Me too, whispered little Jerry Casey, youngest of the lot. Me too. What if you never got back? said Marty Hillek, and no one said anything.

"The probability," lectured the professor to Astronomy 101, "of intelligent life visiting earth covertly is very small. Even if we generously suppose a 50-50 chance of life developing on any planet within a 25-light-year radius of Earth, the next calculation would—"

"You don't *know*," insisted Kara Stine, née Phillips. "Nobody really knows."

Casey took another step forward. Wet leaves squished under his boot. The letter rustled in his hand:

Dear Mr. Casey:

We are happy to inform you that our editorial staff is very impressed with your book, and that we are interested in publishing it. First, however, it is necessary....

The Whatever floated back to Casey a third time. It was humming more loudly now, and in the humming Casey heard a soft urgency.

Moonlight shone on the letter, crumpled where his fist had tightened, fouled at one corner with vomited champagne.

Would You Go? asked Marty Hillek and Carl Nielsen and Billy DeTine. What if you never got back? Nights on the cemetery tombs: Regulus

Formalhaut Betelguese Ri-i-gel. Days at his desk, struggling with stars on the head of a pin. "If Jerry Casey, great unpublished novelist, hasn't personally seen one...." *Me too,* whispered little Jerry Casey. We are happy to inform you... "What are you doing now? I mean your, uh, plans?" Me too. Oh, me too. Happy to inform... "Escapist improbabilities, Mr. Casey. You must see...'galactic empire'!" Happy to inform you....

Casey, battlefield for two warring empires, hiccupped in anguish.

Carefully, as if he might break, he took three steps backward. Then three more.

The Whatever followed him, then reversed direction and floated towards the ship, but only once. It floated inside, and the curved section of hull lowered slowly. The ship started to rise, slowly at first, then more rapidly. For a moment the dark hull stood poised above the birches, blotting out the stars. Then it blurred and was gone. The birch branches snapped back. Something small and furry scuttled away through the leaves, startled by the sudden sharp sobbing that went on and on, the unchecked tearless sobbing of a ten-year-old-boy.

You know the rest. All but Casey's name, which is not Casey. You can read in any standard reference work about the first official UN contact with the Beta Hydrans, fifteen years ago last May. You can read the pages and pages of testimony from the Des Moines dentist and the Portuguese fisherman and the Australian housewife who visited the Beta Hydran spacecraft during their reconnaissance landings. You can read about the shifts of global power and the scientific boons and the interstellar promises of good faith and speedy return by the Beta Hydrans, who were not part of a galactic empire and who seemed bewildered by the entire concept. You can't *not* read it; it's everywhere.

You can look up Casey, too, in the reference works, and read about how he became the most famous "name" in SF before he was forty-five. You can look up his awards, his honorary this-and-thats, his movie credits, the alimony he pays both wives, his bout with alcoholism. If your mind runs that way, you can look up his biographies—written, all, by impoverished Ph.D.'s weary of Keats—which will analyze for you all the early environmental influences on Casey's writing. You can look up the academic critics, also impoverished Ph.D.'s, who have concerned themselves with Casey's novels. They find in all of them, except the first, a "lost, human yearning, a quality almost mythic in the scope of its cosmic rootlessness" (Glasser, Richard J., "Rockets and Wanderjahr: Another Look at SF," PMLA, 122 (1992), 48-76). You can look it all up, or could if you knew Casey's name. You'd recognize it, even if you don't read "that space stuff."

But what you don't know, can't look up, is the loss of Casey's galactic empire. What it was, what it meant, how it felt. You don't know. Unless it has happened to you, you don't know. You can't ever know.

Afterword to "Casey's Empire"

This was a very important story to me, and not only because of its content. It garnered me my very first piece of fan mail: a postcard from James Patrick Kelly, who had the generous habit of telling other pros when he liked a story of theirs. Subsequently I met Jim at a convention; he introduced me to John Kessel; together they introduced me to Connie Willis. Thirty-five years later, we are still friends.

At the time I wrote the story, I had just finished my Master's degree in English, during which I served as a teaching assistant in the English department of the college, teaching freshman composition. Fortunately, several members of that particular department considered science fiction to be genuine literature. Other members did not. In subsequent decades, that situation has changed for the better. Now we are not only accepted but trendy. Who knew?

The process of becoming a writer, for me as for Jerry Casey, is often long and anguished. As for Jerry Casey's long string of rejection slips—well, every writer is familiar with those. I have saved all of mine.

SHIVA IN SHADOW

1. SHIP

I watched the probe launch from the *Kepler's* top-deck observatory, where the entire Schaad hull is clear to the stars. I stood between Ajit and Kane. The observatory, which was also the ship's garden, bloomed wildly with my exotics, bursting into flower in such exuberant profusion that even to see the probe go, we had to squeeze between a seven-foot-high bed of comoralias and the hull.

"God, Tirzah, can't you prune these things?" Kane said. He pressed his nose to the nearly invisible hull, like a small child. Something streaked briefly across the sky. "There it goes. Not that there's much to see."

I turned to stare at him. Not much to see! Beyond the *Kepler* lay the most violent and dramatic part of the galaxy, in all its murderous glory. True, the *Kepler* had stopped a hundred light years from the core, for human safety, and dust-and-gas clouds muffled the view somewhat. But, on the other hand, we were far enough away for a panoramic view.

The supermassive black hole Sagittarius A*, the lethal heart of the galaxy, shone gauzily with the heated gases it was sucking downward into oblivion. Around Sgr A* circled Sagittarius West, a three-armed spiral of hot plasma ten light years across, radiating furiously as it cooled. Around that, Sagittarius East, a huge shell left over from some catastrophic explosion within the last 100,000 years, expanded outward. I saw thousands of stars, including the blazing blue-hot stars of IRS16, hovering dangerously close to the hole, and giving off a stellar wind fierce enough to blow a long, fiery tail off the nearby red giant star. Everything was racing, radiating, colliding, ripping apart, screaming across the entire electromagnetic spectrum. All set against the sweet, light scent of my brief-lived flowers.

Nothing going on. But Kane had never been interested in spectacle.

Ajit said in his musical accent, "No, not much to see. But much to pray for. There go we."

Kane snapped, "I don't pray."

"I did not mean 'pray' in the religious sense," Ajit said calmly. He is always calm. "I mean hope. It is a miraculous thing, yes? There go we."

He was right, of course. The probe contained the Ajit-analogue, the Kane-analogue, the Tirzah-analogue, all uploaded into a crystal computer no bigger than a comoralia bloom. "We" would go into that stellar violence at the core, where our fragile human bodies could not go. "We" would observe, and measure, and try to find answers to scientific questions in that roiling heart of galactic space-time. Ninety percent of the probe's mass was shielding for the computer. Ninety percent of the rest was shielding for the three mini-capsules that the probe would fire back to us with recorded and analyzed data. There was no way besides the mini-caps to get information out of that bath of frenzied radiation.

Just as there was no way to know exactly what questions Ajit and Kane would need to ask until they were close to Sgr A*. The analogues would know. They knew everything Ajit and Kane and I knew, right up until the moment we were uploaded.

"Shiva, dancing," Ajit said.

"What?" Kane said.

"Nothing. You would not appreciate the reference. Come with me, Tirzah. I want to show you something."

I stopped straining to see the probe, unzoomed my eyes, and smiled at Ajit. "Of course."

This is why I am here.

Ajit's skin is softer than Kane's, less muscled. Kane works out every day in ship's gym, scowling like a demon. Ajit rolled off me and laid his hand on my glowing, satisfied crotch.

"You are so beautiful, Tirzah."

I laughed. "We are all beautiful. Why would anyone effect a genetic alteration that wasn't?"

"People will do strange things sometimes."

"So I just noticed," I teased him.

"Sometimes I think so much of what Kane and I do is strange to you. I see you sitting at the table, listening to us, and I know you cannot follow our physics. It makes me sad for you."

I laid my hand on top of his, pushing down my irritation with the skill of long practice. It does irritate me, this calm sensitivity of Ajit's. It's lovely in bed—he is gentler and more considerate, always, than Kane—but then there comes the other side, this faint condescension. "I feel sad for you." Sad for me! Because I'm not also a scientist! I am the captain of this expedition, with master status in ship control and a first-class license as a Nurturer. On the *Kepler*, my word is law, with virtually no limits. I have over fifty standard-years' experience, specializing in the nurture of scientists. I have never lost an expedition, and I need no one's pity.

Naturally, I showed none of this to Ajit. I massaged his hand with mine, which meant that his hand massaged my crotch, and purred softly. "I'm glad you decided to show me this."

"Actually, that is not what I wanted to show you."

"No?"

"No. Wait here, Tirzah."

He got up and padded, naked, to his personal locker. Beautiful, beautiful body, brown and smooth, like a slim, polished tree. I could see him clearly; Ajit always makes love with the bunk lights on full, as if in sunlight. We lay in his bunk, not mine. I never take either him or Kane to my bunk. My bunk contained various concealed items that they don't, and won't, know about, from duplicate surveillance equipment to rarely used subdermal trackers. Precautions, only. I am a captain.

From his small storage locker, Ajit pulled a statue and turned shyly, even proudly, to show it to me. I sat up, surprised.

The statue was big, big enough so that it must have taken up practically his entire allotment of personal space. Heavy, too, from the way Ajit balanced it before his naked body. It was some sort of god with four arms, enclosed in a circle of flames, made of what looked like very old bronze.

"This is Nataraja," Ajit said. "Shiva dancing."

"Ajit—"

"No, I am not a god worshipper," he smiled. "You know me better than that, Tirzah. Hinduism has many gods—thousands—but they are, except to the ignorant, no more than embodiments of different aspects of reality. Shiva is the dance of creation and destruction, the constant flow of energy in the cosmos. Birth and death and rebirth. It seemed fitting to bring him to the galactic core, where so much goes on of all three."

This explanation sounded weak to me—a holo of Shiva would have accomplished the same thing, without using up nearly all of Ajit's weight allotment. Before I could say this, Ajit said, "This statue has been in my family for four hundred years. I must bring it home, along with the answers to my scientific questions."

I don't understand Ajit's scientific concerns very well—or Kane's—but I know down to my bones how much they matter to him. It is my job to know. Ajit carries within his beautiful body a terrible, coursing ambition, a river fed by the longings of a poor family who have sacrificed what little they had gained on New Bombay for this favored son. Ajit is the receptacle into which they have poured so much hope, so much sacrifice, so much selfishness. The strain on that vessel is what makes Ajit's love-making so gentle. He cannot afford to crack.

"You'll bring the Shiva statue back to New Bombay," I said softly, "and your answers, too."

In his hands, with the bright lighting, the bronze statue cast a dancing shadow on his naked body.

I found Kane at his terminal, so deep in thought that he didn't know I was there until I squeezed his shoulder. Then he jumped, cursed, and dragged his eyes from his displays.

"How does it progress, Kane?"

"It doesn't. How could it? I need more data!"

"It will come. Be patient," I said.

He rubbed his left ear, a constant habit when he's irritated, which is much of the time. When he's happily excited, Kane runs his left hand through his coarse red hair until it stands up like flames. Now he smiled ruefully. "I'm not much known for patience."

"No, you're not."

"But you're right, Tirzah. The data will come. It's just hard waiting for the first mini-cap. I wish to hell we could have more than three. Goddamn cheap bureaucrats! At an acceleration of—"

"Don't give me the figures again," I said. I wound my fingers in his hair and pulled playfully. "Kane, I came to ask you a favor."

"All right," he said instantly. Kane never counts costs ahead of time. Ajit would have turned gently cautious. "What is it?"

"I want you to learn to play go with Ajit."

He scowled. "Why?"

With Kane, you must have your logic ready. He would do any favor I asked, but unless he can see why, compliance would be grudging at best. "First, because go will help you pass the time until the first mini-cap arrives, in doing something other than chewing the same data over and over again until you've masticated it into tastelessness. Second, because the game is complex enough that I think you'll enjoy it. Third, because I'm not too bad at it myself but Ajit is better, and I think you will be, too, so I can learn from both of you."

And fourth, I didn't say aloud, because Ajit is a master, he will beat you most of the time, and he needs the boost in confidence.

Ajit is not the scientist that Kane is. Practically no one in the settled worlds is the scientist that Kane is. All three of us know this, but none of us have ever mentioned it, not even once. There are geniuses who are easy for the inferior to work with, who are generous enough to slow down their mental strides to the smaller steps of the merely gifted. Kane is not one of them.

"Go," Kane says thoughtfully. "I have friends who play that."

This was a misstatement. Kane does not have friends, in the usual sense. He has colleagues, he has science, and he has me.

He smiled at me, a rare touch of sweet gratitude on his handsome face. "Thanks, Tirzah. I'll play with Ajit. You're right, it will pass the time until the probe sends back the prelim data. And if I'm occupied, maybe I'll be less of a monster to you."

"You're fine to me," I say, giving his hair another tug, grinning with the casual flippancy he prefers. "Or if you're not, I don't care."

Kane laughs. In moments like this, I am especially careful that my own feelings don't show. To either of them.

2. PROBE

We automatically woke after the hyperjump. For reasons I don't understand, a hyperjump isn't instantaneous. Perhaps because it's not really a "jump" but a Calabi-Yau dimension tunnel. Several days ship-time had passed, and the probe now drifted less than five light years from the galactic core. The probe, power off, checked out perfectly; the shielding had held even better than expected. And so had we. My eyes widened as I studied the wardroom displays.

On the *Kepler*, dust clouds had softened and obscured the view.

Here, nothing did. We drifted just outside a star that had begun its deadly spiral inward toward Sgr A*. Visuals showed the full deadly glory around the hole: the hot blue cluster of IRS16. The giant red star IRS7 with its long tail distended by stellar winds. The stars already past the point of no return, pulled by the gravity of Sgr A* inexorably toward its event horizon. The radio, gamma-ray, and infrared displays revealed even more, brilliant with the radiation pouring from every single gorgeous, lethal object in the bright sky.

And there, too, shone one of the mysteries Kane and Ajit had come to study: the massive, young stars that were not being yanked toward Sgr A*, and which in this place should have been neither massive nor relatively stable. Such stars should not exist this close to the hole. One star, Kane had told me, was as close to the hole as twice Pluto's orbit from Sol. How had it gotten there?

"It's beautiful, in a hellish way," I said to Ajit and Kane. "I want to go up to the observatory and see it direct."

"The observatory!" Kane said scornfully. "I need to get to work!" He sat down at his terminal.

None of this is true, of course. There is no observatory on the probe, and I can't climb the ladder "up" to it. Nor is there a wardroom with terminals, chairs, table, displays, a computer. We are the computer, or rather we are inside it. But the programs running along with us make it all seem as real as the fleshy versions of ourselves on the *Kepler*. This, it was determined by previous disastrous experience in space exploration, is necessary to keep us sane and stable. Human uploads need this illusion, this shadow reality, and we accept it easily. Why not? It's the default setting for our minds.

So Kane "sat at" his "terminal" to look at the preliminary data from the sensors. So did Ajit, and I "went upstairs" to the observatory, where I gazed outward for a long time.

I—the other "I", the one on the *Kepler*—grew up on a station in the Oort Cloud, Sol System. Space is my natural home. I don't really understand how mud-dwellers live on planets, or why they would want to, at the bottom of a murky and dirty shroud of uncontrollable air. I have learned to simulate understanding planetary love, because it is my job. Both Kane and Ajit come from rocks, Ajit from New Bombay and Kane from Terra herself. They are space scientists, but not real spacers.

No mud-dweller ever really sees the stars. And no human being had ever seen what I saw now, the frantic heart of the human universe.

Eventually I went back downstairs, rechecked ship's data, and then sat at the wardroom table and took up my embroidery. The ancient, irrelevant cloth-ornamenting is very soothing, almost as much so as gardening, although of course that's not why I do it. All first-class Nurturers practice some humble handicraft. It allows you to closely observe people while appearing absorbed and harmless.

Kane, of course, was oblivious to me. I could have glared at him through a magnifying glass and he wouldn't have noticed, not if he was working. Back on the *Kepler*, he had explained in simple terms—or at least as simple as Kane's explanations ever get—why there should not be any young stars this close to the core, as well as three possible explanations for why there are. He told me all this, in typical Kane fashion, in bed. Post-coital intimacy.

"The stars' spectra show they're young, Tirzah. And close—SO-2 comes to within eighty AU's of Sgr A*! It's wrong —the core is incredibly inhospitable to star formation! Also, these close-in stars have very peculiar orbits."

"You're taking it personally," I observed, smiling.

"Of course I am!" This was said totally without irony. "Those young stars have no business there. The tidal forces of the hole should rip any hot dust clouds to shreds long before any stars could form. And if they formed farther out, say 100 light years out, they should have died before they get this close in. These supermassive stars only last a few million years."

"But there they are."

"Yes. Why do you still have this lacy thing on? It's irritating."

"Because you were so eager that I didn't have time to get it off."

"Well, take it off now."

I did, and he wrapped my body close to his, and went on fretting over star formation in the core.

"There are three theories. One is that a dust cloud ringing the core, about six light years out, keeps forming stars, which are then blown outward again by galactic winds, and then drawn in, and repeat. Another theory is that there's a second, intermediate medium-sized black hole orbiting Sgr A* and exerting a counterpull on the stars. But if so, why aren't we detecting its radio waves? Another idea is that the stars aren't really young at all, they're composites of remnants of elderly stars that merged to form a body that only looks bright and young."

I said, "Which theory do you like?"

"None of them." And then, in one of those lightning changes he was capable of, he focused all his attention on me. "Are you all right, Tirzah? I know this has got to be a boring voyage for you. Running ship can't take much of your time, and neither can babysitting me."

I laughed aloud and Kane, having no idea why, frowned slightly. It was such a typically Kane speech. A sudden burst of intense concern, which would prove equally transitory. No mention of Ajit at all, as if only Kane existed for me. And his total ignorance of how often I interceded between him and Ajit, smoothed over tensions between them, spent time calming and centering separately each of these men who were more like the stars outside the ship than either of them were capable of recognizing. Brilliant, heated, intense, inherently unstable.

"I'm fine, Kane. I'm enjoying myself."

"Well, good," he said, and I saw that he then forgot me, back to brooding about his theories.

Neither Kane nor Ajit knows that I love Kane. I don't love Ajit. Whatever calls up love in our hidden hearts, it is unfathomable. Kane arouses in me a happiness, a desire, a completeness that puts a glow on the world because he—difficult, questing, vital—is in it. Ajit, through no fault of his own, does not.

Neither of them will ever know this. I would berate myself if they did. My personal feelings don't matter here. I am a captain.

"Damn and double damn!" Kane said, admiringly. "Look at that!"

Ajit reacted as if Kane had spoken to him, but of course Kane had not. He was just thinking aloud. I put down my embroidery and went to stand behind them at their terminals.

Ajit said, "Those readings must be wrong. The sensors were damaged after all, either in hypertransit or by radiation."

Kane didn't reply; I doubt he'd heard. I said, "What is it?"

It was Ajit who answered. "The mass readings are wrong. They're showing high mass density for several areas of empty space."

I said, "Maybe that's where the new young stars are forming?"

Not even Ajit answered this, which told me it was a stupid statement. It doesn't matter; I don't pretend to be a scientist. I merely wanted to keep them talking, to gauge their states of mind.

Ajit said, "It would be remarkable if all equipment had emerged undamaged from the jump into this radiation."

"Kane?" I said.

"It's not the equipment," he muttered. So he had been listening, at least peripherally. "Supersymmetry."

Ajit immediately objected to this, in terms I didn't understand. They were off into a discussion I had no chance of following. I let it go on for a while, then even longer, since it sounded the way scientific discussions are supposed to sound: intense but not acrimonious, not personal.

When they wound down a bit, I said, "Did the mini-capsule go off to the *Kepler*? They're waiting for the prelim data, and the mini-cap takes days to jump. Did either of you remember to record and send?"

They both looked at me, as if trying to remember who I was and what I was doing there. In that moment, for the first time, they looked alike.

"I remembered," Ajit said. "The prelim data went off to the *Kepler*. Kane—"

They were off again.

3. SHIP

The go games were not a success.

The problem, I could see, was with Ajit. He was a far better player than Kane, both intuitively and through experience. This didn't bother Kane at all; he thrived on challenge. But his own clear superiority subtly affected Ajit.

"Game won," he said for the third time in the evening, and at the slight smirk in his voice I looked up from my embroidery.

"Damn and double damn," Kane said, without rancor. "Set them up again."

"No, I think I will go celebrate my victories with Tirzah."

This was Kane's night, but the two of them had never insisted on precedence. This was because I had never let it come to that; it's part of my job to give the illusion that I am always available to both, on whatever occasion they wish. Of course, I control, through a hundred subtle signals and without either realizing it, which occasions they happen to wish. Where I make love depends on whom I need to observe. This direct claim by Ajit, connecting me to his go victories, was new.

Kane, of course, didn't notice. "All right. God, I wish the mini-cap would come. I want that data!"

Now that the game had released his attention, he was restless again. He rose and paced around the wardroom, which doesn't admit too much pacing. "I think I'll go up to the observatory. Anybody coming?"

He had already forgotten that I was leaving with Ajit. I saw Ajit go still. Such a small thing—Ajit was affronted that Kane was not affected by Ajit's game victory, or by his bearing me off like some earned prize. Another man would have felt a moment of pique and then forgotten it. Ajit was not another man. Neither was Kane. Stable men don't volunteer for missions like this.

It's different for me; I was bred to space. The scientists were not.

I put down my embroidery, took Ajit's hand, and snuggled close to him. Kane, for the moment, was fine. His restless desire for his data wouldn't do him any harm. It was Ajit I needed to work with.

I was the one who had suggested the go games. Good captains are not supposed to make mistakes like that. It was up to me to set things right.

By the time the mini-cap arrived, everything was worse.

They would not, either of them, stop the go games. They played obsessively, six or seven times a day, then nine or ten, and finally every waking minute. Ajit continued to win the large majority of the games, but not all of them. Kane focused his formidable intelligence on devising strategies, and he had the advantage of caring but not too much. Yes, he was obsessed, but I could see that once he had something more significant to do, he would leave the go games without a backward glance.

Ajit grew more focused, too. Even more intent on winning, even as he began to lose a few games. More slyly gleeful when he did win. He flicked his winning piece onto the board with a turn of the wrist in which I read both contempt and fear.

I tried everything I could to intervene, every trick from a century of experience. Nothing worked. Sex only made it worse. Ajit regarded sex as an earned prize, Kane as a temporary refreshment so he could return to the games.

One night Ajit brought out the statue of Shiva and put it defiantly on the wardroom table. It took up two-thirds of the space, a wide metal circle enclosing the four-armed dancer.

"What's that?" Kane said, looking up from the game board. "Oh, God, it's a god."

I said quickly, "It's an intellectual concept. The flow of cosmic energy in the universe."

Kane laughed, not maliciously, but I saw Ajit's eyes light up. Ajit said, "I want it here."

Kane shrugged. "Fine by me. Your turn, Ajit."

Wrong, wrong. Ajit had hoped to disturb Kane, to push him into some open objection to the statue. Ajit wanted a small confrontation, some outlet to emphasize his gloating. Some outlet for his growing unease as Kane's game improved. And some outlet for his underlying rage, always just under the surface, at Kane, the better scientist. The statue was supposed to be an assertion, even a slap in the face: I am here and I take up a lot of your space. Notice that!

Instead, Kane had shrugged and dismissed it.

I said, "Tell me again, Ajit, about Nataraja. What's the significance of the flames on the great circle?"

Ajit said quietly, "They represent the fire that destroys the world."

Kane said, "Your turn, Ajit."

Such a small incident. But deep in my mind, where I was aware of it but not yet overtly affected, fear stirred.

I was losing control here.

Then the first mini-cap of data arrived.

4. PROBE

Mind uploads are still minds. They are not computer programs in the sense that other programs are. Although freed of biological constraints such as enzymes that create sleep, hunger, and lust, uploads are not free of habit. In fact, it is habit that creates enough structure to keep all of us from frenzied feedback loops. On the probe, my job was to keep habit strong. It was the best safeguard for those brilliant minds.

"Time to sleep, gentlemen," I said lightly. We had been gathered in the wardroom for sixteen hours straight, Kane and Ajit at their terminals, me sitting quietly, watching them. I have powers of concentration equal in degree, though not in kind, to their own. They do not suspect this. It has been hours since I put down my embroidery, but neither noticed.

"Tirzah, not sleep now!" Kane snapped.

"Now."

He looked up at me like a sulky child. But Kane is not a child; I don't make that mistake. He knows an upload has to shut down for the cleansing program to run, a necessity to catch operating errors before they grow large enough to impair function. With all the radiation bathing the probe, the program is more necessary than ever. It takes a few hours to run through. I control the run cues.

Ajit looked at me expectantly. It was his night. This, too, was part of habit, as well as being an actual aid to their work. More than one scientist in my care has had that critical flash of intuition on some scientific problem while in my arms. Upload sex, like its fleshy analogue, both stimulates and relaxes.

"All right, all right," Kane muttered. "Good night."

I shut him down and turned to Ajit.

We went to his bunk. Ajit was tense, stretched taut with data and with sixteen hours with Kane. But I was pleased to see how completely he responded to me. Afterward, I asked him to explain the prelim data to me.

"And keep it simple, please. Remember who you're talking to!"

"To an intelligent and sweet lady," he said, and I gave him the obligatory smile. But he saw that I really did want to know about the data.

"The massive young stars are there when they should not be...Kane has explained all this to you, I know."

I nodded.

"They are indeed young, not mashed-together old stars. We have verified that. We are trying now to gather and run data to examine the other two best theories: a fluctuating ring of matter spawning stars, or other black holes."

"How are you examining the theories?"

He hesitated, and I knew he was trying to find explanations I could understand. "We are running various programs, equations, and sims. We are also trying to determine where to jump the probe next—you know about that."

Of course I did. No one moves this ship without my consent. It has two more jumps left in its power pack, and I must approve them both.

"We need to choose a spot from which we can fire beams of various radiation to assess the results. The heavier beams won't last long here, you know—the gravity of the superhole distorts them." He frowned.

"What is it, Ajit? What about gravity?"

"Kane was right," he said, "the mass detectors aren't damaged. They're showing mass nearby, not large but detectable, that isn't manifesting anything but gravity. No radiation of any kind."

"A black hole," I suggested.

"Too small. Small black holes radiate away, Hawking showed that long ago. The internal temperature is too high. There are no black holes smaller than three solar masses. The mass detectors are showing something much smaller than that."

"What?"

"We don't know."

"Were all the weird mass-detector readings in the prelim data you sent back to the *Kepler*?"

"Of course," he said, a slight edge in his voice.

I pulled him closer. "I can always rely on you," I said, and I felt his body relax.

I shut us down, as we lay in each other's arms.

It was Ajit who, the next day, noticed the second anomaly. And I who noticed the third.

"These gas orbits aren't right," Ajit said to Kane. "And they're getting less right all the time."

Kane moved to Ajit's terminal. "Tell me."

"The infalling gases from the circumnuclear disk...see...they curve here, by the western arm of Sgr West..."

"It's wind from the IRS16 cluster," Kane said instantly. "I got updated readings for those yesterday."

"No, I already corrected for that," Ajit said.

"Then maybe magnetization from IRS7, or—"

They were off again. I followed enough to grasp the general problem. Gases streamed at enormous speeds from clouds beyond the circumnuclear disk which surrounded the entire core like a huge doughnut. These streaming gases were funneled by various forces into fairly narrow, cone-like paths. The gases would eventually end up circling the black hole, spiraling inward and compressing to temperatures of billions of degrees before they were absorbed by the maw of the hole. The processes were understood.

But the paths weren't as predicted. Gases were streaming down wrong, approaching the hole wrong for predictions made from all the forces acting on them.

Ajit finally said to Kane, "I want to move the probe earlier than we planned."

"Wait a moment," I said instantly. Ship's movements were my decision. "It's not yet the scheduled time."

"Of course I'm including you in my request, Tirzah," Ajit said, with all his usual courtesy. There was something beneath the courtesy, however, a kind of glow. I recognized it. Scientists look like that when they have the germ of an important idea.

I thought Kane would object or ridicule, but something in their technical discussion must have moved him, too. His red hair stood up all over his head. He glanced briefly at his own displays, back at Ajit's, then at the younger man. He said, "You want to put the probe on the other side of Sagittarius A West."

"Yes."

I said, "Show me."

Ajit brought up the simplified graphic he had created weeks ago for me to gain an overview of this mission. It showed the black hole at the center of the galaxy, and the major structures around it: the cluster of hot blue stars, the massive young stars that should not have existed so close to the hole, the red giant star IRS16, with its long fiery tail. All this, plus our probe, lay on one side of the huge, three-armed spiraling plasma remnant, Sagittarius A West. Ajit touched the computer and a new dot appeared on the other side of Sgr A West, farther away from the hole than we were now.

"We want to go there, Tirzah," he said. Kane nodded.

I said, deliberately sounding naive, "I thought there wasn't as much going on over there. And besides, you said that Sgr A West would greatly obscure our vision in all wavelengths, with its own radiation."

"It will."

"Then—"

"There's something going on over there now," Kane said. "Ajit's right. That region is the source of whatever pull is distorting the gas infall. We need to go there."

We.

Ajit's right.

The younger man didn't change expression. But the glow was still there, ignited by Ajit's idea and fanned, I now realized, by Kane's approval. I heated it up a bit more. "But, Kane, your work on the massive young stars? I can only move the probe so many times, you know. Our fuel supply—"

"I have a lot of data on the stars now," Kane said, "and this matters more."

I hid my own pleasure. "All right. I'll move the probe."

But when I interfaced with ship's program, I found the probe had already been moved.

5. SHIP

Kane and Ajit fell on the mini-cap of prelim data like starving wolves. There were no more games of go. There was no more anything but work, unless I insisted.

At first I thought that was good. I thought that without the senseless, mounting competition over go, the two scientists would cooperate on the intense issues that mattered so much to both of them.

"Damn and double damn!" Kane said, admiringly. "Look at that!"

Ajit reacted as if Kane had spoken to him, but of course Kane had not. He was just thinking aloud. I put down my embroidery and went to stand behind them at their terminals.

Ajit said, with the new arrogance of the go wins in his voice, "Those readings must be wrong. The sensors were damaged after all, either in hypertransit or by radiation."

Kane, for a change, caught Ajit's tone. He met it with a sneer he must have used regularly on presumptuous post-grads. "'Must be wrong'? That's just the kind of puerile leaping to conclusions that gets people nowhere."

I said quickly, "What readings?"

It was Ajit who answered me, and although the words were innocuous, even polite, I heard the anger underlying them. "The mass readings are wrong. They're showing high mass density for several areas of empty space."

I said, "Maybe that's where the new young stars are forming?"

Not even Ajit answered this, which told me it was a stupid statement. It doesn't matter; I don't pretend to be a scientist. I merely wanted to keep them talking, to gauge their states of mind.

Ajit said, too evenly, "It would be remarkable if all probe equipment had emerged undamaged from the jump into core radiation."

"Kane?" I said.

"It's not the equipment." And then, "Supersymmetry."

Ajit immediately objected to this, in terms I didn't understand. They were off into a discussion I had no chance of following. What I could follow was the increasing pressure of Ajit's anger as Kane dismissed and belittled his ideas. I could almost see that anger, a hot plasma. As Kane ridiculed and belittled, the plasma collapsed into greater and greater density.

Abruptly they broke off their argument, went to their separate terminals, and worked like machines for twenty hours straight. I had to make them each eat something. They were obsessed, as only those seized by science or art can obsess. Neither of them would come to bed with me that night. I could have issued an executive order, but I chose not to exert that much trust-destroying force until I had to, although I did eventually announce that I was shutting down terminal access.

"For God's sake, Tirzah!" Kane snarled. "This is a once-in-a-species opportunity! I've got work to do!"

I said evenly, "You're going to rest. The terminals are down for seven hours."

"Five."

"All right." After five hours, Kane would still be snoring away.

He stood, stiff from the long hours of sitting. Kane is well over a hundred; rejuves can only do so much, so long. His cramped muscles, used to much more exercise, misfired briefly. He staggered, laughed, caught himself easily.

But not before he'd bumped the wardroom table. Ajit's statue of Shiva slid off and fell to the floor. The statue was old—four hundred years old, Ajit had said. Metal shows fatigue, too, although later than men. The statue hit the deck at just the right angle and broke.

"Oh...sorry, Ajit."

Kane's apology was a beat too late. I knew—with every nerve in my body, I knew this—that the delay happened because Kane's mind was still racing along his data, and it took an effort for him to refocus. It didn't matter. Ajit stiffened, and something in the nature of his anger changed, ionized by Kane's careless, preoccupied tone.

I said quickly, "Ship can weld the statue."

"No, thank you," Ajit said. "I will leave it as it is. Good night."

"Ajit—" I reached for his hand. He pulled it away.

"Good night, Tirzah."

Kane said, "The gamma-ray variations within Sgr A West aren't quite what was predicted." He blinked twice. "You're right, I am exhausted."

Kane stumbled off to his bunk. Ajit had already gone. After a long while I picked up the pieces of Ajit's statue and held them, staring at the broken figure of the dancing god.

The preliminary data, Kane had declared when it arrived, contained enough information to keep them both busy until the second mini-cap arrived. But by the next day, Kane was impatiently demanding more.

"These gas orbits aren't right," he said aloud, although not to either me or Ajit. Kane did that, worked in silence for long stretches until words exploded out of him to no particular audience except his own whirling thoughts. His ear was raw with rubbing.

I said, "What's not right about them?" When he didn't answer, or probably even hear me, I repeated the question, much louder.

Kane came out of his private world and scowled at me. "The infalling gases from beyond the circumnuclear disk aren't showing the right paths to Sgr A*."

I said, repeating something he'd taught me, "Could it be wind from the IRS16 cluster?"

"No. I checked those updated readings yesterday and corrected for them."

I had reached the end of what I knew to ask. Kane burst out, "I need more data!"

"Well, it'll get here eventually."

"I want it now," he said, and laughed sourly at himself, and went back to work.

Ajit said nothing, acting as if neither of us had spoken.

I waited until Ajit stood, stretched, and looked around vaguely. Then I said, "Lunch in a minute. But first come look at something with me." Immediately I started up the ladder to the observatory, so that he either had to follow or go through the trouble of arguing. He followed.

I had put the welded statue of Shiva on the bench near clear hull. It was the wrong side of the hull for the spectacular view of the core, but the exotics didn't press so close to the hull here, and thousands of stars shone in a sky more illuminated than Sol had seen since its birth. Shiva danced in his mended circle of flames against a background of cosmic glory.

Ajit said flatly, "I told you I wanted to leave it broken."

With Kane, frank opposition is fine; he's strong enough to take it and, in fact, doesn't respect much else. But Ajit is different. I lowered my eyes and reached for his hand. "I know. I took the liberty of fixing it anyway because, well, I thought you might want to see it whole again and because I like the statue so much. It has so much meaning beyond the obvious, especially here. In this place and this time. Please forgive me."

Ajit was silent for a moment, then he raised my hand to his lips. "You do see that."

"Yes," I said, and it was the truth. Shiva, the endless dance, the endless flow of energy changing form and state—how could anyone not see it in the gas clouds forming stars, the black hole destroying them, the violence and creation outside this very hull? Yet, at the same time, it was a profound insight into the very obvious, and I kept my eyes lowered so no glimpse of my faint contempt reached Ajit.

He kissed me. "You are so spiritual, Tirzah. And so sweet-natured."

I was neither. The only deceptions Ajit could see were the paranoid ones he assumed of others.

But his body had relaxed in my arms, and I knew that some part of his mind had been reassured. He and I could see spiritual beauties that Kane could not. Therefore he was in some sense superior to Kane. He followed me back down the ladder to lunch, and I heard him hum a snatch of some jaunty tune. Pleased with myself, I made for the galley.

Kane stood up so abruptly from his terminal that his eyes glowed. "Oh, my shitting stars. Oh, yes. Tirzah, I've got it."

I stopped cold. I had never seen anyone, even Kane, look quite like that. "Got what?"

"All of it." Suddenly he seized me and swung me into exuberant, clumsy dance. "All of it! I've got all of it! The young stars, the gas orbits, the missing mass in the universe! All shitting fucking all of it!"

"Wwwhhhaaatttt..." He was whirling me around so fast that my teeth rattled. "Kane, stop!"

He did, and enveloped me in a rib-cracking hug, then abruptly released me and dragged my bruised body to his terminal. "Look, sweetheart, I've got it. Now sit right there and I'm going to explain it in terms even you can understand. You'll love it. It'll love you. Now look here, at this region of space—"

I turned briefly to look at Ajit. For Kane, he didn't even exist.

6. PROBE

"The probe has moved," I said to Ajit and Kane. "It's way beyond the calculated drift. By a factor of ten."

Kane's eyes, red with work, nonetheless sharpened. "Let me see the trajectory."

"I transferred it to both your terminals." Ordinarily ship's data is kept separate, for my eyes only.

Kane brought up the display and whistled.

The probe is under the stresses, gravitational and radiational, that will eventually destroy it. We all know that. Our fleshy counterparts weren't even sure the probe would survive to send one mini-cap of data, and I'm sure they were jubilant when we did. Probably they treated the mini-cap like a holy gift, and I can easily imagine how eager they are for more. Back on the ship, I—the other "I"—had been counting on data, like oil, to grease the frictions and tensions between Ajit and Kane. I hoped it had.

We uploads had fuel enough to move the probe twice. After that, and since our last move will be no more than one-fiftieth of a light year from the black hole at the galactic core, the probe will eventually spiral down into Sgr A*. Before *that*, however, it will have been ripped apart by the immense tidal forces of the hole. However, long before that final death plunge, we analogues will be gone.

The probe's current drift, however, considerably farther away from the hole, was nonetheless much faster than projected. It was also slightly off course. We were being pulled in the general direction of Sgr A*, but not on the gravitational trajectory that would bring us into its orbit at the time and place the computer had calculated. In fact, at our current rate of acceleration, there was a chance we'd miss the event horizon completely.

What was going on?

Kane said, "Maybe we better hold off moving the probe to the other side of Sgr A West until we find out what's pulling us."

Ajit was studying the data over Kane's shoulder. He said hesitantly, "No…wait… I think we should move."

"Why?" Kane challenged.

"I don't know. I just have…call it an intuition. We should move now."

I held my breath. The only intuition Kane usually acknowledged was his own. But, earlier, things had subtly shifted. Kane had said, "Ajit's right. That region is the source of whatever pull is distorting the gas infall." Ajit had not changed expression, but I'd felt his pleasure, real as heat. That had given him the courage to now offer this unformed—"half-baked" was Kane's usual term—intuition.

Kane said thoughtfully, "Maybe you're right. Maybe the—" Suddenly his eyes widened. "Oh my God."

"What?" I said, despite myself. "What?"

Kane ignored me. "Ajit—run the sims for the gas orbits in correlation with the probe drift. I'll do the young stars!"

"Why do—" Ajit began, and then he saw whatever had seized Kane's mind. Ajit said something in Hindi; it might have been a curse, or a prayer. I didn't know. Nor did I know anything about their idea, or about what was happening with the gas orbits and young stars outside the probe. However, I could see clearly what was happening within.

Ajit and Kane fell into frenzied work. They threw comments and orders to each other, transferred data, backed up sims and equation runs. They tilted their chairs toward each other and spouted incomprehensible jargon. Once Kane cried, "We need more data!" and Ajit laughed, freely and easily, then immediately plunged back into whatever he was doing. I watched them for a long time, then stole quietly up to the observation deck for a minute alone.

The show outside was more spectacular than ever, perhaps because we'd been pulled closer to it than planned. Clouds of whirling gases wrapped and oddly softened that heart of darkness, Sgr A*. The fiery tail of the giant red star lit up that part of the sky. Stars glowed in a profusion unimaginable on my native Station J, stuck off in a remote arm of the galaxy. Directly in front of me glowed the glorious blue stars of the cluster IRS16.

I must have stayed on the observation deck longer than I'd planned, because Kane came looking for me. "Tirzah! Come on down! We want to show you where we're moving and why!"

We.

I said severely, gladness bursting in my heart, "You don't show me where we're going, Kane, you ask me. I captain this ship."

"Yeah, yeah, I know, you're a dragon lady. Come on!" He grabbed my hand and pulled me toward the ladder.

They both explained it, interrupting each other, fiercely correcting each other, having a wonderful time. I concentrated as hard as I could, trying to cut through the technicalities they couldn't do without, any more than they could do without air. Eventually I thought I glimpsed the core of their excitement.

"Shadow matter," I said, tasting the words on my tongue. It sounded too bizarre to take seriously, but Kane was insistent.

"The theory's been around for centuries, but deGroot pretty much discredited it in 2086," Kane said. "He—"

"If it's been discredited, then why—" I began.

"I said 'pretty much,'" Kane said. "There were always some mathematical anomalies with deGroot's work. And we can see now where he was wrong. He—"

Kane and Ajit started to explain why deGroot was wrong, but I interrupted. "No, don't digress so much! Let me just tell you what I think I understood from what you said."

I was silent a moment, gathering words. Both men waited impatiently, Kane running his hand through his hair, Ajit smiling widely. I said, "You said there's a theory that just after the Big Bang, gravity somehow decoupled from the other forces in the universe, just as matter decoupled from radiation. At the same time, you scientists have known for two centuries that there doesn't seem to be enough matter in the universe to make all your equations work. So scientists posited a lot of 'dark matter' and a lot of black holes, but none of the figures added up right anyway.

"And right now, neither do the orbits of the infalling gas, or the probe's drift, or the fact that massive young stars were forming that close to the black hole without being ripped apart by tidal forces. The forces acting on the huge clouds have to condense to form stars that big."

I took a breath, quick enough so that neither had time to break in and distract me with technicalities.

"But now you think that if gravity did decouple right after the Big Bang—"

"About 10^{-43} seconds after," Ajit said helpfully. I ignored him.

"— then two types of matter were created, normal matter and 'shadow matter.' It's sort of like matter and antimatter, only normal matter and shadow matter can't interact except by gravity. No interaction through any other force, not radiation or strong or weak forces. Only gravity. That's the only effect shadow matter has on our universe. Gravity.

"And a big chunk of this stuff is there on the other side of Sgr A West. It's exerting enough gravity to affect the path of the infalling gas. And to affect the probe's drift. And even to affect the young stars because the shadow matter-thing's exerting a counterpull on the massive star clouds, and that's keeping them from being ripped apart by the hole as soon as they otherwise would be. So they have time to collapse into young stars."

"Well, that's sort of it, but you've left out some things that alter and validate the whole," Kane said impatiently, scowling.

"Yes, Tirzah, dear heart, you don't see the—you can't just say that 'counterpull'—let me try once more."

They were off again, but this time I didn't listen. So maybe I hadn't seen the theory whole, but only glimpsed its shadow. It was enough.

They had a viable theory. I had a viable expedition, with a goal, and cooperatively productive scientists, and a probability of success.

It was enough.

Kane and Ajit prepared the second mini-cap for the big ship, and I prepared to move the probe. Our mood was jubilant. There was much laughing and joking, interrupted by intense bursts of incomprehensible jabbering between Ajit and Kane.

But before I finished my programming, Ajit's head disappeared.

7. SHIP

Kane worked all day on his shadow-matter theory. He worked ferociously, hunched over his terminal like a hungry dog with a particularly meaty bone, barely glancing up and saying little. Ajit worked, too, but the quality of his working was different. The terminals both connect to the same computer, of course; whatever Kane had, Ajit had, too. Ajit could follow whatever Kane did.

But that's what Ajit was doing: following. I could tell it from the timing of his accesses, from the whole set of his body. He was a decent scientist, but he was not Kane. Given the data and enough time, Ajit might have been able to go where Kane raced ahead now. Maybe. Or, he might have been able to make valuable additions to Kane's thinking. But Kane gave him no time; Kane was always there first, and he asked no help. He had shut Ajit out completely. For Kane, nothing existed right now but his work.

Toward evening he looked up abruptly and said to me, "They'll move the probe. The uploads—they'll move it."

I said, "How do you know? It's not time yet, according to the schedule."

"No. But they'll move it. If I figured out the shadow matter here, I will there, too. I'll decide that more data is needed from the other side of Sgr A West, where the main shadow mass is."

I looked at him. He looked demented, like some sort of Roman warrior who has just wrestled with a lion. All that was missing was the blood. Wild, filthy hair—when had he last showered? Clothes spotted with the food I'd made him gulp down at noon. Age lines beginning, under strain and fatigue and despite the rejuve, to drag down the muscles of his face. And his eyes shining like Sgr A West itself.

God, I loved him.

I said, with careful emphasis, "You're right. The Tirzah upload will move the ship for better measurements."

"Then we'll get more data in a few days," Ajit said. "But the radiation on the other side of Sgr A West is still intense. We must hope nothing gets damaged in the probe programs, or in the uploads themselves, before we get the new data."

"We better hope nothing gets damaged long before that in my upload," Kane said, "or they won't even know what data to collect." He turned back to his screen.

The brutal words hung in the air.

I saw Ajit turn his face away from me. Then he rose and walked into the galley.

If I followed him too soon, he would see it as pity. His shame would mount even more.

"Kane," I said in a low, furious voice, "you are despicable."

He turned to me in genuine surprise. "What?"

"You know what." But he didn't. Kane wasn't even conscious of what he'd said. To him, it was a simple, evident truth. Without the Kane upload, no one on the probe would know how to do first-class science.

"I want to see you upstairs on the observation deck," I said to him. "Not now, but in ten minutes. And you announce that you want me to see something up there." The time lag, plus Kane's suggesting the trip, would keep Ajit from knowing I was protecting him.

But now I had put up Kane's back. He was tired, he was stressed, he was inevitably coming down from the unsustainable high of his discovery.

Neither body nor mind can keep at that near-hysterical pitch for too long. I had misjudged, out of my own anger at him.

He snapped, "I'll see you on the observation deck when I want to see you there, and not otherwise. Don't push me around, Tirzah. Not even as captain." He turned back to his display.

Ajit emerged from the galley with three glasses on a tray. "A celebratory drink. A major discovery deserves that. At a minimum."

Relief was so intense I nearly showed it on my face. It was all right. I had misread Ajit, underestimated him. He ranked the magnitude of Kane's discovery higher than his own lack of participation in it, after all. Ajit was, first, a scientist.

He handed a glass to me, one to Kane, one for himself. Kane took a hasty, perfunctory gulp and returned to his display. But I cradled mine, smiling at Ajit, trying with warmth to convey the admiration I felt for his rising above the personal.

"Where did you get the wine? It wasn't on the ship manifest!"

"It was in my personal allotment," Ajit said, smiling.

Personal allotments are not listed nor examined. A bottle of wine, the statue of Shiva...Ajit had brought some interesting choices for a galactic core. I sipped the red liquid. It tasted different from the Terran or Martian wines I had grown up with: rougher, more full-bodied, not as sweet.

"Wonderful, Ajit."

"I thought you would like it. It is made in my native New Bombay, from genemod grapes brought from Terra."

He didn't go back to his terminal. For the next half-hour, he entertained me with stories of New Bombay. He was a good storyteller, sharp and funny. Kane worked steadily, ignoring us. The ten-minute deadline I had set for him to call me up to the observation deck came and went.

After half an hour, Kane stood and staggered. Once before, when he'd broken Ajit's statue, stiffness after long sitting had made Kane unsteady. That time he'd caught himself after simply bumping the wardroom table. This time he crashed heavily to the floor.

"Kane!"

"Nothing, nothing...don't make a fuss, Tirzah! You just won't leave me alone!"

This was so unfair that I wanted to slap him. I didn't. Kane rose by himself, shook his head like some great beast, and said, "I'm just exhausted. I'm going to bed."

I didn't try to stop him from going to his bunk. I had planned on sleeping with Ajit, anyway. It seemed that some slight false note had crept into his storytelling in the last five minutes, some forced exaggeration.

But he smiled at me, and I decided I'd been wrong. I was very tired, too. All at once I wished I could sleep alone this night.

But I couldn't. Ajit, no matter how well he'd recovered from Kane's unconscious brutality, nonetheless had to feel bruised at some level. It was my job to find out where, and how much, and to set it to rights. It was my job to keep the expedition as productive as possible, to counteract Kane's dismissing and belittling behavior toward Ajit. It was my job.

I smiled back at him.

8. PROBE

When Ajit's head disappeared, no one panicked. We'd expected this, of course; in fact, we'd expected it sooner. The probe drifted in a sea of the most intense radiation in the galaxy, much of it at lethal wavelengths: gamma rays from Sagittarius East, X-rays, powerful winds of ionized particles, things I couldn't name. That the probe's shielding had held this long was a minor miracle. It couldn't hold forever. Some particle or particles had penetrated all the shielding and reached the computer, contaminating a piece of the upload-maintenance program.

It was a minor glitch. The back-up kicked in a moment later and Ajit's head reappeared. But we all knew this was only the beginning. It would happen again, and again, and eventually programming would be hit that couldn't be restored by automatic back-up, because the back-up would go, too, in a large enough hit—or because uploads are not like other computer programs. We are more than that, and less. An upload has back-ups to maintain the shadows we see of each other and the ship, the shadows that keep our captured minds sane. But an upload cannot house back-ups of itself. Even one copy smudges too much, and the copy contaminates the original. It has been tried, with painful results.

Moreover, we uploads run only partly on the main computer. An upload is neither a biological entity nor a long stream of code, but something more than both. Some of the substratum, the hardware, is wired like actual neurons, although constructed of sturdier stuff: thousands of miles of nano-constructed organic polymers. This is why analogues think at the rate of the human brain, not the much faster rate of computers. It's also why we feel as our originals do.

After Ajit's maintenance glitch our mood, which had been exuberant, sobered. But it didn't sour. We worked steadily, with focus and hope, deciding where exactly to position the probe and then entering the coordinates for the jump.

"See you soon," we said to each other. I kissed both Kane and Ajit lightly on the lips. Then we all shut down and the probe jumped.

Days later, we emerged on the other side of Sgr A West, all three of us still intact. If it were in my nature, I would have said a prayer of thanksgiving. Instead I said to Ajit, "Still have a head, I see."

"And a good thing he does," Kane said absently, already plunging for the chair in front of his terminal. "We'll need it. And—Ajit, the mass detectors...great shitting gods!"

It seems we were to have thanksgiving after all, if only perversely. I said, "What is it? What's there?" The displays showed nothing at all.

"Nothing at all," Ajit said. "And everything."

"Speak English!"

Ajit—I doubt Kane had even heard me, in his absorption—said, "The mass detectors are showing a huge mass less than a quarter light year away. The radiation detectors—all of them—are showing nothing at all. We're—"

"We're accelerating fast." I studied ship's data; the rate of acceleration made me blink. "We're going to hit whatever it is. Not soon, but the tidal forces—"

The probe was small, but the tidal forces of something this big would still rip it apart when it got close enough.

Something this big. But there was, to all other sensors, nothing there.

Nothing but shadows.

A strange sensation ran over me. Not fear, but something more complicated, much more eerie.

My voice sounded strange in my ears. "What if we hit it? I know you said radiation of all types will go right through shadow matter just as if it isn't there—" because it isn't, not in our universe "—but what about the probe? What if we hit it before we take the final event-horizon measurements on Sgr A*?"

"We won't hit it," Ajit said. "We'll move before then, Tirzah, back to the hole. Kane—"

They forget me again. I went up to the observation deck. Looking out through the clear hull, I stared at the myriad of stars on the side of the night sky away from Sgr A West. Then I turned to look toward that vast three-armed cloud of turning plasma, radiating as it cools. Nothing blocked my view of Sgr A West. Yet between us lay a huge, massive body of shadow matter, unseen, pulling on everything else my dazed senses could actually see.

To my left, all the exotic plants in the observatory disappeared.

Ajit and Kane worked feverishly, until once more I made them shut down for "sleep." The radiation here was nearly as great as it had been in our first location. We were right inside Sagittarius A East, the huge expanding shell of an unimaginable explosion sometime during the last 100,000 years. Most of Sgr A East wasn't visible at the wavelengths I could see, but the gamma-ray detectors were going crazy.

"We can't stop for five hours!" Kane cried. "Don't you realize how much damage the radiation could do in that time? We need to get all the data we can, work on it, and send off the second mini-cap!"

"We're going to send off the second mini-cap right now," I said. "And we'll only shut down for three hours. But, Kane, we are going to do that. I mean it. Uploads run even more damage from not running maintenance than we do from external radiation. You know that."

He did. He scowled at me, and cursed, and fussed with the mini-cap, but then he fired the mini-cap off and shut down.

Ajit said, "Just one more minute, Tirzah. I want to show you something."

"Ajit—"

"No, it's not mathematical. I promise. It's something I brought onto the Kepler. The object was not included in the probe program, but I can show you a holo."

Somewhere in the recesses of the computer, Ajit's upload created a program and a two-dimensional holo appeared on an empty display screen. I blinked at it, surprised.

It was a statue of some sort of god with four arms, enclosed in a circle of flames, made of what looked like very old bronze.

"This is Nataraja," Ajit said. "Shiva dancing."

"Ajit—"

"No, I am not a god worshipper," he smiled. "You know me better than that, Tirzah. Hinduism has many gods—thousands—but they are, except to the ignorant, no more than embodiments of different aspects of reality.

Shiva is the dance of creation and destruction, the constant flow of energy in the cosmos. Birth and death and rebirth. It seemed fitting to bring him to the galactic core, where so much goes on of all three. This statue has been in my family for four hundred years. I must bring it home, along with the answers to our experiments."

"You will bring Shiva back to New Bombay," I said softly, "and your answers, too."

"Yes, I have begun to think so." He smiled at me, a smile with all the need of his quick-silver personality in it, but also all the courtesy and hope. "Now I will sleep."

9. SHIP

The next morning, after a deep sleep one part sheer exhaustion and one part sex, I woke to find Ajit already out of bed and seated in front of his terminal. He rose the moment I entered the wardroom and turned to me with a grave face. "Tirzah. The mini-cap arrived. I already put the data into the system."

"What's wrong? Where's Kane?"

"Still asleep, I imagine."

I went to Kane's bunk. He lay on his back, still in the clothes he'd worn for three days, smelling sour and snoring softly. I thought of waking him, then decided to wait a bit. Kane could certainly use the sleep, and I could use the time with Ajit. I went back to the wardroom, tightening the belt on my robe.

"What's wrong?" I repeated.

"I put the data from the mini-cap into the system. It's all corrections to the last mini-cap's data. Kane says the first set was wrong."

"Kane?" I said stupidly.

"The Kane-analogue," Ajit explained patiently. "He says radiation hit the probe's sensors for the first batch, before any of them realized it. They fired off the preliminary data right after the jump, you know, because they had no idea how long the probe could last. Now they've had time to discover where the radiation hit, to restore the sensor programs, and to retake the measurements. The Kane analogue says these new ones are accurate, the others weren't."

I tried to take it all in. "So Kane's shadow matter theory—none of that is true?"

"I don't know," Ajit said. "How can anybody know until we see if the data supports it? The mini-cap only just arrived."

"Then I might not have moved the probe," I said, meaning "the other I." My analogue. I didn't know what I was saying. The shock was too great. All that theorizing, all Kane's sharp triumph, all that tension…

I looked more closely at Ajit. He looked very pale, and as fatigued as a genemod man of his youth can look. I said, "You didn't sleep much."

"No. Yesterday was…difficult."

"Yes," I agreed, noting the characteristically polite understatement. "Yes."

"Should I wake Kane?" Ajit said, almost diffidently.

"I'll do it."

Kane was hard to wake. I had to shake him several times before he struggled up to consciousness.

"Tirzah?"

"Who else? Kane, you must get up. Something's happened."

"Wh-what?" He yawned hugely and slumped against the bulkhead. His whole body reeked.

I braced myself. "The second mini-cap arrived. Your analogue sent a recording. He says the prelim data was compromised, due to radiation-caused sensor malfunction."

That woke him. He stared at me as if I were an executioner. "The data's compromised? All of it?"

"I don't know."

Kane pushed out of his bunk and ran into the wardroom. Ajit said, "I put the mini-cap data into the system already, but I—" Kane wasn't listening. He tore into the data, and after a few minutes he actually bellowed.

"No!"

I flattened myself against the bulkhead, not from fear but from surprise. I had never heard a grown man make a noise like that.

But there were no other noises. Kane worked silently, ferociously. Ajit sat at his own terminal and worked, too, not yesterday's tentative copying but the real thing. I put hot coffee beside them both. Kane gulped his steaming, Ajit ignored his.

After half an hour, Kane turned to me. Defeat pulled like gravity at everything on his face, eyes and lips and jaw muscles. Only his filthy hair sprang upward. He said simply, with the naked straightforwardness of despair, "The new data invalidates the idea of shadow matter."

I heard myself say, "Kane, go take a shower."

To my surprise, he went, shambling from the room. Ajit worked a few minutes longer, then climbed the ladder to the observation deck. Over his shoulder he said, "Tirzah, I want to be alone, please. Don't come."

I didn't. I sat at the tiny wardroom table, looked at my own undrunk coffee, and thought of nothing.

10. PROBE

The data from the probe's new position looked good, Kane said. That was his word: "good." Then he returned to his terminal.

"Ajit?" I was coming to rely on him more and more for translation. He was just as busy as Kane, but kinder. This made sense. If, to Kane, Ajit was a secondary but still necessary party to the intellectual action, that's what I was to both of them. Ajit had settled into this position, secure that he was valued. I could feel myself doing the same. The cessation of struggle turned us both kinder.

Kane, never insecure, worked away.

Ajit said, "The new readings confirm a large gravitational mass affecting the paths of both the infalling gas and the probe. The young stars so close to Sgr A* are a much knottier problem. We've got to modify the whole theory of star formation to account for the curvatures of space-time caused by the hole and by the shadow mass. It's very complex. Kane's got the computer working on that, and I'm going to take readings on Sgr A West, in its different parts, and on stars on the other side of the mass and look at those."

"What about the mass detectors? What do they say?"

"They say we're being pulled toward a mass of about a half million suns."

A half million suns. And we couldn't see it: not with our eyes, nor radio sensors, nor X-rays detectors, nor anything.

"I have a question. Does it have an event horizon? Is it swallowing light, like a black hole does? Isn't it the gravity of a black hole that swallows light?"

"Yes. But radiation, including light, goes right through this shadow matter, Tirzah. Don't you understand? It doesn't interact with normal radiation at all."

"But it has gravity. Why doesn't its gravity trap the light?"

"I don't know." He hesitated. "Kane thinks maybe it doesn't interact with radiation as particles, which respond to gravity. Only as waves."

"How can it do that?"

Ajit took my shoulders and shook them playfully. "I told you—we don't know. This is brand-new, dear heart. We know as much about what it will and will not do as primitive hominids knew about fire."

"Well, don't make a god of it," I said, and it was a test. Ajit passed. He didn't stiffen as if I'd made some inappropriate reference to the drawing of Shiva he'd shown me last night. Instead, he laughed and went back to work.

"Tirzah! Tirzah!"

The automatic wake-up brought me out of shut-down. Ajit must have been brought back on-line a few moments before me, because he was already calling my name. Alarm bells clanged.

"It's Kane! He's been hit!"

I raced into Kane's bunk. He lay still amid the bedclothes. It wasn't the maintenance program that had taken the hit, because every part of his body was intact; so were the bedclothes. But Kane lay stiff and unresponsive.

"Run the full diagnostics," I said to Ajit.

"I already started them."

"Kane," I said, shaking him gently, then harder. He moved a little, groaned. So his upload wasn't dead.

I sat on the edge of the bunk, fighting fear, and took his hand. "Kane, love, can you hear me?"

He squeezed my fingers. The expression on his face didn't change. After a silence in which time itself seemed to stop, Ajit said, "The diagnostics are complete. About a third of brain function is gone."

I got into the bunk beside Kane and put my arms around him.

Ajit and I did what we could. Our uploads patched and copied, using material from both of us. Yes, the copying would lead to corruption, but we were beyond that.

Because an upload runs on such a complex combination of computer and nano-constructed polymer networks, we cannot simply be replaced by a back-up program cube. The unique software/ hardware retes are also why a corrupted analogue is not exactly the same as a stroke- or tumor-impaired human brain.

The analogue brain does not have to pump blood or control breathing. It does not have to move muscles or secrete hormones. Although closely tied to the "purer" programs that maintain our illusion of moving and living as three-dimensional beings in a three-dimensional ship, the analogue brain is tied to the computer in much more complex ways than any fleshy human using a terminal. The resources of the computer were at our disposal, but they could only accomplish limited aims.

When Ajit and I had finished putting together as much of Kane, or a pseudo-Kane, as we could, he walked into the wardroom and sat down. He looked, moved, smiled the same. That part is easy to repair, as easy as had been replacing Ajit's head or the exotics on the observation deck. But the man staring blankly at the terminal was not really Kane.

"What was I working on?" he said.

I got out, "Shadow matter."

"Shadow matter? What's that?"

Ajit said softly, "I have all your work, Kane. Our work. I think I can finish it, now that you've started us in the right direction."

He nodded, looking confused. "Thank you, Ajit." Then, with a flash of his old magnificent combativeness, "But you better get it right!"

"With your help," Ajit said gaily, and in that moment I came close to truly loving him.

They worked out a new division of labor. Kane was able to take the sensor readings and run them through the pre-set algorithms. Actually, Ajit probably could have trained me to do that. But Kane seemed content, frowning earnestly at his displays.

Ajit took over the actual science. I said to him, when we had a moment alone, "Can you do it?"

"I think so," he said, without either anger or arrogance. "I have the foundation that Kane laid. And we worked out some of the preliminaries together."

"We have only one more jump left."

"I know, Tirzah."

"With the risk of radiation killing us all—"

"Not yet. Give me a little more time."

I rested a moment against his shoulder. "All right. A little more time."

He put his arm around me, not in passion but in comradeship. None of us, we both knew, had all that much time left.

11. SHIP

Kane was only temporarily defeated by the contamination of the probe data. Within half a day, he had aborted his shadow-matter theory, archived his work on it, and gone back to his original theories about the mysteriously massive young stars near the hole. He used the probe's new data, which were all logical amplifications of the prelim readings. "I've got some ideas," he told me. "We'll see."

He wasn't as cheerful as usual, let alone as manically exuberant as during the shadow-matter "discovery," but he was working steadily. A mountain, Kane. It would take a lot to actually erode him, certainly more than a failed theory. That rocky insensitivity had its strengths.

Ajit, on the other hand, was not really working. I couldn't follow the displays on his terminal, but I could read the body language. He was restless, inattentive. But what worried me was something else: his attitude toward Kane.

All Ajit's anger was gone.

I watched carefully, while seemingly bent over ship's log or embroidery. Anger is the least subtle of the body's signals. Even when a person is successfully concealing most of it, the signs are there if you know where to look: the tight neck muscles, the turned-away posture, the tinge in the voice. Ajit displayed none of this. Instead, when he faced Kane, as he did in the lunch I insisted we all eat together at the wardroom table, I saw something else. A sly superiority, a secret triumph.

I could be wrong, I thought. I have been wrong before. By now I disliked Ajit so much that I didn't trust my own intuitions.

"Ajit," I said as we finished the simple meal I'd put together, "will you please—"

Ship's alarms went off with a deafening clang. *Breach, breach, breach.*

I whirled toward ship's display, which automatically illuminated. The breach was in the starboard hold, and it was full penetration by a mass of about a hundred grams. Within a minute, the nanos had put on a temporary patch. The alarm stopped and the computer began hectoring me.

"Breach sealed with temporary nano patch. Seal must be reinforced within two hours with permanent hull patch, type 6-A. For location of breach and patch supply, consult ship's log. If unavailability of—" I shut it off.

"Could be worse," Kane said.

"Well, of course it could be worse," I snapped, and immediately regretted it. I was not allowed to snap. That I had done so was an indication of how much the whole situation on the Kepler was affecting me. That wasn't allowed, either; it was unprofessional.

Kane wasn't offended. "Could have hit the engines or the living pod instead of just a hold. Actually, I'm surprised it hasn't happened before. There's a lot of drifting debris in this area."

Ajit said, "Are you going into the hold, Tirzah?"

Of course I was going into the hold. But this time I didn't snap; I smiled at him and said, "Yes, I'm going to suit up now."

"I'm coming, too," Kane said.

I blinked. I'd been about to ask if Ajit wanted to go with me. It would be a good way to observe him away from Kane, maybe ask some discreet questions. I said to Kane, "Don't you have to work?"

"The work isn't going anywhere. And I want to retrieve the particle. It didn't exit the ship, and at a hundred grams, there's going to be some of it left after the breach."

Ajit had stiffened at being pre-empted, yet again, by Kane. Ajit would have wanted to retrieve the particle, too; there is nothing more interesting to space scientists than dead rocks. Essentially, I'd often thought, Sgr A* was no more than a very hot, very large dead rock. I knew better than to say this aloud.

I could have ordered Ajit to accompany me, and ordered Kane to stay behind. But that, I sensed, would only make things worse. Ajit, in his present mood of deadly sensitivity, would not take well to orders from anyone, even me. I wasn't going to give him the chance to retreat more into whatever nasty state of mind he currently inhabited.

"Well, then, let's go," I said ungraciously to Kane, who only grinned at me and went to get our suits.

The holds, three of them for redundancy safety, are full of supplies of all types. Every few days I combine a thorough ship inspection with lugging enough food forward to sustain us. We aren't uploads; we need bodily nurturing as well as the kind I was supposed to be providing.

All three holds can be pressurized if necessary, but usually they aren't. Air generation and refreshment doesn't cost much power, but it costs some. Kane and I went into the starboard hold in heated s-suits and helmets.

"I'm going to look around," Kane said. He'd brought a handheld, and I saw him calculating the probable trajectory of the particle from the ship's data and the angle of the breach, as far as he could deduce it. Then he disappeared behind a pallet of crates marked SOYSYNTH.

The breach was larger than I'd expected; that hundred-gram particle had hit at a bad angle. But the nanos had done their usual fine job, and the permanent patch went on without trouble. I began the careful inspection of the rest of the hull, using my hand-held instruments.

Kane cursed volubly.

"Kane? What is it?"'

"Nothing. Bumped into boxes."

"Well, don't. The last thing I want is you messing up my hold." For a physically fit man, Kane is clumsy in motion. I would bet my ship that he can't dance, and bet my life that he never tries.

"I can't see anything. Can't you brighten the light?"

I did, and he bumped around some more. Whenever he brushed something, he cursed. I did an inspection even more carefully than usual, but found nothing alarming. We met each other back by the hold door.

"It's not here," Kane said. "The particle. It's not here."

"You mean you didn't find it."

"No, I mean it's not here. Don't you think I could find a still-hot particle in a hold otherwise filled only with large immobile crates?"

I keyed in the door code. "So it evaporated on impact. Ice and ions and dust."

"To penetrate a Schaad hull? No." He reconsidered. "Well, maybe. What did you find?"

"Not much. Pitting and scarring on the outside, nothing unexpected. But no structural stress to worry about."

"The debris here is undoubtedly orbiting the core, but we're so far out it's not moving all that fast. Still, we should have had some warning. But I'm more worried about the probe—when is the third mini-cap due?"

Kane knew as well as I did when the third mini-cap was due. His asking was the first sign he was as tense as the rest of us.

"Three more days," I said. "Be patient."

"I'm not patient."

"As if that's new data."

"I'm also afraid the probe will be hit by rapidly orbiting debris, and that will be that. Did you know that the stars close in to Sgr A* orbit at several thousand clicks per second?"

I knew. He'd told me often enough. The probe was always a speculative proposition, and before now, Kane had been jubilant that we'd gotten any data at all from it.

I'd never heard Kane admit to being "afraid" of anything. Even allowing for the casualness of the phrase.

I wanted to distract him, and, if Kane was really in a resigned and reflective mood, it also seemed a good time to do my job. "Kane, about Ajit—"

"I don't want to talk about that sniveling slacker," Kane said, with neither interest not rancor. "I picked badly for an assistant, that's all."

It hadn't actually been his "pick;" his input had been one of many. I didn't say this. Kane looked around the hold one more time. "I guess you're right. The particle sublimed. Ah, well."

I put the glove of my hand on the arm of his suit—not exactly an intimate caress, but the best I could do in this circumstance. "Kane, how is the young-star mystery going?"

"Not very well. But that's science." The hold door stood open and he lumbered out.

I gave one last look around the hold before turning off the light, but there was nothing more to see.

The mended statue of Shiva was back on the wardroom table, smack in the center, when Kane and I returned from the hold. I don't think Kane, heading straight for his terminal, even noticed. I smiled at Ajit, although I wasn't sure why he had brought the statue back. He'd told me he never wanted to see it again.

"Tirzah, would you perhaps like to play go?"

I couldn't conceal my surprise. "Go?"

"Yes. Will you play with me?" Accompanied by his most winning smile.

"All right."

He brought out the board and, bizarrely, set it up balanced on his knees. When he saw my face, he said, "We'll play here. I don't want to disturb the Cosmic Dancer."

"All right." I wasn't sure what to think. I drew my chair close to his, facing him, and bent over the board.

We both knew that Ajit was a better player than I. That's why both of us played: he to win, me to lose. I would learn more from the losing position. Very competitive people—and I thought now that I had never known one as competitive as Ajit—relax only when not threatened.

So I made myself non-threatening in every way I knew, and Ajit and I talked and laughed, and Kane worked doggedly on his theories that weren't going anywhere. The statue of the dancing god leered at me from the table, and I knew with every passing moment how completely I was failing this already failing mission.

12. PROBE

Kane was gentler since the radiation corruption. Who can say how these things happen? Personality, too, is encoded in the human brain, whether flesh or analogue. He was still Kane, but we saw only his gentler, sweeter side. Previously that part of him had been dominated by his combative intellect, which had been a force of nature all its own, like a high wind. Now the intellect had failed, the wind calmed. The landscape beneath lay serene.

"Here, Ajit," Kane said. "These are the equations you wanted run." He sent them to Ajit's terminal, stood, and stretched. The stretch put him slightly off balance, something damaged in the upload that Ajit and I hadn't been able to fix, or find. A brain is such a complex thing. Kane tottered, and Ajit rose swiftly to catch him.

"Careful, Kane. Here, sit down."

Ajit eased Kane into a chair at the wardroom table. I put down my work. Kane said, "Tirzah, I feel funny."

"Funny how?" Alarm ran through me.

"I don't know. Can we play go?"

I had taught him the ancient strategy game, and he enjoyed it. He wasn't very good, not nearly as good as I was, but he liked it and didn't seem to mind losing. I got out the board. Ajit, who was a master at go, went back to Kane's shadow-matter theory. He was making good progress, I knew, although he said frankly that all the basic ideas were Kane's.

Halfway through our second game of go, the entire wardroom disappeared.

A moment of blind panic seized me. I was adrift in the void, nothing to see or feel or hold onto, a vertigo so terrible it blocked any rational thought. It was the equivalent of a long, anguished scream, originating in the most primitive part of my now blind brain: lost, lost, lost and...

The automatic maintenance program kicked in and the wardroom re-appeared. Kane gripped the table edge and stared at me, white-faced. I went to him, wrapped my arms around him reassuringly, and gazed at Ajit. Kane clung to me. A part of my mind noted that some aspects of the wardroom were wrong: the galley door was too low to walk through upright, and one chair had disappeared, along with the go board. Maintenance code too damaged to restore. Ajit said softly, "We have to decide, Tirzah. We could take a final radiation hit at any time."

"I know."

I took my arms away from Kane. "Are you all right?"

He smiled. "Yes. Just for a minute I was..." He seemed to lose his thought.

Ajit brought his terminal chair to the table, to replace the vanished one. He sat leaning forward, looking from me to Kane and back. "This is a decision all three of us have to make. We have one mini-cap left to send back to the *Kepler*, and one more jump for ourselves. At any time we could lose...everything. You all know that. What do you think we should do? Kane? Tirzah?"

All my life I'd heard that even very flawed people can rise to leadership under the right circumstances. I'd never believed it, not of someone with Ajit's basic personality structure: competitive, paranoid, angry at such a deep level he didn't even know it. I'd been wrong. I believed now.

Kane said, "I feel funny, and that probably means I've taken another minor hit and the program isn't there to repair it. I think...I think..."

"Kane?" I took his hand.

He had trouble getting words out. "I think we better send the mini-cap now."

"I agree," Ajit said. "But that means we send it without the data from our next jump, to just outside the event horizon of Sgr A*. So the *Kepler* won't get those readings. They'll get the work on shadow matter, but most of the best things on that already went in the second mini-cap. Still, it's better than nothing, and I'm afraid if we wait to send until after the jump, nothing is what the *Kepler* will get. It will be too late."

Both men looked at me. As captain, the jump decision was mine. I nodded. "I agree, too. Send off the mini-cap with whatever you've got, and then we'll jump. But not to the event horizon."

"Why not?" Kane burst out, sounding more like himself than at any time since the accident.

"Because there's no point. We can't send any more data back, so the event horizon readings die with us. And we can survive longer if I jump us completely away from the core. Several hundred light years out, where the radiation is minimal."

Together, as if rehearsed, they both said, "No."

"No?"

"No," Ajit said, with utter calm, utter persuasiveness. "We're not going to go out like that, Tirzah."

"But we don't have to go out at all! Not for decades! Maybe centuries! Not until the probe's life-maintenance power is used up—" Or until the probe is hit by space debris. Or until radiation takes us out. Nowhere in space is really safe.

Kane said, "And what would we do for centuries? I'd go mad. I want to work."

"Me, too," Ajit said. "I want to take the readings by the event horizon and make of them what I can, while I can. Even though the *Kepler* will never see them."

They were scientists.

And I? Could even I, station bred, have lived for centuries in this tiny ship, without a goal beyond survival, trapped with these two men? An Ajit compassionate and calm, now that he was on top. A damaged Kane, gentle and intellectually gutted. And a Tirzah, captaining a pointless expedition with nowhere to go and nothing to do.

I would have ended up hating all three of us.

Ajit took my left hand. My right one still held Kane's, so we made a broken circle in the radiation-damaged wardroom.

"All right," I said. "We'll send off the mini-cap and then jump to the event horizon."

"Yes," Kane said.

Ajit said, "I'm going to go back to work. Tirzah, if you and Kane want to go up to the observation deck, or anywhere, I'll prepare and launch the mini-cap." Carefully he turned his back and sat at his terminal.

I led Kane to my bunk. This was a first; I always went to the scientists' bunks. My own, as captain, had features for my eyes only. But now it didn't matter.

We made love, and afterward, holding his superb, aging body in my arms, I whispered against his cheek, "I love you, Kane."

"I love you, too," he said simply, and I had no way of knowing if he meant it, or if it was an automatic response dredged up from some half-remembered ritual from another time. It didn't matter. There are a lot more types of love in the universe than I once suspected.

We were silent a long time, and then Kane said, "I'm trying to remember pi. I know three point one, but I can't remember after that."

I said, through the tightness in my throat, "Three point one four one. That's all I remember."

"Three point one four one," Kane said dutifully. I left him repeating it over and over, when I went to jump the probe to the event horizon of Sgr A*.

13. SHIP

The second breach of the hull was more serious than the first.

The third mini-cap had not arrived from the probe. "The analogues are probably all dead," Kane said dully. "They were supposed to jump to one-twenty-fifth of a light year from the event horizon. Our calculations were always problematic for where exactly that is. It's possible they landed inside, and the probe will just spiral around Sgr A* forever. Or they got hit with major radiation and fried."

"It's possible," I said. "How is the massive-young-star problem coming?"

"It's not. Mathematical dead end."

He looked terrible, drawn and, again, unwashed. I was more impatient with the latter than I should be. But how hard is it, as a courtesy to your shipmates if nothing else, to get your body into the shower? How long does it take? Kane had stopped exercising, as well.

"Kane," I began, as quietly but firmly as I could manage, "will you—"

The alarms went off, clanging again at 115 decibels. *Breach, breach, breach…*

I scanned the displays. "Oh, God—"

"Breach sealed with temporary nano patch," the computer said. "Seal must be reinforced within one-half hour with permanent hull patch, type 1-B, supplemented with equipment repair, if possible. For location of breach and patch supply, consult—" I turned it off.

The intruder had hit the back-up engine. It was a much larger particle than the first one, although since it had hit us and then gone on its merry way, rather than penetrating the ship, there was no way to recover it for examination. But the outside mass detectors registered a particle of at least two kilos, and it had probably been moving much faster than the first one.

If it had hit us directly, we would all be dead. Instead it had given the ship a glancing blow, damaging the back-up engine.

"I'll come with you again," Kane said.

"There won't be any particle to collect this time." Or not collect.

"I know. But I'm not getting anywhere here."

Kane and I, s-suited, went into the back-up engine compartment. As soon as I saw it, I knew there was nothing I could do. There is damage you can repair, and there is damage you cannot. The back end of the compartment had been sheared off, and part of the engine with it. No wonder the computer had recommended a 1-B patch, which is essentially the equivalent of "Throw a tarp over it and forget it."

While I patched, Kane poked around the edges of the breach, then at the useless engine. He left before I did, and I found him studying ship's display of the hit on my wardroom screen. He wasn't trying to do anything with ship's log, which was not his place and he knew it, but he stood in front of the data, moving his hand when he wanted another screen, frowning horribly.

"What is it, Kane?" I said. I didn't really want to know; the patch had taken hours and I was exhausted. I didn't see Ajit. Sleeping, or up on the observation deck, or, less likely, in the gym.

"Nothing. Whatever that hit was made of, it wasn't radiating. So it wasn't going very fast, or the external sensors would have picked up at least ionization. Either the mass was cold, or the sensors aren't functioning properly."

"I'll run the diagnostics," I said wearily. "Anything else?"

"Yes. I want to move the ship."

I stared at him, my suit half peeled from my body, my helmet defiantly set on the table, pushing the statue of Shiva to one side. "Move the ship?"

Ajit appeared in the doorway from his bunk.

"Yes," Kane said. "Move the ship."

"But these are the coordinates the mini-cap will return to!"

"It's not coming," Kane said. "Don't you listen to anything I say, Tirzah? The uploads didn't make it. The third mini-cap is days late; if it were coming, it would be here. The probe is gone, the uploads are gone, and we've got all the data we're going to get from them. If we want more, we're going to have to go after it ourselves."

"Go after it?" I repeated, stupidly. "How?"

"I already told you! Move the ship closer into the core so we can take the readings the probe should have taken. Some of them, anyway."

Ajit said, "Moving the ship is completely Tirzah's decision."

His championship of me when I needed no champion, and especially not in that pointlessly assertive voice, angered me more than Kane's suggestion. "Thank you, Ajit, I can handle this!"

Mistake, mistake.

Kane, undeterred, plowed on. "I don't mean we'd go near the event horizon, of course, or even to the probe's first position near the star cluster. But we could move much closer in. Maybe ten light years from the core, positioned between the northern and western arms of Sgr A West."

Ajit said, "Which would put us right in the circumnuclear disk! Where the radiation is much worse than here!"

Kane turned on him, acknowledging Ajit's presence for the first time in days, with an outpouring of all Kane's accumulated frustration and disappointment. "We've been hit twice with particles that damaged the ship. Clearly we're in the path of some equivalent of an asteroid belt orbiting the core at this immense distance. It can't be any less safe in the circumnuclear disk, which, I might remind you, is only shocked molecular gases, with its major radiation profile unknown. Any first-year astronomy student should know that. Or is it just that you're a coward?"

Ajit's skin mottled, then paled. His features did not change expression at all. But I felt the heat coming from him, the primal rage, greater for being contained. He went into his bunk and closed the door.

"Kane!" I said furiously, too exhausted and frustrated and disappointed to watch my tone. "You can't—"

"I can't stand any more of this," Kane said. He slammed down the corridor to the gym, and I heard the exercise bike whirr in rage.

I went to my own bunk, locked the door, and squeezed my eyes shut, fighting for control. But even behind my closed eyelids I saw our furious shadows.

After a few hours I called them both together in the wardroom. When Kane refused, I ordered him. I lifted Ajit's statue of Shiva off the table and handed it to him, making its location his problem, as long as it wasn't on the table. Wordlessly he carried it into his bunk and then returned.

"This can't go on," I said calmly. "We all know that. We're in this small space together to accomplish something important, and our mission overrides all our personal feelings. You are both rational men, scientists, or you wouldn't be here."

"Don't patronize us with flattery," Ajit said.

"I'm sorry. I didn't intend to do that. It's true you're both scientists, and it's true you've both been certified rational enough for space travel."

They couldn't argue with that. I didn't mention how often certification boards had misjudged, or been bribed, or just been too dazzled by well-earned reputations to look below the work to the worker. If Kane or Ajit knew all that, they kept it to themselves.

"I blame myself for any difficulties we've had here," I said, in the best Nurturer fashion. Although it was also true. "It's my job to keep a ship running in productive harmony, and this one, I think we can all agree, is not."

No dissension. I saw that both of them dreaded some long, drawn-out discussion of group dynamics, never a topic that goes down well with astrophysicists. Kane said abruptly, "I still want to move the ship."

I had prepared myself for this. "No, Kane. We're not jumping closer in."

He caught at my loophole. "Then can we jump to another location at the same distance from the core? Maybe measurements from another base point would help."

"We're not jumping anywhere until I'm sure the third mini-cap isn't coming."

"How long will that be?" I could see the formidable intelligence under the childish tantrums already racing ahead, planning measurements, weighing options.

"We'll give it another three days."

"All right." Suddenly he smiled, his first in days. "Thanks, Tirzah."

I turned to Ajit. "Ajit, what can we do for your work? What do you need?"

"I ask for nothing," he said, with such a strange, intense, unreadable expression that for a moment I felt irrational fear. Then he stood and went into his bunk. I heard the door lock.

I had failed again.

No alarm went off in the middle of the night. There was nothing overt to wake me. But I woke anyway, and I heard someone moving quietly around the wardroom. The muscles of my right arm tensed to open my bunk, and I forced them to still.

Something wasn't right. Intuition, that mysterious shadow of rational thought, told me to lie motionless. To not open my bunk, to not even reach out and access the ship's data on my bunk screen. To not move at all.

Why?

I didn't know.

The smell of coffee wafted from the wardroom. So one of the men couldn't sleep, made some coffee, turned on his terminal. So what?

Don't move, said that pre-reasoning part of my mind, from the shadows.

The coffee smell grew stronger. A chair scraped. Ordinary, mundane sounds.

Don't move.

I didn't have to move. This afternoon I had omitted to mention to Kane and Ajit those times that certification boards had misjudged, or been bribed, or just been too dazzled by well-earned reputations to look below the work to the worker. Those times in which the cramped conditions of space, coupled with swollen egos and frenzied work, had led to disaster for a mission Nurturer. But we had learned. My bunk had equipment the scientists did not know about.

Carefully I slid my gaze to a spot directly above me on the bunk ceiling. Only my eyes moved. I pattern-blinked: two quick, three beats closed, two quick, a long steady stare. The screen brightened.

This was duplicate ship data. Not a back-up; it was entirely separate, made simultaneously from the same sensors as the main log but routed into separate, free-standing storage that could not be reached from the main computer. Scientists are all sophisticated users. There is no way to keep data from any who wish to alter it except by discreet, unknown, untraceable storage. I pattern-blinked, not moving so much as a finger or a toe in the bed, to activate various screens of ship data.

It was easy to find.

Yesterday, at 1850 hours, the mini-cap bay had opened and received a mini-cap. Signal had failed to transmit to the main computer. Today at 300 hours, which was fifteen minutes ago, the mini-cap bay had been opened manually and the payload removed. Again signal had failed to the main computer.

The infrared signature in the wardroom, seated at his terminal, was Ajit.

It was possible the signal failures were coincidental, and Ajit was even now transferring data from the third mini-cap into the computer, enjoying a cup of hot coffee while he did so, gloating in getting a perfectly legitimate jump on Kane. But I didn't think so.

What did I think?

I didn't have to think; I just knew. I could see it unfolding, clear as a holovid. All of it. Ajit had stolen the second mini-cap, too. That had been the morning after Kane and I had slept so soundly, the morning after Ajit had given us wine to celebrate Kane's shadow-matter theory. What had been in that wine? We'd slept soundly, and Ajit told us that the mini-cap had come before we were awake. Ajit said he'd already put it into the computer. It carried the Kane upload's apology that the prelim data, the data from which Kane had constructed his shadow-matter thesis, was wrong, contaminated by a radiation strike.

Ajit had fabricated that apology and that replacement data. The actual second mini-cap would justify Kane's work, not undo it. Ajit was saving all three mini-caps to use for himself, to claim the shadow matter discovery for his own. He'd used the second mini-cap to discredit the first; he would claim the third had never arrived, had never been sent from the dying probe.

The real Kane, my Kane, hadn't found the particle from the first ship's breach because it had, indeed, been made of shadow matter. That, and not slow speed, had been why the particle showed no radiation. The particle had exerted gravity on our world, but nothing else. The second breach, too, had been shadow matter. I knew that as surely as if Kane had shown me the pages of equations to prove it.

I knew something else, too. If I went into the shower and searched my body very carefully, every inch of it, I would find in some inconspicuous place the small, regular hole into which a sub-dermal tracker had gone the night of the drugged wine. So would Kane. Trackers would apprise Ajit of every move we made, not only large-muscle moves like a step or a hug, but small ones like accessing my bunk display of ship's data. That was what my intuition had been warning me of. Ajit did not want to be discovered during his mini-cap thefts.

I had the same trackers in my own repertoire. Only I had not thought this mission deteriorated enough to need them. I had not wanted to think that. I'd been wrong.

But how would Ajit make use of Kane's stolen work with Kane there to claim it for himself?

I already knew the answer, of course. I had known it from the moment I pattern-blinked at the ceiling, which was the moment I finally admitted to myself how monstrous this mission had turned.

I pushed open the bunk door and called cheerfully, "Hello? Do I smell coffee? Who's out there?"

"I am," Ajit said genially. "I cannot sleep. Come have some coffee."

"Coming, Ajit."

I put on my robe, tied it at my waist, and slipped the gun from its secret mattress compartment into my palm.

14. PROBE

The probe jumped successfully. We survived.

This close to the core, the view wasn't as spectacular as it was farther out. Sgr A*, which captured us in orbit immediately, now appeared as a fuzzy region dominating starboard. The fuzziness, Ajit said, was a combination of Hawking radiation and superheated gases being swallowed by the black hole. To port, the intense blue cluster of IRS16 was muffled by the clouds of ionized plasma around the probe. We experienced some tidal forces, but the probe was so small that the gravitational tides didn't yet cause much damage.

Ajit has found a way to successfully apply Kane's shadow-matter theory to the paths of the infalling gases, as well as to the orbits of the young stars near Sgr A*. He says there may well be a really lot of shadow matter near the core, and maybe even farther out. It may even provide enough mass to "balance" the universe, keeping it from either flying apart forever or collapsing in on itself. Shadow matter, left over from the very beginning of creation, may preserve creation.

Kane nods happily as Ajit explains. Kane holds my hand. I stroke his palm gently with my thumb, making circles like tiny orbits.

15. SHIP

Ajit sat, fully dressed and with steaming coffee at his side, in front of his terminal. I didn't give him time to get the best of me. I walked into the wardroom and fired.

The sedative dart dropped him almost instantly. It was effective, for his body weight, for an hour. Kane didn't hear the thud as Ajit fell off his chair and onto the deck; Kane's bunk door stayed closed. I went into Ajit's bunk and searched every cubic meter of it, overriding the lock on his personal storage space. Most of that was taken up with the bronze statue of Shiva. The mini-caps were not there, nor anywhere else in his bunk.

I tried the galley next, and came up empty.

Same for the shower, the gym, the supply closets.

Ajit could have hidden the cubes in the engine compartments or the fuel bays or any of a dozen other ship's compartments, but they weren't pressurized and he would have had to either suit up or pressurize them. Either one would have shown up in my private ship data, and they hadn't. Ajit probably hadn't wanted to take the risk of too much covert motion around the ship. He'd only had enough drugs to put Kane and me out once. Otherwise, he wouldn't have risked subdermal trackers.

I guessed he'd hidden the cubes in the observatory.

Looking there involved digging. By the time I'd finished, the exotics lay yanked up in dying heaps around the room. The stones of the fountain had been flung about. I was filthy and sweating, my robe smeared with soil. But I'd found them, the two crystal cubes from the second and third mini-caps, removed from their heavy shielding. Their smooth surfaces shed the dirt easily.

Forty-five minutes had passed.

I went downstairs to wake Kane. The expedition would have to jump immediately; there is no room on a three-man ship to confine a prisoner for long. Even if I could protect Kane and me from Ajit, I didn't think I could protect Ajit from Kane. These mini-caps held the validation of Kane's shadow-matter work, and in another man, joy over that would have eclipsed the theft. I didn't think it would be that way with Kane.

Ajit still lay where I'd dropped him. The tranquilizer is reliable. I shot Ajit with a second dose and went into Kane's bunk. He wasn't there.

I stood too still for too long, then frantically scrambled into my s-suit.

I had already searched everywhere in the pressurized sections of the ship. Oh, let him be taking a second, fruitless look at the starboard hold, hoping to find some trace of the first particle that had hit us! Let him be in the damaged back-up engine compartment, afire with some stupid, brilliant idea to save the engine! Let him be—

"Kane! Kane!"

He lay in the starboard hold, on his side, his suit breached. He lay below a jagged piece of plastic from a half-open supply box. Ajit had made it look as if Kane had tried to open a box marked SENSOR REPLACEMENTS, had torn his suit, and the suit sealer nanos had failed. It was an altogether clumsy attempt, but one that, in the absence of any other evidence and a heretofore spotless reputation, would probably have worked.

The thing inside the suit was not Kane. Not anymore.

I knelt beside him. I put my arms around him and begged, cried, pleaded with him to come back. I pounded my gloves on the deck until I, too, risked suit breach. I think, in that abandoned and monstrous moment, I would not have cared.

Then I went into the wardroom, exchanged my tranquilizer gun for a knife, and slit Ajit's throat. I only regretted that he wasn't awake when I did it, and I only regretted that much, much later.

I prepared the ship for the long jump back to the Orion Arm. After the jump would come the acceleration-deceleration to Skillian, the closest settled world, which will take about a month standard. Space physics which I don't understand make this necessary; a ship cannot jump too close to a large body of matter like a planet. Shadow matter, apparently, does not count.

Both Ajit's and Kane's bodies rest in the cold of the non-pressurized port hold. Kane's initial work on shadow matter rests in my bunk. Every night I fondle the two cubes which will make him famous—more famous—on the settled Worlds. Every day I look at the data, the equations, the rest of his work on his terminal. I don't understand it, but sometimes I think I can see Kane, his essential self, in these intelligent symbols, these unlockings of the secrets of cosmic energy.

It was our shadow selves, not our essential ones, that destroyed my mission, the shadows in the core of each human being. Ajit's ambition and rivalry. Kane's stunted vision of other people and their limits. My pride, which led me to think I was in control of murderous rage long after it had reached a point of no return. In all of us.

I left one thing behind at the center of the galaxy. Just before the *Kepler* jumped, I jettisoned Ajit's statue of Shiva dancing, in the direction of Sgr A*. I don't know for sure, but I imagine it will travel toward the black hole at the galaxy's core, be caught eventually by its gravity, and spiral in, to someday disappear over the event horizon into some unimaginable singularity. That's what I want to happen to the statue. I hate it.

As to what will happen to me, I don't have the energy to hate it. I'll tell the authorities everything. My license as a Nurturer will surely be revoked, but I won't stand trial for the murder of Ajit. A captain is supreme law on her ship. I had the legal authority to kill Ajit. However, it's unlikely that any scientific expedition will hire me as captain ever again. My useful life is over, and any piece of it left is no more than one of the ashy, burned-out stars Kane says orbit Sgr A*, uselessly circling the core until its final death, giving no light.

A shadow.

16. PROBE

We remain near the galactic core, Kane and Ajit and I. The event horizon of Sgr A* is about one-fiftieth of a light year below us. As we spiral closer, our speed is increasing dramatically. The point of no return is one-twentieth of a light year. The lethal radiation, oddly enough, is less here than when we were drifting near the shadow matter on the other side of Sgr A West, but it is enough.

I think at least part of my brain has been affected, along with the repair program to fix it. It's hard to be sure, but I can't seem to remember much before we came aboard the probe, or details of why we're here. Sometimes I almost remember, but then it slips away. I know that Kane and Ajit and I are shadows of something, but I don't remember what.

Ajit and Kane work on their science. I have forgotten what it's about, but I like to sit and watch them together. Ajit works on ideas and Kane assists in minor ways, as once Kane worked on ideas and Ajit assisted in minor ways. We all know the science will go down into Sgr A* with us. The scientists do it anyway, for no other gain than pure love of the work. This is, in fact, the purest science in the universe.

Our mission is a success. Ajit and Kane have answers. I have kept them working harmoniously, have satisfied all their needs while they did it, and have captained my ship safely into the very heart of the galaxy. I am content.

Not that there aren't difficulties, of course. It's disconcerting to go up on the observation deck. Most of the exotics remain, blooming in wild profusion, but a good chunk of the hull has disappeared. The effect is that anything up there—flowers, bench, people—is drifting through naked space, held together only by the gravity we exert on each other. I don't understand how we can breathe up there; surely the air is gone. There are a lot of things I don't understand now, but I accept them.

The wardroom is mostly intact, except that you have to stoop to go through the door to the galley, which is only about two feet tall, and Ajit's bunk has disappeared. We manage fine with two bunks, since I sleep every night with Ajit or Kane. The terminals are intact. One of them won't display any more, though. Ajit has used it to hold a holo he programmed on a functioning part of the computer and superimposed over where the defunct display stood. The holo is a rendition of an image he showed me once before, of an Indian god, Shiva.

Shiva is dancing. He dances, four-armed and graceful, in a circle decorated with flames. Everything about him is dynamic, waving arms and kicking uplifted leg and mobile expression. Even the flames in the circle dance. Only Shiva's face is calm, detached, serene. Kane, especially, will watch the holo for hours.

The god, Ajit tells us, represents the flow of cosmic energy in the universe. Shiva creates, destroys, creates again. All matter and all energy participate in this rhythmic dance, patterns made and unmade throughout all of time.

Shadow matter—that's what Kane and Ajit are working on. I remember now. Something decoupled from the rest of the universe right after its creation. But shadow matter, too, is part of the dance. It exerted gravitational pull on our ship. We cannot see it, but it is there, changing the orbits of stars, the trajectories of lives, in the great shadow play of Shiva's dancing.

I don't think Kane, Ajit, and I have very much longer. But it doesn't matter, not really. We have each attained what we came for, and since we, too, are part of the cosmic pattern, we cannot really be lost. When the probe goes down into the black hole at the core, if we last that long, it will be as a part of the inevitable, endless, glorious flow of cosmic energy, the divine dance.

I am ready.

Afterword to "Shiva in Shadow"

There is a lot going on at the heart of the galaxy: a black hole, massive radiation, stars being torn apart. I knew none of this before Robert Silverberg asked me to write a story set there for his anthology *Between Worlds*. I started to research and was astonished at all the activity near Sagittarius A*. No life, however, and no possibility of putting characters there; humans cannot survive anywhere near that environment. So how was I going to set a hard-SF story at the brink of the black hole? I could have used aliens, I guess, but I didn't want to. I wanted humans. Thus were born the computer uploads of Tirzah, Kane, and Ajit, and once I had that, the two tracks of the story grew naturally. The other contributor to this story—one never knows what will spark fiction!—was a statue I have of Shiva, the Hindu god of creation and destruction. To me, Shiva represents the ceaseless flow of energy in the universe.

Chaos theory—and there is a lot of chaos at the heart of the Milky Way—says that even small changes can eventually have large consequences. So does any realistic theory of human relationships.

GRANT US THIS DAY

When I finally found God, he was slumped at the counter in a Detroit diner, stirring his coffee. The dissolving creamer made little spiral galaxies. He had a bad sunburn. I slid onto the next stool.

"God?"

He looked up. A little gray flecked his dark beard but on the whole he looked younger than I'd expected. Maybe thirty. Maybe twenty-eight. His jeans were grimy. "Who wants to know?"

"Daniel Smith." I held out my hand. He didn't take it. "Listen, God, I've been looking for you for a long time."

He said, "You got to read me my rights."

"What?"

"My Miranda rights. I know I screwed up, all right? But at least do it by the local rules. Let's get at least one part of this right."

"I'm not a cop," I said.

"Not a cop?"

"No."

"Just my luck." He slumped even lower on the stool, elbows resting on the counter, which bore some deep indescribable stain the shape of Africa. God traced it with one finger. Two teenage boys banged noisily through the front door; the waitress eyed them warily. "Then you're a divinity student, right? Colgate? Loyola?"

"No."

"You didn't find some ancient manuscript proving I exist in corporeal form?"

"No." The boys slid into a corner booth. Their jackets rode up, and I caught the flash of steel.

"You didn't consult a lama in a monastery on top of a Tibetan mountain—old, most old?"

"Not that either."

God sipped his coffee and made a face. "Then who the hell are you?"

"I'm from the Committee."

Even with his sunburn, he paled. "Oh, man."

"Well, that was one of the problems, certainly."

God slammed his spoon onto the counter and sat up straight. "Look, I know I screwed up. I know the work has problems. I've already admitted that." He glanced around the diner. In the booth opposite the boys, a hooker sat with an enormously fat man eating a taco salad. He talked with his mouth full; she was asleep. The fat man hadn't noticed. The waitress limped past, carrying a platter of greasy burgers. She had one leg shorter than the other.

"Nonetheless," God said, surly now, "from the Committee's viewpoint I did everything right, so why bother me? I filled out the application in triplicate. I listed my previous work. I filed by the deadline. I submitted work that met your bureaucratic guidelines: neatness, originality, aptness of thought. What's more original than kangaroos? Or the Hundred Years' War? A hundred years for a single war! So why hassle me now?"

"Maybe," I said, looking at the fat man, who had noticed the hooker was asleep and was kicking her viciously, "you could have worked a little harder on 'neatness.'"

"Yeah, well, everybody's a critic." He slumped again, his brief surliness over. I couldn't read the expression on his face. "But that still doesn't explain what you're doing here. I know I didn't make the finals. I saw the list."

"Yes and no."

"What's that supposed to mean?" He rubbed his nose; it really was a wicked sunburn. It was going to peel something awful.

I said, "The list's changed. One finalist withdrew. You were the first name on the waiting list."

His eyes opened wide. "Really? Who withdrew?"

"I'm not at liberty to say. But now you're on the short list."

God bent his head to stare into his coffee. The flush on his neck wasn't all sunburn. This means so damn much to some of them. The waitress delivered the burgers to an old couple at a center table, both of them thin and quavery as parchment.

He said, "So what happens now?"

"The rules say you have a thousand years to revise, before the next round of voting. Off the record, let me say I think you should consider fairly substantial revision. The Committee liked certain aspects of your work, but the consensus was that the tone is uneven, and the whole lacks coherence."

"I'm not creating some cheap commercial piece here!"

"I know that. And nobody says you should. But still, any good work has a voice all its own, a coherence, a thematic pattern that clearly identifies the artist. Your work here—well, frankly, son, it's all over the map. The pieces don't adhere. The proportions are skewed. It lacks balance and unity."

God signaled for a piece of pie. The waitress limped over from the center table, where the old couple were holding hands. The fat man spoke low and fast to the hooker, leaning forward, his mouth twisted. The boys passed a plastic bag across the table, smirking at the room, daring anyone to notice.

God said, "I can't just—"

I held up my hand placatingly, "I know, I know—you can't just compromise your artistic integrity. And nobody's asking you to. Just be a little more consistent in tone and imagery."

God said, "No, you don't understand. It's not a question of artistic integrity. Not really." He leaned closer, suddenly earnest. I wondered if he had any ointment for that nose. "See—there's a spectrum you can work along. Call it 'intended meaningfulness.' At one end you have your absurdist pieces. Things happen in an unconnected manner. Nothing is predictable. Nothing is rational. Godot never shows." He smiled.

I didn't get the reference. Probably to his own work. Some of these guys think the grant Committee memorizes their every detail. The door opened on a gust of wind and a cop entered. The waitress brought God cherry pie on a thick beige plate.

"I don't think much of absurdist stuff," he continued. "I mean, where's the art? If literally anything can happen, why bother? But at the other end is all that tight moral order. Punish the bad, reward the good, solve the mysteries, give every act simple-minded motives and rational outcomes. B-o-r-i-n-g. And not all that just or compassionate, either, no matter what those artists say. What's so compassionate about imposing a single pattern on the lion and the ox? Or on the worm in the heart of the rose, for that matter?"

"I wish you wouldn't be so self-referential. It's an annoying mannerism."

"But you get my point."

"Yes, I do. You go for texture. And density. And diversity. All commendable. But not very commercial."

"I didn't think this was supposed to be a commercial competition!"

"It's not," I said. "But do you realize how many mediocre artists out there justify their mediocrity by their lack of accessibility? Just because they're not commercial doesn't mean they're grandly above all standards and judgments. Not every finger twitch is sacred just because it's theirs."

"That's true." God slumped on his stool a third time. He certainly was a volatile kid. But honest. Not many can see the line between self-justification and true originality. I started to like him. The cop took a seat at the end of the counter. The boys flipped the finger at his back. The hooker wept softly. Her mascara smudged under her eyes.

"Look, son," I said, "don't take criticism so hard. Instead, use it. You're still in the running, and you've got a thousand years. Rework the more outré stuff to bring it in line with your major themes. Tone down your use of color. Make the ending a little clearer. That's all I'm suggesting. Give yourself a fighting chance."

He didn't say anything.

"After all, it's a pretty big grant."

Yes," he said tonelessly. He watched the hooker cry. Her fat pimp showed her something in his hand; from this angle I couldn't see what. The old couple rose to go, helping each other up. The waitress put an order of fries in front of the cop and bent to rub her varicose veins.

"If you win, it could mean a major boost to your career. You have a responsibility to your own talent."

"Yes."

"So think about revisions."

"The thing is," God said slowly, "I filled out the application forms a long time ago. Before I began work. It looks pretty different to me now. I do feel a responsibility to the work, but maybe not in the way you mean."

Something in his voice turned me cold. I'd heard that tone before. Recently. I pushed aside his pie, which he hadn't touched, and covered his hand with mine. "Son—"

"Didn't you wonder why I thought at first that you were a cop?"

The real cop turned his head to glance at us. He ate the last of his fries, nodded at the waitress, and made for the door, brushing past the tottering old couple. The codger fumbled in his pocket for a tip.

I could hear the thickness in my voice. "Son—it doesn't work like that."

"Maybe it does for me." He looked directly into my eyes. His own were very dark, with layered depths, like fine ash. I wondered how I could have thought him only twenty-eight. The cop left, banging the door behind him. The fat pimp pulled the hooker to her feet. She was still crying. The old man laid a dollar bill, a quarter, and three pennies on the table.

I said, "So okay, you feel responsible. It's your work, the outlines are yours, even if it got away from you and took off in directions you never intended. That happens. It's still yours. But that doesn't mean it's you. It's your art, son, not your life. There's a difference, and it's crucial. The people who confuse the two aren't thinking straight."

He turned those dark eyes away from me, and shrugged. "I feel responsible, is all. For all of it. Even the part that got away from me."

Suddenly he smiled whimsically. "Accepting responsibility again would actually strengthen the imagery pattern, wouldn't it? A leitmotif. The Committee might actually like that."

They probably would. I said carefully, "A competition is no real reason to go native."

"It isn't my reason." Abruptly he flung out one hand. "Ah, don't you see? I love it. All of it. Even if it's flawed, even if I screwed up, even if I lose. I love it."

He did. I saw that now. He loved it. Loved this. The old couple tottered toward the door. The two teenage boys shot out of their booth. One of them grabbed the tip off the table; the other lunged for the old lady's purse, ripping it off her arm. She fell backwards, thin arms flailing, squeaking "oh oh oh oh…" Instantly the old man raised his cane and brought it down hard on the boy's head. He shrieked, and blood sprang onto his cheek. The boy, outraged, yelled "Fuck! What you go do that for, you old bastard!" Then both boys tore out the door.

The fat pimp helped the old woman up. He was very gentle. "You all right, ma'am?" The hooker, still crying, reached out one deft hand and stole the old man's wallet from his pocket. The old woman stood, shaky but unhurt. The pimp escorted them to the door, stopped, walked back to the hooker. Silently she handed him the wallet. His fat hands curled into fists. He returned the wallet to the old man, and all four of them left. The waitress leaned over in the silent diner and rubbed her varicose veins.

I have never wanted to be an artist myself.

There wasn't much else to say. Maybe God would actually go through with it again, maybe not. Sometimes these guys are more in love with the idea of artistic risk than with the actuality. But he had done it once. All of it, right up to the final artistic sacrifice. That set him apart. I couldn't tell him this—against Committee rules—but that part of his work was what had earned him the first position on the waiting list. It had been an impressive set-piece, especially amidst the uneven emotional tone of the rest of his work. And if he did it again, it would certainly strengthen the imagery pattern in his entry. He was right about that. His chances of winning would increase dramatically. If, of course, he survived.

He had his place on the short list only because another candidate hadn't. "Withdrew" has a lot of meanings.

God grinned at me. Not a smile this time, an actual grin. "I'm sorry to be so stubborn. It's not like I don't appreciate your interest."

"Tell me something. Do you do all your own construction work?"

He rubbed his sunburned nose and laughed. "You know how it is. If you want something done right..."

"Yes. Well." I held out my hand and this time he took it, still grinning. He sat on the counter stool almost jauntily. I'd been right to like him.

Outside, it was just getting dark. Clouds raced across the sky from the west, casting strange shadows. Litter blew in gusts at my feet: newspapers, Styrofoam cups, a torn shirt. The shirt bore brown stains that might have been blood. The shadows lengthened, lying at right angles to each other.

Each work of art has its own internal pace; a thousand years is different here.

I thought I could hear them on the horizon, dragging the heavy wooden cross, howling about the thorned crown. Coming for him.

Afterword to "Grant Us This Day"

I'm very fond of this story (which is why it's included in this volume), although some readers have found the ending obscure. No writer should ever explain what his or her fiction "means"—the meaning should be carried by the story—but sometimes it's difficult to find the right balance between over-explaining ("Don't insult the reader's intelligence") and under-explaining ("Huh?"). Sometimes a writer, in retrospect, wishes she had hit that balance better in the first place. So I'm going to violate best-practices procedure and explain.

God created this universe, with Earth as its most intricate creation and his own crucifixion as a flashy set-piece, in order to win a cosmic universe-creating contest. He didn't win. Now he has a second chance to fix some of the errors and resubmit, and the last lines imply that, despite his own suffering and some less-than-desirable outcomes, he's going to allow himself to be crucified again, for the sake of his art. There. I explained it. This is my resubmission for the story as art.

THE KINDNESS OF STRANGERS

When morning finally dawns, Rochester isn't there anymore.

Jenny stands beside Eric, gazing south from the rising ground that yesterday was a fallow field. Maybe the whole city hasn't vanished. Certainly the tall buildings are gone, Xerox Square and Lincoln Tower and the few others that just last night poked above the horizon, touched by the red fire of the setting September sun. But unlike Denver or Tokyo or Seattle, Rochester, New York, sits—sat—on flat ground and there's no point from which the whole city could be seen at once. And it was such a *small* city.

"Maybe they only took downtown," Jenny says to Eric, "and Penfield is still there or Gates, or Brighton..."

Eric just looks at her and pulls out his cell yet again. Most of the others—other what? refugees?—are still asleep in their cars or tents or sleeping bags on the dew-soaked weeds. There aren't nearly as many refugees as Jenny expected. Faced with the choice of staying in the city—and such a small city!—or leaving it, most had stayed. Devil you know and all that.

She thinks she might be a little hysterical.

Eric walks around the car, cell pressed to his ear. Deirdre will not answer, will never answer again, but that won't stop him from trying. He tried even as he and Jenny hastily packed up her Dodge Caravan yesterday afternoon, even as she drove frantically south, even as they were stopped. When the battery in Eric's cell runs down, he will take hers. Jenny, sure of this if of nothing else, presses her hands to her temple, trying to stop the blood pounding there. It doesn't work.

"Good morning," says an alien, coming up behind her. "Breakfast is ready now."

Jenny whirls around and stumbles backward, falling against the hood of her van. This one is female, a tall Scandinavian-looking blonde. Her pink skin glows with health; her blue eyes shine warmly; her teeth are small and regular. She is dressed like last night's alien, in a ground-length, long-sleeved brown garment. Loose, modest, cultureless, suitable for dissolving cities on any part of the globe.

Definitely a little hysterical.

"No, thank you," Jenny manages.

"Are you sure?" the alien asks. She gestures toward the low, pale buildings at the far end of the sloping meadow. "The coffee is excellent today."

"No, thank you."

The alien smiles and moves on to the next car. Eric turns on Jenny. "Why are you so *polite* to them?"

She doesn't answer. To say anything—anything at all—will be to unleash the rage he's been battling for fourteen hours. So far, Eric has held that rage in check. She can't risk it.

"Here," he says, thrusting a Quaker Oats breakfast bar at her. She isn't hungry but takes it anyway.

"Some of us are going to dig a latrine," he says, not looking at her, and strides off.

Two cars over, a woman with crazy eyes fires a 9 mm at the alien. The bullet ricochets off her, striking another car's hubcap. People wake and cry out. The alien smiles at the crazed human.

"Good morning. Breakfast is ready now."

Probably the aliens aren't even present. If you touch one—or hit it or shotgun it or hurl a Molotov cocktail at it, all of which were tried last night—you encounter a tough, impenetrable shell that doesn't even wobble under impact. *Personal force field*, someone said. *Holographic projection*, said another, *protected by a force field.* Jenny has no idea who's right, and it hardly matters. The same maybe-force-field was what stopped her and Eric's mad drive south last night. Another transparent wall prevented her from retracing her route. A hundred or so cars were thus invisibly herded into this empty field, their drivers leaping out to compare sketchy information, children crying in the backseats and wives hunched over car radios, their faces in white shock.

Bombay and Karachi had been first, vanishing at 2:16 p.m. No explosion, no dust, no blinding light. One moment, reported dazed observers by satellite, the great cities and their vast suburbs had existed and the next they were gone, leaving bare ground that ended in roads sheared off as neatly as if by a very sharp knife, in halves of temples on the shear line, in bisected holy cows. The ground was not even scorched. People standing beyond the vanishing point saw nothing happen.

Fifteen minutes later it was Delhi, Shanghai, and Moscow.

Fifteen minutes after that, Seoul, Sao Paolo, Istanbul, Lima, and Mexico City.

Then Jakarta, New York, Tokyo, Beijing, Cairo, Tehran, and Riyad.

By this time the hysterical media had figured out that cities were vanishing in order of size, and by a progression of prime numbers. At 3:16 p.m. (London, Bogota, Lagos, Baghdad, Bangkok, Lahore, Dacca, Rio de Janeiro, Bangalore, Wuhan, and Tientsin), the panicked evacuations began. Most people were vaporized (except that no vapor remained) long before they reached the end of the murderous city traffic jams.

Canton, Toronto, Jiddah, Abidjan, Chongqing, Santiago, Calcutta, Singapore, Chennai, St. Petersburg, Shenyang, Los Angeles, Ahmadabad.

As soon as he heard, Eric called Deirdre in Chicago, over and over, even as he and Jenny had been packing her car. He hadn't been able to get through by either cell or land line: *All circuits busy. Please try your call again later.*

Pusan, Alexandria, Hyderabad, Ankara, Pyongyang, Yokohama, Montreal, Casablanca, Ho Chi Minh City, Berlin, Nanjing, Addis Ababa, Poona, Medellin, Kano.

Only two United States cities so far. Jenny lived in Henrietta, Rochester's southernmost suburb. The roads were crowded but not impassable. She inched through traffic, the radio turned on, while Eric tried Deirdre over and over again: *All circuits busy.*

At 4:01, Chicago vanished along with Omdurman, Surat, Madrid, Sian, Kanpur, Havana, Jaipur, Nairobi, Harbin, Buenos Aires, Incheon, Surabaya, Kiev, Hangzhou, Salvador, Taipei, Hai Phong, and Dar es Salaam. Eric kept calling. He said, "Maybe she was visiting someone out of the city, shopping at a mall someplace rural.... She doesn't always have her cell turned on!"

Jenny knew better than to answer. She concentrated on the road, on the traffic, on the panicky radio announcer relaying by satellite a report from where Houston used to be.

"Can I have that?"

A small voice at her elbow. Jenny realizes she is still holding the unopened Quaker Oats bar. The little boy is maybe five or six, dirty and snot-nosed, but with wide dark eyes that hold soft depths, like ash. He stares hungrily at the breakfast bar.

"Sure, take it." Her voice is thick. "What's your name?"

"Ricky." He tears off the wrapping and drops it on the grass. Jenny picks it up.

"Where's your mom, Ricky?"

"Over there." He gobbles the bar in three bites. His mother, a voluptuous redhead in pink stretch pants, sits on the ground with her back against an old green SUV. She nurses an infant from one large breast and watches Jenny. All at once she bawls, "Ricky! Get your ass over here!"

Ricky ignores this. "Do you got any more food?"

"No," Jenny lies. Apparently not everyone thought to pack their cars with food. Those that have will run out before long. The low, pale buildings still sit unvisited.

"Ricky!" his mother screams, and this time he leaves.

Jenny pulls off her sweater; the morning sun is turning the day hot. She opens her cell to key in her brother Bob's number. Bob lives with his family in Dundee, a small town fifty miles away; his and Jenny's mother lives with them. Jenny's sister and her family are nearby. "Bob? You all okay?... No, nothing changed since last night.... Jane? You talk to her?.... Okay, look, I don't want to run down the phone too much.... Love you, too...." When she closes the case, Eric is back.

They stare at each other. *Now it will come*, Jenny thinks. She feels as if she's carrying a teacup of nitroglycerin across a tightrope; the fall is only a matter of time. But all Eric says is, "There's a man here who's good at organization. We divided into sections and checked out the whole wall. No breaks, and it extends as far up as anyone can throw a stone and as far underground as we had time to dig. The force field surrounds the buildings, too. Anything new on the radio?"

"No," Jenny says, not telling him that she hasn't been listening. But he knows; his question was not inquisitive but hostile. He can't help that—Jenny knows as much—but she recoils as if he'd struck her. She's always been too sensitive to rejection.

Eric says, "I'm going back to help the tunnel crew."

"Okay." And then she can't stand it anymore. "Eric, I'm so sorry, but it's not my fault that my family is alive and Deirdre and Mary—"

"Don't," he says, so low and dangerous that Jenny is shocked into silence. Eric is not ordinarily a dangerous man. One thing she loved about him was his lighthearted exuberance.

He walks away, his back toward her, and Jenny covers her face with her hands. It is her fault, will always be her fault. Not that Eric's wife and daughter are dead, of course, but that Eric was with Jenny, in bed with Jenny in another city, pumping away on top of Jenny, when it happened. He will never forgive either of them for that.

They met a year ago, at the American Library Association annual conference, in Kansas City. Jenny's attraction to him was instantaneous, and so was her glance at the wedding ring on Eric's left hand. But he was so handsome and so charming, and she was so thrilled by the almost unprecedented masculine attention. They drifted together at the luncheon held between "Reference Tools for the On-Line Generation" and "Collaborative Approaches to Information Literacy." They had a drink in the bar after the obligatory inedible banquet, laughing at the dullness of the speakers. One drink became many. They spent the last night of the conference in Jenny's room, and the next day she'd flown back to Rochester, suspended somewhere between euphoria and dread. Two days later she'd e-mailed him. Eric had replied, and things had gone on from there.

Sometimes, if she hadn't had an e-mail or phone call from him in several days, Jenny let herself imagine that he'd told his wife about the affair. He'd told her, and then he'd moved out of their Evanston home, and he was just waiting to hear from his lawyer before he told Jenny the great news. She let herself imagine all this in exquisite detail—the scene with Deirdre, Eric's complicated emotions, the phone call to Jenny and how understanding she would be—even while she knew it was not going to happen. Very few married men actually left their wives for their mistresses. Eric adored his six-year-old daughter. He had never even said that he loved Jenny.

But she loved him, and she knew it was turning her desperate, which in turn was driving him away. She waited, helpless and all but hopeless, by the phone. She turned up the volume on her computer ("You've got mail!") so that anywhere in the apartment she would know the instant his e-mail came through. She wrote long, eloquent letters giving him tender ultimatums, and never sent the letters because she knew he would not choose her. It took all her strength to never ask him the Fatal Questions: Do we have a future? Are you tired of me? Is there somebody else? Somebody besides Deirdre, she meant. She tried not to think about Deirdre, and the effort further exhausted her. Finally she Googled Deirdre and got over a thousand hits; Deirdre was a successful real estate agent in Evanston. She was slim, tanned, smiling, dressed more stylishly than Jenny had ever managed. She grew roses and played golf. Jenny mailed one of the eloquent ultimatums.

"I think we'd better end this, Jenny," Eric said gently on the phone. "I'm sorry, but this isn't what I'd thought it was. I don't want you to get any more hurt than it seems you already are."

Seems? More hurt? Not "what he thought it was"? What was that? She found a steeliness she didn't know she possessed. "I want to discuss this in person, Eric. I think you owe me that!" And he agreed, from guilt or compassion or fair play or who-knew-what. He flew to Rochester on a Friday morning, a return flight scheduled for that evening, six hours in which to end what had become the center of her life. She lured him—there really was no other word—into a farewell fuck, thinking desperately, stupidly, *Maybe if it's really good, better than Deirdre…* But Friday afternoon Bombay and Karachi disappeared, and a few hours later Chicago took Deirdre (maybe) and little Mary along with three million other people, and now Rochester is gone and Eric can barely look at Jenny.

She gets into the minivan, but even with the passenger door open, the September sun starts to heat up the car. For something to do, she straightens the blankets on top of the mattress that fills the back of the van; she and Eric, not touching, slept here last night. She checks their boxes of food, bottles of water, two flashlights and small hoard of extra batteries. Jenny, no camper, didn't own the tent, Coleman lanterns, or propane stoves she sees blossoming over the field like mushrooms. Communities are forming. Ricky and two other little boys have started a soccer game in the middle of the semicircle of cars. Somebody's dog, barking wildly, chases the boys. In front of the green SUV, three women gossip over coffee bubbling on a campfire. One of them is Ricky's slatternly mother, and the other two look enough like her to be her sisters or cousins. Out of desperation—she will go mad if she just sits here—Jenny fights off her innate shyness and walks over.

The oldest of the women, overweight and sweet-faced in a Redwings T-shirt, says, "Hi, honey. Want some coffee?"

"Yes, please." The small kindness almost brings tears. "Thank you so much. I'm Jenny."

"Carleen, and this here's Sue and Cheri." Carleen hands Jenny coffee in a thick white mug. "I figure we're all in this together, so we better stick together, right?"

"Right," Jenny says unconvincingly. Cheri, Ricky's mother, is studying Jenny as if planning to dissect her. The coffee is hot and wonderful.

Sue is as talkative as Carleen. "Your husband at the big powwow?"

How to answer that? Cheri's gaze sharpens. Jenny finally says, "They investigated the…the wall this morning and found no breaks. Now they're trying to tunnel underneath."

"That's what my Ted said," Sue says. "But he told me he thinks an assault on the ETs' building is gonna have to happen sooner or later."

Jenny nods. *ET* conjures up for her the cuddly and benevolent creature from the old movie, not the beautiful alien megaterrorist who offered her breakfast and who may or may not even be bodily present. And *assault* is an alarming word all by itself. These look like gun people, which Jenny and Eric emphatically are not.

Carleen says, "If the assholes really do have food in there and—Ricky! Be careful!"

The soccer ball has nearly gone into the campfire. Cheri grabs for her son, who wriggles away with the agility of long practice. She bellows, "Ricky!" The child darts behind Carleen and grabs her ample waist.

"There now, he didn't mean nothing, Cheri—don't get your blood in a boil. Ricky, you be good now, you hear?"

Ricky nods and darts off. Desultory chatter reveals that Carleen is Cheri's and Sue's mother, the grandmother of Ricky and the now-sleeping infant, Daniella. Carleen does not, to Jenny's eyes, look anywhere near old enough to be a grandmother. Sue is the mother of the other two little boys, nonidentical twins. Neither Carleen nor Cheri mentions husbands, either present or vaporized in Rochester. Carleen is casually maternal to anyone who enters her radar, including Jenny. Cheri asks fake-nonchalant questions about Eric, which Jenny avoids answering. After a half hour of this, the coffee is gone, the fire is out, and Jenny is emotionally exhausted.

She excuses herself, crawls onto the mattress in the hot van, and falls fitfully asleep. When she wakes, sweaty and unrefreshed, Eric still hasn't returned. She stumbles out of the car into a midafternoon chaos of cooking, unleashed pets, gossiping, worrying, grieving. Radios yammer, although it's clear that groups have pooled electronic resources to save batteries. Women cry. Children either race frantically around or sit in frightened huddles against parents' knees. There are no aliens visible.

Carleen comes over, evidently a response to Jenny's dazed look. "You need the latrine, honey? Over there." She points. "And your husband said to tell you to go ahead and eat without him; he's gonna work on the tunnel and he'll get something later. You got to make sure he eats, Jenny. Some of these men are mad enough to just burn themselves out."

Jenny nods. She finds the latrine, efficiently and deeply dug behind the field's only line of scrub bushes, divided by a blanket on poles into separate pits for males and females. Many of these people, she realizes, are far better at basic survival than she. Not that that's hard. On the way back to the van, she notices a prayer service of some sort under a tarp strung between two cars, a card game around a collapsible table, and a woman reading a book to a toddler on her lap. All the adults wear the resolute, pinched look of people going through funeral rites and determined to do them correctly despite whatever they might be feeling. This should, Jenny thinks, be an inspiring model for her own behavior, but instead it makes her feel even more inadequate.

How long will Eric stay away from her?

The rest of the day, it turns out. Jenny calls her brother Bob on the cell and then sits in the van, waiting. The early September dusk falls, and a few cars, chosen by lottery, train their headlights on the low, pale buildings across the meadow. This hardly seems necessary, since the buildings glow with their own subtle light. People put on sweaters and jackets, and the smell of canned stew fills the air. Three aliens begin to circulate among the cars.

"Good evening. Dinner is ready now."

People turn their backs or glare menacingly. Sue spits, a glob of sputum that slides off the alien's protective shell. This one is a man, tall and brown-skinned, handsome as an African-American movie star. Sue's husband, Ted, snarls, "Get your ass out of here!"

"Are you sure? The chicken Marengo is excellent."

Cheri appears with a shotgun. The alien smiles at her. Carleen says sharply, "Don't you fire that thing with all these people around—what the hell's wrong with you? Jenny, honey, you want some coffee?"

Cheri returns the shotgun to the green SUV. Ricky sits beside Carleen's fire, eating Chef Boyardee ravioli from a plastic bowl, his baby sister asleep in an infant seat on the grass beside him. Cheri has changed from the pink pants and tee dotted with baby spit to tight jeans and a spangled red sweater cut very low. She has spectacular breasts. Jenny accepts the coffee but no ravioli; she's still not hungry, and anyway she doesn't want to deplete their food supply.

"Honey, you got to eat," Carleen says. "Even a bitty thing like you gotta eat."

"I had something in the van," Jenny lies.

Cheri says, "Not into sharing?"

Jenny faces her. "Would you like some organic yogurt? I have some in the cooler."

Carleen laughs and says, "That's telling her!" Cheri smiles, too, but it's a nasty secret smile, as though Jenny has revealed dirty underwear. Cheri says, "No, thanks." Ricky demands more ravioli and Cheri gives it to him, then turns to her mother.

"Will you watch the kids a bit? I'm going to go find Ralph."

Carleen snaps, "You'd do better to stay away from that no-good."

Cheri doesn't answer, just strolls off into the darkness. Carleen says to Jenny, as if Jenny were her own age and not Cheri's, "Kids. Soon as they get tits you can't tell them nothing."

Jenny, whose own tits are negligible, has no idea what to say to this.

"That Ralph'll just break her heart, same as the daddies of these two." She picks up Daniella, who's starting to fuss in her infant seat.

The information that Cheri, too, is having her heart broken by someone should make Jenny feel more kinship with her. It doesn't. She crawls onto the mattress in the van, trying to read Dickens by flashlight while she waits for Eric to come back for dinner. She's fixed him a sandwich from the best of everything thrown hastily into her cooler. Two bottles of beer are as chilled as the melting ice will get them. Jenny knows it's a pathetic offering, but as the hours pass and he doesn't appear to witness her pathos, anger sets in. What right has he to treat her this way? None of this is her fault. Somewhere deep in her bruised and frightened mind she knows that Eric is staying away because he's afraid of what he'll say if he comes back to her, but she doesn't want to look at this. Looking at it would finish her off.

He doesn't come back all night.

In the very early morning, anger replaced by frenzied anxiety, Jenny looks for him. Eric is asleep near the half-dug tunnel, rolled up in somebody's extra sleeping bag. He lies on his back, his dark hair flopping to one side, and in sleep all the anger and guilt and fear have smoothed out. Through the grime on his face snake tear trails. Jenny's heart melts and she crouches beside him. "Eric..."

He wakes, stares at her, and tightens his mouth to a thin, straight line. That's all she sees; all she can bear. She gets up and walks away, making herself put one sneaker in front of the next, moving blindly through the damp weeds. It's over. He will never forgive her, never forgive himself, possibly never even approach the van again. The frenzy of tunnel digging, which will do no good, will eventually be replaced by frenzies of another sort, any other sort, anything to blot out everything he's lost. And she will not be able to change his mind. Eric is not strong enough to fight off his own passions, including the passion for self-destruction. If he were, he wouldn't have become involved with her—or with his other women—in the first place.

All this comes to Jenny in an instant, like a blow. It's all she can do to remain upright, walking. Her cell rings. It will be her brother, but even knowing how cruel she's being, she can't bring herself to answer. As the field comes alive around her, she sits alone in her van, wishing she had died in Rochester.

Another two days and most of the food and water have run out. Except for a few dour loners, mostly armed, people have been remarkably generous with their supplies. There have been no fights, no looting, no theft. Jenny, who hasn't been able to eat, gave most of her food to Carleen, who made it last as long as possible among her small matriarchal band, which now apparently includes Jenny. Jenny doesn't care, not about anything.

Outside help, it's learned through numerous phone calls, was stopped by a second invisible wall about a mile from the camp. Not even a helicopter was able to rise high enough to surmount the barrier. Relatives, cops, and the Red Cross remain parked just outside in case something, unspecified, lets them drive closer. Most cell phones, including Jenny's, have exhausted their batteries, although a few people have the equipment to recharge phones from car cigarette lighters. Jenny doesn't find out if hers can be recharged. Bob knows that Jenny's still alive, and there is nothing else to report. The car radios now pick up only two small-town stations, but these report that cities have stopped disappearing. A schedule has been organized and a track cleared to drive cars around the field, so that the batteries will not run down and both radio and heat will still be available. It's a nice balance between using up gas and preserving batteries. Jenny does not participate.

Three times a day aliens circulate around the field, offering breakfast, lunch, dinner. No one accepts. The aliens are cursed, spat on, attacked, and once—although this is looked on with disfavor—publicly prayed over.

Tunnels of varying depths now ring the field beside the invisible wall. None of them go deeper than the barrier, but digging them has given many people something physical to drain off rage and grief.

Every once in a while Jenny glimpses Eric in the distance, working on yet another futile tunnel, or huddled in desperate conference with other men, or with Cheri. Each of these sightings turns her inside out like a sock, all her vulnerable organs battered by the smallest sound, breeze, photon of light.

"My Cheri never was no good around men," Carleen says, handing Jenny yet another cup of boiled coffee, not meeting her eyes. It's the first time Carleen has mentioned the situation. Jenny doesn't reply. Carleen's kindness is like air, ubiquitous and necessary and equally available to everyone, but even air hurts Jenny now.

"Honey," Carleen adds, "you gotta *eat*."

"Later," Jenny says, the syllable scraping her throat like gritty vomit.

Carleen goes away, but half an hour later Ricky appears beside the van, holding a book. He is incredibly dirty, smells bad, and clearly does not want to be there. "You spozed to read me this."

It's *Treasure Island* in the original, a book whose flowery language and slow pace Ricky will neither understand nor enjoy. Where on Earth did Carleen get it? She must have asked every last person in the camp, must have remembered that Jenny is—was—a librarian, must have cudgeled her slow wits to think of something that might make Jenny feel better. Jenny starts to cry. An old song title fills her head: "Roses from the Wrong Man." Carleen is not a man, and this filthy child with his reluctant offering is about as far from roses as it's possible to get, but Jenny is in too much pain to appreciate the incongruity. She only knows that if it had been Eric who'd arranged this perverse kindness on her behalf, she could have borne anything. But it is not Eric.

Ricky looks at her tears with the same alarm as would any grown man. "Hey! You...you gonna read me that book?"

"No. You'd hate it. Go play."

Released, Ricky gives a whoop and races away, running backward, maybe to fulfill some small-boy notion of paying attention to the adult he's been told to pay attention to. No one else is in the center of the field; the cars are doing their daily promenade to charge up batteries. The red Taurus is not going very fast and the driver slams on her brakes, but not soon enough. Ricky is hit.

He starts shrieking to wake the dead. Carleen and Cheri both scream and dart from beside their SUV, Cheri with Daniella clamped to one naked breast. Sue's husband, Ted, leaps from his car and reaches Ricky just as Jenny does. Ted says, "Ricky! Buddy!"

The child is wailing and writhing on the flattened weeds. His left arm hangs at a strange angle. Ted gently holds down Ricky's shoulders. "Lie still, buddy, till we see what's broken." Cheri thrusts Daniella at Carleen, yells something anguished, and throws herself practically on top of Ricky. Ted shoves her off. "For Chrissake, let me see how bad he's hurt! Don't crush him, Cheri!"

"Ted's an EMT," Sue says at Jenny's elbow. "What happened?"

Jenny shakes her head. She can't speak. Cheri says shakily, "He was just racing around like always and—fuck it, why does everything always happen to me!"

Jenny just stares at her. The statement is so selfish, so inadequate, so stupid, that no response is possible. A thought forms in Jenny's mind: *If this is what Eric prefers to me, the hell with him.* The next second she's ashamed of this thought; it's as self-absorbed as Cheri's. She turns her attention to Ricky.

His arm is broken. There are no doctors or professional nurses among the refugees. Ted sets the arm, using as a splint a piece of wood torn from a chair leg. Ted is obviously no expert at this, but he's resourceful, gentle, and willing to accept responsibility. Everything, Jenny thinks coldly, that Eric is not. Ricky screams like an animal in a steel-toothed trap. The driver of the red Taurus blubbers apologies; no one blames her. The accident is thoroughly discussed at every campfire, in every tent, on every mattress in the back of every van. Ricky is given a hoarded candy bar, a precious comic book, and a hefty slug of cough syrup mixed with whiskey to make him sleep.

Jenny can't sleep. Lying alone on her mattress, she tries to think coldly about her and Eric, about the destroyed cities, about what will happen now. She can't quite manage enough coldness, but it's better than the hell of the last four days. Somewhere in the deep dark there's a tap at the window.

Eric... Hope burns so sudden, so hot, that Jenny feels scorched inside. She nearly cries out as she fumbles for the door, the flashlight.

Carleen stands there, her meaty arms limp by her side. In the upward-slanting glow from the flashlight, she says despairingly, "Ricky."

Jenny stumbles from the van, follows Carleen. Stars shine in a clear, cold sky. Jenny's lighted watch face says 4:18 a.m. The SUV tailgate gapes open, and Jenny sees the usual mattress, a double in this monster vehicle, on which Ricky lies, glassy-eyed. Daniella whimpers softly in her infant seat. Cheri is not here. With Eric?

"He been like this for a coupla hours now," Carleen says in a low, steady voice. "He won't drink or eat or talk. And his arm's swelling up and turning all dark." She trains the flashlight on Ricky's arm.

Jenny bends over the child, who smells as if he's shit his pants. Gangrene—could it set in that fast? She doesn't know, but clearly something is radically wrong.

Carleen goes on in that strange, even voice. "I can't leave Daniella. And Ted don't know enough to deal with this."

"I don't know anything about medical matters, either—certainly not as much as Ted!"

Carleen continues as if Jenny hadn't spoken. "Anyway Sue's got some kind of diarrhea now and Ted can't leave his kids. Not for good. Can't take the risk. And I got Daniella. Can't count on Cheri."

Jenny straightens and turns. The two women stare at each other. For a long moment, it seems to Jenny, her universe hangs in the balance, all of it: Eric and vaporized Rochester, Deirdre and Jenny's job at the vanished public library, the running-down cell phones and Jenny's mother waiting for her in Dundee, the stars far overhead and the trodden-down weeds underfoot in this desperate refugee camp no one planned on.

Jenny nods.

Together they pick up Ricky and situate him in Jenny's arms. Ricky moans, but softly. He's heavy, reeking, only half-conscious. There is nobody else up, or at least nobody that Jenny sees. In the dark she carries Ricky the entire length of the field, trying not to shift him even as he grows heavier and heavier, navigating by the pale glow from the alien buildings.

Up close, they present rough, cream-colored walls like stucco, but no stucco ever shone with its own light. The buildings all seem interconnected, but Jenny sees only one entry, itself filled with light instead of any tangible door. She walks through the light and into a wide space—surely wider than the whole building appears from the outside?—that is absolutely empty.

"Hello," Jenny calls, inadequately, and suddenly she can hold Ricky no longer. She sinks with her burden to the stucco floor. This is as hopeless as everything else in her stupid life. She doesn't even like this kid.

"Hello," an alien says. It's the tall blonde woman in the standard brown robe; she materializes from empty air. "Is this little person hurt?"

Anger rises in Jenny at the cloying pseudo-friendliness of "this little person"—these beings have murdered nine-tenths of the Earth's population!—but for Ricky's sake she holds the anger in check. "Yes. He's hurt. His arm is broken and some kind of infection has set in."

"What's his name?" the alien asks. Her eyes are blue and warm as the Mediterranean.

"Ricky."

"And what's your name?"

What can that possibly matter? "Jenny."

"Jenny, close your eyes, please."

Should she do it? It makes no more sense than anything else, so why not? She has no idea what she's doing here. She closes her eyes.

"You may open them now."

Even before Jenny can do that, Ricky says, "What the fuck!"

He jumps up and gazes wildly around. His arm is whole, the clumsy splint and darkened swelling both gone. His clothes are clean. He shrieks in fear and jumps into Jenny's lap, hiding his face against her neck. His hair smells of sweet grass.

Jenny struggles to stand while holding Ricky, who mercifully is too scared to scream. She must stand; she can't face this terrible being from a sitting position on the ground. A table stands beside the alien: an ordinary picnic table with benches, the surface laden with scrambled eggs, toast, sweet rolls, orange juice, fragrant hot coffee. The plastic plates have a pattern of daisies. Jenny goes weak in the knees. She dumps Ricky onto a bench. He clutches her around the waist but then sees the sweet rolls and looks up at Jenny.

"Eat," she manages to get out. And to the alien, "Why?"

The smiling blue eyes widen slightly. "Didn't you want me to repair him?"

"I mean, why did you kill all those cities? *All those people?*"

The alien nods. "I see. Sit down, Jenny."

"No."

"All right. But the coffee is excellent today."

"Why did you do it?" Bombay, Karachi, Delhi, Shanghai, Moscow...all in strict order of size. The meticulousness alone is monstrous.

The alien says, "Why did that man hurt Ricky when he tried to pull his arm bones back into the correct line?"

For a minute Jenny can't think what the creature means. Then she gets it. "Are you saying you committed massive genocide for our own *good*?"

"There were too many of you," the alien says. She sits gracefully on the picnic bench across from Ricky, who is gobbling eggs and sweet rolls with one hand, the other fastened firmly on Jenny's jacket. "In one more generation you would have had irreversible climate change, starvation, war, and suffering beyond belief. We spared you all that."

Jenny can barely speak. "You did... It was..."

"It was an act of kindness," the alien says, "and I know it seems hard now, but we've spared your species an incredible amount of suffering. In two more generations, your altered world will seem normal to its inhabitants. Two generations after that, you will thank us for our intervention. And you will have learned, and you will do much better this time. We've seen this before, you know."

Jenny doesn't know. She doesn't know anything. The worst is that, with her book-nourished imagination, she can actually see how that monstrous prophecy might come about. The gratitude of the masses in countries where most people never, ever had enough to eat until the cities disappeared.... Religion would help. Saviors from the stars, revered and deified and carrying out the will of God, of Allah, of Shiva in the endless dance of destruction in order for there to be room for creation.

The alien says, as if reading her thoughts, "You humans have a talent for self-destruction, you know. You cause a lot of your own suffering. It's unfortunate."

Jenny picks up a butter knife and hurls it at the woman's eyes.

It doesn't connect, of course. The knife bounces off the alien's face, and the only response is from Ricky, scared all over again, and also full enough with good food to have the energy for response. He wails and wraps himself around the still-standing Jenny.

The alien stands, too. "Don't think we're not sympathetic, Jenny. But we look at things differently than you do. Good-bye."

"Wait!" Jenny cries over Ricky's screams. "One more question! Why keep us here inside this invisible cage? What did you hope to learn?"

The alien answers without hesitation. "Whether you were different in small enough groups. And you are. A few hundred of you outside Rochester and Bogota and Nantes and Chengdu—you're much better beings in smaller groups. It's chaotic out there just now, but you *will* cooperate better on survival, even if you're no happier. We're very glad to know this. It justifies our decision. Good-bye, Jenny."

The alien vanishes. Then the building vanishes. It's not yet dawn outside, but Jenny hears a siren in the distance, drawing closer. Somewhere in the field a car door slams. She sets Ricky down and tugs at him to walk toward Carleen's camp. The siren comes closer still; Eric and his work crew won't need those tunnels now. Jenny can go to Dundee as soon as Bob arrives for her. He may be on his way now.

Ricky tries to break free, but Jenny holds him firmly. He isn't going to get hit by another car, not while he's with her. She has no idea what the future holds for Ricky, for any of them. But now—finally!—hatred of the self-righteous aliens, blithely playing Old Testament God, burns stronger in her than does despair over Eric. *It justifies our decision*... The hell it does! All those innocent lives, all the grief tearing apart the survivors...

Hatred is a great heartener. Hatred, and the knowledge that she is going to be needed (*It's chaotic out there just now*...), as Carleen and Ricky had needed her. These things, hatred and usefulness, aren't much (*...even if you're no happier*...) but they're something. And both are easier than love.

She brings the child back to his grandmother as the camp wakes and the cars drive in.

Afterward to "The Kindness of Strangers"

What is an act of kindness? Some are easy to identify: helping up a stranger who has fallen, donating to disaster relief, not pointing out that your spouse has told the story about the wheelbarrow six times to the same people. But what about more ambiguous acts? Is it a kindness to stop a suicide who desperately wants to die?

My father lives far out in the country, and his woods and field are overpopulated with deer. In the winter, many starve. Culling a deer herd by killing a bunch of them—is that a kindness? Not to the dead ones, but to the survivors, who then will not starve? What about an overpopulated planet?

The mind recoils from the idea, but one of the functions of SF is to examine ideas that the mind recoils from. The result, as here, is often an ambiguous and bleak story. It's bleak for Jenny, too, and I got some negative email about this story's ending. Sometimes, however, hatred *is* "a great heartener," enabling a person to go on when nothing else will.

Perhaps you didn't like "The Kindness of Strangers." It's included in this volume because I think it contains some of my best writing. You, however, will be the judge of that.

END GAME

Allen Dodson was sitting in seventh-grade math class, staring at the back of Peggy Corcoran's head, when he had the insight that changed the world. First his own world and then, eventually, like dominos toppling in predestined rhythm, everybody else's, until nothing could ever be the same again. Although we didn't, of course, know that back then.

The source of the insight was Peggy Corcoran. Allen had sat behind her since third grade (Anderson, Blake, Corcoran, Dodson, DuQuesne...) and never thought her remarkable. Nor was she. It was 1982 and Peggy wore a David Bowie T-shirt and straggly brown braids. But now, staring at the back of her mousy hair, Allen suddenly realized that Peggy's head must be a sloppy mess of skittering thoughts and contradictory feelings and half-buried longings—just as his was. Nobody was what they seemed to be!

The realization actually made his stomach roil. In books and movies, characters had one thought at a time: *"Elementary, my dear Watson." "An offer he couldn't refuse." "Beam me up, Scotty!"* But Allen's own mind, when he tried to watch it, was different. *Ten more minutes of class I'm hungry gotta pee the answer is x+6 you moron what would it be like to kiss Linda Wilson M*A*S*H on tonight really gotta pee locker stuck today Linda eight more minutes do the first sixteen problems baseball after school—*

No. Not even close. He would have to include his mind watching those thoughts and then his thoughts about the watching thoughts and then—

And Peggy Corcoran was doing all that, too.

And Linda Wilson.

And Jeff Gallagher.

And Mr. Henderson, standing at the front of math class.

And everyone in the world, all with thoughts zooming through their heads fast as electricity, thoughts bumping into each other and fighting each other and blotting each other out, a mess inside every mind on the whole Earth, nothing sensible or orderly or predictable.... Why, right this minute Mr. Henderson could be thinking terrible things even as he assigned the first sixteen problems on page 145, terrible things about Allen even or Mr. Henderson could be thinking about his lunch or hating teaching or planning a murder.... You could never know. No one was settled or simple, nothing could be counted on....

Allen had to be carried, screaming, from math class.

I didn't learn any of this until decades later, of course. Allen and I weren't friends, even though we sat across the aisle from each other (Edwards, Farr, Fitzgerald, Gallagher...). And after the screaming fit, I thought he was just as weird as everyone else did. I never taunted Allen like some of the boys, or laughed at him like the girls, and a part of me was actually interested in the strange things he sometimes said in class, always looking as if he had no idea how peculiar he sounded. But I wasn't strong enough to go against the herd and make friends with such a loser.

The summer before Allen went off to Harvard, we did become—if not friends—then chess companions. "You play rotten, Jeff," Allen said to me with his characteristic, oblivious candor, "but nobody else plays at all." So two or three times a week we sat on his parents' screened porch and battled it out on the chessboard. I never won. Time after time I slammed out of the house in frustration and shame, vowing not to return. After all, unlike wimpy Allen, I had better things to do with my time: girls, cars, James Bond movies. But I always went back.

Allen's parents were, I thought even back then, a little frightened by their son's intensity. Mild, hard-working people fond of golf, they pretty much left Allen alone from his fifteenth birthday on. As we moved rooks and knights around the chessboard in the gathering darkness of the porch, Allen's mother would timidly offer a pitcher of lemonade and a plate of cookies. She treated both of us with an uneasy respect that, in turn, made me uneasy. That wasn't how parents were supposed to behave.

Harvard was a close thing for Allen, despite his astronomical SATs. His grades were spotty because he only did the work in courses he was interested in, and his medical history was even spottier: bouts of depression when he didn't attend school, two brief hospitalizations in a psychiatric ward. Allen would get absorbed by something—chess, quantum physics, Buddhism—to the point where he couldn't stop, until all at once his interest vanished as if it had never existed. Harvard had, I thought in my eighteen-year-old wisdom, every reason to be wary. But Allen was a National Merit scholar, and when he won the Westinghouse science competition for his work on cranial structures in voles, Harvard took him.

The night before he left, we had our last chess match. Allen opened with the conservative Italian game, which told me he was slightly distracted. Twelve moves in, he suddenly said, "Jeff, what if you could tidy up your thoughts, the way you tidy up your room every night?"

"Do what?" My mother "tidied up" my room, and what kind of weirdo used words like that, anyway?

He ignored me. "It's sort of like static, isn't it? All those stray thoughts in a mind, interfering with a clear broadcast. Yeah, that's the right analogy. Without the static, we could all think clearer. Cleaner. We could see farther before the signal gets lost in uncontrolled noise."

In the gloom of the porch, I could barely see his pale, broad-cheeked face. But I had a sudden insight, rare for me that summer. "Allen—is that what happened to you that time in seventh grade? Too much...static?"

"Yeah." He didn't seem embarrassed, unlike anybody normal. It was as if embarrassment was too insignificant for this subject. "That was the first time I saw it. For a long time I thought if I could learn to meditate—you know, like Buddhist monks—I could get rid of the static. But meditation doesn't go far enough. The static is still there, you're just not paying attention to it anymore. But it's still there." He moved his bishop.

"What exactly happened in the seventh grade?" I found myself intensely curious, which I covered by staring at the board and making a move.

He told me, still unembarrassed, in exhaustive detail. Then he added, "It should be possible to adjust brain chemicals to eliminate the static. To unclutter the mind. It should!"

"Well," I said, dropping from insight to my more usual sarcasm, "maybe you'll do it at Harvard, if you don't get sidetracked by some weird shit like ballet or model railroads."

"Checkmate," Allen said.

I lost track of him after that summer, except for the lengthy Bakersville High School Alumni Notes faithfully mailed out every single year by Linda Wilson, who must have had some obsessive/compulsiveness of her own. Allen went on to Harvard Medical School. After graduation he was hired by a prestigious pharmaceutical company and published a lot of scientific articles about topics I couldn't pronounce. He married, divorced, married again, divorced again. Peggy Corcoran, who married my cousin Joe and who knew Allen's second wife, told me at my father's funeral that both ex-wives said the same thing about Allen: He was never emotionally present.

I saw him for myself at our twenty-fifth reunion. He looked surprisingly the same: thin, broad-faced, pale. He stood alone in a corner, looking so pathetic that I dragged Karen over to him. "Hey, Allen. Jeff Gallagher."

"I know."

"This is my wife, Karen."

He smiled at her but said nothing. Karen, both outgoing and compassionate, started a flow of small talk, but Allen shut her off in mid-sentence. "Jeff, you still play chess?"

"Neither *Karen* nor I play now," I said pointedly.

"Oh. There's someone I want you to see, Jeff. Can you come to the lab tomorrow?"

The "lab" was sixty miles away, in the city, and I had to work the next day. But something about the situation had captured my wife's eclectic and sharply intelligent interest. She said, "What is it, Allen, if you don't mind my asking?"

"I don't mind. It's a chess player. I think she might change the world."

"You mean the big important chess world?" I said. Near Allen, all my teenage sarcasm had returned.

"No. The whole world. Please come, Jeff."

"What time?" Karen said.

"Karen, I have a job."

"Your hours are flexible," she said, which was true. I was a real estate agent, working from home. She smiled at me with all her wicked sparkle. "I'm sure it will be fascinating."

Lucy Hartwick, twenty-five years old, was tall, slender, and very pretty. I saw Karen, who unfortunately inclined to jealousy, glance at me.

But I wasn't attracted to Lucy. There was something cold about her beauty. She barely glanced up at us from a computer in Allen's lab, and her gaze was indifferent. The screen displayed a chess game.

"Lucy's rating, as measured by computer games anyway, is 2670," Allen said.

"So?" Yes, 2670 was extremely high; only twenty or so players in the world held ratings above 2700. But I was still in sarcastic mode, even as I castigated myself for childishness.

Allen said, "Six months ago her rating was 1400."

"So six months ago, she first learned to play, right?" We were talking about Lucy, bent motionless above the chessboard, as if she weren't even present.

"No, she had played twice a week for five years."

That kind of ratings jump for someone with mediocre talent who hadn't studied chess several hours a day for years—it just didn't happen. Karen said, "Good for you, Lucy!" Lucy glanced up blankly, then returned to her board.

I said, "And so just how is this supposed to change the world?"

"Come see this," Allen said. Without looking back, he strode toward the door.

I was getting tired of his games, but Karen followed him, so I followed her. Eccentricity has always intrigued Karen, perhaps because she's so balanced, so sane, herself. It was one reason I fell in love with her.

Allen held out a mass of graphs, charts, and medical scans as if he expected me to read them. "See, Jeff, these are all Lucy, taken when she's playing chess. The caudate nucleus, which aids the mind in switching gears from one thought to another, shows low activity. So does the thalamus, which processes sensory input. And here, in the—"

"I'm a realtor, Allen," I said, more harshly than I intended. "What does all this garbage mean?"

Allen looked at me and said simply, "She's done it. Lucy has. She's learned to eliminate the static."

"What static?" I said, even though I remembered perfectly our conversation of twenty-five years ago.

"You mean," said Karen, always a quick study, "that Lucy can concentrate on one thing at a time without getting distracted?"

"I just said so, didn't I?" Allen said. "Lucy Hartwick has control of her own mind. When she plays chess, that's all she's doing. As a result, she's now equal to the top echelons of the chess world."

"But she hasn't actually played any of those top players, has she?" I argued. "This is just your estimate based on her play against some computer."

"Same thing," Allen said.

"It is not!"

Karen peered in surprise at my outrage. "Jeff—"

Allen said, "Yes, Jeff, listen to Carol. Don't—"

"'Karen'!"

"—you understand? Lucy's somehow achieved total concentration. That lets her just...just soar ahead in her understanding of the thing she chooses to focus on. Don't you realize what this could mean for medical research? For...for any field at all? We could solve global warming and cancer and toxic waste and...and everything!"

As far as I knew, Allen had never been interested in global warming, and a sarcastic reply rose to my lips. But either Allen's face or Karen's hand on my arm stopped me. She said gently, "That could be wonderful, Allen."

"It will be!" he said with all the fervor of his seventh-grade fit. "It will be!"

"What was that all about?" Karen said in the car on our way home.

"Oh, that was just Allen being—"

"Not Allen. You."

"Me?" I said, but even I knew my innocence didn't ring true.

"I've never seen you like that. You positively sneered at him, and for what might actually be an enormous breakthrough in brain chemistry."

"It's just a theory, Karen! Ninety percent of theories collapse as soon as anyone runs controlled experiments."

"But you, Jeff...you want this one to collapse."

I twisted in the driver's seat to look at her face. Karen stared straight ahead, her pretty lips set as concrete. My first instinct was to bluster...but not with Karen.

"I don't know," I said quietly. "Allen has always brought out the worst in me, for some reason. Maybe...maybe I'm jealous."

A long pause, while I concentrated as hard as I could on the road ahead. Yellow divider, do not pass, thirty-five MPH, pothole ahead...

Then Karen's hand rested lightly on my shoulder, and the world was all right again.

After that I kept in sporadic touch with Allen. Two or three times I phoned and we talked for fifteen minutes. Or, rather, Allen talked and I listened, struggling with irritability. He never asked about me or Karen. He talked exclusively about his research into various aspects of Lucy Hartwick: her spinal and cranial fluid, her neural firing patterns, her blood and tissue cultures. He spoke of her as if she were no more than a collection of biological puzzles he was determined to solve, and I couldn't imagine what their day-to-day interactions were like. For some reason I didn't understand, I didn't tell Karen about these conversations.

That was the first year. The following June, things changed. Allen's reports—because that's what they were, reports and not conversations—became non-stop complaints.

"The FDA is taking forever to pass my IND application. Forever!"

I figured out that "IND" meant "initial new drug," and that it must be a green light for his Lucy research.

"And Lucy has become impossible. She's hardly ever available when I need her, trotting off to chess tournaments around the world. As if chess mattered as much as my work on her!"

I remembered the long-ago summer when chess mattered to Allen himself more than anything else in the world.

"I'm just frustrated by the selfishness and the bureaucracy and the politics."

"Yes," I said.

"And doesn't Lucy understand how important this could be? The incredible potential for improving the world?"

"Evidently not," I said, with mean satisfaction that I disliked myself for. To compensate I said, "Allen, why don't you take a break and come out here for dinner some night. Doesn't a break help with scientific thinking? Lead sometimes to real insights?"

I could feel, even over the phone line, that he'd been on the point of refusal, but my last two sentences stopped him. After a moment he said, "Oh, all right, if you want me to," so ungraciously that it seemed he was granting me an inconvenient favor. Right then, I knew that the dinner was going to be a disaster.

And it was, but not as much as it would have been without Karen. She didn't take offense when Allen refused to tour her beloved garden. She said nothing when he tasted things and put them down on the tablecloth, dropped bits of food as he chewed, slobbered on the rim of his glass. She listened patiently to Allen's two-hour monologue, nodding and making encouraging little noises. Toward the end her eyes did glaze a bit, but she never lost her poise and wouldn't let me lose mine, either.

"It's a disgrace," Allen ranted, "the FDA is hobbling all productive research with excessive caution for—do you know what would happen if Jenner had needed FDA approval for his vaccines? We'd all still have smallpox, that's what! If Louis Pasteur—"

"Why don't you play chess with Jeff?" Karen said when the meal finally finished. "While I clear away here."

I exhaled in relief. Chess was played in silence. Moreover, Karen would be stuck with cleaning up after Allen's appalling table manners.

"I'm not interested in chess anymore," Allen said. "Anyway, I have to get back to the lab. Not that Lucy kept her appointment for tests on...she's wasting my time in Turkistan or someplace. Bye. Thanks for dinner."

"Don't invite him again, Jeff," Karen said to me after Allen left. "Please."

"I won't. You were great, sweetheart."

Later, in bed, I did that thing she likes and I don't, by way of saying thank you. Halfway through, however, Karen pushed me away. "I only like it when you're really here," she said. "Tonight you're just not focusing on us at all."

After she went to sleep, I crept out of bed and turned on the computer in my study. The heavy fragrance of Karen's roses drifted through the window screen. Lucy Hartwick was in Turkmenistan, playing in the Chess Olympiad in Ashgabat. Various websites told of her rocketing rise to the top of the chess world. Articles about her all mentioned that she never socialized with her own or any other team, preferred to eat all her meals alone in her hotel room, and never smiled. I studied the accompanying pictures, trying to see what had happened to Lucy's beauty.

She was still slender and long-legged. The lovely features were still there, although obscured by her habitual pose while studying a chessboard: hunched over from the neck like a turtle, with two fingers in her slightly open mouth. I had seen that pose somewhere before, but I couldn't remember where. It wasn't appealing, but the loss of Lucy's good looks came from something else. Even for a chess player, the concentration on her face was formidable. It wiped out any hint of any other emotion whatsoever. Good poker players do that, too, but not in quite that way. Lucy looked not quite human.

Or maybe I just thought that because of my complicated feelings about Allen.

At two A.M. I sneaked back into bed, glad that Karen hadn't woken while I was gone.

"She's gone!" Allen cried over the phone, a year later. "She's just gone!"

"Who?" I said, although, of course, I knew. "Allen, I can't talk now, I have a client coming into the office two minutes from now."

"You have to come down here!"

"Why?" I had ducked all of Allen's calls ever since that awful dinner, changing my home phone to an unlisted number and letting my secretary turn him away at work. I'd only answered now because I was expecting a call from Karen about the time for our next marriage counseling session. Things weren't as good as they used to be. Not really bad, just clouds blocking what had been a steady marital sunshine. I wanted to dispel those clouds before they turned into major thunderstorms.

"You have to come," Allen repeated, and he started to sob.

Embarrassed, I held the phone away from my ear. Grown men didn't cry like that, not to other men. All at once I realized why Allen wanted me to come to the lab: because he had no other human contact at all.

"Please, Jeff," Allen whispered, and I snapped, "Okay!"

"Mr. Gallagher, your clients are here," Brittany said at the doorway, and I tried to compose a smile and a good lie.

And after all that, Lucy Hartwick wasn't even gone. She sat in Allen's lab, hunched over a chessboard with two fingers in her mouth, just as I had seen her a year ago on the Web.

"What the hell—Allen, you *said*—"

Unpredictable as ever, he had calmed down since calling me. Now he handed me a sheaf of print-outs and medical photos. I flashed back suddenly to the first time I'd come to this lab, when Allen had also thrust on me documents I couldn't read. He just didn't learn.

"Her white matter has shrunk another 75 percent since I saw her last," Allen said, as though that were supposed to convey something to me.

"You said Lucy was gone!"

"She is."

"She's sitting right there!"

Allen looked at me. I had the impression that the simple act required enormous effort on his part, like a man trying to drag himself free of a concrete block to which he was chained. He said, "I was always jealous of you, you know."

It staggered me. My mouth opened but Allen had already moved back to the concrete block. "Just look at these brain scans, 75 percent less white matter in six months! And these neurotransmitter levels, they—"

"Allen," I said. Sudden cold had seized my heart. "Stop." But he babbled on about the caudate nucleus and antibodies attacking the basal ganglia and bi-directional rerouting.

I walked over to Lucy and lifted her chessboard off the table.

Immediately she rose and continued playing variations on the board in my arms. I took several steps backward; she followed me, still playing. I hurled the board into the hall, slammed the door, and stood with my back to it. I was six-one and 190 pounds; Lucy wasn't even half that. In fact, she appeared to have lost weight, so that her slimness had turned gaunt.

She didn't try to fight me. Instead she returned to her table, sat down, and stuck two fingers in her mouth.

"She's playing in her head, isn't she," I said to Allen.

"Yes."

"What does 'white matter' do?"

"It contains axons that connect neurons in the cerebral cortex to neurons in other parts of the brain, thereby facilitating intercranial communication." Allen sounded like a textbook.

"You mean, it lets some parts of the brain talk to other parts?"

"Well, that's only a crude analogy, but—"

"It lets different thoughts from different parts of the brain reach each other," I said, still staring at Lucy. "It makes you aware of more than one thought at a time."

Static.

Allen began a long technical explanation, but I wasn't listening. I remembered now where I'd seen that pose of Lucy's, head pushed forward and two fingers in her mouth, drooling. It had been in an artist's rendering of Queen Elizabeth I in her final days, immobile and unreachable, her mind already gone in advance of her dying body.

"Lucy's gone," Allen had said. He knew.

"Allen, what baseball team did Babe Ruth play for?"

He babbled on about neurotransmitters.

"What was Bobby Fischer's favorite opening move?" Silently I begged him, *Say e4, damn it.*

He talked about the brain waves of concentrated meditation.

"Did you know that a tsunami will hit Manhattan tomorrow?"

He urged overhaul of FDA clinical-trial design.

I said, as quietly as I could manage, "You have it, too, don't you. You injected yourself with whatever concoction the FDA wouldn't approve, or you took it as a pill, or something. You wanted Lucy's static-free state, like some fucking dryer sheet, and so you gave this to yourself from her. And now neither one of you can switch focus at all." The call to me had been Allen's last, desperate foray out of his perfect concentration on this project. No—that hadn't been the last.

I took him firmly by the shoulders. "Allen, what did you mean when you said 'I was always jealous of you'?"

He blathered on about MRI results.

"Allen—please tell me what you meant!"

But he couldn't. And now I would never know.

I called the front desk of the research building. I called 911. Then I called Karen, needing to hear her voice, needing to connect with her. But she didn't answer her cell, and the office said she'd left her desk to go home early.

Both Allen and Lucy were hospitalized briefly, then released. I never heard the diagnosis, although I suspect it involved an "inability to perceive and relate to social interactions" or some such psychobabble. Doesn't play well with others. Runs with scissors. Lucy and Allen demonstrated they could physically care for themselves by doing it, so the hospital let them go. Business professionals, I hear, mind their money for them, order their physical lives. Allen has just published another brilliant paper, and Lucy Hartwick is the first female World Chess Champion.

Karen said, "They're happy, in their own way. If their single-minded focus on their passions makes them oblivious to anything else—well, so what. Maybe that's the price for genius."

"Maybe," I said, glad that she was talking to me at all. There hadn't been much conversation lately. Karen had refused any more marriage counseling and had turned silent, escaping me by working in the garden. Our roses are the envy of the neighborhood. We have Tuscan Sun, Ruffled Cloud, Mister Lincoln, Crown Princess, Golden Zest. English roses, hybrid teas, floribunda, groundcover roses, climbers, shrubs. They glow scarlet, pink, antique apricot, deep gold, delicate coral. Their combined scent nauseates me.

I remember the exact moment that happened. We were in the garden, Karen kneeling beside a flower bed, a wide hat shading her face from the sun so that I couldn't see her eyes.

"Karen," I said, trying to mask my desperation, "Do you still love me?"

"Hand me that trowel, will you, Jeff?"

"Karen! Please! Can we talk about what's happening to us?"

"The Tahitian Sunsets are going to be glorious this year."

I stared at her, at the beads of sweat on her upper lip, the graceful arc of her neck, her happy smile.

Karen clearing away Allen's dinner dishes, picking up his sloppily dropped food. Lucy with two fingers in her mouth, studying her chessboard and then touching the pieces.

No. Not possible.

Karen reached for the trowel herself, as if she'd forgotten I was there.

Lucy Hartwick lost her championship to a Russian named Dmitri Chertov. A geneticist at Stanford made a breakthrough in cancer research so important that it grabbed all headlines for nearly a week. By a coincidence that amused the media, his young daughter won the Scripps Spelling Bee. I looked up the geneticist on the Internet; a year ago he'd attended a scientific conference with Allen. A woman in Oregon, some New Age type, developed the ability to completely control her brain waves through profound meditation. Her husband is a chess grandmaster.

I walk a lot now, when I'm not cleaning or cooking or shopping. Karen quit her job; she barely leaves the garden even to sleep. I kept my job, although I take fewer clients. As I walk, I think about the ones I do have, mulling over various houses they might like. I watch the August trees begin to tinge with early yellow, ponder overheard snatches of conversation, talk to dogs. My walks get longer and longer, and I notice that I've started to time my speed, to become interested in running shoes, to investigate transcontinental walking routes.

But I try not to think about walking too much. I observe children at frenetic play during the last of their summer vacation, recall movies I once liked, wonder at the intricacies of quantum physics, anticipate what I'll cook for lunch. Sometimes I sing. I recite the few snatches of poetry I learned as a child, relive great football games, chat with old ladies on their porches, add up how many calories I had for breakfast. Sometimes I even mentally rehearse basic chess openings: the Vienna Game or the Petroff Defense. I let whatever thoughts come that will, accepting them all.

Listening to the static, because I don't know how much longer I've got.

Afterword to "End Game"

I play chess. I play it a lot (the word "compulsively" has been used). And I do not play well.

Chess has a distinctly dark side. Twentieth-century artist Marcel Duchamp stopped creating art after he discovered chess, in his thirties. He didn't play the game at top ranks even after years of study, but he became obsessed with it to the exclusion of all else, describing himself to a friend as "still a victim of chess." Ordinarily we admire single-minded drive: it's what leads scientists to try experiment after experiment until they find verifiable hypotheses. It enables entrepreneurs to work insane hours to launch new companies. It pushes athletes and dancers to endless practice.

But can you be too single-minded? When this idea occurred to me, the entire story fell into place almost instantly. It wasn't quite as easy to write as "Out of All Them Bright Stars" (for one thing, it's much longer), but it wasn't hard, either. The story is one of the few horror stories I ever wrote. Because it *is* a horror story—as can be too much of any good thing.

Maybe even writing.

MY MOTHER, DANCING

Fermi's Paradox, California, 1950: Since planet formation appears to be common, and since the processes that lead to the development of life are a continuation of those that develop planets, and since the development of life leads to intelligence and intelligence to technology—then why hasn't a single alien civilization contacted Earth?

Where is everybody?

They had agreed, laughing, on a form for the millennium contact, what Micah called "human standard," although Kabil had insisted on keeping hirs konfol and Deb had not dissolved hirs crest, which waved three inches above hirs and hummed. But, then, Deb! Ling had designed floating baktors for the entire ship, red and yellow mostly, that combined and recombined in kaleidoscopic loveliness only Ling could have programmed. The viewport was set to magnify, the air mixture just slightly intoxicating, the tinglies carefully balanced by Cal, that master. Ling had wanted "natural" sleep cycles, but Cal's argument had been more persuasive, and the tinglies massaged the limbic so pleasantly. Even the child had some. It was a party.

The ship slipped into orbit around the planet, a massive subJovian far from its sun, streaked with muted color. "Lovely," breathed Deb, who lived for beauty.

Cal, the biologist, was more practical: "I ran the equations; by now there should be around 200,000 of them in the rift, if the replication rate stayed constant."

"Why wouldn't it?" said Ling, the challenger, and the others laughed. The tinglies really were a good idea.

The child, Harrah, pressed hirs face to the window. "When can we land?"

The adults smiled at each other. They were so proud of Harrah, and so careful. Hirs was the first gene-donate for all of them except Micah, and probably the only one for the rest except Cal, who was a certified intellect donor. Kabil knelt beside Harrah, bringing hirs face to the child's height.

"Little love, we can't land. Not here. We must see the creations in holo."

"Oh," Harrah said, with the universal acceptance of childhood. It had not changed in five thousand years, Ling was fond of remarking, that child idea that whatever it lived was the norm. But, then...*Ling.*

"Access the data," Cal said, and Harrah obeyed, reciting it aloud as hirs parents had all taught hirs. Ling smiled to see that Harrah still closed hirs eyes to access, but opened them to recite.

"The creations were dropped on this planet 273 E-years ago. They were the one-hundred-fortieth drop in the Great Holy Mission that gives us our life. The creations were left in a closed-system rift...what does that mean?"

"The air in the creations' valley doesn't get out to the rest of the planet, because the valley is so deep and the gravity so great. They have their own air."

"Oh. The creations are cyborged replicators, programmed for self-awareness. They are also programmed to expect human contact at the millennium. They..."

"Enough," said Kabil, still kneeling beside Harrah. Hirs stroked hirs hair, black today. "The important thing, Harrah, is that you remember that these creations are beings, different from us but with the same life force, the only life force. They must be respected, just as people are, even if they look odd to you."

"Or if they don't know as much as you," said Cal. "They won't, you know."

"I know," Harrah said. They had made hirs an accommodater, with strong genes for bonding. They already had Ling for challenge. Harrah added, "Praise Fermi and Kwang and Arlbeni for the emptiness of the universe."

Ling frowned. Hirs had opposed teaching Harrah the simpler, older folklore of the Great Mission. Ling would have preferred that the child receive only truth, not religion. But Deb had insisted. Feed the imagination first, hirs had said, and later Harrah can separate science from prophecy. But the tinglies felt sweet, and the air mixture was set for a party, and hirs own baktors floated in such graceful pattern that Ling, not even Ling, could quarrel.

"I wonder," Deb said dreamily, "what they have learned in 273 years."

"When will they holo?" Harrah said. "Are we there yet?"

Our mother is coming.

Two hours more and they will come, from beyond the top of the world. When they come, there will be much dancing. Much rejoicing. All of us will dance, even those who have detached and let the air carry them away. Those ones will receive our transmissions and dance with us.

Or maybe our mother will also transmit to where those of us now sit. Maybe they will transmit to all, even those colonies out of our own transmission range. Why not? Our mother, who made us, can do whatever is necessary.

First, the dancing. Then, the most necessary thing of all. Our mother will solve the program flaw. Completely, so that no more of us will die. Our mother doesn't die. We are not supposed to die, either. Our mother will transmit the program to correct this.

Then the dancing there will be!

Kwang's Resolution, Bohr Station, 2552: Since the development of the Quantum Transport, humanity has visited nearly a thousand planets in our galaxy and surveyed many more. Not one of them has developed any life of any kind, no matter how simple. Not one.

No aliens have contacted Earth because there is nobody else out there.

Harrah laughed in delight. Hirs long black hair swung through a drift of yellow baktors. "The creations look like oysters!"

The holocube showed uneven rocky ground through thick, murky air. A short distance away rose the abrupt, steep walls of the rift, thousands of feet high. Attached to the ground by thin, flexible, mineral-conducting tubes were hundreds of uniform, metal-alloy double shells. The shells held self-replicating nanomachinery, including the rudimentary AI, and living eukaryotes sealed into selectively permeable membranes. The machinery ran on the feeble sunlight and on energy produced by anaerobic bacteria, carefully engineered for the thick atmospheric stew of methane, hydrogen, helium, ammonia, and carbon dioxide.

The child knew none of this. Hirs saw the "oysters" jumping up in time on their filaments, jumping and falling, flapping their shells open and closed, twisting and flapping and bobbing. Dancing.

Kabil laughed, too. "Nowhere in the original programming! They learned it!"

"But what could the stimulus have been?" Ling said. "How lovely to find out!"

"Sssshhh, we're going to transmit," Micah said. Hirs eyes glowed. Micah was the oldest of them all; hirs had been on the original drop. "Seeding 140, are you there?"

"We are here! We are Seeding 140! Welcome, our mother!"

Harrah jabbed hirs finger at the holocube. "We're not your mother!"

Instantly Deb closed the transmission. Micah said harshly, "Harrah! Your manners!"

The child looked scared. Deb said, "Harrah, we talked about this. The creations are not like us, but their ideas are as true as ours, on their own world. Don't laugh at them."

From Kabil, "Don't you remember, Harrah? Access the learning session!"

"I...remember," Harrah faltered.

"Then show some respect!" Micah said. "This is the Great Mission!"

Harrah's eyes teared. Kabil, the tender-hearted, put hirs hand on Harrah's shoulder. "Small heart, the Great Mission gives meaning to our lives."

"I..know..."

Micah said, "You don't want to be like those people who just use up all their centuries in mere pleasure, with no structure to their wanderings across the galaxy, no purpose beyond seeing what the nanos can produce that they haven't produced before, no difference between today and tomorrow, no—"

"That's sufficient," Ling says. "Harrah understands, and regrets. Don't give an Arlbeni Day speech, Micah."

Micah said stiffly, "It matters, Ling."

"Of course it matters. But so do the creations, and they're waiting. Deb, open the transmission again.... Seeding 140, thank you for your welcome! We return!"

Arlbeni's Vision, Planet Cadrys, 2678: We have been fools.

Humanity is in despair. Nano has given us everything, and nothing. Endless pleasures empty of effort, endless tomorrows empty of purpose, endless experiences empty of meaning. From evolution to sentience, sentience to nano, nano to the decay of sentience.

But the fault is ours. We have overlooked the greatest gift ever given humanity: the illogical emptiness of the universe. It is against evolution, it is against known physical processes. Therefore, how can it exist? And why?

It can exist only by the intent of something greater than the physical processes of the universe. A conscious Intent. The reason can only be to give humanity, the universe's sole inheritor, knowledge of this Intent. The emptiness of the universe—anomalous, unexplainable, impossible—has been left for us to discover, as the only convincing proof of God.

Our mother has come! We dance on the seabed. We transmit the news to the ones who have detached and floated away. We rejoice together, and consult the original program.

"You are above the planetary atmosphere," we say, new words until just this moment, but now understood. All will be understood now, all corrected. "You are in a ship, as we are in our shells."

"Yes," our mother says. "You know we cannot land."

"Yes," we say, and there is momentary dysfunction. How can they help us if they cannot land? But only momentary. This is our mother. And they landed us here once, didn't they? They can do whatever is necessary.

Our mother says, "How many are you now, Seeding 140?"

"We are 79,432," we say. Sadness comes. We endure it, as we must.

Our mother's voice changes in wavelength, in frequency. "Seventy-nine thousand? Are you...we had calculated more. Is this replication data right?"

A packet of data arrives. We scan it quickly; it matches our programming.

"The data is correct, our mother. That is the rate of replication. But..." We stop. It feels like another dying ceremony, suddenly, and it is not yet time for a dying ceremony. We will wait another few minutes; we will tell our mother in another few minutes. Instead, we ask, "What is your rate of replication, our mother?"

Another change in wavelength and frequency. We scan and match data, and it is in our databanks: laughter, a form of rejoicing. Our mother rejoices.

"You aren't equipped for visuals, or I would show you our replicant," our mother says. "But the rate is much, much lower than yours. We have one new replicant with us on the ship."

"Welcome, new replicant!" we say, and there is more rejoicing. There, and here.

"I've restricted transmission...there's the t-field's visual," Micah said.

A hazy cloud appeared to one side of the holocube, large enough to hold two people comfortably, three close together. Only words spoken inside the field would now transmit. Baktors scuttled clear of the ionized haze. Deb stepped inside the field, with Harrah; Cal moved out of it. Hirs frowned at Micah.

"They can't be only 79,000-plus if the rate of replication has held steady. Check the resource data, Micah."

"Scanning...No change in available raw materials...no change in sunlight per square unit."

"Scan their counting program."

"I already did. Fully functional."

"Then run an historical scan of replicants created."

"That will take time...there, it's started. What about attrition?"

Cal said, "Of course. I should have thought of that. Do a seismic survey and match it with the original data. A huge quake could easily have destroyed two-thirds of them, poor seedings..."

Ling said, "You could ask them."

Kabil said, "If it's not a cultural taboo. Remember, they have had time to evolve a culture, we left them that ability."

"Only in response to environmental stimuli. Would a quake or mudslide create enough stimulus pressure to evolve death taboos?"

They looked at each other. Something new in the universe, something humanity had not created...this was why they were here! Their eyes shone, their breaths came faster. Yet they were uncomfortable, too, at the mention of death. How long since any of them...oh, yes, Ling's clone, in that computer malfunction, but so many decades ago...Discomfort, excitement, compassion for Seeding 140, yes compassion most of all, how terrible if the poor creations had actually lost so many in a quake...All of them felt it, and meant it, the emotion was genuine. And in their minds the finger of God touched each for a moment, with the holiness of the tiny human struggle against the emptiness of the universe.

"Praise Fermi and Kwang and Arlbeni..." one of them murmured, and no one was sure who, in the general embarrassment that took them a moment later. They were not children.

Micah said, "Match the seismic survey with the original data," and moved off to savor alone the residue of natural transcendence, rarest and strangest of the few things nano could not provide.

Inside the hazy field Harrah said, "Seeding! I am dancing just like you!" and moved hirs small body back and forth, up and down on the ship's deck.

Arlbeni's Vision, Planet Cadrys, 2678: In the proof of God lies its corollary. The Great Intent has left the universe empty, except for us. It is our mission to fill it.

Look around you, look at what we've become. At the pointless destruction, the aimless boredom, the spiritual despair. The human race cannot exist without purpose, without vision, without faith. Filling the emptiness of the universe will rescue us from our own.

Our mother says, "Do you play any games?"

We examine the data carefully. There is no match.

Our mother speaks again. "That was our new replicant speaking, Seeding 140. Hirs is only half-created as yet, and hirs program language is not fully functional. Hirs means, of the new programs you have created for yourselves since the original seeding, which ones in response to the environment are expressions of rejoicing? Like dancing?"

"Yes!" we say. "We dance in rejoicing. And we also throw pebbles in rejoicing and catch pebbles in rejoicing. But not for many years since."

"Do it now!" our mother says.

This is our mother. We are not rejoicing. But this is our mother. We pick up some pebbles.

"No," our mother says quickly, "you don't need to throw pebbles. That was the new replicant again. Hirs does not yet understand that seedings do what they wish, and only what they wish. Your...your mother does not command you. Anything you do, anything you have learned, is as necessary as what we do."

"I'm sorry again," our mother says, and there is physical movement registered in the field of transmission.

We do not understand. But our mother has spoken of new programs, of programs created since the seeding, in response to the environment. This we understand, and now is the time to tell our mother of our need. Our mother has asked. Sorrow floods us, rejoicing disappears, but now is the time to tell what is necessary.

Our mother will make all functional once more.

"Don't scold hirs like that, hirs is just a child," Kabil said. "Harrah, stop crying, we know you didn't mean to impute to them any inferiority."

Micah, hirs back turned to the tiny parental drama, said to Cal, "Seismic survey complete. No quakes, only the most minor geologic disturbances...really, the local history shows remarkable stability."

"Then what accounts for the difference between their count of themselves and the replication rate?"

"It can't be a real difference."

"But...oh! Listen. Did they just say—"

Hirs turned slowly toward the holocube.

Harrah said at the same moment, through hirs tears, "They stopped dancing."

Cal said, "Repeat that," remembered hirsself, and moved into the transmission field, replacing Harrah. "Repeat that, please, Seeding 140. Repeat your last transmission."

The motionless metal oysters said, "We have created a new program in response to the Others in the environment. The Others who destroy us."

Cal said, very pleasantly, "'Others'? What others?"

"The new ones. The mindless ones. The destroyers."

"There are no others in your environment," Micah said. "What are you trying to say?"

Ling, across the deck in a cloud of pink baktors, said, "Oh, oh…no… they must have divided into factions. Invented warfare among themselves! Oh…"

Harrah stopped sobbing and stood, wide-eyed, on hirs sturdy short legs.

Cal said, still very pleasant, "Seeding 140, show us these others. Transmit visuals."

"But if we get close enough to the Others to do that, we will be destroyed!"

Ling said sadly, "It *is* warfare."

Deb compressed hirs beautiful lips. Kabil turned away, to gaze out at the stars. Micah said, "Seeding…do you have any historical transmissions of the Others, in your databanks? Send those."

"Scanning…sending."

Ling said softly, "We always knew warfare was a possibility for any creations. After all, they have our unrefined DNA, and for millennia…" Hirs fell silent.

"The data is only partial," Seeding 140 said. "We were nearly destroyed when it was sent to us. But there is one data packet until the last few minutes of life."

The cheerful, dancing oysters vanished from the holocube. In their place appeared the fronds of a tall, thin plant, waving slightly in the thick air. It was stark, unadorned, elemental. A multicellular organism rooted in the rocky ground, doing nothing.

No one on the ship spoke.

The holocube changed perspective, to a wide scan. Now there were whole stands of fronds, acres of them, filling huge sections of the rift. Plant after plant, drab olive green, blowing in the unseen wind.

After the long silence, Seeding 140 said, "Our mother? The Others were not there for ninety-two years. Then they came. They replicate much faster than we do, and we die. Our mother, can you do what is necessary?"

Still no one spoke, until Harrah, frightened, said, "What is it?"

Micah answered, hirs voice clipped and precise. "According to the data packet, it is an aerobic organism, using a process analogous to photosynthesis to create energy, giving off oxygen as a by-product. The data includes a specimen analysis, broken off very abruptly as if the AI failed. The specimen is non-carbon-based, non-DNA. The energy sources sealed in Seeding 140 are anaerobic."

Ling said sharply, "Present oxygen content of the rift atmosphere?"

Cal said, "Seven point six two percent." Hirs paused. "The oxygen created by these…these 'others' is poisoning the seeding."

"But," Deb said, bewildered, "why did the original drop include such a thing?"

"It didn't," Micah said. "There is no match for this structure in the gene banks. It is not from Earth."

"Our mother?" Seeding 140 said, over the motionless fronds in the holocube. "Are you still there?"

Disciple Arlbeni, Grid 743.9, 2999: As we approach this millennium marker, rejoice that humanity has passed beyond both spiritual superstition and spiritual denial. We have a faith built on physical truth, on living genetics, on human need. We have, at long last, given our souls not to a formless Deity but to the science of life itself. We are safe, and we are blessed.

Micah said suddenly, "It's a trick."

The other adults stared at hirs. Harrah had been hastily reconfigured for sleep. Someone—Ling, most likely—had dissolved the floating baktors and blanked the wall displays, and only the empty transmission field added color to the room. That, and the cold stars beyond.

"Yes," Micah continued, "a trick. Not malicious, of course. But we programmed them to learn, and they did. They had some seismic event, or some interwarfare, and it made them wary of anything unusual. They learned that the unusual can be deadly. And the most unusual thing they know of is us, set to return at 3,000. So they created a transmission program designed to repel us. Xenophobia, in a stimulus-response learning program suited to this environment. You said it yourself, Ling, the learning components are built on human genes. And we have xenophobia as an evolved survival response!"

Cal jack-knifed across the room. Tension turned hirs ungraceful. "No. That sounds appealing, but nothing we gave Seeding 140 would let them evolve defenses that sophisticated. And there was no seismic event for the initial stimulus."

Micah said eagerly, "We're the stimulus! Our anticipated return! Don't you see...we're the 'others'!"

Kabil said, "But they call us 'mother'...They were thrilled to see us. They're not xenophobic to *us*."

Deb spoke so softly the others could barely hear. "Then it's a computer malfunction. Cosmic bombardment of their sensory equipment. Or at least, of the unit that was 'dying.' Malfunctioning before the end. All that sensory data about oxygen poisoning is compromised."

"Of course!" Ling said. But hirs was always honest. "At least...no, compromised data isn't that coherent, the pieces don't fit together so well biochemically..."

"And so non-terrestrially," Cal said, and at the jagged edge in his voice, Micah exploded.

"California, these are not native life! There is no native life in the galaxy except on Earth!"

"I know that, Micah," Cal said, with dignity. "But I also know this data does not match anything in the d-bees."

"Then the d-bees are incomplete!"

"Possibly."

Ling put hirs hands together. They were long, slender hands, with very long nails, created just yesterday. *I want to grab the new millennium with both hands,* Ling had laughed before the party, *and hold it firm.* "Spores. Panspermia."

"I won't listen to this!" Micah said.

"An old theory," Ling went on, gasping a little. "Seeding 140 said the others weren't there for their first hundred years. But if spores blew in from space on the solar wind, and the environment was right for them to germinate—"

Deb said quickly, "Spores aren't really life. Wherever they came from, they're not alive."

"Yes, they are," Kabil said. "Don't quibble. They're alive."

Micah said loudly, "I've given my entire *life* to the Great Mission. I was on the original drop for this very planet."

"They're alive," Ling said, "and they're not ours."

"My entire life!" Micah said. Hirs looked at each of them in turn, hirs face stony, and something terrible glinted behind the beautiful deep-green eyes.

Our mother does not answer. Has our mother gone away?

Our mother would not go away without helping us. It must be they are still dancing.

We can wait.

"The main thing is Harrah, after all," Kabil said. Hirs sat slumped on the floor. They had been talking so long.

"A child needs secure knowledge. Purpose. Faith," Cal said.

Ling said wearily, "A child needs truth."

"Harrah," Deb crooned softly. "Harrah, made of all of us, future of our genes, small heart Harrah..."

"Stop it, Debaron," Cal said. "Please."

Micah said, "Those things down there are not real. They are not. Test it, Micah. I've said so already. Test it. Send down a probe, and try to bring back samples. There's nothing there."

"You don't know that, Micah."

"I know," Micah said, and was subtly revitalized. Hirs sprang up. "Test it!"

Ling said, "A probe isn't necessary. We have the transmitted data and—"

"Not reliable!" Micah said.

"—and the rising oxygen content. Data from our own sensors."

"Outgassing!"

"Micah, that's ridiculous. And a probe—"

"A probe might come back contaminated," Cal said.

"Don't risk contamination," Kabil said suddenly, urgently. "Not with Harrah here."

"Harrah, made of us all..." Deb had turned hirs back on the rest now, and lay almost curled into a ball, lost in hirs powerful imagination. Deb!

Kabil said, almost pleadingly, to Ling, "Harrah's safety should come first."

"Harrah's safety lies in facing truth," Ling said. But hirs was not strong enough to sustain it alone. They were all so close, so knotted together, a family. Knotted by Harrah and by the Great Mission, to which Ling, no less than the others, had given his life.

"Harrah, small heart," sang Deb.

Kabil said, "It isn't as if we have proof about these 'others.' Not real proof. We don't actually *know*."

"*I* know," Micah said.

Cal looked bleakly at Kabil. "No. And it is wrong to sacrifice a child to a supposition, to a packet of compromised data, to a...a superstition of creations so much less than we are. You know that's true, even though we none of us never admit it. But I'm a biologist. The creations are limited DNA, with no ability to self-modify. Also strictly regulated nano, and AI only within careful parameters. Yes, of course they're life forms deserving respect on their own terms, of course, I would never deny that—"

"None of us would," Kabil said.

"—but they're not *us*. Not ever us."

A long silence, broken only by Deb's singing.

"Leave orbit, Micah," Cal finally said, "before Harrah wakes up."

Disciple Arlbeni, Grid 743.9, 2999: We are not gods, never gods, no matter what the powers evolution and technology have given us, and we do not delude ourselves that we are gods, as other cultures have done at other millennia. We are human. Our salvation is that we know it, and do not pretend otherwise.

Our mother? Are you there? We need you to save us from the Others, to do what is necessary. Are you there?

Are you still dancing?

Afterword to "My Mother, Dancing"

This story is one of the few I have ever set in the very far future. Usually I prefer near-future, on-Earth stories; there is less setting to invent and more concrete details I can plunder from reality. However, some stories need far-flung space travel, radically altered human biology, and a much different culture.

Every human culture we know of has had some form of religion. One function of religion is to explain creation. Another is to locate humans in that creation, including our purpose for existence. And all religions eventually face challenges from our growing body of scientific knowledge. Some incorporate new scientific facts; some do not; some do both at different times. The Catholic Church punished Galileo for heliocentrism, but it accepts evolution.

I enjoyed creating both the empty-universe religion of this story and the non-DNA-organism challenge to that religion. My characters, faced with their spiritual crisis, do not behave very well. Perhaps the next ship to come along will show more flexibility, and more courage.

TRINITY

"Lord, I believe; help Thou mine unbelief!"
—Mark 9:24

At first I didn't recognize Devrie.

Devrie—I didn't recognize *Devrie*. Astonished at myself, I studied the wasted figure standing in the middle of the bare reception room: arms like wires, clavicle sharply outlined, head shaved, dressed in that ugly long tent of light-weight gray. God knew what her legs looked like under it. Then she smiled, and it was Devrie.

"You look like shit."

"Hello, Seena. Come on in."

"I am in."

"Barely. It's not catching, you know."

"Stupidity fortunately isn't," I said and closed the door behind me. The small room was too hot; Devrie would need the heat, of course, with almost no fat left to insulate her bones and organs. Next to her I felt huge, although I am not. Huge, hairy, sloppy-breasted.

"Thank you for not wearing bright colors. They do affect me."

"Anything for a sister," I said, mocking the old childhood formula, the old sentiment. But Devrie was too quick to think it was only mockery; in that, at least, she had not changed. She clutched my arm and her fingers felt like chains, or talons.

"You found him. Seena, you found him."

"I found him."

"Tell me," she whispered.

"Sit down first, before you fall over. God, Devrie, don't you eat at all?"

"Tell me," she said. So I did.

Devrie Caroline Konig had admitted herself to the Institute of the Biological Hope on the Caribbean island of Dominica eleven months ago, in late November of 2017, when her age was 23 years and 4 months. I am precise about this because it is all I can be sure of. I need the precision. The Institute of the Biological Hope is not precise; it is a mongrel, part research laboratory in brain sciences, part monastery, part school for training in the discipline of the mind. That made my baby sister guinea pig, postulant, freshman. She had always been those things, but, until now, sequentially. Apparently so had many other people, for when eccentric Nobel Prize winner James Arthur Bohentin had founded his Institute, he had been able to fund it, although precariously. But in that it did not differ from most private scientific research centers.

Or most monasteries.

I wanted Devrie out of the Institute of the Biological Hope.

"It's located on Dominica," I had said sensibly—what an ass I had been—to an unwasted Devrie a year ago, "because the research procedures there fall outside United States laws concerning the safety of research subjects. Doesn't that tell you something, Devrie? Doesn't that at least give you pause? In New York, it would be illegal to do to anyone what Bohentin does to his people."

"Do you know him?" she had asked.

"I have met him. Once."

"What is he like?"

"Like stone."

Devrie shrugged, and smiled. "All the participants in the Institute are willing. Eager."

"That doesn't make it ethical for Bohentin to destroy them. Ethical or legal."

"It's legal on Dominica. And in thinking you know better than the participants what they should risk their own lives for, aren't you playing God?"

"Better me than some untrained fanatic who offers himself up like an exalted Viking hero, expecting Valhalla."

"You're an intellectual snob, Seena."

"I never denied it."

"Are you sure you aren't really objecting not to the Institute's dangers but to its purpose? Isn't the 'Hope' part what really bothers you?"

"I don't think scientific method and pseudo-religious mush mix, no. I never did. I don't think it leads to a perception of God."

"The holotank tapes indicate it leads to a perception of *something* the brain hasn't encountered before," Devrie said, and for a moment I was silent.

I was once, almost, a biologist. I was aware of the legitimate studies that formed the basis for Bohentin's megalomania: the brain wave changes that accompany anorexia nervosa, sensory deprivation, biological feedback, and neurotransmitter stimulants. I have read the historical accounts, some merely pathetic but some disturbingly not, of the Christian mystics who achieved rapture through the mortification of the flesh and the Eastern mystics who achieved anesthesia through the control of the mind, of the faith healers who succeeded, of the carcinomas shrunk through trained will. I knew of the research on focused clairvoyance during orgasm, and of what happens when neurotransmitter number and speed are increased chemically.

And I knew all that was known about the twin trance.

Fifteen years earlier, as a doctoral student in biology, I had spent one summer replicating Sunderwirth's pioneering study of drug-enhanced telepathy in identical twins. My results were positive, except that within six months all eight of my research subjects had died. So had Sunderwirth's. Twin-trance research became the cloning controversy of the new decade, with the same panicky cycle of public outcry, legal restrictions, religious misunderstandings, fear, and demagoguery. When I received the phone call that the last of my subjects was dead—cardiac arrest, no history of heart disease, forty-three Goddamn years old—I locked myself in my apartment, with the lights off and my father's papers clutched in my hand, for three days. Then I resigned from the neurology department and became an entomologist. There is no pain in classifying dead insects.

"There is something there," Devrie had repeated. She was holding the letter sent to our father, whom someone at the Institute had not heard was dead. "It says the holotank tapes—"

"So there's something there," I said. "So the tanks are picking up some strange radiation. Why call it 'God'?"

"Why not call it God?"

"Why not call it Rover? Even if I grant you that the tape pattern looks like a presence—which I don't—you have no way of knowing that Bohentin's phantom isn't, say, some totally ungodlike alien being."

"But neither do I know that it is."

"Devrie—"

She had smiled and put her hands on my shoulders. She had—has, has always had—a very sweet smile. "Seena. Think. If the Institute can prove rationally that God exists—can prove it to the intellectual mind, the doubting Thomases who need something concrete to study...faith that doesn't need to be taken on faith..."

She wore her mystical face, a glowing softness that made me want to shake the silliness out of her. Instead I made some clever riposte, some sarcasm I no longer remember, and reached out to ruffle her hair. Big-sisterly, patronizing, thinking I could deflate her rapturous interest with the pin-prick of ridicule. God, I was an ass. It hurts to remember how big an ass I was.

A month and a half later Devrie committed herself and half her considerable inheritance to the Institute of the Biological Hope.

"Tell me," Devrie whispered. The Institute had no windows; outside I had seen grass, palm trees, butterflies floating in the sunshine, but inside here in the bare gray room there was nowhere to look but at her face.

"He's a student in a Master's program at a third-rate college in New Hampshire. He was adopted when he was two, nearly three, in March of 1997. Before that he was in a government-run children's home. In Boston, of course. The adopting family, as far as I can discover, never was told he was anything but one more toddler given up by somebody for adoption."

"Wait a minute," Devrie said. "I need...a minute."

She had turned paler, and her hands trembled. I had recited the information as if it were no more than an exhibit listing at my museum. Of course she was rattled. I wanted her rattled. I wanted her out.

Lowering herself to the floor, Devrie sat cross-legged and closed her eyes. Concentration spread over her face, but a concentration so serene it barely deserved that name. Her breathing slowed, her color freshened, and when she opened her eyes, they had the rested energy of a person who has just slept eight hours in mountain air. Her face even looked plumper, and an EEG, I guessed, would show damn near alpha waves. In her year at the Institute she must have mastered quite an array of biofeedback techniques to do that, so fast and with such a malnourished body.

"Very impressive," I said sourly.

"Seena—have you seen him?"

"No. All this is from sealed records."

"How did you get into the records?"

"Medical and governmental friends."

"Who?"

"What do you care, as long as I found out what you wanted to know?"

She was silent. I knew she would never ask me if I had obtained her information legally or illegally; it would not occur to her to ask. Devrie, being Devrie, would assume it had all been generously offered by my modest museum connections and our dead father's immodest research connections. She would be wrong.

"How old is he now?"

"Twenty-four years last month. They must have used your two-month tissue sample."

"Do you think Daddy knew where the...baby went?"

"Yes. Look at the timing—the child was normal and healthy, yet he wasn't adopted until he was nearly three. The researchers kept track of him, all right; they kept all six clones in a government-controlled home where they could monitor their development as long as humanely possible. The same-sex clones were released for adoption after a year, but they hung onto the cross-sex ones until they reached an age where they would become harder to adopt. They undoubtedly wanted to study them as long as they could. And even after the kids were released for adoption, the researchers held off publishing until all six were placed and the records sealed. Dad's group didn't publish until April, 1998, remember. By the time the storm broke, the babies were out of its path, and anonymous."

"And the last," Devrie said.

"And the last," I agreed, although of course the researchers hadn't foreseen that. So few in the scientific community had foreseen that. Offense against God and man, Satan's work, natter natter. Watching my father's suddenly stooped shoulders and stricken eyes, I had thought how ugly public revulsion could be and had nobly resolved—how had I thought of it then? So long ago—resolved to snatch the banner of pure science from my fallen father's hand. Another time that I had been an ass. Five years later, when it had been my turn to feel the ugly scorching of public revulsion, I had broken, left neurological research, and fled down the road that led to the Museum of Natural History, where I was the curator of ants fossilized in amber and moths pinned securely under permaplex.

"The other four clones," Devrie said, "the ones from that university in California that published almost simultaneously with Daddy—"

"I don't know. I didn't even try to ask. It was hard enough in Cambridge."

"Me," Devrie said wonderingly. "He's me."

"Oh, for—Devrie, he's your twin. No more than that. No—actually less than that. He shares your genetic material exactly as an identical twin would, except for the Y chromosome, but he shares none of the congenital or environmental influences that shaped your personality. There's no mystical replication of spirit in cloning. He's merely a twin who got born eleven months late!"

She looked at me with luminous amusement. I didn't like the look. On that fleshless face, the skin stretched so taut that the delicate bones beneath were as visible as the veins of a moth wing, her amusement looked ironic. Yet Devrie was never ironic. Gentle, passionate, trusting, a little stupid, she was not capable of irony. It was beyond her, just as it was beyond her to wonder why I, who had fought her entering the Institute of the Biological Hope, had brought her this information now. Her amusement was one-layered, and trusting.

God's fools, the Middle Ages had called them.

"Devrie," I said, and heard my own voice unexpectedly break, "leave here. It's physically not safe. What are you down to, ten percent body fat? Eight? Look at yourself, you can't hold body heat, your palms are dry, you can't move quickly without getting dizzy. Hypotension. What's your heartbeat? Do you still menstruate? It's insane."

She went on smiling at me. God's fools don't need menstruation. "Come with me, Seena. I want to show you the Institute."

"I don't want to see it."

"Yes. This visit you should see it."

"Why this visit?"

"Because you are going to help me get my clone to come here, aren't you? Or else why did you go to all the trouble of locating him?"

I didn't answer. She still didn't see it.

Devrie said, "'Anything for a sister.' But you were always more like a mother to me than a sister." She took my hand and pulled herself off the floor. So had I pulled her up to take her first steps, the day after our mother died in a plane crash at Orly. Now Devrie's hand felt cold. I imprisoned it and counted the pulse.

"Bradycardia."

But she wasn't listening.

The Institute was a shock. I had anticipated the laboratories: monotonous gray walls, dim light, heavy soundproofing, minimal fixtures in the ones used for sensory dampening; high-contrast textures and colors, strobe lights, quite good sound equipment in those for sensory arousal. There was much that Devrie, as subject rather than researcher, didn't have authority to show me, but I deduced much from what I did see. The dormitories, divided by sex, were on the sensory-dampening side. The subjects slept in small cells, ascetic and chaste, that reminded me of an abandoned Carmelite convent I had once toured in Belgium. That was the shock: the physical plant felt scientific, but the atmosphere did not.

There hung in the gray corridors a wordless peace, a feeling so palpable I could feel it clogging my lungs. No. "Peace" was the wrong word. Say "peace" and the picture is pastoral, lazy sunshine and dreaming woods. This was not like that at all. The research subjects—students? postulants?—lounged in the corridors outside closed labs, waiting for the next step in their routine. Both men and women were anorexic, both wore gray bodysuits or caftans, both were fined down to an otherworldly ethereality when seen from a distance and a malnourished asexuality when seen up close. They talked among themselves in low voices, sitting with backs against the wall or stretched full-length on the carpeted floor, and on all their faces I saw the same luminous patience, the same certainty of being very near to something exciting that they nonetheless could wait for calmly, as long as necessary.

"They look," I said to Devrie, "as if they're waiting to take an exam they already know they'll ace."

She smiled. "Do you think so? I always think of us as travelers waiting for a plane, boarding passes stamped for Eternity."

She was actually serious. But she didn't in fact wear the same expression as the others; hers was far more intense. If they were travelers, she wanted to pilot.

The lab door opened and the students brought themselves to their feet. Despite their languid movements, they looked sharp: sharp protruding clavicles, bony chins, angular unpadded elbows that could chisel stone.

"This is my hour for biofeedback manipulation of drug effects," Devrie said. "Please come watch."

"I'd sooner watch you whip yourself in a twelfth-century monastery."

Devrie's eyes widened, then again lightened with that luminous amusement. "It's for the same end, isn't it? But they had such unsystematic means. Poor struggling God-searchers. I wonder how many of them made it."

I wanted to strike her. "Devrie—"

"If not biofeedback, what would you like to see?"

"You out of here."

"What else?"

There was only one thing: the holotanks. I struggled with the temptation, and lost. The two tanks stood in the middle of a roomy lab carpeted with thick gray matting and completely enclosed in a Faraday cage. That Devrie had a key to the lab was my first clue that my errand for her had been known, and discussed, by someone higher in the Institute. Research subjects do not carry keys to the most delicate brain-perception equipment in the world. For this equipment Bohentin had received his Nobel.

The two tanks, independent systems, stood as high as my shoulder. The ones I had used fifteen years ago had been smaller. Each of these was a cube, opaque on its bottom half, which held the sensing apparatus, computerized simulators, and recording equipment; clear on its top half, which was filled with the transparent fluid out of whose molecules the simulations would form. A separate sim would form for each subject, as the machine sorted and mapped all the electromagnetic radiation received and processed by each brain. All that each brain perceived, not only the visuals; the holograph equipment was capable of picking up all wavelengths that the brain did, and of displaying their brain-processed analogues as three-dimensional images floating in a clear womb. When all other possible sources of radiation were filtered out except for the emanations from the two subjects themselves, what the sims showed was what kinds of activity were coming from—and hence going on in—the other's brain. That was why it worked best with identical twins in twin trance: no structural brain differences to adjust for. In a rawer version of this holotank, a rawer version of myself had pioneered the recording of twin trances. The UCIC, we had called it then: What you see, I see.

What I had seen was eight autopsy reports.

"We're so close," Devrie said. "Mona and Marlene"—she waved a hand toward the corridor but Mona and Marlene, whichever two they had been, had gone—"had taken KX3, that's the drug that—"

"I know what it is," I said, too harshly. KX3 reacts with one of the hormones overproduced in an anorectic body. The combination is readily absorbed by body fat, but in a body without fat, much of it is absorbed by the brain.

Devrie continued, her hand tight on my arm. "Mona and Marlene were controlling the neural reactions with biofeedback, pushing the twin trance higher and higher, working it. Dr. Bohentin was monitoring the holotanks. The sims were incredibly detailed—everything each twin perceived in the perceptions of the other, in all wavelengths. Mona and Marlene forced their neurotransmission level even higher and then, in the tanks"—Devrie's face glowed, the mystic-rapture look—"a completely third sim formed. Completely separate. A third presence."

I stared at her.

"It was recorded in both tanks. It was shadowy, yes, but it was there. A third presence that can't be perceived except through another human's electromagnetic presence, and then only with every drug and trained reaction and arousal mode and the twin trance all pushing the brain into a supraheightened state. A third presence!"

"Isotropic radiation. Bohentin fluffed the pre-screening program and the computer hadn't cleared the background microradiation—" I said, but even as I spoke I knew how stupid that was. Bohentin didn't make mistakes like that, and isotropic radiation simulates nowhere close to the way a presence does. Devrie didn't even bother to answer me.

This, then, was what the rumors had been about, the rumors leaking for the last year out of the Institute and through the scientific community, mostly still scoffed at, not yet picked up by the popular press. This. A verifiable, replicable third presence being picked up by holography. Against all reason, a long shiver went over me from neck to that cold place at the base of the spine.

"There's more," Devrie said feverishly. "They felt it. Mona and Marlene. Both said afterwards that they could feel it, a huge presence filled with light, but they couldn't quite reach it. Damn—they couldn't reach it, Seena! They weren't playing off each other enough, weren't close enough. Weren't, despite the twin trance, melded enough."

"Sex," I said.

"They tried it. The subjects are all basically heterosexual. They inhibit."

"So go find some homosexual God-yearning anorexic incestuous twins!"

Devrie looked at me straight. "I need him. Here. He is me."

I exploded, right there in the holotank lab. No one came running in to find out if the shouting was dangerous to the tanks, which was my second clue that the Institute knew very well why Devrie had brought me there. "Damn it to hell, he's a human being, not some chemical you can just order up because you need it for an experiment! You don't have the right to expect him to come here, you didn't even have the right to tell anyone that he exists, but that didn't stop you, did it? There are still anti-bioengineering groups out there in the real world, religious split-brains who—how dare you put him in any danger? How dare you even presume he'd be interested in this insane mush?"

"He'll come," Devrie said. She had not changed expression.

"How the hell do you know?"

"He's me. And I want God. He will, too."

I scowled at her. A fragment of one of her poems, a thing she had written when she was fifteen, came to me: "Two human species/Never one—/One aching for God/One never." But she had been fifteen then. I had assumed that the sentiment, as adolescent as the poetry, would pass.

I said, "What does Bohentin think of this idea of importing your clone?"

For the first time she hesitated. Bohentin, then, was dubious. "He thinks it's rather a long shot."

"You could phrase it that way."

"But *I* know he'll want to come. Some things you just know, Seena, beyond rationality. And besides—" She hesitated again, and then went on. "I have left half my inheritance from Daddy, and the income on the trust from Mummy."

"Devrie. God, Devrie—you'd *buy* him?"

For the first time she looked angry. "The money would be just to get him here, to see what is involved. Once he sees, he'll want this as much as I do, at any price! What price can you put on God? I'm not 'buying' his life—I'm offering him the way to find life. What good is breathing, existing, if there's no purpose to it? Don't you realize how many centuries, in how many ways, people have looked for that light-filled presence and never been able to be sure!? And now we're almost there, Seena, I've seen it for myself—almost there. With verifiable, scientifically-controlled means. Not subjective faith this time—scientific data, the same as for any other actual phenomenon. This research stands now where research into the atom stood fifty years ago. Can you touch a quark? But it's there! And my clone can be a part of it, can be it, how can you talk about the money buying him under circumstances like that!"

I said slowly, "How do you know that whatever you're so close to is God?" But that was sophomoric, of course, and she was ready for it. She smiled warmly.

"What does it matter what we call it? Pick another label if it will make you more comfortable."

I took a piece of paper from my pocket. "His name is Keith Torellen. He lives in Indian Falls, New Hampshire. Address and mailnet number here. Good luck, Devrie." I turned to go.

"Seena! I can't go!"

She couldn't, of course. That was the point. She barely had the strength in that starved, drug-battered body to get through the day, let alone to New Hampshire. She needed the sensory-controlled environment, the artificial heat, the chemical monitoring. "Then send someone from the Institute. Perhaps Bohentin will go."

"Bohentin," she said, and I knew that was impossible; Bohentin had to remain officially ignorant of this sort of recruiting. Too many U.S. laws were involved. In addition, Bohentin had no persuasive skills; people as persons and not neurologies did not interest him. They were too far above chemicals and too far below God.

Devrie looked at me with a kind of level fury. "This is really why you found him, isn't it? So I would have to stop the drug program long enough to leave here and go get him. You think that once I've gone back out into the world either the build-up effects in the brain will be interrupted or else the spell will be broken and I'll have doubts about coming back here!"

"Will you listen to yourself? 'Out into the world.' You sound like some archaic nun in a cloistered order!"

"You always did ridicule anything you couldn't understand," Devrie said icily, turned her back on me, and stared at the empty holotanks. She didn't turn when I left the lab, closing the door behind me. She was still facing the tanks, her spiny back rigid, the piece of paper with Keith Torellen's address clutched in fingers delicate as glass.

In New York the museum simmered with excitement. An unexpected endowment had enabled us to buy the contents of a small, very old museum located in a part of Madagascar not completely destroyed by the African Horror. Crate after crate of moths began arriving in New York, some of them collected in the days when naturalists-gentlemen shot jungle moths from the trees using dust shot. Some species had been extinct since the Horror and thus were rare; some were the brief mutations from the bad years afterward and thus were even rarer. The museum staff uncrated and exclaimed.

"Look at this one," said a young man, holding it out to me. Not on my own staff, he was one of the specialists on loan to us—DeFabio or DeFazio, something like that. He was very handsome. I looked at the moth he showed me, all pale wings outstretched and pinned to black silk. "A perfect *Thysania africana*. Perfect."

"Yes."

"You'll have to loan us the whole exhibit, in a few years."

"Yes," I said again. He heard the tone in my voice and glanced up quickly. But not quickly enough—my face was all professional interest when his gaze reached it. Still, the professional interest had not fooled him; he had heard the perfunctory note. Frowning, he turned back to the moths.

By day I directed the museum efficiently enough. But in the evenings, home alone in my apartment, I found myself wandering from room to room, touching objects, unable to settle to work at the oversize teak desk that had been my father's, to the reports and journals that had not. His had dealt with the living, mine with the ancient dead—but I had known that for years. The fogginess of my evenings bothered me.

"Faith should not mean fogginess."

Who had said that? Father, of course, to Devrie, when she had joined the dying Catholic Church. She had been thirteen years old. Skinny, defiant, she had stood clutching a black rosary from God knows where, daring him from scared dark eyes to forbid her. Of course he had not, thinking, I suppose, that Heaven, like any other childhood fever, was best left alone to burn out its course.

Devrie had been received into the Church in an overdecorated chapel, wearing an overdecorated dress of white lace and carrying a candle. Three years later she had left, dressed in a magenta body suit and holding the keys to Father's safe, which his executor had left unlocked after the funeral. The will had, of course, made me Devrie's guardian. In the three years Devrie had been going to Mass, I had discovered that I was sterile, divorced my second husband, finished my work in entomology, accepted my first position with a museum, and entered a drastically premature menopause.

That is not a flip nor random list.

After the funeral, I sat in the dark in my father's study, in his maroon leather chair and at his teak desk. Both felt oversize. All the lights were off. Outside it rained; I heard the steady beat of water on the window, and the wind. The dark room was cold. In my palm I held one of my father's research awards, a small abstract sculpture of a double helix, done by Harold Landau himself. It was very heavy. I couldn't think what Landau had used, to make it so heavy. I couldn't think, with all the noise from the rain. My father was dead, and I would never bear a child.

Devrie came into the room, leaving the lights off but bringing with her an incandescent rectangle from the doorway. At sixteen she was lovely, with long brown hair in the masses of curls again newly fashionable. She sat on a low stool beside me, all that hair falling around her, her face white in the gloom. She had been crying.

"He's gone. He's really gone. I don't believe it yet."

"No."

She peered at me. Something in my face, or my voice, must have alerted her; when she spoke again it was in that voice people use when they think your grief is understandably greater than theirs. A smooth dark voice, like a wave.

"You still have me, Seena. We still have each other."

I said nothing.

"I've always thought of you more as my mother than my sister, anyway. You took the place of Mother. You've been a mother to at least me."

She smiled and squeezed my hand. I looked at her face—so young, so pretty—and I wanted to hit her. I didn't want to be her mother; I wanted to be her. All her choices lay ahead of her, and it seemed to me that self-indulgent night as if mine were finished. I could have struck her.

"Seena—"

"Leave me alone! Can't you ever leave me alone? All my life you've been dragging behind me; why don't you die and finally leave me alone!"

We make ourselves pay for small sins more than large ones. The more trivial the thrust, the longer we're haunted by memory of the wound.

I believe that.

Indian Falls was out of another time: slow, quiet, safe. The Avis counter at the airport rented not personal guards but cars, and the only shiny store on Main Street sold wilderness equipment. I suspected that the small state college, like the town, traded mostly on trees and trails. That Keith Torellen was trying to take an academic degree here told me more about his adopting family than if I had hired a professional information service.

The house where he lived was shabby, paint peeling and steps none too sturdy. I climbed them slowly, thinking once again what I wanted to find out.

Devrie would answer none of my messages on the mailnet. Nor would she accept my phone calls. She was shutting me out, in retaliation for my refusing to fetch Torellen for her. But Devrie would discover that she could not shut me out as easily as that; we were sisters. I wanted to know if she had contacted Torellen herself, or had sent someone from the Institute to do so.

If neither, then my visit here would be brief and anonymous; I would leave Keith Torellen to his protected ignorance and shabby town. But if he had seen Devrie, I wanted to discover if and what he had agreed to do for her. It might even be possible that he could be of use in convincing Devrie of the stupidity of what she was doing. If he could be used for that, I would use him.

Something else: I was curious. This boy was my brother—nephew? no, brother—as well as the result of my father's rational mind. Curiosity prickled over me. I rang the bell.

It was answered by the landlady, who said that Keith was not home, would not be home until late, was "in rehearsal."

"Rehearsal?"

"Over to the college. He's a student and they're putting on a play."

I said nothing, thinking.

"I don't remember the name of the play," the landlady said. She was a large woman in a faded garment, dress or robe. "But Keith says it's going to be real good. It starts this weekend." She laughed. "But you probably already know all that! George, my husband George, he says I'm forever telling people things they already know!"

"How would I know?"

She winked at me. "Don't you think I got eyes? Sister, or cousin? No, let me guess—older sister. Too much alike for cousins."

"Thank you," I said. "You've been very helpful."

"Not sister!" She clapped her hand over her mouth, her eyes shiny with amusement. "You're checking up on him, ain't you? You're his mother! I should of seen it right off!"

I turned to negotiate the porch steps.

"They rehearse in the new building, Mrs. Torellen," she called after me. "Just ask anybody you see to point you in the right direction."

"Thank you," I said carefully.

Rehearsal was nearly over. Evidently it was a dress rehearsal; the actors were in period costume and the director did not interrupt. I did not recognize the period or the play. Devrie had been interested in theater: I was not. Quietly I took a seat in the darkened back row and waited for the pretending to end.

Despite wig and greasepaint, I had no trouble picking out Keith Torellen. He moved like Devrie: quick, light movements, slightly pigeon-toed. He had her height and, given the differences of a male body, her slenderness. Sitting a theater's length away, I might have been seeing a male Devrie.

But seen up close, his face was mine.

Despite the landlady, it was a shock. He came toward me across the theater lobby, from where I had sent for him, and I saw the moment he too struck the resemblance. He stopped dead, and we stared at each other. Take Devrie's genes, spread them over a face with the greater bone surface, larger features, and coarser skin texture of a man—and the result was my face. Keith had scrubbed off his make-up and removed his wig, exposing brown curly hair the same shade Devrie's had been. But his face was mine.

A strange emotion, unnamed and hot, seared through me.

"Who are you! Who the hell are you?"

So no one had come from the Institute after all. Not Devrie, not any one.

"You're one of them, aren't you?" he said; it was almost a whisper. "One of my real family?"

Still gripped by the unexpected force of emotion, still dumb, I said nothing. Keith took one step toward me. Suspicion played over his face—Devrie would not have been suspicious—and vanished, replaced by a slow painful flush of color.

"You are. You are one. Are you...are you my mother?"

I put out a hand against a stone post. The lobby was all stone and glass. Why were all theater lobbies stone and glass? Architects had so little damn imagination, so little sense of the bizarre.

"No! I am not your mother!"

He touched my arm. "Hey, are you okay? You don't look good. Do you need to sit down?"

His concern was unexpected, and touching. I thought that he shared Devrie's genetic personality, and that Devrie had always been hyper-sensitive to the body. But this was not Devrie. His hand on my arm was stronger, firmer, warmer than Devrie's. I felt giddy, disoriented. This was not Devrie.

"A mistake," I said unsteadily. "This was a mistake. I should not have come. I'm sorry. My name is Dr. Seena Konig and I am a...relative of yours, but I think this now is a mistake. I have your address and I promise that I'll write you about your family, but now I think I should go." Write some benign lie, leave him in ignorance. This was a mistake.

But he looked stricken, and his hand tightened on my arm. "You can't! I've been searching for my biological family for two years! You can't just go!"

We were beginning to attract attention in the theater lobby. Hurrying students eyed us sideways. I thought irrelevantly how different they looked from the "students" at the Institute, and with that thought regained my composure. This was a student, a boy—"you can't!" a boyish protest, and boyish panic in his voice—and not the man-Devrie-me he had seemed a foolish moment ago. He was nearly twenty years my junior. I smiled at him and removed his hand from my arm.

"Is there somewhere we can have coffee?"

"Yes. Dr..."

"Seena," I said. "Call me Seena."

Over coffee, I made him talk first. He watched me anxiously over the rim of his cup, as if I might vanish, and I listened to the words behind the words. His adopting family was the kind that hoped to visit the Grand Canyon but not Europe, go to movies but not opera, aspire to college but not to graduate work, buy wilderness equipment but not wilderness. Ordinary people. Not religious, not rich, not unusual. Keith was the only child. He loved them.

"But at the same time I never really felt I belonged," he said, and looked away from me. It was the most personal thing he had knowingly revealed, and I saw that he regretted it. Devrie would not have. More private, then, and less trusting. And I sensed in him a grittiness, a tougher awareness of the world's hardness, than Devrie had ever had—or needed to have. I made my decision. Having disturbed him thus far, I owed him truth—but not the whole truth.

"Now you tell me," Keith said, pushing away his cup. "Who were my parents? Our parents? Are you my sister?"

"Yes."

"Our parents?"

"Both are dead. Our father was Dr. Richard Konig. He was a scientist. He—" But Keith had recognized the name. His readings in biology or history must have been more extensive than I would have expected. His eyes widened, and I suddenly wished I had been more oblique.

"Richard Konig. He's one of those scientists that were involved in that bioengineering scandal—"

"How did you learn about that? It's all over and done with. Years ago."

"Journalism class. We studied how the press handled it, especially the sensationalism surrounding the cloning thing twenty years—"

I saw the moment it hit him. He groped for his coffee cup, clutched the handle, didn't raise it. It was empty anyway. And then what I said next shocked me as much as anything I have ever done.

"It was Devrie," I said, and heard my own vicious pleasure, "Devrie was the one who wanted me to tell you!"

But of course he didn't know who Devrie was. He went on staring at me, panic in his young eyes, and I sat frozen. That tone I heard in my own voice when I said "Devrie," that vicious pleasure that it was she and not I who was hurting him...

"Cloning," Keith said. "Konig was in trouble for claiming to have done illegal cloning. Of humans." His voice had held so much dread that I fought off my own dread and tried to hold myself steady to his need.

"It's illegal now, but not then. And the public badly misunderstood. All that sensationalism—you were right to use that word, Keith—covered up the fact that there is nothing abnormal about producing a fetus from another diploid cell. In the womb, identical twins—"

"Am I a clone?"

"Keith—"

"Am I a clone?"

Carefully I studied him. This was not what I had intended, but although the fear was still in his eyes, the panic had gone. And curiosity—Devrie's curiosity, and her eagerness—they were there as well. This boy would not strike me, nor stalk out of the restaurant, nor go into psychic shock.

"Yes. You are."

He sat quietly, his gaze turned inward. A long moment passed in silence.

"Your cell?"

"No. My—our sister's. Our sister Devrie."

Another long silence. He did not panic. Then he said softly, "Tell me."

Devrie's phrase.

"There isn't much to tell, Keith. If you've seen the media accounts, you know the story, and also what was made of it. The issue then becomes how you feel about what you saw. Do you believe that cloning is meddling with things man should best leave alone?"

"No. I don't."

I let out my breath, although I hadn't known I'd been holding it. "It's actually no more than delayed twinning, followed by surrogate implantation. A zygote—"

"I know all that," he said with some harshness, and held up his hand to silence me. I didn't think he knew that he did it. The harshness did not sound like Devrie. To my ears, it sounded like myself. He sat thinking, remote and troubled, and I did not try to touch him.

Finally he said, "Do my parents know?"

He meant his adoptive parents. "No."

"Why are you telling me now? Why did you come?"

"Devrie asked me to."

"She needs something, right? A kidney? Something like that?"

I had not foreseen that question. He did not move in a class where spare organs were easily purchasable. "No. Not a kidney, not any kind of biological donation." A voice in my mind jeered at that, but I was not going to give him any clues that would lead to Devrie. "She just wanted me to find you."

"Why didn't she find me herself? She's my age, right?"

"Yes. She's ill just now and couldn't come."

"Is she dying?"

"No!"

Again he sat quietly, finally saying, "No one could tell me anything. For two years I've been searching for my mother, and not one of the adoptee-search agencies could find a single trace. Not one. Now I see why. Who covered the trail so well?"

"My father."

"I want to meet Devrie."

I said evenly, "That might not be possible."

"Why not?"

"She's in a foreign hospital. Out of the country. I'm sorry."

"When does she come home?"

"No one is sure."

"What disease does she have?"

She's sick for God, I thought, but aloud I said, not thinking it through, "A brain disease."

Instantly I saw my own cruelty. Keith paled, and I cried, "No, no, nothing you could have as well! Truly, Keith, it's not—she took a bad fall. From her hunter."

"Her hunter," he said. For the first time, his gaze flickered over my clothing and jewelry. But would he even recognize how expensive they were? I doubted it. He wore a synthetic, deep-pile jacket with a tear at one shoulder and a cheap wool hat, dark blue, shapeless with age. From long experience I recognized his gaze: uneasy, furtive, the expression of a man glimpsing the financial gulf between what he had assumed were equals. But it wouldn't matter. Adopted children have no legal claim on the estates of their biological parents. I had checked.

Keith said uneasily, "Do you have a picture of Devrie?"

"No," I lied.

"Why did she want you to find me? You still haven't said."

I shrugged. "The same reason, I suppose, that you looked for your biological family. The pull of blood."

"Then she wants me to write to her?"

"Write to me instead."

He frowned. "Why? Why not to Devrie?"

What to say to that? I hadn't bargained on so much intensity from him. "Write in care of me, and I'll forward it to Devrie."

"Why not to her directly?"

"Her doctors might not think it advisable," I said coldly, and he backed off—either from the mention of doctors or from the coldness.

"Then give me your address, Seena. Please."

I did. I could see no harm in his writing me. It might even be pleasant. Coming home from the museum, another wintry day among the exhibits, to find on the mailnet a letter I could answer when and how I chose, without being taken by surprise. I liked the idea.

But no more difficult questions now. I stood. "I have to leave, Keith."

He looked alarmed. "So soon?"

"Yes."

"But why?"

"I have to return to work."

He stood, too. He was taller than Devrie. "Seena," he said, all earnestness, "just a few more questions. How did you find me?"

"Medical connections."

"Yours?"

"Our father's. I'm not a scientist." Evidently his journalism class had not studied twin-trance sensationalism.

"What do you do?"

"Museum curator. Arthropods."

"What does Devrie do?"

"She's too ill to work. I must go, Keith."

"One more. Do I look like Devrie as well as you?"

"It would be wise, Keith, if you were careful whom you spoke with about all of this. I hadn't intended to say so much."

"I'm not going to tell my parents. Not about being—not about all of it."

"I think that's best, yes."

"Do I look like Devrie as well as you?"

A little of my first, strange emotion returned with his intensity. "A little, yes. But more like me. Sex variance is a tricky thing."

Unexpectedly, he held my coat for me. As I slipped into it, he said from behind, "Thank you, Seena," and let his hands rest on my shoulders.

I did not turn around. I felt my face flame, and self-disgust flooded through me, followed by a desire to laugh. It was all so transparent. This man was an attractive stranger, was Devrie, was youth, was myself, was the work not of my father's loins but of his mind. Of course I was aroused by him. Freud outlasts cloning: a note for a research study, I told myself grimly, and inwardly I did laugh.

But that didn't help either.

In New York, winter came early. Cold winds whipped whitecaps on harbor and river, and the trees in the Park stood bare even before October had ended. The crumbling outer boroughs of the shrinking city crumbled a little more and talked of the days when New York had been important. Manhattan battened down for snow, hired the seasonal increases in personal guards, and talked of Albuquerque. Each night museum security hunted up and evicted the drifters trying to sleep behind exhibits, drifters as chilled and pale as the moths under permaplex, and, it seemed to me, as detached from the blood of their own age. All of New York seemed detached to me that October, and cold. Often I stood in front of the cases of *Noctuidae*, staring at them for so long that my staff began to glance at each other covertly. I would catch their glances when I jerked free of my trance. No one asked me about it.

Still no message came from Devrie. When I contacted the Institute on the mailnet, she did not call back.

No letter came from Keith Torellen.

Then one night, after I had worked late and was hurrying through the chilly gloom toward my building, he was there, bulking from the shadows so quickly that the guard I had taken for the walk from the museum sprang forward in attack position.

"No! It's all right! I know him!"

The guard retreated, without expression. Keith stared after him, and then at me, his face unreadable.

"Keith, what are you doing here? Come inside!"

He followed me into the lobby without a word. Nor did he say anything during the metal scanning and ID procedure. I took him up to my apartment, studying him in the elevator.

He wore the same jacket and cheap wool hat as in Indian Falls, his hair wanted cutting, and the tip of his nose was red from waiting in the cold. How long had he waited there? He badly needed a shave.

In the apartment he scanned the rugs, the paintings, my grandmother's ridiculously ornate, ugly silver, and turned his back on them to face me.

"Seena, I want to know where Devrie is."

"Why? Keith, what has happened?"

"Nothing has happened," he said, removing his jacket but not laying it anywhere. "Only that I've left school and spent two days hitching here. It's no good, Seena. To say that cloning is just like twinning: it's no good. I want to see Devrie."

His voice was hard. Bulking in my living room, unshaven, that hat pulled down over his ears, he looked older and less malleable than the last time I had seen him. Alarm—not physical fear, I was not afraid of him, but a subtler and deeper fear—sounded through me.

"Why do you want to see Devrie?"

"Because she cheated me."

"Of what, for God's sake?"

"Can I have a drink? Or a smoke?"

I poured him a Scotch. If he drank, he might talk. I had to know what he wanted, why such a desperate air clung to him, how to keep him from Devrie. I had not seen her like this. She was strong-willed, but always with a blitheness, a trust that eventually her will would prevail. Desperate forcefulness of the sort in Keith's manner was not her style. But of course Devrie had always had silent money to back her will; perhaps money could buy trust as well as style.

Keith drank off his Scotch and held out his glass for another. "It was freezing out there. They wouldn't let me in the lobby to wait for you."

"Of course not."

"You didn't tell me your family was rich."

I was a little taken aback at his bluntness, but at the same time it pleased me; I don't know why.

"You didn't ask."

"That's shit, Seena."

"Keith. Why are you here?"

"I told you. I want to see Devrie."

"What is it you've decided she cheated you of? Money?"

He looked so honestly surprised that again I was startled, this time by his resemblance to Devrie. She too would not have thought of financial considerations first, if there were emotional ones possible. One moment Keith was Devrie, one moment he was not. Now he scowled with sudden anger.

"Is that what you think—that fortune hunting brought me hitching from New Hampshire? God, Seena, I didn't even know how much you had until this very—I still don't know!"

I said levelly, "Then what is it you're feeling so cheated of?"

Now he was rattled. Again that quick, half-furtive scan of my apartment, pausing a millisecond too long at the Caravaggio, subtly lit by its frame. When his gaze returned to mine it was troubled, a little defensive. Ready to justify. Of course I had put him on the defensive deliberately, but the calculation of my trick did not prepare me for the staggering naiveté of his explanation. Once more it was Devrie complete, reducing the impersonal greatness of science to a personal and emotional loss.

"Ever since I knew that I was adopted, at five or six years old, I wondered about my biological family. Nothing strange in that—I think all adoptees do. I used to make up stories, kid stuff, about how they were really royalty, or lunar colonists, or survivors of the African Horror. Exotic things. I thought especially about my mother, imagining this whole scene of her holding me once before she released me for adoption, crying over me, loving me so much she could barely let me go but had to for some reason. Sentimental shit." He laughed, trying to make light of what was not, and drank off his Scotch to avoid my gaze.

"But Devrie—the fact of her—destroyed all that. I never had a mother who hated to give me up. I never had a mother at all. What I had was a cell cut from Devrie's fingertip or someplace, something discardable, and she doesn't even know what I look like. But she's damn well going to."

"Why?" I said evenly. "What could you expect to gain from her knowing what you look like?"

But he didn't answer me directly. "That first moment I saw you, Seena, in the theater at school, I thought you were my mother."

"I know you did."

"And you hated the idea. Why?"

I thought of the child I would never bear, the marriage, like so many other things of sweet promise, gone sour. But self-pity is a fool's game. "None of your business."

"Isn't it? Didn't you hate the idea because of the way I was made? Coldly. An experiment. Weren't you a little bit insulted at being called the mother of a discardable cell from Devrie's fingertip?"

"What the hell have you been reading? An experiment—what is any child but an experiment? A random egg, a random sperm. Don't talk like one of those anti-science religious split-brains!"

He studied me levelly. Then he said, "Is Devrie religious? Is that why you're so afraid of her?"

I got to my feet, and pointed at the sideboard. "Help yourself to another drink if you wish. I want to wash my hands. I've been handling specimens all afternoon." Stupid, clumsy lie—nobody would believe such a lie.

In the bathroom I leaned against the closed door, shut my eyes, and willed myself to calm. Why should I be so disturbed by the angry lashing-out of a confused boy? I was handy to lash out against: my father, whom Keith was really angry at, was not. It was all so predictable, so earnestly adolescent, that even over the hurting in my chest I smiled. But the smile, which should have reduced Keith's ranting to the tantrum of a child—there, there, when you grow up you'll find out that no one really knows who he is—did not diminish Keith. His losses were real—mother, father, natural place in the natural sequence of life and birth. And suddenly, with a clutch at the pit of my stomach, I knew why I had told him all that I had about his origins. It was not from any ethic of fidelity to "the truth." I had told him he was a clone because I, too, had had real losses—research, marriage, motherhood— and Devrie could never have shared them with me. Luminous, mystical Devrie, too occupied with God to be much hurt by man. Leave me alone! Can't you ever leave me alone! *All my life you've been dragging behind me—why don't you die and finally leave me alone!* And Devrie had smiled tolerantly, patted my head, and left me alone, closing the door softly so as not to disturb my grief. My words had not hurt her. I could not hurt her.

But I could hurt Keith—the other Devrie—and I had. That was why he disturbed me all out of proportion. That was the bond. My face, my pain, my fault.

Through my fault, through my fault, through my most grievous fault. But what nonsense. I was not a believer, and the comforts of superstitious absolution could not touch me. What shit. Like all nonbelievers, I stood alone.

It came to me then that there was something absurd in thinking all this while leaning against a bathroom door. Grimly absurd, but absurd. The toilet as confessional. I ran the cold water, splashed some on my face, and left. How long had I left Keith alone in the living room?

When I returned, he was standing by the mailnet. He had punched in the command to replay my outgoing postal messages, and displayed on the monitor was Devrie's address at the Institute of the Biological Hope.

"What is it?" Keith said. "A hospital?"

I didn't answer him.

"I can find out, Seena. Knowing this much, I can find out. Tell me."

Tell me. "Not a hospital. It's a research laboratory. Devrie is a voluntary subject."

"Research on what? I will find out, Seena."

"Brain perception."

"Perception of what?"

"Perception of God," I said, torn among weariness, anger, and a sudden gritty exasperation, irritating as sand. Why not just leave him to Devrie's persuasions, and her to mystic starvation? But I knew I would not. I still, despite all of it, wanted her out of there.

Keith frowned. "What do you mean, 'perception of God'?"

I told him. I made it sound as ridiculous as possible, and as dangerous. I described the anorexia, the massive use of largely untested drugs that would have made the Institute illegal in the United States, the skepticism of most of the scientific community, the psychoses and death that had followed twin-trance research fifteen years earlier. Keith did not remember that—he had been eight years old—and I did not tell him that I had been one of the researchers. I did not tell him about the tapes of the shadowy third presence in Bohentin's holotanks. In every way I could, with every verbal subtlety at my use, I made the Institute sound crackpot, and dangerous, and ugly. As I spoke, I watched Keith's face, and sometimes it was mine, and sometimes the expression altered it into Devrie's. I saw bewilderment at her having chosen to enter the Institute, but not what I had hoped to see. Not scorn, not disgust.

When I had finished, he said, "But why did she think that *I* might want to enter such a place as a twin subject?"

I had saved this for last. "Money. She'd buy you."

His hand, his third Scotch, went rigid. "Buy me."

"It's the most accurate way to put it."

"What the hell made her think—" He mastered himself, not without effort. Not all the discussion of bodily risk had affected him as much as this mention of Devrie's money. He had a poor man's touchy pride. "She thinks of me as something to be bought."

I was carefully quiet.

"Damn her," he said. "Damn her." Then, roughly, "And I was actually considering—"

I caught my breath. "Considering the Institute? After what I've just told you? How in hell could you? And you said, I remember, that your background was not religious!"

"It's not. But I...I've wondered." And in the sudden turn of his head away from me so that I wouldn't see the sudden rapt hopelessness in his eyes, in the defiant set of his shoulders, I read more than in his banal words, and more than he could know. Devrie's look, Devrie's wishfulness, feeding on air. The weariness and anger, checked before, flooded me again and I lashed out at him.

"Then go ahead and fly to Dominica to enter the Institute yourself!"

He said nothing. But from something—his expression as he stared into his glass, the shifting of his body—I suddenly knew that he could not afford the trip.

I said, "So you fancy yourself as a believer?"

"No. A believer manqué." From the way he said it, I knew that he had said it before, perhaps often, and that the phrase stirred some hidden place in his imagination.

"What is wrong with you," I said, "with people like you, that the human world is not enough?"

"What is wrong with people like you, that it is?" he said, and this time he laughed and raised his eyebrows in a little mockery that shut me out from this place beyond reason, this glittering escape. I knew then that somehow or other, sometime or other, despite all I had said, Keith would go to Dominica.

I poured him another Scotch. As deftly as I could, I led the conversation into other, lighter directions. I asked about his childhood. At first stiffly, then more easily as time and Scotch loosened him, he talked about growing up in the Berkshire Hills. He became more lighthearted, and under my interest turned both shrewd and funny, with a keen sense of humor. His thick brown hair fell over his forehead. I laughed with him, and broke out a bottle of good port. He talked about amateur plays he had acted in; his enthusiasm increased as his coherence decreased. Enthusiasm, humor, thick brown hair. I smoothed the hair back from his forehead. Far into the night I pulled the drapes back from the window and we stood together and looked at the lights of the dying city ten stories below. Fog rolled in from the sea. Keith insisted we open the doors and stand on the balcony; he had never smelled fog tinged with the ocean. We smelled the night, and drank some more, and talked, and laughed.

And then I led him again to the sofa.

"Seena?" Keith said. He covered my hand, laid upon his thigh, with his own, and turned his head to look at me questioningly. I leaned forward and touched my lips to his, barely in contact, for a long moment. He drew back, and his hand tried to lift mine. I tightened my fingers.

"Seena, no..."

"Why not?" I put my mouth back on his, very lightly. He had to draw back to answer, and I could feel that he did not want to draw back. Under my lips he frowned slightly; still, despite his drunkenness—so much more than mine—he groped for the word.

"Incest..."

"No. We two have never shared a womb."

He frowned again, under my mouth. I drew back to smile at him, and shifted my hand. "It doesn't matter anymore, Keith. Not in New York. But even if it did—I am not your sister, not really. You said so yourself—remember? Not a family. Just...here."

"Not family," he repeated, and I saw in his eyes the second before he closed them the flash of pain, the greed of a young man's desire, and even the crafty evasions of the good port. Then his arms closed around me.

He was very strong, and more than a little violent. I guessed from what confusions the violence flowed but still I enjoyed it, that overwhelming rush from that beautiful male-Devrie body. I wanted him to be violent with me, as long as I knew there was no real danger. No real danger, no real brother, no real child. Keith was not my child but Devrie was my child-sister, and I had to stop her from destroying herself, no matter how...didn't I? "The pull of blood." But this was necessary, was justified... was a necessary gamble. For Devrie.

So I told myself. Then I stopped telling myself anything at all, and surrendered to the warm tides of pleasure.

But at dawn I woke and thought—with Keith sleeping heavily across me and the sky cold at the window—what the hell am I doing?

When I came out of the shower, Keith was sitting rigidly against the pillows. Sitting next to him on the very edge of the bed, I pulled a sheet around my nakedness and reached for his hand. He snatched it away.

"Keith. It's all right. Truly it is."

"You're my sister."

"But nothing will come of it. No child, no repetitions. It's not all that uncommon, dear heart."

"It is where I come from."

"Yes. I know. But not here."

He didn't answer, his face troubled.

"Do you want breakfast?"

"No. No thank you."

I could feel his need to get away from me; it was almost palpable. Snatching my bodysuit off the floor, I went into the kitchen, which was chilly. The servant would not arrive for another hour. I turned up the heat, pulled on my bodysuit—standing on the cold floor first on one foot and then on the other, like some extinct species of water fowl—and made coffee. Through the handle of one cup I stuck two folded large bills. He came into the kitchen, dressed even to the torn jacket.

"Coffee."

"Thanks."

His fingers closed on the handle of the cup, and his eyes widened. Pure, naked shock, uncushioned by any defenses whatsoever: the whole soul, betrayed, pinned in the eyes.

"Oh God, no, Keith—how can you even think so? It's for the trip back to Indian Falls! A gift!"

An endless pause, while we stared at each other. Then he said, very low, "I'm sorry. I should have...seen what it's for." But his cup trembled in his hand, and a few drops sloshed onto the floor. It was those few drops that undid me, flooding me with shame. Keith had a right to his shock, and to the anguish in his/my/Devrie's face. She wanted him for her mystic purposes, I for their prevention. Fanatic and saboteur, we were both better defended against each other than Keith, without money nor religion nor years, was against either of us. If I could have seen any other way than the gamble I had taken...but I could not. Nonetheless, I was ashamed.

"Keith. I'm sorry."

"Why did we? Why did we?"

I could have said: We didn't; I did. But that might have made it worse for him. He was male, and so young.

Impulsively I blurted, "Don't go to Dominica!" But of course he was beyond listening to me now. His face closed. He set down the coffee cup and looked at me from eyes much harder than they had been a minute ago. Was he thinking that because of our night together I expected to influence him directly? I was not that young. He could not foresee that I was trying to guess much farther ahead than that, for which I could not blame him. I could not blame him for anything. But I did regret how clumsily I had handled the money. That had been stupid.

Nonetheless, when he left a few moments later, the handle of the coffee cup was bare. He had taken the money.

The Madagascar exhibits were complete. They opened to much press interest, and there were both favorable reviews and celebrations. I could not bring myself to feel that it mattered. Ten times a day I went through the deadening exercise of willing an interest that had deserted me, and when I looked at the moths, ashy white wings outstretched forever, I could feel my body recoil in a way I could not name.

The image of the moths went home with me. One night in November I actually thought I heard wings beating against the window where I had stood with Keith. I yanked open the drapes and then the doors, but of course there was nothing there. For a long time I stared at the nothingness, smelling the fog, before typing yet another message, urgent-priority personal, to Devrie. The mailnet did not bring any answer.

I contacted the mailnet computer at the college at Indian Falls. My fingers trembled as they typed a request to leave an urgent-priority personal message for a student, Keith Torellen. The mailnet typed back:

TORELLEN, KEITH ROBERT. 64830016. ON MEDICAL LEAVE OF ABSENCE. TIME OF LEAVE: INDEFINITE. NO FORWARDING MAILNET NUMBER. END.

The sound came again at the window. Whirling, I scanned the dark glass, but there was nothing there, no moths, no wings, just the lights of the decaying city flung randomly across the blackness and the sound, faint and very far away, of a siren wailing out somebody else's disaster.

I shivered. Putting on a sweater and turning up the heat made me no warmer. Then the mail slot chimed softly and I turned in time to see the letter fall from the pneumatic tube from the lobby, the apartment house sticker clearly visible, assuring me that it had been processed and found free of both poison and explosives. Also visible was the envelope's logo: INSTITUTE OF THE BIOLOGICAL HOPE, all the O's radiant golden suns. But Devrie never wrote paper mail. She preferred the mailnet.

The note was from Keith, not Devrie. A short note, scrawled on a torn scrap of paper in nearly indecipherable handwriting. I had seen Keith's handwriting in Indian Falls, across his student notebooks; this was a wildly out-of-control version of it, almost psychotic in the variations of spacing and letter formation that signal identity. I guessed that he had written the note under the influence of a drug, or several drugs, his mind racing much faster than he could write. There was neither punctuation nor paragraphing.

Dear Seena I'm going to do it I have to know my parents are angry but I have to know I have to all the confusion is gone xxxxxx Seena Keith

There was a word crossed out between "gone" and "Seena," scratched out with erratic lines of ink. I held the paper up to the light, tilting it this way and that. The crossed-out word was "mother."

all the confusion is gone mother

Mother.

Slowly I let out the breath I had not known I was holding. The first emotion was pity, for Keith, even though I had intended this. We had done a job on him, Devrie and I. Mother, sister, self. And when he and Devrie artificially drove upward the number and speed of the neurotransmitters in the brain, generated the twin trance, and then Keith's pre-cloning Freudian-still mind reached for Devrie to add sexual energy to all the other brain energies fueling Bohentin's holotanks—

Mother. Sister. Self.

All was fair in love and war. A voice inside my head jeered: And which is this? But I was ready for the voice. This was both. I didn't think it would be long before Devrie left the Institute to storm to New York.

It was nearly another month, in which the snow began to fall and the city to deck itself in the tired gilt fallacies of Christmas. I felt fine. Humming, I catalogued the Madagascar moths, remounting the best specimens in exhibit cases and sealing them under permaplex, where their fragile wings and delicate antennae could lie safe. The mutant strains had the thinnest wings, unnaturally tenuous and up to twenty-five centimeters each, all of pale ivory, as if a ghostly delicacy were the natural evolutionary response to the glowing landscape of nuclear genocide. I catalogued each carefully.

"Why?" Devrie said. "Why?"

"You look like hell."

"Why?"

"I think you already know," I said. She sagged on my white velvet sofa, alone, the PGs that I suspected acted as much as nurses as guards, dismissed from the apartment. Tears of anger and exhaustion collected in her sunken eye sockets but did not fall. Only with effort was she keeping herself in a sitting position, and the effort was costing her energy she did not have. Her skin, except for two red spots of fury high on each cheekbone, was the color of old eggs. Looking at her, I had to keep my hands twisted in my lap to keep myself from weeping.

"Are you telling me you planned it, Seena? Are you telling me you located Keith and slept with him because you knew that would make him impotent with me?"

"Of course not. I know sexuality isn't that simple. So do you."

"But you gambled on it. You gambled that it would be one way to ruin the experiment."

"I gambled that it would...complicate Keith's responses."

"Complicate them past the point where he knew who the hell he was with!"

"He'd be able to know if you weren't making him glow out of his mind with neurotransmitter kickers! He's not stupid. But he's not ready for whatever mystic hoops you've tried to make him jump through—if anybody ever can be said to be ready for that!—and no, I'm not surprised that he can't handle libidinal energies on top of all the other artificial energies you're racing through his brain. Something was bound to snap."

"You caused it, Seena. As cold-bloodedly as that."

A sudden shiver of memory brought the feel of Keith's hands on my breasts. No, not as cold-bloodedly as that. No. But I could not say so to Devrie.

"I trusted you," she said. "'Anything for a sister'— God!"

"You were right to trust me. To trust me to get you out of that place before you're dead."

"Listen to yourself! Smug, all-knowing, self-righteous…do you know how close we were at the Institute? Do you have any idea what you've destroyed?"

I laughed coldly. I couldn't help it. "If contact with God can be destroyed because one confused kid can't get it up, what does that say about God?"

Devrie stared at me. A long moment passed, and in the moment the two red spots on her cheeks faded and her eyes narrowed. "Why, Seena?"

"I told you. I wanted you safe, out of there. And you are."

"No. No. There's something else, something more going on here. Going on with you."

"Don't make it more complicated than it is, Devrie. You're my sister, and my only family. Is it so odd that I would try to protect you?"

"Keith is your brother."

"Well, then, protect both of you. Whatever derails that experiment protects Keith, too."

She said softly, "Did you want him so much?"

We stared at each other across the living room, sisters, I standing by the mailnet and she supported by the sofa, needing its support, weak and implacable as any legendary martyr to the faith. Her weakness hurt me in some nameless place; as a child Devrie's body had been so strong. The hurt twisted in me, so that I answered her with truth. "Not so much. Not at first, not until we…no, that's not true. I wanted him. But that was not the reason, Devrie—it was not a rationalization for lust, nor any lapse in self-control."

She went on staring at me, until I turned to the sideboard and poured myself a Scotch. My hand trembled.

Behind me Devrie said, "Not lust. And not protection either. Something else, Seena. You're afraid."

I turned, smiling tightly. "Of you?"

"No. No, I don't think so."

"What then?"

"I don't know. Do you?"

"This is your theory, not mine."

She closed her eyes. The tears, shining all this time over her anger, finally fell. Head flung back against the pale sofa, arms limp at her side, she looked the picture of desolation, and so weak that I was frightened. I brought her a glass of milk from the kitchen and held it to her mouth, and I was a little surprised when she drank it off without protest.

"Devrie. You can't go on like this. In this physical state."

"No," she agreed, in a voice so firm and prompt that I was startled further. It was the voice of decision, not surrender. She straightened herself on the sofa. "Even Bohentin says I can't go on like this. I weigh less than he wants, and I'm right at the edge of not having the physical resources to control the twin trance. I'm having racking withdrawal symptoms even being on this trip, and at this very minute there is a doctor sitting at Father's desk in your study, in case I need him. Also, I've had my lawyers make over most of my remaining inheritance to Keith. I don't think you knew that. What's left has all been transferred to a bank on Dominica, and if I die it goes to the Institute. You won't be able to touch it, nor touch Keith's portion either, not even if I die. And I will die, Seena, soon, if I don't start eating and stop taking the program's drugs. I'll just burn out body and brain both. You've guessed that I'm close to that, but you haven't guessed how close. Now I'm telling you. I can't handle the stresses of the twin trance much longer."

I just went on holding her glass, arm extended, unable to move.

"You gambled that you could destroy one component in the chain of my experiment at the Institute by confusing my twin sexually. Well, you won. Now I'm making a gamble. I'm gambling my life that you can undo what you did with Keith, and without his knowing that I made you. You said he's not stupid and his impotency comes from being unable to handle the drug program; perhaps you're partly right. But he is me—me, Seena—and I know you've thought I was stupid all my life, because I wanted things you don't understand. Now Keith wants them, too—it was inevitable that he would—and you're going to undo whatever is standing in his way. I had to fight myself free all my life of your bullying, but Keith doesn't have that kind of time. Because if you don't undo what you caused, I'm going to go ahead with the twin trance anyway—the twin trance, Seena—without the sexual component and without letting Bohentin know just how much greater the strain is in trance than he thinks it is. He doesn't know, he doesn't have a twin, and neither do the doctors. But I know, and if I push it much farther I'm going to eventually die at it. Soon eventually. When I do, all your scheming to get me out of there really will have failed and you'll be alone with whatever it is you're so afraid of. But I don't think you'll let that happen.

"I think that instead you'll undo what you did to Keith, so that the experiment can have one last real chance. And in return, after that one chance, I'll agree to come home, to Boston or here to New York, for one year.

"That's my gamble."

She was looking at me from eyes empty of all tears, a Devrie I had not ever seen before. She meant it, every demented word, and she would do it. I wanted to scream at her, to scream a jumble of suicide and moral blackmail and warped perceptions and outrage, but the words that came out of my mouth came out in a whisper.

"What in God's name is worth that?"

Shockingly, she laughed, a laugh of more power than her wasted frame could have contained. Her face glowed, and the glow looked both exalted and insane. "You said it, Seena—in God's name. To finally know. To know, beyond the fogginess of faith, that we're not alone in the universe...Faith should not mean fogginess." She laughed again, this time defensively, as if she knew how she sounded to me. "You'll do it, Seena." It was not a question. She took my hand.

"You would kill yourself?"

"No. I would die trying to reach God. It's not the same thing."

"I never bullied you, Devrie."

She dropped my hand. "All my life, Seena. And on into now. But all of your bullying and your scorn would look rather stupid, wouldn't it, if there really can be proved to exist a rational basis for what you laughed at all those years!"

We looked at each other, sisters, across the abyss of the pale sofa, and then suddenly away. Neither of us dared speak.

My plane landed on Dominica by night. Devrie had gone two days before me, returning with her doctor and guards on the same day she had left, as I had on my previous visit. I had never seen the island at night. The tropical greenery, lush with that faintly menacing suggestion of plant life gone wild, seemed to close in on me. The velvety darkness seemed to smell of ginger, and flowers, and the sea—all too strong, too blandly sensual, like an overdone perfume ad. At the hotel it was better; my room was on the second floor, above the dark foliage, and did not face the sea. Nonetheless, I stayed inside all that evening, all that darkness, until I could go the next day to the Institute of the Biological Hope.

"Hello, Seena."

"Keith. You look—"

"Rotten," he finished, and waited. He did not smile. Although he had lost some weight, he was nowhere near as skeletal as Devrie, and it gave me a pang I did not analyze to see his still-healthy body in the small gray room where last I had seen hers. His head was shaved, and without the curling brown hair he looked sterner, prematurely middle-aged. That, too, gave me a strange emotion, although it was not why he looked rotten. The worst was his eyes. Red-veined, watery, the sockets already a little sunken, they held the sheen of a man who was not forgiving somebody for something. Me? Himself? Devrie? I had lain awake all night, schooling myself for this insane interview, and still I did not know what to say. What does one say to persuade a man to sexual potency with one's sister so that her life might be saved? I felt ridiculous, and frightened, and—I suddenly realized the name of my strange emotion—humiliated. How could I even start to slog toward what I was supposed to reach?

"How goes the Great Experiment?"

"Not as you described it," he said, and we were there already. I looked at him evenly.

"You can't understand why I presented the Institute in the worst possible light."

"I can understand that."

"Then you can't understand why I bedded you, knowing about Bohentin's experiment."

"I can also understand that."

Something was wrong. Keith answered me easily, without restraint, but with conflict gritty beneath his voice, like sand beneath blowing grass. I stepped closer, and he flinched. But his expression did not change.

"Keith. What is this about? What am I doing here? Devrie said you couldn't...that you were impotent with her, confused enough about who and what..." I trailed off. He still had not changed expression.

I said quietly, "It was a simplistic idea in the first place. Only someone as simplistic as Devrie..." Only someone as simplistic as Devrie would think you could straighten out impotency by talking about it for a few hours. I turned to go, and I had gotten as far as laying my hand on the doorknob before Keith grasped my arm. Back to him, I squeezed my eyes shut. What in God would I have done if he had not stopped me?

"It's not what Devrie thinks!" With my back to him, not able to see his middle-aged baldness but only to hear the anguish in his voice, he again seemed young, uncertain, the boy I had bought coffee for in Indian Falls. I kept my back to him, and my voice carefully toneless.

"What is it, then, Keith? If not what Devrie thinks?"

"I don't know!"

"But you do know what it's not? It's not being confused about who is your sister and who your mother and who you're willing to have sex with in front of a room full of researchers?"

"No." His voice had gone hard again, but his hand stayed on my arm. "At first, yes. The first time. But, Seena—I felt it. Almost. I almost felt the presence, and then all the rest of the confusion—it didn't seem as important anymore. Not the confusion between you and Devrie."

I whirled to face him. "You mean God doesn't care whom you fuck if it gets you closer to fucking with Him."

He looked at me hard then—at me, not at his own self-absorption. His reddened eyes widened a little. "Why, Seena—you care. You told me the brother-sister thing didn't matter anymore—but you care."

Did I? I didn't even know anymore. I said, "But, then, I'm not deluding myself that it's all for the old Kingdom and the Glory."

"Glory," he repeated musingly, and finally let go of my arm. I couldn't tell what he was thinking.

"Keith. This isn't getting us anywhere."

"Where do you want to get?" he said in the same musing tone. "Where did any of you, starting with your father, want to get with me? Glory… glory."

Standing this close to him, seeing close up the pupils of his eyes and smelling close up the odor of his sweat, I finally realized what I should have seen all along: he was glowing. He was of course constantly on Bohentin's program of neurotransmitter manipulation, but the same chemicals that made the experiments possible also raised the threshold of both frankness and suggestibility. I guessed it must be a little like the looseness of being drunk, and I wondered if perhaps Bohentin might have deliberately raised the dosage before letting this interview take place. But no, Bohentin wouldn't be aware of the bargain Devrie and I had struck; she would not have told him. The whole bizarre situation was hers alone, and Keith's drugged musings a fortunate side-effect I would have to capitalize on.

"Where do you think my father wanted to get with you?" I asked him gently.

"Immortality. Godhead. The man who created Adam without Eve."

He was becoming maudlin. "Hardly 'the man,'" I pointed out. "My father was only one of a team of researchers. And the same results were being obtained independently in California."

"Results. I am a 'result.' What do you think he wanted, Seena?"

"Scientific knowledge of cell development. An objective truth."

"That's all Devrie wants."

"To compare bioengineering to some mystic quest—"

"Ah, but if the mystic quest is given a laboratory answer? Then it, too, becomes a scientific truth. You really hate that idea, don't you, Seena? You hate science validating anything you define as non-science."

I said stiffly, "That's rather an oversimplification."

"Then what do you hate?"

"I hate the risk to human bodies and human minds. To Devrie. To you."

"How nice of you to include me," he said, smiling. "And what do you think Devrie wants?"

"Sensation. Romantic religious emotion. To be all roiled up inside with delicious esoterica."

He considered this. "Maybe."

"And is that what you want as well, Keith? You've asked what everyone else wants. What do you want?"

"I want to feel at home in the universe. As if I belonged in it. And I never have."

He said this simply, without self-consciousness, and the words themselves were predictable enough for his age—even banal. There was nothing in the words that could account for my eyes suddenly filling with tears. "And 'scientifically' reaching God would do that for you?"

"How do I know until I try it? Don't cry, Seena."

"I'm not!"

"All right," he agreed softly. "You're not crying." Then he added, without changing tone, "I am more like you than like Devrie."

"How so?"

"I think that Devrie has always felt that she belongs in the universe. She only wants to find the...the coziest corner of it to curl up in. Like a cat. The coziest corner to curl up in is God's lap. Aren't you surprised that I should be more like you than like the person I was cloned from?"

"No," I said. "Harder upbringing than Devrie's. I told you that first day: cloning is only delayed twinning."

He threw back his head and laughed, a sound that chilled my spine. Whatever his conflict was, we were moving closer.

"Oh no, Seena. You're so wrong. It's more than delayed twinning, all right. You can't buy a real twin. You either have one or you don't. But you can buy yourself a clone. Bought, paid for, kept on the books along with all the rest of the glassware and holotanks and electron microscopes. You said so yourself, in your apartment, when you first told me about Devrie and the Institute. 'Money. She'd buy you.' And you were right, of course. Your father bought me, and she did, and you did. But of course you two women couldn't have bought if I hadn't been selling."

He was smiling still. Stupid—we had both been stupid, Devrie and I, we had both been looking in the wrong place, misled by our separate blinders—or by training in the laboratory brain. My training had been scientific, hers humanistic, and so I looked at Freud and she looked at Oedipus, and we were equally stupid. How did the world look to a man who did not deal in laboratory brains, a man raised in a grittier world in which limits were not what the mind was capable of but what the bank book would stand? "Your genes are too expensive for you to claim except as a beggar; your sisters are too expensive for you to claim except as a beggar; God is too expensive for you to claim except as a beggar." To a less romantic man it would not have mattered, but a less romantic man would not have come to the Institute. What dark humiliations and resentments did Keith feel when he looked at Devrie, the self who was buyer and not bought?

Change the light you shine onto a mind, and you see different neural patterns, different corridors, different forests of trees grown in soil you could not have imagined. Run that soil through your fingers and you discover different pebbles, different sand, different leaf mold from the decay of old growths. Devrie and I had been hacking through the wrong forest.

Not Oedipus, but Marx.

Quick lines of attack came to me. Say: Keith it's a job like any other with high-hazard pay why can't you look at it like that a very dangerous and well-paid job for which you've been hired by just one more eccentric member of the monied class. Say: You're entitled to the wealth you're our biological brother damn it consider it rationally as a kinship entitlement. Say: Don't be so nicey-nice it's a tough world out there and if Devrie's giving it away take it don't be an impractical chump.

I said none of that. Instead I heard myself saying, coolly and with a calm cruelty, "You're quite right. You were bought by Devrie, and she is now using her own purchase for her own ends. You're a piece of equipment bought and paid for. Unfortunately, there's no money in the account. It has all been a grand sham."

Keith jerked me to face him with such violence that my neck cracked. "What are you saying?"

The words came as smoothly, as plausibly, as if I had rehearsed them. I didn't even consciously plan them: how can you plan a lie you do not know you will need? I slashed through this forest blind, but the ground held under my feet.

"Devrie told me that she has signed over most of her inheritance to you. What she didn't know, because I haven't yet told her, is that she doesn't have control of her inheritance any longer. It's not hers. I control it. I had her declared mentally incompetent on the grounds of violent suicidal tendencies and had myself made her legal guardian. She no longer has the legal right to control her fortune. A doctor observed her when she came to visit me in New York. So the transfer of her fortune to you is invalid."

"The lawyers who gave me the papers to sign—"

"Will learn about the New York action this week," I said smoothly. How much inheritance law did Keith know? Probably very little. Neither did I, and I invented furiously; it only needed to sound plausible. "The New York courts only handed down their decision recently, and Dominican judicial machinery, like everything else in the tropics, moves slowly. But the ruling will hold, Keith. Devrie does not control her own money, and you're a pauper again. But *I* have something for you. Here. An airline ticket back to Indian Falls. You're a free man. Poor, but free. The ticket is in your name, and there's a check inside it—that's from me. You've earned it, for at least trying to aid poor Devrie. But now you're going to have to leave her to me. I'm now her legal guardian."

I held the ticket out to him. It was wrapped in its airline folder; my own name as passenger was hidden. Keith stared at it, and then at me.

I said softly, "I'm sorry you were cheated. Devrie didn't mean to. But she has no money, now, to offer you. You can go. Devrie's my burden now."

His voice sounded strangled. "To remove from the Institute?"

"I never made any secret of wanting her out. Although the legal papers for that will take a little time to filter through the Dominican courts. She wouldn't go except by force, so force is what I'll get. Here."

I thrust the ticket folder at him. He made no move to take it, and I saw from the hardening of his face—my face, Devrie's face—the moment when Devrie shifted forests in his mind. Now she was without money, without legal control of her life, about to be torn from the passion she loved most. The helpless underdog. The orphaned woman, poor and cast out, in need of protection from the powerful who had seized her fortune.

Not Marx, but Cervantes.

"You would do that? To your own sister?"

Anything for a sister. I said bitterly, "Of course I would."

"She's not mentally incompetent!"

"Isn't she?"

"No!"

I shrugged. "The courts say she is."

Keith studied me, resolve hardening around him. I thought of certain shining crystals, that will harden around any stray piece of grit. Now that I was succeeding in convincing him, my lies hurt—or perhaps what hurt was how easily he believed them.

"Are you sure, Seena," he said, "that you aren't just trying a grab for Devrie's fortune?"

I shrugged again, and tried to make my voice toneless. "I want her out of here. I don't want her to die."

"Die? What makes you think she would die?"

"She looks—"

"She's nowhere near dying," Keith said angrily—his anger a release, so much that it hardly mattered at what. "Don't you think I can tell in twin trance what her exact physical state is? And don't you know how much control the trance gives each twin over the bodily processes of the other? Don't you even know that? Devrie isn't anywhere near dying. And I'd pull her out of trance if she were." He paused, looking hard at me. "Keep your ticket, Seena."

I repeated mechanically, "You can leave now. There's no money." Devrie had lied to me.

"That wouldn't leave her with any protection at all, would it?" he said levelly. When he grasped the doorknob to leave, the tendons in his wrist stood out clearly, strong and taut. I did not try to stop his going.

Devrie had lied to me. With her lie, she had blackmailed me into yet another lie to Keith. The twin trance granted control, in some unspecified way, to each twin's body; the trance I had pioneered might have resulted in eight deaths unknowingly inflicted on each other out of who knows what dark forests in eight fumbling minds. Lies, blackmail, death, more lies.

Out of these lies they were going to make scientific truth. Through these forests they were going to search for God.

"Final clearance check of holotanks," an assistant said formally. "Faraday cage?"

"Optimum."

"External radiation?"

"Cleared," said the man seated at the console of the first tank.

"Cleared," said the woman seated at the console of the second.

"Microradiation?"

"Cleared."

"Cleared."

"Personnel radiation, Class A?"

"Cleared."

"Cleared."

On it went, the whole tedious and crucial procedure, until both tanks had been cleared and focused, the fluid adjusted, tested, adjusted again, tested again. Bohentin listened patiently, without expression, but I, standing to the side of him and behind the tanks, saw the nerve at the base of his neck and just below the hairline pulse in some irregular rhythm of its own. Each time the nerve pulsed, the skin rose slightly from under his collar. I kept my eyes on that syncopated crawling of flesh, and felt tension prickle over my own skin like heat.

Three-quarters of the lab, the portion where the holotanks and other machinery stood, was softly dark, lit mostly from the glow of console dials and the indirect track lighting focused on the tanks. Standing in the gloom were Bohentin, five other scientists, two medical doctors—and me. Bohentin had fought my being allowed there, but in the end he had had to give in. I had known too many threatening words not in generalities but in specifics: reporters' names, drug names, cloning details, twin trance tragedy, anorexia symptoms, bio-engineering amendment. He was not a man who much noticed either public opinion or relatives' threats, but no one else outside his Institute knew so many specific words—some people knew some of the words, but only I had them all. In the end he had focused on me his cold, brilliant eyes, and given permission for me to witness the experiment that involved my sister.

I was going to hold Devrie to her bargain. I was not going to believe anything she told me without witnessing it for myself.

Half the morning passed in technical preparation. Somewhere Devrie and Keith, the human components of this costly detection circuit, were separately being brought to the apex of brain activity. Drugs, biofeedback, tactile and auditory and kinesthetic stimulation—all carefully calculated for the maximum increase of both the number of neurotransmitters firing signals through the synapses of the brain and of the speed at which the signals raced. The more rapid the transmission through certain pathways, the more intense both perception and feeling. Some neurotransmitters, under this pressure, would alter molecular structure into natural hallucinogens; that reaction had to be controlled. Meanwhile other drugs, other biofeedback techniques, would depress the body's natural enzymes designed to either reabsorb excess transmitters or to reduce the rate at which they fired. The number and speed of neurotransmitters in Keith's and Devrie's brains would mount, and mount, and mount, all natural chemical barriers removed. The two of them would enter the lab with their whole brains—rational cortex, emotional limbic, right and left brain functions—simultaneously aroused to an unimaginable degree. Simultaneously. They would be feeling as great a "rush" as a falling skydiver, as great a glow as a cocaine user, as great a mental clarity and receptivity as a da Vinci whose brush is guided by all the integrated visions of his unconscious mind. They would be white-hot.

Then they would hit each other with the twin trance.

The quarter of the lab which Keith and Devrie would use was softly and indirectly lit, though brighter than the rest. It consisted of a raised, luxuriantly padded platform, walls and textured pillows in a pink whose component wavelengths had been carefully calculated, temperature in a complex gradient producing precise convection flows over the skin. The man and woman in that womb-colored, flesh-stimulating environment would be able to see us observers standing in the gloom behind the holotanks only as vague shapes. When the two doors opened and Devrie and Keith moved onto the platform, I knew that they would not even try to distinguish who stood in the lab. Looking at their faces, that looked only at each other, I felt my heart clutch.

They were naked except for the soft helmets that both attached hundreds of needles to nerve clumps just below the skin and also held the earphones through which Bohentin controlled the music that swelled the cathedrals of their skulls. "Cathedrals"—from their faces, transfigured to the ravished ecstasy found in paintings of medieval saints, that was the right word. But here the ecstasy was controlled, understood, and I saw with a sudden rush of pain at old memories that I could recognize the exact moment when Keith and Devrie locked onto each other with the twin trance. I recognized it, with my own more bitter hyperclarity, in their eyes, as I recognized the cast of concentration that came over their features, and the intensity of their absorption. The twin trance. They clutched each other's hands, faces inches apart, and suddenly I had to look away.

Each holotank held two whorls of shifting colors, the outlines clearer and the textures more sharply delineated than any previous holographs in the history of science. Keith's and Devrie's perceptions of each other's presence. The whorls went on clarifying themselves, separating into distinct and mappable layers, as on the platform Keith and Devrie remained frozen, all their energies focused on the telepathic trance. Seconds passed, and then minutes. And still, despite the clarity of the holographs in the tank, a clarity that fifteen years earlier I would have given my right hand for, I sensed that Keith and Devrie were holding back, were deliberately confining their unimaginable perceptiveness to each other's radiant energy, in the same way that water is confined behind a dam to build power.

But how could *I* be sensing that? From a subliminal "reading" of the mapped perceptions in the holotanks? Or from something else?

More minutes passed. Keith and Devrie stayed frozen, facing each other, and over her skeletal body and his stronger one a flush began to spread, rosy and slow, like heat tide rising.

"Jesus H. Christ," said one of the medical doctors, so low that only I, standing directly behind her, could have heard. It was not a curse, nor a prayer, but some third possibility, unnamable.

Keith put one hand on Devrie's thigh. She shuddered. He drew her down to the cushions on the platform and they began to caress each other, not frenzied, not in the exploring way of lovers but with a deliberation I have never experienced outside a research lab, a slow care that implied that worlds of interpretation hung on each movement. Yet the effect was not of coldness nor detachment but of intense involvement, of tremendous energy joyously used, of creating each other's bodies right then, there under each other's hands. They were working, and oblivious to all but their work. But if it was a kind of creative work, it was also a kind of primal innocent eroticism, and, watching, I felt my own heat begin to rise. "Innocent"—but if innocence is unknowingness, there was nothing innocent about it at all. Keith and Devrie knew and controlled each heartbeat, and I felt the exact moment when they let their sexual energies, added to all the other neural energies, burst the dam and flood outward in wave after wave, expanding the scope of each brain's perceptions, inundating the artificially-walled world.

A third whorl formed in each holotank.

It formed suddenly: one second nothing, the next brightness. But then it wavered, faded a bit. After a few moments it brightened slightly, a diffused golden haze, before again fading. On the platform Keith gasped, and I guessed he was having to shift his attention between perceiving the third source of radiation and keeping up the erotic version of the twin trance. His biofeedback techniques were less experienced than Devrie's, and the male erection more fragile. But then he caught the rhythm, and the holograph brightened.

It seemed to me that the room brightened as well, although no additional lights came on and the consoles glowed no brighter. Sweat poured off the researchers. Bohentin leaned forward, his neck muscle tautening toward the platform as if it were his will and not Keith/Devrie's that strained to perceive that third presence recorded in the tank. I thought, stupidly, of mythical intermediaries: Merlyn never made king, Moses never reaching the Promised Land. Intermediaries—and then it became impossible to think of anything at all.

Devrie shuddered and cried out. Keith's orgasm came a moment later, and with it a final roil of neural activity so strong the two primary whorls in each holotank swelled to fill the tank and inundate the third. At the moment of breakthrough Keith screamed, and in memory it seems as if the scream was what tore through the last curtain—that is nonsense. How loud would microbes have to scream to attract the attention of giants? How loud does a knock on the door have to be to pull a sleeper from the alien world of dreams?

The doctor beside me fell to her knees. The third presence—or some part of it—swirled all around us, racing along our own unprepared synapses and neurons, and what swirled and raced was astonishment. A golden, majestic astonishment. We had finally attracted Its attention, finally knocked with enough neural force to be just barely heard—and It was astonished that we could, or did, exist. The slow rise of that powerful astonishment within the shielded lab was like the slow swinging around of the head of a great beast to regard some butterfly it has barely glimpsed from the corner of one eye. But this was no beast. As Its attention swung toward us, pain exploded in my skull—the pain of sound too loud, lights too bright, charge too high. My brain was burning on overload. There came one more flash of insight—wordless, pattern without end—and the sound of screaming. Then, abruptly, the energy vanished.

Bohentin, on all fours, crawled toward the holotanks. The doctor lay slumped on the floor; the other doctor had already reached the platform and its two crumpled figures. Someone was crying, someone else shouting. I rose, fell, dragged myself to the side of the platform and then could not climb it. I could not climb the platform. Hanging with two hands on the edge, hearing the voice crying as my own, I watched the doctor bend shakily to Keith, roll him off Devrie to bend over her, turn back to Keith.

Bohentin cried, "The tapes are intact!"

"Oh God oh God oh God oh God oh God," someone moaned, until abruptly she stopped. I grasped the flesh-colored padding on top of the platform and pulled myself up onto it.

Devrie lay unconscious, pulse erratic, face cast in perfect bliss. The doctor breathed into Keith's mouth—what strength could the doctor himself have left?—and pushed on the naked chest. Breathe, push, breathe, push. The whole length of Keith's body shuddered; the doctor rocked back on his heels; Keith breathed.

"It's all on tape!" Bohentin cried. "It's all on tape!"

"God damn you to hell," I whispered to Devrie's blissful face. "It didn't even know we were there!"

Her eyes opened. I had to lean close to hear her answer.

"But now...we know He...is there."

She was too weak to smile. I looked away from her, away from that face, out into the tumultuous emptiness of the lab, anywhere.

They will try again.

Devrie has been asleep, fed by glucose solution through an IV, for fourteen hours. I sit near her bed, frowned at by the nurse, who can see my expression as I stare at my sister. Somewhere in another bed Keith is sleeping yet again. His rest is more fitful than Devrie's; she sinks into sleep as into warm water, but he cannot. Like me, he is afraid of drowning.

An hour ago he came into Devrie's room and grasped my hand. "How could It—He—It not have been aware that we existed? Not even have known?"

I didn't answer him.

"You felt it too, Seena, didn't you? The others say they could, so you must have too. It...created us in some way. No, that's wrong. How could It create us and not know?"

I said wearily, "Do we always know what we've created?" and Keith glanced at me sharply. But I had not been referring to my father's work in cloning.

"Keith. What's a *Thysania africana*?"

"A what?"

"Think of us," I said, "as just one more biological side-effect. One type of being acts, and another type of being comes into existence. Man stages something like the African Horror, and in doing so he creates whole new species of moths and doesn't even discover they exist until long afterward. If man can do it, why not God? And why should He be any more aware of it than we are?"

Keith didn't like that. He scowled at me, and then looked at Devrie's sleeping face: Devrie's sleeping bliss.

"Because she is a fool," I said savagely, "and so are you. You won't leave it alone, will you? Having been noticed by It once, you'll try to be noticed by It again. Even though she promised me otherwise, and even if it kills you both."

Keith looked at me a long time, seeing clearly—finally—the nature of the abyss between us, and its dimensions. But I already knew neither of us could cross. When at last he spoke, his voice held so much compassion that I hated him. "Seena. Seena, love. There's no more doubt now, don't you see? Now rational belief is no harder than rational doubt. Why are you so afraid to even believe?"

I left the room. In the corridor I leaned against the wall, palms spread flat against the tile, and closed my eyes. It seemed to me that I could hear wings, pale and fragile, beating against glass.

They will try again. For the sake of sure knowledge that the universe is not empty, Keith and Devrie and all the others like their type of being will go on pushing their human brains beyond what the human brain has evolved to do, go on fluttering their wings against that biological window. For the sake of sure knowledge: belief founded on experiment and not on faith. And the Other: being/alien/God? It, too, may choose to initiate contact, if It can and now that It knows we are here. Perhaps It will seek to know us, and even beyond the laboratory Devrie and Keith may find any moment of heightened arousal subtly invaded by a shadowy Third. Will they sense It, hovering just beyond consciousness, if they argue fiercely or race a sailboat in rough water or make love? How much arousal will it take, now, for them to sense those huge wings beating on the other side of the window?

And windows can be broken.

Tomorrow I will fly back to New York. To my museum, to my exhibits, to my moths under permaplex, to my empty apartment, where I will keep the heavy drapes drawn tightly across the glass.

For—*oh God*—all the rest of my life.

Afterword to "Trinity"

This story comes from my pre-hard-SF days; the "science" in it isn't grounded in much of anything. I hadn't yet discovered how much fun it is to build on actual science to create fiction. Nonetheless, "Trinity" was my first Nebula nomination (I lost, to John Varley) and I was thrilled just to be nominated. A cliché, yes—but nonetheless true when you're young and starry-eyed about the science-fiction universe. At the banquet I sat next to Algis Budrys. I met other luminaries. "Trinity" is about a search for God, but I felt I was already in heaven.

In the decades since, my view of SF has gotten a little battered, like any well-used possession, but it has never disappeared. I love this world: the stories, the conventions, the friends, the debates about what SF "should be." All of it. Unlike Seena, who is at home nowhere, I have been lucky.

PEOPLE LIKE US

Parker brought the car around at seven; George was going to meet the dinner guests at the station. Sarah said incredulously, "They're coming up by *train*?"

"Buddy Calucci broke his wrist last week and can't drive," George said, "and his wife has some kind of phobia about it. And the alien of course can't drive either."

Of course. Of course not. Couldn't drive, couldn't wear pants, probably couldn't eat anything Sarah had had Cook prepare for dinner either. All the alien could do was put her poor old George's firm out of business with its strange advanced fuel products, whatever they were. Sarah stood before the fireplace and regarded her husband as he picked up his coat from a leather chair.

"If it's supposed to be such a discreet meeting that you can't have it in the city, why are they taking the train? Why didn't your Mr. Calucci order a car and driver?"

"I don't think it would occur to him."

"This is going to be horrible, George. It really is. I'd just as soon have Parker and Cook and Cook's criminal brother-in-law. The one in Attica."

George shrugged into his coat, crossed the room, and put his hands on Sarah's shoulders. "I know, darling, it's too bad. But necessary. And if they come by train, they can't stay late. The last train back is the 10:42. That's something, at least."

"At least," Sarah said. But she made herself smile at George; it wasn't his fault, after all, and whining like this was really terribly unattractive. These… people were coming, and that was that. Just the same, with George's florid face inches from her own, she suddenly remembered something Louise

Henderson had said to her just last week at the gallery: *You know, darling, George is getting awfully fat. He should go back to tennis instead of golf. If he's not careful, he'll start to look like that man that runs the hardware store.* Sarah had laughed; Louise had a wicked eye. But Sarah had been stung, too.

George did look a little like the man in the hardware store. The same shape to the brow, the same chin. Friends had joked about it before.

After George left for the station, Denise brought in a tray of canapés and fresh ice. Sarah made herself a Scotch and water, drank half of it, poked at the fire, finally settled on a chair. The living room looked well by firelight, she thought. She loved this house, even if it had seemed a little empty since Emily had gone off to Rosemary Hall four years ago. Brass and mahogany gleamed in the firelight; wainscoting and molding took on subtle curves; the colors of the old Orientals glowed. In the bookcases leather bindings and Chinese vases jumbled comfortably against each other, both slightly dusty. Emily's violin leaned against one corner. Had Emily, home for the weekend, practiced today? Probably not; too busy with the horses. Sarah smiled, finished her Scotch, and considered moving a pile of old *Smithsonians* and *Forbes* off the wing chair beside the violin. She decided against it.

She heard the car, and they were here. Sarah rose to meet her guests. "Hello."

"My wife Sarah," George said. "Darling, Mr. Calucci, Mrs. Calucci, Mr. C'Lanth."

"Call me Buddy," Calucci boomed at the same moment that his wife said, "Pleased to meet you, I'm sure. I'm Mabel."

Buddy Calucci seized Sarah's hand and pumped it. He wore a coat with hugely padded shoulders and a bright yellow tie, carefully knotted, printed with daisies. Mabel Calucci wore heart-shaped glasses and a red satin dress cut so low that Sarah blinked. She avoided altogether looking at the alien. Not just yet.

"Nice place you got here," Calucci boomed. "Looks real homey." His eyes, Sarah saw, missed nothing, scrutinizing the portraits as if appraising them.

"My, yes," Mabel Calucci said. Her mouth pursed slightly at the magazines tossed on the wing chair.

Sarah said, "Would you like a drink?" and started towards the sideboard. Calucci's words stopped her.

"No, no, Mabel and I never touch the stuff. Christian Temperance. But you folks go right ahead—feel free."

"You don't drink?"

"Lips that touch liquor shall never touch mine," Mabel said roguishly. "This must be your dog—let him right into the living room, do you?" Her eyes moved to the spot by the fireplace where Brandy usually lay; Labrador hair clung to the Oriental.

"We got a dog, too," Calucci said. "Doberman. Meanest guard dog you ever saw. Not that we need it now with the new security system on the country home. Del EverGuard. Seven thousand for the fencing alone."

"How interesting," Sarah murmured. George threw her a warning glance. She poured herself another Scotch and water, then one for George.

The alien said, "I'd like one, too, please."

Sarah turned in surprise. She had assumed that an alien wouldn't drink alcohol. Not that she actually knew much about the aliens, really—she hadn't kept up. The television set, a small black and white, had broken a few months ago, and with Emily only home occasional weekends, Sarah hadn't yet gotten around to getting it repaired. She didn't watch TV.

"Scotch and water is fine," the alien said. He had a deep, slightly hoarse voice. Sarah made herself look at him. Standing with his back to the fire, balancing with what looked like careless ease on both legs and the curving, muscular tail, he wasn't quite as bad as Sarah had expected. The aliens she had seen on the now-dead TV had worn odd-looking, shiny clothes on the top halves of their bodies, nothing below. But this one wore a soft white shirt, no tie, and a tweed jacket cut long enough to cover all but his hairy legs. His head hair, too, didn't look as strange as on the TV aliens; she supposed that a barber must have cut it. It fell thickly from a side part to just over the tops of his ears. Sarah handed him the drink.

"Didn't know you folks imbibed," Calucci said to the alien. He sat on the sofa, pulling up his pant legs at the knees: preserving the crease. "Didn't see that on TV."

"We just got a new set," Mabel Calucci said. "Sony. Hundred-inch screen, remotes, stereo, everything."

"Have to have you all to our big Superbowl party in January," Calucci said. "C'Lanth, your folks like football?"

"No," C'Lanth said. Calucci waited, but the alien said no more, sipping his drink and smiling faintly. Sarah smothered a grin.

"Probably not your native pastime," Calucci said. "Stands to reason. What sports do you guys like? Earth sports, I mean. When in Rome, I always say."

"I like tennis."

"Tennis?" George said, looking surprised.

C'Lanth smiled. "Yes. I'm afraid I've become something of a fanatic. But I'm also afraid I have an unfair advantage—something about the joints of our thumbs. Do you play?"

"Not as much as I used to," George said ruefully.

"Mrs. Atkinson?"

"Yes," Sarah said, wondering where C'Lanth had learned such good English. But didn't she remember something in the papers about the aliens being natural mimics as well as shrewd businessmen? And about their avidly studying just everything? "I play, but not very seriously, I'm afraid. I prefer sailing."

"Buddy and I bowled in a league," Mabel Calucci said. Her plump rouged face clouded over. "In St. Pete, I mean. Before we moved to New York. Now—I don't know."

"Are there bowling alleys in this cute little country town of yours, George?" Calucci asked.

"I'm afraid I wouldn't know."

There was a slight pause. Then Calucci and the alien spoke simultaneously: "Well, now, let's get down to business!" and "I met a friend of yours, Mrs. Atkinson, at an art gallery board meeting Tuesday. Louise Henderson."

George said to Calucci, "Oh, I rather think later might be better, Buddy."

Sarah said to C'Lanth, "You were at the gallery board meeting?"

"Not as a member, of course. Kyle Van Dorr was just showing me around. A tourist." He smiled; Sarah would have sworn it was a self-deprecating smile.

"When do we get down to business then?" Calucci said. His big body shifted restlessly. When he lowered his head like that, Sarah thought, it was the exact shape of a garden trowel. "We have to act fast on this one, George, if we're going to have any kind of alliance here. Before your pals—" he nodded at C'Lanth "—have their little rule-making meeting on mergers."

"We believe in competition," C'Lanth said mildly. He finished his drink and held out the glass, mouthing *Please*? George made him another Scotch and water. In front of the fireplace Brandy stretched, turned in a circle, and farted. Mabel Calucci looked delicately away, mouth pursed; C'Lanth smiled. Sarah found herself smiling back. What kind of nitwit acted so affected as to be offended by a dog? Denise came to the door and announced dinner.

Sarah ate little. She watched. C'Lanth also ate sparingly, but he tried everything. Mabel Calucci, in the presence of food, turned garrulous;

each course seemed to swell her verbally, words coming out at the same rate that calories went in. She talked about her little grandson— "Cute as a button, and smart as a whip! He can already tell a Caddy from a Buick;" about the redecoration of her kitchen in apple-blossom pink; about a woman on a game show who had won $100,000, had a heart attack, and had to sell the prizes to pay her medical bills; about the street they used to live on in St. Pete when Buddy and her were first married, where people were so friendly they didn't even knock on each other's doors before visiting. Not like here, where you couldn't even see the houses from the street. Not that that was true in New York, of course, where they had their new penthouse, with the cutest terrace you ever saw, twelve stories up and just filled with fresh flowers. Buddy Calucci let his wife talk, his eyes appraising the room's furniture, pictures, wallpaper, silver. George, good host that he always was, listened to Mabel Calucci, nodding and smiling.

The five of them had just returned to the living room when Emily came in with her boyfriend, the Walker boy, both of them in jeans and sweaters, laughing. Emily's dark hair had escaped its barrette and fallen around her face, thick and shining. She showed no reaction to finding an alien in her parents' living room beyond a friendly smile. Sarah felt her heart swell. Her daughter was beautiful, and smart, and mannerly. She was very lucky in Emily. Some of her friends' daughters had turned just impossible, but Emily was wonderful. George made the introductions.

"Enjoying Princeton, Taylor?"

"It's wicked, sir. Especially calculus." Taylor Walker smiled, an attractive easy flash of teeth. "No head for figures, I'm afraid. Professor Boyden is just out of control."

"Hughes Boyden?" C'Lanth asked.

"Yes, sir," Taylor said. "Do you know him?"

"Slightly. I did a lot of reading at Princeton when I first came here. Some of the professors were very helpful. In fact, I was up to Princeton this year for Bicker and Sign-ins."

Taylor and Emily grinned at each other: some private joke. Emily said, "Totally paralytic. I didn't get to bed until 7 a.m."

Mabel Calucci looked at her. Her voice went slightly shrill. "I was always glad that my daughter Tammy had the chance to attend Bob Jones University. The moral standards there are very high."

Fury rose in Sarah. The sheer smug stupidity...Emily, who was Dean's List and honor committee...this horrible stupid woman...

But all she said was, "Can I get anyone a drink? Taylor? Emily?"

"No, thanks, we're off," Taylor said. "We'll be at the club, Mrs. Atkinson. Nice to have met you, Mr. C'Lanth."

"Pleased, I'm sure," Mabel Calucci said coldly. Taylor and Emily left.

"I liked the young people Hughes Boyden introduced me to at Princeton," C'Lanth said, almost musingly. "There was about them a sort of...playful ease."

Calucci said brusquely, "Not supposed to be easy, is it? Toney school like that. Probably has real high admission standards. Now, George, I really think we got to get down to business. I'm sure the ladies will excuse us."

Sarah looked at Mabel Calucci. She saw that the woman was staring at Brandy, now curled in the wing chair on top of the *Forbes* and *Smithsonians*, half of which had tumbled to the floor. Sarah knew what Mabel thought of that. She knew that Mabel was surreptitiously tugging at her red satin neckline, which had slipped even lower. She even knew that in a moment Mabel would say something conciliatory, bright and sweet and cheerful, from lips still pursed like lemons.

"I'll come and listen," Sarah said.

George looked relieved. Calucci looked annoyed. C'Lanth smiled. "Glad to have you," the alien said.

When George came back from the short drive to the station, Sarah was already in bed. She sat up against the pillows and watched George undress. George said nothing until he had flung his coat on a chair, loosened his tie, kicked off his shoes. Finally it burst out.

"That C'Lanth is a cut-throat."

"Oh, I don't know, I thought he was rather amusing."

"Amusing?"

"I thought of seeing if he'd come down the weekend of the third, when we have the Talcotts and the Hendersons."

George turned slowly towards her.

"You know how John Talcott is always complaining that no one he meets can ever give him a really good tennis game. And Louise so enjoys talking to people who actually know something about art. Really, George. don't look at me like that—it's not such a bizarre idea."

"Sarah—he's an *alien*. And you heard how the business talk went, the part of it you stayed for anyway—where the devil did you go? Mabel

Calucci complained in the car that you never came back to the living room. C'Lanth is going to ruin me if we don't get this deal moving."

"Well, wouldn't a chance to get to know him better help that?" Sarah said reasonably. George went on staring at her; after a moment she looked away. He was a dear, but he got so worked up. Unnecessarily, really. After all, they had her money, which was much more than the firm brought in. And when George wrinkled his face like that, he did look like the hardware store man.

"It would be more useful to get to know Buddy Calucci better," George said heavily. "He's the one holding the real clout here. Although C'Lanth might—"

"Oh, really, darling, do come to bed. It's late, and I don't want to argue. You haven't signed any papers yet, after all. Anything could happen."

George didn't answer. He finished undressing, climbed into bed, turned out the light. Sarah waited. When a few minutes had passed, she said softly, "You might be a little nicer to me, George. I did just spend an evening for you with those two dreadful people."

"I know," George said. She felt him reach for her in the darkness, and she put her head on his shoulder.

"I'm sorry I didn't go back to the living room, darling. Truly I am. But her smugness. And that inane chatter. And those little frizzy dyed curls. And him—that eager, hard-eyed grin."

"I know," George said again.

"I did try."

"Yes, you did."

"And you'll think about having C'Lanth down on the third?"

"Might be a good idea," George said sleepily.

Sarah snuggled in closer against his shoulder. She was glad George thought she had tried, glad he wasn't angry. Because of course the truth was that she *had* been rude to those terrible Caluccis, rude with a sort of reverse-English rudeness of not having been polite enough, not having picked up the cues, not having tried at all to enter into their territory. But, really, with some people you just couldn't, and it was no good pretending. Everybody knew that, really. With some people, do what you might, the gap was just too wide.

Afterword to "People Like Us"

This is an early story, written in 1988, that I still like (not true of all my earlier stories. Or of later ones.) Social class is a touchy subject in America, which is supposed to be a democracy. In addition, class is hard to define, since it's a mixture of wealth, education, taste, and family connections, all of which no two people see in the same way. I have met people who immediately decided I was not in the same social class as they were, and they were probably right. This doesn't bother me, but it does interest me. Can gaps in background be made irrelevant in the name of friendship?

Sometimes, if both people have in common some interest important to both (science fiction, chess, sports, books, history). Often, however, one person will decide that "the gap is too wide," and it is not always the person of a "higher" social class.

The alien in this story, unlike aliens in some of my other work, is neither plausible nor well-developed. I've made no attempt to provide him with a home planet or credible biology. As in "Out of All Them Bright Stars," C'lanth is alien used purely as metaphor, which seems to me an acceptable subgenre of SF. Not everyone would agree. Science fiction, too, has its social classes.

EVOLUTION

"Somebody shot and killed Dr. Bennett behind the Food Mart on April Street!" Ceci Moore says breathlessly as I take the washing off the line.

I stand with a pair of Jack's boxer shorts in my hand and stare at her. I don't like Ceci. Her smirking pushiness, her need to shove her scrawny body into the middle of every situation, even ones she'd be better off leaving alone. She's been that way since high school. But we're neighbors; we're stuck with each other. Dr. Bennett delivered both Sean and Jackie. Slowly I fold the boxer shorts and lay them in my clothesbasket.

"Well, Betty, aren't you even going to *say* anything?"

"Have the police arrested anybody?"

"Janie Brunelli says there's no suspects." Tom Brunelli is one of Emerton's police officers, all five of them. He has trouble keeping his mouth shut. "Honestly, Betty, you look like there's a murder in this town every day!"

"Was it in the parking lot?" I'm in that parking lot behind the Food Mart every week. It's unpaved, just hard-packed rocky dirt sloping down to a low concrete wall by the river. I take Jackie's sheets off the line. Belle, Ariel, and Princess Jasmine all smile through fields of flowers.

"Yes, in the parking lot," Ceci says. "Near the dumpsters. There must have been a silencer on the rifle, nobody heard anything. Tom found two .22 250 semi-automatic cartridges." Ceci knows about guns. Her house is full of them. "Betty, why don't you put all this wash in your dryer and save yourself the trouble of hanging it all out?"

"I like the way it smells line-dried. And I can hear Jackie through the window."

Instantly Ceci's face changes. "Jackie's home from school? Why?"

"She has a cold."

"Are you sure it's just a cold?"

"I'm sure." I take the clothespins off Sean's t-shirt. The front says SEE DICK DRINK. SEE DICK DRIVE. SEE DICK DIE. "Ceci, Jackie is not on any antibiotics."

"Good thing," Ceci says, and for a moment she studies her fingernails, very casual. "They say Dr. Bennett prescribed endozine again last week. For the youngest Nordstrum boy. *Without* sending him to the hospital."

I don't answer. The back of Sean's t-shirt says DON'T BE A DICK. Irritated by my silence, Ceci says, "I don't see how you can let your son wear that obscene clothing!"

"It's his choice. Besides, Ceci, it's a health message. About not drinking and driving. Aren't you the one that thinks strong health messages are a good thing?"

Our eyes lock. The silence lengthens. Finally Ceci says, "Well, haven't *we* gotten serious all of a sudden."

I say, "Murder is serious."

"Yes. I'm sure the cops will catch whoever did it. Probably one of those scum that hang around the Rainbow Bar."

"Dr. Bennett wasn't the type to hang around with scum."

"Oh, I don't mean he *knew* them. Some low-life probably killed him for his wallet." She looks straight into my eyes. "I can't think of any other motive. Can you?"

I look east, toward the river. On the other side, just visible over the tops of houses on its little hill, rise the three stories of Emerton Soldiers and Sailors Memorial Hospital. The bridge over the river was blown up three weeks ago. No injuries, no suspects. Now anybody who wants to go to the hospital has to drive ten miles up West River Road and cross at the interstate. Jack told me that the Department of Transportation says two years to get a new bridge built.

I say, "Dr. Bennett was a good doctor. And a good man."

"Well, did anybody say he wasn't? Really, Betty, you should use your dryer and save yourself all that bending and stooping. Bad for the back. We're not getting any younger. Ta-ta." She waves her right hand, just a waggle of fingers, and walks off. Her nails, I notice, are painted the delicate fragile pinky white of freshly unscabbed skin.

"You have no proof," Jack says. "Just some wild suspicions."

He has his stubborn face on. He sits with his Michelob at the kitchen table, dog-tired from his factory shift plus three hours overtime, and he doesn't want to hear this. I don't blame him. I don't want to be saying it. In the living room Jackie plays Nintendo frantically, trying to cram in as many electronic explosions as she can before her father claims the TV for Monday night football. Sean has already gone out with his friends, before his stepfather got home.

I sit down across from Jack, a fresh mug of coffee cradled between my palms. For warmth. "I know I don't have any proof, Jack. I'm not some detective."

"So let the cops handle it. It's their business, not ours. You stay out of it."

"I am out of it. You know that." Jack nods. We don't mix with cops, don't serve on any town committees, don't even listen to the news much. We don't get involved with what doesn't concern us. Jack never did. I add, "I'm just telling you what I think. I can do that, can't I?" and hear my voice stuck someplace between pleading and anger.

Jack hears it, too. He scowls, stands with his beer, puts his hand gently on my shoulder. "Sure, Bets. You can say whatever you want to me. But nobody else, you hear? I don't want no trouble, especially to you and the kids. This ain't our problem. Just be grateful *we're* all healthy, knock on wood."

He smiles and goes into the living room. Jackie switches off the Nintendo without being yelled at; she's good that way. I look out the kitchen window, but it's too dark to see anything but my own reflection, and anyway the window faces north, not east.

I haven't crossed the river since Jackie was born at Emerton Memorial, seven years ago. And then I was in the hospital less than twenty-four hours before I made Jack take me home. Not because of the infections, of course—that hadn't all started yet. But it has now, and what if next time instead of the youngest Nordstrum boy, it's Jackie who needs endozine? Or Sean?

Once you've been to Emerton Memorial, nobody but your family will go near you. And sometimes not even them. When Mrs. Weimer came home from surgery, her daughter-in-law put her in that back upstairs room and left her food on disposable trays in the doorway and put in a chemical toilet. Didn't even help the old lady crawl out of bed to use it. For a whole month it went on like that—surgical masks, gloves, paper gowns—until Rosie Weimer was positive Mrs. Weimer hadn't picked up any mutated drug-resistant bacteria in Emerton Memorial. And Hal Weimer didn't say a word against his wife.

"People are scared, but they'll do the right thing," Jack said, the only other time I tried to talk to him about it. Jack isn't much for talking. And so I don't. I owe him that.

But in the city—in all the cities—they're not just scared. They're terrified. Even without listening to the news I hear about the riots and the special government police and half the population sick with the new germs that only endozine cures—sometimes. I don't see how they're going to have much energy for one murdered small-town doctor. And I don't share Jack's conviction that people in Emerton will automatically do the right thing. I remember all too well that sometimes they don't. How come Jack doesn't remember, too?

But he's right about one thing: I don't owe this town anything.

I stack the supper dishes in the sink and get Jackie started on her homework.

The next day, I drive down to the Food Mart parking lot.

There isn't much to see. It rained last night. Next to the dumpster lie a wadded-up surgical glove and a piece of yellow tape like the police use around a crime scene. Also some of those little black cardboard boxes from the stuff that gets used up by the new holographic TV cameras. That's it.

"You heard what happened to Dr. Bennett," I say to Sean at dinner. Jack's working again. Jackie sits playing with the Barbie doll she doesn't know I know she has on her lap. Sean looks at me sideways, under the heavy fringe of his dark bangs, and I can't read his expression. "He was killed for giving out too many antibiotics."

Jackie looks up. "Who killed the doctor?"

"The bastards that think they run this town," Sean says. He flicks the hair out of his eyes. His face is ashy gray. "Fucking vigilantes'll get us all."

"That's enough, Sean," I say.

Jackie's lip trembles. "Who'll get us all? Mommy..."

"Nobody's getting anybody," I say. "Sean, stop it. You're scaring her."

"Well, she should be scared," Sean says, but he shuts up and stares bleakly at his plate. Sixteen now, I've had him for sixteen years. Watching him, his thick dark hair and sulky mouth, I think that it's a sin to have a favorite child. And that I can't help it, and that I would, God forgive me, sacrifice both Jackie and Jack for this boy.

"I want you to clean the garage tonight, Sean. You promised Jack three days ago now."

"Tomorrow. Tonight I have to go out."

Jackie says, "Why should I be scared?"

"Tonight," I say.

Sean looks at me with teenage desperation. His eyes are very blue. "Not tonight. I have to go out."

Jackie says, "Why should I—"

I say, "You're staying home and cleaning the garage."

"No." He glares at me, and then breaks. He has his father's looks, but he's not really like his father. There are even tears in the corners of his eyes. "I'll do it tomorrow, Mom, I promise. Right after school. But tonight I have to go out."

"Where?"

"Just out."

Jackie says, "Why should I be scared? Scared of what? Mommy!"

Sean turns to her. "You shouldn't be scared, Jack-o-lantern. Everything's going to be all right. One way or another."

I listen to the tone of his voice and suddenly fear shoots through me, piercing as childbirth. I say, "Jackie, you can play Nintendo now. I'll clear the table."

Her face brightens. She skips into the living room and I look at my son. "What does that mean? 'One way or another'? Sean, what's going on?"

"Nothing," he says, and then despite his ashy color he looks me straight in the eyes, and smiles tenderly, and for the first time—the very first time—I see his resemblance to his father. He can lie to me with tenderness.

Two days later, just after I return from the Food Mart, they contact me.

The murder was on the news for two nights, and then disappeared. Over the parking lot is scattered more TV-camera litter. There's also a wine bottle buried halfway into the hard ground, with a bouquet of yellow roses in it. Nearby is an empty basket, the kind that comes filled with expensive dried flowers at Blossoms by Bonnie, weighted down with stones. Staring at it, I remember that Bonnie Widelstein went out of business a few months ago. A drug-resistant abscess, and after she got out of Emerton Memorial, nobody on this side of the river would buy flowers from her.

At home, Sylvia James is sitting in my driveway in her black Algol. As soon as I see her, I put it together.

"Sylvia," I say tonelessly.

She climbs out of the sports car and smiles a social smile. "Elizabeth! How good to see you!" I don't answer. She hasn't seen me in seventeen years. She's carrying a cheese kuchen, like some sort of key into my house. She's still blonde, still slim, still well dressed. Her lipstick is bright red, which is what her face should be.

I let her in anyway, my heart making slow hard thuds in my chest. *Sean. Sean.*

Once inside, her hard smile fades and she has the grace to look embarrassed. "Elizabeth—"

"Betty," I say. "I go by Betty now."

"Betty. First off, I want to apologize for not being...for not standing by you in that mess. I know it was so long ago, but even so, I—I wasn't a very good friend." She hesitates. "I was frightened by it all."

I want to say, *You* were frightened? But I don't.

I never think of the whole dumb story any more. Not even when I look at Sean. Especially not when I look at Sean.

Seventeen years ago, when Sylvia and I were seniors in high school, we were best friends. Neither of us had a sister, so we made each other into that, even though her family wasn't crazy about their precious daughter hanging around with someone like me. The Goddards live on the other side of the river. Sylvia ignored them, and I ignored the drunken warnings of my aunt, the closest thing I had to a family. The differences didn't matter. We were Sylvia-and-Elizabeth, the two prettiest and boldest girls in the senior class who had an academic future.

And then, suddenly, I didn't. At Elizabeth's house I met Randolf Satler, young resident in her father's unit at the hospital. And I got pregnant, and Randy dumped me, and I refused a paternity test because if he didn't want me and the baby I had too much pride to force myself on any man. That's what I told everyone, including myself. I was eighteen years old. I didn't know what a common story mine was, or what a dreary one. I thought I was the only one in the whole wide world who had ever felt this bad.

So after Sean was born at Emerton Memorial and Randy got engaged the day I moved my baby "home" to my dying aunt's, I bought a Smith & Wesson revolver in the city and shot out the windows of Randy's supposedly empty house across the river. I hit the gardener, who was helping himself to the Satler liquor cabinet in the living room. The judge gave me seven-and-a-half to ten, and I served five, and that only because my lawyer pleaded post-partum depression. The gardener recovered and retired to Miami, and Dr. Satler went on to become Chief of Medicine at Emerton Memorial and a lot of other important things in the city, and Sylvia never visited me once in Bedford Hills Correctional Facility. Nobody did, except Jack. Who, when Sylvia-and-Elizabeth were strutting their stuff at Emerton High, had already dropped out and was bagging groceries at the Food Mart. After I got out of Bedford, the only reason the foster-care people would give me Sean back was because Jack married me.

We live in Emerton, but not of it.

Sylvia puts her kuchen on the kitchen table and sits down without being asked. I can see she's done with apologizing. She's still smart enough to know there are things you can't apologize for.

"Eliz...Betty, I'm not here about the past. I'm here about Dr. Bennett's murder."

"That doesn't have anything to do with me."

"It has to do with all of us. Dan Moore lives next door to you."

I don't say anything.

"He and Ceci and Jim Dyer and Tom Brunelli are the ringleaders in a secret organization to close Emerton Memorial Hospital. They think the hospital is a breeding ground for the infections resistant to every antibiotic except endozine. Well, they're right about that—all hospitals are. But Dan and his group are determined to punish any doctor who prescribes endozine, so that no organisms develop a resistance to it, too, and it's kept effective in case one of *them* needs it."

"Sylvia—" the name tastes funny in my mouth, after all this time "—I'm telling you this doesn't have anything to do with me."

"And I'm telling you it does. We need you, Eliz...Betty. You live next door to Dan and Ceci. You can tell us when they leave the house, who comes to it, anything suspicious you see. We're not a vigilante group, Betty, like they are. We aren't doing anything illegal. We don't kill people, and we don't blow up bridges, and we don't threaten people like the Nordstrums who get endozine for their sick kids but are basically uneducated blue collar—"

She stops. Jack and I are basically uneducated blue collar. I say coldly, "I can't help you, Sylvia."

"I'm sorry, Betty. That wasn't what I meant. Look, this is more important than anything that happened a decade and a half ago! Don't you *understand*?" She leans toward me across the table. "The whole country's caught in this thing. It's already a public health crisis as big as the Spanish influenza epidemic of 1918, and it's only just started! Drug-resistant bacteria can produce a new generation every twenty minutes, they can swap resistant genes not only within a species but across *different* species. The bacteria are *winning*. And people like the Moores are taking advantage of that to contribute further to the breakdown of even basic social decency."

In high school Sylvia had been on the debating team. But so, in that other life, had I. "If the Moores' group is trying to keep endozine from being used, then aren't they also fighting against the development of more drug-resistant bacteria? And if that's so, aren't they the ones, not you, who are ultimately aiding the country's public health?"

"Through dynamiting. And intimidation. And murder. Betty, I know you don't approve of those things. I wouldn't be here telling you about our countergroup if I thought you did. Before I came here, we looked very carefully at you. At the kind of person you are. Are now. You and your husband are law-abiding people, you vote, you make a contribution to the Orphans of AIDS Fund, you—"

"How did you know about that? That's supposed to be a secret contribution!"

"—you signed the petition to protect the homeless from harassment. Your husband served on the jury that convicted Paul Keene of fraud, even though his real-estate scheme was so good for the economy of Emerton. You—"

"Stop it," I say. "You don't have any right to investigate me like I was some criminal!"

Only, of course, I was. Once. Not now. Sylvia's right about that—Jack and I believe in law and order, but for different reasons. Jack because that's what his father believed in, and his grandfather. Me, because I learned in Bedford that enforced rules are the only thing that even half-way restrains the kind of predators Sylvia James never dreamed of. The kind I want kept away from my children.

Sylvia says, "We have a lot of people on our side, Betty. People who don't want to see this town slide into the same kind of violence there is in Albany and Syracuse and, worst case, New York."

A month ago, New York Hospital in Queens was blown up. The whole thing, with a series of coordinated timed bombs. Seventeen hundred people dead in less than a minute.

"It's a varied group," she continues. "Some town leaders, some housewives, some teachers, nearly all the medical personnel at the hospital. All people who care what happens to Emerton."

"Then you've got the wrong person here," I say, and it comes out harsher than I want to reveal. "I don't care about Emerton."

"You have reasons," Sylvia says evenly. "And I'm part of your reasons, I know. But I think you'll help us, Elizabeth. I know you must be concerned about your son—we've all observed what a good mother you are."

So she brought up Sean's name first. I say, "You're wrong again, Sylvia. I don't need you to protect Sean, and if you've let him get involved in helping you, you'll wish you'd never been born. I've worked damn hard to make sure that what happened seventeen years ago never touches him. He doesn't need to get mixed up in any way with your 'medical personnel at the hospital.' And Sean sure the hell doesn't owe this town anything, there wasn't even anybody who would take him in after my aunt died, he had to go to—"

The look on her face stops me. Pure surprise. And then something else.

"Oh my God," she says. "Is it possible you don't know? Hasn't Sean told you?"

"Told me what?" I stand up, and I'm seventeen years old again, and just that scared. Sylvia-and-Elizabeth.

"Your son isn't helping our side. He's working for Dan Moore and Mike Dyer. They use juveniles because if they're caught, they won't be tried as severely as adults. We think Sean was one of the kids they used to blow up the bridge over the river."

I look first at the high school. Sean isn't there; he hadn't even shown up for homeroom. No one's home at his friend Tom's house, or at Keith's. He isn't at the Billiard Ball or the Emerton Diner or the American Bowl. After that, I run out of places to search.

This doesn't happen in places like Emerton. We have fights at basketball games and grand theft auto and smashed store windows on Halloween and sometimes a drunken tragic car crash on prom night. But not secret terrorists, not counter-terrorist vigilante groups. Not in Emerton.

Not with my son.

I drive to the factory and make them page Jack.

He comes off the line, face creased with sweat and dirt. The air is filled with clanging machinery and grinding drills. I pull him outside the door, where there are benches and picnic tables for workers on break. "Betty! What is it?"

"Sean," I gasp. "He's in danger."

Something shifts behind Jack's eyes. "What kind of danger?"

"Sylvia Goddard came to see me today. Sylvia James. She says Sean is involved with the group that blew up the bridge, the ones who are trying to get Emerton Memorial closed, and...and killed Dr. Bennett."

Jack peels off his bench gloves, taking his time. Finally he looks up at me. "How come that bitch Sylvia Goddard comes to you with this? After all this time?"

"Jack! Is that all you can think of? Sean is in trouble!"

He says gently, "Well, Bets, it was bound to happen sooner or later, wasn't it? He's always been a tough kid to raise. Rebellious. Can't tell him anything."

I stare at Jack.

"Some people just have to learn the hard way."

"Jack...this is serious! Sean might be involved in terrorism! He could end up in jail!"

"Couldn't ever tell him anything," Jack says, and I hear the hidden satisfaction in his voice, that he doesn't even know is there. Not his son. Dr. Randy Satler's son. Turning out bad.

"Look," Jack says, "when the shift ends I'll go look for him, Bets. Bring him home. You go and wait there for us." His face is gentle, soothing. He really will find Sean, if it's possible. But only because he loves me.

My sudden surge of hatred is so strong I can't even speak.

"Go on home, Bets. It'll be all right. Sean just needs to have the nonsense kicked out of him."

I turn and walk away. At the turning in the parking lot, I see Jack walking jauntily back inside, pulling on his gloves.

I drive home, because I can't think what else to do. I sit on the couch and reach back in my mind, for that other place, the place I haven't gone to since I got out of Bedford. The gray granite place that turns you to granite, too, so you can sit and wait for hours, for weeks, for years, without feeling very much. I go into that place, and I become the Elizabeth I was then, when Sean was in foster care someplace and I didn't know who had him or what they might be doing to him or how I would get him back. I go into the gray granite place to become stone.

And it doesn't work.

It's been too long. I've had Sean too long. Jack has made me feel too safe. I can't find the stony place.

Jackie is spending the night at a friend's. I sit in the dark, no lights on, car in the garage. Sean doesn't come home, and neither does Jack. At two in the morning, a lot of people in dark clothing cross the back lawn and quietly enter Dan and Ceci's house next door, carrying bulky packages wrapped in black cloth.

Jack staggers in at six-thirty in the morning. Alone. His face droops with exhaustion.

"I couldn't find him, Betty. I looked everywhere."

"Thank you," I say, and he nods. Accepting my thanks. This was something he did for me, not for Sean. Not for himself, as Sean's stepfather. I push down my sudden anger and say, "You better get some sleep."

"Right." He goes down the narrow hallway into our bedroom. In three minutes he's snoring.

I let the car coast in neutral down the driveway. Our bedroom faces the street. The curtains don't stir.

The West River Road is deserted, except for a few eighteen-wheelers. I cross the river at the interstate and start back along the east side. Three miles along, in the middle of farmland, the smell of burned flesh rolls in the window.

Cows, close to the pasture fence. I stop the car and get out. Fifteen or sixteen Holsteins. By straining over the fence, I can see the bullet holes in their heads. Somebody herded them together, shot them one by one, and started a half-hearted fire among the bodies with neatly cut firewood. The fire had gone out; it didn't look as if it was supposed to burn long. Just long enough to attract attention that hadn't come yet.

I'd never heard that cows could get human diseases. Why had they been shot?

I get back in my car and drive the rest of the way to Emerton Memorial.

This side of town is deathly quiet. Grass grows unmowed in yard after yard. One large, expensive house has old newspapers piled on the porch steps, ten or twelve of them. There are no kids waiting for school buses, no cars pulling out of driveways on the way to work. The hospital parking lot has huge empty stretches between cars. At the last minute I drive on through the lot, parking instead across the street in somebody's empty driveway, under a clump of trees.

Nobody sits at the information desk. The gift shop is locked. Nobody speaks to me as I study the directory on the lobby wall, even though two figures in gowns and masks hurry past. CHIEF OF MEDICINE, DR. RANDOLF SATLER. Third floor, east wing. The elevator is deserted.

It stop at the second floor. When the doors open a man stands there, a middle-aged farmer in overalls and work boots, his eyes red and swollen like he's been crying. There are tinted windows across from the elevators and I can see the back of him reflected in the glass. Coming and going. From somewhere I hear a voice calling, "Nurse, oh nurse, oh God..." A gurney sits in the hallway, the body on it covered by a sheet up to the neck. The man in overalls looks at me and raises both hands to ward off the elevator, like it's some kind of demon. He steps backward. The doors close.

I grip the railing on the elevator wall.

The third floor looks empty. Bright arrows lead along the hallways: yellow for PATHOLOGY AND LAB SERVICES, green for RESPIRATORY THERAPY, red for SUPPORT SERVICES. I follow the yellow arrow.

It dead-ends at an empty alcove with chairs, magazines thrown on the floor. And three locked doors off a short corridor that's little more than an alcove.

I pick the farthest door and pound on it. No words, just regular blows of my fist. After a minute, I start on the second one. A voice calls, "Who's there?"

I recognize the voice, even through the locked door. Even after seventeen years. I shout, "Police! Open the door!"

And he does. The second it cracks, I shove it hard and push my way into the lab.

"Elizabeth?"

He's older, heavier, but still the same. Dark hair, blue eyes...I look at that face every day at dinner. I've looked at it at soccer matches, in school plays, in his playpen. Dr. Satler looks more shaken to see me than I would have thought, his face white, sweat on his forehead.

"Hello, Randy."

"Elizabeth. You can't come in here. You have to leave—"

"Because of the staph? Do you think I care about that? After all, I'm in the hospital, right, Randy? This is where the endozine is. This place is safe. Unless it gets blown up while I'm standing here."

He stares at my left hand, still gripping the doorknob behind me. Then at the gun in my right hand. A seventeen-year-old Smith & Wesson, and for five of those years the gun wasn't cleaned or oiled, hidden under my aunt's garage. But it still fires.

"I'm not going to shoot you, Randy. I don't care if you're alive or dead. But you're going to help me. I can't find my son—" *your son* "—and Sylvia Goddard told me he's mixed up with that group that blew up the bridge. He's hiding with them someplace, probably scared out of his skull. You know everybody in town, everybody with power, you're going to get on that phone there and find out where Sean is."

"I would do that anyway," Randy says, and now he looks the way I remember him: impatient and arrogant. But not completely. There's still sweat on his pale face. "Put that stupid thing away, Elizabeth."

"No."

"Oh, for..." He turns his back on me and punches at the phone.

"Cam? Randy Satler here. Could you...no, it's not about that...No. Not yet."

Cameron Witt. The mayor. His son is chief of Emerton's five cops.

"I need a favor. There's a kid missing...I know that, Cam. You don't have to lecture *me* on how bad delay could...But you might know about this kid. Sean Baker."

"Pulaski. Sean Pulaski." He doesn't even know that.

"Sean Pulaski. Yeah, that one...okay. Get back to me...I told you. *Not yet.*" He hangs up. "Cam will hunt around and call back. Now will you put that stupid gun away, Elizabeth?"

"You still don't say thank you for anything." The words just come out. Fuck, fuck, fuck.

"To Cam, or to you for not shooting me?" He says it evenly, and the evenness is the only way I finally see how furious he is. People don't order around Dr. Randy Satler at gun point. A part of my mind wonders why he doesn't call security.

I said, "All right, I'm here. Give me a dose of endozine, just in case."

He goes on staring at me with that same level, furious gaze. "Too late, Elizabeth."

"What do you mean, too late? Haven't you got endozine?"

"Of course we do." Suddenly he staggers slightly, puts out one hand behind him, and holds onto a table covered with glassware and papers.

"Randy. You're sick."

"I am. And not with anything endozine is going to cure. Ah, Elizabeth, why didn't you just phone me? I'd have looked for Sean for you."

"Oh, right. Like you've been so interested and helpful in raising him."

"You never asked me."

I see that he means it. He really believes his total lack of contact with his son is my fault. I see that Randy gives only what he's asked to. He waits, lordly, for people to plead for his help, beg for it, and then he gives it. If it suits him.

I say, "I'll bet anything your kids with your wife are turning out really scary."

The blood rushes to his face, and I know I guessed right. His blue eyes darken and he looks like Jack looks just before Jack explodes. But Randy isn't Jack. An explosion would be too clean for him. He says instead, "You were stupid to come here. Haven't you been listening to the news?"

I haven't.

"The CDC publicly announced just last night what medical personnel have seen for weeks. A virulent strain of staphylococcus aureus has incorporated endozine-resistant plasmids from enterococcus." He pauses to catch his breath. "And pneumococcus may have done the same thing."

"What does that mean?"

"It means, you stupid woman, that now there are highly contagious infections that we have no drugs to cure. No antibiotics at all, not even endozine. This staph is resistant to them all. And it can live everywhere."

I lower the gun. The empty parking lot. No security to summon. The man who wouldn't get on the elevator. And Randy's face. "And you've got it."

"We've all got it. Everyone...in the hospital. And for forcing your way in here, you probably do, too."

"You're going to die," I say, and it's half a hope.

And he *smiles*.

He stands there in his white lab coat, sweating like a horse, barely able to stand up straight, almost shot by a woman he'd once abandoned pregnant, and he smiles. His blue eyes gleam. He looks like a picture I once saw in a book, back when I read a lot. It takes me a minute to remember that it was my high school World History book. A picture of some general.

"Everybody's going to die eventually," Randy says. "But not me right now. At least...I hope not." Casually he crosses the floor toward me, and I step backward. He smiles again.

"I'm not going to deliberately infect you, Elizabeth. I'm a *doctor*. I just want the gun."

"No."

"Have it your way. Look, how much do you know about the bubonic plague of the fourteenth century?"

"Nothing," I say, although I do. Why had I always acted stupider around Randy than I actually am?

"Then it won't mean anything to you to say that this mutated staph has at least that much potential—" again he pauses and gulps air "—for rapid and fatal transmission. It flourishes everywhere. Even on doorknobs."

"So why the fuck are you *smiling*?" Alexander. That was the picture of the general. Alexander the Great.

"Because I...because the CDC distributed...I was on the national team to discover..." His face changes again. Goes even whiter. And he pitches over onto the floor.

I grab him, roll him face up, and feel his forehead. He's burning up. I bolt for the door. "Nurse! Doctor! There's a sick doctor here!"

Nobody comes.

I run down the corridors. Respiratory Therapy is empty. So is Support Services. I jab at the elevator button, but before it comes I run back to Randy.

And stand above him, lying there crumpled on the floor, laboring to breathe.

I'd dreamed about a moment like this for years. Dreamed it waking and asleep, in Emerton and in Bedford Hills and in Jack's arms. Dreamed it in a thousand ridiculous melodramatic versions. And here it is, Randy helpless and pleading, and me strong, standing over him, free to walk away and let him die. Free.

I wring out a towel in cold water and put it on his forehead. Then I find ice in the refrigerator in a corner of the lab and substitute that. He watches me, his breathing wheezy as old machinery.

"Elizabeth. Bring me...syringe in a box on...that table."

I do it. "Who should I get for you, Randy? Where?"

"Nobody. I'm not...as bad...as I sound. Yet. Just the initial...dyspnea." He picks up the syringe.

"Is there medicine for you in there? I thought you said endozine wouldn't work on this new infection." His color is a little better now.

"Not medicine. And not for me. For you."

He looks at me steadily. And I see that Randy would never plead, never admit to helplessness. Never ever think of himself as helpless.

He lowers the hand holding the syringe back to the floor. "Listen, Elizabeth. You have...almost certainly have..."

Somewhere, distantly, a siren starts to wail. Randy ignores it. All of a sudden his voice becomes much firmer, even though he's sweating again and his eyes burn bright with fever. Or something.

"This staph is resistant to everything we can throw it. We cultured it and tried. Cephalosporins and aminoglycosides and vancomycin, even endozine...I'll go into gram-positive septic shock..." His eyes glaze, but after a moment he seems to find his thought again. "We exhausted all points of counterattack. Cell wall, bacterial ribosome, folic acid pathway. Microbes just evolve countermeasures. Like beta-lactamase."

I don't understand this language. Even talking to himself, he's making me feel stupid again. I ask something I do understand.

"Why are people killing cows? Are the cows sick, too?"

He focuses again. "Cows? No, they're not sick. Farmers use massive doses of antibiotics to increase meat and milk production. Agricultural use of endozine has increased the rate of resistance development by over a thousand percent since—Elizabeth, this is irrelevant! Can't you pay attention to what I'm saying for three minutes?"

I stand up and look down at him, lying shivering on the floor. He doesn't even seem to notice, just keeps on lecturing.

"But antibiotics weren't invented by humans. They were invented by the microbes themselves to use...against each other and...they had two billion years of evolution at it before we even showed up...We should have—where are you going?"

"Home. Have a nice life, Randy."

He says quietly, "I probably will. But if...you leave now, you're probably dead. And your husband and kids, too."

"Why? Damn it, stop lecturing and tell me why!"

"Because you're infected, and there's no antibiotic for it, but there *is* another bacteria that will attack the drug-resistant staph."

I look at the syringe in his hand.

"It's a Trojan horse plasmid. That's a...never mind. It can get into the staph in your blood and deliver a lethal gene. One that will kill the staph. It's an incredible discovery. But the only way to deliver it so far is to deliver the whole bacteria."

My knees all of a sudden get shaky. Randy watches me from his position on the floor. He looks shakier himself. His breathing turns raspier again.

"No, you're not sick yet, Elizabeth. But you will be."

I snap, "From the staph germs or from the cure?"

"Both."

"You want to make me sicker. With two bacteria. And hope one will kill the other."

"Not hope. I *know.* I actually saw...it on the electromicrograph..." His eyes roll, refocus. "...could package just the lethal plasmid on a transpon if we had time...no time. Has to be the whole bacteria." And then, stronger, "The CDC team is working on it. But *I* actually caught it on the electromicrograph!"

I say, before I know I'm going to, "Stop congratulating yourself and give me the syringe. Before you die."

I move across the floor toward him, put my arms around him to prop him in a sitting position against the table leg. His whole body feels on fire. But somehow he keeps his hands steady as he injects the syringe into the inside of my elbow. While it drains sickness into me I say, "You never actually wanted me, did you, Randy? Even before Sean?"

"No," he says. "Not really." He drops the syringe.

I bend my arm. "You're a rotten human being. All you care about is yourself and your work."

He smiles the same cold smile. "So? My work is what matters. In a larger sense than you could possibly imagine. You were always a weak sentimentalist, Elizabeth. Now, go home."

"Go *home*? But you said..."

"I said you'd infect everyone. And you will—with the bacteria that attacks staph. It should cause only a fairly mild illness. Jenner...smallpox..."

"But you said I have the mutated staph, too!"

"You almost certainly do. Yes...And so will everyone else, before long. Deaths...in New York State alone...passed one million this morning. Six and a half percent of the...the population...Did you really think you could hide on your side of...the...river..."

"Randy!"

"Go...home."

I strip off his lab coat and wad it up for a pillow, bring more ice from the refrigerator, try to get him to drink some water.

"Go...home. Kiss everybody." He smiles to himself, and starts to shake with fever. His eyes close.

I stand up again. Should I go? Stay? If I could find someone in the hospital to take care of him —

The phone rings. I seize it. "Hello? Hello?"

"Randy? Excuse me, can I talk to Dr. Satler? This is Cameron Witt."

I try to sound professional. "Dr. Satler can't come to the phone right now. But if you're calling about Sean Pulaski, Dr. Satler asked me to take the message."

"I don't…oh, all right. Just tell Randy the Pulaski boy is with Richard and Sylvia James. He'll understand." The line clicks.

I replace the receiver and stare at Randy, fighting for breath on the floor, his face as gray as Sean's when Sean realized it was murder he'd gotten involved with. No, not as gray. Because Sean had been terrified, and Randy is only sick.

My work is what matters.

But how had Sean known to go to Sylvia? Even if he knew from Ceci who was on the other side, how did he know which people would hide him, would protect him when I could not, Jack could not? Sylvia-and-Elizabeth. How much did Sean actually know about the past I'd tried so hard to keep from touching him?

I reach the elevator, my finger almost touching the button, when the first explosion rocks the hospital.

It's in the west wing. Through the windows opposite the elevator banks I see windows in the far end of the building explode outward. Thick greasy black smoke billows out the holes. Alarms begin to screech.

Don't touch the elevators. Instructions remembered from high school, from grade-school fire drills. I race along the hall to the fire stairs. What if they put a bomb in the stairwell? What if *who* put a bomb in the stairwell? *A lot of people in dark clothing cross the back lawn and quietly enter Dan and Ceci's house next door, carrying bulky packages wrapped in black cloth.*

A last glimpse through a window by the door to the fire stairs. People are running out of the building, not many, but the ones I see are pushing gurneys. A nurse staggers outside, three small children in her arms, on her hip, clinging to her back.

They aren't setting off any more bombs until people have a chance to get out.

I let the fire door close. Alarms scream. I run back to Pathology and shove open the heavy door.

Randy lies on the floor, sweating and shivering. His lips move but if he's muttering aloud, I can't hear it over the alarm. I tug on his arm. He doesn't resist and he doesn't help, just lies like a heavy dead cow.

There are no gurneys in Pathology. I slap him across the face, yelling "Randy! Randy! Get up!" Even now, even here, a small part of my mind thrills at hitting him.

His eyes open. For a second, I think he knows me. It goes away, then returns. He tries to get up. The effort is enough to let me hoist him over my shoulder in a fireman's carry. I could never have carried Jack, but Randy is much slighter, and I'm very strong.

But I can't carry him down three flights of stairs. I get him to the top, prop him up on his ass, and shove. He slides down one flight, bumping and flailing, and glares at me for a minute. "For...God's sake...Janet!"

His wife's name. I don't think about this tiny glimpse of his marriage. I give him another shove, but he grabs the railing and refuses to fall. He hauls himself—I'll never know how—back to a sitting position, and I sit next to him. Together, my arm around his waist, tugging and pulling, we both descend the stairs the way two-year-olds do, on our asses. Every second I'm waiting for the stairwell to blow up. Sean's gray face at dinner: *Fucking vigilantes'll get us all.*

The stairs don't blow up. The fire door at the bottom gives out on a sidewalk on the side of the hospital away from both street and parking lot. As soon as we're outside, Randy blacks out.

This time I do what I should have done upstairs and grab him under the armpits. I drag him over the grass as far as I can. Sweat and hair fall in my eyes, and my vision keeps blurring. Dimly I'm aware of someone running toward us.

"It's Dr. Satler! Oh my God!"

A man. A large man. He grabs Randy and hoists him over his shoulder, a fireman's carry a lot smoother than mine, barely glancing at me. I stay behind them and, at the first buildings, run in a wide loop away from the hospital.

My car is still in the deserted driveway across the street. Fire trucks add their sirens to the noise. When they've torn past, I back my car out of the driveway and push my foot to the floor, just as a second bomb blows in the east wing of the hospital, and then another, and the air is full of flying debris as thick and sharp as the noise that goes on and on and on.

Three miles along the East River Road, it suddenly catches up with me. All of it. I pull the car off the road and I can't stop shaking. Only a few trucks pass me, and nobody stops. It's twenty minutes before I can start the engine again, and there has never been a twenty minutes like them in my life, not even in Bedford. At the end of them, I pray that there never will be again.

I turn on the radio as soon as I've started the engine.

"—in another hospital bombing in New York City, St. Clare's Hospital in the heart of Manhattan. Beleaguered police officials say that a shortage of available officers make impossible the kind of protection called for by Mayor Thomas Flanagan. No group has claimed credit for the bombing, which caused fires that spread to nearby businesses and at least one apartment house.

"Since the Centers for Disease Control's announcement last night of a widespread staphylococcus resistant to endozine, and its simultaneous release of an emergency counterbacteria in twenty-five metropolitan areas around the country, the violence has worsened in every city transmitting reliable reports to Atlanta. A spokesperson for the national team of pathologists and scientists responsible for the drastic countermeasure released an additional set of guidelines for its use. The spokesperson declined to be identified, or to identify any of the doctors on the team, citing fear of reprisals if—"

A burst of static. The voice disappears, replaced by a shrill hum.

I turn the dial carefully, looking for another station with news.

By the time I reach the west side of Emerton, the streets are deserted. Everyone has retreated inside. It looks like the neighborhoods around the hospital look. Had looked. My body still doesn't feel sick.

Instead of going straight home, I drive the deserted streets to the Food Mart.

The parking lot is as empty as everywhere else. But the basket is still there, weighted with stones. Now the stones hold down a pile of letters. The top one is addressed in blue Magic Marker: TO DR. BENNETT. The half-buried wine bottle holds a fresh bouquet, chrysanthemums from somebody's garden. Nearby a foot-high American flag sticks in the ground, beside a white candle on a Styrofoam plate, a stone crucifix, and a Barbie doll dressed like an angel. Saran Wrap covers a leather-bound copy of *The Prophet*. There are also five anti-NRA stickers, a pile of seashells, and a battered peace sign on a gold chain like a necklace. The peace sign looks older than I am.

When I get home, Jack is still asleep.

I stand over him, as a few hours ago I stood over Randy Satler. I think about how Jack visited me in prison, week after week, making the long drive from Emerton even in the bad winter weather. About how he'd sit smiling at me through the thick glass in the visitors' room, his hands with their grease-stained fingers resting on his knees, smiling even when we couldn't think of anything to say to each other. About how he clutched my hand in the delivery room when Jackie was born, and the look on his face when he first held her. About the look on his face when I told him Sean was missing: the sly, secret, not-my-kid triumph. And I think about the two sets of germs in my body, readying for war.

I bend over and kiss Jack full on the lips.

He stirs a little, half wakes, reaches for me. I pull away and go into the bathroom, where I use his toothbrush. I don't rinse it. When I return, he's asleep again.

I drive to Jackie's school, to retrieve my daughter. Together, we will go to Sylvia Goddard's—Sylvia James's—and get Sean. I'll visit with Sylvia, and shake her hand, and kiss her on the cheek, and touch everything I can. When the kids are safe at home, I'll visit Ceci and tell her I've thought it over and I want to help fight the overuse of antibiotics that's killing us. I'll touch her, and anyone else there, and everyone that either Sylvia or Ceci introduces me to, until I get too sick to do that. If I get that sick. Randy said I wouldn't, not as sick as he is. Of course, Randy has lied to me before. But I have to believe him now, on this.

I don't really have any choice. Yet.

A month later, I am on my way to Albany to bring back another dose of the counterbacteria, which the news calls "a reengineered prokaryote." They're careful not to call it a germ.

I listen to the news every hour now, although Jack doesn't like it. Or anything else I'm doing. I read, and I study, and now I know what prokaryotes are, and beta-lactamase, and plasmids. I know how bacteria fight to survive, evolving whatever they need to wipe out the competition and go on producing the next generation. That's all that matters to bacteria. Survival of their own kind.

And that's what Randy Satler meant, too, when he said, "My work is what matters." Triumph of his own kind. It's what Ceci believes, too. And Jack.

We bring in the reengineered prokaryotes in convoys of cars and trucks, because in some other places there's been trouble. People who don't understand, people who won't understand. People whose family got a lot sicker than mine. The violence isn't over, even though the CDC says the epidemic itself is starting to come under control.

I'm early. The convoy hasn't formed yet. We leave from a different place in town each time. This time we're meeting behind the American Bowl. Sean is already there, with Sylvia. I take a short detour and drive, for the last time, to the Food Mart.

The basket is gone, with all its letters to the dead man. So are the American flag and the peace sign. The crucifix is still there, but it's broken in half. The latest flowers in the wine bottle are half wilted. Rain has muddied the Barbie doll's dress, and her long blonde hair is a mess. Someone ripped up the anti-NRA stickers. The white candle on a Styrofoam plate and the pile of seashells are untouched.

We are not bacteria. More than survival matters to us, or should. The individual past, which we can't escape, no matter how hard we try. The individual present, with its unsafe choices. The individual future. And the collective one.

I search in my pockets. Nothing but keys, money clip, lipstick, tissues, a blue marble I must have stuck in my pocket when I cleaned behind the couch. Jackie likes marbles.

I put the marble beside the candle, check my gun, and drive to join the convoy for the city.

Afterword to "Evolution"

I wrote this story in 1994. In the twenty years since, the situation it describes has only become more acute. More diseases have become drug-resistant; fewer antibiotics are still effective; hospital-caused infections have risen. Epidemiologists say we are overdue for a major pandemic.

In the past, technological problems have often been cured by technology. In the early 1900's, for example, New York City's major problem was horse manure. It clogged every street, increasing at an alarming rate, and experts prophesied that soon the city would be unlivable. Within a few decades, however, the manure disappeared as horses were replaced with cars—bringing their own problems. And so it goes on. Will drug-resistant diseases be vanquished by some new technological breakthrough? No one knows. We do know, however, that this technological pyramid scheme may not continue forever. And then what?

Science fiction is not prediction of the future; it is rehearsal for possible futures. Perhaps the events of "Evolution" will not happen.

Perhaps.

MARGIN OF ERROR

Paula came back in a blaze of glory, her Institute uniform with its pseudo-military medals crisp and bright, her spine straight as an engineered diamond-fiber rod. I heard her heels clicking on the sidewalk and I looked up from the bottom porch step, a child on my lap. Paula's face was genemod now, the blemishes gone, the skin fine-pored, the cheekbones chiseled under green eyes. But I would have known that face anywhere. No matter what she did to it.

"Karen?" Her voice held disbelief.

"Paula," I said.

"Karen?" This time I didn't answer. The child, my oldest, twisted in my arms to eye the visitor. The slight movement made the porch step creak.

It was the kind of neighborhood where women sat all morning on porches or stoops, watching children play on the sidewalk. Steps sagged; paint peeled; small front lawns were scraped bare by feet and tricycles and plastic wading pools. Women lived a few doors down from their mothers, both of them growing heavier every year. There were few men. The ones there were, didn't seem to stay long.

I said, "How did you find me?"

"It wasn't hard," Paula said, and I knew she didn't understand my smile. Of course it wasn't hard. I had never intended it should be. This was undoubtedly the first time in nearly five years that Paula had looked.

She lowered her perfect body gingerly onto the porch steps. My little girl, Lollie, gazed at her from my lap. Then Lollie opened her cupped hands and smiled. "See my frog, lady?"

"Very nice," Paula said. She was trying hard to hide her contempt, but I could see it. For the sad imprisoned frog, for Lollie's dirty face, for the worn yard, for the way I looked.

"Karen," Paula said, "I'm here because there's a problem. With the project. More specifically, with the initial formulas, we think. With a portion of the nanoassembler code from five years ago, when you were...still with us."

"A problem," I repeated. Inside the house, a baby wailed. "Just a minute."

I set Lollie down and went inside. Lori cried in her crib. Her diaper reeked. I put a pacifier in her mouth and cradled her in my left arm. With my right arm I scooped Timmy from his crib. When he didn't wake, I jostled him a little. I carried both babies back to the porch, deposited Timmy in the portacrib, and sat down next to Paula.

"Lollie, go get me a diaper, honey. And wipes. You can carry your frog inside to get them."

Lollie went; she's a sweet-natured kid. Paula stared incredulously at the twins. I unwrapped Lori's diaper and Paula grimaced and slid farther away.

"Karen—are you listening to me? This is important!"

"I'm listening."

"The nanocomputer instructions are off, somehow. The major results check out, obviously—" Obviously, yes. The media had spent five years exclaiming over the major results. "—but there are some odd foldings in the proteins of the twelfth-generation nano-assemblers."

Twelfth generation. The nanocomputer attached to each assembler replicates itself every six months. That was one of the project's checks and balances on the margin of error. It had been five and a half years. Twelfth generation was about right.

"Also," Paula continued, and I heard the strain in her voice, "there are some unforeseen macro-level developments. We're not sure yet that they're tied to the nanocomputer protein folds. There might not be any connection. What we're trying to do now is cover all the variables."

"You must be working on fairly remote variables if you're reduced to asking me."

"Well, yes, we are. Karen, do you have to do that now?"

"Yes." I scraped the shit off Lori with one edge of the soiled diaper. Lollie danced out of the house with a clean one. She sat beside me, whispering to her frog.

Paula said, "What I need...what the project needs—"

I said, "Do you remember the summer we collected frogs? We were maybe eight and ten. You'd become fascinated reading about that experiment where they threw a frog in boiling water but it jumped out, and then they put a frog in cool water and gradually increased the temperature to boiling until the stupid frog just sat there and died. Remember?"

"Karen—"

"I collected sixteen frogs for you, and when I found out what you were going to do with them, I cried and tried to let them go. But you boiled eight of them anyway. The other eight were controls. I'll give you that—proper scientific method. To reduce the margin of error, you said."

"Karen—we were just kids..."

I put the clean diaper on Lori. "Not all kids behave like that. Lollie doesn't. But you wouldn't know that, would you? Nobody in your set has children. You should have had a baby, Paula."

She barely hid her shudder. But, then, most of the people we knew felt the same way.

She said, "What the project needs is for you to come back and work on the same small area you did originally. Looking for something—anything—you might have missed in the protein-coded instructions to successive generations of nanoassemblers."

"No," I said.

"It's not really a matter of choice. The macro-level problems—I'll be frank, Karen. It looks like a new form of cancer, one nobody's ever seen. Unregulated replication of some very weird cells."

"So take the cellular nanomachinery out." I crumpled the stinking diaper and set it out of the baby's reach. Closer to Paula.

"You know we can't do that! The project's irreversible!"

"Many things are irreversible," I said. Lori started to fuss. I picked her up, opened my blouse, and gave her the breast. She sucked greedily. Paula glanced away. She has had nanomachinery in her perfect body, making it perfect, for five years now. Her breasts will never look swollen, blue-veined, sagging.

"Karen, listen—"

"No—you listen," I said quietly. "Eight years ago you convinced Zweigler I was only a minor member of the research team, included only because I was your sister. I've always wondered, by the way, how you did that—were you sleeping with him, too? Seven years ago you got me shunted off into the minor area of the project's effect on female gametes—which nobody cared about because it was already clear there was no way around sterility as a side effect. Nobody thought it was too high a price for a perfect, self-repairing body, did they? Except me."

Paula didn't answer. Lollie carried her frog to the wading pool and set it carefully in the water.

I said, "I didn't mind working on female gametes, even if it was a backwater, even if you got star billing. I was used to it, after all. As kids, you were always the cowboy, I got to be the horse. You were the astronaut, I was the alien you conquered. Remember? One Christmas you used up all the chemicals in your first chemistry set and then stole mine."

"I don't think trivial childhood incidents matter in—"

"Of course you don't. And I never minded. But I did mind when five years ago you made copies of all my notes and presented them as yours, while I was so sick during my pregnancy with Lollie. You claimed my work. Stole it. Just like the chemistry set. And then you eased me off the project."

"What you did was so minor—"

"If it was so minor, why are you here asking for my help now? And why would you imagine for half a second I'd give it to you?"

She stared at me, calculating. I stared back coolly. Paula wasn't used to me cool, I could see that. I'd always been the excitable one. Excitable, flighty, unstable—that's what she'd told Zweigler. A security risk.

Timmy fussed in his portacrib. I stood up, still nursing Lori, and scooped him up with my free arm. Back on the steps, I juggled Timmy to lie across Lori on my lap, pulled back my blouse, and gave him the other breast. This time Paula didn't permit herself a grimace.

She said, "Karen, what I did was wrong. I know that now. But for the sake of the project, not for me, you have to—"

"You *are* the project. You have been from the first moment you grabbed the headlines away from Zweigler and the others who gave their life to that work. 'Lovely Young Scientist Injects Self With Perfect-Cell Drug!' 'No Sacrifice Too Great To Circumvent FDA Shortsightedness, Heroic Researcher Declares.'"

Paula said flatly, "You're jealous. You're obscure and I'm famous. You're a mess and I'm beautiful. You're—"

"A milch cow? While you're a brilliant researcher? Then solve your own research problems."

"This was your area—"

"Oh, Paula, they were *all* my areas. I did more of the basic research than you did, and you know it. But you knew how to position yourself with Zweigler, to present key findings at key moments, to cultivate the right connections...all that stuff you do so well. And, of course, I was still under the delusion we were partners. I just didn't realize it was a barracuda partnering a goldfish."

From the wading pool Lollie watched us with big eyes. "Mommy..."

"It's okay, honey. Mommy's not mad at you. Look, better catch your frog—he's hopping away."

She shrieked happily and dove for the frog. Paula said softly, "I had no idea you were so angry after all this time. You've changed, Karen."

"But I'm not angry. Not any more. And you never knew what I was like before. You never bothered to know."

"I knew you never wanted a scientific life. Not the way I did. You always wanted kids. Wanted...this." She waved her arm around the shabby yard. David left eighteen months ago. He sends money. It's never enough.

"I wanted a scientific establishment that would let me have both. And I wanted credit for my work. I wanted what was mine. How did you do it, Paula—end up with what was yours and what was mine, too?"

"Because you were distracted by babyshit and frogs!" Paula yelled, and for the first time I saw how scared she really was. Paula didn't make admissions like that. A tactical error. I watched her stab desperately for a way to regain the advantage. A way to seize the offensive.

I seized it first. "You should have left David alone. You already had Zweigler; you should have left me David. Our marriage was never the same after that."

She said, "I'm dying, Karen."

I turned my head from the nursing babies to look at her.

"It's true. My cellular machinery is running wild. Just in the last few months. The nano-assemblers are creating weird structures, destructive enzymes. For five years they replicated perfectly and now...For *five years* it all performed exactly as it was programmed to—"

I said, "It still is."

Paula sat very still. Lori had fallen asleep. I juggled her into the porta-crib and nestled Timmy more comfortably on my lap. Lollie chased her frog around the wading pool. I squinted to see if Lollie's lips were blue; the weather was really too cool for her to be in the water very long.

Paula choked out, "You programmed the assembler machinery in the ovaries to—"

"Nobody much cares about women's ovaries. Only fourteen percent of college-educated women want to muck up their lives with kids. Recent survey result. Less than one percent margin of error."

"—you actually sabotaged...hundreds of women have been injected by now, maybe thousands—"

"Oh, there's a reverser enzyme," I said. "Completely effective if you take it before the twelfth-generation replication. You're the only person that's been injected that long. I just discovered the reverser a few months ago, tinkering with my old notes for something to do in what your friends probably call my idle domestic prison. That's provable, incidentally. All my notes are computer-dated."

Paula whispered, "Scientists don't *do* this—"

"Too bad you wouldn't let me be one."

"Karen—"

"Don't you want to know what the reverser is, Paula? It's engineered from human chorionic gonadotropin. The pregnancy hormone. Too bad you never wanted a baby."

She went on staring at me. Lollie shrieked and splashed with her frog. Her lips were turning blue. I stood up, laid Timmy next to Lori in the portacrib, and buttoned my blouse.

"You made an experimental error twenty-five years ago," I said to Paula. "Too small a sample population. Sometimes a frog jumps out."

I went to lift my daughter from the wading pool.

Afterword to "Margin of Error"

I don't usually write short. Like writing poetry and titles, writing very short stories demands a talent for compression that I lack (nearly all my stories are titled by somebody else). But in 1994, Ellen Datlow, editor of *Omni*, asked me for a story under 2,000 words to run with four others of similar length. I compressed and compressed, but could only get "Margin of Error" down to 2,125 words. Ellen took it anyway.

Every once in a while, a sharp-eyed fan notes that I write a lot about pairs of sisters. Then the question comes: "Do you have a sister?" Yes, I do. However, my relationship with Kate is not murderous, as is Paula's and Karen's. It's not even strained, as with Leisha and Alice in "Beggars in Spain." My sister is terrific, but "terrific" does not make for good fiction.

Kate complains that I never put her in my fiction. Well, if she arranged for my murder, I probably would.

BEGGARS IN SPAIN

ONE

They sat stiffly on his antique Eames chairs, two people who didn't want to be here, or one person who didn't want to and one who resented the other's reluctance. Dr. Ong had seen this before. Within two minutes he was sure: the woman was the silently furious resister. She would lose. The man would pay for it later, in little ways, for a long time.

"I presume you've performed the necessary credit checks already," Roger Camden said pleasantly, "so let's get right on to details, shall we, Doctor?"

"Certainly," Ong said. "Why don't we start by your telling me all the genetic modifications you're interested in for the baby."

The woman shifted suddenly on her chair. She was in her late twenties—clearly a second wife—but already had a faded look, as if keeping up with Roger Camden was wearing her out. Ong could easily believe that. Mrs. Camden's hair was brown, her eyes were brown, her skin had a brown tinge that might have been pretty if her cheeks had had any color. She wore a brown coat, neither fashionable nor cheap, and shoes that looked vaguely orthopedic. Ong glanced at his records for her name: Elizabeth. He would bet people forgot it often.

Next to her, Roger Camden radiated nervous vitality, a man in late middle age whose bullet-shaped head did not match his careful haircut and Italian-silk business suit. Ong did not need to consult his file to recall anything about Camden. A caricature of the bullet-shaped head had been the leading graphic for yesterday's online edition of the Wall Street journal: Camden had led a major coup in cross-border data-atoll investment. Ong was not sure what cross-border data-atoll investment was.

"A girl," Elizabeth Camden said. Ong hadn't expected her to speak first. Her voice was another surprise: upper-class British. "Blonde. Green eyes. Tall. Slender."

Ong smiled. "Appearance factors are the easiest to achieve, as I'm sure you already know. But all we can do about slenderness is give her a genetic disposition in that direction. How you feed the child will naturally—"

"Yes, yes," Roger Camden said, "that's obvious. Now: intelligence. *High* intelligence. And a sense of daring."

"I'm sorry, Mr. Camden, personality factors are not yet understood well enough to allow genet—"

"Just testing," Camden said, with a smile that Ong thought was probably supposed to be lighthearted.

Elizabeth Camden said, "Musical ability."

"Again, Mrs. Camden, a disposition to be musical is all we can guarantee."

"Good enough," Camden said. "The full array of corrections for any potential gene-linked health problem, of course."

"Of course," Dr. Ong said. Neither client spoke. So far theirs was a fairly modest list, given Camden's money; most clients had to be argued out of contradictory genetic tendencies, alteration overload, or unrealistic expectations. Ong waited. Tension prickled in the room like heat.

"And," Camden said, "no need to sleep."

Elizabeth Camden jerked her head sideways to look out the window.

Ong picked up a paper magnet from his desk. He made his voice pleasant. "May I ask how you learned whether that genetic-modification program exists?"

Camden grinned. "You're not denying it exists. I give you full credit for that, Doctor."

Ong held his temper. "May I ask how you learned whether the program exists?"

Camden reached into an inner pocket of his suit. The silk crinkled and pulled; body and suit came from different classes. Camden was, Ong remembered, a Yagaiist, a personal friend of Kenzo Yagai himself. Camden handed Ong hard copy: program specifications.

"Don't bother hunting down the security leak in your data banks, Doctor. You won't find it. But if it's any consolation, neither will anybody else. Now." He leaned forward suddenly. His tone changed. "I know that you've created twenty children who don't need to sleep at all, that so far nineteen are healthy, intelligent, and psychologically normal. In fact, they're better than normal; they're all unusually precocious. The oldest is already four years old and can read in two languages. I know you're thinking of offering this genetic modification on the open market in a few years. All I want is a chance to buy it for my daughter now. At whatever price you name."

Ong stood. "I can't possibly discuss this with you unilaterally, Mr. Camden. Neither the theft of our data—"

"Which wasn't a theft—your system developed a spontaneous bubble regurgitation into a public gate. You'd have a hell of a time proving otherwise—"

"—*nor* the offer to purchase this particular genetic modification lie in my sole area of authority. Both have to be discussed with the Institute's board of directors."

"By all means, by all means. When can I talk to them, too?"

"You?"

Camden, still seated, looked up at him. It occurred to Ong that there were few men who could look so confident eighteen inches below eye level. "Certainly. I'd like the chance to present my offer to whoever has the actual authority to accept it. That's only good business."

"This isn't solely a business transaction, Mr. Camden."

"It isn't solely pure scientific research, either," Camden retorted. "You're a for-profit corporation here. *With* certain tax breaks available only to firms meeting certain fair-practice laws."

For a minute Ong couldn't think what Camden meant. "Fair-practice laws..."

"...are designed to protect minorities who are suppliers. I know it hasn't ever been tested in the case of customers, except for red-lining in Y-energy installations. But it could be tested, Dr. Ong. Minorities are entitled to the same product offerings as non-minorities. I know the Institute would not welcome a court case, Doctor. None of your twenty genetic beta-test families is either Black or Jewish!"

"A court...but you're not Black *or* Jewish!"

"I'm a different minority. Polish-American. The name was Kaminsky." Camden finally stood. And smiled warmly. "Look, it is preposterous. You know that, and I know that, and we both know what a grand time journalists would have with it anyway. And you know that I don't want to sue you with a preposterous case just to use the threat of premature and adverse publicity to get what I want. I don't want to make threats at all, believe me I don't. I just want this marvelous advancement you've come up with for my daughter." His face changed, to an expression Ong wouldn't have believed possible on those particular features: wistfulness. "Doctor, do you know how much more I could have accomplished if I hadn't had to *sleep* all my life?"

Elizabeth Camden said harshly, "You hardly sleep now."

Camden looked down at her as if he had forgotten she was there. "Well, no, my dear, not now. But when I was young...college, I might have been able to finish college and still support...Well. None of that matters now. What matters, Doctor, is that you and I and your board come to an agreement."

"Mr. Camden, please leave my office now."

"You mean before you lose your temper at my presumptuousness? You wouldn't be the first. I'll expect to have a meeting set up by the end of next week, whenever and wherever you say, of course. Just let my personal secretary, Diane Clavers, know the details. Anytime that's best for you."

Ong did not accompany them to the door. Pressure throbbed behind his temples. In the doorway Elizabeth Camden turned. "What happened to the twentieth one?"

"What?"

"The twentieth baby. My husband said nineteen of them are healthy and normal. What happened to the twentieth?"

The pressure grew stronger, hotter. Ong knew that he should not answer; that Camden probably already knew the answer even if his wife didn't; that he, Ong, was going to answer anyway; that he would regret the lack of self-control, bitterly, later.

"The twentieth baby is dead. His parents turned out to be unstable. They separated during the pregnancy, and his mother could not bear the twenty-four-hour crying of a baby who never sleeps."

Elizabeth Camden's eyes widened. "She killed it?"

"By mistake," Camden said shortly. "Shook the little thing too hard." He frowned at Ong. "Nurses, Doctor. In shifts. You should have picked only parents wealthy enough to afford nurses in shifts."

"That's horrible!" Mrs. Camden burst out, and Ong could not tell if she meant the child's death, the lack of nurses, or the Institute's carelessness. Ong closed his eyes.

When they had gone, he took ten milligrams of cyclobenzaprine-III. For his back—it was solely for his back. The old injury was hurting again. Afterward he stood for a long time at the window, still holding the paper magnet, feeling the pressure recede from his temples, feeling himself calm down. Below him Lake Michigan lapped peacefully at the shore; the police had driven away the homeless in another raid just last night, and they hadn't yet had time to return. Only their debris remained, thrown into the bushes of the lakeshore park: tattered blankets, newspapers, plastic bags like pathetic trampled standards. It was illegal to sleep in the park, illegal to enter it without a resident's permit, illegal to be homeless and without a residence. As Ong watched, uniformed park attendants began methodically spearing newspapers and shoving them into clean self-propelled receptacles.

Ong picked up the phone to call the chairman of Biotech Institute's board of directors.

Four men and three women sat around the polished mahogany table of the conference room. *Doctor, lawyer, Indian chief,* thought Susan Melling, looking from Ong to Sullivan to Camden. She smiled. Ong caught the smile and looked frosty. Pompous ass. Judy Sullivan, the Institute lawyer, turned to speak in a low voice to Camden's lawyer, a thin nervous man with the look of being owned. The owner, Roger Camden, the Indian chief himself, was the happiest-looking person in the room. The lethal little man—what did it take to become that rich, starting from nothing? She, Susan, would certainly never know—radiated excitement. He beamed, he glowed, so unlike the usual parents-to-be that Susan was intrigued. Usually the prospective daddies and mommies—especially the daddies—sat there looking as if they were at a corporate merger. Camden looked as if he were at a birthday party.

Which, of course, he was. Susan grinned at him, and was pleased when he grinned back. Wolfish, but with a sort of delight that could only be called innocent—what would he be like in bed? Ong frowned majestically and rose to speak.

"Ladies and gentlemen, I think we're ready to start. Perhaps introductions are in order. Mr. Roger Camden, Mrs. Camden, are of course our clients. Mr. John Jaworski, Mr. Camden's lawyer. Mr. Camden, this is Judith Sullivan, the Institute's head of Legal; Samuel Krenshaw, representing Institute Director Dr. Brad Marsteiner, who unfortunately couldn't be here today; and Dr. Susan Melling, who developed the genetic modification affecting sleep. A few legal points of interest to both parties—"

"Forget the contracts for a minute," Camden interrupted. "Let's talk about the sleep thing. I'd like to ask a few questions."

Susan said, "What would you like to know?" Camden's eyes were very blue in his blunt-featured face; he wasn't what she had expected. Mrs. Camden, who apparently lacked both a first name and a lawyer, since Jaworski had been introduced as her husband's but not hers, looked either sullen or scared, it was difficult to tell which.

Ong said sourly, "Then perhaps we should start with a short presentation by Dr. Melling."

Susan would have preferred a Q&A, to see what Camden would ask. But she had annoyed Ong enough for one session. Obediently she rose.

"Let me start with a brief description of sleep. Researchers have known for a long time that there are actually three kinds of sleep. One is 'slow-wave sleep,' characterized on an EEG by delta waves. One is 'rapid-eye-movement sleep,' or REM sleep, which is much lighter sleep and contains most dreaming. Together these two make up 'core sleep.' The third type of sleep is 'optional sleep,' so-called because people seem to get along without it with no ill effects, and some short sleepers don't do it at all, sleeping naturally only three or four hours a night."

"That's me," Camden said. "I trained myself into it. Couldn't everybody do that?"

Apparently they were going to have a Q&A after all. "No. The actual sleep mechanism has some flexibility, but not the same amount for every person. The raphe nuclei on the brain stem—"

Ong said, "I don't think we need that level of detail, Susan. Let's stick to basics."

Camden said, "The raphe nuclei regulate the balance among neurotransmitters and peptides that leads to a pressure to sleep, don't they?"

Susan couldn't help it; she grinned. Camden, the laser-sharp ruthless financier, sat trying to look solemn, a third-grader waiting to have his homework praised. Ong looked sour. Mrs. Camden looked away, out the window.

"Yes, that's correct, Mr. Camden. You've done your research."

Camden said, "This is my *daughter*," and Susan caught her breath. When was the last time she had heard that note of reverence in anyone's voice? But no one in the room seemed to notice.

"Well, then," Susan said, "you already know that the reason people sleep is because a pressure to sleep builds up in the brain. Over the past twenty years, research has determined that's the *only* reason. Neither slow-wave sleep nor REM sleep serve functions that can't be carried on while the body and brain are awake. A lot goes on during sleep, but it can go on during wakefulness just as well, if other hormonal adjustments are made.

"Sleep served an important evolutionary function. Once Clem Pre-Mammal was done filling his stomach and squirting his sperm around, sleep kept him immobile and away from predators. Sleep was an aid to survival. But now it's a leftover mechanism, a vestige like the appendix. It switches on every night, but the need is gone. So we turn off the switch at its source, in the genes."

Ong winced. He hated it when she oversimplified like that. Or maybe it was the lightheartedness he hated. If Marsteiner were making this presentation, there'd be no Clem Pre-Mammal.

Camden said, "What about the need to dream?"

"Not necessary. A leftover bombardment of the cortex to keep it on semi-alert in case a predator attacked during sleep. Wakefulness does that better."

"Why not have wakefulness instead then? From the start of the evolution?"

He was testing her. Susan gave him a full, lavish smile, enjoying his brass. "I told you. Safety from predators. But when a modern predator attacks—say, a cross-border data-atoll investor—it's safer to be awake."

Camden shot at her, "What about the high percentage of REM sleep in fetuses and babies?"

"Still an evolutionary hangover. Cerebrum develops perfectly well without it."

"What about neural repair during slow-wave sleep?"

"That does go on. But it can go on during wakefulness, if the DNA is programmed to do so. No loss of neural efficiency, as far as we know."

"What about the release of human growth enzyme in such large concentrations during slow-wave sleep?"

Susan looked at him admiringly. "Goes on without the sleep. Genetic adjustments tie it to other changes in the pineal gland."

"What about the—"

"The *side effects*?" Mrs. Camden said. Her mouth turned down. "What about the bloody side effects?"

Susan turned to Elizabeth Camden. She had forgotten she was there. The younger woman stared at Susan, mouth turned down at the corners.

"I'm glad you asked that, Mrs. Camden. Because there are side effects." Susan paused; she was enjoying herself. "Compared to their age mates, the nonsleep children—who have *not* had IQ genetic manipulation—are more intelligent, better at problem-solving, and more joyous."

Camden took out a cigarette. The archaic, filthy habit surprised Susan. Then she saw that it was deliberate: Roger Camden was drawing attention to an ostentatious display to draw attention away from what he was feeling. His cigarette lighter was gold, monogrammed, innocently gaudy.

"Let me explain," Susan said. "REM sleep bombards the cerebral cortex with random neural firings from the brain stem; dreaming occurs because the poor besieged cortex tries so hard to make sense of the activated images and memories. It spends a lot of energy doing that. Without that energy expenditure, nonsleep cerebrums save the wear-and-tear and do better at coordinating real-life input. Thus, greater intelligence and problem-solving.

"Also, doctors have known for sixty years that antidepressants, which lift the mood of depressed patients, also suppress REM sleep entirely. What they have proved in the past ten years is that the reverse is equally true: suppress REM sleep and people don't *get* depressed. The nonsleep kids are cheerful, outgoing...*joyous*. There's no other word for it."

"At what cost?" Mrs. Camden said. She held her neck rigid, but the corners of her jaw worked.

"No cost. No negative side effects at all."

"So far," Mrs. Camden shot back.

Susan shrugged. "So far."

"They're only four years old! At the most!"

Ong and Krenshaw were studying her closely. Susan saw the moment the Camden woman realized it; she sank back into her chair, drawing her fur coat around her, her face blank.

Camden did not look at his wife. He blew a cloud of cigarette smoke. "Everything has costs, Dr. Melling."

She liked the way he said her name. "Ordinarily, yes. Especially in genetic modification. But we honestly have not been able to find any here, despite looking." She smiled directly into Camden's eyes. "Is it too much to believe that just once the universe has given us something wholly good, wholly a step forward, wholly beneficial? Without hidden penalties?"

"Not the universe. The intelligence of people like you," Camden said, surprising Susan more than anything else that had gone before. His eyes held hers. She felt her chest tighten.

"I think," Dr. Ong said dryly, "that the philosophy of the universe may be beyond our concerns here. Mr. Camden, if you have no further medical questions, perhaps we can return to the legal points Ms. Sullivan and Mr. Jaworski have raised. Thank you, Dr. Melling."

Susan nodded. She didn't look again at Camden. But she knew what he said, how he looked, that he was there.

The house was about what she had expected, a huge mock-Tudor on Lake Michigan north of Chicago. The land was heavily wooded between the gate and the house, open between the house and the surging water. Patches of snow dotted the dormant grass. Biotech had been working with the Camdens for four months, but this was the first time Susan had driven to their home.

As she walked toward the house, another car drove up behind her. No, a truck, continuing around the curved driveway to a service entry at the side of the house. One man rang the service bell; a second began to unload a plastic-wrapped playpen from the back of the truck. White, with pink and yellow bunnies. Susan briefly closed her eyes.

Camden opened the door himself. She could see his effort not to look worried. "You didn't have to drive out, Susan; I'd have come into the city!"

"No, I didn't want you to do that, Roger. Mrs. Camden is here?"

"In the living room." Camden led her into a large room with a stone fireplace, English country-house furniture, and prints of dogs or boats, all hung eighteen inches too high; Elizabeth Camden must have done the decorating. She did not rise from her wing chair as Susan entered.

"Let me be concise and fast," Susan said, "I don't want to make this anymore drawn-out for you than I have to. We have all the amniocentesis, ultrasound, and Langston test results. The fetus is fine, developing normally for two weeks, no problems with the implant on the uterine wall. But a complication has developed."

"What?" Camden said. He took out a cigarette, looked at his wife, and put it back unlit.

Susan said quietly, "Mrs. Camden, by sheer chance both your ovaries released eggs last month. We removed one for the gene surgery. By more sheer chance the second was fertilized and implanted. You're carrying two fetuses."

Elizabeth Camden grew still. "Twins?"

"No," Susan said. Then she realized what she had said. "I mean, yes. They're twins, but non-identical. Only one has been genetically altered. The other will be no more similar to her than any two siblings. It's a so-called normal baby. And I know you didn't want a so-called normal baby."

Camden said, "No. I didn't."

Elizabeth Camden said, "I did."

Camden shot her a fierce look that Susan couldn't read. He took out the cigarette again, and lit it. His face was in profile to Susan, and he was thinking intently; she doubted he knew the cigarette was there, or that he was lighting it. "Is the baby being affected by the other one's being there?"

"No," Susan said. "No, of course not. They're just...coexisting."

"Can you abort it?"

"Not without aborting both of them. Removing the unaltered fetus would cause changes in the uterine lining that would probably lead to a spontaneous miscarriage of the other." She drew a deep breath. "There's that option, of course. We can start the whole process over again. But as I told you at the time, you were very lucky to have the *in vitro* fertilization take on only the second try. Some couples take eight or ten tries. If we started all over, the process could be a lengthy one."

Camden said, "Is the presence of this second fetus harming my daughter? Taking away nutrients or anything? Or will it change anything for her later on in the pregnancy?"

"No. Except that there is a chance of premature birth. Two fetuses take up a lot more room in the womb, and if it gets too crowded, birth can be premature. But the—"

"How premature? Enough to threaten survival?"

"Most probably not."

Camden went on smoking. A man appeared at the door. "Sir, London calling. James Kendall for Mr. Yagai."

"I'll take it." Camden rose. Susan watched him study his wife's face. When he spoke, it was to her. "All right, Elizabeth. All right." He left the room.

For a long moment the two women sat in silence. Susan was aware of disappointment; this was not the Camden she had expected to see. She became aware of Elizabeth Camden watching her with amusement.

"Oh, yes, Doctor. He's like that."

Susan said nothing.

"Completely overbearing. But not this time." She laughed softly, with excitement. "Two. Do you...do you know what sex the other one is?"

"Both fetuses are female."

"I wanted a girl, you know. And now I'll have one."

"Then you'll go ahead with the pregnancy."

"Oh, yes. Thank you for coming, Doctor."

She was dismissed. No one saw her out. But as she was getting into her car, Camden rushed out of the house, coatless. "Susan! I wanted to thank you. For coming all the way out here to tell us yourself."

"You already thanked me."

"Yes. Well. You're sure the second fetus is no threat to my daughter?"

Susan said deliberately, "Nor is the genetically altered fetus a threat to the naturally conceived one."

He smiled. His voice was low and wistful. "And you think that should matter to me just as much. But it doesn't. And why should I fake what I feel? Especially to you?"

Susan opened her car door. She wasn't ready for this, or she had changed her mind, or something. But then Camden leaned over to close the door, and his manner held no trace of flirtatiousness, no smarmy ingratiation. "I better order a second playpen."

"Yes."

"And a second car seat."

"Yes."

"But not a second night-shift nurse."

"That's up to you."

"And you." Abruptly he leaned over and kissed her, a kiss so polite and respectful that Susan was shocked. Neither lust nor conquest would have shocked her; this did. Camden didn't give her a chance to react; he closed the car door and turned back toward the house. Susan drove toward the gate, her hands shaky on the wheel until amusement replaced shock: It *had* been a deliberate, blatant, respectful kiss, an engineered enigma. And nothing else could have guaranteed so well that there would have to be another.

She wondered what the Camdens would name their daughters.

Dr. Ong strode the hospital corridor, which had been dimmed to half-light. From the nurse's station in Maternity a nurse stepped forward as if to stop him—it was the middle of the night, long past visiting hours—got a good look at his face, and faded back into her station.

Around a corner was the viewing glass to the nursery. To Ong's annoyance, Susan Melling stood pressed against the glass. To his further annoyance, she was crying.

Ong realized that he had never liked the woman. Maybe not any women. Even those with superior minds could not seem to refrain from being made damn fools by their emotions.

"Look," Susan said, laughing a little, swiping at her face. "Doctor—*look*."

Behind the glass Roger Camden, gowned and masked, was holding up a baby in a white undershirt and pink blanket. Camden's blue eyes—theatrically blue—a man really should not have such garish eyes—glowed. The baby's head was covered with blond fuzz; it had wide eyes and pink skin. Camden's eyes above the mask said that no other child had ever had these attributes.

Ong said, "An uncomplicated birth?"

"Yes," Susan Melling sobbed. "Perfectly straightforward. Elizabeth is fine. She's asleep. Isn't she beautiful? He has the most adventurous spirit I've ever known." She wiped her nose on her sleeve; Ong realized that she was drunk. "Did I ever tell you that I was engaged once? Fifteen years ago, in med school? I broke it off because he grew to seem so ordinary, so boring. Oh, God, I shouldn't be telling you all this. I'm sorry. I'm sorry."

Ong moved away from her. Behind the glass Roger Camden laid the baby in a small wheeled crib. The nameplate said BABY GIRL CAMDEN #1. 5.9 POUNDS. A night nurse watched indulgently.

Ong did not wait to see Camden emerge from the nursery or to hear Susan Melling say to him whatever she was going to say. Ong went to have the OB paged. Melling's report was not, under the circumstances, to be trusted. A perfect, unprecedented chance to record every detail of gene alteration with a non-altered control, and Melling was more interested in her own sloppy emotions. Ong would obviously have to do the report himself, after talking to the OB. He was hungry for every detail. And not just about the pink-cheeked baby in Camden's arms. He wanted to know everything about the birth of the child in the other glass-sided crib: BABY GIRL CAMDEN #2. 5.1 POUNDS. The dark-haired baby with the mottled red features, lying scrunched down in her pink blanket, asleep.

TWO

Leisha's earliest memory was flowing lines that were not there. She knew they were not there because when she reached out her fist to touch them, her fist was empty. Later she realized that the flowing lines were light: sunshine slanting in bars between curtains in her room, between the wooden blinds in the dining room, between the crisscross lattices in the conservatory. The day she realized the golden flow was light she laughed out loud with the sheer joy of discovery, and Daddy turned from putting flowers in pots and smiled at her.

The whole house was full of light. Light bounded off the lake, streamed across the high white ceilings, puddled on the shining wooden floors. She and Alice moved continually through light, and sometimes Leisha would stop and tip back her head and let it flow over her face. She could feel it, like water.

The best light, of course, was in the conservatory. That's where Daddy liked to be when he was home from making money. Daddy potted plants and watered trees, humming, and Leisha and Alice ran between the wooden tables of flowers with their wonderful earthy smells, running from the dark side of the conservatory where the big purple flowers grew to the sunshine side with sprays of yellow flowers, running back and forth, in and out of the light. "Growth," Daddy said to her, "flowers all fulfilling their promise. Alice, be careful! You almost knocked over that orchid!" Alice, obedient, would stop running for a while. Daddy never told Leisha to stop running.

After a while the light would go away. Alice and Leisha would have their baths, and then Alice would get quiet, or cranky. She wouldn't play nice with Leisha, even when Leisha let her choose the game or even have all the best dolls. Then Nanny would take Alice to bed, and Leisha would talk with Daddy some more until Daddy said he had to work in his study with the papers that made money. Leisha always felt a moment of regret that he had to go do that, but the moment never lasted very long because Mamselle would arrive and start Leisha's lessons, which she liked. Learning things was so interesting! She could already sing twenty songs and write all the letters in the alphabet and count to fifty. And by the time lessons were done, the light had come back, and it was time for breakfast.

Breakfast was the only time Leisha didn't like. Daddy had gone to the office, and Leisha and Alice had breakfast with Mommy in the big dining room. Mommy sat in a red robe, which Leisha liked, and she didn't smell funny or talk funny the way she would later in the day, but still breakfast wasn't fun. Mommy always started with The Question.

"Alice, sweetheart, how did you sleep?"

"Fine, Mommy."

"Did you have any nice dreams?"

For a long time Alice said no. Then one day she said, "I dreamed about a horse. I was riding him." Mommy clapped her hands and kissed Alice and gave her an extra sticky bun. After that Alice always had a dream to tell Mommy.

Once Leisha said, "I had a dream, too. I dreamed light was coming in the window and it wrapped all around me like a blanket and then it kissed me on my eyes."

Mommy put down her coffee cup so hard that coffee sloshed out of it. "Don't lie to me, Leisha. You did not have a dream."

"Yes, I did," Leisha said.

"Only children who sleep can have dreams. Don't lie to me. You did not have a dream."

"Yes I did! I did!" Leisha shouted. She could see it, almost: the light streaming in the window and wrapping around her like a golden blanket.

"I will not tolerate a child who is a liar! Do you hear me, Leisha—I won't tolerate it!"

"You're a liar!" Leisha shouted, knowing the words weren't true, hating herself because they weren't true but hating Mommy more and that was wrong, too, and there sat Alice stiff and frozen with her eyes wide, Alice was scared and it was Leisha's fault.

Mommy called sharply, "Nanny! Nanny! Take Leisha to her room at once. She can't sit with civilized people if she can't refrain from telling lies!"

Leisha started to cry. Nanny carried her out of the room. Leisha hadn't even had her breakfast. But she didn't care about that; all she could see while she cried was Alice's eyes, scared like that, reflecting broken bits of light.

But Leisha didn't cry long. Nanny read her a story, and then played Data Jump with her, and then Alice came up and Nanny drove them both into Chicago to the zoo where there were wonderful animals to see, animals Leisha could not have dreamed—nor Alice *either.* And by the time they came back Mommy had gone to her room and Leisha knew that she would stay there with the glasses of funny-smelling stuff the rest of the day and Leisha would not have to see her.

But that night, she went to her mother's room.

"I have to go to the bathroom," she told Mamselle. Mamselle said, "Do you need any help?" maybe because Alice still needed help in the bathroom. But Leisha didn't, and she thanked Mamselle. Then she sat on the toilet for a minute even though nothing came, so that what she had told Mamselle wouldn't be a lie.

Leisha tiptoed down the hall. She went first into Alice's room. A little light in a wall socket burned near the crib. There was no crib in Leisha's room. Leisha looked at her sister through the bars. Alice lay on her side with her eyes closed. The lids of the eyes fluttered quickly, like curtains blowing in the wind. Alice's chin and neck looked loose.

Leisha closed the door very carefully and went to her parents' room.

They didn't sleep in a crib but in a huge enormous bed, with enough room between them for more people. Mommy's eyelids weren't fluttering; she lay on her back making a hrrr-hrrr sound through her nose. The funny smell was strong on her. Leisha backed away and tiptoed over to Daddy. He looked like Alice, except that his neck and chin looked even looser, folds of skin collapsed like the tent that had fallen down in the back yard. It scared Leisha to see him like that. Then Daddy's eyes flew open so suddenly that Leisha screamed.

Daddy rolled out of bed and picked her up, looking quickly at Mommy. But she didn't move. Daddy was wearing only his underpants. He carried Leisha out into the hall, where Mamselle came rushing up saying, "Oh, sir, I'm sorry, she just said she was going to the bathroom—"

"It's all right," Daddy said. "I'll take her with me."

"No!" Leisha screamed, because Daddy was only in his underpants and his neck had looked all funny and the room smelled bad because of Mommy. But Daddy carried her into the conservatory, set her down on a bench, wrapped himself in a piece of green plastic that was supposed to cover up plants, and sat down next to her.

"Now, what happened, Leisha? What were you doing?"

Leisha didn't answer.

"You were looking at people sleeping, weren't you?" Daddy said, and because his voice was softer Leisha mumbled, "Yes." She immediately felt better; it felt good not to lie.

"You were looking at people sleeping because you don't sleep and you were curious, weren't you? Like Curious George in your book?"

"Yes," Leisha said. "I thought you said you made money in your study all night!"

Daddy smiled. "Not all night. Some of it. But then I sleep, although not very much." He took Leisha on his lap. "I don't need much sleep, so I get a lot more done at night than most people. Different people need different amounts of sleep. And a few, a very few, are like you. You don't need any."

"Why not?"

"Because you're special. Better than other people. Before you were born, I had some doctors help make you that way."

"Why?"

"So you could do anything you want to and make manifest your own individuality."

Leisha twisted in his arms to stare at him; the words meant nothing. Daddy reached over and touched a single flower growing on a tall potted tree. The flower had thick white petals like the cream he put in coffee, and the center was a light pink.

"See, Leisha—this tree made this flower. Because it *can*. Only this tree can make this kind of wonderful flower. That plant hanging up there can't, and those can't either. Only this tree. Therefore the most important thing in the world for this tree to do is grow this flower. The flower is the tree's individuality—that means just *it*, and nothing else—made manifest. Nothing else matters."

"I don't understand, Daddy."

"You will. Someday."

"But I want to understand *now*," Leisha said, and Daddy laughed with pure delight and hugged her. The hug felt good, but Leisha still wanted to understand.

"When you make money, is that your indiv...that thing?"

"Yes," Daddy said happily.

"Then nobody else can make money? Like only that tree can make that flower?"

"Nobody else can make it just the way I do."

"What do you do with the money?"

"I buy things for you. This house, your dresses, Mamselle to teach you, the car to ride in."

"What does the tree do with the flower?"

"Glories in it," Daddy said, which made no sense. "Excellence is what counts, Leisha. Excellence supported by individual effort. And that's *all* that counts."

"I'm cold, Daddy."

"Then I better bring you back to Mamselle."

Leisha didn't move. She touched the flower with one finger. "I want to sleep, Daddy."

"No, you don't, sweetheart. Sleep is just lost time, wasted life. It's a little death."

"Alice sleeps.

"Alice isn't like you."

"Alice isn't special?"

"No. You are."

"Why didn't you make Alice special, too?"

"Alice made herself. I didn't have a chance to make her special."

The whole thing was too hard. Leisha stopped stroking the flower and slipped off Daddy's lap. He smiled at her. "My little questioner. When you grow up, you'll find your own excellence, and it will be a new order, a specialness the world hasn't ever seen before. You might even be like Kenzo Yagai. He made the Yagai generator that powers the world."

"Daddy, you look funny wrapped in the flower plastic." Leisha laughed. Daddy did, too. But then she said, "When I grow up, I'll make my specialness find a way to make Alice special, too," and Daddy stopped laughing.

He took her back to Mamselle, who taught her to write her name, which was so exciting she forgot about the puzzling talk with Daddy. There were six letters, all different, and together they were *her name*. Leisha wrote it over and over, laughing, and Mamselle laughed too. But later, in the morning, Leisha thought again about the talk with Daddy. She thought of it often, turning the unfamiliar words over and over in her mind like small hard stones, but the part she thought about most wasn't a word. It was the frown on Daddy's face when she told him she would use her specialness to make Alice special, too.

Every week Dr. Melling came to see Leisha and Alice, sometimes alone, sometimes with other people. Leisha and Alice both liked Dr. Melling, who laughed a lot and whose eyes were bright and warm. Often Daddy was there, too. Dr. Melling played games with them, first with Alice and Leisha separately and then together. She took their pictures and weighed them. She made them lie down on a table and stuck little metal things to their temples, which sounded scary but wasn't because there were so many machines to watch, all making interesting noises, while they were lying there. Dr. Melling was as good at answering questions as Daddy.

Once Leisha said, "Is Dr. Melling a special person? Like Kenzo Yagai?" And Daddy laughed and glanced at Dr. Melling and said, "Oh, yes, indeed."

When Leisha was five she and Alice started school. Daddy's driver took them every day into Chicago. They were in different rooms, which disappointed Leisha. The kids in Leisha's room were all older. But from the first day she adored school, with its fascinating science equipment and electronic drawers full of math puzzlers and other children to find countries on the map with. In half a year she had been moved to yet a different room, where the kids were still older, but they were nonetheless nice to her. Leisha started to learn Japanese. She loved drawing the beautiful characters on thick white paper. "The Sauley School was a good choice," Daddy said.

But Alice didn't like the Sauley School. She wanted to go to school on the same yellow bus as Cook's daughter. She cried and threw her paints on the floor at the Sauley School. Then Mommy came out of her room—Leisha hadn't seen her for a few weeks, although she knew Alice had—and threw some candlesticks from the mantelpiece on the floor. The candlesticks, which were china, broke. Leisha ran to pick up the pieces while Mommy and Daddy screamed at each other in the hall by the big staircase.

"She's my daughter, too! And I say she can go!"

"You don't have the right to say anything about it! A weepy drunk, the most rotten role model possible for both of them...and I thought I was getting a fine English aristocrat!"

"You got what you paid for! Nothing! Not that you ever needed anything from me or anybody else!"

"Stop it!" Leisha cried. "Stop it!" There was silence in the hall. Leisha cut her fingers on the china; blood streamed onto the rug. Daddy rushed in and picked her up. "Stop it," Leisha sobbed, and didn't understand when Daddy said quietly, "*You* stop it, Leisha. Nothing *they* do should touch you at all. You have to be at least that strong."

Leisha buried her head in Daddy's shoulder. Alice transferred to Carl Sandburg Elementary School, riding there on the yellow school bus with Cook's daughter.

A few weeks later Daddy told them that Mommy was going away to a hospital, to stop drinking so much. When Mommy came out, he said, she was going to live somewhere else for a while. She and Daddy were not happy. Leisha and Alice would stay with Daddy and they would visit Mommy sometimes. He told them this very carefully, finding the right words for truth. Truth was very important, Leisha already knew. Truth was being true to yourself, your specialness. Your individuality. An individual respected facts, and so always told the truth.

Mommy—Daddy did not say but Leisha knew—did not respect facts.

"I don't want Mommy to go away," Alice said. She started to cry. Leisha thought Daddy would pick Alice up, but he didn't. He just stood there looking at them both.

Leisha put her arms around Alice. "It's all right, Alice. It's all right! We'll make it all right! I'll play with you all the time we're not in school so you don't miss Mommy!"

Alice clung to Leisha. Leisha turned her head so she didn't have to see Daddy's face.

THREE

Kenzo Yagai was coming to the United States to lecture. The title of his talk, which he would give in New York, Los Angeles, and Chicago, with a repeat in Washington as a special address to Congress, was "The Further Political Implications of Inexpensive Power." Leisha Camden, eleven years old, was going to have a private introduction after the Chicago talk, arranged by her father.

She had studied the theory of cold fusion at school, and her global studies teacher had traced the changes in the world resulting from Yagai's patented, low-cost applications of what had, until him, been unworkable theory: the rising prosperity of the Third World; the death throes of the old communistic systems; the decline of the oil states; the renewed economic power of the United States. Her study group had written a news script, filmed with the school's professional-quality equipment, about how a 1985 American family lived with expensive energy costs and a belief in tax-supported help, while a 2019 family lived with cheap energy and a belief in the contract as the basis of civilization. Parts of her own research puzzled Leisha.

"Japan thinks Kenzo Yagai was a traitor to his own country," she said to Daddy at supper.

"No," Camden said, "*some* Japanese think that. Watch out for generalizations, Leisha. Yagai patented and licensed Y-energy in the United States because here there were at least the dying embers of individual enterprise. Because of his invention, our entire country has slowly swung back toward an individual meritocracy, and Japan has slowly been forced to follow."

"Your father held that belief all along," Susan said. "Eat your peas, Leisha." Leisha ate her peas. Susan and Daddy had only been married less than a year; it still felt a little strange to have her there. But nice. Daddy said Susan was a valuable addition to their household: intelligent, motivated, and cheerful. Like Leisha herself.

"Remember, Leisha," Camden said, "a man's worth to society and to himself doesn't rest on what he thinks other people should do or be or feel, but on himself. On what he can actually do, and do well. People trade what they do well, and everyone benefits. The basic tool of civilization is the contract. Contracts are voluntary and mutually beneficial. As opposed to coercion, which is wrong."

"The strong have no right to take anything from the weak by force," Susan said. "Alice, eat your peas, too, honey."

"Nor the weak to take anything by force from the strong," Camden said. "That's the basis of what you'll hear Kenzo Yagai discuss tonight, Leisha."

Alice said, "I don't like peas."

Camden said, "Your body does. They're good for you."

Alice smiled. Leisha felt her heart lift; Alice didn't smile much at dinner any more. "My body doesn't have a contract with the peas."

Camden said, a little impatiently, "Yes, it does. Your body benefits from them. Now eat."

Alice's smile vanished. Leisha looked down at her plate. Suddenly she saw a way out. "No, Daddy, look—Alice's body benefits, but the peas don't! It's not a mutually beneficial consideration, so there's no contract! Alice is right!"

Camden let out a shout of laughter. To Susan he said, "Eleven years old...*eleven*." Even Alice smiled, and Leisha waved her spoon triumphantly, light glinting off the bowl and dancing silver on the opposite wall.

But even so, Alice did not want to go hear Kenzo Yagai. She was going to sleep over at her friend Julie's house; they were going to curl their hair together. More surprisingly, Susan wasn't coming either. She and Daddy looked at each other a little funny at the front door, Leisha thought, but Leisha was too excited to think about this. She was going to hear *Kenzo Yagai*.

Yagai was a small man, dark and slim. Leisha liked his accent. She liked, too, something about him that took her a while to name. "Daddy," she whispered in the half-darkness of the auditorium, "he's a joyful man."

Daddy hugged her in the darkness.

Yagai spoke about spirituality and economics. "A man's spirituality, which is only his dignity as a man, rests on his own efforts. Dignity and worth are not automatically conferred by aristocratic birth; we have only to look at history to see that. Dignity and worth are not automatically conferred by inherited wealth. A great heir may be a thief, a wastrel, cruel, an exploiter, a person who leaves the world much poorer than he found it. Nor are dignity and worth automatically conferred by existence itself. A mass murderer exists, but is of negative worth to his society and possesses no dignity in his lust to kill.

"No, the only dignity, the only spirituality, rests on what a man can achieve with his own efforts. To rob a man of the chance to achieve, and to trade what he achieves with others, is to rob him of his spiritual dignity as a man. This is why communism has failed in our time. *All* coercion—all force to take from a man his own efforts to achieve—causes spiritual damage and weakens a society. Conscription, theft, fraud, violence, welfare, lack of legislative representation—*all* rob a man of his chance to choose, to achieve on his own, to trade the results of his achievement with others. Coercion is a cheat. It produces nothing new. Only freedom—the freedom to achieve, the freedom to trade freely the results of achievement—creates the environment proper to the dignity and spirituality of man."

Leisha applauded so hard her hands hurt. Going backstage with Daddy, she thought she could hardly breathe. Kenzo Yagai!

But backstage was more crowded than she had expected. There were cameras everywhere. Daddy said, "Mr. Yagai, may I present my daughter Leisha," and the cameras moved in close and fast—on *her*. A Japanese man whispered something in Kenzo Yagai's ear, and he looked more closely at Leisha. "Ah, yes."

"Look over here, Leisha," someone called, and she did. A robot camera zoomed so close to her face that Leisha stepped back, startled. Daddy spoke very sharply to someone, then to someone else. The cameras didn't move. A woman suddenly knelt in front of Leisha and thrust a microphone at her. "What does it feel like to never sleep, Leisha?"

"What?"

Someone laughed. The laugh was not kind. "Breeding geniuses..."

Leisha felt a hand on her shoulder. Kenzo Yagai gripped her very firmly, and pulled her away from the cameras. Immediately, as if by magic, a line of Japanese men formed behind Yagai, parting only to let Daddy through. Behind the line, the three of them moved into a dressing room, and Kenzo Yagai shut the door.

"You must not let them bother you, Leisha," he said in his wonderful accent. "Not ever. There is an old Asian proverb: 'The dogs bark but the caravan moves on.' You must never let your individual caravan be slowed by the barking of rude or envious dogs."

"I won't," Leisha breathed, not sure yet what the words really meant, knowing there was time later to sort them out, to talk about them with Daddy. For now she was dazzled by Kenzo Yagai, the actual man himself who was changing the world without force, without guns, by trading his special individual efforts. "We study your philosophy at my school, Mr. Yagai."

Kenzo Yagai looked at Daddy. Daddy said, "A private school. But Leisha's sister also studies it, although cursorily, in the public system. Slowly, Kenzo, but it comes. It comes." Leisha noticed that he did not say why Alice was not here tonight with them.

Back home, Leisha sat in her room for hours, thinking over everything that had happened. When Alice came home from Julie's the next morning, Leisha rushed toward her. But Alice seemed angry about something.

"Alice—what is it?"

"Don't you think I have enough to put up with at school already?" Alice shouted. "Everybody knows, but at least when you stayed quiet it didn't matter too much! They'd stopped teasing me! Why did you have to do it?"

"Do what?" Leisha said, bewildered.

Alice threw something at her: a hard-copy morning paper, on newsprint flimsier than the Camden systems used. The paper dropped open at Leisha's feet. She stared at her own picture, three columns wide, with Kenzo Yagai. The headline said, "Yagai and the Future: Room For the Rest of Us? Y-Energy Inventor Confers With 'Sleep-Free' Daughter of Mega-Financier Roger Camden."

Alice kicked the paper. "It was on TV last night too—on *TV.* I work hard not to look stuck-up or creepy, and you go and do this! Now Julie probably won't even invite me to her slumber party next week!" She rushed up the broad curving stairs to her room.

Leisha looked down at the paper. She heard Kenzo Yagai's voice in her head: *The dogs bark but the caravan moves on*. She looked at the empty stairs. Aloud she said, "Alice—your hair looks really pretty curled like that."

FOUR

"I want to meet the rest of them," Leisha said. "Why have you kept them from me this long?"

"I haven't kept them from you at all," Camden said. "Not offering is not the same as denial. Why shouldn't you be the one to do the asking? You're the one who now wants it."

Leisha looked at him. She was fifteen, in her last year at the Sauley School. "Why didn't you offer?"

"Why should I?"

"I don't know," Leisha said. "But you gave me everything else."

"Including the freedom to ask for what you want."

Leisha looked for the contradiction, and found it. "Most things that you provided for my education I didn't ask for, because I didn't know enough to ask and you as the adult did. But you've never offered the opportunity for me to meet any of the other sleepless mutants—"

"Don't use that word," Camden said sharply.

"—so you must either think it was not essential to my education or else you had another motive for not wanting me to meet them."

"Wrong," Camden said. "There's a third possibility. That I think meeting them is essential to your education, that I do want you to, but this issue provided a chance to further the education of your self-initiative by waiting for *you* to ask."

"All right," Leisha said, a little defiantly; there seemed to be a lot of defiance between them lately, for no good reason. She squared her shoulders. Her new breasts thrust forward. "I'm asking. How many of the Sleepless are there, who are they, and where are they?"

Camden said, "If you're using that term—'the Sleepless'—you've already done some reading on your own. So you probably know that there are 1,082 of you so far in the United States, more in foreign countries, most of them in major metropolitan areas. Seventy-nine are in Chicago, most of them still small children. Only nineteen anywhere are older than you."

Leisha didn't deny reading any of this. Camden leaned forward in his study chair to peer at her. Leisha wondered if he needed glasses. His hair was completely gray now, sparse and stiff, like lonely broom straws. The *Wall Street Journal* listed him among the hundred richest men in America; *Women's Wear Daily* pointed out that he was the only billionaire in the country who did not move in the society of international parties, charity balls, and social secretaries. Camden's jet ferried him to business meetings around the world, to the chairmanship of the Yagai Economics Institute, and to very little else. Over the years he had grown richer, more reclusive, and more cerebral. Leisha felt a rush of her old affection.

She threw herself sideways into a leather chair, her long slim legs dangling over the arm. Absently she scratched a mosquito bite on her thigh. "Well, then, I'd like to meet Richard Keller." He lived in Chicago and was the beta-test Sleepless closest to her own age. He was seventeen.

"Why ask me? Why not just go?"

Leisha thought there was a note of impatience in his voice. He liked her to explore things first, then report on them to him later. Both parts were important.

Leisha laughed. "You know what, Daddy? You're predictable."

Camden laughed, too. In the middle of the laugh Susan came in. "He certainly is not. Roger, what about that meeting in Buenos Aires on Thursday? Is it on or off?" When he didn't answer, her voice grew shriller. "Roger? I'm talking to you!"

Leisha averted her eyes. Two years ago Susan had finally left genetic research to run Camden's house and schedule; before that she had tried hard to do both. Since she had left Biotech, it seemed to Leisha, Susan had changed. Her voice was tighter. She was more insistent that Cook and the gardener follow her directions exactly, without deviation. Her blond braids had become stiff sculptured waves of platinum.

"It's on," Roger said.

"Well, thanks for at least answering. Am I going?"

"If you like."

"I like."

Susan left the room. Leisha rose and stretched. Her long legs rose on tiptoe. It felt good to reach, to stretch, to feel sunlight from the wide windows wash over her face. She smiled at her father, and found him watching her with an unexpected expression.

"Leisha—"

"What?"

"See Keller. But be careful."

"Of what?"

But Camden wouldn't answer.

The voice on the phone had been noncommittal. "Leisha Camden? Yes, I know who you are. Three o'clock on Thursday?" The house was modest; a thirty-year-old colonial on a quiet suburban street where small children on bicycles could be watched from the front window. Few roofs had more than one Y-energy cell. The trees, huge old sugar maples, were beautiful.

"Come in," Richard Keller said.

He was no taller than she, stocky, with a bad case of acne. Probably no genetic alterations except sleep, Leisha guessed. He had thick dark hair, a low forehead, and bushy black brows. Before he closed the door Leisha saw him stare at her car and driver, parked in the driveway next to a rusty ten-speed bike.

"I can't drive yet," she said. "I'm still fifteen."

"It's easy to learn," Richard said. "So, you want to tell me why you're here?"

Leisha liked his directness. "To meet some other Sleepless."

"You mean you never have? Not any of us?"

"You mean the rest of you know each other?" She hadn't expected that.

"Come to my room, Leisha."

She followed him to the back of the house. No one else seemed to be home. His room was large and airy, filled with computers and filing cabinets. A rowing machine sat in one corner. It looked like a shabbier version of the room of any bright classmate at the Sauley School, except there was more space without a bed. She walked over to the computer screen.

"Hey—you working on Boesc equations?"

"On an application of them."

"To what?"

"Fish migration patterns."

Leisha smiled. "Yeah, that would work. I never thought of that." Richard seemed not to know what to do with her smile. He looked at the wall, then at her chin. "You interested in Gaea patterns? In the environment?"

"Well, no," Leisha confessed. "Not particularly. I'm going to study politics at Harvard. Pre-law. But of course we had Gaea patterns at school."

Richard's gaze finally came unstuck from her face. He ran a hand through his dark hair. "Sit down, if you want."

Leisha sat, looking appreciatively at the wall posters, shifting green on blue, like ocean currents. "I like those. Did you program them yourself?"

"You're not at all what I pictured," Richard said.

"How did you picture me?"

He didn't hesitate. "Stuck up. Superior. Shallow, despite your IQ."

She was more hurt than she had expected to be.

Richard blurted. "You're one of only two Sleepless who're really rich. You and Jennifer Sharifi. But you already know that."

"No, I don't. I've never checked."

He took the chair beside her, stretching his stocky legs straight in front of him, in a slouch that had nothing to do with relaxation. "It makes sense, really. Rich people don't have their children genetically modified to be superior—they think any offspring of theirs is already superior. By their values. And poor people can't afford it. We Sleepless are upper-middle class, no more. Children of professors, scientists, people who value brains and time."

"My father values brains and time," Leisha said. "He's the biggest supporter of Kenzo Yagai."

"Oh, Leisha, do you think I don't already know that? Are you flashing me or what?"

Leisha said with great deliberateness, "I'm *talking* to you." But the next minute she could feel the hurt break through on her face.

"I'm sorry," Richard muttered. He shot off his chair and paced to the computer and back. "I *am* sorry. But I don't...I don't understand what you're doing here."

"I'm lonely," Leisha said, astonished at herself. She looked up at him. "It's true. I'm lonely. I am. I have friends and Daddy and Alice. But no one really knows, really understands—what? I don't know what I'm saying."

Richard smiled. The smile changed his whole face, opened up its dark planes to the light. "I do. Oh, do I. What do you do when they say, 'I had such a dream last night?'"

"Yes!" Leisha said. "But that's even really minor. It's when I say, 'I'll look that up for you tonight' and they get that funny look on their face that means, 'She'll do it while I'm asleep.'"

"But that's even really minor," Richard said. "It's when you're playing basketball in the gym after supper and then you go to the diner for food and then you say, 'Let's have a walk by the lake,' and they say, 'I'm really tired. I'm going home to bed now.'"

"But that's really minor," Leisha said, jumping up. "It's when you really are absorbed by the movie and then you get the point and it's so goddamn beautiful you leap up and say, 'Yes! Yes!' and Susan says, 'Leisha, really, you'd think nobody but you ever enjoyed anything before.'"

"Who's Susan?" Richard said.

The mood was broken. But not really; Leisha could say, "My stepmother," without much discomfort over what Susan had promised to be and what she had become. Richard stood inches from her, smiling that joyous smile, understanding, and suddenly relief washed over Leisha so strong that she walked straight over to him and put her arms around his neck, only tightening them when she felt his startled jerk. She started to sob—she, Leisha, who never cried.

"Hey," Richard said. "Hey."

"Brilliant," Leisha said, laughing. "Brilliant remark."

She could feel his embarrassed smile. "Wanta see my fish migration curves instead?"

"No," Leisha sobbed, and he went on holding her, patting her back awkwardly, telling her without words that she was home.

Camden waited up for her, although it was past midnight. He had been smoking heavily. Through the blue air he said quietly, "Did you have a good time, Leisha?"

"Yes."

"I'm glad," he said, and put out his last cigarette, and climbed the stairs—slowly, stiffly, he was nearly seventy now—to bed.

They went everywhere together for nearly a year: swimming, dancing, the museums, the theater, the library. Richard introduced her to the others, a group of twelve kids between fourteen and nineteen, all of them intelligent and eager. All Sleepless.

Leisha learned.

Tony Indivino's parents, like her own, had divorced. But Tony, fourteen, lived with his mother, who had not particularly wanted a Sleepless child, while his father, who had, acquired a red sports car and a young girlfriend who designed ergonomic chairs in Paris. Tony was not allowed to tell anyone—relatives, schoolmates—that he was Sleepless. "They'll think you're a freak," his mother said, eyes averted from her son's face. The one time Tony disobeyed her and told a friend that he never slept, his mother beat him. Then she moved the family to a new neighborhood. He was nine years old.

Jeanine Carter, almost as long-legged and slim as Leisha, was training for the Olympics in ice skating. She practiced twelve hours a day, hours no Sleeper still in high school could ever have. So far the newspapers had not picked up the story. Jeanine was afraid that if they did, they would somehow not let her compete.

Jack Bellingham, like Leisha, would start college in September. Unlike Leisha, he had already started his career. The practice of law had to wait for law school; the practice of investing required only money. Jack didn't have much, but his precise financial analyses parlayed six hundred dollars saved from summer jobs to three thousand dollars through stock-market investing, then to ten thousand dollars, and then he had enough to qualify for information-fund speculation. Jack was fifteen, not old enough to make legal investments; the transactions were all in the name of Kevin Baker, the oldest of the Sleepless, who lived in Austin. Jack told Leisha, "When I hit eighty-four percent profit over two consecutive quarters, the data analysts logged onto me. Just sniffing. Well, that's their job, even when the overall amounts are actually small. It's the patterns they care about. If they take the trouble to cross-reference data banks and come up with the fact that Kevin is a Sleepless, will they try to stop us from investing somehow?"

"That's paranoid," Leisha said.

"No, it's not," Jeanine said. "Leisha, you don't *know*."

"You mean because I've been protected by my father's money and caring," Leisha said. No one grimaced; all of them confronted ideas openly, without shadowy allusions. Without dreams.

"Yes," Jeanine said. "Your father sounds terrific. And he raised you to think that achievement should not be fettered—Jesus Christ, he's a Yagaiist. Well, good. We're glad for you." She said it without sarcasm. Leisha nodded. "But the world isn't always like that. They hate us."

"That's too strong," Carol said. "Not hate."

"Well, maybe," Jeanine said. "But they're different from us. We're better, and they naturally resent that."

"I don't see what's natural about it," Tony said. "Why shouldn't it be just as natural to admire what's better? We do. Does any one of us resent Kenzo Yagai for his genius? Or Nelson Wade, the physicist? Or Catherine Raduski?"

"We don't resent them because we are better," Richard said. "Q.E.D."

"What we should do is have our own society," Tony said. "Why should we allow their regulations to restrict our natural, honest achievements? Why should Jeanine be barred from skating against them and Jack from investing on their same terms just because we're Sleepless? Some of them are brighter than others of them. Some have greater persistence. Well, we have greater concentration, more biochemical stability, and more time. All men are not created equal."

"Be fair, Jack—no one has been barred from anything yet," Jeanine said.

"But we will be."

"*Wait,*" Leisha said. She was deeply troubled by the conversation. "I mean, yes, in many ways we're better. But you quoted out of context, Tony. The Declaration of Independence doesn't say all men are created equal in ability. It's talking about rights and power; it means that all are created equal *under the law.* We have no more right to a separate society or to being free of society's restrictions than anyone else does. There's no other way to freely trade one's efforts, unless the same contractual rules apply to all."

"Spoken like a true Yagaiist," Richard said, squeezing her hand.

"That's enough intellectual discussion for me," Carol said, laughing. "We've been at this for hours. We're at the beach, for Chrissake. Who wants to swim with me?"

"I do," Jeanine said. "Come on, Jack."

All of them rose, brushing sand off their suits, discarding sunglasses. Richard pulled Leisha to her feet. But just before they ran into the water, Tony put his skinny hand on her arm. "One more question, Leisha. Just to think about. If we achieve better than most other people, and if we trade with the Sleepers when it's mutually beneficial, making no distinction there between the strong and the weak—what obligation do we have to those so weak they don't have anything to trade with us? We're already going to give more than we get; do we have to do it when we get nothing at all? Do we have to take care of their deformed and handicapped and sick and lazy and shiftless with the products of our work?"

"Do the Sleepers have to?" Leisha countered.

"Kenzo Yagai would say no. He's a Sleeper."

"He would say they would receive the benefits of contractual trade even if they aren't direct parties to the contract. The whole world is better fed and healthier because of Y-energy."

"Come on!" Jeanine yelled. "Leisha, they're ducking me! Jack, you stop that! Leisha, help me!"

Leisha laughed. Just before she grabbed for Jeanine, she caught the look on Richard's face, and on Tony's: Richard frankly lustful, Tony angry. At her. But why? What had she done, except argue in favor of dignity and trade?

Then Jack threw water on her, and Carol pushed Jack into the warm spray, and Richard was there with his arms around her, laughing.

When she got the water out of her eyes, Tony was gone.

Midnight. "Okay," Carol said. "Who's first?"

The six teenagers in the brambly clearing looked at each other. A Y-lamp, kept on low for atmosphere, cast weird shadows across their faces and over their bare legs. Around the clearing Roger Camden's trees stood thick and dark, a wall between them and the closest of the estate's outbuildings. It was very hot. August air hung heavy, sullen. They had voted against bringing an air-conditioned Y-field because this was a return to the primitive, the dangerous; let it be primitive.

Six pairs of eyes stared at the glass in Carol's hand.

"Come *on*," she said. "Who wants to drink up?" Her voice was jaunty, theatrically hard. "It was difficult enough to get this."

"How *did* you get it?" said Richard, the group member—except for Tony—with the least influential family contacts, the least money. "In a drinkable form like that?"

"Jennifer got it," Carol said, and five sets of eyes shifted to Jennifer Sharifi, who two weeks into her visit with Carol's family was confusing them all. She was the American-born daughter of a Hollywood movie star and an Arab prince who had wanted to found a Sleepless dynasty. The movie star was an aging drug addict; the prince, who had taken his fortune out of oil and put it into Y-energy when Kenzo Yagai was still licensing his first patents, was dead. Jennifer Sharifi was richer than Leisha would someday be, and infinitely more sophisticated about procuring things. The glass held interleukin-1, an immune-system booster, one of many substances which as a side effect induced the brain to swift and deep sleep.

Leisha stared at the glass. A warm feeling crept through her lower belly, not unlike the feeling when she and Richard made love. She caught Jennifer watching her, and flushed.

Jennifer disturbed her. Not for the obvious reasons she disturbed Tony and Richard and Jack: the long black hair, the tall, slim body in shorts and halter. Jennifer didn't laugh. Leisha had never met a Sleepless who didn't laugh, nor one who said so little, with such deliberate casualness. Leisha found herself speculating on what Jennifer Sharifi wasn't saying. It was an odd sensation to feel toward another Sleepless.

Tony said to Carol, "Give it to me!"

Carol handed him the glass. "Remember, you only need a little sip."

Tony raised the glass to his mouth, stopped, and looked at them over the rim from his fierce eyes. He drank.

Carol took back the glass. They all watched Tony. Within a minute he lay on the rough ground; within two, his eyes closed in sleep.

It wasn't like seeing parents sleep, siblings, friends. It was Tony. They looked away, avoided each other's eyes. Leisha felt the warmth between her legs tug and tingle, faintly obscene. She didn't took at Jennifer.

When it was Leisha's turn, she drank slowly, then passed the glass to Richard. Her head turned heavy, as if it were being stuffed with damp rags. The trees at the edge of the clearing blurred. The portable lamp blurred, too. It wasn't bright and clean anymore but squishy, blobby; if she touched it, it would smear. Then darkness swooped over her brain, taking it away: *taking away her mind*. "Daddy!" She tried to call, to clutch for him, but then the darkness obliterated her.

Afterward, they all had headaches. Dragging themselves back through the woods in the thin morning light was torture, compounded by an odd shame. They didn't touch each other. Leisha walked as far away from Richard as she could.

Jennifer was the only one who spoke. "So now we know," she said, and her voice held a strange satisfaction.

It was a whole day before the throbbing left the base of Leisha's skull, or the nausea her stomach. She sat alone in her room, waiting for the misery to pass, and despite the heat, her whole body shivered.

There had not even been any dreams.

"I want you to come with me tonight," Leisha said, for the tenth or twelfth time. "We both leave for college in just two days; this is the last chance. I really want you to meet Richard."

Alice lay on her stomach across her bed. Her hair, brown and lusterless, fell around her face. She wore an expensive yellow jumpsuit, silk by Ann Patterson, which rucked up around her knees.

"Why? What do you care if I meet Richard or not?"

"Because you're my sister," Leisha said. She knew better than to say "my twin." Nothing got Alice angry faster.

"I don't want to." The next moment Alice's face changed. "Oh, I'm sorry, Leisha — I didn't mean to sound so snotty. But...but I don't want to."

"It won't be all of them. Just Richard. And just for an hour or so. Then you can come back here and pack for Northwestern."

"I'm not going to Northwestern."

Leisha stared at her.

Alice said, "I'm pregnant."

Leisha sat on the bed. Alice rolled onto her back, brushed the hair out of her eyes, and laughed. Leisha's ears closed against the sound. "Look at you," Alice said. "You'd think it was *you* who was pregnant. But you never would be, would you, Leisha? Not until it was the proper time. Not you."

"How?" Leisha said. "We both had our caps put in...."

"I had the cap removed," Alice said.

"You wanted to get pregnant?"

"Damn flash I did. And there's not a thing Daddy can do about it. Except, of course, cut off all credit completely, but I don't think he'll do that, do you?" She laughed again. "Even to me?"

"But Alice...why? Not just to anger Daddy!"

"No," Alice said. "Although you would think of that, wouldn't you? Because I want something to love. Something of my *own*. Something that has nothing to do with this house."

Leisha thought of herself and Alice running through the conservatory, years ago, her and Alice, darting in and out of the sunlight. "It hasn't been so bad growing up in this house."

"Leisha, you're stupid. I don't know how anyone so smart can be so stupid. Get out of my room! Get out!"

But Alice—a *baby*—"

"Get out!" Alice shrieked. "Go to Harvard! Go be successful! Just get out!"

Leisha jerked off the bed. "Gladly! You're irrational, Alice. You don't think ahead, you don't plan, a *baby*—" But she could never sustain anger. It dribbled away, leaving her mind empty. She looked at Alice, who suddenly put out her arms. Leisha went into them.

"You're the baby," Alice said wonderingly. "You *are*. You're so...I don't know what. You're a baby."

Leisha said nothing. Alice's arms felt warm, felt whole, felt like two children running in and out of sunlight. "I'll help you, Alice. If Daddy won't."

Alice abruptly pushed her away. "I don't need your help."

Alice stood. Leisha rubbed her empty arms, fingertips scraping across opposite elbows. Alice kicked the empty, open trunk in which she was supposed to pack for Northwestern, and then abruptly smiled a smile that made Leisha look away. She braced herself for more abuse. But what Alice said, very softly, was, "Have a good time at Harvard."

FIVE

She loved it.

From the first sight of Massachusetts Hall, older than the United States by a half century, Leisha felt something that had been missing in Chicago: Age. Roots. Tradition. She touched the bricks of Widener Library, the glass cases in the Peabody Museum, as if they were the grail. She had never been particularly sensitive to myth or drama; the anguish of Juliet seemed to her artificial, that of Willy Loman merely wasteful. Only King Arthur, struggling to create a better social order, had interested her. But now, walking under the huge autumn trees, she suddenly caught a glimpse of a force that could span generations, fortunes left to endow learning and achievement the benefactors would never see, individual effort spanning and shaping centuries to come. She stopped, and looked at the sky through the leaves, at the buildings solid with purpose. At such moments she thought of Camden, bending the will of an entire genetic research institute to create her in the image he wanted.

Within a month, she had forgotten all such mega-musings.

The work load was incredible, even for her. The Sauley School had encouraged individual exploration at her own pace; Harvard knew what it wanted from her, at its pace. In the past twenty years, under the academic leadership of a man who in his youth had watched Japanese economic domination with dismay, Harvard had become the controversial leader of a return to hard-edged learning of facts, theories, applications, problem-solving, and intellectual efficiency. The school accepted one of every two hundred applicants from around the world. The daughter of England's prime minister had flunked out her first year and been sent home.

Leisha had a single room in a new dormitory, the dorm because she had spent so many years isolated in Chicago and was hungry for people, the single so she would not disturb anyone else when she worked all night. Her second day a boy from down the hall sauntered in and perched on the edge of her desk.

"So you're Leisha Camden."

"Yes."

"Sixteen years old."

"Almost seventeen."

"Going to outperform us all, I understand, without even trying."

Leisha's smile faded. The boy stared at her from under lowered downy brows. He was smiling, his eyes sharp. From Richard and Tony and the others Leisha had learned to recognize the anger that presents itself as contempt.

"Yes," Leisha said coolly, "I am."

"Are you sure? With your pretty little-girl hair and your mutant little-girl brain?"

"Oh, leave her alone, Hannaway," said another voice. A tall blond boy, so thin his ribs looked like ripples in brown sand, stood in jeans and bare feet, drying his wet hair. "Don't you ever get tired of walking around being an asshole?"

"Do you?" Hannaway said. He heaved himself off the desk and started toward the door. The blond moved out of his way. Leisha moved into it.

"The reason I'm going to do better than you," she said evenly, "is because I have certain advantages you don't. Including sleeplessness. And then after I outperform you, I'll be glad to help you study for your tests so that you can pass, too."

The blond, drying his ears, laughed. But Hannaway stood still, and into his eyes came an expression that made Leisha back away. He pushed past her and stormed out.

"Nice going, Camden," the blond said. "He deserved that."

"But I meant it," Leisha said. "I will help him study."

The blond lowered his towel and stared. "You did, didn't you? You meant it."

"Yes! Why does everybody keep questioning that?"

"Well," the boy said, "I don't. You can help me if I get into trouble." Suddenly he smiled. "But I won't."

"Why not?"

"Because I'm just as good at anything as you are, Leisha Camden."

She studied him. "You're not one of us. Not Sleepless."

"Don't have to be. I know what I can do. Do, be, create, trade."

She said, delighted, "You're a Yagaiist!"

"Of course." He held out his hand. "Stewart Sutter. How about a fish burger in the Yard?"

"Great," Leisha said. They walked out together, talking excitedly. When people stared at her, she tried not to notice. She was here. At Harvard. With space ahead of her, time, to learn, and with people like Stewart Sutter who accepted and challenged her.

All the hours he was awake.

She became totally absorbed in her class work. Roger Camden drove up once, walking the campus with her, listening, smiling. He was more at home than Leisha would have expected: he knew Stewart Sutter's father and Kate Addams's grandfather. They talked about Harvard, business, Harvard, the Yagai Economics Institute, Harvard. "How's Alice?" Leisha asked once, but Camden said he didn't know; she had moved out and did not want to see him. He made her an allowance through his attorney. While he said this, his face remained serene.

Leisha went to the Homecoming Ball with Stewart, who was also majoring in pre-law but was two years ahead of Leisha. She took a weekend trip to Paris with Kate Addams and two other girlfriends, taking the Concorde III. She had a fight with Stewart over whether the metaphor of superconductivity could apply to Yagaiism, a stupid fight they both knew was stupid but had anyway, and afterward they became lovers. After the fumbling sexual explorations with Richard, Stewart was deft, experienced, smiling faintly as he taught her how to have an orgasm both by herself and with him. Leisha was dazzled. "It's so *joyful*," she said, and Stewart looked at her with a tenderness she knew was part disturbance but didn't know why.

At mid-semester she had the highest grades in the freshman class. She got every answer right on every single question on her midterms. She and Stewart went out for a beer to celebrate, and when they came back Leisha's room had been destroyed. The computer was smashed, the data banks wiped, hard copies and books smoldered in a metal wastebasket. Her clothes were ripped to pieces, her desk and bureau hacked apart. The only thing untouched, pristine, was the bed.

Stewart said, "There's no way this could have been done in silence. Everyone on the floor—hell, on the floor *below*—had to know. Someone will talk to the police." No one did. Leisha sat on the edge of the bed, dazed, and looked at the remnants of her Homecoming gown. The next day Dave Hannaway gave her a long, wide smile.

Camden flew east, taut with rage. He rented her an apartment in Cambridge with E-lock security and a bodyguard named Toshio. After he left, Leisha fired the bodyguard but kept the apartment. It gave her and Stewart more privacy, which they used to endlessly discuss the situation. It was Leisha who argued that it was an aberration, an immaturity.

"There have always been haters, Stewart. Hate Jews, hate Blacks, hate immigrants, hate Yagaiists who have more initiative and dignity than you do. I'm just the latest object of hatred. It's not new, it's not remarkable. It doesn't mean any basic kind of schism between the Sleepless and Sleepers."

Stewart sat up in bed and reached for the sandwiches on the night stand. "Doesn't it? Leisha, you're a different kind of person entirely. More evolutionarily fit, not only to survive but to prevail. Those other objects of hatred you cite—they were all powerless in their societies. They occupied *inferior* positions. You, on the other hand—all three Sleepless in Harvard Law are on the *Law Review*. All of them. Kevin Baker, your oldest, has already founded a successful bio-interface software firm and is making money, a lot of it. Every Sleepless is making superb grades, none has psychological problems, all are healthy, and most of you aren't even adults yet. How much hatred do you think you're going to encounter once you hit the high-stakes world of finance and business and scarce endowed chairs and national politics?"

"Give me a sandwich," Leisha said. "Here's my evidence you're wrong: you yourself. Kenzo Yagai. Kate Addams. Professor Lane. My father. Every Sleeper who inhabits the world of fair trade and mutually beneficial contracts. And that's most of you, or at least most of you who are worth considering. You believe that competition among the most capable leads to the most beneficial trades for everyone, strong and weak. Sleepless are making real and concrete contributions to society, in a lot of fields. That has to outweigh the discomfort we cause. We're *valuable* to you. You know that."

Stewart brushed crumbs off the sheets. "Yes. I do. Yagaiists do."

"Yagaiists run the business and financial and academic worlds. Or they will. In a meritocracy, they *should*. You underestimate the majority of people, Stew. Ethics aren't confined to the ones out front."

"I hope you're right," Stewart said. "Because, you know, I'm in love with you."

Leisha put down her sandwich.

"Joy," Stewart mumbled into her breasts, "you are joy."

When Leisha went home for Thanksgiving, she told Richard about Stewart. He listened tight-lipped.

"A Sleeper."

"A *person*," Leisha said. "A good, intelligent, achieving person!"

"Do you know what your good intelligent achieving Sleepers have done, Leisha? Jeanine has been barred from Olympic skating. 'Genetic alteration, analogous to steroid abuse to create an unsportsmanlike advantage.' Chris Devereaux has left Stanford. They trashed his laboratory, destroyed two years' work in memory-formation proteins. Kevin Baker's software company is fighting a nasty advertising campaign, all underground of course, about kids using software designed by nonhuman minds. Corruption, mental slavery, satanic influences: the whole bag of witch-hunt tricks. Wake up, Leisha!"

They both heard his words. Minutes dragged by. Richard stood like a boxer; forward on the balls of his feet, teeth clenched. Finally he said, very quietly, "Do you love him?"

"Yes," Leisha said. "I'm sorry."

"Your choice," Richard said coldly. "What do you do while he's asleep? Watch?"

"You make it sound like a perversion!"

Richard said nothing. Leisha drew a deep breath. She spoke rapidly but calmly, a controlled rush: "While Stewart is asleep I work. The same as you do. Richard—don't do this. I didn't mean to hurt you. And I don't want to lose the group. I believe the Sleepers are the same species as we are. Are you going to punish me for that? Are you going to *add* to the hatred? Are you going to tell me that I can't belong to a wider world that includes all honest, worthwhile people whether they sleep or not? Are you going to tell me that the most important division is by genetics and not by economic spirituality? Are you going to force me into an artificial choice, us or them?"

Richard picked up a bracelet. Leisha recognized it; she had given it to him in the summer. His voice was quiet. "No. It's not a choice." He played with the gold links a minute, then looked at her. "Not yet."

By spring break, Camden walked more slowly. He took medicine for his blood pressure, his heart. He and Susan, he told Leisha, were getting a divorce. "She changed, Leisha, after I married her. You saw that. She was independent and productive and happy, and then after a few years she stopped all that and became a shrew. A whining shrew." He shook his head in genuine bewilderment. "You saw the change."

Leisha had. A memory came to her: Susan leading her and Alice in "games" that were actually controlled cerebral-performance tests, Susan's braids dancing around her sparkling eyes. Alice had loved Susan then, as much as Leisha had.

"Dad, I want Alice's address."

"I told you up at Harvard, I don't have it," Camden said. He shifted in his chair, the impatient gesture of a body that never expected to wear out. In January Kenzo Yagai had died of pancreatic cancer; Camden had taken the news hard. "I make her allowance through an attorney. By her choice."

"Then I want the address of the attorney."

The attorney, a quenched-looking man named John Jaworski, refused to tell Leisha where Alice was. "She doesn't want to be found, Ms. Camden. She wanted a complete break."

"Not from me," Leisha said.

"Yes," Jaworski said, and something flickered in his eyes, something she had last seen in Dave Hannaway's face.

She flew to Austin before returning to Boston, making her a day late for classes. Kevin Baker saw her instantly, canceling a meeting with IBM. She told him what she needed, and he set his best datanet people on it, without telling them why. Within two hours she had Alice's address from Jaworski's electronic files. It was the first time, she realized, that she had ever turned to one of the Sleepless for help, and it had been given instantly. Without trade.

Alice was in Pennsylvania. The next weekend Leisha rented a hover car and driver—she had learned to drive, but only ground cars as yet—and went to High Ridge, in the Appalachian Mountains.

It was an isolated hamlet, twenty-five miles from the nearest hospital. Alice lived with a man named Ed, a silent carpenter twenty years older than she, in a cabin in the woods. The cabin had water and electricity but no newsnet. In the early spring light the earth was raw and bare, slashed with icy gullies. Alice and Ed apparently worked at nothing. Alice was eight months pregnant.

"I didn't want you here," she said to Leisha. "So why are you?"

"Because you're my sister."

"God, look at you. Is that what they're wearing at Harvard? Boots like that? When did you become fashionable, Leisha? You were always too busy being intellectual to care."

"What's this all about, Alice? Why here? What are you doing?"

"Living," Alice said. "Away from dear Daddy, away from Chicago, away from drunken, broken Susan—did you know she drinks? Just like Mom. He does that to people. But not to me. I got out. I wonder if you ever will."

"Got out? To *this*?"

"I'm happy," Alice said angrily. "Isn't that what it's supposed to be about? Isn't that the aim of your great Kenzo Yagai—happiness through individual effort?"

Leisha thought of saying that Alice was making no efforts that she could see. She didn't say it. A chicken ran through the yard of the cabin. Behind, the mountains rose in layer upon layer of blue haze. Leisha thought what this place must have been like in winter, cut off from the world where people strived toward goals, learned, changed.

"I'm glad you're happy, Alice."

"Are you?"

"Yes."

"Then I'm glad, too," Alice said, almost defiantly. The next moment she abruptly hugged Leisha, fiercely, the huge, hard mound of her belly crushed between them. Alice's hair smelled sweet, like fresh grass in sunlight.

"I'll come see you again, Alice."

"Don't," Alice said.

SIX

"Sleepless Mutie Begs for Reversal of Gene Tampering," screamed the headline in the Food Mart. "'Please Let Me Sleep Like Real People!' Child Pleads."

Leisha typed in her credit number and pressed the news kiosk for a printout, although ordinarily she ignored the electronic tabloids. The headline went on circling the kiosk. A Food Mart employee stopped stacking boxes on shelves and watched her. Bruce, Leisha's bodyguard, watched the employee.

She was twenty-two, in her final year at Harvard Law, editor of the *Law Review*, clearly first in her graduating class. The closest three contenders were Jonathan Cocchiara, Len Carter, and Martha Wentz. All Sleepless.

In her apartment she skimmed the printout. Then she accessed the Groupnet run from Austin. The files had more news stories about the child, with comments from other Sleepless, but before she could call them up Kevin Baker came online himself, on voice.

"Leisha. I'm glad you called. I was going to call you."

"What's the situation with this Stella Bevington, Kev? Has anybody checked it out?"

"Randy Davies. He's from Chicago but I don't think you've met him; he's still in high school. He's in Park Ridge, Stella's in Skokie. Her parents wouldn't talk to him—they were pretty abusive, in fact—but he got to see Stella face-to-face anyway. It doesn't look like an abuse case, just the usual stupidity: parents wanted a genius child, scrimped and saved, and now they can't handle that she is one. They scream at her to sleep, get emotionally abusive when she contradicts them, but so far no violence."

"Is the emotional abuse actionable?"

"I don't think we want to move on it yet. Two of us will keep in close touch with Stella—she does have a modem, and she hasn't told her parents about the net—and Randy will drive out weekly."

Leisha bit her lip. "A tabloid shitpiece said she's seven years old."

"Yes."

"Maybe she shouldn't be left there. I'm an Illinois resident, I can file an abuse grievance from here if Candy's got too much in her briefcase…." *Seven years old.*

"No. Let it sit a while. Stella will probably be all right. You know that."

She did. Nearly all of the Sleepless stayed all right, no matter how much opposition came from the stupid segment of society. And it was only the stupid segment, Leisha argued, a small if vocal minority. Most people could, and would, adjust to the growing presence of the Sleepless, when it became clear that that presence included not only growing power but growing benefits to the country as a whole.

Kevin Baker, now twenty-six, had made a fortune in microchips so revolutionary that Artificial Intelligence, once a debated dream, was yearly closer to reality. Carolyn Rizzolo had won the Pulitzer Prize in drama for her play *Morning Light*. She was twenty-four. Jeremy Robinson had done significant work in superconductivity applications while still a graduate student at Stanford. William Thaine, *Law Review* editor when Leisha first came to Harvard, was now in private practice. He had never lost a case. He was twenty-six, and the cases were becoming important. His clients valued his ability more than his age.

But not everyone reacted that way.

Kevin Baker and Richard Keller had started the datanet that bound the Sleepless into a tight group, constantly aware of each other's personal fights. Leisha Camden financed the legal battles, the educational costs of Sleepless whose parents were unable to meet them, the support of children in emotionally bad situations. Rhonda Lavelier got herself licensed as a foster mother in California, and whenever possible the Group maneuvered to have young Sleepless who were removed from their homes assigned to Rhonda. The Group now had three licensed lawyers; within the next year it would gain four more, licensed to practice in five different states.

The one time they had not been able to remove an abused Sleepless child legally, they kidnapped him.

Timmy DeMarzo, four years old. Leisha had been opposed to the action. She had argued the case morally and pragmatically—to her they were the same thing—thus: If they believed in their society, in its fundamental laws and in their ability to belong to it as free-trading productive individuals, they must remain bound by the society's contractual laws. The Sleepless were, for the most part, Yagaiists. They should already know this. And if the FBI caught them, the courts and press would crucify them.

They were not caught.

Timmy DeMarzo—not even old enough to call for help on the datanet, they had learned of the situation through the automatic police record scan Kevin maintained through his company—was stolen from his own back yard in Wichita. He had lived the last year in an isolated trailer in North Dakota; no place was too isolated for a modem. He was cared for by a legally irreproachable foster mother who had lived there all her life. The foster mother was second cousin to a Sleepless, a broad cheerful woman with a much better brain than her appearance indicated. She was a Yagaiist. No record of the child's existence appeared in any data bank: not the IRS's, not any school's, not even the local grocery store's computerized checkout slips. Food specifically for the child was shipped in monthly on a truck owned by a Sleepless in State College, Pennsylvania. Ten of the Group knew about the kidnapping, out of the total 3,428 sleepless born in the United States. Of those, 2,691 were part of the Group via the net. An additional 701 were as yet too young to use a modem. Only thirty-six Sleepless, for whatever reason, were not part of the Group.

The kidnapping had been arranged by Tony Indivino.

"It's Tony I wanted to talk to you about," Kevin said to Leisha. "He's started again. This time he means it. He's buying land."

She folded the tabloid very small and laid it carefully on the table. "Where?"

"Allegheny Mountains. In southern New York State. A lot of land. He's putting in the roads now. In the spring, the first buildings."

"Jennifer Sharifi still financing it?" It had been six years since the interleukin-1 drinking in the woods, but the evening remained vivid to Leisha. So did Jennifer Sharifi.

"Yes. She's got the money to do it. Tony's starting to get a following, Leisha."

"I know."

"Call him."

"I will. Keep me informed about Stella."

She worked until midnight at the *Law Review*, then until 4:00 A.M. preparing her classes. From four to five she handled legal matters for the Group. At 5:00 A.M. she called Tony, still in Chicago. He had finished high school, done one semester at Northwestern, and at Christmas vacation had finally exploded at his mother for forcing him to live as a Sleeper. The explosion, it seemed to Leisha, had never ended.

"Tony? Leisha."

"The answers are yes, yes, no, and go to hell."

Leisha gritted her teeth. "Fine. Now tell me the questions."

"Are you really serious about the Sleepless withdrawing into their own self-sufficient society? Is Jennifer Sharifi willing to finance a project the size of building a small city? Don't you think that's a cheat of all that can be accomplished by patient integration of the Group into the mainstream? And what about the contradictions of living in an armed restricted city and still trading with the Outside?"

"I would never tell *you* to go to hell."

"Hooray for you," Tony said. After a moment he added, "I'm sorry. That sounds like one of *them*."

"It's wrong for us, Tony."

"Thanks for not saying I couldn't pull it off."

She wondered if he could. "We're not a separate species, Tony."

"Tell that to the Sleepers."

"You exaggerate. There are haters out there, there are *always* haters, but to give up…"

"We're not giving up. Whatever we create can be freely traded: software, hardware, novels, information, theories, legal counsel. We can travel in and out. But we'll have a safe place to return *to*. Without the leeches who think we owe them blood because we're better than they are."

"It isn't a matter of owing."

"Really?" Tony said. "Let's have this out, Leisha. All the way. You're a Yagaiist—what do you believe in?"

"Tony…"

"Do it," Tony said, and in his voice she heard the fourteen-year-old she had been introduced to by Richard. Simultaneously, she saw her father's

face: not as he was now, since the bypass, but as he had been when she was a little girl, holding her on his lap to explain that she was special.

"I believe in voluntary trade that is mutually beneficial. That spiritual dignity comes from supporting one's life through one's own efforts, and from trading the results of those efforts in mutual cooperation throughout the society. That the symbol of this is the contract. And that we need each other for the fullest, most beneficial trade."

"Fine," Tony bit off. "Now what about the beggars in Spain?"

"The what?"

"You walk down a street in a poor country like Spain and you see a beggar. Do you give him a dollar?"

"Probably."

"Why? He's trading nothing with you. He has nothing to trade."

"I know. Out of kindness. Compassion."

"You see six beggars. Do you give them all a dollar?"

"Probably," Leisha said.

"You would. You see a hundred beggars and you haven't got Leisha Camden's money. Do you give them each a dollar?"

"No."

"Why not?"

Leisha reached for patience. Few people could make her want to cut off a comlink; Tony was one of them. "Too draining on my own resources. My life has first claim on the resources I earn."

"All right. Now consider this. At Biotech Institute—where you and I began, dear pseudo-sister—Dr. Melling has just yesterday—"

"Who?"

"Dr. Susan Melling. Oh, God, I completely forgot she used to be married to your father!"

"I lost track of her," Leisha said. "I didn't realize she'd gone back to research. Alice once said...never mind. What's going on at Biotech?"

"Two crucial items, just released. Carla Dutcher has had first-month fetal genetic analysis. Sleeplessness is a dominant gene. The next generation of the Group won't sleep either."

"We all knew that," Leisha said. Carla Dutcher was the world's first pregnant Sleepless. Her husband was a Sleeper. "The whole world expected that."

"But the press will have a field day with it anyway. Just watch. Muties Breed! New Race Set to Dominate Next Generation of Children!"

Leisha didn't deny it. "And the second item?"

"It's sad, Leisha. We've just had our first death."

Her stomach tightened. "Who?"

"Bernie Kuhn. Seattle." She didn't know him. "A car accident. It looks pretty straightforward; he lost control on a steep curve when his brakes failed. He had only been driving a few months. He was seventeen. But the significance here is that his parents have donated his brain and body to Biotech, in conjunction with the pathology department at the Chicago Medical School. They're going to take him apart to get the first good look at what prolonged sleeplessness does to the body and brain."

"They should," Leisha said. "That poor kid. But what are you so afraid they'll find?"

"I don't know. I'm not a doctor. But whatever it is, if the haters can use it against us, they will."

"You're paranoid, Tony."

"Impossible. The Sleepless have personalities calmer and more reality-oriented than the norm. Don't you read the literature?"

"Tony—"

"What if you walk down that street in Spain and a hundred beggars each want a dollar and you say no and they have nothing to trade you but they're so rotten with anger about what you have that they knock you down and grab it and then beat you out of sheer envy and despair?"

Leisha didn't answer.

"Are you going to say that's not a human scenario, Leisha? That it never happens?"

"It happens," Leisha said evenly. "But not all that often."

"Bullshit. Read more history. Read more *newspapers*. But the point is: What do you owe the beggars then? What does a good Yagaiist who believes in mutually beneficial contracts do with people who have nothing to trade and can only take?"

"You're not—"

"*What*, Leisha? In the most objective terms you can manage, what do we owe the grasping and nonproductive needy?"

"What I said originally. Kindness. Compassion."

"Even if they don't trade it back? Why?"

"Because..." She stopped.

"Why? Why do law-abiding and productive human beings owe anything to those who neither produce very much nor abide by just laws? What philosophical or economic or spiritual justification is there for owing them anything? Be as honest as I know you are."

Leisha put her head between her knees. The question gaped beneath her, but she didn't try to evade it. "I don't know. I just know we do."

"Why?"

She didn't answer. After a moment, Tony did. The intellectual challenge was gone from his voice. He said, almost tenderly, "Come down in the spring and see the site for Sanctuary. The buildings will be going up then."

"No," Leisha said.

"I'd like you to."

"No. Armed retreat is not the way."

Tony said, "The beggars are getting nastier, Leisha. As the Sleepless grow richer. And I don't mean in money."

"Tony—" she said, and stopped. She couldn't think what to say.

"Don't walk down too many streets armed with just the memory of Kenzo Yagai."

In March, a bitterly cold March with wind whipping down the Charles River, Richard Keller came to Cambridge. Leisha had not seen him for three years. He didn't send her word on the Groupnet that he was coming. She hurried up the walk to her townhouse, muffled to the eyes in a red wool scarf against the snowy cold, and he stood there blocking the doorway. Behind Leisha, her bodyguard tensed.

"Richard! Bruce, it's all right, this is an old friend."

"Hello, Leisha."

He was heavier, sturdier-looking, with a breadth of shoulder she didn't recognize. But the face was Richard's, older but unchanged: dark low brows, unruly dark hair. He had grown a beard.

"You look beautiful," he said.

Inside, she handed him a cup of coffee. "Are you here on business?" From the Groupnet she knew that he had finished his master's and had done outstanding work in marine biology in the Caribbean but had left that a year ago and disappeared from the net.

"No. Pleasure." He smiled suddenly, the old smile that opened up his dark face. "I almost forgot about that for a long time. Contentment, yes. We're all good at the contentment that comes from sustained work. But pleasure? Whim? Caprice? When was the last time you did something silly, Leisha?"

She smiled. "I ate cotton candy in the shower."

"Really? Why?"

"To see if it would dissolve in gooey pink patterns."

"Did it?"

"Yes. Lovely ones."

"And that was your last silly thing? When was it?"

"Last summer," Leisha said, and laughed.

"Well, mine is sooner than that. It's now. I'm in Boston for no other reason than the spontaneous pleasure of seeing you."

Leisha stopped laughing. "That's an intense tone for a spontaneous pleasure, Richard."

"Yup," he said, intensely. She laughed again. He didn't.

"I've been in India, Leisha. And China and Africa. Thinking, mostly. Watching. First I traveled like a Sleeper, attracting no attention. Then I set out to meet the Sleepless in India and China. There are a few, you know, whose parents were willing to come here for the operation. They pretty much are accepted and left alone. I tried to figure out why desperately poor countries—by our standards anyway; over there Y-energy is mostly available only in big cities—don't have any trouble accepting the superiority of Sleepless, whereas Americans, with more prosperity than any time in history, build in resentment more and more."

Leisha said, "Did you figure it out?"

"No. But I figured out something else, watching all those communes and villages and *kampongs*. We are too individualistic."

Disappointment swept Leisha. She saw her father's face: *Excellence is what counts, Leisha. Excellence supported by individual effort....* She reached for Richard's cup. "More coffee?"

He caught her wrist and looked up into her face. "Don't misunderstand me, Leisha. I'm not talking about work. We are too much individuals in the rest of our lives. Too emotionally rational. Too much alone. Isolation kills more than the free flow of ideas. It kills joy."

He didn't let go of her wrist. She looked down into his eyes, into depths she hadn't seen before. It was the feeling of looking into a mineshaft, both giddy and frightening, knowing that at the bottom might be gold or darkness. Or both.

Richard said softly, "Stewart?"

"Over long ago. An undergraduate thing." Her voice didn't sound like her own.

"Kevin?"

"No, never—we're just friends."

"I wasn't sure. Anyone?"

"No."

He let go of her wrist. Leisha peered at him timidly. He suddenly laughed. "Joy, Leisha." An echo sounded in her mind, but she couldn't place it, and then it was gone and she laughed too, a laugh airy and frothy as pink cotton candy in summer.

"Come home, Leisha. He's had another heart attack."

Susan Melling's voice on the phone was tired. Leisha said, "How bad?"

"The doctors aren't sure. Or say they're not sure. He wants to see you. Can you leave your studies?"

It was May, the last push toward her finals. The *Law Review* proofs were behind schedule. Richard had started a new business, marine consulting to Boston fishermen plagued with sudden inexplicable shifts in ocean currents, and was working twenty hours a day. "I'll come," Leisha said.

Chicago was colder than Boston. The trees were half-budded. On Lake Michigan, filling the huge east windows of her father's house, whitecaps tossed up cold spray. Leisha saw that Susan was living in the house; her brushes were on Camden's dresser, her journals on the credenza in the foyer.

"Leisha," Camden said. He looked old. Grey skin, sunken cheeks, the fretful and bewildered look of men who accepted potency like air, indivisible from their lives. In the corner of the room, on a small eighteenth-century slipper chair, sat a short, stocky woman with brown braids.

"Alice."

"Hello, Leisha."

"Alice. I've looked for you..." The wrong thing to say. Leisha had looked, but not very hard, deterred by the knowledge that Alice had not wanted to be found. "How are you?"

"I'm fine," Alice said. She seemed remote, gentle, unlike the angry Alice of six years ago in the raw Pennsylvania hills. Camden moved painfully on the bed. He looked at Leisha with eyes which, she saw, were undimmed in their blue brightness.

"I asked Alice to come. And Susan. Susan came a while ago. I'm dying, Leisha."

No one contradicted him. Leisha, knowing his respect for facts, remained silent. Love hurt her chest.

"John Jaworski has my will. None of you can break it. But I wanted to tell you myself what's in it. The past few years I've been selling, liquidating. Most of my holdings are accessible now. I've left a tenth to Alice, a tenth to Susan, a tenth to Elizabeth, and the rest to you, Leisha, because you're the only one with the individual ability to use the money to its full potential for achievement."

Leisha looked wildly at Alice, who gazed back with her strange remote calm. "Elizabeth? My...mother? Is alive?"

"Yes," Camden said.

"You told me she was dead! Years and years ago!"

"Yes. I thought it was better for you that way. She didn't like what you were, was jealous of what you could become. And she had nothing to give you. She would only have caused you emotional harm."

Beggars in Spain...

"That was wrong, Daddy. You were *wrong*. She's my mother..." She couldn't finish the sentence.

Camden didn't flinch. "I don't think I was. But you're an adult now. You can see her if you wish."

He went on looking at her with his bright, sunken eyes, while around Leisha the air heaved and snapped. Her father had lied to her. Susan watched her closely, a small smile on her lips. Was she glad to see Camden fall in his daughter's estimation? Had she all along been that jealous of their relationship, of Leisha...?

She was thinking like Tony.

The thought steadied her a little. But she went on staring at Camden, who went on staring back implacably, unbudged, a man positive even on his deathbed that he was right.

Alice's hand was on her elbow, Alice's voice so soft that no one but Leisha could hear. "He's done talking now, Leisha. And after a while you'll be all right."

Alice had left her son in California with her husband of two years, Beck Watrous, a building contractor she had met while waiting on tables in a resort on the Artificial Islands. Beck had adopted Jordan, Alice's son.

"Before Beck there was a real bad time," Alice said in her remote voice. "You know, when I was carrying Jordan I actually used to dream that he would be Sleepless? Like you. Every night I'd dream that, and every morning I'd wake up and have morning sickness with a baby that was only going to be a stupid nothing like me. I stayed with Ed—in the Appalachian Mountains, remember? You came to see me there once for two more years. When he beat me, I was glad. I wished Daddy could see. At least Ed was touching me."

Leisha made a sound in her throat.

"I finally left because I was afraid for Jordan. I went to California, did nothing but eat for a year. I got up to 190 pounds." Alice was, Leisha estimated, five-foot-four. "Then I came home to see Mother."

"You didn't tell me," Leisha said. "You knew she was alive and you didn't tell me."

"She's in a drying-out tank half the time," Alice said, with brutal simplicity. "She wouldn't see you if you wanted to. But she saw me, and she fell slobbering all over me as her 'real' daughter, and she threw up on my dress. And I backed away from her and looked at the dress and knew it *should* be thrown up on, it was so ugly. Deliberately ugly. She started screaming how Dad had ruined her life, ruined mine, all for you. And do you know what I did?"

"What?" Leisha said. Her voice was shaky.

"I flew home, burned all my clothes, got a job, started college, lost fifty pounds, and put Jordan in play therapy."

The sisters sat silent. Beyond the window the lake was dark, unlit by moon or stars. It was Leisha who suddenly shook, and Alice who patted her shoulder.

"Tell me..." Leisha couldn't think what she wanted to be told, except that she wanted to hear Alice's voice in the gloom, Alice's voice as it was now, gentle and remote, without damage any more from the damaging fact of Leisha's existence. Her very existence as damage. "Tell me about Jordan. He's five now? What's he like?"

Alice turned her head to look levelly into Leisha's eyes. "He's a happy, ordinary little boy. Completely ordinary."

Camden died a week later. After the funeral, Leisha tried to see her mother at the Brookfield Drug and Alcohol Abuse Center. Elizabeth Camden, she was told, saw no one except her only child, Alice Camden Watrous.

Susan Melling, dressed in black, drove Leisha to the airport. Susan talked deftly, determinedly, about Leisha's studies, about Harvard, about the *Law Review.* Leisha answered in monosyllables, but Susan persisted, asking questions, quietly insisting on answers: When would Leisha take her bar exams? Where was she interviewing for jobs? Gradually Leisha began to lose the numbness she had felt since her father's casket was lowered into the ground. She realized that Susan's persistent questioning was a kindness.

"He sacrificed a lot of people," Leisha said suddenly.

"Not me," Susan said. "Only for a while there, when I gave up my work to do his. Roger didn't respect sacrifice much."

"Was he wrong?" Leisha said. The question came out with a kind of desperateness she hadn't intended.

Susan smiled sadly. "No. He wasn't wrong. I should never have left my research. It took me a long time to come back to myself after that."

He does that to people, Leisha heard inside her head. Susan? Or Alice? She couldn't, for once, remember clearly. She saw her father in the old conservatory, now empty, potting and repotting the exotic flowers he had loved.

She was tired. It was muscle fatigue from stress, she knew; twenty minutes of rest would restore her. Her eyes burned from unaccustomed tears. She leaned her head back against the car seat and closed her eyes.

Susan pulled the car into the airport parking lot and turned off the ignition. "There's something I want to tell you, Leisha."

Leisha opened her eyes. "About the will?"

Susan smiled tightly. "No. You really don't have any problems with how he divided the estate, do you? It seems reasonable to you. But that's not it. The research team from Biotech and Chicago Medical has finished its analysis of Bernie Kuhn's brain."

Leisha turned to face Susan. She was startled by the complexity of Susan's expression. It held determination, and satisfaction, and anger, and something else Leisha could not name.

Susan said, "We're going to publish next week, in the *New England Journal of Medicine*. Security has been unbelievably restricted—no leaks to the popular press. But I want to tell you now, myself, what we found. So you'll be prepared."

"Go on," Leisha said. Her chest felt tight.

"Do you remember when you and the other Sleepless kids took interleukin-1 to see what sleep was like? When you were sixteen?"

"How did you know about that?"

"You kids were watched a lot more closely than you think. Remember the headache you got?"

"Yes." She and Richard and Tony and Carol and Brad and Jeanine... no, not Jeanine. Jennifer. It had been Jennifer in the woods with them.

"Interleukin-1 is what I want to talk about. At least partly. It's one of a whole group of substances that boost the immune system. They stimulate the production of antibodies, the activity of white blood cells, and a host of other immuno-enhancements. Normal people have surges of IL-1 released during the slow-wave phases of sleep. That means that they were getting boosts to the immune system during sleep. One of the questions we researchers asked ourselves twenty-eight years ago was: will Sleepless kids who don't get those surges of IL-1 get sick more often?"

"I've never been sick," Leisha said.

"Yes, you have. Chicken pox and three minor colds by the end of your fourth year," Susan said precisely. "But in general you were all a very healthy lot. So we researchers were left with the alternate theory of sleep-driven immuno-enhancement: that the burst of immune activity existed as a counterpart to a greater vulnerability of the body in sleep to disease, probably in some way connected to the fluctuations in body temperature during REM sleep. In other words, sleep *caused* the immune vulnerability that endogenous pyrogens like IL-1 counteracted. Sleep was the problem, immune-system enhancements were the solution. Without sleep, there would be no problem. Are you following this?"

"Yes."

"Of course you are. Stupid question." Susan brushed her hair off her face. It was going gray at the temples. There was a tiny brown age spot beneath her right ear.

"Over the years we collected thousands, maybe hundreds of thousands, of Single Photon Emission Topography scans of you kids' brains, plus endless EEGs, samples of cerebrospinal fluid, and all the rest of it. But we couldn't really see inside your brains, really know what's going on in there. Until Bernie Kuhn hit that embankment."

"Susan," Leisha said, "give it to me straight. Without more buildup."

"You're not going to age."

"What?"

"Oh, cosmetically, a little—sagging due to gravity, maybe. But the absence of sleep peptides and all the rest of it affects the immune and tissue-restoration systems in ways we don't understand. Bernie Kuhn had a perfect liver. Perfect lungs, perfect heart, perfect lymph nodes, perfect pancreas, perfect medulla oblongata. Not just healthy, or young-perfect. There's a tissue regeneration enhancement that clearly derives from the operation of the immune system but is radically different from anything we ever suspected. Organs show no wear and tear, not even the minimal amount expected in a seventeen-year-old. They just repair themselves, perfectly, on and on…and on."

"For how long?" Leisha whispered.

"Who the hell knows? Bernie Kuhn was young. Maybe there's some compensatory mechanism that cuts in at some point and you'll all just collapse, like an entire fucking gallery of Dorian Grays. But I don't think so. Neither do I think it can go on forever; no tissue regeneration can do that. But a long, long time."

Leisha stared at the blurred reflections in the car windshield. She saw her father's face against the blue satin of his casket, banked with white roses. His heart, unregenerated, had given out.

Susan said, "The future is all speculative at this point. We know that the peptide structures that build up the pressure to sleep in normal people resemble the components of bacterial cell walls. Maybe there's a connection between sleep and pathogen receptivity. We don't know. But ignorance never stopped the tabloids. I wanted to prepare you because you're going to get called supermen, *homo perfectus*, who-all knows what. Immortal."

The two women sat in silence. Finally Leisha said, "I'm going to tell the others. On our datanet. Don't worry about the security. Kevin Baker designed Groupnet; nobody knows anything we don't want them to."

"You're that well organized already?"

"Yes."

Susan's mouth worked. She looked away from Leisha. "We better go in. You'll miss your flight."

"Susan…"

"What?"

"Thank you."

"You're welcome," Susan said, and in her voice Leisha heard the thing she had seen before in Susan's expression and had not been able to name: it was longing.

Tissue regeneration. A long, long time, sang the blood in Leisha's ears on the flight to Boston. *Tissue regeneration*. And, eventually: *immortal*. No, not that, she told herself severely. Not that. The blood didn't listen.

"You sure smile a lot," said the man next to her in first class, a business traveler who had not recognized Leisha. "You coming from a big party in Chicago?"

"No. From a funeral."

The man looked shocked, then disgusted. Leisha looked out the window at the ground far below. Rivers like microcircuits, fields like neat index cards. And on the horizon, fluffy white clouds like masses of exotic flowers, blooms in a conservatory filled with light.

The letter was no thicker than any hard-copy mail, but hard-copy mail addressed by hand to either of them was so rare that Richard was nervous. "It might be explosive." Leisha looked at the letter on their hall credenza. MS. LIESHA CAMDEN. Block letters, misspelled.

"It looks like a child's writing," she said.

Richard stood with head lowered, legs braced apart. But his expression was only weary. "Perhaps deliberately like a child's. You'd be more open to a child's writing, they might have figured."

"'They'? Richard, are we getting that paranoid?"

He didn't flinch from the question. "Yes. For the time being."

A week earlier the *New England Journal of Medicine* had published Susan's careful, sober article. An hour later the broadcast and datanet news had exploded in speculation, drama, outrage, and fear. Leisha and Richard, along with all the Sleepless on the Groupnet, had tracked and charted each of four components, looking for a dominant reaction: speculation ("The Sleepless may live for centuries, and this might lead to the following events...."); drama ("If a Sleepless marries only Sleepers, he may have lifetime enough for a dozen brides, and several dozen children, a bewildering blended family...."); outrage ("Tampering with the law of nature has only brought among us unnatural so-called people who will live with the unfair advantage of time: time to accumulate more kin, more power, more property than the rest of us could ever know...."); and fear ("How soon before the Super-race takes over?")

"They're all fear, of one kind or another," Carolyn Rizzolo finally said, and the Groupnet stopped its differentiated tracking.

Leisha was taking the final exams of her last year of law school. Each day comments followed her to the campus, along the corridors and in the classroom; each day she forgot them in the grueling exam sessions, in which all students were reduced to the same status of petitioner to the great university. Afterward, temporarily drained, she walked silently back home to Richard and the Groupnet, aware of the looks of people on the street, aware of her bodyguard Bruce striding between her and them.

"It will calm down," Leisha said. Richard didn't answer.

The town of Salt Springs, Texas, passed a local ordinance that no Sleepless could obtain a liquor license, on the grounds that civil rights statutes were built on the "all men were created equal" clause of the Declaration of Independence, and Sleepless clearly were not covered. There were no Sleepless within a hundred miles of Salt Springs and no one had applied for a new liquor license there for the past ten years, but the story was picked up by United Press and by Datanet News, and within twenty-four hours heated editorials appeared, on both sides of the issue, across the nation.

More local ordinances were passed. In Pollux, Pennsylvania, the Sleepless could be denied an apartment rental on the grounds that their prolonged wakefulness would increase both wear-and-tear on the landlord's property and utility bills. In Cranston Estates, California, Sleepless were barred from operating twenty-four hour businesses: "unfair competition." Iroquois County, New York, barred them from serving on county juries, arguing that a jury containing Sleepless, with their skewed idea of time, did not constitute "a jury of one's peers."

"All those statutes will be thrown out in superior courts," Leisha said. "But God! The waste of money and docket time to do it!" A part of her mind noticed that her tone as she said this was Roger Camden's.

The state of Georgia, in which some sex acts between consenting adults were still a crime, made sex between a Sleepless and a Sleeper a third-degree felony, classing it with bestiality.

Kevin Baker had designed software that scanned the newsnets at high speed, flagged all stories involving discrimination or attacks on Sleepless, and categorized them by type. The files were available on Groupnet. Leisha read through them, then called Kevin. "Can't you create a parallel program to flag defenses of us? We're getting a skewed picture."

"You're right," Kevin said, a little startled. "I didn't think of it."

"Think of it," Leisha said, grimly. Richard, watching her, said nothing.

She was most upset by the stories about Sleepless children. Shunning at school, verbal abuse by siblings, attacks by neighborhood bullies, confused resentment from parents who had wanted an exceptional child but had not bargained for one who might live centuries. The school board of Cold River,

Iowa voted to bar Sleepless children from conventional classrooms because their rapid learning "created feelings of inadequacy in others, interfering with their education." The board made funds available for Sleepless to have tutors at home. There were no volunteers among the teaching staff. Leisha started spending as much time on Groupnet with the kids, talking to them all night long, as she did studying for her bar exams, scheduled for July.

Stella Bevington stopped using her modem.

Kevin's second program cataloged editorials urging fairness toward Sleepless. The school board of Denver set aside funds for a program in which gifted children, including the Sleepless, could use their talents and build teamwork through tutoring even younger children. Rive Beau, Louisiana, elected Sleepless Danielle du Cherney to the City Council, although Danielle was twenty-two and technically too young to qualify. The prestigious medical research firm of Halley-Hall gave much publicity to their hiring of Christopher Amren, a Sleepless with a Ph.D. in cellular physics.

Dora Clarq, a Sleepless in Dallas, opened a letter addressed to her and a plastic explosive blew off her arm.

Leisha and Richard stared at the envelope on the hall credenza. The paper was thick, cream-colored, but not expensive, the kind of paper made of bulky newsprint dyed the shade of vellum. There was no return address. Richard called Liz Bishop, a Sleepless who was majoring in criminal justice in Michigan. He had never spoken with her before, and neither had Leisha—but she came on the Groupnet immediately and told them how to open it. Or, she could fly up and do it if they preferred. Richard and Leisha followed her directions for remote detonation in the basement of the townhouse. Nothing blew up. When the letter was open, they took it out and read it:

Dear Ms. Camden,

You been pretty good to me and I'm sorry to do this but I quit. They are making it pretty hot for me at the union not officially but you know how it is. If I was you I wouldn't go to the union for another bodyguard I'd try to find one privately. But be careful. Again I'm sorry but I have to live too.

Bruce

"I don't know whether to laugh or cry," Leisha said. "The two of us getting all this equipment, spending hours on this setup so an explosive won't detonate…."

"It's not as if I at least had a whole lot else to do," Richard said. Since the wave of anti-Sleepless sentiment, all but two of his marine consulting clients, vulnerable to the marketplace and thus to public opinion, had canceled their accounts.

Groupnet, still up on Leisha's terminal, shrilled in emergency override. Leisha got there first. It was Tony Indivino.

"Leisha. I need your legal help, if you'll give it. They're trying to fight me on Sanctuary. Please fly down here."

Sanctuary was raw brown gashes in the late-spring earth. It was situated in the Allegheny Mountains of southern New York State, old hills rounded by age and covered with pine and hickory. A superb road led from the closest town, Conewango, to Sanctuary. Low, maintenance-free buildings, whose design was plain but graceful, stood in various stages of completion. Jennifer Sharifi, unsmiling, met Leisha and Richard. She hadn't changed much in six years but her long black hair was uncombed and her dark eyes enormous with strain. "Tony wants to talk to you, but first he asked me to show you both around."

"What's wrong?" Leisha asked quietly.

Jennifer didn't try to evade the question. "Later. First look at Sanctuary. Tony respects your opinion enormously, Leisha; he wants you to see everything."

The dormitories each held fifty, with communal rooms for cooking, dining, relaxing, and bathing, and a warren of separate offices and studios and labs for work. "We're calling them 'dorms' anyway, despite the etymology," Jennifer said, and even in this remark, which from anybody else would have been playful, Leisha heard the peculiar combination of Jennifer's habitual deliberate calm with her present strain.

She was impressed, despite herself, with the completeness of Tony's plans for lives that would be both communal and intensely private. There was a gym, a small hospital—"By the end of next year, we'll have eighteen board-certified doctors, you know, and four of them are thinking of coming here"—a daycare facility, a school, and an intensive-crop farm. "Most of the food will come in from the outside, of course. So will most people's jobs, although they'll do as much of them as possible from here, over datanets. We're not cutting ourselves off from the world, only creating a safe place from which to trade with it." Leisha didn't answer.

Apart from the power facilities, self-supported Y-energy, she was most impressed with the human planning. Tony had interested Sleepless from virtually every field they would need both to care for themselves and to deal with the outside world. "Lawyers and accountants come first," Jennifer said. "That's our first line of defense in safeguarding ourselves. Tony recognizes that most modern battles for power are fought in the courtroom and boardroom."

But not all. Last, Jennifer showed them the plans for physical defense. For the first time, her taut body seemed to relax slightly.

Every effort had been made to stop attackers without hurting them. Electronic surveillance completely circled the 150 square miles Jennifer had purchased. Some *counties* were smaller than that, Leisha thought, dazed. When breached, a force field a half-mile within the E-gate activated, delivering electric shocks to anyone on foot—"but only on the *outside* of the field. We don't want any of our kids hurt," Jennifer said. Unmanned penetration by vehicles or robots was identified by a system that located all moving metal above a certain mass within Sanctuary. Any moving metal that did not carry a special signaling device designed by Donald Pospula, a Sleepless who had patented important electronic components, was suspect.

"Of course, we're not set up for an air attack or an outright army assault," Jennifer said. "But we don't expect that. Only the haters in self-motivated hate."

Leisha touched the hard-copy of the security plans with one finger. They troubled her. "If we can't integrate ourselves into the world...Free trade should imply free movement."

Jennifer said swiftly, "Only if free movement implies free minds," and at her tone Leisha looked up. "I have something to tell you, Leisha."

"What?"

"Tony isn't here."

"Where is he?"

"In Cattaraugus County jail in Conewango. It's true we're having zoning battles about Sanctuary—zoning! In this isolated spot! But this is something else, something that just happened this morning. Tony's been arrested for the kidnapping of Timmy DeMarzo."

The room wavered. "FBI?"

"Yes."

"How…how did they find out?"

"Some agent eventually cracked the case. They didn't tell us how. Tony needs a lawyer, Leisha. Bill Thaine has already agreed, but Tony wants you."

"Jennifer—I don't even take the bar exams until July!"

"He says he'll wait. Bill will act as his lawyer in the meantime. Will you pass the bar?"

"Of course. But I already have a job lined up with Morehouse, Kennedy & Anderson in New York…." She stopped. Richard was looking at her hard, Jennifer inscrutably. Leisha said quietly, "What will he plead?"

"Guilty," Jennifer said, "with—what is it called legally? Extenuating circumstances." Leisha nodded. She had been afraid Tony would want to plead not guilty: more lies, subterfuge, ugly politics. Her mind ran swiftly over extenuating circumstances, precedents, tests to precedents…. They could use *Clements v. Voy*….

"Bill is at the jail now," Jennifer said. "Will you drive in with me?" She made the question a challenge.

"Yes," Leisha said.

In Conewango, the county seat, they were not allowed to see Tony. William Thaine, as his attorney, could go in and out freely. Leisha, not officially an attorney at all, could go nowhere. This was told to them by a man in the D.A.'s office whose face stayed immobile while he spoke to them, and who spat on the ground behind their shoes when they turned to leave, even though this left him with a smear of spittle on his courthouse floor.

Richard and Leisha drove their rental car to the airport for the flight back to Boston. On the way Richard told Leisha he was leaving. He was moving to Sanctuary, now, even before it was functional, to help with the planning and building.

She stayed most of the time in her townhouse, studying ferociously for the bar exams or checking on the Sleepless children through Groupnet. She had not hired another bodyguard to replace Bruce, which made her reluctant to go outside very much; the reluctance in turn made her angry with herself. Once or twice a day she scanned Kevin's electronic news clippings.

There were signs of hope. The *New York Times* ran an editorial, widely reprinted on the electronic news services:

PROSPERITY AND HATRED: A LOGIC CURVE WE'D RATHER NOT SEE

The United States has never been a country that much values calm, logic, and rationality. We have, as a people, tended to label these things "cold." We have, as a people, tended to admire feeling and action: We exalt in our stories and our memorials—not the creation of the Constitution but its defense at Iwo Jima; not the intellectual achievements of a Linus Pauling but the heroic passion of a Charles Lindbergh; not the inventors of the monorails and computers that unite us but the composers of the angry songs of rebellion that divide us.

A peculiar aspect of this phenomenon is that it grows stronger in times of prosperity. The better off our citizenry, the greater their contempt for the calm reasoning that got them there, and the more passionate their indulgence in emotion. Consider, in the past century, the gaudy excesses of the roaring twenties and the antiestablishment contempt of the sixties. Consider, in our own century, the unprecedented prosperity brought about by Y-energy—and then consider that Kenzo Yagai, except to his followers, was seen as a greedy and bloodless logician, while our national adulation goes to neo-nihilist writer Stephen Castelli, to "feelie" actress Brenda Foss, and to daredevil gravity-well diver Jim Morse Luter.

But most of all, as you ponder this phenomenon in your Y-energy houses, consider the current outpouring of irrational feeling directed at the "Sleepless" since the publication of the joint findings of the Biotech Institute and the Chicago Medical School concerning Sleepless tissue regeneration.

Most of the Sleepless are intelligent. Most of them are calm, if you define that much-maligned word to mean directing one's energies into solving problems rather than to emoting about them. (Even Pulitzer Prize winner Carolyn Rizzolo gave us a stunning play of ideas, not of passions run amuck.) All of them show a natural bent toward achievement, a bent given a decided boost by the one-third more time in their days to achieve. Their achievements lie, for the most part, in logical fields rather than emotional ones: Computers. Law. Finance. Physics. Medical research. They are rational, orderly, calm, intelligent, cheerful, young, and possibly very long-lived.

And, in our United States of unprecedented prosperity, they are increasingly hated.

Does the hatred that we have seen flower so fully over the past few months really grow, as many claim, from the "unfair advantage" the Sleepless have over the rest of us in securing jobs, promotions, money, and success? Is it really envy over the Sleepless' good fortune? Or does it come from something more pernicious, rooted in our tradition of shoot-from-the-hip American action. Hatred of the logical, the calm, the considered? Hatred in fact of the superior mind?

If so, perhaps we should think deeply about the founders of this country: Jefferson, Washington, Paine, Adams—inhabitants of the Age of Reason, all. These men created our orderly and balanced system of laws precisely to protect the property and achievements created by the individual efforts of balanced and rational minds. The Sleepless may be our severest internal test yet of our own sober belief in law and order. No, the Sleepless were not "created equal," but our attitudes toward them should be examined with a care equal to our soberest jurisprudence. We may not like what we learn about our own motives, but our credibility as a people may depend on the rationality and intelligence of the examination.

Both have been in short supply in the public reaction to last month's research findings.

Law is not theater. Before we write laws reflecting gaudy and dramatic feelings, we must be very sure we understand the difference.

Leisha hugged herself, gazing in delight at the screen, smiling. She called the *New York Times* and asked who had written the editorial. The receptionist, cordial when she answered the phone, grew brusque. The Times was not releasing that information, "prior to internal investigation."

It could not dampen her mood. She whirled around the apartment, after days of sitting at her desk or screen. Delight demanded physical action. She washed dishes, picked up books. There were gaps in the furniture patterns where Richard had taken pieces that belonged to him; a little quieter now, she moved the furniture to close the gaps.

Susan Melling called to tell her about the *Times* editorial; they talked warmly for a few minutes. When Susan hung up, the phone rang again.

"Leisha? Your voice still sounds the same. This is Stewart Sutter."

"Stewart." She had not seen him for four years. Their romance had lasted two years and then dissolved, not from any painful issue so much as from the press of both their studies. Standing by the comm-terminal, hearing his voice, Leisha suddenly felt again his hands on her breasts in the cramped dormitory bed: all those years before she had found a good use for a bed. The phantom hands became Richard's hands, and a sudden pain pierced her.

"Listen," Stewart said, "I'm calling because there's some information I think you should know. You take your bar exams next week, right? And then you have a tentative job with Morehouse, Kennedy & Anderson."

"How do you know all that, Stewart?"

"Men's room gossip. Well, not as bad as that. But the New York legal community—that part of it, anyway—is smaller than you think. And you're a pretty visible figure."

"Yes," Leisha said neutrally.

"Nobody has the slightest doubt you'll be called to the bar. But there is some doubt about the job with Morehouse, Kennedy. You've got two senior partners, Alan Morehouse and Seth Brown, who have changed their minds since this...flap. 'Adverse publicity for the firm,' 'turning law into a circus,' blah blah blah. You know the drill. But you've also got two powerful champions, Ann Carlyle and Michael Kennedy, the old man himself. He's quite a mind. Anyway, I wanted you to know all this so you can recognize exactly what the situation is and know whom to count on in the infighting."

"Thank you," Leisha said. "Stew...why do you care if I get it or not? Why should it matter to you?"

There was a silence on the other end of the phone. Then Stewart said, very low, "We're not all noodleheads out here, Leisha. Justice does still matter to some of us. So does achievement."

Light rose in her, a bubble of buoyant light.

Stewart said, "You have a lot of support here for that stupid zoning fight over Sanctuary, too. You might not realize that, but you do. What the Parks Commission crowd is trying to pull is...but they're just being used as fronts. You know that. Anyway, when it gets as far as the courts, you'll have all the help you need."

"Sanctuary isn't my doing. At all."

"No? Well, I meant the plural you."

"Thank you. I mean that. How are you doing?"

"Fine. I'm a daddy now."

"Really! Boy or girl?"

"Girl. A beautiful little bitch named Justine, drives me crazy. I'd like you to meet my wife sometime, Leisha."

"I'd like that," Leisha said.

She spent the rest of the night studying for her bar exams. The bubble stayed with her. She recognized exactly what it was: joy.

It was going to be all right. The contract, unwritten, between her and her society—Kenzo Yagai's society, Roger Camden's society—would hold. With dissent and strife and yes, some hatred. She suddenly thought of Tony's beggars in Spain, furious at the strong because the beggars were not. Yes. But it would hold.

She believed that.

She did.

SEVEN

Leisha took her bar exams in July. They did not seem hard to her. Afterward three classmates, two men and a woman, made a fakely casual point of talking to Leisha until she had climbed safely into a taxi whose driver obviously did not recognize her, or stop signs. The three were all Sleepers. A pair of undergraduates, clean shaven blond men with the long faces and pointless arrogance of rich stupidity, eyed Leisha and sneered. Leisha's female classmate sneered back.

Leisha had a flight to Chicago the next morning. Alice was going to join her there. They had to clean out the big house on the lake, dispose of Roger's personal property, put the house on the market. Leisha had had no time to do it earlier.

She remembered her father in the conservatory, wearing an ancient flat-topped hat he had picked up somewhere, potting orchids and jasmine and passion flowers.

When the doorbell rang she was startled; she almost never had visitors. Eagerly, she turned on the outside camera—maybe it was Jonathan or Martha, back in Boston to surprise her, to celebrate—why hadn't she thought before about some sort of celebration?

Richard stood gazing up at the camera. He had been crying.

She tore open the door. Richard made no move to come in. Leisha saw that what the camera had registered as grief was actually something else: tears of rage.

"Tony's dead."

Leisha put out her hand, blindly. Richard didn't take it.

"They killed him in prison. Not the authorities—the other prisoners. In the recreation yard. Murderers, rapists, looters, scum of the earth—and they thought they had the right to kill *him* because he was different."

Now Richard did grab her arm, so hard that something, some bone, shifted beneath the flesh and pressed on a nerve. "Not just different—*better.* Because he was better, because we all are, we goddamn just don't stand up and shout it out of some misplaced feeling for *their* feelings...God!"

Leisha pulled her arm free and rubbed it, numb, staring at Richard's contorted face.

"They beat him to death with a lead pipe. No one even knows how they got a lead pipe. They beat him on the back of the head and then they rolled him over and—"

"Don't!" Leisha said. It came out a whimper.

Richard looked at her. Despite his shouting, his violent grip on her arm, Leisha had the confused impression that this was the first time he had actually seen her. She went on rubbing her arm, staring at him in terror.

He said quietly, "I've come to take you to Sanctuary, Leisha. Dan Jenkins and Vernon Bulriss are in the car outside. The three of us will carry you out, if necessary. But you're coming. You see that, don't you? You're not safe here, with your high profile and your spectacular looks. You're a natural target if anyone is. Do we have to force you? Or do you finally see for yourself that we have no choice—the bastards have left us no choice—except Sanctuary?"

Leisha closed her eyes. Tony, at fourteen, at the beach. Tony, his eyes ferocious and shining, the first to reach out his hand for the glass of interleukin-1. Beggars in Spain.

"I'll come."

❋

She had never known such anger. It scared her, coming in bouts throughout the long night, receding but always returning again. Richard held her in his arms, sitting with their backs against the wall of her library, and his holding made no difference at all. In the living room Dan and Vernon talked in low voices.

Sometimes the anger erupted in shouting, and Leisha heard herself and thought, *I don't know you.* Sometimes it became crying, sometimes talking about Tony, about all of them. Neither the shouting nor the crying nor the talking eased her at all.

Planning did, a little. In a cold, dry voice she didn't recognize, Leisha told Richard about the trip to close the house in Chicago. She had to go; Alice was already there. If Richard and Dan and Vernon put Leisha on the plane, and Alice met her at the other end with union bodyguards, she should be safe enough. Then she would change her return ticket from Boston to Conewango and drive with Richard to Sanctuary.

"People are already arriving," Richard said. "Jennifer Sharifi is organizing it, greasing the Sleeper suppliers with so much money they can't resist. What about this townhouse here, Leisha? Your furniture and terminal and clothes?"

Leisha looked around her familiar office. Law books, red and green and brown, lined the walls although most of the same information was online. A coffee cup rested on a printout on the desk. Beside it was the receipt she had requested from the taxi driver this afternoon, a giddy souvenir of the day she had passed her bar exams; she had thought of having it framed. Above the desk was a holographic portrait of Kenzo Yagai.

"Let it rot," Leisha said.

Richard's arm tightened around her.

"I've never seen you like this," Alice said, subdued. "It's more than just clearing out the house, isn't it?"

"Let's get on with it," Leisha said. She yanked a suit from her father's closet. "Do you want any of this stuff for your husband?"

"It wouldn't fit."

"The hats?"

"No," Alice said. "Leisha—what is it?"

"Let's just *do* it!" She yanked all the clothes from Camden's closet, piled them on the floor, scrawled FOR VOLUNTEER AGENCY on a piece of paper, and dropped it on top of the pile. Silently, Alice started adding clothes from the dresser, which already bore a taped paper bearing the words, ESTATE AUCTION.

The curtains were already down throughout the house; Alice had done that yesterday. She had also rolled up the rugs. Sunset glared red on the bare wooden floors.

"What about your old room?" Leisha said. "What do you want there?"

"I've already tagged it," Alice said. "A mover will come Thursday."

"Fine. What else?"

"The conservatory. Sanderson has been watering everything, but he didn't really know what needed how much, so some of the plants are—"

"Fire Sanderson," Leisha said curtly. "The exotics can die. Or have them sent to a hospital, if you'd rather. Just watch out for the ones that are poisonous. Come on, let's do the library."

Alice sat slowly on a rolled-up rug in the middle of Camden's bedroom. She had cut her hair; Leisha thought it looked ugly, like jagged brown spikes around her broad face. She had also gained more weight. She was starting to look like their mother.

Alice said, "Do you remember the night I told you I was pregnant? Just before you left for Harvard?"

"Let's do the library!"

"Do you?" Alice said. "For God's sake, can't you just once listen to someone else, Leisha? Do you have to be so much like Daddy every single minute?"

"I'm not Daddy!"

"The hell you're not. You're exactly what he made you. But that's not the point. Do you remember that night?"

Leisha walked over the rug and out the door. Alice simply sat. After a minute Leisha walked back in. "I remember."

"You were near tears," Alice said implacably. Her voice was quiet. "I don't even remember exactly why. Maybe because I wasn't going to college after all. But I put my arms around you, and for the first time in years—years, Leisha—I felt you really were my sister. Despite all of it—the roaming the halls all night and the showoff arguments with Daddy and the special school and the artificially long legs and golden hair—all that crap. You seemed to need me to hold you. You seemed to need me. You seemed to *need*."

"What are you saying?" Leisha demanded. "That you can only be close to someone if they're in trouble and need you? That you can only be a sister if I was in some kind of pain, open sores running? Is that the bond between you Sleepers? 'Protect me while I'm unconscious, I'm just as crippled as you are'?"

"No," Alice said. "I'm saying that *you* could be a sister only if you were in some kind of pain."

Leisha stared at her. "You're stupid, Alice."

Alice said calmly, "I know that. Compared to you, I am. I know that."

Leisha jerked her head angrily. She felt ashamed of what she had just said, and yet it was true, and they both knew it was true, and anger still lay in her like a dark void, formless and hot. It was the formless part that was the worst. Without shape, there could be no action; without action, the anger went on burning her, choking her.

Alice said, "When I was twelve Susan gave me a dress for our birthday. You were away somewhere, on one of those overnight field trips your fancy progressive school did all the time. The dress was silk, pale blue, with antique lace—very beautiful. I was thrilled, not only because it was beautiful but because Susan had gotten it for me and gotten software for you. The dress was mine. Was, I thought, me." In the gathering gloom Leisha could barely make out her broad, plain features. "The first time I wore it a boy said, 'Stole your sister's dress, Alice? Snitched it while she was sleeping?' Then he laughed like crazy, the way they always did.

"I threw the dress away. I didn't even explain to Susan, although I think she would have understood. Whatever was yours was yours, and whatever wasn't yours was yours, too. That's the way Daddy set it up. The way he hard-wired it into our genes."

"You, too?" Leisha said. "You're no different from the other envious beggars?"

Alice stood up from the rug. She did it slowly, leisurely, brushing dust off the back of her wrinkled skirt, smoothing the print fabric. Then she walked over and hit Leisha in the mouth.

"Now do you see me as real?" Alice asked quietly.

Leisha put her hand to her mouth. She felt blood. The phone rang, Camden's unlisted personal line. Alice walked over, picked it up, listened, and held it calmly out to Leisha. "It's for you."

Numb, Leisha took it.

"Leisha? This is Kevin. Listen, something's happened. Stella Bevington called me, on the phone, not Groupnet; I think her parents took away her modem. I picked up the phone and she screamed, 'This is Stella! They're hitting me, he's drunk—' and then the line went dead. Randy's gone to Sanctuary—hell, they've *all* gone. You're closest to her, she's still in Skokie. You better get there fast. Have you got bodyguards you trust?"

"Yes," Leisha said, although she hadn't. The anger, finally, took form. "I can handle it."

"I don't know how you'll get her out of there," Kevin said. "They'll recognize you, they know she called somebody, they might even have knocked her out...."

"I'll handle it," Leisha said.

"Handle what?" Alice said.

Leisha faced her. Even though she knew she shouldn't, she said, "What your people do. To one of ours. A seven-year-old kid who's getting beaten by her parents because she's Sleepless—because she's *better* than you are—" She ran down the stairs and out to the rental car she had driven from the airport.

Alice ran right down with her. "Not your car, Leisha. They can trace a rental car just like that. My car."

Leisha screamed, "If you think you're—"

Alice yanked open the door of her battered Toyota, a model so old the Y-energy cones weren't even concealed but hung like drooping jowls on either side. She shoved Leisha into the passenger seat, slammed the door, and rammed herself behind the wheel. Her hands were steady. "Where?"

Blackness swooped over Leisha. She put her head down, as far between her knees as the cramped Toyota would allow. It had been two—no, three—days since she had eaten. Not since the night before the bar exams. The faintness receded, swept over her again as soon as she raised her head.

She told Alice the address in Skokie.

"Stay way in the back," Alice said. "And there's a scarf in the glove compartment—put it on. Low, to hide as much of your face as possible."

Alice stopped the car along Highway 42. Leisha said, "This isn't—"

"It's a quick-guard place. We have to look like we have some protection, Leisha. We don't need to tell him anything. I'll hurry."

She was out in three minutes with a huge man in a cheap dark suit. He squeezed into the front seat beside Alice and said nothing at all. Alice did not introduce him.

The house was small, a little shabby, with lights on downstairs, none upstairs. The first stars shone in the north, away from Chicago. Alice said to the guard, "Get out of the car and stand here by the car door—no, more in the light—and don't do anything unless I'm attacked in some way." The man nodded. Alice started up the walk. Leisha scrambled out of the back seat and caught her sister two-thirds of the way to the plastic front door.

"Alice, what the hell are you doing? *I* have to—"

"Keep your voice down," Alice said, glancing at the guard. "Leisha, *think*. You'll be recognized. Here, near Chicago, with a Sleepless daughter—these people have looked at your picture in magazines for years.

They've watched long-range holovids of you. They know you. They know you're going to be a lawyer. Me they've never seen. I'm nobody."

"Alice—"

"For Chrissake, get back in the car!" Alice hissed, and pounded on the front door.

Leisha drew off the walk, into the shadow of a willow tree. A man opened the door. His face was completely blank.

Alice said, "Child Protection Agency. We got a call from a little girl, this number. Let me in."

"There's no little girl here."

"This is an emergency, priority one," Alice said. "Child Protection Act 186. Let me in!"

The man, still blank-faced, glanced at the huge figure by the car. "You got a search warrant?"

"I don't need one in a priority-one child emergency. If you don't let me in, you're going to have legal snarls like you never bargained for."

Leisha clamped her lips together. No one would believe that, it was legal gobbledygook.... Her lip throbbed where Alice had hit it.

The man stood aside to let Alice enter.

The guard started forward. Leisha hesitated, then let him. He entered with Alice.

Leisha waited, alone, in the dark.

In three minutes they were out, the guard carrying a child. Alice's broad face gleamed pale in the porch light. Leisha sprang forward, opened the car door, and helped the guard ease the child inside. The guard was frowning, a slow puzzled frown shot with wariness.

Alice said, "Here. This is an extra hundred dollars. To get back to the city by yourself."

"Hey..." the guard said, but he took the money. He stood looking after them as Alice pulled away.

"He'll go straight to the police," Leisha said despairingly. "He has to, or risk his union membership."

"I know," Alice said. "But by that time we'll be out of the car."

"*Where?*"

"At the hospital," Alice said.

"Alice, we can't—" Leisha didn't finish. She turned to the back seat. "Stella? Are you conscious?"

"Yes," said the small voice.

Leisha groped until her fingers found the rear-seat illuminator. Stella lay stretched out on the seat, her face distorted with pain. She cradled her left arm in her right. A single bruise colored her face, above the left eye. Her red hair was tangled and dirty.

"You're Leisha Camden," the child said, and started to cry.

"Her arm's broken," Alice said.

"Honey, can you…" Leisha's throat felt thick, she had trouble getting the words out "…can you hold on till we get you to a doctor?"

"Yes," Stella said. "Just don't take me back there!"

"We won't," Leisha said. "Ever." She glanced at Alice and saw Tony's face.

Alice said, "There's a community hospital about ten miles south of here."

"How do you know that?"

"I was there once. Drug overdose," Alice said briefly. She drove hunched over the wheel, with the face of someone thinking furiously. Leisha thought, too, trying to see a way around the legal charge of kidnapping. They probably couldn't say the child came willingly. Stella would undoubtedly cooperate but at her age and in her condition she was probably *non sui juris*, her word would have no legal weight….

"Alice, we can't even get her into the hospital without insurance information. Verifiable online."

"Listen," Alice said, not to Leisha but over her shoulder, toward the back seat, "here's what we're going to do, Stella. I'm going to tell them you're my daughter and you fell off a big rock you were climbing while we stopped for a snack at a roadside picnic area. We're driving from California to Philadelphia to see your grandmother. Your name is Jordan Watrous and you're five years old. Got that, honey?"

"I'm seven," Stella said. "Almost eight."

"You're a very large five. Your birthday is March 23. Can you do this, Stella?"

"Yes," the little girl said. Her voice was stronger.

Leisha stared at Alice. "Can *you* do this?"

"Of course I can," Alice said. "I'm Roger Camden's daughter."

Alice half-carried, half-supported Stella into the Emergency Room of the small community hospital. Leisha watched from the car: the short stocky woman, the child's thin body with the twisted arm. Then she drove

Alice's car to the farthest corner of the parking lot, under the dubious cover of a skimpy maple, and locked it. She tied the scarf more securely around her face.

Alice's license plate number, and her name, would be in every police and rental-car databank by now. The medical banks were slower; often they uploaded from local precincts only once a day, resenting the governmental interference in what was still, despite a half-century of battle, a private-sector enterprise. Alice and Stella would probably be all right in the hospital. Probably. But Alice could not rent another car.

Leisha could.

But the data file that would flash to rental agencies on Alice Camden Watrous might or might not include that she was Leisha Camden's twin.

Leisha looked at the rows of cars in the lot. A flashy luxury Chrysler, an Ikeda van, a row of middle-class Toyotas and Mercedes, a vintage '99 Cadillac—she could imagine the owner's face if that were missing—ten or twelve cheap runabouts, a hover car with the uniformed driver asleep at the wheel. And a battered farm truck.

Leisha walked over to the truck. A man sat at the wheel, smoking. She thought of her father.

"Hello," Leisha said.

The man rolled down his window but didn't answer. He had greasy brown hair.

"See that hover car over there?" Leisha said. She made her voice sound young, high. The man glanced at it indifferently; from this angle you couldn't see that the driver was asleep. "That's my bodyguard. He thinks I'm inside, the way my father told me to, getting this lip looked at." She could feel her mouth swollen from Alice's blow.

"So?"

Leisha stamped her foot. "So I don't want to be inside. He's a shit and so's Daddy. I want out. I'll give you four thousand bank credits for your truck. Cash."

The man's eyes widened. He tossed away his cigarette and looked again at the hover car. The driver's shoulders were broad, and the car was within easy screaming distance.

"All nice and legal," Leisha said, trying to smirk. Her knees felt watery.

"Let me see the cash."

Leisha backed away from the truck, to where he could not reach her. She took the money from her arm clip. She was used to carrying a lot of cash; there had always been Bruce, or someone like Bruce. There had always been safety.

"Get out of the truck on the other side," Leisha said, "and lock the door behind you. Leave the keys on the seat, where I can see them from here. Then I'll put the money on the roof where you can see it."

The man laughed, a sound like gravel pouring. "Regular little Dabney Engh, aren't you? Is that what they teach you society debs at your fancy schools?"

Leisha had no idea who Dabney Engh was. She waited, watching the man try to think of a way to cheat her, and tried to hide her contempt. She thought of Tony.

"All right," he said, and slid out of the truck.

"Lock the door!"

He grinned, opened the door again, and locked it. Leisha put the money on the roof, yanked open the driver's door, clambered in, locked the door, and powered up the window. The man laughed. She put the key into the ignition, started the truck, and drove toward the street. Her hands trembled.

She drove slowly around the block twice. When she came back, the man was gone, and the driver of the hover car was still asleep. She had wondered if the man would wake him, out of sheer malice, but he had not. She parked the truck and waited.

An hour and a half later Alice and a nurse wheeled Stella out of the Emergency entrance. Leisha leaped out of the truck and yelled, "Coming, Alice!" waving both her arms. It was too dark to see Alice's expression; Leisha could only hope that Alice showed no dismay at the battered truck, that she had not told the nurse to expect a red car.

Alice said, "This is Julie Bergadon, a friend that I called while you were setting Jordan's arm." The nurse nodded, uninterested. The two women helped Stella into the high truck cab; there was no back seat. Stella had a cast on her arm and looked drugged.

"How?" Alice said as they drove off.

Leisha didn't answer. She was watching a police hover car land at the other end of the parking lot. Two officers got out and strode purposefully toward Alice's locked car under the skimpy maple.

"My God," Alice said. For the first time, she sounded frightened.

"They won't trace us," Leisha said. "Not to this truck. Count on it."

"Leisha." Alice's voice spiked with fear. "Stella's *asleep*."

Leisha glanced at the child, slumped against Alice's shoulder. "No, she's not. She's unconscious from painkillers."

"Is that all right? Normal? For...her?"

"We can black out. We can even experience substance-induced sleep." Tony and she and Richard and Jennifer in the midnight woods.... "Didn't you know that, Alice?"

"No."

"We don't know very much about each other, do we?"

They drove south in silence. Finally Alice said, "Where are we going to take her, Leisha?"

"I don't know. Any one of the Sleepless would be the first place the police would check—"

"You can't risk it. Not the way things are," Alice said. She sounded weary. "But all my friends are in California. I don't think we could drive this rust bucket that far before getting stopped."

"It wouldn't make it anyway."

"What should we do?"

"Let me think."

At an expressway exit was a pay phone. It wouldn't be data-shielded, as Groupnet was. Would Kevin's open line be tapped? Probably.

There was no doubt the Sanctuary line would be.

Sanctuary. All of them were going there or already there, Kevin had said. Holed up, trying to pull the worn Allegheny Mountains around them like a safe little den. Except for the children like Stella, who could not.

Where? With whom?

Leisha closed her eyes. The Sleepless were out; the police would find Stella within hours. Susan Melling? But she had been Alice's all-too visible stepmother, and was a co-beneficiary of Camden's will; they would question her almost immediately. It couldn't be anyone traceable to Alice. It could only be a Sleeper that Leisha knew, and trusted, and why should anyone at all fit that description? Why should she risk so much on anyone who did?

She stood a long time in the dark phone kiosk. Then she walked to the truck. Alice was asleep, her head thrown back against the seat. A tiny line of drool ran down her chin. Her face was white and drained in the bad light from the kiosk. Leisha walked back to the phone.

"Stewart? Stewart Sutter?"

"Yes?"

"This is Leisha Camden. Something has happened." She told the story tersely, in bald sentences. Stewart did not interrupt.

"Leisha—" Stewart said, and stopped.

"I need help, Stewart." *'I'll help you, Alice.' 'I don't need your help.'*

A wind whistled over the dark field beside the kiosk and Leisha shivered. She heard in the wind the thin keen of a beggar. In the wind, in her own voice.

"All right," Stewart said, "this is what we'll do. I have a cousin in Ripley, New York, just over the state line from Pennsylvania, the route you'll be driving east. It has to be in New York; I'm licensed in New York. Take the little girl there. I'll call my cousin and tell her you're coming. She's an elderly woman, was quite an activist in her youth. Her name is Janet Patterson. The town is—"

"What makes you so sure she'll get involved? She could go to jail. And so could you."

"She's been in jail so many times you wouldn't believe it. Political protests going all the way back to Vietnam. But no one's going to jail. I'm now your attorney of record, I'm privileged. I'm going to get Stella declared a ward of the state. That shouldn't be too hard with the hospital records you established in Skokie. Then she can be transferred to a foster home in New York. I know just the place, people who are fair and kind. Then Alice—"

"Stella's resident in Illinois. You can't—"

"Yes, I can. Since those research findings about the Sleepless lifespan have come out, legislators have been railroaded by stupid constituents scared or jealous or just plain angry. The result is a body of so-called law riddled with contradictions, absurdities, and loopholes. None of it will stand in the long run or at least I hope not—but in the meantime it can all be exploited. I can use it to create the most goddamn convoluted case for Stella that anybody ever saw, and in the meantime she won't be returned home. But that won't work for Alice. She'll need an attorney licensed in Illinois."

"We have one," Leisha said. "Candace Holt."

"No, not a Sleepless. Trust me on this, Leisha. I'll find somebody good. There's a guy in—are you crying?"

"No," Leisha said, crying.

"Ah, God," Stewart said. "Bastards. I'm sorry all this happened, Leisha."

"Don't be," Leisha said.

When she had directions to Stewart's cousin, she walked back to the truck. Alice was still asleep, Stella still unconscious. Leisha closed the truck door as quietly as possible. The engine balked and roared, but Alice didn't wake.

There was a crowd of people with them in the narrow and darkened cab: Stewart Sutter, Tony Indivino, Susan Melling, Kenzo Yagai, Roger Camden.

To Stewart Sutter she said: You called to inform me about the situation at Morehouse, Kennedy. You are risking your career and your cousin for Stella. And you stand to gain nothing. Like Susan telling me in advance about Bernie Kuhn's brain. Susan, who lost her life to Daddy's dream and regained it by her own strength. A contract without consideration for each side is not a contract: Every first-year student knows that.

To Kenzo Yagai she said: Trade isn't always linear. You missed that. If Stewart gives me something, and I give Stella something, and ten years from now Stella is a different person because of that and gives something to someone else as yet unknown—it's an ecology. An ecology of trade, yes, each niche needed, even if they're not contractually bound. Does a horse need a fish? Yes.

To Tony she said: Yes, there are beggars in Spain who trade nothing, give nothing, do nothing. But there are *more* than beggars in Spain. Withdraw from the beggars, you withdraw from the whole damn country. And you withdraw from the possibility of the ecology of help. That's what Alice wanted, all those years ago in her bedroom. Pregnant, scared, angry, jealous, she wanted to help *me*, and I wouldn't let her because I didn't need it. But I do now. And she did then. Beggars need to help as well as be helped.

And finally, there was only Daddy left. She could *see* him, bright-eyed, holding thick-leaved exotic flowers in his strong hands. To Camden she said: You were wrong. Alice is special. Oh, Daddy—the specialness of Alice! You were wrong.

As soon as she thought this, lightness filled her. Not the buoyant bubble of joy, not the hard clarity of examination, but something else: sunshine, soft through the conservatory glass, where two children ran in and out. She suddenly felt light herself, not buoyant but translucent, a medium for the sunshine to pass clear through, on its way to somewhere else.

She drove the sleeping woman and the wounded child through the night, east, toward the state line.

Afterword to "Beggars in Spain"

This novella and the novel that grew from it are my most commercially successful pieces. The idea for the Sleepless originated in envy (I need a lot of sleep, and resent that) and took a long time to turn into a story: thirteen years. My first attempt at people who did not need to sleep was rejected by every editor in the field. Robert Silverberg, who had changed editorial hats during the story's long submission period, rejected it twice ("I didn't like this the first time, and I still don't"). I retired the piece.

Eight years later, I tried again. This time even I could see that the story was bad. I never sent it out.

Five years after that I received a very stern lecture from Bruce Sterling about the need to include realistic economics in my fiction. The lecture resulted from a novelette without realistic economics, which I'd unwisely subjected to his scrutiny at a workshop. After licking my wounds, I decided that Bruce was right, and wrote "Beggars in Spain." It won both the Nebula and the Hugo. Thank you, Bruce.

COPYRIGHT INFORMATION

"And Wild For to Hold" Copyright © Nancy Kress, 1991, first appeared in *Isaac Asimov's Science Fiction Magazine*, July, 1991

"Out of All Them Bright Stars" Copyright © Nancy Kress, 1985, first appeared in *Fantasy and Science Fiction*, March, 1985

"Pathways" Copyright © Nancy Kress, 2013, first appeared in *Twelve Tomorrows*, ed. Stephen Cass, M.I.T. Tech Review, October, 2013

"Dancing on Air" Copyright © Nancy Kress, 1993, first appeared in *Isaac Asimov's Science Fiction Magazine*, July, 1993

"Unto the Daughters" Copyright © Nancy Kress, first appeared in *Sisters in Fantasy*, ed. Susan Shwartz and Martin H. Greenberg, Roc/New American Library, 1995

"Laws of Survival" Copyright © Nancy Kress, 2007, first appeared in *Jim Baen's Universe*, December, 2007

"Someone To Watch Over Me" Copyright © Nancy Kress, 2014, first appeared in *Ieee Spectrum*, June, 2014

"The Flowers of Aulit Prison" Copyright © Nancy Kress, 1996, first appeared in *Isaac Asimov's Science Fiction Magazine*, October/November, 1996

"The Price of Oranges" Copyright © Nancy Kress, 1989, first appeared in *Isaac Asimov's Science Fiction Magazine*, April, 1989

"By Fools Like Me" Copyright © Nancy Kress, 2007, first appeared in *Isaac Asimov's Science Fiction Magazine*, September, 2007

"Casey's Empire" Copyright © Nancy Kress, 1981, first appeared in *Fantasy and Science Fiction*, November, 1981

"Shiva in Shadow" Copyright © Nancy Kress, 2004, first appeared in *Between Worlds*, ed. Robert Silverberg, Science Fiction Book Club, 2004

"Grant Us This Day" Copyright © Nancy Kress, 1993, first appeared in *Isaac Asimov's Science Fiction Magazine*, September, 1993

"The Kindness of Strangers" Copyright © Nancy Kress, 2008, first appeared in *Fast Forward 2*, ed. Lou Anders, Pyr, 2008

"End Game" Copyright © Nancy Kress, 2007 first appeared in *Isaac Asimov's Science Fiction Magazine*, April-May, 2007

"My Mother, Dancing" Copyright © Nancy Kress, 2004, first appeared in *Isaac Asimov's Science Fiction Magazine*, June, 2004